About the author

Like my main character, I liked girls and benefitted from some early success, initially with the help of a slightly older woman. Unlike my namesake, I was never in commerce or industry but was fascinated by those who were and who used their power and position to further their personal success with women.

I have always loved nature, rivers and hills, fishing and camping, and loved a spell when I lived on a mixed farm.

I made my living and eventually my career, with a pen in my hand and used my "gift of the gab" to good effect, progressing well enough to help a large family.

I always wanted to write, although early attempts were just not good enough. But now I feel, after plenty of experience in life and particularly in employing the written word, I am ready to try again.

To Ange,
I hope you enjoy
my story.

THE MISTRESS

with love,

James Hinton-Hunt.

James Hinton-Hunt
17th January
2023.

JAMES HINTON-HUNT

THE MISTRESS

Vanguard Press

A CIP catalogue record for this title is
available from the British Library.

ISBN 978 1 80016 131 3

Vanguard Press is an imprint of
Pegasus Elliot MacKenzie Publishers Ltd.
www.pegasuspublishers.com

First Published in 2022

Vanguard Press
Sheraton House Castle Park
Cambridge England

Printed & Bound in Great Britain

Chapter 1

I always liked girls and women more than men, and not just for the obvious reason, for many reasons. Bottom line (forgive the unintended pun) is they seem to like me a lot more than boys and men, partly I figured because I wasn't competition to girls, whereas to men I was. Not physically, but character-wise, well able to defend myself verbally perhaps, more intelligent in many cases, who knows? Probably, it was a combination of these and other factors.

I have learnt, perhaps belatedly, that I am, and maybe have always been, thought of as a sexy person. Again, nothing to do with looking handsome, athletic, manly or whatever may be regarded as sexy. I just was, and I believe even now still, although let's say a bit old, I believe I still have maybe a little of what is known as charisma.

But for a number of years, I actually thought of myself as inferior in looks and personality to my peers at school, and later at work, to most of my fellow males. I was wrong it now seems, but it didn't stop me feeling inadequate at that time. I can laugh about it now, but as a teenager I suffered some serious, albeit probably misplaced, feelings of inadequacy. Needless to say, those feelings have long gone or been banished to my subconscious.

Women never, or rather rarely, made me feel that way, quite the reverse in fact, but even so it was many years before I felt truly confident in my own powers of communication and began to believe that I might actually be attractive. Not just to the opposite sex, but also occasionally I would be approached by boys and men and propositioned.

They didn't push too hard and I always smilingly declined politely, and no harm was done to either side. In fact, although I can honestly state that although I was never attracted to men or boys in that way, I had a certain sympathy for them and never felt the need to ridicule or criticise their occasional error of judgement in my regard. In fact, I was a bit flattered by this attention; to me, it helped to prove I was attractive to other human beings, although I naturally took more cognisance of female appreciation of my talents than those of men.

But I was definitely very interested not only in sex, but in relationships including friendship and comradeship, and although many of my friends were women, I did have and always have had a few special men friends, not more than four or five at any given period. My definition of those who would be my special friends was simple. There had to be a fair amount of mutual respect as well as liking; we had to have similar views about many things, but always be open to discussion and amendment where mutually in agreement, but the most important factor for me was trust.

My best friend during teenage years was Horace. He was the same age as me, same approximate height and physique, same poor economic background and with a very similar attitude to authority and critics that I had. We did everything together during school terms but as we lived a good distance away from each other on different sides of the town, involving at least two bus rides, out of term time we saw each only other rarely.

At school in the second year of seniority when we were 12/13 years of age, we played hooky together, absenting ourselves from class in the afternoons by simply disappearing after the morning register call and usually at lunchtime, and spent our afternoons roaming the town looking for things to do rather than stupid lessons with even more stupid teachers. But gradually we both became more interested in sex and would take delight surreptitiously masturbating in class under the cover of the two seated desks at which we always sat side by side.

It's amazing how many in a class of 12/13 year old boys (no girls in our school) also masturbated during lessons. I would say about a quarter of those present did it, although more surreptitiously than us generally. I remember one guy who amazed me because he looked so unlike a secret masturbator: he was fat, wore glasses and was very strait-laced and studious in appearance. But one day I glanced in his direction a couple of rows in front of me and had the perfect angle to see that he had his stumpy member in his right hand tugging away under the desk assuming, I guess, that he could not be seen, until he finally ejaculated and carefully produced his handkerchief from his left-hand pocket and mopped up the mess.

Another more mature thirteen-year-old who was practically an adult man in appearance was quietly wanking away while pretending to read the German textbook on his desk, when the teacher, a frumpy fifty-plus unmarried German or Austrian lady, seeing him fiddling with something, made a grab for whatever it was he was playing with! She must clearly have grabbed his erect penis and a look of surprised horror crossed her face and she turned and ran out of class.

But she obviously did not report the incident and came back after ten minutes or so looking and acting normally and subsequently this habit of hers of confiscating toys, small knives, etc., ceased. But I observed that despite her dry unsexy appearance, dowdy old-fashioned clothes, and no makeup, she would surreptitiously look at the mature student whose member she had inadvertently grabbed, looking away quickly when observed. Who knows, it may have been the one and only time in her life she had held an erect penis in her hand, however briefly.

Incidentally, I believe the vast majority of men, and perhaps women for that matter, who turn their noses up at this subject and pretend that they never think of such things, with very few exceptions, I think are not being honest with themselves. I accept that one person's libido may be greater or lesser than another's from time to time especially as sexual interest is affected by stress, diet, and many other things. I also accept that some people simply have low testosterone or other hormones or may have been abused early on in their life for example, and therefore have a reduced libido which may become so embedded that they remain that way all their life. I have read supposedly informed opinions on this subject which holds that if a child is starved of demonstrable affection by a parent or guardian, i.e., hugging, etc., such children often grow up with sexual and emotional inhibitions. And conversely those who are raised with open and uninhibited affection and contact from the parents or guardians, are much more open in their adult relationships with partners, lovers, and spouses generally.

But from my own experience with, and talking in depth about this subject to, friends of both sexes, I believe most have masturbated regularly in their life, starting in and even before their teens. And many continue to do so even when they have a good sexual relationship with their partner. It's back again to one's individual libido and sexual needs. Often a man might say that knowing his wife prefers sex only about once a week or even once a month or less, while he would like sex say, three or four times a week or more, the man prefers to masturbate regularly out of respect for his wife not from lack of interest on his part. And vice versa of course. Women have told me that they either don't get an orgasm with normal sex with their husband because he ejaculates too quickly or lacks technique, so they fake an orgasm so that he is not disappointed and have a leisurely perfectly timed orgasm or two when alone and undisturbed, either just using their fingers or with the help of a vibrator. Like me, they enjoy it more if they are able to look at nice soft pornographic pictures or videos.

As for me, I guess I have a greater interest in sexual matters than most and I am aware that my father and several of my brothers were much the same, and at least one of my sisters too. It's natural, I guess that there is a general interest in sex; otherwise, how come there are something like 8 billion of us humans now living on this planet? Sex is and always has been one of the main drivers for all mammals certainly, but also reptiles and birds I guess, in creating the massive populations of all these creatures on this planet which are still alive and thriving today.

Obtaining food and shelter of course have always played a big part in survival as well. But for the human race, food and shelter have not been too difficult for much of our recent history with our highly developed brains, which must leave sex and maybe power, as the two main drivers after the bare essentials are catered for.

Even so, with all these hormones, sex drive and power trips, sex can still become humdrum; but given that both regular parties remain sufficiently motivated and 'in love' — or at least hold a strong attraction for each other, and with other substantial bonds to bind them like careers, property and children and the fact that losing any of these things is a big deterrent for most people, they don't tend to look for alternative sexual experiences. And yet it does still happen.

Then there is the matter of ego as well. Many people of both sexes when they are young attach an achievement status to the number of times they make love a week for example, how many orgasms achieved per session, length of time achieving those orgasms and their perceived attractiveness of the partner to whom they are currently attached.

This sort of score card attitude is quite juvenile and normally fades away with experience of life. But not for everybody.

Chapter Two

I have clear memories of being interested in sexual matters very early on at about six or seven years of age, although of course I was years away from puberty. This I believe was partly due to having older brothers and sisters around during most of my early years and overhearing quiet conversations on the subject while I shared a bedroom and a bed in the earlier years, with one or more sisters. I would of course be sent to bed before my older siblings and so was often asleep when one or more of them arrived and quietly got into bed with me or into one of the other two beds in our bedroom. I never saw any actual sexual activities between my siblings, but I do remember hearing their whispered conversations about matters revolving around the subject, from which I soon learnt what was involved. In any case as a small boy, I often witnessed horses and cattle being mated at the farm where one of my pals lived, as well as seeing dogs mating in the streets, getting 'tied' or 'knotted' which I soon learnt meant a successful mating of canines. I also witnessed many different wild animals and birds copulating and in my day such things were commonplace in the countryside, where I was brought up.

At school, even junior school, there was a high level of sexual awareness amongst country raised boys and girls, many of whom lived on farms. Also, many were members of large families; it was a comparative rarity to know a boy or girl who had only one or two siblings, most had five, six or seven siblings and a few like me had more than that. So particularly when out roaming the countryside looking for birds' nests, mushrooms and catching sticklebacks to keep in jars, with a group of maybe six or seven pals aged between seven and ten years of age, sexual conversation often took place. This moved on to the slightly more mature ones amongst us, who, although still sexually immature, had already masturbated. We were happy to demonstrate our achievement where, although there was no ejaculation, an orgasm of sorts was achieved which we called 'the itch' and I recall it was a nice feeling.

Then a year or two of these activities led to the most developed boys amongst us not only masturbating but ejaculating. This was often achieved at pre-puberty when there was little or no pubic hair displayed and their penis was still quite small, but erection and masturbation was possible, and those who could 'come' were ahead of the pack and boasted about it. As a few had bigger penises and started to grow pubic hair, the rest of us sometimes felt left behind and somewhat inadequate.

I have been told by women that they too had learnt to masturbate and achieved orgasms before puberty in some cases, but mainly seemed to do this alone, not in the company of a group of other girls.

So I would say that the majority of young people start experimenting in sexual activity at a relatively young age and certainly pre-puberty, and boys definitely exhibited greater overt interest than girls, but it is quite likely that they too were similarly disposed but girls were more discreet about it.

Chapter Three

By the time I left secondary school at sixteen, I had certainly grown up quite a bit but still had many doubts and uncertainties about my ability to actually develop a relationship sufficient to continue on my path to full sexual maturity. But I was starting to attract a few girls — not in my village where we all knew each other too well and me as hardly a prize package! I was still quite small and thin and had no money for nice clothes, or to take a girl to the cinema, so I concentrated on developing my hairstyle and trying to get to know girls from other places.

This was hampered somewhat by the fact that having escaped school and completed my GCE examinations, I was in no hurry to enslave myself in a factory or farm, or indeed down the local coal mine. I knew I was educationally a cut above most of my pals because despite no real application, I had passed a good selection of GCE O levels at the 'tech' and none of my pals in the village possessed an O level between them.

But eventually I reluctantly sought employment, telling the recruitment person that any office job would do and when she recovered from learning that this uncouth youth in front of her indeed had a selection of GCEs including the magical English and Mathematic passes, a must for any decent office job, she set about finding me a suitable post.

When I started work at a large manufacturing company, I was in the procurement department with about twenty others, mostly men, but situated alongside were several other departments, accounts, sales, research, etc. Over the whole open floor of this one-storey building were over two hundred staff of all shapes and sizes including several attractive girls and women. I soon learnt that I could patrol my territory with a few documents under my arm and check out the talent.

I didn't make any conquests, but I honed my walking and nonchalance skills and picked up a few passable items of clothing at weekends which helped.

But after a few months I realised that I was making slow progress at the office because nearly all the girls were married or courting, etc., and really not interested in the lowest member of the male pecking order, a filing clerk, which I realised I had inadvertently become.

I thought to myself that I had better move on to something further away from my home town and preferably with better pay, as the weekly pay packet at this place was bare minimum. I scouted around.

The next phase of my sexual education and development happened quite unexpectedly when, working late one day to earn a little extra money, I found myself alone in the vast office with a lady who looked about thirty or perhaps more, who I knew and liked as a person. However, I never considered her from a sexual point of view, not only because she was so much older than me, but she was also a very serious person, had a good job as a personal secretary to one of the managers, was plain looking and tall with a slight stoop, a poor complexion, wore glasses and just didn't register with me as any sort of prospect.

How wrong I was. She saw me beavering away photographing records on a huge Kodak machine as she passed en route to the ladies' toilets, and she paused, smiled and asked how I was getting on. I was surprised as although I was often near her when moving around the office, I had only spoken to her once or twice before.

I said, "OK, thanks, but this microfilming job is a bit boring." She stopped, looked more closely at what I was doing and leant over me while she straightened up the pile of documents on the feeder and I noticed how when she bent forward, I could see right down her blouse and realised what a nice pair of tits she had. She saw me looking and leaned a little further over and placed her hand on my shoulder and whispered, "Do you like my blouse?"

Never being backward in coming forward I said, "Nice tits."

She rested one hand on my shoulder and putting her hand on my chin turned my face towards her and kissed me full on the lips. I was gobsmacked but I kissed her back then slid my free hand down her blouse and cupped one breast in my hand. I squeezed it gently and then twiddled her large pink nipple a bit and she gasped and said, "Follow me to the sick room; nobody else is here so we have plenty of time before the cleaners come."

15

I left the machine on and followed her, and she was now wiggling her arse and standing more upright with her tits stuck out more than usual and I realised that she was actually quite sexy looking, and I thought *wow, this could be it my boy!* I followed her past the two toilet doors to the sick room further down towards the back of the office and in we went. As soon as the door closed behind me, she put her arms around me and kissed me again and I got an instant hard-on and felt it pushing against her thighs, as she was taller than me by about four inches and had long legs. She pushed towards me making it clear she had felt my dick against her thighs and then she reached down and opened my flies. Out sprang my tool.

She just touched it a bit feeling the way as it were then she stopped kissing me, knelt on the floor and took my dick in her mouth and started to suck it gently, moaning all the time. It was wonderful but only for a minute or two as with her hand round my shaft and balls, I got so excited I ejaculated in her mouth and thought, *oh God, she won't like that* and tried belatedly to pull it out in time. She held me firmly in her hand and kept me in her mouth as months of sexual frustration made me have a huge orgasm and I squirted everything I had in her mouth, and she just moaned and kept me there until it started to go soft. But she simply kept tugging and sucking slowly and sure enough up my dick came, hard again after only about five minutes. She kept stroking him with one hand while she removed her skirt and knickers leaving her stockings and suspenders in place and exposing her lovely black bush.

She told me to take my trousers and my underpants off and then slipped off her shoes, lifted up one long leg so her knee was above her waist. She moved me nearer to where she was standing like a stork with one leg and her back to the wall and bent her standing leg just a bit and guided me into her secret lips hidden in that lovely bush where her fanny was all juiced up and waiting and she thrust forward so I could slide my once again rigid cock inside her. Wow, the sight of those long white thighs, the black lacy suspenders, and her lovely fanny, were more exciting than I ever imagined and by now she had her blouse open and with those wonderful tits, like ripe melons, swaying in front of my eyes, I was in heaven. This was beyond all expectations and hopes. She stood on one leg holding the other apart to make room as I thrust back and forth, in as far as I could reach, and every moment was bliss.

This time I must have made love to her for about ten minutes before she shouted out, "Oh yes! Come on, come in me again!" and I squirted my second load inside her. Her orgasm seemed to go on and on and her vaginal muscles gripped me in spasms lasting what must have been a full minute at least. Then she lowered her leg, leant against the wall with her head back and a huge smile on her face and I just stood there, bollock naked against her as the juice ran down her legs and onto mine.

She asked, was that my first time and I said yes, but not the last. She said, "I promised myself to have you almost a year ago and boy it was worth waiting for. You are a very sexy boy and thank you, that's the best I have had in many years."

I said, "What about your husband?" and she said that he was useless in bed and preferred other things.

I said can we do this again and she said yes but only when she says and never to tell anyone and don't talk to her any different in the office. I said, "Don't worry, I will not let you down, but make it soon please."

Chapter 4

Thus, began a joyous three or four months of wonderful, regular, and totally satisfying sex with this lady. She changed her appearance not at all, nor her clothes or habits. I would look casually at her walking about her business and marvelled at her composure; no one could have guessed what she was up to or what a fantastic, sexy person she was. I knew I would look on women differently from now on and assume nothing.

She would walk by my position and casually say hello and with a straight face say "tonight at five" or whatever and I would nod and say, "Thank you for asking," and on she would go. We used the sick room bed after the first time and I learnt that height difference doesn't matter when you are laid down. My face was level with her tits as we made love so I moved up and down her kissing first her lips then her neck and tits and back up again entering her at all different angles so that I explored all her vaginal cavity which she loved as she told me parts had never been touched by her husband or anyone else, and I was her first since she was married twelve years before! Another position was only possible because of her long legs, and I introduced that to her one day by picking up her legs while I was on top of her and first holding them in the crooks of my arms so that when I pushed up inside her there was more contact with the clitoris as well as higher up. Then while still inside her, I released one leg, took her ankle, and slowly pushed it higher halfway up her chest, then took the other leg and pushed them both slowly higher until her ankles were alongside her face, and she loved that as she was folded up double and without my dick straightening it out a fair bit it meant her vaginal canal was doubled up. So, she found that we achieved deeper penetration and more sensation all the way. Not to be recommended unless the person involved is fit and supple and then only a bit at a time slowly rising the legs and pushing gently up the vagina. But after doing it a few times, it became our favourite position as she achieved internal orgasms which she said were different to clitoral only and much more intense and long-lasting.

She also liked it from the back with a cushion under her front so that her vagina was clearly visible, and I liked to see it as I entered her slowly. I pushed it up as far as I could then withdrew each stroke until my knob end was almost visible before plunging it back up to the hilt again.

She loved that especially if I put my thumb up her arse at the same time and she would say, "Yes, yes, I like that, keep doing it 'til I come, I'm coming, I'm comiiiiing!"

And sometimes I was able to hold back, especially if it was the second or third barrel of course and then I would keep it going until she came again twice or even three times before saying, "Enough, enough." But even then, if I lay still hard inside her and just moved a little, she would start again and say, "Come on, please." She told me some things, but I think I quickly learnt to adapt and introduced her to new manoeuvres I had read about or just through experiments, some of which she didn't like much such as anal sex, although the thumb trick while up her vagina was OK.

I asked her once if the fact that she was making love with me two or three times a week, and having multiple orgasms, affected her relationship with her husband and she said no, in fact it had improved generally as she was taking the initiative more and using practice with me to make things more interesting for her, so he liked that, but only at most once a week and only one quick orgasm and he was snoring. She even masturbated on days she didn't see me as her libido had increased and she felt like sex almost every day. So like an idiot I said, "I suppose you fancy other blokes more now," and she reacted angrily saying, "Don't say that stupid! I told you I had no one else in twelve years and you were special. I won't ever be doing this again if and when you get tired of me as you are sure to one day."

I said sorry and promised her I would not be looking at anyone else while I had her to make love to. She just said, "We shall see."

Big lesson learnt, don't ask questions which might indicate a lack of belief or mistrust. Jealousy is destructive and futile.

She was I suppose my first mistress in the sense that she was married; I was not in love with her, I liked her a lot and admired her as a

19

person and was very fond of her as she was of me. But there was no love. She was using me, and I was using her, both for similar reasons. When I achieved a job transfer out of there, I felt a huge void in my life for a while, and I often thought of her but never tried to contact her and to this day I believe only I know.

I learnt a lot from the experience and had a great sexual awakening thanks to her and now knew what all the fuss this little subject of sex, without love or marriage or commitment was about, at least! That was way in the future, I thought, I wanted more of what I had and with different girls or women. But I did not want to be thought of by anyone as a randy airhead. I realised sex can be destructive as well as great fun and all women need to feel there is respect and that you care, even if it's not love, but I wasn't sure what love would be like or affect sexual relations; who does at eighteen years of age? I knew that I could not expect similar sex with any young girl of my age group and didn't seek that. I was still idealistic enough to want a conventional relationship with a girl, courtship, love maybe, getting to know someone and taking a new relationship step by step. I would not like to feel in any future relationship that my girl, fiancée, or wife would feel it necessary or desirable to have the sort of affair I had experienced. But at the same time, I delved in my store of memories of the affair and relived parts of it many times.

I found a job through a newspaper advert and started in my new position in a large company once again, but at trainee executive level which not only gave me more salary but offered the chance of career development and greater responsibility, something I felt a need for. The job was interesting enough for the time being and sufficiently well paid so that I could get some decent clothes and it took me away from my home town which I wanted to do so that I could develop new approaches to life in general and particularly in my relationships with the opposite sex. I also quickly forgot how my first affair had started, intending that any future relationships would be broader based and perhaps last longer and be out in the open. But I had been introduced to some pretty good, interesting, and satisfying sexual techniques as well as developing some myself and within a few months I was actively seeking a relationship, but this time not setting the bar too high.

I had a couple of unsatisfactory dates and some fumbled attempts at sex, but I discovered that the girls I was dating were either totally inexperienced and a bit scared of having full sex or were virgins, and I was definitely past the knee trembler stage and not satisfied with being tossed off or sucked off inexpertly. They were either too keen on a 'relationship' or were looking to keep their virginity until they were married or perhaps just plain stupid as well as naive.

So I thought I would try one or two slightly older girls, ones who looked like they might have experience without being sluts or were clearly not the marrying types at that stage, and I immediately got more interest, especially as by this stage disco dancing and pubbing were possible as I was over eighteen and had a few pounds in my pocket, and some half-decent gear.

My first bit of success was with a 22-year-old blonde hairdresser who had a good figure and a sexy look about her and was not currently dating anyone else. Rosy was her name, and she was not too fussy about dating a guy without a car, liked just going to the local town for a few drinks, maybe see a movie or even be content with a walk in the countryside, it being summer. She realised I was about three or four years younger than her and laughed when I mentioned her friends might accuse her of cradle snatching. She said, "Let them, I don't care; I think you are a bit of all right and know what's what!"

We had a couple of dates and went to the pub and then the cinema and I kissed her but didn't push it too hard and she seemed happy with that. Then I suggested we make a picnic, take a blanket and a couple of beers maybe and walk down a lane into the countryside which I had done alone before and knew there were a few nice-looking paths by the river. She said great idea, so we arranged to do it the following Saturday and I bought a packet of three, not bothered if they were not needed but thought it better to be prepared.

We held hands and walked a good distance from the town and down the riverbank to a little nook at a bend with some nice short grass and high hedgerows and spread our picnic. She had packed a bottle of wine wrapped in a towel so after we had a beer each and the cold chicken salad, we opened the wine and sat on the blanket relaxed and chatting. I decided it was time to make a move so I leaned on one elbow alongside her and kissed her on the lips making my lips soft and gentle like I had practised with my first lover and just rubbed the back of her neck and her bare arms. She started to breathe heavily and moaned a little so, taking that as a good sign, I progressed to feeling her tits and massaged them a little until I could feel her nipples hardening. I unbuttoned her blouse slowly and unhooked her bra and exposed her splendid breasts and then moved to kissing the nipples and nibbling them a little and she definitely liked that.

Suffice it to say that taking far more time than necessary I undressed her, touching and feeling her all the while until she only had small briefs on which were very sexy, and she hadn't bikini shaved I was pleased to see and so a small fringe of blonde pubic hair was visible, I liked that. I had removed my shoes and socks, trousers and shirt by this time and she was totally relaxed and lapping it all up. I masturbated her slowly just the outside lips and her clitoris, which was getting quite swollen by this time, as was my dick and she was moaning and groaning so I kept it up until she had a good strong orgasm, but I didn't stop there. I kept rubbing her gently on the little button even though her thighs were clenched shut at this point until she slowly opened them again and was clearly building up for a second orgasm when she breathlessly said, "Put it in, it's OK I'm on the pill!" So, I got my leg over her and slowly pushed my dick into her up to the hilt and after only about three full length strokes, she screamed and had a huge shuddering orgasm.

We lay there a few minutes while she panted her recovery, and I was still hard inside her not having yet come. I then started to slowly resume my rhythm, and she gasped at every stroke then I gradually increased the tempo until I knew I had to come soon, and I doubled my speed. We had a crashing simultaneous orgasm which lasted for several slower strokes until we were both finished. I didn't just roll off her, I settled down between her open thighs with her arms tight around me and we fell asleep!

"Well Rosy," I said when we awoke about half an hour later, "That was very nice, lovely day, lovely girl and a great fuck!"

She laughed and said, "Not bad for a beginner, I thought you looked like you knew what you were about, and you seem to. But what's for encores or are you ready to go now?"

I said, "Let's see, shall we?" and bit her nipple, not hard but enough that she said, "Ow," and grabbed my dick and squeezed it quite hard to which it responded immediately. She said, "Mmm, life in the old dog yet," and started to wank me off slowly pushing my foreskin up and back with one hand and cupping my balls with the other. I lay back so she could see what she was doing, and she took me in her mouth and slowly wanked me and ran her tongue all round my bell end just nibbling a bit to show who was boss. Her hair was loose and hanging over my tackle and I loved that. Then when she thought the end was swelling and getting ready to come again, she straddled me, put it in and rocked back and forth for a few strokes until she got a bit tired, and I took over and rolled her right over on her back and kept up a slow rhythmic movement until she came again. Then, as I was still hard I turned her over and thrust it up from the back which made her gasp and I reached round underneath her and put the end of my finger in her fanny so that it was in contact with her clitoris to ensure she was getting the best of two worlds and after about another two or three minutes, we both came again and this time I did collapse on her back with my finger still on her clitoris and my dick getting softer but still hard enough to stay inside her.

We lay like that a while until I said quietly in her ear, "Had enough for now?"

And she just nodded and fell asleep again. Phew, what a first sexual experience with my new woman! I felt drained but so satisfied as I hadn't had anything much since my last tryst in the sick room! And what a woman this little blonde turned out to be. I thought, this one will last a bit longer and I intend to nurture the relationship as long as the fun lasted. Or wait and see if it developed further than I anticipated.

Rosy and I had become a recognisable couple after a few weeks of great sex in all sorts of places, and she indicated that she might like us to meet up with her friends occasionally. I asked her if she was embarrassed to have a young boyfriend and she said not, she was proud of me, and I acted more her age anyway. So, we all met up in a pub one evening and they were all interested in me as a person and as Rosy's boyfriend. It seemed she had not told them much about me or discussed our private affairs, although one girlfriend of hers was looking at me speculatively and I wondered! But made an immediate mental note not to react to any come-on from her and to pay her just normal polite respect. Maybe it was a test, if so it didn't work, and Rosy seemed happy.

She was popular among the group, and we made sure we gave everyone more or less equal attention and didn't get too close or familiar in their company. Afterwards we held no post-mortem, it wasn't necessary, and our dating and lovemaking continued unabated, but a bit more in comfort as I had a small flat by this time with a king-sized bed squeezed into the one bedroom and a decent three-piece suite, record player and TV. We took it in turns when staying in to make something to eat or paid for a takeaway. This was a period of consolidation of our relationship, me getting used to my new job and colleagues and generally growing up, I guess. But I am sure that although we got on great together and had a fantastic sex life, neither of us was in love with each other, just really good mates all round.

This went on, this affair, for almost a year before we had our first spat and it wasn't anything very serious, just about what to watch on the box and we both had a laugh about it, made extra passionate love and forgot it, until the next time something caused a rift and I said, "Look, do we have a problem, are we beginning to get like all couples seem to or what?"

She said, "I don't think so but let's discuss it like adults shall we?"

So, we had a good conversation and I pointed out that although we were at my flat most nights, she still kept a room at her parents' and hadn't moved in exactly and that was OK with me but how did she feel about it? She said that although our relationship had everything she wanted, and she wasn't looking around or anything, but she was now twenty-five and getting a little bit concerned about her future but she didn't want to move out altogether and she didn't think I was 'the one' necessarily. I told her I felt the same other than the fact that I was only nineteen and felt it would be years before I wanted a permanent relationship and I respected her feelings and suggested we both pulled back a couple of steps, did some different things with different people. I, for example, was thinking about joining my pals at a pub as a member of their dart team, and taking up fishing again, something I had done at fifteen and sixteen years of age. She said she was thinking along similar lines but really wanted to maintain a sexual relationship and said how great we were in bed so that was something she definitely wanted to continue, and I agreed with that. "But," I said, "if you fancied someone else then you should maybe give it a go and see what happens."

I didn't mind a bit as long as she told me about it and was with a sensible person, no silly risky stuff.

She said she had nobody at all in mind and she doubted she could find someone as good as me but yes, she would consider it. However, unlike me, she didn't want to know if I had a dip into something else, no reports and no comparisons and that she would have to see what her feelings were should she learn or feel I was seeing another woman.

I said, "Well let's just carry on as we are, think about things and see how we get on, but if you do meet a bloke and end up in the sack with him, not in my flat of course, but elsewhere, I would like you to tell me honestly how it was and how you feel about us afterwards."

She said, "Fair enough, but if you do the same, I don't want to know unless it becomes serious."

Chapter 5

So began a different phase in my life. Job still good, pay not bad, I bought a little car, passed my driving test, and kept seeing Rosy on a regular basis at least three or four times week. Sometimes we would go out and see our friends, others to a film and at least twice a week she stayed over, and we had our usual great sex.

She didn't appear to have any other dates, or not sexually related at any rate. I didn't question her at all nor she me, and for a couple of months there was no discernible difference in our relationship. Then I noticed a new girl in the office who definitely interested me. She was demure and reserved but sexy in a non-provocative way. She was nicely dressed and sounded quite well educated and she seemed about the same age, or a bit older, than me.

Her name was Sarah and I learnt that she had come straight from college so I calculated she must be about twenty or twenty-one. I also was coming up to twenty so we were pretty evenly matched in years but not, I thought, in experience. She didn't particularly turn me on or get me horny at any time; she was cool and relatively undemonstrative and keen to get on with her job which involved style and fashion relating to production of clothing and female accessories.

I thought, *Hmm, could be a virgin, obviously well brought up and educated and had a degree in design or something like that, and keen to get on with making her job work for her.* I only spoke to her very occasionally in, for me, quite a restrained manner, and she seemed a bit shy but also quite confident and self-assured, a strange mixture, and for the first time with a girl I thought *"I'd like to get to know you"*, rather than *"I'd like to get in your knickers"*.

No way however was I going to try to seduce her, I was still in an excellent relationship with Rosy and sexually satisfied so there was no point in rocking that boat just because I was intrigued by another type of girl, especially as I still didn't see her in that way at all. I kept my distance, said nothing suggestive or crude and just observed her at work, and that was that.

Then one day Sarah stopped me as I was passing and said, "James, (everybody else called me Jim) would you like to take me to coffee today, my friend is away and I rather like going with someone I know, if only a little, rather than alone. I hope you don't mind me asking?"

I said, "Not at all, I usually go about ten-thirty across the road to the cafe, rather than the staff restaurant."

She said, "That would be fine thank you, see you at the entrance door here then if that's OK?"

So, she was not too shy to ask me for coffee, the question in my mind though, was she telling the truth that her friend was away today? Very interesting, I thought.

I freshened up, straightened my tie, and made sure my teeth were clean and mouth fresh. I was in the habit of keeping a toothbrush bag in my desk drawer as Rosy and I often met straight after leaving the office. At exactly ten-thirty, I sauntered up to our main office exit where I found Sarah waiting and looking exactly as she always did, cool calm and collected. I took her elbow to cross the street then dropped it as soon as we hit the kerb outside the cafe and just touched her lightly as I guided her through the door to a table near the window where I usually sat. I pulled out her chair and saw her seated before I sat opposite her and said, "Well, this was a nice surprise, I normally just read the *Daily Mail* while I have a late breakfast as I usually don't have time at my flat before work, late riser I'm afraid."

She laughed and said, "I sometimes have toast or a small cake with my coffee, because I too am a bit rushed in the mornings and my mum always says 'Sarah, bad habit skipping breakfast'." We had a nice friendly chat, and she had her cake and I had bacon and fried egg sandwich and a pot of tea, and she had coffee. And that was that. I didn't push at all on any subject outside work, and I didn't try to convert this innocent little meeting into a date. I thought, *I'm not even sure I want a date quite yet, if at all.* She was a very nice person, fresh and quite interesting and very correct and polite, so I was not at all sure this was going anywhere.

Then she said, "How would you like to take me to the annual office dinner and dance on Tuesday week? I would like to go but don't have a partner to take me and I would be grateful for you to escort me there and back, and of course sit with me at dinner and have a dance or two. I know you have a car if you don't mind driving me there and I have two tickets for the dinner, which is smart casual not dinner suit. I believe there will be a small band playing as well as a disco so a bit of jiving is about all I can do except a straightforward waltz."

This little speech left her a bit breathless as she waited anxiously for my reaction.

I said what a nice thought, I would love to take her but that I would certainly pay for my ticket, and I was quite happy to drive her there and home, so her parents needn't worry about her. She said how had I guessed that this was a worry for her, and she wanted them to be secure in the knowledge that she was in good hands so just to cement that, would I kindly come to dinner at their house say on Friday night so that they could see this nice colleague she had told them about?

Thinking quickly, I realised that, as luck would have it, I was not committed to either the Friday coming or the week Tuesday: and as I knew nothing about the staff dinner and dance party I had not mentioned it to Rosy so all was well, and I could explain exactly what had happened and how I was effectively being vetted as a suitable escort for this sweet young girl. Perfect, except Rosy had said she didn't want to know about any dates I might have and let's face it, this was a date!

In the event I chose to say nothing to Rosy, and she had things on those two days, so it all seemed fine.

On the Friday, having been given directions to her parents' house, I dressed smart casual, picked up a decent bottle of wine and presented myself at the front door of their very nice four-bedroom detached house in a good area and a quiet street, with plenty of parking. Most houses had small drives and double or single garages. About what I would have guessed from observing Sarah's manners, clothing, and education, I thought.

She met me at the door when I walked up the short drive and welcomed me in with a big smile and a little peck on the cheek. We went through to the sitting room where her parents and a younger brother were seated waiting.

Her father stood and said, "Hello, I'm George. You must be James, and this is my wife Felicity and our son William."

He welcomed me to their home and accepted the bottle of wine saying, "Ah a good Rioja, just the job, this will go well with dinner. What would you like to drink?"

I replied, "Very nice to meet you all; have you any alcohol-free beer so that I can have a glass of wine without worrying about driving later?"

He beamed his approval and said, "Sure, I often have one and so does William, although we are happy for him to have the odd beer or glass of wine."

Felicity was an older version of Sarah with a trim figure and a ready smile but sexier (watch yourself Jim) and I thought, *don't look too interested in her figure or anything*, but I had immediate thoughts of my first affair with an older woman and said to myself, *I bet this lady can go a bit!* She leaned forward so I followed Sarah's meeting by giving Felicity a kiss on the cheek and shook hands with George and William.

We had a pleasant evening and a very nice dinner of beef stroganoff and steamed chocolate pudding with cream, fruit and nuts on the table if desired. I had one glass of the Rioja and then just coffee afterwards and went home leaving about ten p.m., congratulating myself on a good evening's performance as a sensible reliable chap, etc. I was thinking though, that if anything, I would rather have the mother than the daughter, given the choice!

The following day was Saturday, and I was meeting Rosy at lunchtime as we had arranged to go for a pub lunch by the river, then go for a walk along the riverbank. Then we planned a night in at my flat watching TV and having a light supper and then the usual romp in the sack afterwards. We had a nice day and evening, and the sex afterwards was very good as always, but I did catch myself thinking of Felicity and speculating how good she might be as I made love with Rosy.

So for the next week I saw Rosy once again on the Wednesday and said I was going to the works 'do' on the Saturday and apologised that I hadn't got a ticket for her. She said it was fine as she had a date with a girlfriend and two blokes whom she had not met, but she was sure it was just a friend type thing with no set ideas as to what was happening, other than going for a drink or two at the local pub.

I said, "That's cool, let me know how you got on when we meet at Sunday lunchtime and I will tell you about my date as well, with a colleague from work who I have volunteered to escort, as she was new and a bit shy."

Chapter 6

I was reflecting one day about life in general and was quite pleased with the way things had gone both work-wise and socially. Here I was only twenty and had a steady fulfilling sex life with my regular squeeze Rosy, a wonderful first experience behind me with the older secretary at my previous job, who I had not tried to contact at all, preferring to respect her sufficiently not to want to rock her boat or cause her any problems. Having said that, I often thought about all she had shown me almost two years before and for sure I would never forget her.

Not only that, but I had a possibility of a new type of relationship with Sarah, although it was Felicity, her mother, who I really fancied, so any relationship with Sarah was fraught with potential difficulties. I didn't want to get into a situation which could become embarrassing. Plus, it might affect Sarah's career and mine, not to mention the sheer morality of it all by the possibility of me making love to mother and daughter, not a good idea, but hard to ignore Felicity's appeal. It might turn out that Felicity did not fancy me at all, and Sarah might not want to get into a sexual relationship with me or anyone else at this stage of her life.

I reasoned, however, that there was no harm in having a few dates with Sarah if she wanted to, and I could re-evaluate as it went along and either kick it into touch if it became boring or too complicated. I had Rosy to keep the lid on my sexual kettle meantime. But I told myself it was all good practice for what I fully expected one day, to meet the woman of my dreams and 'forsaking all others' as the refrain goes. But I honestly could not see myself being celibate other than with one chosen partner, for years at a time. But I liked and respected women enough not to want to hurt anyone and determined to avoid that if at all possible.

For the time being it was steady as you go with Rosy, keep an eye on Sarah and ask her out for a couple of dates, and keep my eyes open for any new and interesting crumpet as well. I considered these reasonable objectives under current circumstances and smiled at a memory of an older brother once saying to me, "You look at life through the eye of your penis my lad."

My reply had been, "Well I'm only following your example," and he laughed and said, "Perhaps, but look where it got me!" referring I think to the fact he was not terribly happy in his marriage and had certainly been pretty indiscriminate with his extracurricular activities. I was determined not to follow his path and play the game a bit more intelligently, or at least thoughtfully and carefully. Ah, the best-laid plans of mice and men.

After a fairly boring day at the office, I saw Sarah coming in my direction at about a quarter to five. She smiled, and I waved to her, and she came to my workplace. I pulled out a chair and asked how things were. She said fine but a bit slow regarding her ambitions involving some new designs she was working on, so I grasped the opportunity and said, "I've had a fairly boring day on my latest project today, so how about you call your mum and say you are going straight out with me tonight, we will eat out, home before, say, ten-thirty?"

She said, "Great idea where shall we go?"

I said, "How about a walk first along the river and call at the Green Dragon after, as I know they do good food there?"

"Great," she said, "I've got flat shoes on so no problems, I will call her and go and freshen up and see you about twenty minutes at the door, OK?"

I replied, "Fantastic, see you then." I went to the loo, cleaned my teeth and had a quick shave with a throw-away razor. Then I straightened my tie, combed my hair, etc., and we met at the door after I had waited only a couple of minutes. As always, she looked as cool and fresh as a cucumber.

I cautioned myself mentally not to rush her in any way, just wait and see what happens and certainly don't make any silly moves sexually as that might be a premature end to what was becoming a very nice little relationship.

We parked in the pub car park, and I popped in and told them my car number and said we would be back between seven-thirty and eight. I reserved a nice table for two by a window overlooking the river and they said, "No problem, sir, is it a special occasion?"

I laughed and said, "Could be."

We held hands and meandered down the riverbank where there was lots of wildlife, the odd fisherman or dog walker and just a few other couples strolling like us. I had found holding hands is one test of warmth and compatibility, and this time it felt good. She talked a bit about her current project, and I filled her in on mine and then we moved on to discuss things of mutual interest, wildlife being one. I discovered she knew a fair bit about the species seen as did I, and we both saw and recognised various wild fowl like a great crested grebe, moorhens, mallard ducks, swans, and river martins (like the swallows who nest up against our house eaves and in barns) who make their nest in holes in the steeper parts of the eroded riverbank. She, like me, knew about predators like cormorants, wild mink — escapees from farms, pike, and suchlike, and I was surprised when she also was knowledgeable about the kinds of fish in the river such as chub, roach, eels, perch, carp and tench, even barbel, a very elusive fish, difficult to catch by anglers and fierce fighters when hooked. I never had known a woman to know all these fish were there, and she was not an angler, and neither were her father or brother. Turns out she was very interested in ecology, the environment, especially river and sea pollution. She was a bit concerned that I was a fisherman until I explained I used barbless hooks and put all the fish back at the end of the day except for large pike which kill so many other fish, and she accepted some control over their numbers was probably justifiable.

We got a couple of miles along the river when I suggested we should think about turning back but first, I suggested we sat on the dry shorn grass of a meadow, which had already been cut for silage some weeks before.

She said, "OK how long have we got?" and I replied, "Oh about twenty minutes I guess; we shall be quicker going back, and I have booked a table for seven-thirty to eight if you think you can last that long."

We climbed a five barred gate and I spread my jacket and we sat under an oak tree, and I immediately put my arm round her shoulders. I said how lovely it had been and how I would never have guessed she was so knowledgeable about wildlife and river fish. She blushed with pleasure and looked directly at me and said, "You too, most boys I have known are really ignorant on these subjects."

She was only inches from my face, and I couldn't resist trying a kiss. I kissed her on the lips slowly and softly and she did the same. Then we both pulled reluctantly away, and she looked me right in the eyes and said, "And I certainly would never have thought you could kiss like that," and she moved to kiss me again soft lips moving a little but no tongue and nothing too hurried. For the first time with her I felt a stirring in my loins, not an embarrassing thumping hard-on, thank God.

We embraced and had a nice snogging session for about ten minutes, and it was lovely, no panting breath no wriggling about with fear or suppressed sexuality that I could detect, just very, very nice. I looked at my watch and said reluctantly that we should make a move and helped her to her feet, back over the gate and hand in hand we meandered back to the pub arriving about ten minutes to eight. On our reserved table was a nice bunch of fresh flowers and a chilled bottle of white wine in a bucket!

She said, "Oh you shouldn't."

I replied, "I didn't, I just replied to his question was it a special day, said could be, and it is."

She said, "I think you were right, a day to remember."

I smiled and said I agreed.

I had a beer as I was thirsty and Sarah asked for a bottle of sparkling water to mix with the Beaujolais and mixed herself a spritzer, and after I had downed the beer, I joined her in the same.

We looked at the menu and she chose avocado vinaigrette, so I said, "And me." That was followed by fresh Dover sole, highly recommended by the landlord, and fresh strawberries and cream for dessert. It was wonderful and we both really enjoyed it so much. We both had coffee afterwards and she had a small vodka liqueur, but I declined a brandy as I was driving. What a meal, and Sarah insisted on paying half, so I reluctantly accepted.

We left the pub a bit later than expected at quarter to eleven so Sarah phoned her mum and explained. Her mother said, "Don't worry, you have your key, and we are going to bed shortly, so glad you had such a pleasant time and hope to see James again soon."

We kissed in the car, this time leaving us both a little breathless and I watched her get through the front door. She waved before she closed it, and I went back to my flat a very thoughtful Jim.

I slept like a log and woke up thinking of the date last night and thought to myself that I had better take this new affair very slowly and carefully so as not to get too involved, at least until I was pretty sure where we were going with it.

But at work my eyes sought her out as I got near enough and approached my workstation, and she was looking over and gave me a cheery wave.

The next couple of months were interesting as my long-term affair with Rosy continued unabated and still, we had very good sexual relations but we neither of us was too bothered about seeing our so-called mutual friends or socialising much with anyone else. On the other side of the equation my slow-paced relationship with Sarah continued to develop along a more conventional path with the occasional visit to the parents or a cinema and, while the weather remained good, our favourite walk along the river and to the pub.

I decided to try out a proposal to introduce Sarah to coarse fishing and she agreed albeit a bit reluctantly at first, so I gave her the use one of my lighter rods and took a fold-up camp stool for her to sit on while I sat on my fishing kit box. She was a bit squeamish about putting live maggots or worms on a hook, so I made small bread pellets for her and took a tin of sweet corn and some luncheon meat, and we baited her up for roach, bass, carp, rudd and so on while I used maggots and worms. I made sure her line was strong enough to pull in a fair-sized fish without too much risk of her inexperience causing a loss of a fish and/or tackle.

I also put her fishing on the bottom while I trotted with the flow of the river, and I threw some ground bait near her float to attract feeding fish. Typically, she had beginners' luck and got a stupendous bite straight away and I helped her land a very nice tench weighing about 4 lbs which is quite a good size on these waters for a tench. She was really excited about landing the fish but also concerned about its welfare. I had already put the keep net into the river attached to an aluminium rod with a spike on the bottom and a screw attachment for the top hoop of the keep net, and I showed her how to hold the fish properly without distressing it, detach the barbless hook from its lip, and put it in the keep net where it could be seen happily swimming round.

Then she re-baited the hook and cast in again, while I missed a bite and re-baited mine and continued trotting for a while and, sure enough I caught two or three smallish roach on maggot which joined the tench in the keep net. Then a bit of excitement as a pike took a fish I had been landing and I carefully reeled him alongside where I gaffed him in his gill and pulled him onto the bank. It was a jack, or juvenile pike of about 5 or 6 lbs weight, and I allowed it back into the river a few yards downstream.

Then I changed the tackle a bit and put heavier lines and tackle on both rods and baited them up; one with a large chunk of luncheon meat about 2 cm square, and the other with several sweet corn kernels on the one hook. And heavier lead weights, so that they could be cast further out, and both with the hooks and baits sitting on the bottom of the river. I shot a few pieces of meat and sweet corn out into the area where we had cast as ground bait, using a special angler's catapult with a large pouch with holes in on the end, and put two little bells secured with clamps onto the ends of our two rods. Then we got the picnic and cool box out for lunch. Cool beer and lemonade and pork pie, potato salad and pickled onions and some cheese and a couple of wholemeal buns we had buttered earlier, great fisherman's lunch!

We had our drinks and consumed the rest, apart from a couple of chocolate bars and an apple or pear each, when a bell started to ring and my rod was jumping up and down on its rest, secured fortunately with a clamp to the rest. I released the clamp, grabbed the rod, and struck upwards straight away and I hooked a fine fish which I knew was a carp by the way it set off like a train towards the far riverbank. I slowed him down a bit using the flexibility of the rod so he couldn't snap the line and he eventually ran out of river, and steam. I reeled him back to our side of the river, allowing him to make a couple more breaks for freedom, while keeping the line tight, so that the hook didn't get spat out. He tired gradually to the point where I was able to bring him gently sliding into the landing net. What a beauty, a common carp with silver scales and reddish fins and the typical large rubber-lipped mouth.

He was about two feet long and nearly a foot deep, but my scales were not suitable for weighing him, but I guessed he was about 25 lbs in weight. Far short of any record, but a very large carp for this stretch of the river, probably about fifteen years old, judging from the size and number of scales, and his body depth. He was in perfect condition. We took a photo of him, and I picked him up with both hands correctly positioned under him and slid him straight back into the river. With one lash of his tail, he disappeared down to the bottom, heading for the middle of the river I guessed, the safest part.

Sarah was fascinated and said that she had never seen such a fish before and never imagined there were any like it each time we had walked down the bank together. I asked her if that meant she might like to come again sometime and she said yes, but not on a rainy or windy day when bad weather gear might be needed. She confessed that she may only become a fair-weather fisherman.

On another date we went looking for mushrooms down a lane I knew, where there were many old mature trees alongside the cow pastures there, and I had found some great big mushrooms growing in the long grass right under the trees where the cattle gathered for shade, and inevitably left their cow pats scattered around, ideal compost for mushrooms. We didn't find any large ones, but further out in the shorter grass, we found about a dozen pink gilled mushrooms, some at button stage and others fully opened to three or four inches across. We took them back to my flat and I cooked a mixed grill with bacon, kidney, a small lamb chop each, a couple of eggs fried with the mushrooms using the fat from the grill, and new potatoes. We had a bottle of beer and some good red wine — a Rioja, and then after washing up, we sat and watched an old movie on TV and kissed and cuddled on the sofa.

We were very comfortable together with our relationship and I was not expecting it when one such evening after a nice pub meal and a few drinks Sarah looked me in the eyes and said, "Don't you really fancy me, Jim?"

I said, "Of course but I—" and she interrupted me with a very passionate kiss and started to open my flies. I said, "You do realise that this will lead us to bed; are you sure that's what you want?"

She replied, "Yes if it's also what you want."

I said yes, I did want, but said also what about protection and she said, "I have been on the pill since the first time you kissed me; I'm ready for it."

I simply kissed her and began to undress her, and she helped me out of my clothes as well until we were both naked and kissing and touching and I said, "Let's get into bed," and we walked together and did just that. No big fireworks, just very nice gentle lovemaking, and she appeared to have made love before, although was no expert, so I modified my usual approach a bit but made her come before I entered her, and she came again a couple of times in the next hour as did I.

She was expected home, although by this time there was no problem checking with mum, she would have gone to bed happy, knowing that Sarah was with me but even so, after a quick shower I took her home by midnight and all was well. I went back to the flat somewhat gobsmacked. She had planned this to a T, I was being very slow as I feared deep involvement at this point and thought she might be a virgin. Wrong but happily wrong, but now I had a dilemma: continue with both my lovers? Or finish with one of them? And the sex with Sarah, while good, was not earth-shattering and certainly not so intense as with Rosy, but I really liked Sarah and enjoyed her company, so rationalised that sex was only part of a complete relationship and was in any case quite satisfactory, and of course may get better with practice!

Chapter 7

I knew it was a dangerous game to play but I had not reached a firm decision when my next date with Rosy came around and I justified my action by saying to myself that I was not in love with either of them and wanted to give time for sex and my relationship with Sarah to develop and mature, and I also didn't want to give up my long relationship with Rosy or the great sexual relationship we still had.

So I met Rosy at a different pub to the one I used with Sarah and in a completely different area so there was little chance of our paths crossing. We greeted each other affectionately as always and had our usual bantering, joking, non-serious conversation, had a nice meal and back to my place for a good session in bed. off she went home at about one a.m. without a care in the world. And so, my relationship with both my ladies continued in similar vein for a few weeks with sex occurring with them both about once or twice a week and both experiences remaining as before, intense, and more overt passion with Rosy, and slower gentler sex with Sarah, but no change in range or intensity, which was fine.

Then a huge change in my routine happened unexpectedly one afternoon, when I called to see Sarah at home as she had a day off, and I wondered if she was unwell because she hadn't mentioned anything to me. Not that it was so unusual, as we didn't always talk every day at work and were quite relaxed about each other's movements. I left work at lunchtime saying I had an appointment with a dentist and drove round to Sarah's house. I parked in the drive, knocked on the door and after a short delay I heard Felicity say, "Who is it?"

I said, "It's James, everything OK?"

And she said, "Oh James, yes, just a moment." She opened the front door in a dressing gown and slippers, gave me a big hug and a nice kiss on the cheek, and invited me in saying, "Sorry about the robe, I was just about to have a shower after my workout."

I said, "Oh sorry, I was just checking Sarah was OK and don't want to disturb anybody." She laughed and said there was nobody to disturb but her, as George and William had gone to an event at George's college and Sarah had gone to London for the day with an old girlfriend and wouldn't be back "'til late.

"Oh," I said, "I was a bit concerned not to see her at work that's all."

She said, "Well, as you are here, would you like a coffee or a beer and a sandwich maybe? I was just going to have a bite of lunch before I showered."

I said, "Are you sure?" and she said she certainly was, as it was the first time we had been alone together, so we could have a proper conversation without worrying about other people's ideas or interruptions, giving me a very big smile. As she passed me on her way to the kitchen her slipper caught on something and she almost fell and I caught her in my arms; her robe opened, and she had nothing on underneath! Wow, I just couldn't resist it, I drew her towards me and kissed her full on the lips and she responded immediately with a passionate kiss and let her robe drop to the floor. I ran my hands down her back and then cupped her firm muscular buttocks and she thrust her groin towards me and so I responded by pulling one hand back and put a finger straight into her slit. She abandoned the kiss and gave a huge groan as I masturbated her while she hung round my neck, groaning, and she came very quickly with three loud gasps.

She then opened my fly without any hesitation and took out my member, which was hard, and said, "Put it in me please now."

So I backed her against the kitchen wall put my hands under her thighs and lifted her up and put it where she asked, and I was surprised because was a very tight fit and we had great passionate sex standing in the kitchen. She came again with more groans, and I did too.

I put her on her feet and said, "Wow where did that come from?"

She replied, "I saw the way you looked at me on the first day we met, and I have wanted this to happen so much. Don't worry, there is no problem, I will explain to you after lunch, but I will shower first. I want you to come in the shower with me please, you are not finished yet I am sure, as this is the first real sex I have had for years, so please just do it for me."

How could I refuse? the die was cast, we were now very involved and had to sort out exactly how we were going to treat this massive change in our relationship, and I wanted to know why. What the hell was going on, but more importantly I wanted more of it.

But first things first, the shower together and whatever else she wanted. Suffice it to say I enjoyed it immensely. She had a superb body, toned and athletic and she obviously worked hard at it and the result was that she looked and felt like twenty-five not forty-five, which she must be I reckoned. Not that I cared about that; I really fancied her a lot and had fantasised about having her, many times but never dreamed I would. We soaped and fondled each other and made love in the shower and again on her bed, and finally she said, "I knew you fancied me, and I fancied you from the moment I set eyes on you, but I honestly had no idea you could do what you have done for me today. You have more than fulfilled my expectations. I only dreamed of sex like that and really thought it would never happen."

We showered again and dressed and tidied up everything before going down for a late lunch about three p.m., a sandwich and a beer followed by a coffee and a chat!

"So," I said, "Tell me all about it please and leave nothing out. I really need to know what has made this happen and where therefore we go from here, not so much because of George, but I do not want to hurt Sarah in any way."

She replied, "Of course, and we won't. First, she must never even suspect us, and second you must keep seeing her for a while at least as I believe your relationship with her will not last, at least as a lover, possibly as a friend but never more than that."

I said, "How can you say that? We are having sex and get on really well."

She said, "Well, that may be so, but tell me, is it great sex? Like you have had with others I am sure, and you just had several times with me? Or is it just, OK?"

I looked at her hard and said, "What exactly are you getting at? It's fine and we enjoy it together; not all sex can be like you mention, so what's the subtext?"

41

She said, "I had hoped by now you and she would have reached what is to me an obvious conclusion: that she is not turned on by you. You want to know why, it's because she is more turned on by her female friend."

I said, "Are you trying to tell me she is a lesbian, because I just don't believe it?"

"Not necessarily a lesbian," she replied, "but she has definitely had affairs with three different girls, and they have used a sex toy, including penetration of one or both of them, of that I am certain. That is why, I am sure, you discovered she was not a virgin, even though she might have seemed like one, she has been struggling with gender problems from puberty and we have talked about this a lot, but not specifically about you of course."

I was gobsmacked and said feebly, "Well you are right that I suspected she might be a virgin and that is why I didn't just get on with the job. It was she who precipitated sex with me, and it's also true that there were no fireworks, but she had orgasms and enjoyed the sex, I thought."

"Well of course, she had no comparison to measure herself against. And there is no doubt you are both very fond of each other, have much in common and enjoy each other's company immensely. But do you love each other in a man-woman way; is there ever going to be fireworks? Is she a suitable long-term partner for a man with your appetites? I very much doubt it."

I said, "Put like that, probably not, but it would destroy her to know about us."

And she replied, "I know, and we must make sure she never does, not for a long time anyway."

"So, tell me" I said, "What is the problem with George; don't tell me he is otherwise inclined?"

"No, he is relatively normal, not confused about his gender and happy and content with life, but he is totally unaware of my frustration that his idea of a sex life is based on his need to have sex maybe once a month, lasting about five minutes, when he ejaculates then that's it. He just doesn't know, because I was the first one he had reached that position with, and I was too young and inexperienced to understand or to try to change him."

"Bloody hell!" I said. "So you haven't tried it with anybody else until now?"

"No, I haven't; believe me, I have been tempted, but I just couldn't risk destroying our marriage, which, sex apart, is nigh on perfect. You have released me from a self-imposed prison, for which I shall always be grateful, but I beg you, do not let me down. I have trusted you as no other and I just hope my judgement is right."

I thought about this for a few minutes, and I said, "Thank you, and yes I believe you are right, but one never knows what may happen, as this is not just up to me, it's equally up to you Sarah, and serendipity."

She said, "Thank God; I will make you very glad you said that, and I trust you to do everything you can to protect my family from what would be disaster. It's a big ask but believe me I will more than repay you in the way you like, for as long as you want me to." I kissed her and said, "It's a big responsibility, so let's get it right first time of asking. I will continue to date Sarah and make love with her as long as she clearly wants to, and I don't care about her seeing her female friends for whatever she wants to see them about. I will assume an attitude of complete ignorance, and if she chooses to tell me I will go along with whatever scenario she likes, for a while at least. But that is conditional on you doing the same with me as we just have today, whenever it is safe and sensible to do so, and making sure George never finds out, and all will be well."

She said, "You are a very mature young man for your age, a fantastic lover and a very good person. I will not disappoint you I promise."

We sat and chatted for a bit and George and William arrived for our first big test, having had a great day at William's College, and neither of them was particularly surprised to see me there alone with Felicity, because they both knew Sarah was in London and it didn't take a genius to realise that I had come round looking for her, as I hadn't been aware of her outing. Being such nice, ordinary, happy people, they never suspected a thing, so it was relatively easy to play the part, have dinner with them, and await Sarah's return from London.

We had a pleasant evening chatting and laughing, and Felicity was clearly happy with everything and at one point George said, "You are on good form, darling, Jim must come and entertain you again in our absence as he has clearly made it a good day for you." We all laughed and I said, "I would be delighted to, but I'm not sure Sarah would be so pleased."

"Don't be silly," said Felicity, "she will be very happy that we have entertained each other in her, and the rest of the family's, absence."

"Hear, hear!" said George. Bless him, it was very clear right then that she was fully capable of feeding him the right lines to keep him happy; good on her I thought.

Sarah arrived exhausted by taxi at close to midnight and was very surprised to find all the family up and me clearly awaiting her arrival. She looked a bit shocked at first then realised we were all happy and smiling and she immediately relaxed. Felicity said, "Have a nice day darling with Patty?"

Sarah replied, "Yes, fantastic, she is such a good sport, and we had a great time together seeing everything we wanted to, a nice lunch and then dinner on the train as a treat."

Great, we all said and then I said that she looked a bit tired so that now we all knew she was safe and sound back home, I thought I would get home too and catch up on my beauty sleep! Sarah saw me to the front door, and after a cheery call goodnight to the others I gave her a goodnight kiss and off I went to my flat, breathing a huge sigh of relief.

Chapter 8

We entered the most significant development of all our lives although all but Felicity and I were unaware this was the case. I was determined to change nothing until I had chance to evaluate all the options and difficulties, so I saw Rosy the following night and relaxed with her, as there were no apparent concerns in our relationship, and I thought not seeing her without a good reason which I could talk about, was the best option pro tem.

She, by this time had bought a flat of her own with a deposit from her parents — probably glad to see the back of her at almost twenty-eight years of age, or was it twenty-nine? — And she proudly took me back there, where I admired all she had done, and we christened her king-sized bed. We stayed the night together as it was a Friday, so no work tomorrow and despite my exertions with Felicity and the emotional turmoil, I performed as usual and so did she, what a gal! In the morning we had a light breakfast and a pub lunch and said goodbye, as she had another date with her girl pal and the two blokes they had been seeing. Rosy said that there was nothing going on with them so far worth talking about, but it was a change and a bit of fun, so I responded saying, "Way to go Gal," and left it at that.

I confess I had thoughts of Felicity when I was making love with Rosy, but not primarily for comparison purposes, just thinking how lucky I was and how different the sex was, both good, but Felicity had the edge probably due to the urgency and long, long time of relative abstinence she had endured. Be interesting whether it remained at that level of intensity or not! And Felicity, despite her age, was tighter and more muscular and yes, more grateful!

So now for the first time in my short life at age almost twenty-one, I had three lovely women to contend with. One 45-ish, well preserved and really sexy, the second her daughter who was tight also and fit but not nearly so sexy as her mother, and Rosy, number three and my long-term squeeze, who was performing as well as ever she did. All content with the situation bearing in mind only Felicity was aware of Sarah being taken care of as well as her, but neither Rosy nor Sarah was aware of either of the other two, and Felicity knew nothing about Rosy. Hmmm, not ideal but potentially manageable, for a while at lease. Certainly, I was not minded to actively seek a further sexual commitment.

In fact, for the first time since I was a teenager, I was not looking at every bit of crumpet I saw with thoughts of having them. But I did happen to notice a few who were speculatively looking at me, and I thought, no way baby, but thank you.

Life went on more or less as usual regarding Rosy and Sarah, odd dates and trips and occasional lovemaking when it was remotely possible without risk. Rosy was scrumptious as always and Sarah maintained her cool but pleasant lovemaking, quite a nice contrast I suppose. So far nothing more from Felicity, so I began to worry a bit. I shouldn't have because she called me one day and said, "I can't wait for another similar opportunity at home, so how about you book a room at a Travelodge or similar, say at lunchtime tomorrow and take a half day off, and I will meet you wherever it is for lunch and an afternoon in the room. Then we just go our separate ways and bobs your uncle!"

And I replied, "And Fannie's your aunt, or rather your fanny will be mine for the day."

She laughed and said, "Deal, call me with the time and place, and we will take it from there. I have my car so no problems with transport, and no one need be any the wiser."

I booked at a Premier Lodge, near a motorway junction, in a false name and paid cash in advance. I took the key and went to the hotel bar and phoned Felicity who said, "I know it; I will be there at twelve-thirty, OK?"

I said, "Great I will be sitting in the restaurant bar waiting for you, business meeting so be smart and maybe have a folder or briefcase or similar."

She agreed she would, and it was a good plan and we both said see you later and rang off.

I had a pint of bitter while I waited, and in she came looking the part, with a smart skirt and blouse and a small, zipped bag under one arm. She walked straight up to me and offered her cheek which I gave an air kiss and we sat at the bar while I ordered a gin and tonic, which we then took to a table in the restaurant and settled in. She was dazzling and fully made up with earrings, the whole works, and I complimented her and told her she looked fantastic. She replied that I didn't look too bad myself considering the heavy load I was carrying! I replied that I intended to shift a good part of that load onto or into her! She liked that. We looked at the menu and I ordered a sirloin steak with new potatoes and salad, and she had the surf and turf, a portion of king prawns in shell and a 6-oz steak, with just salad. We decided a bottle of wine was in order and she chose a light crisp Bordeaux white which she said was good for her, and I replied that I would get a large glass of Rioja to be going on with, and added, "What time have we got?"

She indicated no fixed time, it was all covered until ten p.m. at least, as she was meeting old business acquaintances at a conference on health and exercise in town somewhere. I thought great and said I was good until whenever she was, and she smiled.

This was the thing I particularly liked about her; she was fit, smart, educated and very sexy as well. It was a shame, but poor old George just had no idea what he had, and never would. But credit to her, she was going to stick with him for everyone's sake, but she sure wasn't going to act like a nun any more. And she was ageless, could be anything between thirty and forty and good even at that age. But of course, my first lover who took my cherry was twelve years or so older than me at the time, so I knew age meant nothing.

We savoured every mouthful of the meal and the wine, and I had a glass from her bottle to finish my meal with and then we had coffee, she with a port and me with a good old brandy. I asked her if she had brought any drinks and she said not so I ordered another bottle of the same Bordeaux, and we went to our room.

This time we both knew what to expect and had plenty of time, so we kissed a while and then slowly undressed each other on the king-size bed. and then I took time kissing her all over including the secret lips, which she liked. Then we made love for the first time that day very slowly at first, then gathering speed as we both got into the mood, ending the first session with a crashing mutual orgasm lasting long for me, and a similar long three spasms from her.

Then we rested a little with a glass each of wine and shared a bottle of water, and I casually leaned over and tweaked her nipples and she equally casually leant down and after licking my balls and taking each one carefully into her mouth for a while, she knelt between my thighs and kissed my knob and ran her tongue round the circumference and then slowly took it in her mouth to the bottom of my shaft, before pulling back for a breath. Then she demonstrated her superb fitness and her muscular thighs by squatting over me and putting the end in her vulva, slowly started to rise and fall on it to its full extent, mainly with her thigh and calf muscles. She kept this up for about five minutes and then I took over, settling her down on me and I flexed my buttocks, into the soft bed and thrust up and back, steadying her so she didn't slip out until once again we both came. Fabulous, really fabulous.

After that we just lazed and talked, had another brief session, and then fell asleep for a while. We then showered and got dressed and went down to my car, where I deposited my small bag, having put the room keys in the box provided in reception. We kissed and said goodbye until the next time, and drove off our separate ways, speaking for myself, very content with our re-acquaintance. A quick phone call was made to me as I went to bed to say all was well and thanks, see you soon.

When I woke up the following morning, I immediately thought I don't believe this is happening, how lucky can a man get? Even though there were risks, with Felicity on the case I was pretty confident she would protect her family whatever happened, and I was equally determined not to hurt anyone if I possibly could manage that. Still, no room for complacency; I must be alert to all possibilities and ready to react accordingly.

First things first, negotiate my next meeting with Sarah in as casual a manner as I could but being wary all the time not to let anything slip out which might indicate something untoward. That morning I was a bit late getting into the office and a glance in Sarah's direction confirmed she was in and looking cheerful and relaxed. I gave her a little wave; we were an item of course in the office, so no harm there and my phone rang as I sat at my desk and Sarah just said, "Coffee at ten-thirty usual place," and I replied sure, and put the phone down. I got through the first work session and met her at the door as usual at ten-thirty prompt and off we toddled over the road to our favourite cafe where she had an 'Americano' and a toasted tea cake and I had a pot of tea with a bacon, sausage and fried egg sandwich. I was pretty hungry having had no breakfast and a strenuous evening the day before!

She looked calm and relaxed as always, but I knew that meant nothing. She was like the proverbial serene swan on the calm river, floating along quietly but against the current so the legs were paddling furiously beneath the surface, but I had no reason to think this was so, just my cautious thinking.

She said, "I had been meaning to ask you, how did you and Mum get on that day when you discovered she was all alone? No embarrassing moments?"

I calmly took a big bite of my toasted sandwich, licked some yolk off my lips, took a sip of tea and replied, "No everything was fine, she is a really nice person and I get on as well with her alone as when you are there, no difference really." I followed that up immediately with "How did your day with your friend go in London, did you do anything special?"

"Well London is always special but no, we shopped a bit, had some lunch and then went to an exhibition of contemporary clothing, including some new stuff from a house where I know people through design work."

I persisted and said, "So this is an old friend" from university days?"

She said, "Yes, I've known her since I started university and we have kept in touch. I'm hoping to introduce you sometime, I'm sure she will like you."

"Great," I said, "I will look forward to that."

I then went on about something relating to my work and she replied with similar 'in-house' gossip and we left the subject behind without a ripple.

So, I thought no revelations, no drama, business as usual. I said, "So when are you going to come and see my new flat? It's more or less shipshape now so either we can have a meal in or go out to eat. Tomorrow night suit you?"

"Yes, that's good," she said, "I am dying to see it. Are you pleased you have bought now rather than renting; such a waste of money renting, isn't it? I am hoping to get my own place soon if Mum and Dad will help with the deposit. I'm still paying off education loans, but they should be history quite soon. Then we will have choices of where to get together in our own environment rather than in some sleazy hotel."

I almost choked on my sandwich, but managed to reply "Absolutely, wouldn't want that, but meantime I have a new bed I'd like you to check out."

She laughed and said, "I thought you would never get round to that offer; it seems ages since we last made love, can't wait!"

I puzzled over this latest change of attitude in Sarah, actually talking about sex like this and I wondered what had, in fact, happened in London, not that I cared about the fact she might have had sex with her female friend, but if so, what had precipitated a change in her regard for our lovemaking? Then I thought, *hold on Jim boy, bit premature old chap, wait and see what happens rather than speculating about the unknown.* So, I tried to put it from my mind and didn't bother contacting Rosy or Felicity, preferring instead, and for a change, to think about other matters like fishing, flat decoration, etc. I had elicited a preference to going out from Sarah, as she rightly observed that I probably didn't know where everything was as yet, so suggested that we wait a while on that one. I thought, fishing no, but the same pub where we went after the first walk along the river might be a good idea, and I booked the same table.

Work was interesting at this point, and I was having to embrace a new computer system. I was given a young assistant, male thankfully, who I was training up, and who came for coffee with me the next morning, so no Sarah this time. I left Sarah a message that I would pick her up at home, to save her driving, and I didn't tell her where I had booked, thinking it might be a nice surprise.

I called for her at seven p.m. and she wasn't quite ready so I had a nice chat with the family while I waited, and all seemed absolutely normal, no signs of drama there and Felicity looked happy that I was taking Sarah out. However, I could tell she was itching for a good session herself, and I tipped her a discreet wink as we left saying, "See you soon."

As soon as we turned off to go down to the river of course, Sarah knew where we were going, and I could tell by the sparkle in her eyes that she approved of my choice. We got there a bit early and had a short walk along the riverbank, but nights were drawing in now, so it was a bit cool, but the pub had a blazing log fire burning in the grate and it looked and felt really cosy and warm.

The landlord recognised us and said, "Another special night sir?" and I replied, "Could be."

We ordered a pint for me and a spritzer for Sarah and looked at the specials on the chalk board as well as the main menu and decided to have the Dover sole again as it was freshly available, with spinach and mashed potato, and a white sauce with mushrooms. We also had one starter of garlic prawns from the board and ordered the same wine as last time, with a large bottle of soda water to mix 'spritzers with and ice.

She said, "This is lovely. Thanks for booking this, I really appreciate it and there is nothing better than a good meal together before we make love."

I thought, *wow that makes twice she has freely mentioned the lovemaking, let's hope it lives up to expectations.* I doubted it would but was quite prepared to keep an open mind. And I was going to try to let her make the pace and choose her options.

Great meal, good conversation with nothing contentious, and she is a good-looking girl I thought, what more could a man want? It was as if she was auditioning for the number one spot ahead of her mother, although I was sure she was totally unaware of all that. Or maybe, I hypothesised, when she was in the ladies' loo, the final fling with her female friend and her vibrator had cleared Sarah's vision a bit. Then I chastised myself for such thoughts and concentrated on the rest of the meal, and what I felt was sure to follow.

We got to my new place about ten p.m. and she said, "I would like another drink please and to stay the night if that's OK?"

I said, "Sure thing; have you told Mum?"

She said, "More or less, nothing specific, just said I don't know when I will be back, don't like Jim having to drive after a drink, and she said, 'Whatever, I am sure you will be in good hands, enjoy'. That's what I'm going to do, enjoy everything on the menu."

As it turned out, literally I gave her everything I had in my locker and her limited experience. She was like a different woman, unbelievable. Uninhibited, vocal, wanted everything twice at least, shouted and screamed at her every orgasm, sucked me off completely and wanted every variation I could think of, including my famous sandwich trick with her ankles alongside her face, thumb up the bum, everything. She also rode me like a horse and goaded me into having a total of five orgasms, a new record I think, over the space of about five hours admittedly before, completely exhausted, we slept until about seven-thirty a.m.

I was sore and felt like I had been in a brawl the minute I crawled out of bed. She was tight anyway and the sandwich trick, the bucking bronco and the vigorous blow job left me aching and sore in a score of places. I had bite marks on my nipples and on my member! She looked pretty knackered when she surfaced as well, but hardly surprising.

After showering and phoning the office to say we both had a bug, we had some breakfast and coffee and sat looking at each other for a bit until I cracked and said, "Do you want to talk about all this or not?"

She said, "Yes somewhat, but not everything just yet, OK?"

I said, "Whatever you want to tell me, nothing more than you feel you need to. I accept you just as you are even though I am really knocked out by your performance last night in comparison to before, and I certainly could not cope with all that too often."

"Well, I think you deserve an explanation, no apologies, just explanations," she said.

I replied, "Go ahead, I'm listening.".

"For a long time, I was unsure if I was sexually-oriented 100% female, because I fancied both men and women. And as you have hinted, I had a long-term affair with Jane, starting at age eighteen at university. I had not had sex with anyone else male or female, but I was pretty proficient with Mum's dildo, which I gather she needs because Dad has a low libido; once a month I guess from observation and deduction, and that clearly is not enough for Mum. It was fun with Jane, a bit of a laugh; neither of us was sure but felt we were not out and out lesbians, and it was safe, convenient, and better than just doing it alone. I was relatively happy with all that, tried a couple of other girls, one was a dyke and wanted to dominate; the other needed a dyke not a play partner. So, I stuck with my friend, even though she had acquired a boyfriend and had started having sex with him, which she thought was pretty cool. And then I met you, and everything changed, I really liked you as a person and I gradually fancied you more and more as well, but I was worried I would not come up to your expectations. When we finally had sex, it was very good, but I still held something back because of my past history I suppose. This came to a head when I saw Jane this time. She was in love with her bloke and wanted to call our little arrangement off, but didn't want to lose me as a friend. So, I told her about you and said, "Me too, let's just be friends." She was delighted and that is it in a nutshell. I don't think I am in love with you, but I am certainly in lust. Now I will quite understand if you want to drop our relationship or maybe take a break to think about it, but I happen to believe in honesty wherever humanly possible."

"OK all taken on board," I said. "It takes some bottle to tell me all that. But what I would now like to know is how it was for you this night of passion? Was it different, same, or worse or better? And where do you see us going, bearing in mind I definitely want to continue seeing you?"

She replied, "It was amazing, I don't want to know how you acquired all that knowledge and experience unless of course, you feel it is a good idea, you know, skeletons in cupboards and all that. But I never thought one person could do all those things and have so many beautiful fulfilling orgasms, especially men. I knew I could have multiples because I became quite expert at it by myself, but I had no idea a man could come more than say two or possibly three times and I counted five, or were you faking?"

"Never faked one yet and don't think I ever will," I said.

"Where do we go from here you ask," she said, "I want us just to carry on as if this didn't happen, use our newfound knowledge to advantage, and suck it and see," then she laughed like a drain at her own joke.

"I agree," I said, "on the accepted condition that if either of us has second thoughts we discuss it and react accordingly."

"Condition accepted. Now I know you are a bit tired and sore poor thing, but I really would like you inside me just one more time, nice and gentle and no fireworks and then just hold me while we have another couple of hours' sleep."

"I will try," I said, "but I may need a little encouragement, but don't bite it this time please."

She said, "It wasn't a bite, it was a love bite."

I replied, "OK, thank God for that then."

Chapter 9

I saw Rosy again after a period of almost two weeks and she was not her usual self. I asked was she OK and she said, "Not really, I'm beginning to think things are going nowhere with you and I will be thirty next month. I think it's time I settled down and found a regular type of man who will marry me and have a couple of kids. I am not complaining; it's been great knowing you and I have enjoyed it all, but maybe it's the time to move on." I replied, "I can understand that. I've been very happy with our arrangement, but all good things must come to an end, and I am certainly not ready for wife and children, and can't see it happening to me for a good few years yet. But if you like, I am happy to see you occasionally for our usual, and I won't make a fuss if you see other blokes in the meantime and see how it goes."

"I was hoping you would say something like that because I have never sustained as long a relationship before and was getting worried that I might be left high and dry."

I said, "Don't be silly, I wouldn't just abandon you like that; let's just phone when we need a break from others and a good shag."

She replied, "Great, I would like to think I can always come back to you for that."

I said, "What, even if you were married?" and she said, "Well obviously it would depend how good he was in bed, but I can easily imagine giving you a call to come and cheer me up."

"I'm your man," I said. "You know I would never abandon you."

So, we had one last session and said goodbye, and I made her promise to call me if she needed me and we parted, a bit sadly, but still good pals.

This meant that I could put all my energy and thoughts, apart from work, into keeping Sarah and Felicity happy.

All this time I had been living too far from where I was brought up to involve my parents, but I did visit them occasionally, although I had no time for my father who was a lazy old bugger, and Mum was too in thrall to him ever to grumble or complain and lived a very narrow existence in his shadow.

Really since I left home at seventeen, there had not been much contact either way, so I felt no loss there and my siblings who were all married bar one, really didn't know my kind of life at all. I liked calling on my sisters, but my brothers were like my father in the main, self-centred, and selfish and I felt close to none of them. So, my life with my various female acquaintances and just one or two male pals, based as it was around work, entertainment, and sex, was quite sufficient for me at twenty-one years of age, and I sought nothing more. I had, however, joined an angling club and entered competitions sometimes or just fished alone, mainly river fishing, as my main way of switching off. The one exception being Sarah who I really enjoyed taking out for a day's fishing, with or without sex!

My career was doing OK too as I appeared to be progressing well at the office; the boss liked me, and said I had potential as a future section leader in junior management, so that was good, and I had a couple of pay rises as well.

But I admit my main preoccupation was Sarah and her mother, neither of whom I wanted to give up, and it was obviously a bit more difficult to arrange to see Felicity, but she seemed happy enough to have me sporadically after years of frustration. She was happy also that Sarah and I were getting along fine, and her gender situation no longer seemed a problem.

What Felicity wanted was to get away with me somewhere alone for a weekend maybe, so we could really enjoy ourselves without fear of discovery. The opportunity came by means of her having a training course for the new job she had landed as a publicity manager at a medium sized PR firm in the town, which meant occasional trips to London and other cities where events took place marketing their services. It had been years since she had a good job appropriate to her education and experience, and now William was old enough to take care of himself, everyone agreed it was a good thing.

So when she was required to go to Manchester for a four-day course on Business Management and Public Relations as their new office manager to be, in the local town where she lived, it was a golden opportunity for us to get together for a couple of nights anyway.

I spoke to my manager and said, "Is there anything coming up in the training line from which I might benefit?"

He looked at me speculatively and said, "There might just be a place on the coming Buyers Symposium in Stockport during the week starting 11th November, would that interest you?"

I replied, "Perfectly," as I knew Felicity's course was the 12th to the 16th of November.

Felicity decided that she would book a different hotel from the one pre-booked for the other attendees, saying they were younger in the main, and she preferred somewhere quiet when there would be no late-night sessions or other activities. I booked my own accommodation as well, as I knew nobody from other companies who were attending the symposium. This meant that, as I arrived in Stockport a day before Felicity was due in Manchester, I was able to check out where her hotel was, and it was only about ten minutes' drive from where I was staying on the outskirts of Stockport, on the Manchester side.

My room was fine, in a good position on the 2nd floor near to the lifts, and with a decent outlook across a park, and had a very nice bed, tea trolley and minibar, so apart from main meals I could happily stay in there watching TV or reading, when not otherwise engaged. Felicity called my room when she arrived on the Monday afternoon, and I had just got back from my first full meeting with all the other 'would-be' buyers. She told me she had just checked in so after a shower and a change how about meeting somewhere in Manchester for a drink and a meal and take it from there? I said that was great and I had already had a test run so I would meet her at the Corn Exchange bar, not far from Deansgate and her hotel, and she said this was fine.

I parked on the road nearby where there were meters and we met up at the bar I mentioned, but it was all blokes drinking after a big meeting nearby, so we walked around a bit and spotted a nice Spanish restaurant at the back of Deansgate towards the Irwell. It was large and noisy but there were plenty of tables and a great atmosphere, so we grabbed a table, and a waiter was with us in a couple of minutes. We ordered a couple bottles of San Miguel beer and studied the menu which was in Spanish and English so no problems there although I had taken Spanish at school so could understand most things.

There was a small group playing Spanish music with a guitar, drums and an accordion and singing Spanish songs and it seemed quite authentic and exciting after our local small restaurants and pubs back home. We decided to have a selection of tapas to start with followed by grilled whole snapper fish, and papas bravas: chopped up potatoes fried and covered in a spicy sauce, and it was all excellent if a bit hot and greasy. The beer went down well so we had another one then a couple of glasses of Rioja, which suited the spicy nature of nearly all the food. Plus, a litre of still water to keep the fires from burning too hot.

It was only nine-thirty when we made it back to her hotel, and we went straight up to her room and locked the door. We were undressed and in each other's arms in about three minutes and kissing and reacquainting ourselves and making sure we were on the same base as when we last met over three weeks before. Needless to say, the first orgasm came pretty quickly but that was the first of several and we both wasted no time in small talk, just concentrated on each other's needs and wants, which required no explanation at all. She was as before, very passionate and sexy and showed great appreciation for everything I did, and we eventually had a break after about an hour and made a coffee and consumed a couple of miniatures from the minibar. Then we had a chat touching each other as we talked, and lay on the bed facing each other.

"So," she said, "how was it with Sarah after her split with her long-term friend, any better?"

I said, "Yes much more relaxed and participative, but I don't really want to discuss that if you don't mind." Felicity said that she didn't seek details, just an idea as to how she seemed in general, and in particular asked did she tell me all about her past relationship?

I said, "Well she certainly made great efforts to put all that behind her and did tell me all, and what I will say is that she equalled, and even exceeded at times, my appetite for energetic sex. In fact, I felt like I had been in a rugby scrum afterwards."

Felicity laughed and said that Sarah looked much the same the following day when she finally got home, but nobody had said anything about it and she looked happy, but exhausted, so it was assumed it went well.

"Yes, it did, but I feel that was her getting the long bottled-up suppression of her emotions off her chest and am sure there will not be a repeat performance like that. So, I will see her again soon and we shall have to see how we get on. But I definitely want to continue with her relationship as well as with you if that is at all possible."

"It's not only possible, but also what I want for both of you, and I will never step in your way regarding whatever relationship you have with her. If that means giving you up, I am prepared to do that."

I said, "No, never; as long as you and she are happy and both want to continue with this relationship, I do too. Let's just forget about that for now and enjoy these nights we have together."

And we did. We had a great three nights, leaving the last night for Felicity to spend with her new colleagues at their hotel, and I joined my fellow travellers at their hotel, ignoring the sly digs and winks as to where I had been hiding all week. Despite the distractions, I still learnt a lot at the symposium and was able to give a good account of myself when debriefed by my boss on return to the office. Sarah was keen also to know how it all went and made no mention of her mother's absence and the fact that Manchester and Stockport are very close, etc. We appeared to have managed that situation well with no one any the wiser.

Chapter 10

The next few months went surprisingly smoothly as both Sarah and I continued our regular dates and sex was very good. She appeared to have put the past behind her and was embracing a much freer and easier, more relaxed relationship with me. More importantly, she obviously had no suspicions regarding Felicity, although she remarked that she had never seen her mother so relaxed and happy, and wondered if the new job and maybe someone she had met there was "seeing her".

I said, "Probably the job is stimulating her or has George entered a more active period of his life?"

Sarah laughed and said, "No way, he will never change in that respect I'm afraid."

I was seeing Felicity about once or twice a week, but not at my flat, too risky, so we had found a small motel just ten minutes out of town where I could book a room and we could just disappear late at night without a problem. Sarah also continued her relationship with me without major change, just adding a few variations to our routine as did I from time to time. It was a period of great stability and happiness as they were not in competition with each other. Sarah had no idea and Felicity loved the sex sessions and was very happy that Sarah was getting it too and had stabilised her life.

But of course, a little bit of complacency was bound to creep in and having the same performance with the same two people every time, however good, eventually made me start looking at other women again, just wondering of course.

I couldn't look too interested in anyone in our office building of course, because Sarah would spot it immediately. But I had started to play darts with the team at my local pub near the new flat and the wife of one of the team members, who often accompanied him, especially to the away matches at other pubs and clubs all around the area which took place every alternate week. These were fun because the host landlord was required to put on some bar food for the opposing team and provide a free drink to all the visiting team and its supporters on arrival. Dora, Pete's wife, was a bit of a tart, had huge tits and an athletic body which she showed off with tight sweaters and jeans. She really was an eyeful and flaunted it, and her husband, who was a bit of a slob, smoked and drank heavily and clearly couldn't care less who ogled his wife. She flirted with all the men, and it was rumoured that one young dart player called Ivan was a regular visitor at their house when Pete was there as well as when he had occasional trips to Portsmouth, where his skill as a fitter was employed in the naval dockyards I was told, on emergency repair jobs.

She wiggled her bottom at me, thrust out her huge tits and gave me the come-on, just like she did with most men, but I kind of liked the idea of shagging her rigid, no holds barred so to speak, just because I could. My ego was getting in the way of common sense.

Then one such dart match took place at our pub, and we entertained a pub from a village nearby and Dora was there as usual, but no Pete. And Ivan was hanging on her every word as were several others and I heard her say, "Back to my house, got a chicken and some cans in; we can have a little party while Pete's away." I thought, *no thanks, not with an audience,* but she specifically asked me to come and tipped me a wink. So foolishly I went along with some of the gang to see what would happen. The house was a somewhat untidy council house where her two small children were in bed and the babysitter was sent home. We all relaxed with a beer and waited for the chicken to finish cooking and had that, and then several left, leaving me, Dora, a guy called Steve and Ivan. But she made it clear she was interested in me on this occasion and Steve and Ivan both left leaving just me and Dora sitting on the floor watching TV and drinking. She said that she had seen me admiring her tits so why not have a closer look, so I took off her sweater and bra and boy they were magnificent, big but firm, very white with large pink nipples, which I readily took in my mouth for a few minutes. Then I took her jeans off and her knickers and exposed her large ginger bush. I put a couple of fingers in, and she liked that, but asked me to put them in further as she liked them right up so I complied and worked her off just with fingers, but she didn't come at all and I only had a semi-hard-on, not really fit for purpose. She didn't try to excite me, didn't suck it or wank me off, nothing, just laid back and made some remark about, "Suppose it's time to have your wicked way." At which point I completely lost interest, said must be going and got dressed and left. She turned out to be the least sexy woman I have ever known, and thought she only had to wiggle her bum, expose those wonderful breasts, and then lay back and wait for it to happen. No wonder Pete wasn't bothered and Ivan looked pretty gormless to me. At last, a failure to my name, thank God!

It served one good purpose; it focussed my mind on what could be and was with Felicity and Sarah. But on the other hand, I don't like failure, if that is what it was. And very shortly afterwards another woman involved with the dart team, the landlady, although about fifty, indicated she was definitely interested in me, especially after seeing me go off with Dora and the gang. I thought Edna was a low-risk possibility, her husband was older and ex-navy with a huge moustache, but Edna, who had a teenage daughter, was a different proposition and she had quietly been looking at me and giving subtle hints for a time. When her husband and daughter had gone away for some reason, she and her barmaid were in sole charge, it happened. It was another home match and she made sure I had two free pints and the best bits of food and said quietly, "Hang around a bit and help me clear up, will you?"

I just nodded and she then ignored me for the rest of the evening, and I helped collect glasses and put the stools up on the bar as she got rid of the barmaid and sorted out behind the bar. Then after the last customer left, she locked the front and the back doors and said, "Come with me."

We went behind the bar and up the stairs to the living accommodation above.

She turned and kissed me as she reached the top of the stairs and I got an immediate hard-on, and she reached down and fondled it and whispered, "Nice, very nice."

Then she went into the lounge asked me what I would like to drink, gave me a brandy, and said, "Enjoy that, I will just have a shower and get ready."

Ten minutes later she appeared in a black basque, suspenders and stockings and nothing else, her bush was black and curly and matched the outfit, she twirled round showing she had a good firm figure and said, "You like?"

I said, "Yes I like."

I stood up, kissed her first on the lips then moving the bra part of the basque out of the way I nibbled her nipples and then I dropped to my knees and stuck my tongue up her fanny, licking her secret lips and nibbling her surprisingly large clitoris, which grew even larger as I sucked it. She shivered and groaned and came in my face — something I had never experienced before, two jets of cum right in my face as she spasmed.

She then helped me off with my togs, and left hers on, and pulled me down on the carpet. She put her legs over my face so I could continue sucking her clit while she sucked my member, position 69 for the first time too, and this time I was able to hold off for about twenty strokes until we did it again! As before, she came in my face as I shot mine into her mouth. We both swallowed the juices and carried on, me sucking her clit and her my bobby's helmet until we both came again! Incredible, I had never known anything like it.

We then got into bed and just cuddled and kissed for a while and then she said, "One for the road, a brandy and a proper fuck."

The brandy was good, and the proper fuck was magnificent. She got me going easily and slid it in for me and I shagged her slowly, enjoying the feel of her fanny gripping me, then she moved a little faster against me and put her finger up my arse and urged me to go faster and her finger really made me go like a rabbit for a few minutes until we both came one last time, and we flopped down, exhausted.

This was new territory for me, I thought I knew a lot, but this proved I knew next to nothing.

This had certainly made up for my disappointment with Dora and had also provided me with a wakeup call as well as a wonderful new friend. Fifty she might be, but believe me, age really means very little providing one is fit enough.

I went back to my routine with Felicity and Sarah, and it was quite a while before I thought of anyone else, then I had another invitation from Edna after a home match. This time it wasn't for the same day, but for a daytime trip to the seaside starting at eight a.m. and returning late.

She had all the details and we drove to the station and got on a train to Cleethorpes of all places, and just sat and behaved like normal passengers and had a snack and a coffee at the buffet car and chatted away about life in general. Then at Cleethorpes station she guided me to a small out of season hotel she knew, and we booked in no problem for one night. We went out for a quick fish-and-chip lunch at a seaside cafe, picked up a carry-out at the off-licence and back to the hotel and to our room.

Suffice it to say we had a very interesting afternoon and had a shower and wandered off to the train station in time to catch the one we had planned on and arrived back in our local town station at nine p.m. and went our separate ways, leaving the train apart and ignoring each other all the way out to the car park.

I thought all this lovemaking with such an experienced and capable not to say very sexy woman might have affected my attitude to my other two lovers, but not at all. I was somehow able to compartmentalise the three of them and forget them when with one of the others. Not entirely, but enough to enjoy things and certainly felt no guilt. I was a single man, a free agent, and the two older women were clearly glad to have my attentions, and Sarah I felt OK about in all the circumstances, and so long as I was able to control things, no one should get hurt. Maybe I was overly optimistic, but I truly believed I was in control of my own destiny and with care and attention, just as with Rosy, when any one of the relationships failed so be it. Certainly, I felt that Felicity was well pleased with our arrangement, as she would have still been frustrated and unfulfilled sexually. She had a caring and thoughtful husband and two caring and loving children, and she knew one day our thing would end, and what she and I wanted was that it ended amicably, with no fallout for Sarah and herself.

As for Edna, she was very happy with her toy boy and expected nothing more than what she was getting, so I wasn't worried about her at all and knew that the number of times I would be able to see her were likely to be pretty limited.

I carried on my merry way, well satisfied with my existing situation, and focussed more on my job and career and just getting on with life. You could say I had not a care in the world at that point of my life.

Chapter 11

I felt this could not last, but I was going to do my darndest to keep it going as long as I could. Although it may seem from this account that I was obsessed with sex, I do not believe I was, not more than many others like me anyway. I read somewhere that men think about sex once every ten minutes for about two minutes and women slightly more than that. Well, I certainly didn't. When I thought about sex was when I was on my way to have it, during and for a short time afterwards, so I guess that maybe I thought about sex on average about ten hours in a week. So there are say sixteen hours in a waking day, times seven equals 112 hours per week, of which I probably thought about it for sixteen hours based on my known times per week having sex: four at an average of four hours before during and after sex. Which I calculate works out at 16 hours per 112 which is 14.28% of my waking hours. Hmmm, two minutes every ten is 20% of the free waking time spent by men thinking of sex, much more than my figure. I rest my case.

But anyway, I would argue that I am no more obsessed with sex than I am with food, for example. And I am in fact more interested in the whole relationship, not just the sex. I also believe that people who aren't getting it, or not very much or of a sufficiently high quality, are the ones who are obsessed by getting more and better sex, rather like I was at fifteen. *Ipso facto*, and all that. Whatever, I liked the subject, I liked pursuing the subject with suitable people especially women, slightly older women, and I felt I was perfectly normal in this respect.

I recognised of course that one cannot spend one's whole life just chasing fanny and at some point, one had to accept responsibility for bringing new life into the world, providing food on the table and a roof over one's families heads. But not for ages yet. I was not yet twenty-one, for God's sake, give me a break.

So, I was coasting along nicely, everyone seemed to be enjoying things like I was, and no need to change anything at all in the foreseeable future but wham! Things suddenly went pear- shaped! Not Sarah who was on the pill, but Felicity, who it turned out was forty-three and who wasn't on the pill, got pregnant! Oh shit! What was going to happen now?

She told me about it and seemed really pleased and I responded saying, "Surely not, you will have to get rid of it won't you?". "Never!" she said, "I do not believe in abortion and neither do Sarah or George."

"But," I protested, "surely it cannot be George's child, can it?"

She said, "Why not, he has managed it twice before, and you don't imagine I was stupid enough to stop having it with him once a month, and that's all it takes. It might not be yours at all and I do still love him you know."

That really put me in my place, and I said, "OK fair enough, but will you have it genetically tested, see if it is his or mine?"

"Not on your life," she said, "if it's yours what would you want me to do, divorce him and marry you? Of course not, so the only option is to announce the happy news and for you to keep away from me except when Sarah is present, at least for a while, and see what transpires."

Bloody nightmare, but she was right, who knows anyway except me and her, nobody. And maybe it was George's, maybe I am infertile.

But for all my rationalisation, this really threw a spanner in the works. George was over the moon, Sarah was so pleased for both of them, and I kept quiet and smiled and made appropriate noises and concentrated very hard on work, mates, fishing and thankfully Edna, when she was available. I couldn't face sex with Sarah for a while and made up an excuse about a hernia I had picked up at the gym. But eventually I had to face the music and we met at my flat and I tentatively, because my hernia was still a bit painful, made love with Sarah and she was most considerate. It worked out OK with me managing to remember to show some discomfort in certain positions.

Meanwhile Felicity bloomed and so did George; a nursery was prepared, baby clothes and prams and cots were purchased all over again and Felicity swelled noticeably at the front, and I was a severely chastened man.

With Edna being unreliable due to being the landlady of a pub and Sarah also not as frequently around at my disposal, I was feeling the pinch a bit, so I rang Rosy and asked her how she was. She was pregnant too, married and very happy and so that was that. I decided rather than put pressure on Sarah, I would try to find another outlet for my average libido. Then one day who should I bump into but my old mistress and first lover who had taken my cherry in the sick room at my old employers! I couldn't remember her name but she saw my dilemma and quietly said, "It's me Heather."

I said, "Of course, so sorry. How are you Heather, where are you working now?"

And she told me the name of a firm not far from ours where she was now office manager. I asked after her husband and she indicated that nothing had changed so I took the plunge and said, "How about we have a date for old times' sake, catch up with life's happenings?"

She looked at me and said, "Still a randy little bugger then?" and I said, "More so, how about you?"

She smiled and said, "It would be very nice thanks, have you a flat or something?"

I said, "Yes, what time do you finish work?" and she told me, and we made a date for the following day at five-thirty at the wine bar, near where I had just bumped into her.

Chapter 12

Well, what a turn up for the books, Heather looked exactly the same, same type of clothes, almost no makeup, looked about thirty-five, much younger than either Felicity or Edna, how had I ever thought of her as old? I was quite excited because what had happened with Heather had changed my life and she was such a nice, good person who had a strange, probably bisexual husband and no children, oh shit, better make sure she doesn't get pregnant as well! No, she must be OK we had made love regularly for several months and no problem, she must be on something, but I would ask just in case.

We met outside the wine bar at five-thirty and I said, "Would you like to go for a meal, I would like to do that if you are OK with time, etc."

She said, "Why not, quite the man of the world now, aren't you? And I would like to hear about your life since we first met, as well as see how your skills have progressed. My husband has gone away on a hiking trip with some mates, so no problem there, but I didn't think it a good idea to go to my house as it's a fair way from here, so I've brought a few necessities. I could stay the night maybe, and go straight to work tomorrow, leaving yours about eight-thirty?"

"Great, I said, I am so glad we bumped into each other." We started at the wine bar as we were outside it and went in and ordered a couple of drinks although it was too early to eat there and wasn't my idea of a good place for a meal anyway.

Strange really because in my memory she had seemed about fifteen or sixteen years older than me and now it felt only a few years especially when I thought of Edna and Felicity, good examples of mature womanhood, but definitely not old, and Heather was at least eighteen years younger than Edna and about twelve years younger than Felicity. How perspective changes as you get out of your teens, I thought.

We were not an unusual couple at all now I felt and both of us were totally relaxed in each other's company, after all we knew exactly what was coming! And I guessed that Heather had been without good sex for a while.

We sat at the window and sipped our drinks and I said, "So Heather, how has it been, new job, hubby still not much interested, have you had any other boyfriends to alleviate your needs which of course I know very well?"

"No, I told you that you were a one-off and that is still true. Honestly, most of the time it doesn't bother me too much, although I confess, I often think of you and remember our sessions in the sick room and masturbate, which helps."

I said with real feeling, "Poor you."

But she said, "Not really, I managed OK before you happened, and I will manage OK again when you disappear again."

Ouch.

"I will definitely be seeing you if you want to and I will explain my position if you like."

"Spare me the gory details, just tell me what partners you have now and how you see these relationships going so that I can decide whether I want to be part of it or not."

"OK," I said, "I will. I am in a couple of relationships neither very serious, the younger one is called Sarah and she is great company, a nice girl, but not exceptional in bed, and I have also had a relationship with her mother, which is now very much on hold because she has had a late pregnancy and wants the baby, which may in fact be her husband's. The daughter knows nothing and neither does the husband. Really nice people who I wouldn't hurt for the world. But clearly there is no future in either relationship and the one with her mother is over and she is six months pregnant, I'm a friend of the family. Her husband is a once-a-month man which is how I fitted in."

She said, "Bloody hell, sounds complicated but you have clearly now got good relationship skills and have matured a lot to be able to handle all that. Go on, and?"

"Yes," I continued, "there is one other relationship, with a fifty-year-old pub landlady who has a boring older husband who cannot deliver what she needs, and boy does she have needs. Purely sexual, no affection, no pretence, just really hot sex and only infrequently because of her occupation and family, and she basically provides the sort of sex that Sarah is incapable of."

"And that's it, no proper girlfriend or lover, just sex partners and Sarah is like a friend, not a future wife?"

"No way she will ever be my wife, and with the other complications I think I will try to cool it and extricate myself when I decently can."

"So, if we are still compatible, how do you see me fitting in to this scene?"

"I don't know yet, but I think if you are up for it, I would like you to be my long-term mistress I suppose even though I am not married and no plans to be so for a few years yet. But why don't we see how we get on tonight and have a few more dates and re-evaluate our positions then?"

She replied,"

"Good thinking; I could do with you in my office, but that is not really a possibility, so I will be happy for now to be your unofficial mistress."

We laughed at all that and went arm in arm to a pub, about 150 metres away on the opposite side of the road to the wine bar, which Heather said was good. As I had never been in there should work out all right, but just in case, we agreed a story about her company possibly doing some business with mine, blah blah.

The pub was warm and lively, but we got a table in an alcove, and I had a pint of bitter and Heather had a sherry. We sat and stared at each other for a bit, speechless, and then I said, "I'm really pleased to see you again," and she smiled and said, "Me too."

We held hands over the table like a couple of teenagers for a bit. Then she said, "Right what shall we have?" so we consulted the specials of the day and the main menu and I chose a sirloin steak medium rare with a jacket potato and green beans, and Heather also had the sirloin but with chips and peas and asked for medium to well. We didn't talk too much over the meal, just ordered a bottle of Rioja and concentrated on eating the meal and looking at each other and quietly smiling. Then I had treacle sponge and custard and she ordered the same. Coffee and a brandy followed, so a bit risky driving to my flat, but as it was only about half a mile, we decided to walk. It was a fine night and not too cold once we had walked about the first hundred metres. I said that we could either walk back to my car or get a taxi in the morning if it was raining.

She said, "Whatever."

We arrived at my flat and she admired it and said it was very nice, and we were in no hurry as we had all night. We had another coffee and a nice brandy I had bought for special occasions, Hennessy Antique, and settled down for a chat on the sofa. She told me about her new management job, how much she liked the responsibility for several staff and the more complicated computer work she had been taking on, as well as being PA to the MD, quite a job and with a commensurate salary. I said that she well deserved it and how glad I was for her. Then I told her about my bit of progress at work and how my boss liked me and said I was promotion material, etc. After about half an hour we kissed, tenderly and slowly, feeling our way a little, but I soon undid her blouse and looked once again at her wonderful tits and played with and sucked her nipples and then it was, "Let's go to bed," and we did.

I wanted so much for her to enjoy every minute and I also wanted to try some of my new skills on her, so first I laid her across the bed and undressed her so that I could give her oral sex. She opened her thighs and displayed her lovely bush and labia which I was really seeing properly for the first time. I kissed and nibbled her labia and tongued her clitoris which was also quite big, and she loved it and just tousled my hair and moaned a little as I slowly increased the tempo, which she liked, and she gave a huge moan and climaxed.

Then without me saying anything, she rearranged us to the 69 position so she could return the compliment and sucked my dick gently and cupped my balls in her hand while I continued where I had left off, starting with the clitoris, and working up to the tongue going in as far as I could, and she came again, and I ejaculated in her mouth. We continued in similar fashion, and I did all I could to please her for all she had done for me the first time around.

We paused for refreshment, a glass of sparkling wine and water, and then lay down again with her in the crook of my arm and cuddled and she said,

"My you have certainly come on since you last made love to me," and I said, "You seemed to like it."

She said, "Very much; I look forward to the teacher being taught."

I laughed and reached over and put my glass down and turned her over and we continued with her education!

This was the best sex I had had since I first had her standing up in the sick room at work, and it was so good that I could pay her back a little for what she had done for me then. We had another drinks break, and resumed and did the sandwich thing where I folded her double, put her ankles round my neck, getting penetration not otherwise possible and she came again and again but I didn't. We did the ride-em cowboy where she straddled me and rocked back and forth and then laid forward so I could put my finger up her anus and keep her going longer and she had more orgasms. By this time, it was three a.m. and we were both pretty knackered, but very happy. Great reunion, couldn't have been better. Off to sleep.

Chapter 13

I awoke very happy the next morning. No more sex, nobody had anything to prove; we were both very tired but happy to be together again and with how it had turned out. Life was good, and I was determined to keep it that way. Back to having three women to make love with and not only that, to be good company in two out of three cases, was I, a lucky man? You bet!

I think the sexual experience and dealing with several women in tandem and managing the situations was probably character building, although some puritanical souls would doubtless say I was depraved. I would respond that they were envious and lacked the spirit to attempt such things but hey! We are in the 20th century not dealing with Dickensian morality, and we have no workhouses now to underline that fact. And I believed I was, in the main, giving good advice and counsel not to mention great sexual satisfaction and help in keeping fit!

Yes, a little tongue in cheek but not much.

My increasing maturity and application certainly were impressing my boss, and he called me in and said that he was going to give me temporary promotion to head a small new team involved in the strategic forward planning of materials for our manufacturing arm. This would be so that we didn't need to carry huge stocks of everything but had adequate reserves and fast supply structures in place to deal with the occasional surge in production. Not quite a 'just in time' supply but undoubtedly a precursor to what he believed would become the norm for big manufacturing in the future, he said.

I had my own small office and a team of six men and women to command, and an outline planning document drawn up by higher management. I looked at this and immediately said to the boss, "Fine so far, but I am concerned it's all a bit too incestuous." He said, "How?" and I explained that while all the higher management and in-house planners were undoubtedly good company men and women, they were by definition predisposed to what they knew, and were experienced in, but we were looking for a new and perhaps even revolutionary approach to production materials procurement, with the focus being on slimming down stock piles, keeping our materials and subcontract parts manufacturers up to date, and saving money on materials, handling and production in due course. He looked very hard at me then smiled and said, "OK, explain to me how we may have got this wrong and how you think we can improve the approach we have decided on."

I said, "With respect, sir, I do not believe that is what I am saying; perhaps we cannot improve on your plan, but I think we should have brought in a specialist company, or a small team of professionals, to look at our existing system and our objectives, before setting our approach in concrete. Maybe any further savings would be smallish but could be significantly larger than we thought; to then look carefully at any suggestions and ideas they might come up with, evaluate them and then, if necessary, setting out the final guidelines for my team."

He looked hard at me again and then he smiled again and said, "That's why I have nurtured you and trusted you with this new project, because I always thought you had a brain under that posh haircut of yours and, contrary to some who thought all you were interested in was crumpet, I have always taken the view that, risk-taker that you might be, this was tempered by your unusual maturity for a boy of your age, your quick and analytical mind and your drive, determination and ambition. So right or wrong, I like your ideas and your spirit, and I am going to recommend a pause in the launch of this new project while I put someone on getting these experts in. I shall recommend to the MD that you are the person who should spearhead and drive this consultation forward. Are you up for it, yes, or no?"

I replied that I was ready and prepared and already had two target groups for who I was preparing a brief so that in this event I could get cracking within 48 hours.

He smiled again and said, "Take it as read you will be doing just that, or I'm going to resign."

Bugger me, Heather's advice had helped me a lot, and I was going to make sure she got my full appreciation for that.

The MD approved. My boss — who was also a director, and the "in-house" team leader whose plan had been effectively vetoed, seeing which way the wind was blowing — fully endorsed my proposals saying, somewhat mealy-mouthed I thought in passing, that he had some doubts about a totally 'in-house' appraisal of this project from the start. Lying bastard, but I didn't care because I knew he had exposed our boss to potential problems by not saying this if he in fact ever believed it was the case, and, in trying to cover his arse, had actually exposed it fully. He in fact only lasted a few more months before 'moving on'.

I got the team Heather had recommended of the two I put forward and after a day's briefing, they set to work and looked at all our existing procurement systems, stock levels and average draw down times, etc., including, at my written suggestion, an analysis of waste from outdated stock disposals. They also addressed the 'bring-in' times of new products and price history, and projected future purchase figures. This particular analysis ultimately led to the conclusion that overstocking of certain items produced an ultimate cost increase of around 20% on those goods affected, over a one-year period.

Other wrinkles in the proposed procurement strategy now indicated faster production of our end products, better utilisation of standards parts and complete modules, and of a greater preponderance of up-to-date technology. These advantages, together with an altogether slimmed down, computer controlled, stock monitoring, and generally less current capital outlay, freed up cash for other projects. The net projected result therefore was, year on year, overall savings of nearly 40%, as opposed to costs under the old system. Of course the costs of our studies and new computer programmes, retraining of staff, etc., bit into the first year savings, but this was off — set by a reduction of numbers of receiving staff, the costs of storage control and the 'as needed' issuing of parts and materials, were all significant factors making the implementation costs negligible. Going forward, the savings over the next five years were forecast to be over 4 million pounds.

Needless to say, yours truly's promotion was made permanent with added responsibilities and a mandate to recruit more members on my team from time to time, plus a wider remit to look at any systems related to production and subcontracting in general, with a view to streamlining and modernisation across the board. So, within one year of my joyful resuming of my old relationship with Heather, I had been appointed as a Senior Manager Projects to the whole company, achieved a salary increase of several thousand per annum, a company car and free medical and life insurance. Not bad at twenty-four years of age.

But during all of this I had not lost sight or touch of my three lovers, Heather *numero uno*, Sarah *numero dos* and Edna, my lovely sexy landlady.

Meanwhile, Felicity bloomed and gave birth to her second son to be called David, 8lb 6oz with jet-black hair and a dimple, and she and George were absolutely over the moon, especially as George's dimple had been faithfully reproduced. The fact that I had a dimple didn't matter, especially since I had grown a small beard to cover the thing! Sarah was equally enamoured with David, but she never knew I was serving her mother at the time she got pregnant, or indeed at all. And there was no way I would ever try to get together with Felicity again even if I did sever relations with Sarah. She was a happy and completely different woman, and I was glad to be able to leave it that way.

Heather was superb in and out of bed. She was a fountain of knowledge and had vast experience; she had a rock steady but totally boring relationship with her useless husband and was forever grateful for my choosing her as my main squeeze. She knew about the other two and didn't give a damn, as long as I continued to demonstrate my fascination with her and her wonderful sexy body and sought her counsel and advice. Plus, she knew instinctively that Sarah was no competition in that department, that Edna was getting on a bit, and her career experience as a pub landlady was immaterial, so all in all she knew I was more than fully occupied sexually between the three of them and with my career taking off, there was no need to look over her shoulder.

I was enjoying work very much nowadays and the perks, but I also was enjoying the new responsibilities I had been given, and was determined to prove to Charles, the Production Director, that he was right to have faith in me. I decided I would do whatever it took to deliver on the promises I had made, using sound management skills and looking all the time at different aspects of the whole works systems from maintenance through to new systems and methods which would deliver further cost gains and efficiency.

The trade unions didn't like me because I had reduced staffing with my ideas, but I sweet-talked them and discussed their perceived problems, made one or two minor concessions, and gradually convinced them that I had enhanced the long-term future of the company in the UK, thereby safeguarding jobs.

I volunteered to take a management course which dealt not just with the staff and their training and general well-being, but also helped me understand the dynamics of system management as well, including the increasing role of computers, use of new materials, and the like. One result was that I suggested we install our own painting plant for the larger equipment we produced rather than subcontract this work which often led to frustrating delays in delivery of products. This meant we kept the standards of paintwork high by ensuring we used the best quality paints and that they were applied to high professional standards, not something you can know or be sure of when such work is subcontracted. No immediate gain of course but I convinced Charles that the pay back would come in increased market share once the higher quality and durability of our finished products became recognised.

But on the contrary, I axed one out-of-date metal pressing plant which used old heavy machines which would soon need replacing, and the recruitment and training of some new staff as the older employees in that department approached retirement age. This time I convinced Charles that to move the metal pressing and body forming to a young contracting company who had all the latest high-tech equipment, fully trained and young operatives, and a keen desire to get our business. This meant I could negotiate a five-year contract for all our metal pressings and forming body shells without any new capital equipment being necessary. No extra staff and no retraining, which would deliver significant savings in the five years and still be very competitive in the full ten-year capital plant renewal cycle. And I pointed out to Charles, that in five, or more importantly, in ten years' time, there would be an opportunity to either set up a new department if it could be done competitively, or invite a range of tenders from similar companies to the one we were set to use, and either get another good 5/10 year contract or move to another competitor on equal or better terms. Showing I could think long-term and strategically, contracting out where it made sense, and bringing in new functions and staff where it was justified.

This sort of thing kept me and the top management on their toes, and all departments were subject to my scrutiny and recommendations which kept the department heads on their toes as well. It was challenging but fun and when things went well, I got praise, prospects of further promotion and bonuses sometimes. The trick was to make sure things continued to go well.

The next couple of years seemed to fly by with my involvement in middle and top management making it very interesting and exciting at work, so I had no incentive to move on or change anything other than to try to improve what I was doing and gain recognition so that options within the company and maybe in the future in other companies, might materialise.

Chapter 14

Outside work, I had a full life as well, and continued seeing all my ladies regularly with no major incidents or changes. At work they of course heard all about my success as Sarah was still employed there although I rarely saw her at work, not even for coffee as I tended to be in meetings where coffee was consumed during working moments, so no coffee break as such. I kept Heather up to speed of course and she continued to offer opinions and insights on a wide range of work-related topics, but we neither of us let that spoil our continuing love affair, which it had quietly become. In fact, although we were not living together, we were to a large extent rather like a married couple, although neither of us voiced that thought. Sex was just as good; we both liked to introduce new ideas for fun in bed and laughed over some and found minor peaks of enjoyment in others. But really our basic methods of making love, well-honed and practised, were stimulus enough for us both to obtain and maintain a high degree of satisfaction.

I of course continued to see Edna occasionally and she kept herself fit and was always ready for a good session whenever we both found time to fit it in. And she was so down to earth, glad she had my attention and appreciation and of course getting exactly what she wanted, great sex, no real risks involved and nobody hurting. We both knew it must end one day, but at fifty-three, she was still one hell of a woman and would put many a much younger woman to shame with her performance, enthusiasm, and sheer joy of it all, not to mention her special skills.

As for Sarah, it was becoming a bit repetitive and slightly boring. Although I was still very fond of her and she performed well enough, I got the feeling she was going through the motions a bit on occasion.

So, it was no surprise when at one such event, at my flat, she said, "You know Jim, I don't think our relationship is going anywhere, do you?"

I paused and thought a bit and said, "I'm not sure exactly what you mean by that, do you mean we are not getting engaged or married because if so, that's right. I am no nearer settling down to such a firm commitment as that, I am very much enjoying my job and career enhancement, and I am still only twenty-six. Really I don't see me being interested enough to marry anyone in the foreseeable future; how about you?"

"I agree," she said, "I don't want that either, my career, while not as stellar has yours has been, is going well too, and I certainly don't want what Mum has now, a two-year-old toddler who still shits his nappies, cries in the night, and throws his food and toys all over the place. I really don't understand why Mum and Dad find that all fun, especially as they have done it all before. And I don't really want to live with you or any other man full time; I think I would find that too restrictive, and I do actually like my privacy quite a bit. On the other hand, I enjoy our outings and pub meals and fishing and of course the sex, but I sometimes feel you are getting a bit bored with it all." I replied, "Well I don't think any long-term relationship can be maintained 100 percent fulfilled, happy and joyful, but as things are I am quite content, and if I needed some extra excitement, I am sure I could find it. Do you feel you get a bit bored at times? Do you feel an urge to try something different?"

"Yes and no. I like you a lot and I admire your grip on life and everything else you touch. But I would hate to feel I wasn't enough of a challenge for you, that you hanker after something more exciting, another woman I mean not work."

I said, "What man doesn't think from time to time. Hmm that looks a bit of all right, but that's just physical sex we are talking about. I think we have a broader relationship than just sexual, and I am not complaining about that. And what about you, don't you ever think he looks bit of all right, wouldn't mind a romp with him, or don't girls think like that?"

She replied, "Oh yes I think women do think like that, but include things like nice hair, slim hips or whatever, not just tits, arses and fannies, like most men do I imagine."

I laughed at that and said, "Fair comment, now how about you show me your tits, arse and fanny, the lot, and let's see who remains bored then."

She laughed and the tension disappeared, and she provocatively removed her jeans and top, reached around her back and unhooked her bra and wiggled her tits about, slowly pulled down her knickers and bent down in front of me with her arse in the air and her bush, labia and clit staring me in the face, only inches away. I needed no encouragement. I leaned forward and licked her lips and her clit and reached round and cupped her tits and she pushed against my face as I stuck my tongue up her vagina as far as I could and proceeded to tongue her from the back, and I reached round and fingered her clit at the same time, and she was really turned on and groaning by now and she quickly came. I licked her juices and then pulled off my trousers and underpants and put my cock straight in her where she knelt, doggy fashion reaching around and manipulating her clit and outer lips so I could feel my cock going in and out and, in short order, we both orgasmed and she gripped my cock really tightly with her vaginal muscles as she came.

I then turned her over, got astride her with my head between her thighs and she grabbed my cock and sucked it back to life and we had a really nice slow 69 until we both came again, and she took my cum in her mouth, as I did hers.

We both lay spent on the rug, and I said, "We must have more of these serious talks if that's what happens," and she said, "Yes, it was very nice thank you. We must do it like that again; it really turns me on."

So another mini phase in our relationship began where I paid a bit more attention to her wants and needs and introduced her to other ways to make love and our relationship was effectively rekindled, and the lovemaking all round with my three leading ladies seemed to benefit as well. Long may it last, I thought.

Chapter 15

My team at work had grown to nine people now excluding me, and we continued to seek new ways of doing things throughout every department in the company. Although this brought some disgruntled looks, when any of the managers involved complained to Charles or even the MD, they got short shrift.

Bulletins went up on notice boards and an order went out from the MD that the board expected full compliance with our economy driven search for change of methods, personnel, equipment or whatever else my team chose to focus on. A brief resume of our work so far and the benefits flowing from our projects, and the financial gains already made, and in the pipeline, was circulated to all team leaders with an order to make discussion on this drive compulsory at their management meetings, and it was made clear that full cooperation was required.

People listened more carefully, and a small stream of ideas and suggestions started to arrive on my desk, which I always answered and followed up if I thought there was any mileage at all in them.

Consequently, this was a dynamic situation and change was sweeping across our whole operation. We even had a prominent journalist interested who came and interviewed selected groups and individuals terminating with me and Charles and the MD. They gave me fulsome praise and I became the focus of the article which was published in a leading broadsheet with photos and charts showing, in broad terms what had been taking place.

Our public relations manager made a point of inviting me and three of my team to a very nice lunch where the press was invited. We made a presentation of our methods and progress, and I was invited to a TV interview. We also were asked to lecture at two universities on our project which was sufficiently impressive that it then became part of the educational policy objective committee's plan for innovative industrial methods and processes and was due to be introduced in eight selected universities and polytechnics for the next full education year.

Not long after all this, my public profile had led to a lot of interest in our methods by several key industrial groups in the UK and abroad, and I started to have people putting out feelers about my availability should an offer be made to recruit me to their company. In short, I was headhunted.

I drew all this to Charles' and the MD's attention and they thanked me for my openness regarding all this.

They said, "What do you want in order that we can give you a binding contract here for a minimum of five years?"

I said, "I have no intention of leaving and in any case, I do not know what is on offer out there, not just financially for me, but in terms of what I could hope to achieve elsewhere and how interesting any proposals might be from a development of my skills point of view and of course, would I fit in with a crowd I knew nothing about? So let me explore what is on offer please and then I can come back to you with some reasonable requests I might have to ensure my loyalty to you, but rest assured I am very happy here with both of you and my team and would not lightly abandon you at this juncture."

They both said this was sensible and fair but would just like to give me a big incentive before we knew anything about other company's objectives. A directorship and a seat on the board was a distinct possibility, higher salary of course and shares in the company plus a better car and a cheap loan, if I wanted to upgrade my house and location. Bugger me, I thought. Wow. But I kept cool and thoughtfully said, "Sounds very interesting, and I might just have stayed regardless of all that, but it will certainly focus my mind, and I suppose similar incentives, 'Golden Handcuffs' I hear they are called, might well already be discussed at several board meetings around the UK and one or two in the USA, and other countries. But I say again, my first loyalty is with you, particularly you Charles, no offence to my MD of course, so it would take something quite extraordinary to make me want to move."

I repeated all this to Heather that very night, and she was not surprised, being fully aware of my achievements, not least as in part they were thanks to her, but she brushed that aside, saying that was nothing.

She ran over several scenarios I had not fully considered and advised me to look very carefully at any offers, particularly from much bigger companies who could offer even bigger incentives and also greater advancement prospects within a much larger organisation or even a group of companies might be interested. However, she tempered those comments by also pointing out that the bigger the organisational pool, the bigger the sharks who swam there, and I was still relatively inexperienced. So, might be better to get an excellent new deal, guaranteed five years as a director with a team I knew and no real competition. Certainly, safer, and still a big enough challenge once I was on the board.

We made love and Heather stayed after for a brandy and talked some more and I said, teasing her, "Maybe you just want me to stay here so I still have you nearby?"

She smiled and said, "It never crossed my mind, I know I will always be special to you whatever happens, and I certainly would never stand in your way if it was something you really wanted, and I believed you would benefit by in the long term."

I said, "You really trust me, don't you?"

"Yes," she said, "I do, but you don't get as far and as fast as you have by accident, you are a very fast and mature thinker, courageous but not reckless, and I think that you would never leave me behind wherever you went, not that I'm saying I would go, but I might, for you!"

I kissed her and we made love again and I thanked her for everything she had done for me and said, "I will do nothing without first consulting you."

I knew that if I stayed at the same firm, Sarah would have to go, I couldn't fulfil my role as a board director I felt, if I was still an item with her. Unless of course I married her and that would be hypocritical.

Also, Edna, she was great, but again I couldn't take the risk of maintaining a relationship with her either, whereas Heather would be perfect, the soul of discretion, totally loyal, intelligent and could, if required, fit into almost any role she wanted to.

Lots to think about, but first things first, let's see what offers, if any, came up, and evaluate them before even thinking of any other issues.

Things started moving fast with the MD of a well-known international agricultural manufacturer's UK plant calling me by telephone, and he asked if I could meet him soon for a private discussion concerning an important development his company were planning in the UK. I had already cleared with my boss that it was OK for me to go where I liked and meet anyone concerned with the project business, providing I told him in advance who, where and when. So, I said to this other MD, "Sure, I assume you are interested in me, rather than just a product. If so, name a place and a time and I will check my diary."

He said, "Can you meet me in the lobby of the Savoy Hotel in London for lunch say arriving at twelve-thirty tomorrow or as soon after as possible?"

I asked him to hold while I checked my diary, put his call on the recorded music standby and called Charles who immediately said, "Yes, do it and stay overnight if necessary." I picked up the caller again and said, "Yes I will be there at twelve-thirty tomorrow; I take it you will recognise me?" He laughed and said he would and thanked me for my quick response and had the nerve to also ask if he was the first to ask, but I said that I had no comment to make at this point.

By the time I left the office that night I had three further dates made with big and bigger companies, two in London which I could fit in after the lunch appointment, the second for dinner at Langan's and the third for lunch the day after at another well-known restaurant. The fourth was to be in Manchester on the next free day, two days after the first. I decided there and then that four would be quite sufficient for now and in any case, I could easily accommodate further trips if it seemed necessary. I booked first-class rail tickets to London so that I had breakfast on the train at about nine a.m. and arrived in London at quarter to twelve. A short taxi ride would take me to the Savoy for twelve-thirty, and I also booked that night at The Savoy Hotel, and with the following night optional and reserved a seat first-class to Manchester the following day. I knew I could get back from Manchester by taxi if necessary or book another room there if required.

This was going to be quite a demanding session of interviews and I decided that if she would come, I would take Heather with me as my PA. She loved the idea but said she needed to get herself properly organised but would come with me for the whole trip. So, I altered the bookings accordingly after clearing it with Charles, and I thought, if this works out, I will offer her a permanent position if she would consider such a move. If this took place, I knew the situation with Sarah and Edna were history and Heather's husband would have to swallow it or bugger off. I also contacted the four suitors and told them I would require my PA to be with us for all the meetings so please make sure she is booked for meals as well.

Heather must have done some pretty quick shopping as she came in a very smart dark two-piece suit and mid-height heels making her a very imposing figure. She had an upmarket travel case and a portable computer/typewriter/printer all in one. She had tidied up her hair and put on a bit of makeup and she really looked and acted the part.

Heather stayed at my flat the night before and lo and behold, after just one nice but short love session we were both asleep by midnight and ready and fresh to go to get the early train to London the following morning.

I had decided to refer to the four meetings as A B C & D for ease of reference. Heather fired up her computer and researched all four outfits and the main players and she prepared briefings for me which she printed out and put in four matching vellum folders simply marked A to D. After breakfast in the Pullman of grapefruit, smoked salmon and scrambled eggs and a pot of tea and a pot of coffee, we got to work. By the time we reached London I had a good working knowledge of each company and a profile of the main man we were meeting from each one.

We rolled into the station a little early and were deposited at The Savoy at 12.10 p.m. and so had time to book in and put our bags in the room. We were back in the lobby at 12.25 p.m. where we were immediately spotted and approached by two men, and one woman, carrying briefcases.

I walked towards the main man who was called Henry Smythe; I had seen a photo of him so was confident enough to hold my hand out to him and say, "Henry, so pleased to meet you; this is my PA Heather, I do hope it's no problem to have her with me."

I think he was surprised I picked him out, knew his name and took the initiative but didn't flicker an eyelid as he smoothly shook my hand saying, "James, a pleasure and you too Heather, glad you came along too and absolutely no problem, we have altered the booking for lunch which will be me and my colleagues here, and another colleague will join us shortly so six in all. I do hope that's aright with you?"

"Of course," I replied, "the more the merrier." Making it clear I was not easily intimidated and, in reality, was in the driving seat anyway, at least for now.

Henry was a mature man of probably fifty-plus and his team were not much younger than him.

I was therefore considerably younger than any of them as was Heather, but if they thought that might be an advantage they were mistaken. What that said to me was, old fashioned maybe, stuck in the mud possibly, but smart and clever operators, for sure. But it also explained why they were eager to get me, they were in catch-up mode.

By this time, I was accustomed to handling mixed groups of men and women in meetings, and I was a pioneer of this new approach; I was super confident that I could more than hold my own here. But at the same time, I cautioned myself to take things slowly, as advised by Heather and listen carefully, and not to hog any conversation and above all not to make any firm commitments at this meeting. And most importantly, to part on amicable terms with a positive attitude rather than make a rapid decision which might turn out to be the wrong one. I called that 'Keeping my powder dry'.

After a brief chat in the lobby, Henry said that he hoped that for this meeting to keep it informal, so he thought that having a table for six in a secluded part of the restaurant, we could be sufficiently private to discuss matters openly but, as they had no fixed agenda this was more exploratory than setting a fixed plan, and there was a need for both sides to look at options in broad rather than specific terms. I agreed and saw no problems with a semi-public meeting providing we were to keep things general and establish a few possible parameters and terms of reference. But I said that we had other groups who were interested and of course I would perhaps need one or two important commitments made for a fair analysis to take place and decide who, if anybody, reached a point where we could talk serious business, with specific requirements and needs. In code I was saying I would draw up a shortlist and maybe a couple of front runners for a final play off, so don't be backward in making some pretty clear ballpark commitments or you might risk not reaching the quarter finals!

Henry knew exactly what I was saying and said that he felt enough would be said in order for me to appreciate the level of their interest without fear of misunderstanding. But first for drinks, start the meal and see what sort of people we all were before getting into the serious stuff.

Heather had said nothing so far, but when we all sat down with Heather on my left and Henry on my right, she listened carefully to all we both said, and the rest just listened as well as Henry and I held the floor. He explained about their core business, plant infrastructure, levels of staff, sales and destination countries and so on, until Heather interjected politely and said, "James and I have already learnt much of this from our research and reading on the Pullman to London this morning. With respect I suggest we get down to not what you are now, but what you would like to be in the future and in broad terms, your strategy for that. Is that about right James?"

I said with a short laugh, "I can always trust Heather to put her finger on the button and move things along a bit."

And to his credit Henry also laughed and said, "Well said, Heather. Is it all right if we use first names here?" and Heather smiled and nodded.

So Henry said, "In general terms, both our Chairman and a majority of our directors have agreed that we have fallen a little behind in sales of new equipment, particularly in the home market. We have been watching and listening to you on TV and reading about your lectures and your portrayal of the modus operandi and have studied your project's apparent effect on costs and delivery times, not to mention improved quality as well, in what is a comparable business, albeit a bit smaller than us, and we see a need to do something similar."

"Like your clear and unambiguous statement there, Henry, it's what I prefer to do, although Heather tries to make sure I don't shoot from the hip too much. Just a small comment on what you said about being a bit bigger than us, that will rapidly not be the case, I would suggest, if you carried on as you are, and we are certainly not standing still."

"Absolutely James, you put that in a nutshell. So, what I need to know is, what can we do to attract you into our set-up, just general stuff not specific figures, more strategic rather than tactical, or the identification of targets. I am thinking in the area of being a board member; you are already a director I know, and with a bigger all-round remuneration package of course. Choosing the size and constitution of your team, location you would like, help with re-housing, index linked non-contributory pension, free medical insurance, whatever it takes, frankly. I can put some flesh on bone if we get to that stage, but I can assure you we would take some beating."

"All sounds good and interesting, but I am also interested in the breadth and scope of my remit. It is no secret that I have carte blanche to look at all functions across the whole company, not just production related, marketing, accounting, procurement of everything including service and maintenance, security, sales, the lot. No individual director or manager should be able to cramp my style."

One of the group muttered, "Impossible, people are not going to swallow all that."

"In that case," I said, "we may as well just enjoy the rest of our lunch and say goodbye."

Henry looked daggers at the person who had spoken and said, "I think you may have spoken rather hastily there Mathew; kindly go and organise your trip back, you have finished here for the day." Shit, Henry was a tough cookie, no doubt, and totally in charge. Mathew went bright red, then pale and muttered, "Sorry and goodbye," and fled.

Henry turned to me and smiled, "Sorry about that, I feared he might say something out of turn. I know about the scope and breadth of your powers in your current set-up and I will just say you would have exactly the same powers as you have now and, more importantly you would be the most powerful director beneath me and the chairman, with the full backing of a comfortable majority on the board of which of course you would be a member." I said that he had missed one very important part of any putative deal, which was for how long? I told him that I wanted at least a five-year contract, possibly longer, enshrining my terms which included as a central plank, the cross-company scrutiny and, subject to no veto.

"Unusual," he said, "but we could put our legal team on that and satisfy your needs I am sure, perhaps tied to an agreed level of cost reduction achievements."

"Hmm. Possible," I said.

We had almost finished lunch and I said, "All good so far as it goes. I confirm that you are the very first ones to get this interview possibility, and clearly, I have several to go through before I can begin to make any sort of commitment. I will say however, that I have no doubt I could work with you, and you have covered the bigger issues. But I want you also to talk to your chairman about shares being part of any package, plus maybe an interest-free loan to facilitate the purchase of a house. And I am sure there may be other offers not yet envisaged which I will need to take into consideration. Not least will be that I may want Heather to come with me as my PA, if she wants to, of course."

Thanks were given and positive noises made, but I couldn't resist a quiet aside to Henry that I hoped not to see the idiot who had been sent home again, and that their head of personnel or whatever they were called — human resources, perhaps — should be tasked to look a bit more carefully at long-term staff and their ongoing suitability. A bit cheeky, but I wanted everything I could get so that if I did move to them, I would hit the ground running, with dead wood underfoot already cleared.

After lunch, when everyone had departed, Heather and I had a coffee and a brandy in our room and went to bed for an hour before preparing for tonight's meeting with contestant B at Langan's. Another nice short session just to relax properly seemed in order, so we kissed and cuddled, which worked well, and we both had a good nap before changing into smart casual for Langan's. I gave Team A 7 out of 10 overall with a big 9 out of 10 for Henry, my type of guy. Heather agreed but was a bit disappointed that the oik who disgraced himself was ever allowed at the meeting. That defect alone might scupper a deal.

Langan's was great, glad they were picking up the tab, and Michael Caine was at his table near the door only two tables from us. The food was excellent; the wine too and the Hennessy XO with coffee was as usual superb. We went through a similar but smoother performance by the team the company brought, and they were a younger and sharper band, more subtle than Team A, but I liked them all and the right noises were made. Just a bit concerned that they were too smooth and there was not much specificity about what might be on offer. They tried to be very laid back, but I knew that this was all an act, and they were just as desperate as team A were to get me and my package, and if they thought Langan's would make any difference whatsoever, they were wrong.

Heather too was similarly unimpressed by their approach and like me would have liked a bit more honest desire to be shown. It seemed to her that they thought we were from the sticks and could easily be soft-soaped. Big mistake. We gave the team 7 out of 10, and the same mark for their leader. I said, "Unless things get worse, I can't see them in the quarter finals at this stage."

Heather said, "I think we should take phase 2 on the road and look at the candidates at their head offices and tour some of their plants, to see if the rhetoric gels with the bullshit." I concurred.

We went to our room and relaxed after what had been a hectic day but were well satisfied with matters so far.

I asked Heather for any points she might have from observing all that happened, and she said, "Nothing major, you did pretty well, and it did no harm that team B allowed your youthful looks and eagerness to make them feel a little superior so that they relaxed their guard a bit and may have missed the boat. You are playing this about right and more gravitas would not work coming from you. Plenty of time to show your teeth in the later stages. But tell me, are you any nearer to staying than before or further away?"

I thought a moment and said, "My gut tells me that any slight advantage I might gain from bargaining would be eroded by the need for a complete change of staff and management above me as well and might get in the way of progress. So, I think I lean towards the status quo at present. However, should a decisive and significant advantage emerge from one of the candidates, I could easily change my position on that. After all, it's the job and the thrill and power it gives me, not so much the money or status as such."

She said, "Well put and good thinking, you don't really need me at this point."

I said, "Always need you, you know that."

Breakfast at the Savoy was superb, everything anyone could want and top quality. I gave Charles a quick call and updated him and said that we have lunch in London with group C then were training up to Manchester for group D for an evening dinner meeting, and might come back tonight, but probably would get a room and come back early tomorrow. I said, "I did clear with you about Heather's temporary appointment as my PA, didn't I? If not, she shared my room anyway, so just the extra transport costs involved which I will pay, but more importantly, I am making it a condition, go or stay, that she will be my PA in a permanent position, if she agrees that is!"

He replied, with a chuckle, that she makes a very good PA for sure, and said, "You know you can virtually write your own cheque here."

Nice to hear.

So, to Browns Hotel where the restaurant specialised in fresh fish to meet group C. And this was a different type of company, very large, with extensive international operations and with plant and offices in several countries. They had a group consisting of several nationalities to greet us, eight in all! They were clearly keen to make an impact. I was pretty laid back and cool by now in the process, but I was watching who I considered to be the number-two player who sat on Michael's right. Heather of course sat on my left. Introductions took a while as they clearly sought to impress me with their size and scope, and I looked straight at each one in turn and gave them my full attention as they were introduced. All were MDs or Chief Execs of different parts of the group, other than the one who I spotted as the number-two man, who was the Finance Director for the whole group, and sat on the main board with Michael who was Chief Executive Director of the group. Some team!

I said at the outset, "Ladies and gentlemen (nodding to the two women in their party and of course including Heather), I confess I am impressed by how important you clearly believe this meeting to be, and I am grateful to have the opportunity to meet you all. But today, we cannot cover all you might desire, and rather I wish to get a good general feel of your group's wishes relating to my particular project perhaps being reproduced, with variations, in your group. So, if I may I would like to start by giving you a few pointers as to what I would aspire to achieve at whichever company or group I join, if, in fact, I am minded moving at all. Clearly more detailed meetings will be appropriate later perhaps. Then I would like you to give some general information about the sort of package and the scope of my remit should I join you, rather than get into specifics. If at any point you wish for a little more clarification don't hesitate to stop me. Heather will, I assure you, if she feels the need."

This produced chuckles all round and an outright laugh from Michael. Heather just smiled and said nothing.

"My general purpose will be to look at change to systems, in all departments, in order to produce a cleaner, meaner, machine. Habits and machinery will change. Systems of purchasing and procurement of services within and without the existing group structure will be looked at, analysed, tested and whatever is necessary to produce not just cost and efficiency improvements but better quality and service all round. The bottom line will be to produce more, sell more and in a relatively short time, say one year, will yield measurable positive results overall. I will need the right team or teams, the full support of the top management and directors, I will need my personal authority enhanced by a directorship at the best level possible and only be answerable to Michael and your Chairman, subject to a supporting main board majority, and I want to be on that main board. The monetary reward I simply say will be commensurate and need not be dwelt on here as my main concern is the job, the power to deliver results, freedom of action and movement around the whole group, and my personal decision on all candidates who would join me. And Heather shall be offered the job of continuing as my PA plus a significant management role, and again pay, etc. will be commensurate. She will tell you herself that until she sees exactly what the final package is for me and her, she will not commit herself."

"I am happy to elucidate wherever necessary, but no detailed specifics please just ballpark figures and outline information on any issue at this meeting please. We have one more meeting tomorrow making four so far, I do not rule out more as there is great interest and I anticipate eight meetings minimum in total, then I shall decide which candidates to take forward to the second round of meetings at which point more specifics will be made available. Thanks for your attention and patience."

Heather interjected at this point and quietly said, "Do excuse me interrupting please, what James has said is, as you know, just a broad general scenario, but I can tell you that he is very determined to get exactly what he wants, no ifs, no buts, and will need the final commitment to at least a five-year binding contract for the first phases of the grand scheme, with an option to renew for a further five years. I, for my part already have a demanding and interesting management career which I would be reluctant to throw away unless I received similar contractual assurances to James and a significant salary increase and other incentives. But I am in principle amenable to this opportunity alongside James although, as a married woman, I have other commitments, so the money side does matter perhaps a bit more to me than it does to James." And Heather looked to me for acceptance of what she had said, not at anyone else. I smiled at her, then looked around and said, "So you see ladies and gentlemen, what you are up against!" Laughter and a little applause all round. "Just one more point neither of us mentioned in this meeting so far, I will be looking to be given shares in your group, as will Heather, and medical insurance and good index linked pensions too."

Michael said, "Well James and Heather, I am sure you make a formidable team all by yourselves, and thank you both for your opening speeches, most refreshing and enlightening. I for one applaud your directness and transparent sincerity and honesty, not to mention courage and I say here and now, you will get whatever you want if you choose us as your next move. Subject of course to the Chairman's thoughts and the main board's majority approval, which I am confident of delivering. And in the spirit of honesty and openness, James and Heather, I have taken the liberty of recording this meeting up to this point for the Chairman's ears only and I beg your indulgence as I wish the Chairman to hear what we have all said, which after your introductory speech I believe is doubly important. However, I will undertake to destroy this tape as soon as the Chairman has heard it and there will be no copies unless you yourselves would like one."

I said, "Well that's fine Michael and thanks for telling me all that. I have a recording as well don't I Heather? We can hardly complain, and I think for the rest of the meetings we hold we shall declare our intention to record beforehand. So, can we move on please and have lunch and continue the discussion informally from here, as we do have a train to catch for our final meeting of this phase."

We moved from the private room we had been into the restaurant and had a superb meal of various shellfish including lobster, and a choice of fish including Dover sole, red snapper, halibut and sea bream. There were lots of fresh vegetables and a delicious raspberry sorbet, with various cakes and puddings for those who wanted them, plus an excellent Chardonnay and also Moet Champagne followed by coffee and cognac. I joked with Michael saying that all future meetings in the UK should be here and he said, "I shall see to it."

The Finance Director, Peter, collared me and asked a few pertinent questions and I confirmed that I wanted access to all the companies and plant and offices throughout the world in order to draw up a suitable strategic plan for implementing cross-border changes to production, parts manufacture, and the like. It would have to be a carefully coordinated plan so that no uncalled- for disruption to production and markets were experienced. He said it could be done with top management backing, but we would have to tread very carefully and have an in-house international lawyer for the whole period of planning and implementation."

"Make it happen," I said.

I got the impression that the FD was a very important part of this process as he admitted he saw the TV show I did and had followed matters including my lectures at universities, etc. and he clearly thought we were a winning team, with potential to improve his group's profitability and long-term desire for growth.

We caught the train, just, and chatted on the way up to Manchester about our first three candidates and had a quick look at candidate 4. They were bigger than our company but not multinational, concentrating on home markets, but were run by a hard-headed group of directors and managers predominantly from the Northwest of England. We didn't know how ambitious they were or how far their budget could stretch, that we could discover in some measure today. The main man was at this meeting, the Chairman and Chief Executive and also a large shareholder Sir Philip, was a very well-known entrepreneur and industrialist who did not suffer fools gladly but was renowned for standing up for his own people as well as being ruthless if they failed. Most importantly he was no bullshitter and called a spade a shovel, and what he promised he invariably delivered. I liked him already.

We made it to the venue at a suite in a conference centre based on one of the new quayside hotels, which already had a reputation for comfort, good communications, and facilities. Turned out that Sir Philip built it!

We entered the conference suite at quarter to seven, fifteen minutes early and had not decided at that point if we would stay the night. They were already seated and waiting, obviously being briefed by Sir Philip who was easily recognisable as he was a large bluff-looking man with power oozing from him.

He saw us coming in and leapt up shouting, "You are early, well done, come in and take a seat and I will introduce you both. Gentlemen," he said to his team of six men, "this is James and Heather, and these men are all from my team." He named them even though they had thoughtfully provided both lapel badges and placed name plates in front of each of them. "Welcome to Manchester both; I know that you are from not too far away but have come straight up from London where you were entertained by our well-known competitors, and right royally I am told. Can't compete on that front I'm afraid, but you will have a nice supper for the second part of the meeting of good, simple, local food and our hospitality includes locally brewed real ale if desired, or whatever else you may want. So how about we have a drink right away as you must be thirsty after all that talking and rich food."

I laughed and said, "I haven't had a Northern welcome like that until now on this particular trip and I warn you a couple of drinks might make me more boisterous, but not careless. So, I will try a pint of your famous ale please; what would you like Heather?"

She said, "I will have a gin and tonic with ice and lemon please."

A waiter was summoned and most of his team had a half of beer, but Sir Philip joined me having a pint, as I knew he would. When the drinks had been served and we had taken a swallow, I asked Sir Philip, "How would you like to play this? I am happy to set out my position, but I would be even happier to let you tell me in general terms, nothing too specific at this stage, what you are offering me, not money or rank or sweeteners. I want to know what you believe is the job that I can do for you and why."

"I like it, a man after my own heart, straight to the point, let's get down to business. I have, of course, heard all about you, your company, your project, and the excellent results so far. I also have seen your TV show and read about your lectures at the universities, and I confess I have also done some due diligence on you. Frankly, I like what I have seen and heard, and I want you to come and join me and do the same or better for our company. I am also aware of your shopping list both in terms of position, responsibility, powers you will need, team of your choice, five-year minimum contract, shares in the company, everything, and I say to you I can match or better anything you have been, or may be offered to move your team, (nodding towards Heather) be it two or twenty, to our camp. You will have complete autonomy for five years and I will have the option of renewal for a further five years. But, in those first five years no one, not even me, will be able to veto or undermine your efforts in any way. Only a man in my position in a company of our size or greater, can offer the freedom I have outlined. This is because I am a major shareholder. The rest of the package is whatever you make it, and the same goes for you, Heather, if you choose to come as PA to James, General Manager of all offices, personnel, support systems and staff and a directorship is yours. And if I have missed anything just say and it will be added. "Let's eat,"

I said, "I think I have heard enough. You amaze me and you also interest me. Naturally, I will want to look at your whole operation and see what's to be done and test a few people in situ, and take legal advice, but I can tell you now that I am strongly minded putting you straight on the next phase list, the first I may add to which I have said this. But first, Heather, what is your immediate reaction?"

Heather looked at her notes, put her head back and looked at the ceiling, took a sip of her drink, deliberated a few more seconds and, looking just at me, said, "It sounds very good; I have no doubt that Sir Philip is a man of his word and in a very strong position to deliver what he says he will deliver. I will need to think very carefully about all the implications for me, but I believe, subject as you say to legal advice, this decision to put this offer straight through to the second-level scrutiny is sound for you and probably also for me, but I will need a bit of time for further consideration. Not of incentives or money, all the rest of it, including my own personal position."

Sir Philip answered, "Splendid, let's eat and drink to that." And he led the happy team, none of whom had even spoken, into the hotel restaurant where, amongst other delights, was a huge baron of beef sitting on a massive grill and there were displays of partridge, guinea fowl, pheasant and other game and meats. Plus, a refrigerated fresh fish cabinet and assorted seafood on display. The chefs were dressed in striped, blue aprons and had on white hats and gloves and there was a quiet murmur from the other diners, all of whom knew the hotel owner had walked in with ten other people to the central table, which was already laid out with all the cutlery and glassware imaginable, plus several iced buckets containing wine and Champagne and candelabra with real lighted candles. On the stage was a small band playing typical Palm Court numbers, but not loudly. What a scene, fantastic. I turned to Heather and mouthed "A room" and she nodded.

I said to Sir Philip, "Can you order us a nice suite for the night, I don't think we will be going home."

"Already done my boy," he said with a twinkle in his eye, "And your luggage is already in it and the head waiter will organise you when the time comes."

He then directed me to sit at his right and Heather on his left which she gracefully accepted.

We had a great evening with Sir Philip and his team and went happily to bed where we both gratefully went straight to sleep, well content with what we had achieved so far.

The following morning, we were up, breakfasted and went to pay our bill only to find it was already settled. I asked the desk manager to give our thanks to Sir Philip when he saw him, and we took a taxi to the station and train back home where I had left my car. Then we went into the office together and gave a first-hand verbal report on everything we had done so far to Charles, and he naturally said, "Very impressive; so, are you in a position to make any decisions yet?"

I said, "Not yet, except for the one we made about putting Sir Philip's company into the next round, but no one else at present, and I note that I have several messages from other suitors which Heather and I will look at this afternoon and I will keep you informed."

He said, "And am I to take it that we also are in the next round?" I laughed and said, "You will be in the final play-off, that's for sure, and that will be the time for us to review all the options and form our decision, and I can tell you this, there will have to be a considerable advantage if I am to abandon my team here and your company, but clearly I cannot rule that out. I hope you understand that position and respect my wishes, and Heather's of course. She will almost certainly be a large factor in my final decision. Meanwhile I will keep you advised of all developments so that you have the maximum time and sufficient detail with which to formulate your final offer."

"Fair enough," he said.

Chapter 16

We sifted the calls and messages from people who said they wanted to meet to discuss an offer with me about the project and just sent acknowledgements and thanks to most, selecting six more for further analysis. We gathered data on these, and Heather ruled out one straight away as too small, and I ruled out another for being full of vague bullshit, despite the size and scope of the company involved. This left four to look more closely at and make appointments with, but this time I decided to take longer and space them out so that no more than one per day was to be booked over the next week.

I asked Heather, "Now we have come this far, I think you should now try to make a decision at least in principle, give your current employer fair notice and join me here as my permanent PA in the sure and certain knowledge of what sort of future lies ahead for you. Larger salary, a directorship, a separate management function within the company if that's what you want; better pension and free medical insurance; help if you need to move home, with or without your husband, and more. You will want to have a talk with him I'm sure, but if you prefer to stay with him, or alone, I can live with that, but if you will, I am prepared and happy to live with you in a new home as a couple, regardless of whether you two divorce or not. Big decisions I know, and I will respect whatever you decide providing you will stick with me in my future career at least for the five-year contract."

"Wow Jim, she said, "it's a huge move for anyone to consider, but I will immediately agree to the last part, sticking with you in the new company, or the old, along the lines you lay out, which I am certain you can deliver. I am really fed up with my other half and I think I will suggest a trial separation for two years, live alone or with you, the latter is great for me. I don't particularly want a divorce, messy things, but I have not slept with him since the day we bumped into each other outside the wine bar. Really our marriage is effectively over. So, in principle, yes, yes, and yes, subject to my breaking all this to him at home, and I really don't think he will be a problem. I will not insist on selling our house at present, and he has his own life to lead. But let's just see what he says before jumping ship altogether. I do see my future with you at least for five years; I don't want to tie you down or marry you; I don't want children. I want what we have now but a bit more official, so living together in a new place would be good, and I would like to own half of it and make a 50% contribution to all costs so that we both know exactly where we stand. But first let's get these next meetings organised; I will send my resignation to my current employer, and I want a temporary contract here with the things we have discussed put in place, subject only to the first five-year contract being ratified. Do you think they will do that?"

"Yes, I do," I said, "if they want any chance of retaining me, but then if we both move on, I will ensure we get all we want from a new employer, that's a given."

"It's a deal," we both said, and we shook hands and kissed.

Then we went to work contacting the would-be suitors, making appointments and working out the logistics and also researching each one of them. They were all quite major players, three with just UK offices and plants; the fourth was truly international with their head office in London and their UK factory, and other depots situated in the South and the Midlands and their overseas sites were in Italy, Spain, France and one in the USA. But they were looking to get into the Far East markets and scouting for a production site in Malaysia and Australasia generally with offices and maybe even a new HQ in that area to cover that region. But it was anticipated that the General HQ would remain in London where the Metals and Stock Markets and Finance majors were all situated.

I said to Heather that I thought the international one was in a state of flux and so it might not be suitable, but we should see their UK operation in the first instance and leave the foreign bases until the next round of the selection process if they got that far. So, we asked to see all the UK plants of all four candidates first with morning appointments, followed by afternoon or next day appointments for the actual meetings. I also asked Heather to make a plant visit and HO appointment with Sir Philip's company, as we were already committed to the next round of talks with them.

I left all the transport and hotel bookings to her to attend to in my office and went to see Charles in his office to talk about Heather and the overall situation as things now stood. I called him first and he set aside half an hour after coffee in the directors' lounge. He was there with the Chairman and a couple of other directors but we three split off into a corner for a more private chat over coffee and éclairs. The MD wasn't around so Charles, who as Production Director stood in as MD when he was away, introduced me to the Chairman who said that he was totally aware of what I had achieved and was up to date regarding the first four candidates. He insisted that I call him David.

I brought them up to date regarding the second wave of would-be suitors, explained my slight reluctance concerning the international company and their Far East foray, and that we were in the process of making a series of plant inspections as well as setting up meetings over the next week or so. David immediately said that I was to take all the time I wanted, and that Heather and I should put all costs through our office.

I said, "This brings us to an interesting point in all the negotiations and potential future for both me and Heather, and as you know, I am telling all parties that she is an integral part of my future planning. Go or stay, she would get a similar package to me including being made a director and so we had arrived at a position where I had asked her to commit herself to a future with me, wherever that might be,"

"That's no problem, James, it is fully understood."

"Good," I said, "but I have asked her if she wants to not only commit to me as my PA and fellow director for at least the next five years, but also on a personal level, to become my partner and she has agreed and will be severing her connections with a two-year separation from her husband, with whom she has not really had a proper relationship for some time. She asks therefore, that she is given a contract starting very soon to be my PA but also, should we both stay with you, that the various incentives are written in provisionally, which would be confirmed at the point where she and I signed the five-year contract we have talked about and agreed in principle. I shall be asking all other candidates to commit similarly so all are on a level playing field from that point of view."

Charles began to say something and was not smiling but David immediately grasped the implications and said with a big smile on his face, "Of course, subject to our lawyer's advice we will commit to what you want for Heather and if you went that would cease of course, but if you stay, would be fully ratified in the five-year contact. I see no difficulty with that, and it leaves you both free to concentrate on the job in hand, don't you agree Charles?"

"Yes, I do," said Charles, "I confess I was a little surprised and wrong-footed there, but I see clearly now that the Chairman has clarified, it is quite logical and understandable, and I shall ensure it gets priority attention. But meantime take it as read, I will speak to personnel and accounts and get everything put in place. I will see our lawyers this afternoon. But tell me James, will you be moving in together? If so, our offer of a cheap or even interest-free loan in order to purchase a new home should become a priority once we have the contracts signed."

"Thanks," I said, "that is most helpful, do not bother about changing anything for me at present, I am content to continue as I am until it is all settled."

"Fine," said David, "that's very sensible, but I insist you are appointed as a director with immediate effect and will minute the board about this immediately after this meeting, so your salary will be automatically upgraded appropriately from today and I will look forward to you joining board meetings in due course so that you can keep us all up to date with negotiations. Excellent, know where we are now, don't we, Charles? I will also brief the MD at the first opportunity."

I went back and told Heather the good news and she was delighted and said, "I have spoken to my husband, and I will be meeting him to discuss matters more fully this evening, if that's OK."

"Yes, that's fine; the sooner you are sorted the better, and you can move in with me now if you wish."

She said that things wouldn't take long to sort out, as she was not bothered about anything at their house and she could go and pick stuff up anytime; for now, she just wanted him to know, and then to get on with our project, so yes, she would regard us as cohabiting as of tonight.

We went to a series of meetings similar to the first four and we also saw most of the new candidates' factories and offices, as well as Sir Philip's and it proved a good thing as we were able to see vast scope for improvements and changes which would keep them, and possibly us, busy for much more than five years. It made me consider leaving all the companies and instead setting up a consultancy which could send teams to all the protagonists, but that would take a lot of time to set up and be unacceptably risky, we both agreed. But this was something to bear in mind for the future perhaps. We both felt we needed the security this five-year contact would bring at this juncture in our lives.

We labelled the new contestants F, G H and I, and were variously impressed by all their presentations and selected two, G and I, from this group to join Sir Philip. Then I went back to the one who impressed me most after Sir Philip, which was Henry and his outfit, despite the inclusion of the dissenting member who was sent home.

They all were ready to do whatever we wanted, but none of them came up with a special reason to go for them in particular, so as the packages looked very similar, it was going to boil down to our personal preferences, plus the prospects for the future and location involved. But I still felt on balance that all things being pretty equal, my home team, who I knew very well, had the slight advantage over the rest, despite the size and scope of the two largest groups. With Sir Philip's company a close second. But a lot would depend on what came out at the second phase of meetings, almost semi-finals!

We informed the successful companies that they were into the next phase and invited them to make more comprehensive cases concerning monetary and contractual incentives but also to state why the future would be brighter with their individual companies or groups, from a work angle and scope perspective, what period in years they anticipated the contract might ultimately last, giving their reasons. We asked for all this to be presented in documentary form for our consideration prior to the ultimate meetings which would be just us and them individually not an open competition because we were sworn to secrecy and full confidentiality by this point. One outfit pulled out at this stage, so we just included our own company in at this phase maintaining the four semi-finalists, rather than just have our own company facing one other in the final eliminator. And we asked our company to do exactly as we had asked the others.

Semi-final's day would be one week after receiving their submissions, which we allowed two weeks to prepare, as they came in, Heather and I looked them over and some draft legal documents included. We engaged our own independent firm of solicitors, who specialised in company contract law, to scrutinise the submissions, giving them only a few days, but they managed that OK. They gave their opinions which, in general were pretty complimentary about how we had exploited our position, and approved in principle all which had been submitted, subject of course, to final scrutiny of the five-year contract when we had decided which company we would proceed with. Our company had a distinct and obvious advantage over the rest, but we promised nothing at this point other than fair and open competition and in so doing achieved an overall package which was on a par or better than all the rest, the key point being that we would decide on the second five-year contract not just them. Plus, our company made a house loan not only interest-free but would pay for all the legal and other related costs and fees and the removal as well as a grant of 10,000 pounds for fixtures, fittings and amenities saying, "We want our directors to have a home commensurate with their position within the company and in the community."

And the icing on the cake was an immediate issue of 25,000 shares each, and a further 10,000 for each of the five years of the initial contract.

So, we entered the final with just one outside company against ours, that of Sir Philip, and he tried valiantly with some very nice offers, but at the end of the day home advantage won out and Heather and I decided to stay put. But I promised Sir Philip privately that I would ensure that we would provide a consultancy package, for an appropriate fee, to help him catch up.

Chapter 17

The next five years passed like a dream. All went well; Heather and I were a very busy team and we both were allowed to run what amounted to a consultancy, but remained legally part of the company where I had achieved this breakthrough and, first Sir Philip and then one by one the other main protagonists were allowed to catch up by stages; with our state-of-the-art management structure, which controlled all systems and procurement, along the same lines as before, but with new innovations coming on stream on a regular basis, keeping us ahead of the pack. The company grew in size and complexity and made good profits and Heather and I benefitted proportionally. We were very happy in our beautiful new home with its large garden, a BBQ area, a small outdoor pool, a jacuzzi and a triple garage.

We entertained very rarely, preferring just a few close friends and the occasional invitation to fellow directors' houses for informal meals, especially in the summer when I could indulge my favourite outside occupation, the BBQ!

I never for one single moment had any doubts or complaints about our taking on the industry in general while staying put at the company that gave me the opportunity, space, and support to develop what had become an industry leader in dynamic and reforming industrial support systems for all mid to large companies.

On the personal level, I had stopped seeing any other women at all in terms of a sexual relationship, although I still saw Felicity, Sarah, and George occasionally, and all were doing well and were fulsome in praise for what Heather and I had achieved together. I never saw Edna or Rosy again and heard nothing about them at all. Heather and I were a couple in every sense of the word, and we both were committed to our work projects and each other, and there was no time or reason for any other relationship.

The first year as a full director had been quite tough. I had a lot to learn and all the other directors were very helpful, but gradually I became a fully contributing board member and after three years, when the Chairman moved on, Charles took over as Chairman and I was offered MD, which I accepted. Heather and I were now significant shareholders in the company, dividends were paid every year and were growing in size as our shares increased, added incentive to keep performing well for the company.

In addition, Heather had divorced her husband and bought his half of their house which she decided to keep and let out for extra income and for long-term capital gain. I had done the same thing, kept my smaller house and let that out, and we had both bought three further small properties each, which we let through just one local agent, so we had no responsibilities there to occupy our valuable time. Property prices were rocketing, and we both made significant capital gains and salted the income away, which added to our bonuses and dividends from the company, plus our very significant salaries and the interest-free loan we had, meant we had a fairly large surplus of income over expenditure. Heather had her property portfolio including half of our home as did I, so we were both very content with that situation.

My salary was significantly higher than Heather's now I was MD, as were share allocations, but she said she was fine with all that as I had done the lion's share of the initial project work and put the company and her in the position, we were in.

The consultancy income was shared half with the company and half between Heather and me. That pulled in further significant income for us all. Sir Philip tried a few times to get me to jump ship, but as our consultancy was doing the trick for his company, he was well content with us staying there, in competition, but giving guidance and advice from time to time and he made sure we were well rewarded for it.

Heather and I knew that the momentum of the project changes would eventually diminish, although remain significant for many years to come, and me being MD meant I had a much bigger all-round role to play for the company as time went on, so our positions were secure, barring some unforeseen catastrophe. In any case our assets in property, shares and other investments we were making in the stock market, using our extensive knowledge to select likely winners, were getting to the point where, if we wanted to, we could step back and do something completely different, but neither of us wanted that.

As we approached the end of the initial five-year contract and started to formulate the succeeding five-year deal, which had been enshrined at the outset as part of the cost of retaining us, we started to take stock of our position and look further ahead.

By this time, the years between us hadn't changed of course, Heather was approaching forty and I was in my thirty-first year, a nine-year difference in our ages, not that anyone would have guessed it. Heather was a very different woman to when I first met her. She had, through physiotherapy and a special programme with her fitness specialist at the local health club, corrected her slight stoop so she stood a couple of inches taller than me and with heels she was almost six feet tall. She had maintained a superb figure and as a director and leading consultant, she had acquired quite an aura of competence and authority about her. She was a formidable woman and highly respected throughout the industry. She had continued lecturing at colleges and universities and had found time to add a BSc to her BA through the Open University. What a woman, and fantastic still in bed, which was good for both of us and reduced the possibility of me straying, as I had in my earlier years. Never say never I thought, I was only thirty and kept pretty fit myself, but I never gave a thought to my misspent youthful activities at all.

Then the unthinkable happed: Heather was pregnant! Oh shit, not again I thought, Felicity did it at thirty-eight I think it was; Heather was thirty-nine, and this time there could be no doubt whatever who the father was, unless she had completely bamboozled me, and I knew deep down that was impossible. We sat and looked at each other stupefied and I said, "Well, what shall we do about this?"

She said, "You tell me; I have been on the pill for years then for the last three years I have been fitted with a coil, but neither is fool proof and to be honest, I am gobsmacked. I never wanted children primarily because I didn't want to be tied to that idiot I married, but also because I felt I had something to contribute other than children. But look at what we have already achieved."

"Heather," I said, "I never wanted children either, or to get married, but I confess that the last five years with you have been wonderful and I believe getting married would in itself be no problem, no different than our partnership. And I don't think I would want this baby aborted or adopted. So, in short, will you marry me, have my baby and we will just adapt our life to it and carry on as before. We can well afford an au pair, a nanny, child minders, whatever, or you could take a sabbatical if that appealed to you, whatever you think is best for you and me and the baby."

Heather was gobsmacked, "You really mean all that don't you?"

"The answer is yes. Yes, I would love to marry you and have this baby, the rest I won't even think about right now." And she was in my arms, crying and I was crying too, such a shock for both of us, it was incredible how we had both decided instantly that marriage and a baby were both fine with us after so many disavowals through the years since we first met. We decided not to tell anyone else yet, to make sure, as sure as we could, that this pregnancy was viable, and make some plans before we broke the news. She said how she very much wanted to continue with the second phase of the project and nothing on earth would stop her, even if part of the time she worked from home. I knew if she said that, she was right, she was unstoppable once embarked on a course of action. We laughed and cried some more then opened a bottle of Champagne and I allowed her two glasses, and I quaffed the rest, and we went on to eat the meal she had prepared, with me offering numerous toasts to our future together, our baby, our work, everything. So, I confess I got a bit pissed and went to bed singing, but she just laughed and said, "Don't think you can change anything in the morning, or you are in big trouble."

Chapter 18

The scan proved the baby, a boy, was looking very good and there were no problems with Heather's general health and fitness to carry to term, so that was that.

I told the Chairman Charles all about it and he was delighted saying, "Absolutely no problem, write your own agenda, take whatever steps you want within reason and common sense, and you know I will back you both to the hilt. You are the main reason I am here as Chairman today. Yes, I chose you to back and push, and thank goodness I was right, and you and Heather have contributed hugely to this company's current very competitive and profitable position in the UK market."

"And in any case," he continued, you have a cast-iron successor five-year contract to fulfil, and I am certain that you will succeed as well as you have in the first five years."

I said, "That's a nice thought Charles, but as I am sure you are aware, the competition is slowly catching up, partly thanks to our skills they are getting through our consultancy project."

He replied, "Yes, but even a part-time Heather and you are more than a match for any of them and I am confident you will keep us ahead of the game and will in any case think up some other plan which will compensate for whatever improvement they are managing."

So we appeared to be pretty sure of carrying on as we were, but I was already working, together with Heather, on a couple of promising new ideas for greater efficiency and quality improvement. Our huge customer base, was very pleased with our product and would remain loyal for many years to come with only a modest improvement, and we intended that it would in fact be far better than modest.

So on we went, Heather was getting more noticeably pregnant all the while and we were forever getting words of wisdom and encouragement from all around us. We redoubled our efforts as we entered the first year of our second five-year plan. We both had parents still alive, and we shared our happy knowledge of our impending nuptials and birth of our son, and they were all delighted. We planned a simple registry office wedding soon, followed by a low-key celebration party at our house for about fifty guests, hired a catering company and had a marquee ordered for a date only about three weeks hence.

I did not invite any of my old female friends of course and there were no press articles or other public announcements, and the day soon came. Heather and I wanted it as low-key as possible so only close family came to the registry office and then it was straight back home where the rest of the guests waited and straight into the garden and the marquee, where we had organised a sit-down meal for fifty-six. There was a small band to play suitable music, some modern some old and there was a small wooden-floored dance area, and it all went very well. Just a few speeches and then the band played requests while people danced, and it all went very much to plan. After suitable farewells all round, the bride and groom retired to their quarters, the caterers quickly tidied up and the marquee was left until the following morning so by the time we surfaced and had breakfast, all was more or less back to normal, except we were man and wife!

It had been great that our parents could all come, and we had made sure they were looked after and that they were given lots of polite attention from our friends and colleagues. They went off to their hotel which we had booked for them and were clearly very happy for us both and 'the bump' and couldn't wait to meet him, etc. I had a sudden thought, which I knew I must keep to myself, that Felicity and George's boy whose name I had forgotten or perhaps I never knew — but hold on yes, it was David I was practically certain, would be about ten years old, and if he were mine? Then I put that right out of my mind and focussed on what was in front of me family and my career, no room for anything else.

We had a week in Sardinia, where no one knew us, and relaxed totally in a small but discreet and well-appointed hotel where we lazed about, swimming in the pool, eating al fresco at the everyday BBQ at lunch, and in the candlelit restaurant at night and came back refreshed and invigorated to our desks on the following Monday. We got straight into our backlog of paperwork and had it all cleared by mid-afternoon.

We went home early, ready for our first board meeting as a man and wife team at ten on Tuesday morning.

Nothing changed; we were welcomed and applauded by the full board and then it was just business as usual with both my wife and I contributing an update of the almost ready for publishing first five-year plan report and set out some of our ideas and plans going into the next phase, and if anyone ever doubted our commitment and capability, I think we put any such doubts to bed.

The one small difference was that from here on in until at least a month or two after the baby was born, all conferences were held at our office or by telephone and video if they involved Heather. I went out and about as usual and took up some of her commitments to lectures and so on, using briefing material Heather had prepared for me. I found it refreshing to go back to these and everybody was pleased to see me and hear the news about our marriage and impending baby.

Eventually I persuaded Heather to stay at home and to only do a fraction of the work she normally did, but of course I had no real control, and she did what she wanted to and there were no obvious problems like getting overtired. She swam in the pool when it was warm enough and attended her gym club where her fitness coach provided her with a special programme for first-time mothers of her vintage!

In no time it seemed, she had contractions and her waters broke and she was admitted immediately into a private hospital paid for by our employers. The baby was born, weighed 8lb 12 oz and was healthy and normal and he began breast feeding almost immediately. They insisted she stay in for three days and then he and she came home where of course all amenities and facilities had been planned and prepared by Heather. The girl she had chosen as part nurse, part PA, part cleaner and cook, had moved in with us and took up the reins of her new job. Even so, Heather insisted on doing the night feed and changes herself, but with minimal disturbance to me as she chose to feed sitting in a rocking chair in the nursery.

We decided to call him Nathanial James after my father and me and booked his christening for a few weeks hence at our local parish church and registered his birth at the office situated in the County Council

Offices. He thrived under the expert care of Heather and her PA, and had all the usual checks, inoculations, etc. although I couldn't tell you what!

Meanwhile I forged ahead with our work plans, consulting Heather most days so she remained very much in touch with everything and in about ten weeks, she resumed full-time service to the company, sometimes calling in at home for lunch and to ensure Nat was fine. The general factotum, Kath, was superb, completely unflappable, and competent, so Heather stopped the midday visits pretty quickly, being satisfied with telephone reports and not daily even then. Kath was Miss Super-efficient and was a plain dumpy girl with no interests other than her own family in the village and ours, so that meant I was not distracted by her becoming part of our family. We made sure that she got appreciation on a regular basis, and she loved us all. We were able to take her with us on away visits bringing Nat of course and all his equipment which we managed quite comfortably as I had purchased a seven-seater 4X4 Mercedes for UK use and we would hire similar if we went abroad.

Our clients soon became accustomed to our family appearing at their premises and made sure we had a separate room near to their meeting rooms for Kath and Nat and all his gear, and staff would find excuses to come and see them, a most unusual site in what was still very much a male bastion in many firms, but as always, we were pioneering. The trade unions and minority groups loved it and quoted our example to assist their own workers' emancipation.

Work went well and our second phase plan was bearing fruit, so all round things were going very smoothly and then Heather broke the news that number two was on the way! I protested that it couldn't be as I had hardly seen her long enough to get her pregnant again and she laughed — pointing out that by her calculations meaningful cohabitation with me must average four times a week minimum! And furthermore, she had taken no precautions at all since the coil had been removed as she believed the guff about Nat being a "late pre-menopausal surge" and in any case she wanted at least two now she had one, so there! Secretly I was really pleased about it, but of course Heather realised that almost immediately.

So we went through the same procedures which had worked so well the first time around and it all worked like clockwork and Joanna Heather was born not quite as big as Nat but long in the body and legs like her mother, and with the same hair colouring. Kath was delighted and very happy and prepared to deal with the doubling of her baby-oriented duties.

But after Jo was born, Heather had another coil fitted and we decided to call it a day regarding babies, unless of course another miracle happened. By this time everyone in our company and all our clients knew about the caravan coming to town when we needed to visit their various plants around the country and scarcely an eyebrow was raised. They all knew Heather well and liked her a lot but, in any case, they knew how formidable she could be if aroused.

So we progressed through the next couple of years with our growing family and Kath remained happily with us, but Heather took on a work-related PA so that aspect was relinquished somewhat reluctantly, but really she had her hands full and deep down minded not at all.

We had expanded our consultancy-based work so that it incorporated more general business organisational advice packages, relatively unconnected to the efficiency-based structure of the project work we had spearheaded the two five-year plans with. And I pushed the board to allow us to launch our own company selling different packages of advice and implementation of our general business model. They agreed providing I gave a free copy of all the advice packages we sold independently from the main company, to which we readily acceded.

I said, "And if we expand further into any area remotely similar to yours, we will undertake to provide you with full information and advice, but I will reserve the right, in consultation with Heather, to make some sort of charge where such a package is adopted by this board."

They all murmured assent, but I insisted that I wanted this all put in an outline planning and implementation document by my own lawyers because, I pointed out, this board's constitution might change significantly enough that informal assurances minuted here would not be the sort of protection we feel we need. I said, "Come on fellow board members, you have nothing to lose and everything to gain. I will guarantee full disclosure and make everything we introduce available to you at below market rate; what could be fairer than that and, when, if ever, have Heather or I let this company down?"

Charles interjected at his point and said, "Ladies and gentlemen, I do not want to see anything half-hearted about this response to what I see as an excellent and well-balanced proposal from which we stand to gain, as we have from everything the MD and his wife Heather have done for us for the last eight years or more. I want 100% commitment to this plan in entirety here and now, including the obtaining of a suitable contractual document being prepared by James' own lawyers as he proposes. I now call on you to vote yea or nay, no abstentions accepted."

They all looked a bit sheepish and immediately all put up their hands for a unanimous yea vote, which was declared and accepted and minuted by the Chairman.

I had made a note of the two members who had muttered when I proposed this first and made a promise to myself that they would not survive if I ever became Chairman. Although, judging from the scowl Charles gave them maybe they would not be my problem soon.

I smiled at them all however and graciously accepted their full and unequivocal acceptance of my plan and Heather chipped in with a "Hear, hear!" so we moved to the next business.

Afterwards Charles apologised for the mealy-mouthed support of members X and Y and said, "If I get them off the board, have you any candidates in mind to replace them?"

I asked him if he had any and he indicated one such who I readily agreed to and then I suggested the man who had supported us completely throughout the last eight years, and was a senior manager in the Production, Development & Research Division, called Arthur.

Charles immediately said, "Good choice, very sound man, I will approach him myself and make sure he wants it, as I will the other candidate. Furthermore, my intention is to make your informal Vice Chairmanship an actual ratified appointment at the same time, so if anything like this comes up again, you can jump on it like I did. And take it as read, if I have anything to do with it and I will, you will be my natural successor, although not for some time yet I hope."

"Thanks Charles, much appreciated, and can I take it my share and bonus calculations will reflect my new formal status? I ask this because as you will be well aware, I have significant holdings of shares now as does Heather as we have bought quite a lot on the stock market as well as the ones we have earned. At the last look I had, she and I now own about 12% of the company."

"Good heavens James, you have been very shrewd about all this, and I will not only ensure your allocation equals mine, but privately I can tell you that if I sell mine for any reason I will offer you first refusal, and sell them to you direct, cutting out the brokers' share. And just between you and me I currently hold 10% so that together with any more we may get, will make you and Heather very significant shareholders in the future."

"Noted and many thanks Charles, I am sure we will be open to such a proposal when the time comes."

Chapter 19

We did consult our lawyers and had a contract drawn up between Heather and me, owners of our new company we called H & J Industrial Consultants Limited or HJIC Limited for short, to supply packages developed by our new company to the original company on which we were board members. There was no conflict of interests as it was all laid out exactly what type of packages were envisaged and we undertook to supply these packages to the main company at a discounted rate of 25% from current market value, determined by the last year's aggregate sale of similar packages on the open market. Charles, together with the new board, which had changed two of its members, who had also decided to leave the company with a very generous farewell deal, and with me as Vice Chairman, had received legal clearance and ratified the deal there and then.

So Heather and I took on a small staff of four people *pro tem* and pushed out our pre-prepared marketing material. We started taking calls almost immediately from medium to small companies, partnerships, and even one-man outfits. We drew up a visiting and appraisal plan and put two of our new staff straight on the road, trained and briefed and equipped with lots of pamphlets and charts, to evaluate the market and make outline proposals for Heather and me to consider.

We rented a small unit in a nearby office building and the remaining two personnel manned the phones and fax machine and handled the logistics of the salesmen, fielded enquiries and anything else they or we could think of at that early time. Word got around fast, and a number of medium-to-small businesses, were getting in touch who wouldn't have been listened to before, but we made it clear from the start saying, "We can help your bottom line whether you are a large or a small company; no job is too small to consider or too large." And our company name incorporating my first initial and Heather's was all the pedigree we needed.

The main work for our employees continued unabated, and the twenty-strong team we had there ensured that we were kept totally in touch and of course Heather and I made all the big decisions, but our Division Manager ran the show on a day-to-day basis. As we had recruited and trained him, he knew very well what was required of him. We still gave our personal attention to any new contracts and guided the team as to how we wanted matters to proceed, but really it was a well-oiled machine which, with the occasional touch from the tiller, sailed on serenely.

It was more fun however for Heather and me to put a lot of energy into growing our own fledgling company and we derived much satisfaction from each little gain and progress generally, and when one or two good-sized contracts were won, we personally visited the clients and looked first-hand at their situations and made sound comments regarding what to do and when. This was much appreciated and our reputation as a caring company grew exponentially.

I was increasingly drawn to different parts of the UK on projects large and small and Heather became more involved locally as this helped her to keep tabs on the children and their upbringing was, of course, the most important thing on our horizon. She still attended all main board meetings at what we regarded as our parent company even though we were 100 % shareholders of our own company. She had lost none of her steel or control and was still universally respected. And on a few occasions, she stood in for me as MD with Charles' support and approval when I was away, particularly if I was abroad which was happening more now that we had contracts with an increasing number of international clients and our 'parent' company.

Heather was now forty-four and still very attractive and quite fit but I confess that at thirty-five, found myself looking occasionally at some striking younger woman when they were thrust, as it were, in front of me. I reasoned that this was to be expected but I vowed to myself that however much I was attracted by some younger possibly more nubile woman, I would not let any relationship get out of hand or threaten my wife's and my relationship. I suppose it was bound to happen and it did. I was in the lift one day with a particularly attractive young married woman who I had dealings with on an irregular basis and I became aware that she was giving me the sort of attention that years ago I took for granted, but for some years had not affected me at all. There was no one in the lift but us, with three floors to go, and I suddenly leaned forward and kissed her on the lips, and she responded by opening her lips and giving me a clear indication that it was an acceptable thing to do.

I didn't apologise, I simply said, "Get in your car if you have one and follow me, discreetly please."

She nodded and we arrived at the basement car park, and I went to my car and noted she went to a Mini Cooper, and I exited the car park, turned left, and headed towards the countryside looking for a suitable stop for a discreet chat.

We parked under some spreading chestnut trees at the side of a shady and little used lane and she locked her car up and came round and got in my passenger seat and I drove on about 500 yards to a suitable similar stopping point, parked up and killed the engine and said, "Well Janet, if I offended you, I'm sorry, if I didn't then let's see where we are at."

She leaned over and kissed me and said, "This is where we are at, I am married, so are you and I have fancied you for some time, so here we are, your move."

I said, "You are a very attractive woman and I have not trodden this particular path for some years, but I think I am ready to do it again if you are. But let us understand each other: I love my wife and children and if we are to have a relationship, nothing, but *nothing*, must affect them at all, is that accepted and understood?"

She replied, "Absolutely, and I feel the same; my husband is a good guy, we have no children yet, but we intend to. He goes away on business almost every week, so I feel I need more than that and I think you are the man to help me here."

I said, "Maybe I am, we shall see."

I kissed her again and put my hand up her skirt and found smooth thighs and suspenders and stockings, quite unusual in younger women, and I immediately got an erection. I pushed her very brief panties out of the way and touched her pubic hair, her lips and finally I located her clitoris and started to massage it. She stopped me and said, "No not like this, I want to really make love to you, but not in a car like this please. My husband is away next week, Wednesday would be good, take me to

119

lunch and I will take you to my bed afterwards and make love with you properly." I agreed without hesitation, we parted company and went our separate ways, after I had dropped her back at her car.

I felt a bit guilty that night but aroused and made love to Heather and all was well, and we both slept soundly as usual and breakfasted as we always did, absolutely not a smidgeon of any sign of a problem. I was at it again, could I control it sufficiently well to avoid real problems? I believed I could, so it was game on.

I made sure I was available for the whole of Wednesday afternoon, went to a local meeting in the morning and met Janet in a pub we both knew. I parked at a little distance from her Mini Cooper and sauntered into the lounge bar where there were tables one could eat at with the usual number plates, and there she sat, cool as a cucumber, looking very nice indeed and with a big smile on her face as I approached the table. We said hello and she didn't get up or touch me and I sat opposite her and said, "Fancy meeting you here! Are you meeting anybody, or can I join you?"

She replied it's OK I've checked there is no one we know from your firm or ours here at present and we can see both entrance doors from here. But in any case, we can say we had an informal arrangement to meet privately so I could discuss a possible move to your company."

"Well thought out," I said, "good plan. What can I get you to drink while we study the menu?"

And she said, "Gin and tonic, lemon, and ice please, but I will drive to my house in my car and you can follow me and park round the corner until I ensure its OK to come in, is that OK?" I said fine, so we had both better not have more than a couple of drinks as we don't want to be pulled for drink driving, do we?"

I went to the bar and got myself a pint of bitter and her the G & T and put a couple of menus under my arm and re-joined her at table 24.

I said, "So, when did you first think you fancied me? I seem to remember bumping into you when I came to your firm first about six months ago."

"That's right," she said, "you literally bumped into me, and it felt good, and I thought yes I could fancy him, shame he's a bit out of my league though."

120

I laughed and said, "With your looks, body and cheek, nobody is safe or out of your league, nobody who likes sex as much as I do that is."

"I will be surprised if you like sex more than me, but we shall see, maybe you are all talk."

I said, "If you believed that you wouldn't be here, unless you are a prick teaser and somehow, I don't think you are."

She said, "What do you think I am then?"

I replied, "Exactly what you intimated, a highly sexed young woman who is not getting enough from her husband and wants more, but not just with anybody. You judge, and quite rightly, that you can afford to pick and choose but also you need somebody who is not going to fall in love with you and become a problem."

"Flattery will get you everywhere," she said, "but you missed one vital part which is that I will get my kicks out of giving you a really good seeing-to and you getting really turned on by me. That's why no car jobs, no messing about in dark hotel rooms; I want the comfort and thrill of having you in my own bed and making you want more."

We ordered our food, cod in beer batter with chips and peas for me and a chicken salad for Janet.

She said, "I suppose you are used to more exotic food in posh hotels, but I quite like this local pub grub thing."

"Yes," I said, "I do like good food served properly, but this is fine and makes a nice change for me. Plus, I will need some fuel for later I'm hoping!"

"So am I," she said. We had another drink, no sweets but she had a liqueur coffee and I had a small brandy with my coffee. Then we both looked at each other as if to say, *let's get moving, shall we?*

She was good, she did get me aroused more than once and she had her fair share of orgasms as well. We both made the most of what was on offer, had a shower and I was on my way by four-thirty p.m. very satisfied with my afternoon efforts and she certainly seemed pretty pleased too.

I said, "Let's leave it a couple of weeks to see if we are both OK to continue and do this again, but I will take you to a different pub and drop you back for your car after lunch, OK?"

She replied "Yes, that's a good plan, I will call you at your office and make a discreet reference to our appointment being fine and confirm the date and time. But it will probably be three weeks I think."

"Good, and thanks, it was a very worthwhile meeting," I said.

I went back to my office and did another couple of hours' work and called Heather to confirm that I would be home for dinner about seven-thirty.

She said, "Fine, I will keep the children up if I can but it's likely they will be shattered and have gone up by then."

I came home to find that as predicted they were both fast asleep and I made a promise that I would see them at six p.m. tomorrow and Heather said that it didn't matter they were used to only one of us and sometimes just 'Nanny', as they called Kath, so it was no big deal. The main thing we both agreed was that when we were at home we would devote as much time as we could spend with them, especially playing games and then reading to them at bedtime. Quality, Heather insisted, was more important than quantity in terms of time spent in their company.

This affair with Janet was sporadic and unpredictable but we both enjoyed each other's company, and the sex was pretty good and made no difference at all to the way I felt about Heather in or out of bed. Janet was pure lust and sex nothing more or less and we both agreed on that. This lasted about a year and then Janet said, "That's it, it's been great fun, but I am coming off the pill this month so do not want to risk any complications as we are starting to try for a family now. It's been great and I have appreciated everything you have done for me including getting me promoted in my company, but it's got to stop now, I am sure you understand."

I said, "Of course I understand; I've really enjoyed it all and have no regrets and respect your position and honesty. And when you do have a child, I want to get it a little present so please keep in touch."

Back to my normal routine and really, I was not looking round for a replacement, it was after all just sex and I had plenty of that with Heather and finally the ego thing was beginning to fade, I thought. I still looked at a nice face and figure but saw nothing to attract me sufficiently to make me approach anyone and they all seemed a bit in awe of me. Therefore, it just didn't happen for a couple of years by which time Nat was at the infants' school and Jo was at pre-school classes and both getting some tuition at home through Kath.

Our own company grew slowly with a clientele mainly in the small to medium bracket, but it was good training for our small staff, and we gradually found the niche we could exploit without treading on our "parent" company's toes, so to speak. Charles was hanging in there as Chairman waiting for age sixty to retire but made it clear to one and all that I would be his successor and a couple of the longer-term directors were making subtle bids to be considered as MD when I did become Chairman. Heather had decided it was too incestuous for her to be made MD and in reality, what with the growing family and our own company, she had quite enough on her plate.

We made one of our employees a director of our company and gave him some shares and appointed a woman who had managed the office for some time, as Company General Manager. The team were getting well into the whole corporate thing and learning all the time and it would be relatively easy for us to step back if we wanted to. But we both felt a few more years of consolidation were in order. I had no intention of retiring so young anyway and even if we sold the business and I resigned from the main company, which I had no intention of doing, I would definitely be looking for another challenge, perhaps in another sphere. But I wanted to stay as Chairman for many more years and increasingly becoming a significant shareholder. Heather too said she was minded to continue at our company until at least fifty-five, depending of course on continued good health and maintaining her current level of interest in what we were doing.

Heather, however, at age forty-seven (I was thirty-eight) with the children Nat and Jo (being seven and five respectively) even though we were retaining Kath, decided she would like to take more of an interest in our own company and resign from the 'parent'. We had enough assets in property, shares and cash investments such that we really needed little income, so she did resign and received a golden farewell package of an index-linked pension, continued free medical insurance and a smaller allocation of shares for ten years to come and we had a great farewell party for her where almost every person who had ever worked with her came and gave her an emotional send-off.

Charles retired six months later, and I became Chairman, and we appointed a new MD whom I particularly liked, admired, and respected. He was several years older than me, but that did not seem to affect our mutual regard at all.

I hardly went to our own company now except for occasional board meetings and any major changes where Heather though my input important, so we saw less of each other during the day, but of course, if I wasn't travelling, we were together almost every evening, the first hour being with the children whenever possible.

I don't think it was the being apart that sharpened my renewed interest in the opposite sex; it certainly was not because I was neglected in that way by Heather. It might have been a reaction to my approaching forty I suppose, but I didn't really think that was a factor as my libido hadn't shrunk so to speak. No, I reasoned, it was just a natural phase I was going through and thought no more about it.

There was one woman who intrigued me however, who on the face of it was most certainly not exhibiting any signs of overt sexuality or undue interest in men, quite the contrary. She was a British-born Indian woman of around thirty who had a husband who worked somewhere in the infrastructure industry. They had two children, owned their own house and another which they let out. Her name was Plainer or something sounding very similar; she wore normal European dress and she worked in a consultancy we used sometimes as a subcontractor. I remarked to myself that she had beautiful very long, straight black hair. She was lively and always smiling and laughing and very popular with men and women alike, but I thought of her as very sexy with large brown eyes and a full figure and I fantasised a bit about getting her in bed one day, but knew it was extremely unlikely that I could or would.

I saw her on one occasion where she was part of a team employed on a project for us. Then I had occasion to sit by her at a small dinner party one evening after a day's work in a town about a hundred miles from home. I had arranged to spend the night with them in their modest hotel and was invited to dinner with them. We had a few drinks as there was no need to drive and it was a lively little group and Palvinder was enjoying talking to me as well as others, but I felt she was happy to be in close contact with me and felt her thigh alongside my thigh and she made no move to pull it away. So, I casually reached under the tablecloth and put my hand on her thigh and squeezed it a little through the denim jeans she was wearing, while she laughed at what someone else was saying and made no attempt to remove my hand and exhibited no other obvious reaction at all. I removed my hand and continued eating and drinking normally but just dropping my hand down now and again and giving another gentle squeeze and again she showed no reaction at all, just carried on talking and laughing with everybody as before. There was no chance to take matters any further and, in any case, she might have been just ignoring what I was doing as the best way of dealing with an unwanted advance, however small.

I said to her after we closed business the following afternoon, "That was nice last night, I really enjoyed your company, as well as the others of course."

She smiled and said, "I enjoyed your company as well, maybe we can do it again sometime."

And off she went without a backward look. When I next saw her some months later in an office, I noticed that she was visibly pregnant, and I congratulated her and said, a bit tongue in cheek, "Shame, I was hoping to get to spend a little time with you alone this time."

To my amazement she replied, "There will be plenty of time for that after I have this baby, say in about five- or six-months' time when we have our autumn get-together in Manchester at the hotel we usually go to, the Holiday Inn on West Street, or Edgbaston Road I'm not sure. Someone else will be able to tell you and I will look forward perhaps to meeting you again."

Work went on and I forgot about our possible meeting until a member of the consultancy she worked for said to me one day, "By the way James, I believe you expressed an interest in our annual get-together at the Holiday Inn, near Edgbaston and I would like to invite you to address our AGM and stay the night if you can on July 5th." I thought, *maybe this is an invitation engineered by Palvinder, surely not? But if so, I must not let her down.*

I wrote to them saying how nice it was to be invited to speak and looking forward to seeing them all again etc and booked the 5th of July at the hotel and thought no more about it. Things went on as usual both at the office and at home and life was good. No one else tickled my fancy and I concentrated on our main projects being pursued at the 'parent' company. There was still a fairly constant stream of new and growing businesses who still felt the need of the possible competitive edge our company offered and with our now quite longstanding reputation, with me still at the helm, business kept coming in. We did our best to stay ahead of the game by constantly upgrading our technology and searching for new angles in an ever-developing field. And I constantly reminded the Board and all staff I came into contact with, "It's no good standing still, maintaining the status quo, you must be forever looking for new ideas, new techniques, new angles and above all, in this increasingly computer driven world, new programmes and hardware as well."

Then July approached and I began to picture Palvinder and wondered if I was just imagining it, or did she really fancy me and would she overcome her position and background to accept an approach from a white European, married at that, as a possible lover or not? Probably a pipe dream I thought, but what the hell I didn't get where I had by faint heartedness and lack of bottle! I realised it was risky, for me, but more so for her, as I had read about reprisals against unfaithful ethnic minority wives who strayed from their universally accepted path. I rationalised that we will have to be ultra-careful and I wouldn't make any move at all unless a green light was definitely showing. So when the time came and I was at the hotel, booked in and registered as the guest speaker at the AGM, I wandered down to the restaurant at about seven-thirty p.m. and there she was, standing calmly in the queue at the buffet.

I said, "Hello," and she smiled and said, "Nice to see you," and moved away to sit with her fellow workers, so I took my plate and joined another group.

Then about half an hour later at the sweet and coffee counter, there she was again, and I went up behind her and said, "I hope I'm not mistaken, or that you are not getting cold feet," and she replied, "Of course not."

So I said, "OK what's your room number? I am going out shortly to meet a friend for a drink and I will knock on your door when I am back, probably after eleven p.m. Will you be ready for me by then?"

She simply said, "Four-oh-seven; yes, I will be ready."

And I turned away back to my seat with some fruit and a coffee.

I was so excited, it was so unusual, and she obviously wanted it to happen but did not want anyone else to become aware, for obvious reasons, and we had both waited so long for this to happen, it seemed to me. I had arranged to meet an old pal of mine who lived in a town nearby, partly as I wanted to anyway, and partly as a fall-back thing to occupy my evening. He picked me up in his Range Rover and we went to a nearby pub. I had four pints of bitter and, just in case, got a packet of condoms from the machine in the pub toilet. My pal Rob knew me well and I trusted him completely, so I told him a bit about Palvinder and life in general and his reaction was, "Go for it, mate, you only live once, just don't get involved and vulnerable."

I said that was absolutely good advice, thanked him and he dropped me back at my hotel and went home.

I was a bit pissed but feeling good and her room by chance was immediately above mine at the end of a corridor linked by a fire escape stairway. Perfect.

By this time, it was about quarter to twelve so I tapped gently on the door. No response. I knocked a little harder and the door opened a couple of inches showing her face. She let me in and shut and locked the door immediately. She was in a cotton nightgown down to her ankles and her beautiful hair was down to her waist. I kissed her for the first time, and it was clear she was not used to being kissed, so I kissed her again, gently, and gradually with a little coaching, she relaxed her lips and returned my kiss.

She took off her nightdress after a bit of persuasion and I was already naked by then. She had on old-fashioned knickers, which I took off and finally we were naked together under the sheets in bed. I took it very slowly and kissed her dark brown, almost purple, nipples and eventually found her large black bush. I gazed at the dark purple lips of her vulva with the pale pink interior lips, so exciting. She clearly liked being masturbated and in fact showed me, with her painted fingernails glowing in the dim bedside light, exactly where she wanted my fingers to go to give her the right buzz. When I finally entered her, after she had three or four orgasms, I found she was surprisingly tight for a woman with three children, and I said so. She told me that she had lots of stitches after the last baby but had always been quite tight. I realised some considerable time later in our relationship that she must have thought her husband was quite small in that department, because she told me after making love to her several times, that he had commented that it went in much more easily than before and hinted she was up to something. She reported to me that she just laughed at that and said that she was just stretching again after all the stitches!

Long story short, that first night together lasted until four-thirty a.m. when I finally left her for a couple of hours sleep before the AGM! But it was an incredible experience which we both enjoyed enormously, and I knew we would see each other again, not just for breakfast or the meeting!

The meeting was a bit of a blur; although she looked fine, I felt knackered, but I knew that no one would know that I had let the side down. She was cool, calm and collected and no one appeared to give either of us any special attention. I thought, yes this is a great discovery for me and her, and with due care, almost risk-free.

We parted mid-afternoon and I managed to say to her that I hoped I would be seeing her very soon. I had her mobile phone number so I could call or message her as well as her office contact number, but neither of us wanted to risk that too often. She had told me that she did once have a European boyfriend, but her parents disapproved, and her family more or less chose her husband for her. She said that he was an OK guy but a bit of a stick-in-the-mud, old fashioned but a good, hardworking father to their children. My attention, however, had woken her up a bit and she was going to make the most of it without in any way endangering their marriage.

Chapter 20

This new relationship was both interesting and satisfying for both of us and not something I had consciously sought but I was glad I had taken the risk. We had a good all-round relationship, it wasn't just sex, although we did have sex every time we met. She was insatiable and she confessed to having sex with her husband in the mornings before leaving to go into town on a little shopping trip with a girlfriend, partly to allay any suspicion he might have but also because knowing she was going to have me later that day turned her on more with her husband, and he wasn't complaining about that. She would take a local bus to the train station and then I would meet her at the busy main station in town and we would walk through town barely touching, just chatting. Then we would find a busy town centre pub where there were usually to be found many mixed groups and couples of various ethnic origins and we were both of an age where it aroused no interest whatsoever. We would usually have lunch, which strangely she insisted on paying for every time despite my protests, and then we went to her girlfriend's flat to which Palvinder had a key where we would make love. She liked to show off her large breasts and nipples and her long dark hair would hang like a veil around her breasts, and she liked to feel me between them. She would bend her neck and receive the end in her mouth as I moved back and forth between her breasts.

She also liked to masturbate herself during sex; this seemed to give her more intensive orgasms. But a lot of the time, over lunch and later after we had made love, she liked just to talk about life, and she was very interested in my experiences as I was in hers. She was undoubtedly intelligent as well as sensual and sexy; one would never have guessed from her normal demeanour what a raver she really was.

This mutually satisfactory arrangement went on for about two years, until one day, out of the blue, she said, "It's over, I must get on with my life now. It's been great and thanks for everything, but this is goodbye."

I was surprised, but I knew she meant it and I accepted her decision and that was the end of what was a very interesting and very satisfying couple of years. She told me in a brief conversation we had some time later, that she had been quite infatuated with me for almost all of those two years but that was over. She had gained so much thanks to me, she added.

So, slightly pensive, I entered a more mature period of my life as I approached forty, and concentrated on the two main businesses I was involved in. We continued building our own consultancy into quite a good size, with two offices and over fifty staff, with Heather being the main mover in that. I was putting most of my energies into the 'parent' company as Chairman and Chief Executive. By this time Heather and I, with the addition of Charles' 12% he sold us when he retired, and continued accumulation through our directorships and purchasing more shares on the open market, now owned 42% of the 'parent' company and we still held more than 90% of our consultancy company; the rest of the shares being ones we had given senior employees.

At this stage of my life, I did feel a bit flat at times and wondered if I was reaching some sort of watershed. Heather was, approaching fifty and that changed things a little but not much, yet I felt somehow unfulfilled, in particular in my physical love life, and I began to think I would never experience the thrills and excitement of my earlier love life again and later what Palvinder had also given me. But I didn't sit and feel sorry for myself, I just got on with life and enjoyed it all, only occasionally wondering if anything else might somehow happen to rekindle the former joys.

Our children were growing up fast and enjoyed school as well as the activities they pursued out of school hours. Jo was a Brownie and Nat a Cub Scout and they had many friends who they delighted in bringing home to share in the many activities they pursued there. We took them on interesting trips and holidays with a cultural element in them, but also fishing and camping which we all enjoyed, as I gradually introduced them into country life pursuits. Both had an interest in languages too and we encouraged them to learn two each and they both chose German and Spanish, so were able to study them together as well as at school.

My father died after a fairly short illness; I had never been really close to him — much more so with my mother. I asked Heather what she thought of bringing Mother nearer to us so we could keep an eye on her as there were no other siblings at home by this time and they all lived more remotely, and didn't have the financial resources to assist in any significant way. Mother had the small house they had lived in for years, but it was somewhat rundown and needed a lot doing to it, so I floated the idea of helping her buy something more suitable, a bungalow perhaps near to us and her grandchildren. She was very enthusiastic about that idea and definitely wasn't ready for sheltered accommodation or a place or a home and was still keen on doing a bit of gardening.

So Heather and I looked around our locality and found a nice little bungalow with a decent size garden only about five or six minutes' walk away from us. We funded the difference in the value of the one she sold and the bungalow and made sure it had all the necessary equipment and furniture as most of the stuff they had before was old and worn out. She moved in about five months after Father died and was delighted with everything including a small conservatory for plants and sunny days, and the garden soon took shape to her liking with a little judicious help from our gardener. She could walk to our house safely and easily in under ten minutes and did so on an almost daily basis. The children loved their grandma and took pleasure in her company and answered her questions about school more readily than if Heather or I asked them.

We also had occasional visits from other members of my family who I hadn't seen much of for years. They appreciated what we had done for Mum and there was no rancour or jealousy we could detect. We entertained quite a few of the family one weekend when it was Mum's 73rd birthday by providing a BBQ and hired some games equipment for about a dozen youngsters. We also put up a small marquee in case of inclement weather, but it was fine and sunny, so the pool cover came off and they all enjoyed that. Several stayed overnight with us and a few with Mum, so only a small minority went home that night. It was weekend of joy for Mum with almost all her family together.

At work we had been improving our 'in-house' repairing and renovation of large equipment facilities and publicised this. As a result, were getting quite a few decent orders for this service with new plants being so expensive it made sense to have older machines repaired and renovated up to standard. We had persuaded two big-name manufacturers to give us agency rights and be nominated as dealers in their plant, providing we sold new plants as well as second-hand renovated machines. We dedicated a part of our grounds and a workshop just for this purpose alongside a marked off and fully equipped exposition of new machinery. We also agreed that a member of their own sales department and an engineer be seconded to us, initially for a year, to ensure standards were maintained and we paid 50% of their salaries. It helped of course that we had previously dealt with these two companies over the years selling them our consultancy package and improving their bottom-line profitability with our plans for streamlining their internal operations. We successfully agreed that in reality we had a symbiotic relationship which would benefit both of us.

We were always looking for ways to improve our services and sell our methods to new clients and this sort of public exhibition of cooperation between our companies helped our reputation and encouraged related enquiries about similar ideas in new contact areas.

Then I was headhunted! Yes, at the time when I was thinking my life as a businessman and entrepreneur was maybe coming to a natural sort of close, gradually maybe but in that direction. I was approached by one of the big outfits I had considered as targets for our expansion ambitions some years back, who had apparently been monitoring my progression to Chairman and Chief Executive Director of our 'parent company' and felt it was a good time to sound me out as a potential Chief Executive of their group of companies!

I had no intentions of moving from my pretty comfortable position as big fish in a relatively small pool into what amounted to a shark-infested ocean! But I was flattered and intrigued, so I thought why don't I play along for a bit just to see what this was all about? How could they be aware that I was having some doubts about my future, my interest was maybe waning a bit, and I was looking around, maybe? Or were they really interested in acquiring my services; could I still keep what was virtually full control of our company; what was their game?

Chapter 21

So, I talked it over with Heather and she said, "You have nothing to lose, play along and see what you can figure out, maybe there will be a good angle for us to exploit, maybe not, but knowledge is everything, and you have probably got a lot more of that than even you realise after twenty years of successfully promoting yourself and your ideas and skills and, very successfully. Here you are owner of one smallish but thriving company, together with me of course, but we also are now approaching 50% ownership of the company you were only a lowly employee of not that long ago. That says quite a lot — for both of us. So, what might my role be? I am not finished yet by a long way."

"Wow," I said, "you never cease to amaze me. Here am I thinking you were a settled, contented mother and wife and underneath you have been continuing to nurture ambitions."

She laughed and said, "No, I just love it when you get excited and fired up and anything I can do to nurture that in you I will. But at the same time, I do feel I have energy and ambition left enough to continue to support you actively in whatever you want to do, and if that means a further shimmy up the greasy pole, and it's what you want, then fine."

I accepted an invitation for exploratory talks with XYZ Corporation, HQ in London, with factories and offices in several countries, a turnover of approximately fifty times ours and ten times as many personnel. They were publicly listed in the top 100 Companies in the UK. They said that we should meet first informally for lunch and meet a few key personnel including the retiring CE and several Main Board Members (MBM) and a couple of other foreign directors and furthermore, having clearly done their homework, they invited Heather too. Smart people.

We made the appropriate arrangements and booked a suite at a good hotel so that we arrived the day before the lunch meeting and left the day after, intending to do a bit of shopping maybe in London and take in a show, or whatever we fancied. Grandma and Nanny were in charge at home and our MD at the main business. All was covered, and, in any case, we could easily be contacted in case of emergency. We decided to take no briefcases, no computers, just ourselves and our combined experience, knowledge and instincts and be very laid back, open to ideas and in listening mode.

We arrived at our favourite hotel, booked in and went out to dinner in China Town at the Wong Kei restaurant where the informality was far exceeded by the superb quality of their traditional Cantonese Food. I loved it there and had visited many times with a dear friend, now deceased so had particularly poignant memories. The place was spread over several floors, and you might be on a table for two or four or more commonly ten or twelve and all strangers.

I recall a story I have told many times of the quite aggressive staff there, who were used to all sorts using their restaurant but would tolerate no dissent or problems from customers. One evening I had been there with my old friend and a loud-mouthed Englishman was complaining about something so the nearest head waiter of that floor came over and asked what the problem was. The man persisted in making a fuss over something he didn't like so the head waiter took up his and his partner's plates and said, "OK, you no like our food, you fuck off, now!" and the two people involved looked around them at laughing customers and at the several grim-looking waiters who had gathered round, and they left. The man's partner did not look impressed. '

Heather laughed even though she had heard the story several times, she still thought it was funny. Then we had a couple of drinks at pubs on the walk back to our hotel and a coffee with brandy in my case and a liqueur for Heather. We retired happy but tired.

The next morning after a sumptuous breakfast, we wandered around the shops locally for an hour and picked up a couple of things for the children, Mum and Nanny and went back to our rooms to prepare for the lunch meeting at a well-known restaurant in Piccadilly. We were picked up at our hotel entrance at precisely one p.m. as arranged. The chauffeur-driven blacked-out limo was a bit much but what the heck, so we settled in the back for the short ride to the restaurant. We were met at the car door by a smiling young man who said, "James and Heather, so pleased to meet you, please come with me."

We followed this extremely nice young man into the restaurant and were shown to a table with a dozen seats with nine people standing behind their chairs awaiting our arrival. I noted an approximately 70/30 split male to female which, for such high-ranking people within their organisation, was pretty progressive for that era.

The leader of this group whom I recognised as the retiring CE of the XYZ Corp., immediately came forward and first introduced himself to Heather and then to me, nice touch. We then went slowly round the table being introduced and we urged them all to be seated once we had said hello.

I guess that at least half the people present other than Heather and I were in the forty to fifty-five age group, so I was one of the youngest present. But there were about three who were around my age or slightly younger or older and they all looked very sharp customers. Why wouldn't they be? If I was the preferred candidate to be your new CE, wouldn't you be fully on the ball?!

We had the knowledge that we could walk away from this at any time of our choosing to help us, although after all our experiences together over the last almost twenty years I'm not sure it made that much difference. We sat down and looked around us, taking it all in and liking what we saw, and then ordered our particular appetiser drinks: Pernod with ice and water for Heather and a bottle of Belgian beer for me. The rest took mainly water, but a few joined us with a glass of something containing alcohol. The CE said, as soon as glasses were charged, "A toast please to our very welcome guests here today. I propose that we all have a good meeting, enjoy the food and that this will be the first of many such gatherings."

We all dutifully sipped our drinks and said words like Cheers, *Prost*, *Skål* or whatever and then started talking to our immediate neighbours.

They were serious, they were trying to sell me the job; the bottom line was they wanted me and were prepared to pay a good price to get me. *How very flattering*, I thought; *how exciting*, I thought; *what is the hidden agenda?* I thought. Then it dawned on me, they knew we had virtual control of the company through our combined shares, and they knew there was no way they could get the company without our blessing! Bingo!

I gave Heather a signal we had perfected years ago, "I need to talk to you now!" in code.

She gave a very slight nod and turned to me and said, "Darling, we promised to call the children about now. Is it possible we can just retire for five minutes please?" she asked the table.

And of course, they assented readily.

We made our way slowly to the restroom area and managed a quick conference where I unveiled my suspicions and she immediately said, "So that's it! I have been trying to think what this is all about. Well fine, let's consider it tonight and meantime play along, there could be some big mileage in this, and we could still come out on top."

"Agreed," I said.

We did just that; discussed all sorts of things from the makeup of the Group, its plans and ambitions, the numbers of staff and higher executives, the profitability, how our input might enhance that, etc., etc. We didn't get near to discussing incentives, salaries, benefits, nothing so crude. Just nice general stuff about our input enhancing their profile, improving their bottom line, initiating expansion into new markets, and so on. It was superbly done but had not fooled us one bit. But we gave no hint of our suspicions or thoughts, just enjoyed basking in their admiration and praise and taking it all with a very large pinch of salt.

We discussed all this later and we agreed that we would see what we could get from them in return for delivering our company on a plate so to speak. We produced a wish list which ran something like this:

1. Initial award of a significant number of shares in whole group for both of us.
2. Heather to become a director and me CE.
3. Minimum of five years binding contracts for both of us.
4. Annual dividend minimum each.
5. Annual minimum share allocations each.
6. Good index-linked pensions for both.
7. First-class medical insurance for both.
8. Free house movement and 'children's education allowance to private schools of our choice in the country we were based. UK preferably.
9. Club Class minimum; First-class airfares to official meetings.

10. Minimum option to buy further shares at 10% discount.

11. Keep our consultancy company totally private.

We could probably have done more, but this seemed a good starting point and we wanted to throw it at them at the least expected moment at a time of our choosing, and fairly soon so that they were aware how long we had been on to them.

They came back to us in about one week and asked had we considered our position and we replied, "What position are you referring to, James as the new CE, Heather as a main board director, both with a suitable package of incentives, but in exchange for what? We felt," we said, "that our meeting last week, although very nicely done, told us little of your specific goals and objectives; couched, we both thought, in very general terms. We need much more specific detail before we could seriously consider our position. Clearly with the right package in contract form and containing all the necessary incentives and safeguards we would both need, this was worthy of consideration but, based on what we had heard so far, we really could not, and would not, commit ourselves to anything."

We had a couple of exploratory phone calls from the old CE and others which led nowhere and eventually I said that I was running out of patience with their rather woolly proposal — if indeed it was a proposal at all in a defined sense, and basically told them, "Put up or shut up," but obviously not in those words.

Within one further week reality had clearly dawned on them, that we were on to their plan to try to get our company with us on board fairly cheaply. They, rather belatedly, said that maybe, if they came out publicly and said they were looking on our company as an acquisition which was conditional on our agreeing me being appointed as the new CE for a minimum of three years and Heather as a senior main board member also for three years, provided a fair price was set on the share values. Heather and I felt insulted! Had they really believed people who had achieved what we had were so naive? We replied that we wanted five years (minimum) contracts for us both, plus we both were to be allocated 10% shares in the new group and be paid the going rates for all our existing shares in our company. That, we said, we might consider was a realistic offer. Plus of course — we sent them our prepared list of wants with a proviso that this was for openers and subject to our legal advisors' scrutiny and approval. And we wanted recognition that these negotiations could need further amendments in either direction, subject, of course to mutual satisfaction and agreement.

They sat on this another week during which time we said nothing at all to anyone and our company shares had risen 25% in value. They finally cracked and effectively said, "OK, you win, stop this now and agree within 48 hours or the deal is off."

We replied, "No, we will not negotiate or consent to a 'takeover' except in a completely free and open manner. We pointed out that they had been the ones to obfuscate and try to delude us in the first instance; this was not the way Heather, or I were accustomed to dealing with such important matters, so if they were really sincere and open about their acquisition of our company, of which Heather and I were now majority shareholders, we would not do this anyway with a gun pointed at our heads. We suggested a target date of three weeks hence to iron out difficulties and come to a sensible, rational, fair, and fully acceptable deal, which would not sour our ongoing relationship and would help set the Group on a new footing, led by us. Take it or leave it.

They swallowed their collective pride and conceded practically everything we asked for and convened a final meeting of all the top personnel on both sides which would, if acceptable equally to both sides, mean a completely new rancour-free beginning to our relationship. Finally, the elder statesmen and biggest shareholders of the Group were seen to accept everything and several actually said that we had proved we were needed in the Group and their plan was good but not good enough to start with. They now saw a bright future for the enhanced Group with me as CE and Heather alongside me on the main board.

We had played hardball having been provoked by their underhand way of going about things and we felt we needed to set the scene for a future shaped differently from that. We could have comfortably walked away from the deal but having achieved all or most of our objectives and being reinvigorated by this massive new challenge, we decided to embrace the whole situation in a positive manner and try to create a new ethos within the expanded Group.

On the day of the public announcement there was a flurry of press releases and briefings, and Heather and I were headline news in the industry and across the wide range of companies we had become associated with over the past twelve years. We had gained significantly from their overconfident, and somewhat underhanded attempt to get our company on the cheap and they had now paid the full price for their ineptitude. I called an early main board meeting and put right at the top of the agenda: 1. Open and inclusive management of the Group. This, I believed, set the tone for the meeting and the future in that way. We recognised that we still had a lot to learn, but we were both pretty experienced campaigners by now and made a formidable team, and we knew it. But we were determined to carry on as we had before and try to fit our methods and attitudes into a template for managing this now moderately large group of companies.

But publicly we smiled a lot, appearing relaxed but in command, and encouraged all present to give their opinions about the takeover and anything else they wanted to raise at this, our first General Group Main Board Meeting. I made sure that the meeting progressed however and wasn't used to bring out old grudges and arguments and strove to put a positive slant on anything I could but made notes all the time for future actions and reactions. Heather came in quite strongly at times, showing her mettle, but she demonstrated that she was also very good at conciliation, feather smoothing, and giving positive constructive criticism where she thought it was appropriate. We were not overawed; in fact, as far as we were concerned, this was just a larger version of what we had been doing for years. Heather and I conferred afterwards, and both felt it went well and augured well for the future, and that we had already identified a few major issues to deal with.

What undoubtedly helped our sanguine feelings was the fact that, already very comfortably off both in capital and monetary assets, with very good income and privileges, before the takeover, we were now (taken together or separately) rich. And it felt good, no need to fool ourselves or anyone else, we had achieved in our almost twenty years together, what most people would never equal in a lifetime, and we hadn't finished yet!

We were determined, however, that none of this would go to our heads, we would still have a comparatively modest lifestyle, preferring to grow our assets rather than spend them on flashy or overpriced cars or houses or whatever. Very comfortable lifestyle yes, ostentatious, and showy, no. Mum was still our near neighbour; our children, although at private schools, lived at home and we maintained the same group of friends and did the same sort of things we always did. In reality, Heather and I agreed that we felt just the same as when we started.

I still loved a day out on the riverbank fishing, and now I had introduced not only Heather, who went along with it, but also both children, who, suitably equipped, took to it like, yes, a fish to water. They also exhibited a keen interest in the river wildlife, and it encouraged them to add biology to their long list of study subjects. We went on camping holidays in Britain, Spain and France and loved the free and easy lifestyle adopted for such trips, which we as parents felt was so important to inculcate early.

Domestic bliss, yes pretty much; work interests, totally as interesting as always; family events and commitment, total. But I confess the wild streak I had always had in relation to the opposite sex was never far beneath the surface and I knew I was not yet finished in that department, but I was as determined as ever to never allow any other relationship to impinge on all of the main objectives.

Heather and I never discussed this subject, but I was fully aware that she knew me better than anyone, and therefore she was aware that I always had the potential to stray off the straight and narrow and I guess she just lived with that knowledge, confident that she was capable of dealing with whatever arose. I didn't think of it often but occasionally I would feel the urge to look at an attractive woman and speculate a little on how she might be in bed. Things were so busy transforming the public image of the group and also looking closely at existing systems and seeking improvements, not to mention the huge manpower resources we now controlled and all their needs, education and training, personal and domestic, the list was endless. Heather and I both were well aware how important the human resources are to the success of any large organisation such as ours and we put early emphasis and focus on staff, personnel of all grades, managers and the makeup of the individual boards of each component company within the group.

I had enjoyed my time as Chairman and Chief Executive of our original company, and I enjoyed this bigger beast even more. I liked the power, but I also liked giving good guidance and counsel to all my board members and as many of our employees as I could but clearly much had to be delegated. I did, however, in the first year as group CE, make a point of touring all our offices and factories and meeting as many shop floor people as I could as well as directors, managers and foremen, etc. and it was always surprising how much very ordinary work men and women knew about the struggle we had gone through to form the new group and in general they were enthusiastic and interested.

I saw a lot of women and girls as well as men and boys in all my visits and meetings and steered clear of obvious dangerous potentially close relationships with females like directors, managers and PAs, as indicating potential affairs. So that limited my scope quite bit, and in any case, I wasn't actively looking for any involvement, just fancied a quiet and discreet shag if such an animal still existed at my level. And after one year had passed by nothing of note had reared its head in the crumpet sense, or at least nothing risk-free enough for me to even consider it.

But then one day a girl in a tight lycra gym outfit caught my eye at the private club where I tried to work out at least once a week. The gym was almost empty at ten a.m. when I was in the weights, cross trainer, bicycle, treadmill part and I was on a rowing machine. I liked these machines because they exercised most of the muscle groups and you could either focus on a problem or just listen to music in your headphones or whatever as you mindlessly clocked up the kilometres and noted the calories you were burning.

The only other occupant of this part of the club facility was a well-built girl of about twenty-five to thirty, who was cycling away, and she started to moan, and gasp and I thought she might be in trouble. But she just pedalled harder and the noises became louder. Then I realised she was working herself off on the saddle wedged firmly between her substantial thighs and she reached a crescendo with her head thrown back, obviously having a tremendous orgasm.

Phew, I had never witnessed anything like it before, amazing. She slowly came round from wherever she was and glanced around and saw me, momentarily paused, working away on my rowing machine in the far corner. She went bright red and started to get off the machine obviously with thoughts of an immediate escape. I casually arose after my ninety-minute workout rowing during which, according to the display, I had travelled twenty kilometres and burned off a thousand calories!

And I sauntered over towards her and said, "I have to confess I have never seen such a thing before, but you appeared to have reached your target."

She was flustered but countered, "I didn't know anyone was there."

So I said, "Don't worry, your secret is safe with me, but I have to admit that was quite an orgasm you had there just with a bicycle seat between your thighs, and I very much envied the saddle."

She laughed at that and said, "Well sometimes beggars can't be choosers."

I said, "I think I know what you mean. How about we both, as it were, put some flesh on that particular expression? But wait, don't feel under pressure, I only ask, but I am interested if you are. After a short sauna and a shower, I will be in the club bar in about half an hour if you would care to join me for a cool drink?"

She said, "I might just do that."

I took my time, didn't want to appear too eager and went to the bar about thirty-five minutes later and there she was looking a bit disappointed, until I walked in at which her face literally lit up.

I strolled up to her and said, "I'm James but you may call me Jim; what's your name?"

"Pauline," she replied, "and I don't care what you call me if you are half as serious as you appear to be."

I considered that, looked at her very closely, and said no I'm not half as serious, I am twice as serious."

"Fuck me!" she replied, "You really are, aren't you?"

"Yes, and I have every intention of fucking you until you have at least as good an orgasm as that wretched saddle did for you."

And she said, "That's a certainty if you perform half as well as you talk."

"Where and when?" I replied.

"Tomorrow morning at ten, outside. I will be in a red Maserati Sports, waiting for you."

I said, "It's a deal."

She had a lager, and I had a beer, and we were both looking at each other as if we couldn't believe our luck. We both said we were looking forward to tomorrow and went our separate ways.

Chapter 22

I was ready and raring to go at eight-thirty a.m. as usual and Heather said, could I drop her off at the local garage to pick up her car which she had left the day before so naturally I said yes. She said, "Very smart today, and the aftershave. Is there an attractive woman in today's meeting?"

"Can't deny it". I said, "But it's just my male 'peacock thing'." And she just laughed, not at all concerned; in fact, I suspected, proud.

I dropped her off at the garage and went on to the office and then at the appointed hour I was at the gym car park and sure enough there she was the lovely Pauline in her Maserati in the car park.

I walked over and she said, "Get in."

So, I did.

She drove off at quite a speed towards a residential area known as 'The Gates' for obvious reasons and swept into a gravelled driveway in front of an imposing Georgian style mansion, pulled to a halt and literally threw herself on me.

I responded OK, if a bit surprised and she said, "Come on," and led me through the front door into what was a magnificent house. It appeared we were the only one's present.

No time to pause and think, she literally dragged me up the stairs to the master bedroom and threw off her clothes and started to remove mine.

"Hold on a minute" I said, let's take this slowly, and as I think you might just enjoy it more."

"Fuck that," she said, "I haven't had a good fuck for weeks and that stops right here. We can talk and take things slowly later, right now I want you inside me as far as it will go."

How can a man refuse such a request? I still tried to slow it down a little, but this lady was a big, powerful woman and she wanted it bad. I rose to the occasion and gave her just about all I had which, after a fairly abstemious period for me, was quite a lot!

She was an athlete, pure and simple, and she had a large well-developed clitoris, and the secret was simple, get it in at the right angle, push it fast and hard for maybe five or six minutes and bingo, she exploded with groans and shrieks and an enormous "YES!" punctuated orgasm.

The second and third time I was able to employ my various arts a little more and she finally got the message, 'Wham Bam Thankyou Ma'am', wasn't the only game in town.

And to give her credit, after the finale, she was done, and said, "Thank you, that was absolutely fantastic. I am so glad I met you yesterday, you are an amazing man, and I am so grateful. I'm sorry I can't promise to see you as often as I would like; I am married to an absolute ogre who is away in the USA today and tomorrow, so God knows when I can see you again, but please, I really want to."

I told her I was also tied up a lot of the time, but I would do my best to see her as and when and she gave me her contact details, but I warned her I was happily married with two children. To which she replied, "Perfect!"

It wasn't perfect, but it was certainly demanding, interesting, and satisfying. What more could a man in my position want? Well frankly, after the first two or three times of what amounted to a wrestling match complete with groans, even though I knew these groans were not an act; I had heard them when she thought she was alone with her saddle! Even so, apart from the risk of injury, I had enough past experience to be well aware there was more to sexual satisfaction than she had so far achieved in her life. And I was willing to educate her a little if she permitted it of course. She was not a fool; she had just been very frustrated as I was about to discover, by her beast of a husband, whose system amounted to complete control of his wife, body, and soul, and she must deliver what he wanted and when he wanted it and no questions asked. I was minded to destroy this son of a bitch and make her really enjoy the kind of sex I for one was used to having. Having sex where nobody was in charge, just a mutual search for the right techniques, the appropriate attitude, and a little loving kindness.

"Otherwise divorce him and join a circus," I said. Risky, but it got her attention.

I set about reconstructing her ideas of a good satisfying, interesting and enjoyable sexual relationship; with a person who showed some respect, consideration, and tenderness as well as seeking, as a primary objective, to make their partner happy and fulfilled. A tall order but achievable if the partner wants that as well.

She was a quick learner but handicapped by alternate sessions with her Stone Age husband and me, modern man, I liked to think. Had she not been so eager and willing, not to mention having a superb but slightly muscular figure, youth on her side and so grateful, I don't think we would have survived more than a couple of weeks. But she exhibited all that tenacity and drive which enabled her to survive her hopeless marriage so far. But one thing was certain, short of completely breaking her spirit, he could not win. I was able to observe him in public when she tipped me off where they would be one day having lunch at a restaurant in town with which I was not familiar. It was only then it dawned on me, he was not a typical UK sort of man, he was it seemed, a Russian type of minor oligarch of dubious origins. Dark and swarthy, build like an all-in wrestler, 5ft 9in or 5ft 10in maximum but very wide and with a considerable gut. But he looked and sounded tough and harsh, and he required obedience. She, give her credit where it was due, did not appear afraid of him and stood her ground, but he was unrelenting, demanding complete attention and truly as horrible a specimen of manhood as you could imagine.

His English was very poor, and she appeared not to have any Russian or whatever it was he spoke to his countrymen and I thought, *I'm out of here, this man is dangerous. If he finds out about me, he could have me beaten up or worse.* But then, I thought, *can you just walk away and abandon her to him? Hardly.*

I did the next best thing I could think of which was to get as much detail as I could on him and try to have him investigated. Maybe he was an illegal immigrant, a wanted criminal even, in his own country. Maybe we could get him deported. But then I had second thoughts. This man had obvious wealth, better to discover his business dealings and partners, associates, whatever. Get details of his full name and date of birth and nationality, maybe she could even copy his passport or birth certificate. Note down any companies he appeared involved with, the names and vehicle registrations of his visitor's, etc., yes this was the way to go, no confrontation, no overt surveillance, soft-shoe stuff. Let me think, did I know anybody in that line of business. I would put out some discreet feelers and see what could be done and by whom. I thought I would be safe providing I used a reputable detective agency or well-known and reputable PI perhaps.

Meanwhile I determined not to speak of my ideas to Pauline as yet, the last thing I wanted was an attack of guilt, a beating maybe and she might confess and tell him about me. So, I thought carefully and apart from the gym club, we had nothing else in common, she only knew my first name and I used different company cars on different days as well as my own and I didn't recall taking her out in my personal car at all.

I reviewed my contacts with her, and I got rid of my usual mobile phone and bought what I believe they call in the trade a 'burner'. Just buy one with a pre-paid sim card for cash and no names used and dump it after using it for anything which might give identification to me. They were very cheap so I could get a dozen for about two hundred pounds. She wouldn't think a thing about it, I would explain that my employer provided them, I wouldn't tell her my real company or status, no home address, nothing through which I could easily be traced. I would use cash in restaurants and pubs, no cards. *Yes*, I thought, *let's put all these measures in place gradually and act calmly and see what transpired when I gently pumped her for information about him.* And if she got too suspicious or started enquiring too much, I would simply ditch her.

It worked fine and she showed no suspicion whatever. I said I was worried about her safety when I saw what he was and so this led to me gently getting quite a lot of information from her about him including her copying his passport, birth certificate and driving licence and copies of some of his credit and debit cards, the banks which he used, the details of his companies and associates and much more. He was not a high-class crook that was for sure because this stuff was lying around their home in a variety of places, bedroom, office, kitchen almost anywhere in the house and of course in his cars of which he had four and I got all four makes type, colour, and most important number plates.

There were no staff at the house, bodyguards, or servants; he obviously had a very high opinion of himself and considered he needed no protection. And he valued his privacy in the home, so he had total command there whenever he was in the house. But he did have a gun! A Walther PPK she thought, in his bedside table in a box, and a box of ammunition in a drawer underneath. I thought I'm never going into that house again, any meetings we have will have to be where I say and when, I would say that I was suspicious my wife might put a PI on my trail, so we would have to be careful, and she liked that.

So began a very strange affair and really, I *should* perhaps have just walked away, but I found that difficult to do. Pauline was not some con merchant, she had met this crook — and I was certain he was crooked although I had no evidence of that at the moment. He had been charming and persuasive and admired her strong physique and youth of course and he wanted a respectable wife to front up his organisation, I felt sure. He certainly had a lot of money at his disposal. The mansion had cost him around 3 million pounds I guessed, with the grounds, security perimeter with 24-hour staff, and it had an indoor pool and gymnasium with sauna and a TV/cinema room, sports room for snooker and pool and all mod cons like air conditioning and sound proofing, satellite TV and communication systems, everything you could wish for if that was your desire. So, like a fool she had swallowed all his story and married him, but she was definitely having second thoughts now. I cautioned her not to let this show, who knew what he might do if she tried to break away. Go with the flow I told her, I know what he is, and I am looking into his affairs so play dumb and don't ask any more questions and keep as low a profile as she could without changing so much that he noticed.

Chapter 23

I kept seeing her and continued with her education and she appeared calmer and more relaxed. He almost treated her as a human being for a while and allowed her to make love to him rather than him just dominate everything and, for a time, it worked fine, until the penny appeared to have dropped, and he accused her of having an affair — who was he? etc. She convincingly denied all this, merely admitting to seeing a sex therapist that had been helping her with her bedroom techniques and only so she could please him more. He appeared to swallow all this, but I insisted in not seeing her for a few weeks while I got a PI surveillance team, who a friend had found for me, on his trail to see where he was going and what was he doing. And lo and behold, it was *he* who was having an affair! And covering it the best way he knew, by accusing her of the same thing. That was the final straw for her, and she was determined to be rid of him, but in her own time and such a way that when it happened it would be too late for him to retaliate, and she would be far away and out of his control.

He was not mean, he had loads of money and flaunted it and any wife of his must be seen to be the same, so she had her own cards and a bank account, and he gave her a very generous allowance and over time she had deposited over 20,000 pounds in a separate account he knew nothing about but was now determined to get more before she fled. She quietly sold many of the baubles he had bought her, and some were quite valuable, with an assortment of precious stones, and he had never looked in her drawers and wardrobes, etc., so apart from having a good memory, he had no control at all over her financial status.

She meanwhile had discovered where his wall safe was and even managed to memorise the numbers when he casually opened it one day to take out a huge roll of cash and his top-of-the-range Rolex Oyster, which was gold and platinum and with jewels encrusting it and must have been worth 100,000 pounds at least. He only wore it at big meetings where he needed to impress "people".

She picked a day when he was away again in New York for three nights, sold her Maserati for cash, took all her cash out of the known account and deposited it with a different bank in her mother's maiden name, and bought a second hand 4x4 truck for cash. She loaded up all her favourite clothes and other things. She then cleaned out his wall safe, including the Rolex, and put all the contents except the cash in a deposit box at yet another bank, this time in her mother's married name. She had already obtained all the necessary documents, copied from her mother's home without her knowledge, and she then performed her master stroke. She had found out where the garbage truck and other service vehicles entered and left the compound and their normal entry to departure habits, so she set a bonfire in the middle of the house, piled it high with flammable stuff and obscured the surveillance camera with an old shirt of his. Before she departed one night in her anonymous 4x4 truck, she set a simple slow fuse and lit it. She quietly drove out unseen after the night watchman had turned on his TV and was stuffing his face with a takeaway and a couple of beers.

There was a huge house fire at about one a.m. in the gated compound but it was already way out of control before the watchman woke up from his regular nap after his beer and takeaway supper, and most neighbours were fast asleep or away. By the time the fire service attended and brought the fire under control it was a smoking pile of debris about ten feet high with nothing left at all to show what had happened.

When her husband came home two days later, he found the pile still much as it was awaiting his return, and the police arrested him, following a tip-off, for alleged insurance fraud said to be millions of pounds in scope. They carried out further investigations while holding him in custody, which ultimately uncovered a massive drug distribution business of which the ogre was a main player. He also was operating on false passports and identification, and was actually a Romanian wanted for serious crimes, including insurance fraud and murder. His Walther was recovered from the ruined house, but the investigators could find no sign of the Rolex or anything else of real value. He was eventually tried and convicted and after five years would be deported back to Romania to serve out the rest of his sentences.

How did I know all this? Well, a lot was in the newspapers and on TV and I saw Pauline, in tears, being interviewed when she said she had feared for her life and gone to stay with her old mother in Wales the evening of the tragedy and made much of her very lucky escape from certain death.

I never attempted to contact her nor she me, and I was relieved to read some time later that she had obtained her divorce and married her new next-door neighbour, who had a farm in West Wales not too far from her mother's place. The happy couple had turned it into a stud farm for pedigree horses and her greatest delight was riding them with a specially made saddle, and she was a very contented lady.

It was incredible, the whole thing, and I thanked my lucky stars I had come out of the affair in one piece and relatively unscathed. But I vowed I would never chat up another gym user again whatever she was up to. Was I used? Maybe. 'It's probable nobody will ever know the whole truth; if so, she was a very clever lady. I prefer to believe that she was genuine, but intelligent and a fast learner and had a very strong mind and was a resourceful woman who initially saw me as a potential means of escape, but in reality, I had done very little, just provided a few ideas.

It was exciting if a little scary at times, but I resolved that I should perhaps modify my inclinations a little, at least choose someone who might be thought of as more normal. But how on earth can you tell? It is very much suck it and see but be ready to back-pedal rapidly. Above all else, if I had another relationship, stop naively using normal phones provided by the company, my own or a private car and my company and private credit cards. I had learnt a bit and I fully intended to be extra careful if I ever strayed from the beaten path again. Until the next time anyway.

The Group CE role was demanding but exciting too in its own way. I still had a lot to learn, especially about boardroom politics and realised that I tended to be too open and trusting in my relationships on the board and throughout the management structures within the group members. Heather was good, but she was pretty fully occupied with her directorship, for our consultancy company, as well as managing the domestic household and two teenage children. But after about two years as CE, I was pretty well bedded into the role and beginning to use a little more force than had been my normal approach to higher management hitherto. I felt it was expected of me, leadership, strong and decisive management, and so increasingly, that's what I gave them, and they seemed to like it.

They also seemed to like how Heather and I were restructuring each company within the group as well as the group as a whole. We used the same methods and principles as always and they still worked. The key was choosing the right team leaders to carry out the various systems and practice reviews, and we had a core of good people whom we had brought on over the years to draw on and incentivised them in the same way. Bonuses, share issues, salary increases and good quality medical insurance, etc. Just as we had insisted on for ourselves from the outset, 'Do as you would be done by' might have been our motto, if we had one. What we had was a group of key members of our former review and implementation groups who were totally loyal and dependable and knew that as a result they would be properly rewarded.

As a consequence, the old group board members who survived, felt fully justified in what was a bit of a bloodbath in the lead-up to our taking over the group, and the benefits were now there to be seen in bottom line production increases and profits. So, there were no mutterings or "I told you so's". On the contrary, the boardroom was a happy place to be and to work and Heather and I were determined that it stay that way for our remaining time there.

After another year, my third as CEO, I was turning forty-five and Heather fifty-four, but we both were fit and well and enjoying life and our children. Nat and Jo were now fourteen and twelve (almost thirteen) respectively and were at senior school, although still preferred living at home and when offered boarding. They said, "No way, Dad", we like our life here with you, fishing, rambling, playing tennis and pool with you guys at weekends and there are always interesting colleagues of yours to meet and much to learn just by listening at the dinner table." Nuff Sed.

I did still go to the gym as I was confident lightning does not strike twice in the same place, and I wanted to keep fit and not to develop a pot belly from excessive good eating and drinking. In summer there was the pool to help in my daily fitness routine. But I was prevailed upon to build an indoor pool and gymnasium at home, so that these events could continue throughout the year. Heather said, "We can afford it, why not?"

So, we got quotes and dissected them and chose a suitable contractor, neither the dearest nor the cheapest, and had the extension built as an L at the end of the house, with glass walls on three sides. The gymnasium had blinds for the sensitive ones and all of the huge windows could easily be screened off as required, but in good weather or foul, if you wanted to, you could believe you were outside with all the glass around.

I still went to the gym club as I liked the different machines available and didn't want too much of that stuff around at home. But I preferred swimming at home and was quite happy with our own sauna and jacuzzi. Also, it was good if the kids brought a gang home to enjoy our facilities, I would slope off to the gym and let them all hang out.

This happy life went on until my first five-year tenure as CEO was due to end and then a 'would-be' future CEO made a bid to oust me. He knew, and I knew, he had no chance, but he was intent on laying down a marker for a future contest, which by my reckoning was at least another five years away, but it was to be a fatal mistake, for him that is. He was part of the residual hierarchy remaining from the old main board, but he had only about a third of current directors remotely on his side, and the remaining two thirds were our men and women. In any case, they knew which side of their bread was buttered. He lost badly and was out of the boardroom within six months. We all liked loyalty, certainty and good incomes and fringe benefits and profits tend to go along with a happy and industrious main board, and our people either were our people previously or very decent converts. I was picking up the politics quite fast with Heather's help, plus my loyal Vice Chair and MD, so there was never a real danger, but I wanted to know 'who put him up to that and why'. Know that and I might learn who my real opponent was. It only took a week or two and Mr Nice & Smarmy emerged, and was duly ousted, and not even allowed to join one of the group boards. Loyalty is all.

Another even bigger group of companies came after us and we agreed unanimously "enough was enough" for the foreseeable future. I was busy ensuring that all main board members focussed on accumulating group shares so that if it came to a hostile takeover, it could be prevented from happening. Heather's and my shares alone should prevent that, but I would be more comfortable, I let it be known, if together we had more than 50% of the whole group shares in the main board's hands.

Somebody in the press had been talking down our share price for a few weeks, then I said in open board, "Don't know about you people, but I think it might be a good time to take advantage of the 10% discount offered on new shares to all directors. there are public indications in the press that our share prices are quite low right now and with our team in control that might change soon."

All open and above board, all the main board members used their recent bonuses and share allocations to boost their overall holdings of our group shares and it was nice to see that we collectively now owned 58% of the stock and it was rising in value, as the press had predicted it would. So good, these press financial journalists, must invite a few of them to a BBQ party I was having soon as the celebration of our Grand Extension Opening. And the whole main board of course, they so enjoyed our little parties and enjoyed talking to our children!

We went from strength to strength over the next year or two and took on a couple more companies who said they were happy to join us. We had already approached a few board members and told them how much we liked their set-up, etc. They already knew our background and how well our group was performing, so this made for happy marriages and two MDs joined our main board and were immediately made welcome in our, by now, well known, and trusted way. Discounted shares, bonuses, share issues, etc.

We were fast becoming one of the leading UK based international companies and were not far short of Top 100 listing. But Heather and I decided to put a gentle brake on our expansion to ensure we remained in control and didn't excite too much attention which can become a problem even with a group as diverse as ours. It is all too easy to become a victim of your own success, so we quietly let our feelings be known and took some of the potential heat out of the equation.

Then at age forty-seven, I met a very unusual woman who was thirteen years younger in age and about twenty years older in experience. She was Swedish and divorced with two children and already had a string of boyfriends, associates, lovers, and friends. She was tall and blonde and quite fit without any gym work. And she was not a businesswoman, she was a nurse, not fully qualified, but could easily get work in whatever area she wanted. She was not looking to be rich or well-connected in the normal sense; she was her own woman living in a style and fashion of her own choosing. She did some private upmarket caring type nursing; she was a very able PR person; she did tour-guide work. She did what she wanted just enough to provide a reasonable income, but with the sort of friends she had, she needed to do nothing. She chose what she wanted to do. When I met her, she had just thrown the latest suitor's engagement ring away, was once again totally free, and she was completing some sort of nursing diploma course and earning a few bucks as a tour guide in Europe. She spoke Swedish, Finnish, English, German, and a couple of other languages, but more importantly she understood and could talk upper middle-class English and was familiar with all the social etiquettes necessary in that echelon. For all I knew she might have even known some minor Royal!

Chapter 24

Her name was Ronja, and she fascinated me from about the second time I met her at a pal's house where she stayed in between affairs long and short. She had been the 'Hostess' for a county-type millionaire businessman of not very high repute, whom she eventually rejected as she felt she was mainly there to be used to enhance his status among his particular peer group. A sort of superior maid/housekeeper and bed warmer! She would not tolerate any such position, despite his money and promises, and had recently kicked him into touch before getting involved with the rejected engaged man.

Enter yours truly, comparatively speaking, really wet behind the ears despite all my experience. She was happy for the mutual friend, whose house it was, to pretend she and he had a thing going, but in reality, all he really had going was a nice, relaxed easy-going manner. He was never capable, I was soon to learn, of being her lover if anyone's at all. He was himself divorced and had got burned emotionally when his 'first girlfriend marriage' foundered after about twenty years, primarily because he had a drinking problem and someone with a bit more spine had made a play for her and won. He entertained old pals and new in his quite reasonable house not too far from London where he worked, and he pretended he was happy with normal appetites, etc. but anybody with an ounce of nous could see he was borderline alcoholic and was basically a 'never-grown-up' schoolboy of forty-five.

I was actually visiting him with an old girlfriend I had known for quite a few years, nothing serious, just a night away as it were, in the safety of our mutual friends' house. We had a quiet couple of drinks in the nice old pub over the road and a meal cooked by our host and off to bed. Ronja with my male friend in one bedroom and me and my casual girlfriend in another, even though we had not got a sexual thing going at all by this point. Even so, we laughingly shared a room. I instinctively knew the friend and Ronja thing was a sham, but because she used his house as one of her boltholes, she happily let him hint she was his girlfriend and, in a sense, she was, but not in the accepted sense. I was only mildly interested in her at this point and enjoyed my night with my old friend even though we did not make love. Yet I wondered about Ronja, and I actually thought, she's too sophisticated for me, and maybe too young, got plenty bigger fish to fry no doubt. But there was something about her which intrigued me, I just couldn't quite figure out quite what. Apart from the fact she was about thirteen years younger than me and was very attractive and interesting.

In the morning, after my old girlfriend had left to wherever she was en route for, and our host had gone off to work in London, I stayed in bed a bit catching up on a few zzzz's and Ronja came into my room with a knock and an 'excuse me' but could she pick up a few items she needed? This clearly demonstrated to me that this normally was her room not Fred's bedroom. She had on a loose housecoat or dressing gown showing part of her breasts as she bent over to retrieve something as I lay in bed just waiting for her to go. Then she apologised and withdrew to the bathroom. I thought to myself, that was deliberate, a message maybe. But I did nothing about it. My old fear of rejection raising its head at my age!

We had breakfast together and she was then going off to some training appointment in Guildford and I was meeting an important client at Royal Ascot Racecourse for a track-side private 'cabin lunch', overlooking the finishing post. I was due to return home on the Wednesday afternoon after the last race had been run, catching the local train to Sunningdale. I had left my car there because I was being picked up this morning by my host on the main road nearby Fred's house for the short drive to Ascot where his company had parking slots connected to their private suite.

I had on my tweed jacket and cavalry twills, suitable I thought for a private box at Ascot and for walking out to the bookmakers to place a few bets, but I had no real idea of the required protocol as I had never done Ascot before. I mentioned this to Ronja, and she laughed and said, "You'll be fine, it's only the toffs who bother with penguin suits and their ladies wear funny hats and things, but in a private box you will be fine."

157

We just chatted normally, nothing much personal talked about and no mention of last night's sleeping arrangements, or me sleeping with my friend in her normal room, she was very discreet. Fred, normally called FB as his surname was Bramley and he even had a number plate on his car with FB prominent on it, was due back about six p.m. but Ronja said, "You never know with FB, he could be back anytime, depends on who he ends up drinking with."

I said, before we parted company, her to Guildford in her car, me to stand on the verge of the main road at the allotted hour, "Well it's been great meeting you again, and I think you were here for part of an evening when I was here a few months ago. I often wondered how you were getting on." Then I leaned casually over and gave her a little kiss on the lips and said, "Hope to see you again sometime."

And she appeared gobsmacked for a moment, then recovered and said, "Me too, it's really nice to know that FB has at least one normal friend."

And I smiled, waved as she drove off. I walked fifty metres up the road with my small attaché overnight case and after about five minutes, my client rolled up and picked me up and off we went to Royal Ascot.

I had a great day there, the weather was very good, and the box turned out to be a suite, old-fashioned, but with a perfect view of the finishing post on the racetrack from a balcony which had glazed sections to be rolled back when the weather was good. The main salon seated about twelve around a central oval-shaped table and there was a small kitchen and a toilet suite so you could spend all afternoon in there if you didn't want to visit the bookmakers.

Champagne was opened at the outset, followed by whatever drink took your fancy from a very well-stocked bar arrangement. Hot and cold food was prepared for serving from the kitchen and the maid ensured there was quite enough of everything you could possibly want. Salads, quail eggs, fresh poached salmon, hot or cold cuts of beef, lamb and ham, vegetables of all kinds, a real feast, and all the different wines you could want chilled or not, opened at the drop of a hat.

This was followed by a variety of desserts from fresh strawberries and cream to hot apple pie and custard; several different cakes, and a huge bowl of assorted fruits. And more wine of course.

I really enjoyed the whole experience and went with the host to the bookmakers and had a quick lesson on the procedures and placed several twenty-pound bets on what he called second favourites and finished the afternoon about £160 up on the day! But I realised after I had bid a farewell to my generous host, and consulted my watch and train timetables, that I was in no state to drive and still had to get to the main railway station.

I called FB's number, thinking he would be home by then as it was quarter to seven and Ronja answered. She said that FB wasn't home yet how could she help. I explained that I was a bit pissed and had missed the train I wanted and wondered if FB would mind if I extended my stay for another night. She replied, "Of course not, no one else is coming tonight and he might not be back until late. Just wait there and I will come and pick you up in about twenty minutes, OK?"

I said a heartfelt thank you, phoned and left a message with Heather's PA that I had been detained and would not be back tonight but would see her after work tomorrow, and gave my love to the kids and that was that.

Ronja picked me up and we went back to FB's and he was still absent, so we both sat at the dining table in his sitting room. She opened a bottle of red wine which I agreed was a good idea, then we looked each other in the eye and started to talk.

We were into the important stuff straight away as I looked at her and said, "This morning when you came into my room for some things, I looked at you and thought, pull her into bed now, you've nothing to lose."

She didn't even pause for breath, leaned forward, and took my hand across the table and said, "Why didn't you?"

It was my turn to be gobsmacked, I was a bit pissed and so less inhibited than in the morning, but I half expected either a laugh or a 'How dare you' but instead got an immediate strong indication that she really fancied me. I liked that and wanted her as soon as it could be arranged to our mutual satisfaction.

She gazed into my eyes and said, "When you kissed me this morning, it was wonderful; I wanted you right away but didn't know for sure and didn't want to spoil anything and in any case, I knew you had this important meeting at Ascot. So when you rang this evening, I was thrilled."

I said, quite happy, but cautiously, "You know that I am married, and you know I slept with another woman last night and you are still interested?"

She half climbed over the table, and I took her in my arms and gave her my full-on best, most sensuous kiss, lingering for a minute or two, and we both sat back somewhat breathless. She said, "I knew there was something about you that was different from most men; boy was I right, you are some kisser! If you fuck like you kiss that would be amazing. But it's better FB is not aware of this. He warned me about you and is terribly jealous even though I am not his woman, just a good friend. I only ever tried sex with him once and he is hopeless, an alcoholic in the making and no technique at all, pathetic really, but I like him, and he loves people thinking we are an item. It doesn't bother me at all because I know we are not. If he takes it too far, I put him in his place, gently and move on."

I said, "I guessed all that and wasn't in the least bit concerned. I have known about him many years and I met his ex-wife and her new husband, and I know he is hopeless with women as lovers but has many women friends."

"Oh, that's perfect. Just play along with me and don't upset him, let's take my dog for a walk and we can have a few kisses and come back and act like we are just friends, is that OK?"

"Absolutely," I said, "I will come to your bed after he is gone to work tomorrow morning, if that's what you would like?"

"I like very much," she said, "I can't wait."

At that point FB came in the front door and there we were sitting with a bottle of wine and clearly enjoying each other's company and he looked a bit put out until she explained my problem nicely to him and he immediately relaxed and said, "Of course it's no problem, same bed; Ronja can sleep with me again."

"Great," I said, "you're a pal. We are about to take Ronja's dog for a little walk then how about we all go over the road and I buy us dinner and we have a couple of pints?"

"Perfect," FB said. "Save me cooking again. I'll have a bath and see you here in about twenty minutes then."

Off Ronja and I went with her dog on a lead and only got about twenty metres through an alleyway of bushes alongside FB's house before we were half in a bush kissing frantically with me groping her through the fly of her blue jeans, where I discovered she had no pants on under the jeans. She was gasping as I massaged her between the legs and saying, "Fuck me, fuck me now!"

"Not now," I said, "I can't with your dog on the lead and anyone could come along, even FB." She calmed down at that and we contented ourselves with holding hands and taking it in turns to hang on to the dog lead with the other hand. We just kept talking and turning to look at each other and laugh and stop for a little kiss every now and then.

She then explained that she had been a bit down the last few days after throwing her boyfriend's engagement ring at him and breaking up the relationship. She said that this was the latest of several relationships she'd had after separating from and then divorcing her husband and meeting me was such a pleasant surprise as she had fancied me the first time we met, but I hardly looked at her, and now wow!

Strange, but I was just content at that point to hold her hand and kiss a little, I knew she would be special, but was prepared to wait and play it her way and just see what happened. She made it clear that she was not looking for a long-term relationship, she had had enough of those for a while and was concentrating on her nursing thing at present, filling in with her foreign trips as a tourist guide, usually of middle aged and older Brits visiting the continent. It was well-paid in cash and sporadic, which suited her current lifestyle staying at FB's free for as long as she wanted in the meantime. We picked up FB and deposited her dog in the house and strolled over the road to the pub where FB and Ronja were obviously well known by the landlord and ordered a couple of pints and a red wine and looked at the fairly limited bar menu and I ordered steaks for Ronja and me and FB had sausages and mash with gravy, most of which he left on the plate.

Ronja and I were careful not to look at each other quite so much and she made a bit of a fuss of FB, and he sank his pint quickly and ordered a bottle of red wine. The evening went very pleasantly with he and I reminiscing about old times and mutual friends and generally playing the game Ronja wanted us to play, with the certain knowledge we would get together, all being well, as soon as he had gone to work, expected to be about seven-thirty or so in the morning. When we returned, we opened another bottle of wine and after FB had downed a couple more glasses, he went yawning to bed saying to Ronja, "Don't be long coming up Ronja; I have to be up early tomorrow."

She just said OK and off he went to bed, but we heard no snoring so didn't risk anything silly, just talked quietly for a bit and finished the bottle and a quick kiss goodnight and she went off to her side of his double bed. After I had made and consumed a coffee and a brandy, I went up too about midnight.

In the morning I stayed in bed and Ronja got up to see him off and then she went back to his bed, and we waited about ten minutes more to be sure he was truly gone and had caught his train up to London. Then I walked into his room and slid into bed alongside Ronja who was also naked, ready, and waiting. There were no fireworks this time, just a long slow build-up of hugging and kissing and touching each other all over and then I made her come with my finger on her spot before getting inside her and slowly worked her up to a crescendo and she had about four more orgasms before I allowed myself one. It was very nice and satisfying but a new experience for both of us, I think. Neither of us was trying to prove anything, just two experienced lovers using all their knowledge and skills to please each other, and that I am certain, we did.

About ten-thirty a.m. in between sessions as it were, the phone rang and she said, "That will be FB don't make a sound," so I pulled away and lay still while she answered the phone in a sleepy voice saying, "Yes."

It was clearly FB I could hear his voice, and she replied, "Yes I'm still in bed, a bit tired after yesterday, how are you? When can I expect you for dinner?"

I didn't get all his response but she obviously put his mind at rest, and he rang off. She explained that he was possessive and jealous, even though there was no real relationship with him, and she just went along with it. I indicated it bothered me not at all and we carried on where we had left off. I discovered that Ronja loved sex as much if not more than

I did, and she was capable of multi-orgasms which appeared to continue as long as I was capable of performing.

I eventually left after lunch which Ronja made, and we both knew this relationship was going to go on for some considerable time, and we needn't even mention the fact. We ran over our individual commitments for the next few weeks and swapped mobile phone numbers, promised only that we would see each other as and when it was possible, and off we went with her driving me as far as the station where I had left my car, a quick kiss goodbye and we then departed in opposite directions.

I was happy with the new relationship, but never expected it to last because I believed she had the confidence and looks and was at an age when she could pull any man she desired. I just counted my blessings and toddled off back to my office for an hour and then home to the welcome of my wife and children, and my mother who was visiting from just down the road. I was surprised some time later when Ronja said to me almost the same words, I had thought about her, that I could have any woman I wanted if I really wanted to. What a thought, what a compliment.

I was part right and part wrong. She could pull other men as and when she wished and did so from time to time, and I too still had my moments with other women very occasionally, but our relationship was to be destined to be far longer than I anticipated and far more complex and at times nerve-racking. But I digress, let me continue on how the relationship developed, its highs and lows and how I knew jealousy and fear, but also what love really was.

I can say that now with absolute certainty and confidence. The test of true love is the desire to be with the other person always and at all times, regardless. Just be with. All the rest is trimmings.

I already had an arrangement with a small private hotel in a back street not a half mile from Madame Tussauds in London where I could visit discreetly for clandestine meetings of several kinds. When I wanted to carry out a surprise visit to a group members office early in the morning for example, I could go to my hotel the previous evening without anyone being aware I was in town and appear on the group office doorstep with the first arrivals in the morning, which could cause a stir, but I learnt a lot this way and it kept people on their toes. I could also have a private business meeting with a client or supplier or legal adviser and stay on for dinner or whatever and slip into my small private hotel at any hour and even without notice, my room would always be available. I knew the part owner/manager very well and she was very reliable and discreet, and we had just a business relationship, but I think circumstances being different we might well have had a small affair, but this never happened.

But for meeting Ronja discreetly from both our points of view, it was ideal. I stayed there on several occasions when I had business in London, often real meetings happened when it was appropriate to stay the night, but it was relatively simple to arrange a night or two there more or less at will. I would travel by train to London and then tube and taxi wherever I wanted, and no one was ever absolutely certain where I was or when I might appear or in whose company. For almost a year that arrangement applied on a very regular basis and as far as I ever knew no one but Ronja and I were aware of it, apart from the hotelier of course. And she made sure we had Champagne and a good selection of wines available and occasionally we had meals out as there were many restaurants in this part of London.

During the first six months of my relationship with Ronja it was incredible the lengths we would go to meet, not just in London but further away in the Home Counties where I had various group interests. Ronja and I found a couple of hotels — one as far away as Guildford — which were convenient, reasonable quality and had a decent restaurant and where there was a constant flow of clients, who were similar to us. I was a mobile, senior director and shareholder of a pretty fair-sized group of companies with lots of contacts and many reasons to be almost anywhere I chose. Ronja could act the part required with ease, both in dress sense, demeanour and languages. She could fit in at a board meeting, a fashion show, theatre, restaurant, a local pub; almost any venue you might imagine, with ease.

Certain regular clients and colleagues got to know about her and just assumed she was some sort of freelance diplomat, PR exec. or similar, who we employed on a day-to-day basis as required. They all knew it was best not to query her presence with me, or to ask her any untoward questions. We kept our real relationship pretty much under wraps and even if seen having dinner or at a club, it would not be too out of the ordinary to justify anything other than a private thought on the subject, best kept to 'oneself.

We were making love on a regular basis often well into the night and we were both probably drinking too many late-night brandies, but we were fired up for each other and really enjoying the ride.

One such night after a long session in bed, she was sitting up in bed as was I and she suddenly said, "You are an incredible man, I don't think I have ever known anybody like you."

I said, "Thanks, I feel the same about you."

She responded, "Well you know by now I have had a lot of different lovers, but with you it's different, sex I mean, why it is so different with you?"

I replied with a laugh, "It's because we are in love."

We both looked at each other, a bit shocked I think, and she said nothing to that statement, and I added nothing more and it was dropped. But later I was to reflect, could this be right? Am I in love with Ronja? Is she also in love with me? Big questions, because if this were so it could change everything, I thought.

But there were downs as well as ups, and I was to be consumed with jealousy for a while when she dallied with other men. I recall one very poignant such occasion when FB reported to me (and he knew about our affair by this time and did not like it). He said to me that he had seen Ronja with a colleague of his whom I also knew, who worked in London. He went on that he had seen them leaving a hotel together and Ronja put her bag in his car boot at about nine a.m. after an evening when I had an arrangement with Ronja which she never appeared for. I was furious and jealous, especially as this man was even older than me and I knew he was a womaniser too. So, I tackled her about him, and she just said, "So you prefer to believe a story from FB rather than me? Yes, I was putting my bag in his car because I had been meeting someone else not him, but as you know he stays at FB's often and I know him quite well. He was helping me out of a difficult situation, and you knew what he calls me?"

"No," I said.

"The ice maiden," she said, "I wouldn't fuck him for any reason whatever, but in any case, I can see who I want when I want OK?"

165

"But we had an arrangement that night!" I protested.

"Yes, we did, but things happen, and I don't have to explain myself to you or anyone else. I am sorry I didn't make it but I can tell you there was a very good personal reason why not and that will have to do. So, if you are going to be like all the other men I have known and act like a jealous teenager, let's just forget all about us eh!"

So, I apologised, said how stupid I was and swallowed my pride and said I was an idiot, but I was in love with her, and it was my fault too for not waiting for her to explain and jumping to conclusions, etc. She smiled, kissed me, and said, "OK now let's move on, what is the plan. If there isn't one let's just go to The Cricketers. We can book a room, have a meal and forget all about this. I have things going on which are family related, don't forget I have two children still living with their father and his parents. And let us be open about this, you have a wife and two children too but in much happier circumstances and, like me you also still see other women, yes?"

"True, all true, I'm being a selfish, possessive, jealous prick and I will cease to be that as of now, or at least I will try."

The crucial part of this exchange was the expression "I love you" came out. She never said anything at that time but forever afterwards when I said I love you, or just love you at the end of a telephone conversation she would chuckle and say, "Love you too" and I know we both meant it. I was in love, really at that intensity and maturity, for the first time in my life at age forty-seven.

Chapter 25

I continued to function as CE etc., no problem at all; in fact, I felt more alive than at any comparable period of my life. But the fact is I really did this time have a mistress, although neither of us referred to her in that way for a long, long time, until she eventually said that was what she was she was, my mistress.

But I digress, there was a lot of things going to happen over the coming years, but at the point I was at recalling all this, we were, as it were, still in the honeymoon phase. And although I said to Ronja that I loved her, and wanted at some point to marry her, and I really believed that, it was not going to happen. Not in the sort of timescale I was putting on it at that stage, after almost one year had elapsed since our very intense affair had begun. It was like starting from scratch in one sense for both of us.

Ronja told me about some of her adventures and I told her of some of mine, but none were like this. I remember one specific week where we had managed to arrange three consecutive nights together at 'our' hotel and we both packed medium-size bags and were greatly looking forward to it. I had arranged to meet her at the main train station serving her area at something like six-thirty p.m. I watched one train from Sunningdale arrive and no Ronja. I waited for the next due in half an hour and again no Ronja. She was often unpunctual but my anticipation and all meant I was pretty wound up, so when she wasn't on the second train I thought, *Here we go again, if she lets me down this time THAT IS IT!* I got the tube back to the area where the hotel was and went straight to the bar and ordered a pint and sat there thinking *fuck her, I am not going to put up with this being jerked around any more*, etc. But after about half an hour a taxi pulled up at the hotel and Ronja struggled through the entrance doors with two bags looking frazzled and said, "Why didn't you meet me?"

I replied, "Very nice to see you darling but I met the train you said you would be on and waited for the next one, but you didn't make that one either, so I came here to wait."

She explained about the delay and in about ten minutes we were at the bar gazing into each other's eyes. We sat at the bar for about an hour having a few drinks and getting in the mood and then we went out to a Greek restaurant and had a typical Greek meal. Halfway through, a small dance floor was brought in to play, not just Greek music but pop and we were doing the new dance which I forget the name of but involves a lot of actions where the man puts his right thigh between the woman's and you sway back and forth to the music leaning back and gyrating and soon there were just three couple at it in the small floor and the rest of the diners were standing round in a ring watching and making comments. It got faster and we were both well in the mood and Ronja was leaning further and further back with her head thrown back and her eyes closed, and I knew what was going to happen, she went into a multiple orgasm as I controlled the dance with my right leg wedged between her thighs. As the music stopped or changed tempo she came to basically and stood more upright very flushed and worked up and laughing and a guy who was also dancing with a woman said to us, "That looked pretty good."

And Ronja said, "It was."

We finished our meal and then people started throwing their plates to the floor, smashing them against a stone fireplace at one end in a mounting crescendo of noise and complete bedlam. But it was all orchestrated and apparently a regular thing after a full house for food and drink, music, and dancing. Then on the walk back to the hotel on this the first night of three, she started to cry. I said, "What's wrong?" and she, sobbing replied, "I'm missing you already."

I said, "But we are here until Friday; we haven't even been to bed yet."

She said that she knew all that, but she was still dreading it ending and I replied that there would be many more such days and night and basically don't be silly. With hindsight I knew what she meant, there was no doubt about it we were in love and couldn't bear to be apart, her perhaps more than me, but this being a woman who had so many male friends and yes, perhaps lovers, past and maybe present, I found incredible then and now.

I went to a couple of meetings and made some phone calls but basically it was three days and nights of fun and laughter and much lovemaking. Then came the last day and we went together on the tube, she to transfer to her main station and me to mine, which meant parting company at one of the tube stations where our lines crossed, each with our suitcase or bag, and Ronja was again in tears. Some Indian guy gave her a helping hand as we parted and she didn't know which way to go for her tube. Whatever happened after that time, and many things did which I will relate, I always had faith it was me she really loved and wanted, but she never pushed for me to take any firm steps to make it happen but just kept hoping perhaps.

So that first year of our relationship was filled with joy and laughter and sometimes a few tears and a lot of lovemaking. But neither of us could keep up that pace for ever and so our relationship developed along slightly different lines after that year ended. I was in love with Ronja without a doubt, and still am, even though much time has now passed.

Chapter 26

The children were now growing quickly, and Nat was starting university in the September at Reading. He was interested in linguistics and business studies and having a good time as well. He was sure he would be a businessman like me, but I had my doubts because I knew you have to be very committed, flexible, hardworking and a bit ruthless in order to do well in my chosen occupation, not to mention ambitious. And let's face it, comparatively he, in common with two previous generations, had had quite a stress-free, want-for-nothing, upbringing in what, by almost any standard, was quite a privileged position. He kind of knew it, but to some extent took it all for granted as well, so I talked his future over with Heather and told her my thoughts saying that I believed we should not be too generous with his budget, let him experience his university life more on a par with the majority rather than the privileged few.

She agreed and we worked out what we thought was a reasonable income for him in Halls at Reading the first year, thinking he could branch out to private accommodation, perhaps share a small house with other students, for his second of a scheduled four years there. He said four years, because he wanted to leave with a Masters in Linguistics, Spanish and German probably, as well as have a BSc in Business Studies. When we gave him the news about his fairly meagre budget, he seemed a bit surprised but completely unfazed saying, "Whatever, if I need to earn some money I will, and I have my savings of course."

We both said, "What savings?" and he informed us that he had been saving from about twelve years old, had a bank account and put in half his monthly pocket money allowance and some casual earnings, together with cash gifts for birthdays, etc., and had about 6,000 pounds in the bank. We were both gobsmacked. Maybe he would make a businessman after all!

Jo was in the lower-sixth class from that autumn, so had two years to go to her A levels but was already talking about doing something in music and art, design maybe, not sure where though, but liked the idea of Oxford. She too was a budding linguist but not so advanced as Nat was nor so committed to becoming an MA linguist, or businesswoman. She quite liked the idea of teaching, but we believed that deep down she wanted to have an acting career. But there were two years to go before this would eventually become clear. Kath, their Nanny for their earlier years, was still with us and was treated more or less like part of the family. She had boyfriends from time to time, but never anything serious and was quite content as our housekeeper, cook and general factotum. She had her own car paid for by us and was always available for taking people places or picking them up from the station or a pub if too many drinks had been indulged in.

My mother was still hale and hearty and very contented in her retirement bungalow and walked round our place most days and ended up staying for lunch and/or dinner. Heather and I were as close as ever and still made love fairly frequently as well as going on fishing or hiking jaunts with or without one or both of the children, and we all now went to the pub about twice a month for a nice meal in very informal surroundings in our favourite riverside hostelry.

So, life was good, and I was able as I always had been to compartmentalise my work and extracurricular sexual relationships from my everyday life as husband and father, and never got down or depressed about the situation. In fact, it felt more normal to me than straight monogamy would, I imagined. The difference was the acknowledgement to myself that for the very first time in my life I truly felt that I loved a woman, but I was not going to sacrifice all Heather and I had together because of that and indeed I was sure that Ronja would never have let me, not with her anyway. It seems that we both liked our freedom to have a second relationship but also to retain the right to play the field a little as well!

We did discuss the possibility of me divorcing and marrying Ronja, but I think we both knew it would not work out, it just wouldn't be so exciting and dangerous and it might even get boring! Or that one or both of us might look around for something new anyway. In any case, Ronja had started seeing another man, whom she didn't love, but who was mad keen on her and wanted to marry her, or at least live with her full time.

And I had been pulling back a little at that time and had also seen another woman myself, but nothing serious. However, Ronja was looking for a more permanent relationship than it seemed we were ever going to have and this guy who was keen on her was being posted to some African Country, I was never sure quite which one, and he was in security for a multinational company, head honcho I believe. Anyway, he needed a woman to take with him, a white woman as he was South African or Rhodesian or whatever of European descent, and she liked the idea of the tropics, great beaches, lots of nightlife in the capital city, etc. But really, I thought she just wanted to test me out to see how far I was prepared to take our relationship, and I knew she had form for testing relationships to destruction, but I wasn't so easily manipulated as her other men might have been. I asked why? She said she was unsettled by our relationship, it wasn't going anywhere, she needed some sort of commitment, no marriage but something a bit more stable than we had. So, I made it clear I would not leave Heather and my family; the risks and other downsides were too great. I said she had better grasp this opportunity and I would not try to dissuade her, the decision was hers. But that I did love her, didn't want to lose her and believed that I wouldn't and because I loved her, I wanted her to be happy.

We met for what might be the last time for an evening with me and my pal Simon who had a large apartment in London, and had dinner together, basically to say goodbye and I could see she was very emotional, and we parted that night, maybe forever and she was flying to Botswana or wherever the next day with her new man. But she promised to write to me and give me a contact number and keep me abreast of her affairs and that was that.

I knew it was not the end of our relationship, I knew this guy was going to get let down, Ronja's men always did, except me. For I believe the first time in her life she was no longer totally in charge of a man, i.e., me, and she didn't know what to do about it other than run. Sure, she had let me down temporarily many times, but I learnt not to react, not to be jealous, to quietly get on with life and take another woman on if I felt like it and not hide the fact. To do exactly what she was used to doing with sometimes disastrous effect on the poor bugger she was manipulating at that time. Take her husband as an example. She had two children with him and there can be no doubt he was in love with her, and then she had an affair. He fell in love with her and ultimately, she effectively destroyed them both. She had been seeing the guy often and exchanged letters, etc., where explicit stuff was written, and the guy sent one such letter to their house and hubby picked it up one morning after Ronja had gone to work. When she came through the door he just snapped and attacked Ronja at the door injuring her seriously enough to put her in intensive care in hospital for a night or two. He was devastated and had a bit of a breakdown. She left him and went to live elsewhere, leaving him with their two children and his mother and father. When she told me all of this, I was totally on her side because of the level of violence he used on her, but when I reflected how she told me that both of the men involved had effectively had their lives destroyed by her, I began to have some doubts.

She told me that her husband was still basically living day-to-day at his mother's house and had not moved on at all some three or four years later. But she was so softly spoken, so kind and tender a person, it was easy to forget the downside stuff and instead just focus on the 'real' Ronja, the one I loved.

So, I did just that, and when she went off to Africa, I rationalised that I was doing the right thing for her, not just hanging on selfishly to a relationship I could not, or would not, allow to destroy my marriage as she had destroyed her own and I don't know how many others.

So, I got on with my comfortable, demanding but satisfying life and although I thought about her almost every day, I could handle that without too much trouble after the first two years had passed with a variety of minor disappointments where arrangements with Ronja had time and time again left me high and dry and alone when I should have been meeting her. I had grown used to that happening and I started to ensure I had a fall-back person I could turn to in order to assuage my sorrows and disappointments.

So, when Ronja got in touch from the gated compound where rich Europeans lived in this African city, with their local black servants, gardeners, drivers, etc. I was delighted to speak to her, but I began to realise that although with her servants she could go out shopping and visit a beach and suchlike, it was always potentially dangerous and the circle of similar white immigrants who lived there was quite small. Alcohol was the main distraction and dinner parties, but her man was often away on business trips, and I got the impression she was a bit disappointed all round. It was always good to hear her voice of course and we always ended with "Love you", and the reply "Love you too".

So a year or two passed where there was only telephone contact until, after a nasty experience where she became quite ill after falling asleep in the hot sun on a beach, and I guess an increasing frustration with the narrow existence there in Africa, she persuaded her bloke to transfer back to the UK. They went to live near Kew, and I guess he was working in London. That changed matters a bit and I made my mind up that if opportunities arose, I would see her again, and it seemed, knowing her as well as I did, that the man, who she told me was an ex-rugby player, and a huge man it appears, was gradually losing his appeal as I knew was inevitable.

I was still visiting all sorts of places and of course the London area was the easiest in terms of logistics and cover stories, but I had no idea if our relationship would be the same after so long apart and she with the big man. Then I was talking to her on my mobile phone and mentioned that I might be coming to London, and she said, "When?"

And I replied, "When is a good day for you?" and she replied, "Tomorrow; he goes off early to Birmingham and out that night there, so you could stay the night here if you come tomorrow."

I told her that I would look into it and get back to her and something I had in the pipeline made it possible so I said, "Give me your address and I will be there at about five or six p.m. and will be able to stay the night, that is, if you are sure he won't be back unexpectedly."

She assured me he had to stay the night in Birmingham for an early appointment the next day and no way would he suddenly appear; he always telephoned her every day, sometimes twice a day!

I made my plans and took my car this time and drove down to Kew which I was familiar with and eventually found the house, an ordinary semi-detached house which they were renting for his UK spell. I was familiar with her ways and reflected this was exactly the sort of thing I could expect from her if we had got together, yes, she was a great Mistress, but a poor wife or permanent partner. But I was used to all that and I loved her and there was no one in bed like she was, and I loved her company.

We went straight to bed and made love after a glass or two of red wine, and it was just like always, fantastic. Then we walked to a pub not too far away and had a couple more drinks and a very average pub meal and back to bed for dessert. In the morning, she woke me about eight a.m. and told me it would be better if I went by say eleven at the latest, just in case he turned up early.

I said, "What's the big hurry? Are you afraid of him because I'm not?"

She said that I would be if I saw him, he was a huge man and could break me in two if he caught me there. I realised then that he must know something about me and might be suspicious; in fact, knowing Ronja like I do, it's inevitable that she must have taunted him at some point with stories about me. She may have even told him it was me she loved. So rather than be on the receiving end of a casualty submission and in intensive care myself, I swallowed my pride, kissed her, and drove off by eleven a.m. as she wished. I talked to her the following day, and she said he came back at about noon in a foul temper having abandoned his early meeting and coming straight back from Birmingham, probably hoping to catch her out. History repeating itself.

Needless to say, things carried on for a while before she finally took pity on the poor bloke and put him out of his misery, and off he went, back to Africa or wherever with his tail between his legs. I continued to see her from time to time, meeting at a hotel near Bristol on one occasion and at another in Bristol itself for another. She had many friends in Bristol and area and eventually went to live with an old girlfriend and her husband for a while and I even visited her there one day when both were out. Then she moved into her own little house which she had purchased 50/50 I think with the African guy, but they had rented it out. But although they were now split up, he still owned half and hoped perhaps they would get back together again, poor sucker, I knew he never would, not once he had been put out like he had, there was no way back. The thing was that the rent had paid the mortgage on their property, so I assumed she had got round him to pay that off or continue making the payments. Anyway, she loved the little house and I straightened out the small back garden for her on one visit.

This mistress thing is never straightforward and to survive as the male part you have to be as strong and committed as the female partner and prepared to use the same or similar tactics in order to survive. But I suppose at the end of the day, love comes into it, and that is the real glue, I guess. But you could never feel sorry for Ronja, she was what she chose to be. She enjoyed it, or most of it anyway, and it was going to be a long time before she stopped doing it, if ever.

It seems to me now with 20/20 hindsight, a kind of symbiotic relationship; to be happily married to one woman and happily having a knowledgeable and relatively compliant mistress as well, you both need each other, but not full time. Permanent maybe, but not permanently together otherwise you are no longer a happy married man with a compliant and happy mistress, you become the latest conquest of a predatory female species, or she loses her independence, and you end up not so happily as her husband or long-term partner and the fizz goes.

There has to be love and a modicum of respect and even admiration for the other person, male or female, for being able to go through a large part of your adult life in this way, successfully. So yes, you can have a mistress, but that normally seems to involve an aspiring woman who would really like to be married to you, and a man who is prepared to foster that illusion just to maintain his regular extracurricular sex. Neither of us truly wanted to be married to each other, certainly not after the first year in a relationship like ours. But we liked toying with the idea and loved just being together, part time.

The thing was, it was fun. The risk-taking, the clandestine meetings and outings together, they were actually irregular, but much anticipated sexual activity which neither of us ever tired of, with each other that is. That feeling of being very special for someone, and secretly, it gave the sort of kick I imagine some drug might. Although, apart from the odd cannabis roll-up, I had never indulged in drug taking of any other kind. I heard tales of mad sex sessions fuelled by cocaine and heroin but neither of us had ever done that, I don't think; I certainly had not. A few glasses of wine, a couple of snifters of brandy was our preference although, as I say we had a cannabis smoke about two or three times in all, I think. And quite honestly a puff at a grass tube was no more stimulating than a couple of pints of beer and a sexy partner, for me anyway.

So, although this may all sound a bit debauched, I believe it was nothing of the kind. It was fun, but it endangered our families not at all. Ronja was seeing more of her fast-growing children as time went on and enjoying having them to herself, mostly. I loved being with my family although, Nat was in his third year at Reading University now. Jo had passed the entrance procedures for Oxford and was doing Modern Art and Theatre or something like that, which could lead to an MA and maybe the teaching profession, or some special post in a major Art Gallery. But those decisions were still in the melting pot, and she was just enjoying the whole experience, living with several other girls in a large house owned by a parent who collected the rent from their daughter and her fellow guests as and when she took the trouble to gather it in!

I liked the sound of that arrangement and suggested to Nat that maybe he and Heather and I should buy a suitable property and he could do something similar to Jo as a future investment for the period after he had to leave university. And if he stayed on for further years, so be it. If not, he could still retain the house and get an agent to manage it for him. He said he had similar thoughts and within a week had located a suitable property and we put in an offer which was accepted. We agreed that we form a small company where he and us could be one-third owners each, Heather, and I to pay the deposit and he to fund the mortgage repayments from rents.

Having heard all this, Jo said she wanted the same if we could afford it, so we did something similar except Jo preferred a small modern apartment block with just six units and a common area for lounging in, a large kitchen, a separate study, a dining room, and a small fitness room. Each flat had its own kitchenette and bathroom, but we liked this purpose-built block which was designed for sharing by six students or teachers and could sleep twelve if needed, with ample space for communal get-together as well as providing privacy. This cost more than Nat's, but the rent potential was far more and in addition a service charge was due from each flat for the extra amenities. After factoring in these points, a similar deposit was required, and the mortgage would still be adequately covered by the rents. Furthermore, we learnt that if a student signed a contract (or their parents did) this meant a smaller monthly rent but for the whole twelve months of each yearly contract. Better for parental cash flow and for us to fund the mortgage and no worries about people losing their rooms to others. Under the contract, the room was theirs for that year and they were reminded a couple of months in advance of when the contract would expire to avoid disappointment.

Although both our children were away for most of the year at university, they visited us often and stayed the weekend, sometimes with others in tow, and of course our facilities were much more commodious and with the gym, the sports room, and the indoor heated pool, in winter, it was a given that we would have a full house at weekends more often than not. And why not? This is what we had planned for, and we loved having them home at weekends with all their young friends about.

I still found time for genuine business trips and important board meetings as well as seeing Ronja occasionally, and should I happen to be away for one reason or another at weekend, there was more than enough going on normally at home to keep Heather and the gang fully occupied!

And you know what? I actually calculated that since I had Ronja as my mistress, I had seen fewer other females for any sort of extracurricular activity, than at any other comparable period since Heather and I were married! Hardly justification of course, but still a source of some moral comfort, for me. I ignored the fact that I was now fast approaching fifty and that Heather was nine years older than me. But really that had never mattered to us and still didn't. I had always preferred to have sex at least four times a week and that was never difficult to achieve married to Heather and still wasn't now, whether or not I saw Ronja, or anyone else for that matter. In fact, I was as active sexually if not more so during my forties than at any comparable period before and fully intended that it remain that way for as long as possible. So it seemed as I turned fifty, that nothing much changed except availability and opportunity, especially as I was busier at work than at any time previously. Someone had told me many years ago regarding any muscle in which category they included the penis and the brain! "Use it or lose it!" And I was determined to keep both organs active as long as possible.

Chapter 27

The group, our group of companies of which we had a controlling interest these days, was going from strength to strength by consistent attention to the market, the recruitment and retention of high-quality job applicants for almost all levels now, not just higher management. We also included, as always, share and bonus incentives and first-class medical insurance for all grades down to junior executives and team leaders, and good holiday breaks for all. We rewarded loyalty and industry and were remorseless in rooting out slackers and troublemakers paying particular attention to the elected union leaders and including them on a rota basis to attend senior management meetings.

Our reform and modernisation of equipment usage and selling our industrial and management expertise to other companies and providing key persons to implement the packages we sold still worked well. And we rarely had any adverse feedback but if we did, we attempted to remedy whatever situation may have developed quickly and cheaply but providing our best people to attend the crisis site and sort matters out.

We had an excellent reputation by this time and guarded it carefully. We acted upon any complaints or allegations made against us as a group or against our individual representatives to get to the root of any such complaints and if unfounded we totally backed the people publicly. If fault were found, we tried to educate and instruct but if that produced no real improvement, contracts were ended. But by and large we were a happy and contented group, well paid and looked after by top management who themselves were also very well paid and rewarded by the directors, and ultimately by Heather and me.

I often attended lower group meetings and workshops and listened carefully and only interfered when invited to. Almost always I was able to say truthfully that I was well pleased with everything and keep it up, etc.

We had stopped actively searching for companies to approach in order to expand our group. Heather and I agreed that we were large enough to remain efficient and viable, and if we got any bigger, we felt that we would have difficulty keeping tabs and making valuable input and decisions designed to keep everything running smoothly. In fact, one of our group, who I had thought some time ago was not a really good fit with the rest of our group, had been approached by another group about joining forces with them and sought my advice. Heather and I looked at the whole scenario and agreed it wasn't a perfect fit, but with a few modifications to product control and marketing, getting rid of some underperforming products and adding one or two new lines, adjusting our manufacturing set-up to accommodate some new technology and a small recruiting drive and we could produce leaner, meaner machine which would fit better into our group as a whole. We were aware that the Managing Director of this particular group member had been cosying up to the rival group, so we offered him a demotion to director only or to terminate his contact on quite good terms, freeing him to join our rivals if he chose and he opted for the latter and was gone in a month. We then promoted his former Deputy to MD, and he embraced our proposed overhaul of the group company wholeheartedly. So we gave the job of completing the reform independently of Heather and me, just asking him to keep us well advised on any large issues and make monthly progress reports. He loved it and made a great success of the big alterations we had set in train. We noted that he should get a particularly good bonus at year end, plus extra shares and an upgrade of his salary and perks package. When the rest of the group welcomed him to our main board meeting, he was greeted with cheers and congratulations. We thought this proved a very good example to all the others and sharpened up their attitude to change and reform, not that much was needed, but we felt it kept them on their toes.

The accounts for the group at year end showed that there was a marked improvement both in productivity and profitability across the group, the leading member being the one we had considered offloading, but who instead had reformed. Our accounts were published of course, and our opposition were quick to note what we had done and new enquiries for our reform packages were coming in thick and fast within days of publication of our accounts and our joint Chairman and CE report concerning the changes that we had implemented.

This once again led to predators sniffing around as our dividends and share price was both up on the previous year's. We politely saw them off and they knew without my and Heather's support they were going nowhere. We both felt that we had our best years yet to come and were enjoying it as well and certainly weren't interested in selling up and sitting on a cash pile wondering what to do with ourselves. I wanted to continue exactly as before and a busy group of companies to manage was as good a way as any to allow me to pursue my hobbies as I pleased! Including fishing and shooting, a new hobby I had become interested in after being invited to a pheasant shoot at a well-known politician's country estate. I quite liked clay pigeon shooting as well. But I had been told that grouse shooting was even more fun although I don't really like killing things. Then a gillie explained to me that 90% of grouse and pheasant were raised only for the shoots and if there were no shoots, there would be 90% less of them to be seen, and a good percentage of the farm-reared grouse and pheasant survived, he said. I wondered how these town birds as I called them, fared against natural predators other than man.

Having seen all the predators of the human kind off our manor so to speak, I was still keen to do business with them, and they with me. A bit hypocritical you might say, maybe so, but amongst fellow businessmen it was just par for the course. That's something I never had the time for, nor saw the point in: golf. Chasing a little white ball around a field and trying to put it into holes. For people with nothing better to do was my opinion, although I could see some merit when too old to work effectively, in strolling round a golf course and having a few beers afterwards in the club. But again, I thought, only if I had nothing better to do, and that was a long time in the future as far as I could see.

Ronja and I kept in touch by messages and calls on a regular basis and an opportunity to meet up happened when I had a meeting in the West Country with a prospective major client whose HO was in Bristol. He lived in the heart of the countryside about forty miles away and I was invited to stay at his place for a night or two, maybe have a spot of trout fishing on the river which snaked through his estate, possibly a little shooting, rabbits, hares, that sort of thing and some excellent British home cooking. I asked in coded language if I could bring 'someone' who was well versed in these things and definitely wouldn't let the side down as an 'associate'.

He said, "Quite understand old boy, bring her along, there will be no one there from your set, so don't worry. I will explain to Sarah and have you put in adjoining rooms."

I thought Sarah must be his wife, another Sarah! Mustn't get them mixed up, but in fact I didn't see the first Sarah at all nowadays. I explained to Ronja, and she was thrilled. It was ages since she had been to such a gathering but she knew the rules well and she assured me that she would not let me down.

So the weekend in question drew nearer and I explained to Heather that she would not like the gathering likely to be at this particular person's estate and she readily agreed as she had all the rest of the family there that weekend and they would all understand.

So off I went in my newish Range Rover with my guns and clobber in the back, plus fours, hacking jacket, etc. Plus, dinner jacket and smart casual clothes as well and I had primed Ronja so she had all the necessary stuff and had done shoots and fly fishing but would need waders, etc., as did I, but we had been assured everything we needed would be provided.

I picked her up at her house and off we went arriving at the magnificent Estate at around six p.m. on the Friday and pulled into the huge circular gravelled drive at the front of the main house where a butler met us, took our bags, and told a boy to park our car at the back near the stables. We entered the huge hall filled with statuary and gilt-framed mirrors, and suchlike and were met before we had progressed far by our host whom I referred to as Michael without any of his titles, as I had been advised to do.

After he said, "James, so glad to see you here at last," we were introduced to his wife Sarah as James and Ronja and that was that.

Michael said to the butler, "Take them to the 4.5 suite and bring them back to the oak drawing room whenever they ask, say in half an hour?"

I merely nodded.

Up we went, two men carrying our baggage including my guns, up a long curved spiral staircase, and up again and along about half a mile of corridor to a large door numbered 4 where Simon, the butler, let us in and deposited our baggage in a small room immediately to the left of the entrance door, said, "Please call me when Sir is ready on 111." And departed.

What a suite, two bedrooms and two bathrooms, a changing room and a huge balcony overlooking the gardens, trees, and fields all around. Each bedroom had a king-sized bed and all the usual side tables, wardrobes, etc., All in oak. There was a large piece of oak furniture at one side which I quickly found out had a fridge and lots of different drinks in it as well as a magnificent array of crystal glassware.

I said, "What should we wear do you think? Meeting in half an hour must mean pre-dinner drinks, so we won't be back for a change of clothing before dinner."

"That's right, I think we should dress for dinner you in your tuxedo and I will wear a long dress for tonight. If we are overdressed, which I doubt, we can modify that for tomorrow, but this is where we shall be judged, by the wife at least. So, not too familiar at this stage, OK? Do we know who else might be here?"

"Not a clue," I said. "Probably an upmarket neighbour or two, no one else of our class. But I am sure we can hold our own."

We called Simon on 111 as directed and he appeared in about two minutes looking approvingly at my tailormade tuxedo and black bow tie and Ronja's cream shimmering silk floor length dress with the sapphire necklace I had given her, and her white-blonde hair in a chignon. She looked fantastic as with four-inch heels, she was about six feet one inch tall, way above me.

There was our host Michael and his wife Sarah; he in his dinner jacket, complete with black tie, and she in floor-length satin of a regal purple, and a simple diamond tiara in her hair. Both looked splendid and I could see by their very slight reaction, that they were pleasantly surprised at our similar turnout. There were two other couples similarly in slightly less stylish apparel, so Ronja was spot on as usual. Turned out that one couple spoke one of the several languages Ronja spoke so that provoked some interest, but the rest of us stuck with English and I believe we more than held our own. Ronja was a model of appropriate behaviour as was I of course being a wealthy, self-made, captain of business. And the guests had been well briefed so that they could take part in most of the conversation that Michael and I indulged in for a while. Then it was on to tomorrow's shoot: what guns had I brought in their leather bags?

I said, "A matching pair of twin barrel Holland & Holland 12 bore and 16 bore, with walnut stocks, made about fifty years ago I believe, but I'm no expert, I just load, point and fire."

"And you, Ronja, do you shoot?" asked another.

She replied, "Only when I need to, but yes I quite like shooting and will use whatever is offered from 410 to 12 bore. I am happy with anything really, and I have brought my shooting trousers just in case."

"Splendid," said Michel, "I will show you my gun collection and you can choose one to suit you."

Then we moved on to fishing and of course I had plenty of coarse fishing experience but next to none on fly fishing so Michael promised a man to guide me tomorrow as to the finer arts of tying the right fly and how to cast properly, etc. I asked if we needed waders and was told ideally yes but you can also fish from the safety of the bank if preferred. I asked if any size 9 waders might be available and there would be and Ronja wanted the same size, but longer legs!

After a sumptuous dinner, with five courses and as many wines we retired to our suite of rooms very happy with the way things had gone. I told Ronja that she exceeded even my high expectations of her, and it was clear that both the host and his wife as well as their guests had been intrigued and impressed by her knowledge and understanding of the British upper-class way of life. We didn't pretend we were sleeping separately; it was clear that no one at this house would be talking to anyone else about my special guest and the host made no reference to Heather and her potential role in any deal we might do at all. Not because he didn't know all about her, everyone in our line of business knew about our marriage and partnership at the helm of our own and the group of companies we were leading.

As usual Ronja and I made full use of all the splendid facilities, made coffee with the equipment provided and had a couple of snifters of excellent brandy before making love in the magnificent bed. Then we slept like babies, only awakening when our maid came in quietly and drew the blinds back, said good morning and enquired if we would join the others at breakfast in approximately thirty or forty minutes. We said we would and thanked her.

Today we had, or rather *I* had, an appointment with Michael alone to discuss our business ideas and the plan was to have a light lunch and then go shooting some pheasant and partridge in the vast grounds surrounding the house. Then later we had a choice of looking at the magnificent house and gardens, the orangery and hot and cool green houses and the stables. And to have an hour or two fishing if we preferred and if time allowed, but Michael said that fishing tomorrow morning would be better as that was when the flies were around, and the trout would likely be rising. Ronja was invited to go riding while we had our meeting and she accepted providing they had some suitable riding gear for her as she was unaware that might be needed. Sarah assured her there was quite collection of riding gear available for occasions such as this despite Ronja's height and very long legs, and Sarah herself rode as did one of the other couples and their groom would accompany them on the ride.

We said our thanks and agreed with Michael that tomorrow morning might be best for the trout and that we looked forward to the shoot, and again the groom and his assistant were in control of the pheasant-rearing and would supervise the gun arrangements. He was, I realised, their gamekeeper.

We all then had breakfast, and what a breakfast it was. Cereals and fruits fresh from the hothouse, milk and cream from the home farm, bacon cured by themselves from their own pigs, fresh farm eggs, home-made bread and pastries, kippers or smoked haddock for fish lovers, sautéed kidneys, home-made black pudding, field mushrooms and more. Home-made jams and marmalades and various other preserved fruits, what a spread and mostly home produce and home cooked and baked. And Ronja and I did justice to this feast making our hosts laugh with our childish enthusiasm. I said to Michael, "You are going to take advantage of me as I shall be soporific after this splendid breakfast."

But he pointed out he was having much the same as me, so honours even.

Off went the riders to get acquainted with their steeds and sort out equipment and Michael and I went to the library where, at one corner, was a fully equipped modern office set up with everything you might need including printers and scanners, fax machine, a full-size desk top computer and a couple of laptops were available. But Michael and I knew we had most of what we needed in our heads, had prepared for this meeting well and were both confident and experienced businessmen.

Although Michael lived on his splendid estate almost permanently, he was head of several companies, some in London, a couple abroad and a few more spread about the UK. They were quite a disparate mixture as some had been started by Michael's father who was in textiles and his father before him had owned woollen and cotton mills in what was Victorian Britain. Michael himself had worked in the City and was both a member of Lloyds Insurance Group and The Stockbrokers Association and he was also a stockbroker of some note. He ran and controlled not just the estate where we were, which his grandfather had renovated many years ago from an old almost ruined mansion, with its satellite farms, a dairy, a pig producing unit, the herd of pedigree Holstein Friesian cows one could see in distant fields, but he also had control of an estate in Scotland tenanted by his uncle's family, and another in Ireland similarly controlled by Michael and tenanted by another more distant relation.

Plus, there was a considerable group of companies who were into manufacture, importation and leasing out of large machinery, industrial and agricultural, and were a big client and receiver of JCB tractors and ancillary machinery and John Deere equipment. So, many irons in several fires, and of course, although Michael was a very large shareholder in almost all these companies, he also was the Chairman and Chief Executive of the main group of companies. Clearly, he had to have a large management team to enable overall control, with smaller localised teams on the various boards and committees. However, they all ultimately answered to Michael and his son Robert, whom we had not met at this point, but whom, it seemed, Michael was training with a view to taking over one day.

I knew most of this from research done when I was first approached by Michael about a possibly quite large contract which might be on offer to the right people at an appropriate time later this year. I had an inkling as to what he might be interested in, but I sat back and waited for him to talk, set the scene, and explain exactly what he had in mind. I knew that was why we were getting the treatment as it were, not because he doubted our ability, in the area I felt he must be thinking of, but to have a good look at me over a couple of days on what was his home territory. So I figured Heather must come into this equation at some point although she had made one or two small hints that she might want to reduce her several demanding roles rather than expand them, and she was getting towards sixty now, although you would never guess it.

All of this was going through my mind as Michael ordered fresh pots of tea and coffee and we settled into our seats, he in a huge old carver at the back of an oak desk fully eight feet long and three feet wide and I sat in a smaller but still impressive captain's chair opposite him, with my back to the remainder of the library. He smiled at me and sat back sipping his tea and helping himself to a dark chocolate from an open box placed at our disposal in the centre of the desk.

He said, "Tell me James, why do you think you might be the person I want to assist our group and indeed our family, to look at our set-up and perhaps make sweeping recommendations for changing the shape and our general *modus operandi?*"

I said, "I could just reply, you tell me, you have brought me here, but I won't." And I smiled back at him as I spoke. "I think that, knowing our history, having looked at what we have done not just to build our own group, but to assist many others in a similar manner, you wonder if we are big enough and experienced enough to be able to do something similar in what admittedly is a much bigger organisation with many disparate parts to it. And I think that you must have quite a good level of confidence that we have the necessary knowledge and expertise and have a very good team of experts within our companies, otherwise I would not be sat here. I think your main concern this weekend is to see if the man who you have looked at carefully from a distance and by consulting others and analysing what we have achieved over the past twenty years, fits the profile. Is he a man I can trust to get the job done, both timeously and thoroughly; does he measure up to our expectations and reports? And since you do not interject at this point, I say the answer is yes, decidedly so. But I have one addition I would like to make which you may not have yet considered fully, although that would surprise me."

"And what might that be, may I hazard a guess?"

"Certainly," I said.

"You are substantially right in your opening remarks, and I like a man who can speak his mind without fear or favour. But I believe the addition you refer to is, do I want to do this? Is this a man I want to work with? What you would like to do before giving this whole matter more serious consideration, is to be allowed to carry out a tour of inspection, so to speak. Meet all the main players and visit a few of the bigger and/or most complex units, a sort of due diligence in reverse. Am I right?"

"Substantially, yes. A few extra wrinkles; some meat on the bones, to mix metaphors, but I repeat, substantially correct. So, let me ask you Michael, why do you think I am here?"

He actually laughed at this and said, "Touché; I will reply equally straightforwardly. I believe you accepted my invitation because you were intrigued and interested. But I also believed that you too would need convincing by me, as I by you. You were not afraid of the size or complexity of this task, just not totally sure if you really wanted or needed such a large and complex task. Not through fear of failure, you don't know what that is, but more a question of the huge commitment in time and effort, of you and your wife Heather, who I recognise is a very important part of your team. Did you really want that, or need it?"

"Very good" I replied, "Very good and to borrow your phrase, substantially correct! But," I went on, "although Heather is fit and well, I have a feeling, no more than that, she might not relish such a big commitment from her at this stage, I could be wrong. I know she is quite happy being my MD on the main board and continuing to run our small company offering smaller deals as well. But I would have to sound her out about a big one like this and I think the answer might be, you go ahead darling, I will always be on hand for opinion and advice, but I don't really want such a big commitment myself as to be a full partner in this, if it happens. Furthermore, she may well say, I think I have trained you well enough to be confident of tackling this alone, or perhaps with one or two other persons, and by recruiting and co-opting the other people you will certainly need, if this is anywhere near as big as I imagine, having read all your briefing papers."

"Splendid speech which answers about five of the questions I had in mind," said Michael. "Might I ask a very personal question; I shall not be offended if you decline?"

"Yes, you may and the answer, strictly confidential to you and me only, agreed?" And he simply nodded. "Ronja is my long-standing mistress; she is very talented as you have seen but is not well versed in business matters nor would she want to be, of that I am certain. She is, however, apart from being my very special friend and lover, a great social asset and very astute. Also, she might well have her uses for both of us, intellectually and other skills I mean of course, in a variety of situations. I haven't even told her why I am here, but she is no fool and will have worked out that there is a big deal afoot, and she will want to help me in any reasonable way she can. She is not, in the ordinary sense employable by us, but would no doubt be interested in some foreign travel on an ad hoc basis, and she has several languages which could be useful. She can mix, I am sure you would agree, at almost any level she chooses. But actually, I cannot, nor would I wish to, speak for her on this. I suggest, if you were thinking along these lines, that we, that is just you and I, could deal with this sort of thing as we went along. She will always be glad to see me, and after this weekend, assuming Sarah wouldn't mind, I am certain Ronja would like the odd invitation for purely social reasons and I would have thought you could easily imagine such, and like. She will not let you down. Maybe timed with when I may need to come and meet for good reason?"

"Very well anticipated my dear chap, you have exceeded my expectations. I can tell you here and now that you will be offered the contract, which you would probably like to assist in writing, after you have, and your core team have decided what we need to do. It will be a very substantial contract and I have in mind a sum of around 4 million GBP to cover preparations for the first five- year phase, but you may convince me with your analysis that might not be enough. Let's leave it there for now, meanwhile I will think a little more before I write to you formally and I have a feeling that you may want to bring Heather down, just for introductions etc., but that weekend you shall have a different suite and there will be no reference whatever by anyone to this current weekend. But may we pencil in another weekend of say three weeks from now, to further our discussions? Of course, should you like Ronja to be invited that weekend, it would be absolutely fine. All the top people interested in our businesses are already aware of your good friend Ronja and they have taken the trouble to learn a little about you as a pair as any good far-sighted possible client or partner might wish to do. And I can tell you that they will be very interested in my opinions on this matter and that they will be very positive."

"Thank you, Michael; I really appreciate your openness and honesty and welcome your views, not that any of that will influence my business decisions in any way; this is my personal thank you for so readily accepting Ronja here and your clear liking for her. Now I look forward to the shooting and fishing and just hope Ronja's bottom is not too sore from riding, I had no idea she rode until now, or shot, she never ceases to amaze me."

"Good," said Michael, "Let's see how good a shot you both are and how about a little private wager? I will back Ronja to get more bird hits than you and you to catch more trout than she. Say 100 pounds each bet?"

"Taken," I said, "although it is pure chance as I have no idea of her level of skills in either sport, but I anticipate she will be pretty good!"

The riding party had returned with no major spills and Ronja did indeed have a bit of a sore bottom as it had been some years since she rode last, but she assured me it would not affect her other performances! I didn't tell her about our wager nor about her potential role in the future contract, plenty of time for that, if it actually happened; but I intended to sound her out about an occasional bit of help she might profitably wish to give, especially if it meant some visits to other countries, and also let her know that she now had what amounted to a general open invitation, subject obviously to specific invitation when circumstances suggested. No one walks into a place like this without a specific invitation from Michael or Sarah.

We all got together for a light lunch before changing and preparing for the shoot and then we piled into a variety of vehicles, land rovers and other 4x4 farm vehicles, for our overland trip to the prepared shooting hides alongside an area of coppiced woodland and a small stream which ran down and joined the river. The beaters had already gone to their positions, and we were warned about only shooting in an upward trajectory as the pheasant rose from cover, never horizontally and always against a clear sky background. The hunt captain checked all guns and ammunition — only light shot and no repeaters, only single or double barrels and manual loading allowed — so it was fair to all, including some birds!

The captain admired my guns and asked where I had obtained them and I told him and he said, beautiful, must be 50 years old at least. Ronja was given a 16 bore, big enough to bring a fast-flying pheasant down, but not quite the kick of a 12 bore. We all got in position and waited for the signal for the beaters to start and there were assistants behind each group of shooters to reload and handle spare guns. We had four retrievers controlled by the kennel keeper, but these would not be released until the orders were given and guns put down.

A close eye was kept on Ronja and me, but we soon showed them that we could handle a gun and although I was not aware of it, we were up with the better shots in birds downed. It was hectic and great fun and it seemed to be over in no time but in fact we had been shooting sporadically for nearly forty-five minutes. I had won the first bet; the trout would either even my win to nothing or double it!

There were forty-six pheasant killed cleanly and retrieved, and Ronja had got seven and me eight. Our host had seven also and nobody beat my eight, so I was the leading shot. How hard they tried of course I don't know, or care. I was happy, Ronja was happy, and Michael was happy. Good enough for now. We decided yes there was still time for some trout fishing, but Michael overruled that, saying by the time we went back, showered, and changed into fishing gear and got all set up at the oxbow bend he favoured on the river. We would only get about half an hour's actual fishing and dusk was not a good time to be wading waist-deep in the river. And in any case, he had ordered an early dinner and wanted us all to have time to prepare and have aperitifs, etc. So, we all laughingly agreed and meandered back to the house with our bags of game and went to our rooms to clean up and prepare for the evening's entertainment.

No pheasant from today's shoot of course would be cooked and eaten today. They, like all game, are better hung in a cool place for up to three weeks in order for the full flavour to develop. I remember seeing a brace of pheasant an old friend had hung in his garden shed for a month in winter fortunately, and apart from the corn having been eaten by mice straight from the bird's gizzards, the meat was untouched. The feathers all peeled off with the skin and the meat was stewed, not roasted and was absolutely delicious.

The dinner was quite something and we all dressed for it as before and this time there were several more guests at the table. Michael had invited a small ensemble to play while we ate: seven musicians on a small stage which had been hidden by curtains or panelling last night, and the dining room was altogether much bigger than I had realised.

Michael made a toast to all the guests and introduced Ronja and me to a few who we did not already know us and said, "This is very probably an auspicious occasion because, although nothing is yet formally agreed, I think there is a strong possibility that James and I will be going into a joint business venture of some magnitude. He will, I hope, bring all his undoubted expertise to bear in a study of our whole business concerns with a view to improving our systems, reforming our practices, reviewing all our procedures, and generally bringing all the companies I am associated with, both within our group and perhaps beyond, into the 21st century. I am not just talking about computers and the like, but basic business methods and practice. I would like all of those present to raise their glasses and drink to the future!"

All raised their glasses and chorused, "To the future!"

I stood and replied, "Thank you Michael and all your guests here tonight for your warm endorsement of Michael's toast to our future relationship. This relationship is not just business, although that is of course very important, but is also the cementing of a friendship we hope to share. So that not only shall we be successful if and when we join forces in this venture, like Michael, I believe it will lead to a brighter, better and more prosperous future for us all."

Several "Hear Him, Hear Him" calls were made by people I guessed were future protagonists. I then raised my glass as did everyone and took a sip of my drink and sat down.

Formalities over, and with music playing quietly in the background, we set about the magnificent meal before us. There were various cold and hot starter dishes and salads. Local fresh crawfish, guinea fowl and partridges and olives, anchovies, and whitebait with sauces of many kinds. Followed by suckling pig, crown of lamb, baron of beef, the main roasts. Lots of fresh home-grown vegetables with roast and early new potatoes. There was sea bream and halibut for fish main course if desired; asparagus out of season, and a host of side dishes to tempt one's palate. Followed by the hothouse fruit selection, sorbets, and hot and cold puddings; it was a veritable feast. Ronja and I, who were sitting next to Michael and Sarah as guests of honour, praised the kitchen and other staff and marvelled at the selection of dishes available. We then gave the food our full attention, as they did, pausing occasionally to take a sip of wine and exchange the odd comment, but basically really enjoying this fantastic meal.

I paused after one particular course and dabbed my mouth with a pure Irish linen napkin and said, "Michael, and Sarah, this is really very good food and beautifully prepared and presented; you must both be very proud of your housekeeper, head cook and all your staff. My only concern is all the exercise I shall need to take in order to try to not put on too much weight."

And Ronja added, "May I add that I have had some excellent dinners in different parts of the world, and I must add to Jim's comments that I too am very aware of the sort of preparation and work that goes to make a meal of this breadth and scope, not to mention magnitude."

"Thank you my dear," said Sarah, "You are right, but it is worth it to see how much you and Jim — may I call you Jim also James? — enjoy our meagre offerings so much."

I laughed out loud and replied, "Certainly call me Jim if you like, and meagre offerings! May I say Sarah that is the biggest misnomer I have heard in a long time! Meagre offerings indeed; a feast fit for a king is nearer the mark."

I confess that after a full and active day on and off field so to speak, then the magnificent dinner, after our usual coffee and brandy, Ronja I went to bed, and both promptly fell asleep! I did however have a very nice dream, which I could not be certain was while waking or sleeping when I recalled it in the morning.

Another wonderful breakfast after an early call, and we trooped off to the river. With our guides and experts helping, we set up our kit and waded out on the gravel riverbed about one third of the way across and positioned ourselves just near a bend in the river. I knew about the theory of fly fishing, but it took me a while to get the knack of whipping enough silk airborne to send the fly sailing out across the river to alight gently on the surface in order to tempt a trout. With weighted coarse fishing lines and floats attached one can flick the rod and the weight on the end will take the fine nylon line easily off a front-loaded reel. With trout fishing, there is little or no weight at the end and so the bulkier line has to be persuaded to go far enough with a series of jerks with the rod until the fly has reached the position you wish it to. Then you look on and let out more line as the fly floats downstream and hopefully until, with a splash, a trout takes the fly, and you need then to strike immediately to ensure the hook gets embedded in its mouth. If there is no bite you reel in the line and start again.

At my third or fourth cast I hit a fish immediately and reeled him in to my side where I netted him in a short-handled landing net and put him wriggling into my carry net on my belt at the other side. He was a beauty of around 2 lbs. in weight and would make a splendid dinner, but I was intent on getting more. Once bitten as they say, twice shy. By the time a break was called for refreshments I had bagged six nice trout of varying size, all big enough to eat. Ronja had four and the others had varying quantities, but I suspected we had been put by the best lies, where trout hover in one place flicking their tails to keep in one spot, and where they know there is often food to be had due to the current and swirls created by the bend in the river. I certainly wasn't going to grumble about the position I had been allotted, because I was enjoying it too much to care.

After a biscuit or two, a hot coffee or tea and a snifter for those who wanted one, we re-entered the river, but changing places to make it fair. However, it made no difference to me as I bagged another six trout in the ensuing hour, and was well satisfied, but I had not necessarily won my bet because I learnt, rather belatedly, and I suspected after a swift rule change, that number of trout was irrelevant, total gross weight caught was the deciding factor for who became top rod that day. But as it happened not only had I scored the most fish, but also the heaviest gross weight as well. I was going to win both my bets with Michael and collect two hundred pounds!

We happily trundled back to the house for more coffee and tea and changed and smartened up for lunch which was going to be the last meal for most of the guests before heading back to wherever they came from. Ronja and I had already accepted an invitation to stay that night and after consulting with Heather and giving her a big hint of our progress, she readily consented, but she wouldn't have minded anyway, the children were already gone and she could see me any old time she wanted, except tonight of course.

Ronja and Sarah had decided to play some card games after lunch and have a few ladies' drinks together while Michael and I had another informal meeting in the billiards room this time, so after another excellent meal we said our goodbyes to all the leavers and tentatively accepted a couple of invites to their homes, and wished each other all the very best of luck, wonderful to make your acquaintances, etc. Then Michael and I, brandy decanter and cigars in one hand and cut-glass balloons in another, went to the billiards room, and put our bits and pieces down and decided snooker was favourite. Of course, Michael offered me double or quits, which I accepted. I forgot to mention that I had been college champion two years in a row when I did my mature students' course on forward business planning, so it was with some surprise on his part when I whipped him on his home table with a borrowed cue by sixty points in our first game.

He thought this was hilarious as he was the house champion, but he never knew how much of that was due to sycophancy or what. But he did say that I might have warned him and given him a three-black start as a handicap.

I said, "Really, and what about you disclosing that you are house champion and that you have a custom-made cue and took lessons from a professional?"

He laughed and said fair enough. But I did give him three blacks start the next frame, this time for 800 pounds and still beat him easily.

"You bugger" he said. "Now I know that you don't normally play billiards so how about 1600 pounds or nothing?"

"OK," I said, "but I will warn you that although I am not a billiards player, class like mine will out in any comparable cue and balls game."

He smiled, certain that he was on a winner this time, what I didn't tell him was, that although I almost never play billiards, I am an ace at pool, which involves skills similar to billiards, in that cannoning and blocking holes and avoiding in-offs when you need to, are very similar parts of both games, and after all a cue is a cue, a pocket is a pocket, it's only in the accruing points by cannoning and going in off in billiards that things differ from pool.

I let him build a sizeable lead and then I kept the break and continued stroking in pots and in-offs and so on until I had amassed double his points.

"Double bugger you, you scoundrel, you are a master of the cue and ball game obviously, but never mind, I know when I am beaten, and you shall get your 1,600 pounds and I won't deduct it from your fees."

"Now, to more serious matters my boy, let us talk a little about how best to start this thing moving, have you any suggestions?"

"Yes, I have," I said, "first I want to personally see lots of people and places and methods and machinery and the best way for me to plan that is to get from you a comprehensive list of key personnel, locations, with contact details and marry them to their particular work responsibilities, together with a complete list of all significant machinery, products, materials stores, shipping contracts and agreements with suppliers. Including at JCB and John Deere if that is possible, and an introduction to them all specifying absolute free access and compliance and swearing me to total confidentiality etc. It is imperative if I am to really make an impact here, that I get full and open access to all of these people, and they are made fully aware of my needs and purpose. And I don't need to tell you I am sure, but if anyone, and I mean anyone, at whatever level, however big his organisation, commercial clout, whatever criteria you wish to apply, demurs in any way, mark them down for my special attention please."

"Good God," he said, "you don't take prisoners, do you? People may run a mile rather than agree to all this access; people from other companies outside the group I mean."

"Then," I said, "maybe that's where they should be, maybe not. I am sure you can wrap it up in such a way that it is acceptable, and it may be pivotal in them remaining on your 'favoured client' or 'favoured supplier' lists. You have a lot of clout and with my help that is going to grow. They should realise that this is a new world market, favoured status has to be earned and maintained, the Americans have proved that. And if it means taking a very small risk in opening up to me, after any due diligence they wish to carry out, I am happy with that. But this is going to be good for most if not all of your supplier and customer chains in the short to medium term and much better after that. If people really won't cooperate, ask yourself and them, why? What have they got to hide? Yes, commercial secrets of course, but general operating methods, stock-control procedures, last-minute delivery chains strategies, many of these things are quite routine and not state or company secrets."

"Anyway, in my opinion that's where you should start, providing me with all the information I need regarding your main suppliers and clients. I am not bothered too much at this stage about smaller concerns although we may come back on a few of those much later on. You could just ask these people to come and see me, but they will be much better at fulfilling their purpose if you have a private word with the key people along the lines we have discussed, don't you think? I can also wander around your own company operations and chat to people but no special preparation is needed for that at this point I wouldn't have thought, so I can start there and then when I get the dossiers you put together later on, I can work out a visiting strategy and don't worry, it will go round on the grapevine like wildfire so that I am almost expected wherever I go, and I know how to handle this and people, alone at first."

"I do believe you do, and I have great confidence in your abilities, but I will have to think very carefully how I approach people like the Bamford family and the John Deere top echelon. And that might take a little time."

"Of course it will, but meanwhile, give me your internal key personnel, locations and contact details and ask them to expect me at any time any day I choose. Tell them you expect total compliance, assistance and above all, all information labelled sensitive or secret or whatever, I really must have total access within your organisation please."

"When would you like to start and what sort of contract do you require at this point?"

I replied, "Just a basic study of business practice and methods survey of your entire group, and your other satellites as well if you wish, which I know you control. In particular, I think you should bring your son into this early on so he is fully apprised of my remit and feels he is in the loop, and I will ensure he will be, if that is your wish of course."

"I can send you a typical draft for your legal people to skim over, just covering Phase 1 as discussed. Then if that goes to plan, we can work on a Phase 2 contract and so on, stopping or withdrawing with minimal penalties if things don't go to yours or my liking. Won't be needed, but it will make your legal team happy."

"Right, take it as read, that I will do my best to set up what you require for Phase 1, you send me a suitable draft contract as outlined. My secretary Rosemary will fill in any details you need, and I will start my MD on those lists of internal personnel and our plant and offices to see as and when you like, and I will agree a start date as soon as we have signed that first phase contract."

"Great," I said, "I feel once we start you will be amazed at the momentum generated, and I promise you that you will not be disappointed."

Chapter 28

I took Ronja home after a very full and interesting weekend and she told me that she had enjoyed it very much and what a lovely couple Michael and Sarah were, making her so very welcome. I told her I had enjoyed it all too, but as I thought she knew something big and important had been discussed by me and Michael and wanted to know if this might mean we could see more of each other and especially would there be more visits to their beautiful home again. She said likewise in effect and also wondered how I was going to play it regarding Heather and the danger of them meeting her inadvertently. I reassured her that Michael and Sarah knew about our relationship and that it was unlikely Heather would have a major role in any business deal we made, although a weekend there at least once was on the cards, but that she, Ronja, was to be a regular guest if she would like that.

"Would I?" she said, "That's wonderful and thanks so much for making it all possible, I really appreciate that."

Off I went home to my usual warm welcome, and I reported to Heather a brief synopsis of what I had discussed with Michael and the rough outline of my proposed business plan.

Then I asked her straight, "Are you interested in playing a major part in this or would you rather focus on your current commitments and leave it to me, just giving advice when I think it is necessary?"

She didn't hesitate, "No I think it will be too demanding for me, especially all the travelling, and so much to think about. No, I will be quite happy looking after the home front so to speak, that is if you are quite OK with that?"

I admitted that I had more or less forecast what her attitude might be, and Michael would still like to meet her and for her to come down for a weekend if she could, to talk first-hand with him, because he would value an input from her, knowing as he does just about everything she and I had done together. And I told her that he said also that he might like her opinion from time to time on matters arising.

"That's very thoughtful of you both and I would like to see his set-up and meet him and Sarah; she sounds my type of woman. I am totally confident of you darling, but I do like to keep tabs on the opposition!"

I laughed and indicated that Sarah, though a charming lady, was not my type in that way, and in any case this project, easily the biggest we had taken on, was going to be a major challenge for which I would need all my energies. So, I arranged with Michael that the weekend after next might be a good time for Heather and me to come down and discuss things and to pick up any papers etc, and he immediately concurred.

I said, "Thanks a lot, Heather will not be interested in riding or shooting but maybe in some fishing if that included some coarse fishing tackle," as I had spotted barbel and roach in the river and was pretty certain of several other species being there as well as trout.

I arranged for a suitable draft Phase 1 contract to be drawn up and sent to Michael's lawyers, and set about preparing an itinerary, as far as I could, for the coming weeks by cancelling minor meetings and inspections and clearing my diary generally. Then I looked at lists of Michael's companies, plants and offices and his other majority interests, all available publicly, and started pencilling in a few targets as potential warm-up visits I could make.

Michael was doing something similar I had no doubt but would have different criteria than I and I intended doing things my way from the outset. But it would be interesting to see how our priorities might differ and at some point, analyse those differences. Ronja called me to tell me she was invited down to their place again this coming weekend and that Sarah had made it clear that should I be able to join them for a night or two, I was also welcome. I thought, why not, Heather will be there the following weekend, and so it might be several weeks before Ronja and I had another such opportunity. I contacted Michael who was aware of the tentative arrangements and immediately indicated it was fine with him also and he already had some material for me to discuss anyway.

I arrived there on the Friday evening about p.m. to find Ronja already there, having arrived at lunchtime, and after a brief hello in our suite, we changed for dinner and down we went. This time the only people there in the dining room were our hosts, the servants, and their son Robert. Michael introduced us to Robert who was a slimmer, younger version of his father and about thirty years old I guessed, and he was a very likeable young man only a few years younger than Ronja. He was not yet married, and his girlfriend was many miles away in Edinburgh. I apologised if I had been the cause of his visit from far away in Scotland, but he immediately reassured me that this visit he had fitted in while he had meetings in London and the south of England, so no major drama. He went on to say that his father had given him a rough outline of my history and of the major task I had been asked to perform for their family companies, businesses, and properties, and he looked forward to helping me in any way he could.

"Excellent," I said, "I am glad to hear that, and I look forward to talking to you about things in general and your particular role in those companies and properties in which your family have a major interest."

So a very nice dinner was had, with all the usual home produced meats and fruits and we all concentrated on that for a while. Then we gradually conversed about the project as this was just family and us, so no need for quite the level of confidentiality as the first dinner there in which we had partaken. I went to some lengths to explain my general plan of approach, gathering information and data about all the main systems employed by all the larger members of the group. How, having formed a good picture of the current organisation, of their suppliers, manufacturers, buyers of their products and services and the group's sales methods, not to mention control systems, stock level controls and long-term supply contracts, I would start to produce outline plans of how things could be changed or developed. Greater efficiency with significant cost savings would flow from that, which would lead to more production and a more profitable future.

We all had another memorable weekend with Michael and Sarah and Ronja was in her element. Although she was as down to earth as anybody, she had developed such style and knowledge about the sort of people she had worked for. This included an old lady she had looked after in her large apartment situated on the ground floor of an old mansion in Surrey. The woman had been bedridden and must have been late 90s in age. She was from a good family and had two sons in their late fifties early sixties and she paid for a cook and general companion. Ronja got to know one of the sons, don't ask me how or what the relationship was, and she always denied any intimacy with him. But hearing on a trip to the races one weekend, that Ronja had nursing experience and was not employed at that time, he asked her if she would like to help look after his mother and explained the situation. Ronja went and saw the set-up and met the cook/housekeeper Bertha. She got on with her OK and she also met the aged parent and was quite interested in her background and so agreed to give it a try and become her attendant and nurse and deal with bed-baths, toilet necessities, etc. Part of the deal was she had free accommodation and food there and although she was on call 24 hours a day, Bertha would stay to cook and clean and could stand in for Ronja when she might have to go out and in any case when she had her weekend breaks once a month.

The old lady, called Mrs Timperley, had a room on the ground floor of what was the main apartment in the building, with the main entrance to the old house being her apartment's entrance. There was a kitchen and a huge hall space, a dining room and a lounge plus another small bedroom and a bathroom all on that level. Down at what had been the servants' quarters below ground level, there were several other rooms and a bathroom, and Bertha lived down there.

I was familiar with the place because after a time, Bertha was dismissed or left of her own volition and Ronja had voluntarily taken on her role as cook/housekeeper as well as the 24-hour nursing aspect. I was therefore able to visit her as her trips out now were very limited, and she would cook a meal for Mrs Timperley and for her and me. We would have a nice evening eating, drinking, and making love on Ronja's bed or on the carpeted lounge floor or wherever we fancied. It was sometimes interrupted by Mrs Timperley shouting for Ronja to attend her, usually to use the bed pan, but it was fun. But this was an example of the sort of people she worked for and often that work included nice visits to the theatre, abroad, the races and mixing with high-class families and other well-to-do people, so she was capable of acting comfortably in many different situations.

Back to the weekend with Michael and Sarah. We talked a bit of business but basically it was a fun weekend and our friendship with

Michael and Sarah developed very positively and we were all very relaxed around each other. Heather was mentioned at some point, but we all knew the position and it made no difference whatever to their attitude to Ronja who, of course, was charming to them. I thought fleetingly, I wouldn't be surprised if she does get offered a job here, but maybe not. It would be interesting, I thought, how things turned out for Heather's visit next weekend!

During the following week I received a list of companies, their office and works locations and a list of the key contacts for each and a note from Michael telling me all had been notified that I might visit without warning and to offer me total assistance and cooperation. I looked through the list of locations and chose a few which it might be possible to visit as they were within a reasonable driving distance both of our group HQ and our home. I took no briefing material, just the lists, a portable tape recorder and video camera, an ordinary camera for still shots and a supply of notepads and sleeves, pencils, and pens.

I explained to Heather my initial plans and she approved and packed my bag for up to three nights away. I said my goodbyes and off I went in the Range Rover so I could take some kit in case I diverted to Michael's place at some point. I arrived at my first destination, a factory with offices on site only about an hour's drive away and was greeted by a security guard at the main gates who was obviously expecting me or my Range Rover to appear at any moment. Big smile and "Welcome, sir," and I was directed to where the offices were situated. I parked in a reserved bay and was met at the entrance by a smart middle-aged man in a business suit and his PA or secretary in a nice two-piece blue outfit. They called me 'Sir' and I insisted James or Jim would be fine. In return they said their names were Peter and Anne. I was ushered into Peter's office where we all sat and exchanged a few words over a welcome cup of coffee with biscuits.

Then I said, "Right, let's get down to business. I will be looking at your management systems, and methods of control of stock today, have a general look at the site and look at office systems on another occasion. All I would like to do now is have someone who knows the plant well and all, or most, of the middle and lower management, and can accompany me as I walk around the plant."

Peter made a call and a man of about forty appeared in a suit with a cover all over it and a dustcoat and gloves for my use. I accepted and put on the coat but not the gloves and thanked Peter and Anne.

I said to Joe my guide, "Let's just start at goods inwards please Joe, and just call me Jim. I don't need any running commentary as I normally like to look at things before I ask questions, but please tell me of any dangers or protocol, etc., of course."

Joe nodded and off we went in a golf buggy as he briefly explained that the plant sprawled over several acres when you included stocks and materials for manufacture and workshops, etc.

We arrived at receiving where a man in his sixties was in charge; a former Army RSM I would guess, and he also wore a dust jacket over a suit. He immediately shook my hand, told me he was pleased to meet me, having heard all about me, from people who delivered things, and knew our group and its reputation.

He said, "Right, sir, what can I show you"? And I knew he would not be comfortable with first names as he had a nameplate on his lapel — *Mr Jones. Goods Inwards* — so I said, "Thank you Mr Jones, am I right in thinking you are ex-Army, possibly a former RSM?"

He was a bit shocked but immediately replied, "Yes sir, correct, but I told no one here so how did you know?"

"I didn't know," I said, "but I have met one or two who were heads of receiving in plants like this, it seems your Army experience at RSM level is invaluable in the physical control of so many disparate items, and the discipline of your storemen is paramount in ensuring ready access to all your thousands of stock items, am I right?"

"Spot on, sir, spot on. Some items are small but vital from time to time and a delay in finding a spare part for a lathe or milling machine can cost many hours and lose us thousands of pounds and it's no good, if I may say so, out housing such stock to 'just in time' suppliers and will not do for certain things which must be available at all times of day or night and at the drop of a hat, and my job is to ensure that happens."

"Excellent Mr Jones, I am glad to hear it. But how are you able to distinguish which items which fall into that very important category and those which do not, and do you have a separate way of dealing with them?"

"Yes sir, I can, and I do have a different coding system to cover that very point. I advise higher management which stock items lend themselves to lighter control, but also ensure fast location and delivery to the place needed within the plant."

"And can you identify where these stocks are kept for immediate access regardless of ultimate usage points?"

He looked a bit blank at that one, so I added, "Let me explain my thinking, I sometimes forget that my head is full of data from dozens of visits like this. Suppose you have a permanent and regular need of certain sprockets used in machinery manufacture, then your 'just in time' scenario bites, so in that case you need to ensure that the parts are able to be obtained firstly from your stores, but ultimately from the suppliers, correct?" He nodded. "So, what system do you have which triggers reordering these parts regardless of the buyer's actions? Are you proactive in ensuring the parts are on order and will be delivered in good time?"

"I put all stocks on a computer programme, or my staff do to be correct, but I still maintain my old card system for a lot of important items, and so not only can buyers look at the computer stock which they need to order in a timely fashion, but they know that if there is any doubt or the system is compromised, they can turn to me and my staff to access the old card system. I find this sometimes is the only way to be sure I can keep the levels of stock under control."

"Have you ever been caught out with no stock of an important part when needed?" I asked.

"Yes, in the very early days when I first took over this job ten years ago, but I instituted an alarm system which redlines all important stock which must be maintained at a minimum level. If the buyers have not provided new stock when the stock level of an item reaches my red line, I contact the head buyer immediately and inform him."

"Very good," I said, "but it depends on you being here, doesn't it? What if you are off sick or on holiday?"

"My number two here is fully briefed and does what I would do, but in fact now that the buyers are aware that I go straight to their boss, it very rarely happens. In any case we have agreed with all our suppliers that they must ensure adequate back-up stocks of certain key parts and items otherwise they risk losing their contract with us."

"Thank you, Mr Jones, I would now like someone to show me some of these redline items and see exactly how your system works."

"I would like to show you that myself, sir if you have no objections?"

"Not at all," I said.

I did a tour of receiving, the office and the mighty parts racks containing thousands of items and also looked at huge hoppers and bins full of larger stuff and also stock replacements of complete machines kept in case of major breakdown.

I thanked Mr Jones for all his help, told him I was impressed with his systems and iron control, and moved on with Joe to the massive foundry building where they made their own engine blocks and other castings to be fitted into finished engines and smaller kit into the range of industrial and agricultural tractors and earth movers, dump trucks, etc. These they manufactured on site and displayed for sale and demonstration to clients. Alongside they had a separate compound not only for their own tractors and implements stock, but also kept a fair stock of JCBs and John Deere products as well, which they were entitled to supply alongside their own products. I spoke briefly with their two sales reps who clearly knew who I was and were very open and friendly.

This was one of my main reasons for visiting this particular complex as I wished to put down a marker for when I visited the two giant companies named above and I was pleased to see that Michael had already laid some of the foundations for those visits.

I toured the whole plant, made a few notes, asked a few questions, and drew a couple of rough flow charts and the like. By the time I had finished it was mid-afternoon and I was pretty hungry, but management had ensured that Joe and I, together with a few other people, had access to a cold buffet in the plant restaurant, which was open to all the staff normally, but had shut its doors at two-thirty in preparation for our late lunch!

After lunch, I toured the main offices and spoke with the head buyer and a few of his staff and looked at their computerised stock books and at the card index system they too maintained as a fall back. They took the job of ensuring that stocks of key items were always online very seriously and had different buyers for different products. There was even a maintenance buyer who had all the information and contacts relating to plant repairs and maintenance, details of the subcontractors who were available and all the wholesalers and manufacturers who supplied materials and parts relating to maintenance.

The production buyer had his own specialism's and knew all the suppliers of parts that were needed in production, and which were not manufactured in-house. He kept tabs, as did the maintenance buyer, on all his section staff who did most of the buying and record keeping. The larger contracts were the direct responsibility of the section buyers and their systems were replicated by his section staff, so that if he were absent, they could take over immediately and fill the breach. It was a good safe system, but my initial impressions of the buying department and receiving was that they had striven to keep their old card-based systems intact in a belt and braces fashion, rather than evolving a new stand-alone system with appropriate back up computer files kept in a secure environment and with an independent power supply. Food for thought; it could be that an analysis might conclude the savings in time and staff of doing away the old card system might not justify the additional risks.

I toured the rest of the offices having a brief chat here and there and spoke briefly to the office manager and the head of accounts and then called it a day. I departed with smiles and handshakes all round and off I went back home as I hadn't reached my second destination and I felt the need to touch base with Heather. I thought as I drove, this was a bigger and better organised complex than I had expected. Clearly well run with not much wrong that was obvious and may only need a bit of an IT upgrade and a new dedicated IT head. But it was early days and I didn't want to jump the gun and perhaps cause ripples at this point, so apart from chatting to Heather, I would keep my powder dry as regards Michael.

When I discussed my first foray with Heather, she immediately said that she thought I had jumped to conclusions a bit and needed to have another day there at some point looking at more of the many sections I hadn't yet seen. In any case, when we put our specialist team in, they would dig much deeper, and would no doubt come up with a list of things that could be improved sufficiently to be of cost saving and therefore of bottom-line figures importance.

I admitted she was right; it was just that I had expected more red meat I suppose, whereas we both knew that a valid picture often only becomes clear after a lot of analysis. After all, if it were that easy, they wouldn't need us in the first place! I also confessed that being CE at our enhanced group was demanding, and I perhaps had not done as much of the 'on the ground' work these last few years. She agreed and said that is exactly her impression. So, an early conference with my better half helped me refocus and removed any complacency I might have inadvertently developed.

The following day I went to number two on my list, about two hours' drive away from home, which was quite a bit smaller than the first plant and specialised in smaller machinery product manufacture for industrial and farming use, but also for stocking in large stores who specialise in retailing these products amongst many others.

I received the same warm welcome and complete cooperation and wandered round alone this time with my trusty dustcoat and a safety helmet and goggles which I was prevailed upon to wear. Nevertheless, each section or building I went to immediately attached someone to me to ensure my safety and act as guide if required.

This time I didn't try to anticipate the team to come so much and concentrated instead, as maybe I should have first time round, and just tried to put a picture together of the overall activity and methods of manufacture. I looked at actual stockpiles and made few notes and generally got the feel of the place and its workers and management. What I came away with was similar to my overall impressions in the first plant, but I began to sense that both plants had a certain amount of 'hanging on' to old methods while attempting to implement new! That can lead to mistakes and repeating of old bad habits so, perhaps together with updated IT and control methods, maybe the organisation as a whole needed to look at their entire staff a little more closely with a view to a few redundancies a possibility. They would have to consider some retraining as well as bringing in some new blood especially at management and branch-head levels. This whole task was going to have to be thoroughly planned, prepared, and executed, and there might not be one plan fits all, but several plans each with a different main priority list. But I would wait for some of the analysis reports which would follow lengthy inspections by my team or teams before I started to give Michael any real indication of how far we thought we might go towards the sort of restructuring he clearly hoped would bring them up to par and fully competitive, plus more long-term security and higher ongoing profits.

After this somewhat chastening start, I took stock and realised that I was not going to develop any magic plan, but I still wanted to get the feel of as many of the businesses in the group as possible, as well as visit the family estates under management in Scotland and Ireland. And I needed to look at Michael's current strategy which he employed to keep control of his empire, because that might need to change as well.

I ploughed on visiting plant and offices far and wide across the country over the next ten days or so and had quite a stack of notes and plans by the time we got to the weekend when Heather and I were invited to Michael's house. I had sufficient material and knowledge now to begin putting some thoughts together on an overall strategy for development further as and when I had drawn together my teams and briefed them on my needs and expectations. But before all that I wanted to run some of my ideas past Heather before we actually went to Michael's, even though I would stress to him that these were only impressions and ideas at this stage, and that nothing was set in concrete and wouldn't be for a long time to come. But I would give him the bare bones of my plan for the team's visits so that all was prepared and everything they needed could be provided.

So before we departed for our weekend with Michael and Sarah, Heather and I sat down at home and I ran through a condensed version of my visits, the thoughts I had developed and the notes and plans I had sketched out. I also gave her a rough cast list of who should be on those teams and who the two leaders would be.

Heather listened carefully and made a few notes of her own and when I had finished, she said, "Well James, you've got a big fish on your line now haven't you? But I think you are on the right track, and we will need to choose our teams very carefully and make sure they really understand the size and complexity of this task. We must have very

reports and updates as they continue with their visits and you
t seen the estates yet."

True," I said, "but they will be relatively simple tasks to deal with
and only a part of their activities impinges on the group's activities as a
whole."

"Well let's go," she said, "I can't wait to see this place and talk to
Michael and Sarah; will Robert be there as well?"

"I doubt it, he lives in Scotland and in any case, this is only a small
curtain-raiser at present, designed to allow Michael to say go ahead or
not."

So off we went, and I drove the Range Rover while Heather
continued to riffle through the papers I had prepared. I knew from
experience that she would have all she needed in her head by the time we
arrived. And she knew about the dressing for dinner, etc. and had packed
accordingly.

When we turned into the huge cast iron gates and up the long drive
to the circular part by the main entrance, Heather said, "Wow, even
bigger and grander than I thought."

Then the butler and Michael, met us at the car and Michael
summoned a young man lurking alongside the pillared portico to carry
our bags to our room. Michael then stepped forward smiling, took
Heather's gloved hand in his and said, "At last we meet Heather! I have
heard so much about you and admire your work and it is a real pleasure
to welcome you here to our home."

He received a nod from Heather before he turned to me and said,
"Well Jim, here you are again after your travels, good to see you and I
look forward to a debriefing later. But that will keep; now come in and
get comfortable and then perhaps join me in the library for coffee or
whatever suits in about half an hour?"

We followed the butler up the grand staircase and along corridors to
our suite and Heather once again was clearly suitably impressed. We
were left alone by the butler and his assistant to unpack.

Heather soon had us organised and we both stood at the massive bay
windows looking out at the land, farm buildings and copses as well as
ornamental and walled in vegetable gardens and were almost beyond our
vision to the left. The orangery and hot and cool greenhouses were not

visible from here, nor the garages and stables, the hound compound, the dairy and other outbuildings.

Heather said, "Makes our place seem quite small by comparison, but what a place, it's fabulous! Thank you for ensuring I got the opportunity to look at it in more detail over the weekend."

I explained also about the shooting facilities which Heather was not minded to sample, but also about the fishing to be had on their own section of river and that did interest her, but not the horse riding, all much as I expected. They also had an indoor pool and gymnasium, and the billiards and snooker room where I had fooled Michael and won handsomely. If the weather was poor, there was the huge conservatory with espalier fruit trees against the house wall and an enormous selection of potted palms and tropical plants including, in one special part, a collection of orchids. We put that on our list for later and I was beginning to think *what else have I so far missed?*

So, although this was essentially a pleasure trip, I was primed to give Michael something of an idea about my early thinking based on what I had looked at so far, no concrete programme of work as yet; we hadn't even done sufficient to determine what we wanted to do in Phase 1 never mind Phase 2, the more in-depth evaluations to be made by our project teams, to say nothing of the analysis we needed to perform once we had gathered most of the information we required.

Then we went down to the library and into the office Michael had there in a corner, for a brief resume of what I had seen and my thoughts so far. Michael spoke for a while mainly to Heather, reiterating much of what he had said to me when I arrived, and she asked a couple of pertinent questions based on what she heard from him but also based on the study of my notes and research she herself had carried out. He was clearly impressed by her acute understanding of the big picture; what was needed to do and how, and where it all might lead. She also made it clear from the start that she did not wish total involvement; rather, she would be content to look at different aspects as the information began to flow in from our teams and to have discussions with the teams but primarily with me, more or less on demand.

Michael said he quite understood her position which was largely what I had anticipated but thanked her for offering the level of commitment she had and, he added, if at some future date she wanted a greater participation it would always be welcome.

I then ran through the limited work I had done, gave him a taste of some options which suggested themselves to me and an overall summary of what I had identified; no major root-and-branch reforms, but there was a plethora of small- to medium-size reforms which, taken together would by themselves lead to a leaner, meaner machine, more efficient and better structured. This would also require, potentially at least, a few redundancies and some new recruits, as well as upgraded and better IT. I went on to explain that my feeling was just that, only a feeling at this point, that several old systems had been retained alongside newer ones largely, it seemed to me as a 'belt-and-braces' exercise, and to allow some staff a comfort zone. I summarised by saying that in general things were already working quite well, with no obvious beartraps to be seen. He could no doubt carry on as before, and save himself some money in the short term, but eventually it would start to break down and then major surgery might be necessary which could not only be very costly but lead at least to a loss of market share and profitability in the short to medium term.

Michael said, "That is what I myself felt, hence calling on you when I could find no one who had any satisfactory answers for my questions. I applaud you for having done so much to understand the group's dynamic so quickly, and I believe pretty accurately. That's a partial diagnosis you have given me; I look forward to your teams arriving and getting into more detail and your analysis to follow which we hope produces a clear picture of where we are and more importantly, how we rectify the situation and produce a more modern, more productive, and cleaner animal all round, which will carry us all into the future for many years to come. And I have a feeling the longer-term plans will include a permanent or semi-permanent core of your team members on a seconded or part-time basis, to ensure we continue to progress rather than slip back to older habits."

I looked at Heather and said what I always have in these circumstances, "What do you think, Heather?" and she replied, "While I agree in general terms with much of what you have both said, I think it is far too early to be considering such actions as redundancies because the teams may put a completely different slant on things by their much more detailed and in-depth enquiries. Although there is undoubtedly something in what you say about "belt and braces" and "comfort zones", this after all is what full computerisation of data with secure backup systems and data storage will do: provide that security and comfort. So that is just an example of forming preconceived ideas about a study which hasn't even started yet. Yes, your observations and analysis have merit, but only in deciding what to do with the teams, not in deciding outcomes. I believe an open mind is needed by both of you and you should not allow your gut reactions or long-held views to dictate otherwise."

I looked at Michael who was sitting with his hands in steeple fashion up to his chin and looking a bit pensive, but he was only absorbing and thinking.

He looked up, smiled and said, "That's why I wanted to see Heather; she has obviously not lost her touch over the past years and with no disrespect to you at all Jim, she has some very good points to make and is clearly unafraid to make them, and I like that. But, more importantly, I agree with what she has said. I propose therefore that we finish this meeting on that note and the next will be when you have formulated your plan of attack and chosen your teams and perhaps, we should have the two team leaders there at the meeting, and I hope Heather that you could come too, as it is clearly the pivotal point of all this project and needs to be right first time around.

Chapter 29

The rest of the weekend went like a dream, the tour of all the other buildings around and attached to the main house and all the wonderful ornamental and specimen trees and plants, and the fruit trees and exotics was marvellous. Both Heather and I were very impressed and told the head gardener so. It certainly gave us food for thought about getting a larger house with a conservatory and more grounds, although I pointed out to Heather that this kind of set-up cost millions and had evolved over many years. Nevertheless, I liked the idea of a library and an orangery and maybe a hothouse to try growing the same sort of things they had here. But I cautioned, we would need a gardener with the right background and knowledge as neither of us has it. Money wasn't a problem, we had decent cash reserves and bonds and stocks and shares and together with our other properties which were rented out at present, we had a capital base of around 20 million pounds in equity. This project would enhance that of course but I said that we should hold fire on any major changes until we had this project safely well on its way, so at least a year maybe more.

We went fishing, and both tried our hand at trout with the fly tackle and also had a session coarse fishing and found that as no one normally bothered with that type of fishing here, it was comparatively easy to hook some fine specimens, all of which we returned to the river.

Heather wore a black-and-silver gown to dinner the first night and I, my tuxedo. Sarah was splendid as usual in a pale lemon dress and her tiara, and she and Heather, who sat next to each other, were in animated conversation all through dinner.

Heather marvelled at the breakfast spread especially all the home-grown, home-made, and organic produce. We both agreed that we could not sustain a diet like this without taking some serious exercise and I confided to her that I suspected Michael used the gym and pool rather more than he admitted, to stay as slim as he did.

But Heather said, "I think not, I think Sarah puts him back on starvation rations as soon as the guests depart."

I said that I couldn't believe she had that much power over him, but Heather told me that all may not be what it seemed. Sarah came from a very old and wealthy background and Heather hinted that her money had in fact brought about a lot of the changes made to make their estate what it was today. Heather believed that Sarah in fact still held the purse strings and so had much more power and control than you and I might imagine.

I decided to pay a little more attention to Sarah and see if I could glimpse this woman as my wife had seen her; it could make a difference in our negotiations and in any case, I was intrigued.

We left on Sunday afternoon and arrived home in time to see our two grown-up children departing back to their places having spent the weekend at ours with a few friends. I made plans with Heather where I should visit next, and she made a couple of suggestions about how I approached them which involved trying to be totally open-minded and putting aside my earlier, perhaps hasty, impressions about old and new systems and belts and braces.

I decided also to put a hold on visiting Michael and Sarah the next weekend to coincide with Ronja's next visit there because the next few places I wanted to look at were much more remote and included Robert's Scottish estate and he had suggested I make that at the weekend depending on where I found myself later in the week. After informing Heather, I made the travel plans, not driving everywhere this time but travelling by rail. I booked first-class seats on the overnight sleeper up to Edinburgh on the Thursday night. I could always alter the booking if it became necessary, and I could also hire a car if needed. I called Ronja and told her I was not able to make it to Michael's place this weekend, and she said, "No problem, they have invited me anyway, so I am quite happy to go alone, but try to fit me in at some point, will you?"

I laughed and said, "Of course, so long as you fit me in!"

She just replied, "Always, love you."

And I replied, "Love you too."

I travelled to four more different sites where the group had significant assets and activity and spent time roaming around them and asking questions of all types of employees from storekeeper to MDs and making notes as I went, as well as reviewing them each day in my hotel room. And a picture was beginning to form in my mind but was still far from totally clear. But I reminded myself, this is only strategic planning for the teams to ensure they were each very clear what they were looking at and our overall objectives, no real difference from other projects they had carried out, but writ large and complicated by so many disparate functions.

I formed a conclusion that we needed a large room somewhere to put all the various plants and offices on a massive wall chart, so that we could draw lines of communication and goods and services flowing in and through each one to what we would probably designate as head office, which at present was universally accepted as Michael's office in his library. However, I was thinking that will have to just be his office and whoever was really running the show needed a separate office away from Michael's house, where a small staff of very senior people would spend most of their time. I had to be careful not to appear to be side-lining Michael, but I was beginning to think he himself might, inadvertently, become part of the reason they were in need of reform and total reorganisation of top management structures.

I also began to wonder if I should try to engage Sarah in this thought process and discreetly sound her out about both Michael's and her present and future roles. Could be risky, but if Heather were right in what she surmised, maybe not. Might just make things easier to manage while not upsetting Michael too much. I decided to take the bull by the horns and approach Sarah direct and tactfully suggest a meeting just with me to discuss aspects of their home estate, which I was due to look at anyway, as I was the Scottish and Irish estates. She would have a lot of knowledge about all three estates I guessed.

So I rang the house and asked to speak with Sarah and after a few pleasantries I said, "Sarah, I am putting together quite a lot of notes and observations I have made, and I thought as you effectively seem to run your estate there, forgive me if I am wrong, but it occurred to me that I would like to have a meeting with you about my thoughts and other ideas, sooner rather than later. These will be ideas from which Michael and you and Robert might stand to gain, as what I have in mind is the possibility of a new top management leadership for the group and the Estates, in a dedicated office not situated necessarily in your house but obviously with very close links.

She paused only briefly and said,"

"I wondered when you might realise that I am not just a pretty face and I was in a sense waiting and hoping you would call me direct, but I thought you may be held back because you wouldn't want to offend Michael. But rest assured that will not be a problem. I admire the calculated risk you have taken in making this call, but never fear. Michael shall know everything in due course, but not until I decide the time is right. Do you accept that?"

"Yes, absolutely I will rely on your superior judgement in that regard. I am going to see Robert's set up tomorrow for the weekend, so can you name a day when I might visit you there at your house next week perhaps."

"Yes, I can as a matter of fact, Michael is going to Scotland after you have left, to arrive on Tuesday and scheduled to come back Thursday so Tuesday overnight here until Wednesday would be good. Even if he came back early Wednesday it wouldn't matter; I shall just say you came at my invitation to talk about this estate and a few other related matters, no more than that. And please say nothing of all this to Robert. Bless him but all he really knows relates to the Scottish estate."

"Perfect for me. And I will look forward to having you alone so to speak."

"Good, me likewise," she said. "Until say Tuesday then; if you can make it for lunch do so, otherwise dinner, and smart casual will be fine. Let's be informal for this one."

"Until Tuesday then," I said.

I explained to Heather my new thoughts and how I had asked Sarah for a private meeting to discuss the main estate and a few other ideas and she had more or less said it was about time. It would reveal things I believed which might take forever to discover otherwise.

Heather said, "Great idea, I thought you might, well done. But remember she is a powerful woman and will be very used to always getting her way, so tread carefully and be prepared for any indication she doesn't like a particular idea or suggestion. Pull back a bit if signs look like you are treading on dangerous ground. Having said that, I know how persuasive and smooth you can be as well as decisive and a bit abrupt; tend towards the former rather than the latter. If she fancies you, play along a bit and see what happens. Not a licence to kill, just as much as is necessary, but don't let Michael catch you en flagrante!" I didn't say he wouldn't be there, that would really have aroused her suspicions, not that I thought for one minute Sarah was the fancying type. But I knew from long experience, you often just never know until it happens and then it's sink or swim.

Off I went on the longest part of my travels to group companies and factories, offices, etc. And I was more hopeful this time of nailing down some firm objectives for the teams to work on.

I saw four of the targets before entraining up to Edinburgh and thanks to British Rail's sleeping car, after a modest but good dinner in the restaurant car, I had a good seven hours in my cabin sleeping. And there to greet me was Robert and his ghillie, both in kilts, waiting with a battered old Rolls Royce, at the station. Robert was all smiles and came forward hand extended to greet me and said how pleased he was to welcome me to Scotland and his home here, and his ghillie — actual name Hamish — was also full of welcome and shook my hand. No dour looks, no sign of disapproval, very much the opposite. He said also that he had heard about my winning the shoot and the trout fishing contest and asked had I brought any of my tackle. I pointed out it is bit difficult lugging guns and rods around on foot and rail.

He laughed and said, "Never you mind sir, I have more than enough for everybody, if you can find the time."

So, to the estate house, which was almost a castle with turrets and was built in granite with narrow windows at strategic points but modified on the ground floor with large, mullioned windows and a magnificent huge iron studded main entrance door. It was like a film set and it transpired had indeed been used a couple of times for just that purpose. I admired it and said which particular family member had acquired this fantastic place and when. Good job I was prepared for it because he said, "It was my maternal great-great-grandfather who modified it, but the original castle was in my 'mother's family since about 1350 I think."

"Ah, so your mother is a Scot and, so are you?"

"Mother certainly is, and she lived here in the summers in her childhood and then spent the winters with another part of the family in England and also in the South of France at a vineyard and chateau owned by Grandpa and his branch of the family which also goes back centuries."

"But" he said, "enough of the history lesson for now; how about we tour the estate while the weather and light are so good?"

I concurred and another younger man also in a kilt took my bags. We climbed into a Range Rover and set off to see the estate. It too had river rights on the section which passed though the estate where salmon were to be had in season and it also had a large mere or lake, fed by a stream and overflowing by means of an outlet channelled to the river. Robert said, "Please call me Bob," and asked the ghillie to tell me about the fishing as he himself had never developed the habit having actually come here to live and manage the estate only a few years ago and just hadn't the time, nor the inclination, I guessed. The ghillie, Hamish, told me all about the magnificent salmon and trout he had caught, and also the huge common and mirror carp found in the lake and a whole spectrum of other fish, most but not all of which I was familiar with.

We then saw the woodland, mixed soft and hardwood for better all year-round appearance and cover for the abundant wildlife he said were to be found here. Plus, a fenced off patch of about twenty acres or so with a complete herd of red deer including the top stag and his harem of does plus a large selection of young and half-grown deer and one other stag; he was old and a bit lame and no competition for the leading male. Hamish was in fact Game and Fish Keeper and in addition to an old Land Rover, there was a truck for transferring produce to market; two or three tractors of various sizes and ages, and a couple of shaggy fell ponies for getting about the estate when the snow was on the ground. Not attached to the house but nearby was a stable and forage barn, a workshop for repairs and maintenance and an assortment of farm implements to attach to the tractors for hay and silage making, ploughing, drilling and the like.

The main crops were turnips and mangolds, barley, wheat, sugar beet, and kale and these were all for cattle and deer feed. The cattle, roaming the hillsides at present, were the long-haired variety with long pointed horns and these were for meat only other than being for sale when in surplus; no dairy herd here, although a solitary cow or two were kept in a barn for fresh milk, butter, and cheese for the house.

Higher up were hill sheep which, unless there was very bad weather, stayed where they felt safe up on higher ground and only came down when there was no fodder for them in mid-winter and also when brought down by Land Rover and trailer for the market.

This was altogether a much smaller operation than that at the main house where his parents lived, but quite enough for Bob, he confided. Bob was about thirty years of age and had a girlfriend who lived in Edinburgh and came occasionally to stay but found it all too simple and perhaps boring to actually want to live there. I remarked he should be playing the field a bit more and going to young farmers' meetings and events where he might find a partner who would love it here, but he just laughed that off and it seems for now at any rate he was enjoying the peace and solitude up here.

I had a quick look at his books, and it really was a small-scale operation albeit with a large parcel of land, and a house which would be the envy of many and the whole estate was worth millions to the right buyer. But with the set up as it was at present there was going to be no need of an in-depth study or a reform plan, other than to suggest putting in a golf course and making a barn into a club house and letting out say ten of the spare bedrooms to golfers, walkers and so on. But even then, it would probably not need to be incorporated into the master plan, I felt.

There was one other possibility I thought of after talking to Hamish about a derelict stone building alongside a stream running through a peat bog and then on to join the river: start a distillery for malt whisky, in the ruin of what had once been just that! It would need a good sum of capital investment to renovate the old still house and equip it with a decent size still and create stowage vaults for maturing the whisky. Malt could be produced on site from the barley home-grown or bought in, at least for the first production or two. But if you were in no hurry, I could see such an operation being completed in say, a year and then perhaps half the whisky could be sold to the big distilleries and the other half laid down at the estate to mature. I suggested all this, a bit tongue-in-cheek to Bob in Hamish's presence. Bob pooh-poohed it, but Hamish looked very thoughtful and later on at dinner he brought the subject up again. He said that the original malt whisky produced there was excellent and sold well, and he personally would be delighted to be a part of its revival. I said I would mention it in my report to Bob's mother and father and asked him not to tell them of my idea as yet, and he agreed. I was going to do some research on this defunct distillery and its produce to see just what level of investment might be needed bring it back to life, and what sort of market it might reach and unit prices.

The following morning after a real Scottish treat, haggis and home-cured ham, fried potatoes and turnip, and farm fresh eggs with home-made wholegrain flour bread and fruit from the small orchard preserved in Kilner Jars, Hamish asked if I would like to try my hand for a salmon.

I said that I thought that was seasonal, and in any case, would any be running at this time of year and Hamish explained that the owner of the land had all the rights associated with that; we, in fact, could do more or less as we pleased. But in any case, if we did see a salmon at all, it would not be part of a big run, just a straggler who had left it too late to find a mate but was carrying on through a sheer inherited homing device in his brain. He went on to explain that the salmon would die anyway either after spawning or because he would get stuck in a shallow streamlet and would perish from being frozen when the first snows of winter started. How much of this was just to please me I don't know, but I accepted the invitation and was kitted out in much the same gear as for trout fishing but, with a sturdier rod and reel, heavier line and different flies with bigger hooks concealed in them, and off he and I went. Bob had declined and it was clear he was not a fisherman and never would be it seemed.

He led us to a stretch of the river which ran clear and turbulence free with a level gravel bottom good for walking in waders on. He set up the kit and in we went about five yards apart, he towards the centre of the river and me nearer the bank. He demonstrated the casting technique, again similar to trout fishing and away we went. Cast, allow the fly to float freely a while, then reel in and start again. After about ten casts, I was beginning to think this is a waste of time until Hamish hissed through his teeth and nodded to a large ship heading upriver exactly in line with my current cast. He held a finger to his lips and motioned me to keep as still as I could. I thought he had passed my lure but with a swish of his tail, he grabbed the fly. I pulled up sharply and the hook got him in his mouth, and I had a large salmon on my line.

"Keep it taut!" he shouted, "but also let him run a little to tire him out."

I played the fish up and down my part of the river for about ten or fifteen minutes and finally got him near enough for Hamish to gaff him behind his gill and we took him ashore.

What a beauty he was, long and fat, not a mark on him, and Hamish said he would be about 12 lbs in weight and would make excellent eating. We continued for a while and Hamish actually hooked a large trout on his salmon fly; not unusual he said, he half expected that was all we might see so he was delighted I had caught the salmon and his sea trout was at least 5 lbs in weight he thought and would make a nice meal for us all.

Back to the house to show off my salmon and everyone was delighted for me.

The cook said, "Salmon steaks for supper and shall we and have the trout tomorrow at lunch?"

We all readily agreed to this plan and then after a glass of beer we sat down to a delicious cold lunch with home-cured meats, home-grown vegetables and a glass of Chardonnay to wash it down.

I was determined to try to get a bit more information about his side of the family and asked him about the Irish estate, and again it was linked to his mother's family, and the current occupant was Irish-born and had married into Sarah's family but Sarah was the owner as she was of the Scottish estate. Bob didn't know much about the estate other than it too was in considerable acreage of land, had a large country mansion at its heart and owned several farms around it tenanted for many years by local well-to-do farming families. They simply paid a fixed rent for their farms. The rents and the produce, mainly a large dairy herd which produced milk by the tanker load, and there were butter and cheesemaking houses situated near the main house provided much of the income. Bob wasn't sure but guessed that the Irish estate, although much bigger than his, would not yield enough to make it necessary to include it in my plans, although perhaps on the book work and admin side, it might be useful.

So, what Helen had surmised was turning out to be right: most of the estate holdings emanated from Sarah's side and it would not surprise me to find that she had considerable investments in other companies as well as stocks and bonds and cash deposits.

But I had not yet seen the group's accounts, so didn't know who owned what, and where the balance of power lay, although I was beginning to think Sarah was much more involved than I had initially thought; this made my meeting with her in private all the more interesting. If it turned out that she held the major block of shares in all or most of the group constituent companies, then clearly, she would be getting the 'lion's share of dividends to add to her cash pile.

I stayed there until Sunday evening and after the lovely salmon with all the trimmings, Hamish and Bob drove with me to catch my sleeper train from Edinburgh and I was back home just in time for lunch on Monday. I filled Heather in on what I had done and seen, and she said, it was much as she thought from the bits and pieces Sarah had told her, so even more important to carry this coming meeting off well. She agreed it seemed unlikely that the Irish or the Scottish estates and even Michael's and Sarah's estate, would need to be included in the same way as all the companies in the group, but there might be some mileage in getting them to follow the same accountancy practices and to include their profits, such as they were, into the group's balance sheet. This would give the estates an advantage because they could then call for financial assistance for any new projects like the distillery idea, and there might be some scope for expansion in Ireland too, but we would need to check on the position with Ireland being a separate country with its own fiscal laws. Might even be scope for suggesting ownership of the whole group and taxation could be Irish! We would need expert advice on that but worth including as a possibility.

However, I would not have time to visit the Irish estate before my planned meeting with Sarah, but I needed to see the set-up there before making my recommendations and a closer look at the home estate as well.

I completed my notes as far as I could but there were still a couple of other group sites I really needed to see before beginning to put some real shape to my Phase 1 outline plans for all to consider before finalising them sufficient to lay them before our two teams in order to obtain their understanding and also hear any points they might make at the meeting we planned with them, Heather, and me.

So much depended on what I learnt from Sarah and how far she might be prepared to go on letting Michael call the shots, if indeed he was!

First, I wanted to see if I could find any information about the small distillery which had existed at the Scottish estate up until about 1925 according to Bob and Hamish. It had been called Castle McLeish Distillery in its day; no one knew who McLeish was, but I surmised he must have owned all or part of the estate a century or more ago, or perhaps he was just the incumbent who lived there and paid rent to Sarah's family. But it was believed that 50% or so of the whisky production was taken by a bigger outfit who must have been trading and might still be, although they could themselves been taken over by a bigger distillery group by now.

I started with The Scottish Whisky Distillers Association, and they had a museum, so I extended my search to the archives and found no references relating to Castle McLeish Distillery at all. But I was able to establish a rough cost of a decent size pot still and a source for the right casks for maturation. I soon came to the conclusion that more time to find the right entity who could advise us was needed, and certainly the old building which housed the original still would need surveying and estimates of costs and permits or licences, etc., before we could even begin to explore this as a viable objective. That said, I culled some ballpark figures to consider. It would be £150,000 to renovate and prepare the Still House, £60,000 to buy a good-sized pot still with all the attachments and ancillary equipment, £8,000 for a first supply of barrels or casks for maturation of the whisky and another £60,000 to update the barley harvester, storage barn and malt production floor. Not to mention the development of the peat bog for our own supply of peat without disturbing the stream which ran through it, from which we would need to get our water for sparging and mashing the malted barley for distillation. Malting requires some underfloor heat, and this can be achieved with peat burning, but nowadays it is much easier using underfloor electric cables.

In short, we needed expert advice from the outset and another expert to be employed to help set it all up and ultimately to manage every aspect of the production, as well as an experienced cooper to get and keep the casks in trim. Still, I liked the idea and put a ballpark figure on start-up to be around 300,000 pounds, not including any staff taken on. No good clearly as a profit-making scheme in the short term, and with minimum maturation in casks at three years and at least a year to rebuild and set up, plus possibly buying the first shipment of malt, we would need to set aside enough capital to take up to five years before we produced a saleable product. By then, we would need our own bottling plant and a storage house for finished product, plus an advertising campaign. Nevertheless, I intended raising this with Sarah, feeling I had nothing to lose.

Chapter 30

Off I went, by car this time, to arrive on Tuesday at Sarah's house as promised in time for lunch. I arrived at twelve-thirty and received a warm welcome from Sarah at the door with the trusty butler on hand to take my boxes and bag to my room, while I followed Sarah to the library. We didn't go to Michael's office, just to a round mahogany table with four leather upholstered seats. Sarah sat me down first and said, "Well you have been very busy, so let's relax over a beer or a glass of wine perhaps, what do you prefer?"

"I would love a draft beer if you have one. From a bottle would be fine if it's from a decent brewery, maybe an IPA."

She rang for service and the maid who came said she was pretty sure that there was such a beer to be found in the fridge in the billiards room and Sarah said, "Bring me one as well please, I will try this famous brew. I'm pretty dry after a nice long walk around the fields looking for mushrooms."

We sat and I took a good pull of the beer which was from a local micro-brewery and was excellent. Sarah said she liked it too. Then we only had time for pleasantries before lunch was upon us, so we went to the small dining room normally reserved for family only and were served with the usual first-class home-produce lunch and had a couple of glasses of wine to accompany it. We sat back while the table was cleared, and coffee served, and all the staff had disappeared and then the fun started.

Sarah said, "Never mind the gory details, give me your gut impressions and a glimpse of your possible strategy, and I will answer as many of your questions as I can."

I told her roughly what I had told Heather and said that in general, things were pretty good as they were, but it was high time for this review to prevent what might be a gradual falling-off of both turnover and profits, hence lower share value and dividends. If that happened, I said, it would be a harder job and take a lot longer to put things back where they should be. She nodded and asked me to go on. I told her I thought there might be elements of hanging on to older systems even when some reforms and modernisation had taken place and cited the RSM's disclosure about him falling back on his old card system for stock control, whereas all the buyers' records were computerised. I added that some of the buyers had done the same thing, spending time updating their old card systems as well as inputting the data into the computer records. This was understandable for a period, but probably not longer term. But I stressed I was only formulating my overall strategic plan for my two teams of people who between them had done this sort of thing quite a number of times, perhaps with not so large a group of companies but the principles didn't change.

I went on to describe some reforms which could well speed up processes and might lead to a few redundancies and the recruitment of more people technically proficient in certain areas. I also mentioned the in-house foundry and castings plant, one of the group had for making engines for their tractors, and other agricultural as well as industrial needs. I said that was one plant that I would like the team to focus on, as the machinery in the foundry was quite dated and would need replacing before long, and at a high cost. So I wanted the team to study whether it might be better in both the short and the long term, to contract out this work, saving a lot of investment capital and losing about fifty jobs, but the product would be first-class and competitively priced. However, I stressed again that this idea was just one of many for the team to investigate only at this point, stressing that these were just my initial thoughts only at present. The thing was I told her, that there might be a few such operations throughout the group, where this same criterion may apply.

Sarah just nodded and made a couple of notes. I continued, saying that effectively the whole exercise was to explore areas for improvement and to research and suggest just what improvements could be made with some ballpark loss and gain figures. Moving more stocks of parts and finished products bought in to a 'just in time' basis affected the bottom line significantly and yes, there was a risk of an occasional delay from the supply chain being interrupted, but experience has shown that this is a small percentage of the potential gain and can be tolerated. I outlined one or two more specific scenarios I had witnessed, and which were on my list for the teams to prioritise but, I stressed that I would not be riding shotgun on this. I was interested in the big picture; all I was doing at this point, apart from familiarising myself as much as was possible with the whole group's methods, was to ensure the teams were as fully primed as could be, so that twelve experts did not have to waste time finding out the general layout and methods in the group as they went along.

Sarah said, "Thanks for all that. I don't think I need more detail about the plant and main offices; your report is much as I anticipated, and it was I who commissioned this project, so I already knew some of the things you have mentioned. What about the three estates? How should they fit in within all this if at all?"

"Very good question," I said. "Exactly what I have been asking myself after my visit to your old castle! The Scottish estate is relatively small beer when compared with most if not all other components of the group, and I take it they are not part of your central accounting set up but are stand-alone businesses which in Scotland's case is pretty small. But I do have a couple of things which you may not have thought about which might in both the short and longer term make the Scottish estate more viable as a group member."

"Oh," she said, "do tell, I am quite surprised to hear that."

"Well in the first place, I will expound the possibility of rising from the dead so to speak. What, if anything, do you know about the old Castle McLeish Distillery?"

"Ah, well not much, but we have some old books and ledgers and photographs and maybe even some historical records going back over a hundred years ago. But it was taken over by a larger distillery with whom my grandfather was in competition, and they promptly shut it down and that is how it was left. The old pot still was sold, and the still house was allowed to deteriorate I'm afraid."

I said, "Am I right in saying that you personally are the owner of the estate there, handed down to you by either your mother or father or of course both?"

"Yes, that is true, and because it is so remote and very little actual profit is made there, I have allowed Robert to handle it, to cut his teeth on you might say."

"Well," I said, "I have looked at the situation, the old distillery building, the growing of barley on the farm, the existence of a pure peaty water source running through your very own peat bog and I have looked at the trade a little. I feel, subject to a more professional examination and assessment, that there is a good possibility that for around £300,000 initial capital outlay, you might be able to have a functioning distillery fit to make a special single malt whisky. But there would be no income other than already exists on the farm, for at least five years allowing for rebuilding and equipping and maturation of the whisky for minimum of three years in cask. It entails planting more barley, building a small malting floor and employing a decent still man and a cooper. But if you could not afford to do that personally, the estate could be made into a limited company, with say you and Robert as shareholders and then become part of the group, which, I presume would have those sorts of resources."

"Interesting, very interesting," she said. "And the other idea for the castle?"

"I thought also of a golf course, with club house and facilities and you have at least twelve spare bedrooms in the castle, which with the promise of a distillery going to happen, plus the golf, well-to-do tourists from the rest of the UK and abroad might well be interested in a vacation at such an unspoiled and unique former castle. That idea could be developed quietly alongside the major project, but I feel certain it is the sort of place you could get year-round clientele, with for example a honeymoon suite and a heated pool with all the trimmings in the grounds in a stand-alone barn conversion. But you would probably not want all this, these are just ideas. And there is the salmon fishing on the river, and carp fishing in the mere. The list can go on."

"What about this estate here, and the Irish one? You probably have already worked out that I own all three estates, as well as a controlling share in all of the group's companies, so you are talking to the right person, but again I am certain you have already worked that out too."

"I have yet to visit Ireland, and I haven't really looked very closely at this magnificent estate but is it a limited company already?"

"No, but I am open to ideas on that, although reluctant to give anyone else a share in my family inheritance."

"You don't need to, if you made all three estates separate limited companies or indeed just one such company, and you held all or most of those shares, no one can touch it, or you. Just one other point while we are on this subject, have you entertained the idea that with say, the Irish estate as a limited company, and the other two as well perhaps, and indeed this would apply to all the group companies, if you registered the whole business or businesses in Ireland, the tax advantages would be very significant? And I believe, subject to advice, that apart from submitting Irish annual accounts, you would only need to go to Ireland yourself once a year for an AGM, or perhaps not even that. And one final question while we are both at this point, assuming you have significant cash capital in banks, might I simply enquire if the majority is already offshore? I just want to know — yes or no, nothing more — it can affect my recommendations significantly, but I accept readily that you may not want to share that information at this point."

"Well James, you have excited my interest in the project enormously, and I would like to think about it all before we go any further in this. How about you and I have a swim and a sauna and relax with a bottle of bubbly?"

"I didn't bring my swim gear," I said.

"Oh, don't worry about that there are plenty of towels and robes and things and there will not be any staff anywhere we tread I can assure you."

I thought, *crikey I don't believe this, but Heather had said do what you have to do, didn't she?* And now my mind was focussed differently I could see that like Heather, Sarah was probably in her middle to late fifties only a few years older than me and very well kept.

So, I mentally shifted a couple of gears and smiled and said, "What a good idea! Do you know any massage techniques, I am rather stiff from so many hours on trains and could do with a few kinks ironing out?"

"As a matter of fact, I do, but let's see how the swim and sauna do the trick first shall we?"

We disrobed and I picked a towelling kimono type thing up and she had a bathrobe on. We went to the pool, and I just dropped my robe and dived in stark naked and she did the same. It was a lovely way to get to know someone better, and I figured she had so much more than me to lose, and so I was totally confident no one would ever know but us. We splashed around a bit and then climbed out of the pool. Sarah was glowing and her figure was very good, lovely pale smooth skin and a small reddish bush showing. I grabbed her and put my arms around her, and we kissed long and sensuously, and I sought out the bush and put a finger in. She gasped and said, "Not here, to my bedroom. Follow me, don't worry, we will see no one and no one will see us."

Suffice it to say it was much more exciting than I thought it would be and we made love for around two hours on and off, before falling asleep, rousing ourselves in time to get showered and changed for dinner… the show must go on.

Dinner with more wine, followed by a brandy for me and a liqueur for Sarah and coffee and she was ready to say a bit more.

"James, I knew you must be good in bed having seen the other two women in your life and their attitude towards you, but I confess you really amazed me this afternoon and I am so glad we took the plunge. However, I am sure you will realise that however much I like you, that will not affect my judgement regarding the project at all. I happen to also think that I can trust you and that you are very shrewd and have a good business brain. I am going to be pretty candid with you so long as you understand that only you and Heather, whom I admire enormously, can know the things I will and have already told you today. Is that understood and accepted?"

I replied, "Thank you and yes fully understood and accepted, but Michael will surely realise that you have told me a lot by my actions, reports and my programme of work, etc."

"Of course, he will, and I will brief him fully, have no fear. He will be very happy to let me lead this behind the scenes while he acts as my spokesman and CEO of the companies. But what happens to the three estates is entirely my decision.

I want you to look quite closely at the Irish estate and I will brief my cousin Bertram, known as Bertie, on cooperation and providing all information and assistance to you. Let's see if you can come up with any suggestions there, and here of course I can answer anything you ask and allow you access to all our records and archives, especially regarding Scotland. I intend taking advice from our family lawyers and another

231

lawyer who is an expert on these matters and will also be well versed in Irish company registrations and tax positions which we may wish to adopt. I can also tell you that yes, I have considerable cash assets partly offshore in, Switzerland, Isle of Man, British Virgin Islands (BVI) and Luxembourg amounting in total, to about 20 million pounds in several currencies. But I also have several UK accounts as well which hold between them a further 20 twenty million pounds, so roughly 40 million all told. So there is no need to go limited with the estates just for capital purposes, but I am minded making the three estates into limited companies, after we get some more expert advice on the advantages and disadvantages. As you intimated, I could still hold say sixty or even ninety percent of the shares, and Robert, Michael and a couple of members of my family could hold the balance. Now I am quite tired, and I think another session on all this can wait until tomorrow. If you would like it too, I would like you to sleep with me tonight please."

I agreed of course and didn't question how she could manage all this without Michael getting to know because I was sure she had that covered. It was good, and we both had an excellent night's sleep and woke up refreshed and after a little "nice knowing you" session we showered and dressed for breakfast and went down together to the family breakfast room. We both had a very good breakfast before retiring to her corner of the library. There we went over all that we had discussed, and I made a date to return to look more closely at this estate and also confirmed dates to see the Irish estate. In the meantime, Sarah would see her expert advisers and lawyers and seek some guidance on the matters we had discussed, so that I had time to complete my preliminary investigations and prepare the Phase 1 proposal.

I spent a couple of hours in the library and Sarah pointed me in the direction of the old files on the Scottish estate where an account of the takeover was and all the trademarks and brand names for the estate whisky had been sold to the larger distillers so were lost to us now. That didn't worry me too much as a new name could be dreamed up based on the geographical area of the proposed still and there were so few new single malt stills coming on stream so little or no competition at our level. Whatever the trademark situation the fact was this was a revival of an old malt and we could get round the trademark issue and still present the new still as a genuine successor to the old.

Then I spent an hour looking through the current books and noted all the revenue makers and assets in the estate and again it seemed clear to me that this home estate had been ticking over for years with no real attempts to find new revenue streams. There was clearly scope for setting up an "upmarket" attraction as a unique holiday venue, and the estate was big enough to keep the public confined to just parts of the estate leaving the main house undisturbed. There were many buildings, old and not so old, including barns, a granary, and the food stores for the deer and the equipment storage for the home farm. This was situated about half a mile from the mansion and hidden from view by rising fields and woodland as the mansion was situated at the bottom of a large but shallow valley and the home farm was in its own slight depression as well.

I needed to consult the Ordnance Survey maps for the entire estate to assess the potential for development which, as far as possible would only involve existing buildings suitably altered for holiday use. The sort of attractions we could offer were obvious; fishing, both game (trout) and coarse (tench, bream, carp, etc.) Shooting, including actual game shooting at limited times of the year, clay pigeon shooting, riding lessons and more challenging paths for accomplished riders, swimming, inside and out in heated pools and cold; plus, the river if it could be made safe for a stretch and fenced to keep out cattle. Indoor and outdoor games facilities such as tennis, snooker and pool tables, beauty salon and massage rooms with a couple of qualified staff, and I was sure a consultant who dealt in this sort of holiday facility would come up with other activities which would attract the sort of people we wanted. The price would help in that by keeping out riff-raff. But there was little point in addressing this idea any further without first talking to Sarah because she may just refuse to do anything which might change the nature of the estate, although I believed if done well, with a separate entrance from the road about a mile back along the main access road, would do much to alleviate potential disturbance and most of the activities could be situated where little or no such disturbance would happen.

A different approach could be an acceptable idea, make a conference centre with some of the attractions listed above for a discerning few, which could provide some good income with almost no disturbance at all. But I favoured the complete package.

Another idea I had was to develop the already prolific production of organic food, venison, lamb, beef and pork as well as vegetables and fruit, so that the food offered to holidaymakers and event organisers like conference people was organic and all home produced on the estate. Surplus could be marketed to the better supermarkets and restaurants.

So to supplement the above ideas, a restaurant could be made in one of the barns with open beams where top quality organic home-grown meats, vegetables and salads could be offered not just to holidaymakers and conferences, but open to the public as well, again at prices pitched high to encourage a good standard of clientele.

There would be no need to try to develop all these options in one go; instead, we could start with just one or two like the special holiday attraction and move gradually to include some or all of the other options as well as consider any suggestions made by expert analysis from people who were specialists in setting up this type of enterprise.

One more thought I had, in addition to some from the above, was to consider looking at a wildlife enclosure, not a zoo, more like a mini version of Longleat, but not necessarily contain large carnivores, more an extension of farm animals into some wild but easily handled species. Donkeys and mules, or perhaps introduce rare breeds of sheep, goats, and pigs. Rare cattle like the Highland cattle in Scotland; we could bring a few down here. Also, rare breeds of exotic pheasants and guinea fowl, quail were a favourite, and the eggs are all good for special salads, etc.

I drew up a list of possibilities and at that point, Sarah walked into the library and asked how I was getting on. I first stressed that these were very much just ideas, and in any case, she would probably not want any changes which compromised the overall ambience and look of the main house, or the disturbance, limited though that might be with careful and imaginative handling. She smiled and said, "Good time to tell me as I have been enjoying your company so much and Michael will not now be back until the day after tomorrow. So, if you can stretch your visit another night or two, I would be very grateful."

I laughed and said, "Bribery will get you everywhere, so providing I clear it with Heather first, the answer is yes of course."

I then ran through all my list adding a few more details and ideas as I went and she didn't stop me, or interrupt in any way apart from the occasional arching of an eyebrow and a pout or two.

Then she said, "Well that's far too much to take in and digest in one fell swoop, so I will give you a qualified and simply overall gut reaction and then you will have to be patient until I have had my advice on the other matters. In principle, I am not against change per se and of course very careful management would be needed so that there was minimum disturbance of our life here in the house and immediate environs. That said, I am certainly open to your general thrust subject to analysis, advice, consultation and the rest. Mini Longleat indeed! However, we would have to have a very thorough screening of the types who come here for holidays or conferences and we would need strict 'out of bounds' markers and even some discreet surveillance cameras and enhanced security. But why not! I'd love to see some of the Highland cattle down here and I like the idea of rare breeds protection. The shooting and fishing both sound fine if controlled properly, and some extra games facilities, their own pools, etc., also sound fine to me, but you haven't said where all these people are going to sleep., Not in this house for sure. And a restaurant, accessible a mile away also sounds OK. I wonder if we could get planning consent for a motel type hotel, but more upmarket and only accessible through a careful booking procedure; no passing trade, the clients must be vetted to a degree. Although pitching the prices high would undoubtedly help."

"Well, that's enough of a green light for me to at least study the ideas a bit more and as you say take advice, and I believe the organic food production is the way forward and is profitable and is a big factor in considering a holiday with this food on offer, as well as a range of activities."

"Yes, and if you can stay as I have asked there will be much of this we can discuss, but what of your research into the distillery angle in Scotland?"

"Well, we cannot revive the old brand as it was sold with the still, etc. but that's not important in my opinion, it is a rare event for a new single malt whisky distiller to come on stream in this day and age, and I believe the location, the history of a single malt being produced here fifty years ago, and again now using the same barley, the same peat bog and water from it, and exact same location, will intrigue all single malt aficionados. It will sell first because of the story but afterwards because it will be a unique new malt, based on an old and tried and tested recipe with the same materials and will sell well. I prophesy that you would not only be selling locally and to bigger outfits but there will be a big potential market in the USA, Japan and around the world. Yes, it will take a few years to reach that point, but your ancestors have done it all before many times and maybe you are the one to kick start a new era."

"You are a persuasive bugger, that you are, so if I go for these two projects — and we haven't even looked at Ireland yet — and assuming you fulfil your contract, will I be able to keep you as my advisor afterwards, for a few years maybe?"

I laughed and said, "Assuming you still want me then, yes. But it won't all be plain sailing, you will hit snags and problems until all the new activities are well bedded in, so I may not be totally in your favour by then."

"Perhaps so, but am I just a fair-weather friend?"

"Not on your life, If I cannot overcome these problems, with your help or without it, I don't deserve to be the person my family all believe I am."

We had a very busy and enjoyable two more days and nights together and decided I would stay a third night so that we could all have dinner after Michael came home and so we could apprise him of our ideas for his consideration, comment, and approval. Sarah said that he will approve whatever we have decided although he may come up with a few valid criticisms and ideas. He will also have heard what Robert has had to say about my ideas for the Scottish estate and spoken to Hamish and others in Scotland so would be well prepared to hear something similar coming from here.

Although I had my hands full these past few days, in more ways than one, I still found time to touch base with Ronja and explain what was going on. She was fine about it, realising what a big deal this one was, and we made a tentative arrangement to meet up soon, but with no date.

I thought it best to ask Sarah if Ronja was still welcome and she said, "Of course, providing you also make the odd arrangement alone on dates to suit me. But don't worry she will not suspect anything and that goes for Heather too."

I thanked her and told her I was sure she was as up for the challenge as was I.

Chapter 31

After going home for a couple of nights where everything was calm and normal, I made arrangements to go to Ireland through Sarah to ensure I was met, as I had little or no idea where the Irish estate actually was, so decided to ask someone to come to Dublin Airport and meet my flight. I had told Heather all about my development ideas for Scotland and the home estate and she was quite surprised I had managed to do this alone, but I pointed out it was mostly common sense, and everything would have to be looked at by experts to ensure they were both feasible and potentially viable and also to arrive at suitable budget requirements, pointing out to Heather that Sarah had considerable cash assets as well as being the outright owner of all three estates. I also gave my opinion that this whole exercise was long overdue, and Sarah was straining at the leash to do something substantial to plan for the future of the trust she controlled and to get her only child, Robert, a lot further along the road of learning to be the future controller of what, by any measure, was a very considerable legacy. The more we modernised and set the schemes well along their tracks and in as short a time as was possible (consistent with quality and function ability) the better. Sarah was about my age or a little older and in the normal course of events ought to have ten or fifteen years of active participation in all of these potential plans if she wanted to carry on that long, but the future is always untellable regarding health and possible accidents. Therefore, she was very keen to make plans and get things moving, and so far, seemed confident of my ability to orchestrate the whole show, together of course with lawyers, architects possibly and a few more important experts.

So, in order to complete my preparations and then present my master plan, I first needed to look at the Irish estate and see what, if anything, needed to be done in order for it to progress as envisaged with the other two estates. The group company reform plan was almost formed and ran along the same lines as a dozen or more similar — if a bit smaller —

projects our teams had completed before, so it was largely a matter of scale and adaption.

I went straight from home to Manchester Airport, left my car there and caught an early flight to Dublin arriving at ten-thirty a.m. where I was met by a young man called Sean (pronounced Shorn) who told me he was Sarah's second cousin, his father Bertram being her cousin. It was he who ran the Irish estate on behalf of Sarah, the effective head of the family. Young Sean was a bright and chatty young man and a very competent driver of the five-year-old Range Rover he had brought to pick me up, although with me coming by air, no guns or fishing rods this time, as I had been assured everything I might need would be provided. It was a good two hours' drive, much of this on country roads and lanes after we left the major roads around Dublin behind, and Sean was a great talker so no awkward silences. In fact, he was very knowledgeable about the estates business, or seemed to be, so by the time we arrived, together with my own briefing papers and Sean I felt pretty well primed.

This was another castle by the look of it, complete with drawbridge (non-functioning) dry moat and thick stone walls surrounding the majority of houses, barns, and other buildings. At its centre stood the quite magnificent turreted castle which looked in excellent condition and was really quite large, much bigger than I expected. There was a huge keep blocking any unwanted entrance by anyone who had already penetrated the outer defensive walls and the moat, but the huge old iron-banded doors looked as if they had not been closed and barred for many a long year. However, I was assured by Sean that they did in fact function and had certainly been in regular use in wartime. Bertram met me and his son at the entrance to the main castle together with his wife Hannah, and a retainer in dark clothing who I suppose was whatever the Irish equivalent of butler or ghillie would be. All were smiling and very welcoming and handshakes or cheek kisses were the order of the day, and I was welcomed into their home, and what a home!

Stone walls visible everywhere; some were covered with plaster, others with wood panelling or tapestries and many had shields and ancient weapons displayed on them plus portraits of family past. What a place! It really was like a film set but clearly the real thing, and I was spellbound for a long time by all that I saw. Bertram (insisted on being called Bertie) said that I must be a bit tired so how about we postpone any sort of tour and as it was now after one o clock, how about a drink and some lunch and just chat for a while as I adapted to the surroundings. We all agreed and went to a large dining hall with massive furniture fit for banqueting on, but which also had smaller long tables with normal sized chairs situated to one side. One such table was already laid for lunch. Bertie sat us all down with me seated between him and Hannah and asked what I would like to drink. I replied asking if he had Guinness or porter. I love a nice pint of Guinness and felt in need of something to quench my thirst. "Certainly, we have, and I will join you," said Bertie and the usual for the others he said to the man in black. He didn't serve us though, that was for one of his staff, a delightful young lady in a bright check dress and headband who brought in a trolley loaded with two crystal pint mugs of Guinness with a half an inch of cream on top and a variety of other glasses and bottles for everyone else.

Once everyone was served, Bertie said, "Here's a very warm welcome James to our humble abode; may your visit be fruitful and enjoyable." He raised his mug as did I and we all took a sip of our drinks to 'Welcome' from all.

I took the top two inches off my Guinness, and it was beautiful, easily the best I had ever tasted, and I said so. Bertie said that they had an arrangement with the Dublin brewery which made the Guinness to ship a barrel once a month to them and it always came in perfect condition. It was kept in a deep cellar where the temperature never varied from about 55° F. We sat in our allotted seats and were served the most interesting lunch I had experienced for many years. Fresh crayfish from a stream nearby, freshwater mussels, and baby eels with a shallot salad for starters and a choice of guinea fowl or quail for the main course, with an assortment of potatoes done three different ways and beautiful vegetables, all clearly collected that morning from their own gardens.

I asked Bertie if, like his cousin, he tried to be self-sufficient in fruit and vegetables and were they also organic.

And he replied, "Very similar, we too have a hothouse, a cool greenhouse, and an orangery; in fact, we go further than Sarah as we have bananas and mangoes growing successfully here in the hothouse, as well as most temperate fruit in the cool greenhouse and orangery and in the walled garden. But I believe she grows pineapples as well."

I said that I would look forward to a tour of all these sights as well as the whole castle and the farms and I asked, "Apart from the home farm I could see on the way in here, how many other farms are there under tenancies?"

Bertie replied, "Six more: four large ones and two smaller ones which are on the hillsides and are mainly for sheep and lamb production. The larger farms are situated along the valley floor and have rich soil manured by several herds of beef cattle and two herds of milking cows which produce a full tanker of 5,000 litres each day for much of the year. This, together with the lamb, beef and pork sales, form the backbone of our income. Flanking the lower bottom fields, we grow different cereals for animal feedstock, and beet, kale, turnip and mangolds also for animal feed. For the cattle brought indoors, we chop up and mix it with wheat straw for winter feed."

Bertie continued, "This is in fact the biggest of the three estates in acreage, and in productive arable land and also in numbers of animals kept. We take not only rent from the tied farms but also a percentage of their produce, either in cash or kind, depending on the overall situation of the entire estate. The rents are relatively cheap having been so long in the tenant's families, and they have made numerous attempts to buy their farms, but Sarah and her mother and father before her were adamant that they remain ours. So, in order to compensate for the low rents a tithe system was agreed many years ago to limit any other payments with a formula which took account of good and bad years, and which will remain permanently. Unless the estate were broken up, or a tenant voluntarily left or died intestate with no direct heirs, at which point we could intervene and either take that farm over ourselves or offer it for tenancy to a new person or family, and then we could introduce a different system from the current way out of date rents and the tithe compromise, which always causes some ripples. But generally, we get on well with all the tenants and cooperate at peak times of the year in helping each other by loaning workers and machinery."

I asked, "What currently happens to profits made? Do they go automatically to Sarah or is there a local fund you maintain here which take a percentage first?"

He replied, "Ultimately Sarah's word is law; she owns everything albeit a lot of it is in trust for the future generations. She nevertheless controls a majority stake the methodology of which I am uncertain of, but it's all written down and authenticated by the trustees, nearly all of which are family members, plus lawyers and an accountant; both firms used by our family for generations and passed on one to the next in their companies. But, as I say, I am not an expert on these matters and am content to leave it to those who are."

"I'm sure it's all in the books, but give me a feel for turnover, running costs and gross profits before taxation if you can," I said.

He replied, "Certainly I can, I do the books on a weekly basis and send a monthly summary to Michael and Sarah. I can easily give you say twelve months of these summaries which will then cover a typical year's activity. But in round figures we turnover about 800,000 PA including all sales and rents, and running costs are round about half of that, exceptions excluded. So, a gross average profit of around 400,000 PA would cover most years, I think. The enormous advantage we have over the average farmer, or any other company, is that we have no mortgages to service or overdrafts at the banks and we produce much of what we need ourselves. We occasionally buy a substantial piece of equipment, like a tractor, a lorry or a combine harvester, but such big items are few and far between and sometimes we get bargains at repossession sales or bankruptcies for example."

I said, "Have you thought about any activity or product which you might introduce which would swell the turnover and profitability, such as opening part of the estate up to a limited form of tourism? Do you, for example, hold shoots? Is there a river running through your lands which can be fished? Is there scope for turning part of the castle into accommodation for let us say, the right types, to stay on a holiday? Have any of these sorts of activities ever crossed your minds? You must have what, fifty bedrooms here at your disposal not including your own floors?"

He sat back, looked across at his wife and said, "Hannah, would you like to take this one please?"

She replied, "Of course I will. This is the sort of thing I have said many times but we both felt that Sarah would be against this sort of activity in such a place as this. Clearly there would need to be some pretty firm guidelines agreed if one were to undertake such a radical change from working farms to part holiday resort. However, I certainly think it would be possible and also stimulating and interesting as well as becoming profitable in just a year or two. But we don't have the capital for that sort of project and would need finance from Sarah or whoever."

Bertie said, "Yes well put Hannah, but also to answer you earlier questions: yes we hold pheasant shoots, yes we have a river which holds game and coarse fishing and yes we could make a suitable part of the castle into a separate hotel-type accommodation block with its own dining room, games room and even an indoor pool and gym I would say. And I agree that certain tourists would enjoy a tour of the farms to see the where and how we get all our meat, fruit and vegetables from."

"Right," I said, "let me tell you that Sarah and I are currently looking at doing something similar in Scotland but involving possibly a golf course, and the rebuilding and operation of the still which once made fine malt whisky, in addition to hunting, shooting, and fishing activities, and they have a smaller castle than this. But this is all at the early planning stage so not a murmur please. We are also considering another larger project at the English estate, and Sarah is very interested what I might find here to mirror or supplement what we have already discussed with Robert, and I am now discussing with you, and it seems you both might be interested, doesn't it?" They were both amazed and clearly excited to hear this and leaned forwards in their seats to hear more.

I outlined all the different ideas which Sarah and I had previously discussed and got lots of nods and exclamations of surprise and interest in every aspect I mentioned from Hannah and Bertie, so I knew that they would be 100% behind almost anything I suggested, subject of course to all the same parameters discussed by Sarah and me. So, I said that what I would like to do was a complete tour of everything and talk to the tenants and the key staff and make some notes and see any archived documents or deeds held at the castle, and they confirmed that they had an old library as well, and the general office was also put at my disposal. It seemed that the castle was such a large building, having been extended and modified several times over many years and the more up to date parts could relatively more easily be segregated into suites of rooms and lend themselves generally to adaptation as hotel type accommodation. Some in fact had been out of use for more than a generation but kept maintained. Similarly, there were numerous houses and buildings within the castle walls which were under used or completely empty, but all had been maintained and equipped with electricity and water and the houses in particular I thought would make excellent family or group accommodation.

Over the next two days, I toured the whole estate and met the tenants, some of whom were a little nervous at my interest but relaxed once they realised that any changes would be for the better for all concerned, with more revenues to the family possibly making their rents and tithes stable at least. Plus, there was going to be the possibility of members of the tenants' families obtaining gainful employment with better wages without having to travel many miles to occupations in the towns or Dublin. I saw no immediate need to attempt to get any of the farmhouses involved for guest accommodation as there was more than enough scope at the castle, and they were generally content with the idea of guided tours of their operations providing they were properly managed, never carried out unaccompanied and always by appointment. Each farm had direct telephone link to the castle so this could be easily sorted out.

The farms were all well-kept and prosperous looking, as Sarah had always made it clear that funds were available for maintaining the standard of the houses and outbuildings where justified. The families had been tenants for generations and it was very likely to be the case that this state of affairs was going to continue into the foreseeable future.

I looked at the shooting area, both the hides and driving facility for the pheasants and the clay-shooting traps as well as the stretch of river with its several streams feeding it, and it was clear there was plenty of scope to develop both activates to accommodate the sorts of numbers of participants anticipated. This whole estate was quite remote so would tend to attract people seeking the countryside and activities commensurate with isolation, although there was an attractive old pub I learnt in the village immediately beyond the estate borders which would make nice alternative evening walks and a meal, surrounded only by village locals in the main. In short, the rural idyll.

I calculated with Bertie and Hannah that there ought to be sufficient space for about twenty-five rooms, including some suites, plus four cottages with at least two or three bedrooms each within the castle walls. There could be a maximum probably of about eighty beds but comfortably fifty. So I floated the idea that conferences for up to sixty people could be considered, as there were several large rooms in the castle which would accommodate such a number for their meetings. Furthermore, it could prove a very attractive venue for a medium-sized company taking its staff there for a conference break treat, as well as catering for more general conferences where participants would be able to take part in the other activities as well, if desired. My guess was that the managing director and other senior people at such companies would be very attracted by the shooting and fishing facilities.

Organic farming had been taken up to a degree and I decided to let them sort that out themselves, just give them a spreadsheet of the economics involved in the English estate, but I was unsure of the potential take up of the produce in Ireland even though high quality organic produce was already shipped from Ireland to the bigger supermarket chains in the UK as a whole. My feeling was once they saw the potential yields and the much healthier state of the soil resulting from organic manure and no inorganic spraying, and the prices achieved for organic meat from organic home-produced feedstuff, it would attract those not yet growing organically to reconsider their position.

I felt I had enough after three days and nights there to make a suitable outline plan for further examination and expert appraisal — alongside the English and Scottish plans — for an overall strategic plan to be formulated so that no unnecessary duplication of effort, planning time and materials purchasing took place. I had discovered enough to enable the experts to look at the big picture regarding in particular whether or not the existing legal framework was tax efficient in the context of one or more Limited Companies being formed and looking at possible Tax Domicile in Ireland and other tax issues relating to the trust which I understood was English-law based. Also, to Sarah's personal fortune as opposed to that part merely where she acted as a guardian of the trust properties and capital reserves. I considered an integrated team of experts ought to be possible to deal with all the legal, accountancy and taxation issues as a whole. It might be expensive, but I believed would pay handsomely over time.

I said a grateful goodbye to Bertie and family and to the staff with whom I had become acquainted, promising to keep in touch and return at the soonest opportunity, and off I went with Sean to the airport to catch the afternoon Dublin to Manchester flight and then straight back to Sarah's house to give my reports. I had already talked this through with Heather and Sarah and it was agreed that this was the best plan, then I would come home once Michael and Sarah had been suitably briefed and all relevant matters discussed and with an outline plan drafted for me to work on the main phase 1 proposal for our teams.

Chapter 32

I arrived in my car, which I picked up at Manchester Airport, at Michael and Sarah's house at four p.m. and was met by Sarah at the door alone. Michael would not be home until dinner if then, as he had been attending a lunch in town which might go on a bit, so we had three hours at least before he arrived.

"So," Sarah said, "come upstairs and debrief me!"

"My pleasure," I replied.

So, an extra warm welcome from Sarah to cement our ongoing relationship before Michael came home, what could I do? Oblige of course.

Then we sat in the conservatory, and I gave her a brief rundown on what I had found in Ireland, how surprised I was at the size and scope of the castle and the surrounding acreage, and told how Bertie and Hannah were all for it, including, if she agreed, converting parts of the castle, and using at least four of the old cottages within the castle walls and having holidaymakers as well as conferences, etc. I also said about the shooting, fishing and organic foods and meat production, and the advisability that a team of professionals including lawyers, accountants and tax specialists were employed to examine all three estates and give opinion on formation of one or more limited companies and an appraisal of the advantages of Irish domiciliary.

"Summing up," I said, "my immediate thoughts are that taken together, the utilisation of the three estates in a similar pattern of commercial activity, possibly with integrated accounting and taxation, should be a passport to a more prosperous and certain future for them all including your tenants. It will also secure the main interests of the trust, as well as substantially enhancing your own personal fortune."

"As I have already said James, you are a persuasive bugger and I admire your grasp of this whole project even though not an acknowledged expert and I have faith that you are substantially right. But of course, we shall have to take all the advice we need and not rush into this without careful appraisal and planning. But we know that both the trust and I have more than sufficient capital to cover this expansion of our activities, and I would of course make my personal contribution commensurate with my potential share of the additional profits in the same sort of ratios as are employed already on our existing businesses. And I think we are long overdue for this study, but maybe we were just waiting for the right man to come along. I can tell you now that I have had people look at this before, but no one has been half as imaginative or thorough as you, and you are only mapping the way as yet, so I anticipate some serious plans to emanate from your teams and then we shall engage our experts and take it from there. And the personal benefit has already been felt by me I can tell you and I want to say a big thank you for all you have done so far, and as yet have received not a penny."

"Please don't worry about that. Heather and I are not as rich as you, but we are not poor either, so I am happy to wait until I get the go-ahead for the Phase 1 detailed survey and plan to start at an agreed fee from our group, and then I will add my invoice from Heather and my company for time and expenses to date and I warn you that it will be quite a large invoice!"

"Have no fear, it will be paid. And I am sure, short of an unseen and hardly credible adverse report from the expert team of lawyers, etc. who we shall engage, your Phase 1 will be accepted. After that, Phase 2 with more detailed and costed plans, drawings, etc. will follow and that too will also be accepted, subject to whatever modifications prove necessary. That budget too will be provided, and then we will be into choosing subcontract companies for the building and outfitting stages. I find the whole project exciting and stimulating and cannot wait to see it all happen. I just hope your personal interest in what must be your biggest commission yet continues to the finish line and beyond."

"Me too," I said, "it will take a few years to get all the wrinkles ironed out and all the three estates functioning fully and becoming more profitable, and I would not desert you part way through. In fact, I probably will have to have frequent return visits to make sure the wheels and gears are oiled, so to speak!"

"Ah I think I hear Michael arriving just in time for dinner. Just give him the barest of bones please; he will be tired, and he knows already the essence of your plans and I have his complete support. So just enough to show respect and allay any suspicions, although I am certain there will be none, he doesn't know me in that way at all."

"Ah Michael darling, so glad you made it for dinner, James and I have gone over all the essential stuff, and you must be tired. Why don't you freshen up and then come and sit down with us and have a little drink and meantime I will ensure dinner is ready in about half an hour."

"Oh, perfect my sweet; I am a little tired, these business lunches are so boring but very tiring I find. James, so good to see you, I will pop upstairs and be right down and we can have a little chat. So long as it's not too complicated, I will be fine."

She winked at me as she followed him out of the room and I relaxed over my glass of beer and thought, *James, you are a lucky man, but you deserve it.*

So, it seemed that Michael was another of these men who were not too bothered about sex, more of a duty than a pleasure perhaps, and he had no idea what a very sexy wife he had and wouldn't know what to do if he did. Probably brought up to make a good match which he certainly had. I understood he too had a reasonable fortune himself, which he inherited from his parents, but at the time of his wedding he probably just had a salaried job, awaiting his inheritance, so marrying Sarah was his big day; he was a very nice man and suited her perfectly in many ways so good luck to him.

Michael came down first and sighed as he dropped into a deep armchair and ordered a whisky and soda from the maid and I asked for another of his special pale ales.

Michael smiled and said, "Ah you have found my secret store I see; I hope you enjoy it."

I then gave him a potted version of my travels and findings together with a brief outline plan of my recommendations and he nodded sagely and said, "Sounds just the ticket and I am sure we will progress along the lines you suggest as Sarah has already briefed me on most of it and is clearly quite excited by the whole plan. So am I, and I will look forward to your Phase 1 proposal regarding the more in-depth study by your teams. In particular I am very pleased you have already recommended re-building the old still in Scotland and looking into a new golf course there amongst other projects. Robert is very excited too at the ideas you have brought forward and looks to the future when he will have a sizeable operation to manage, and this will be very good experience for him."

At this point Sarah returned having changed her dress, but we stayed in our business suits and when I murmured about changing, she said not to be silly it was only the three of us and we should dress how we like. We had a very nice dinner together and only referred to one or two of the more interesting parts of my report. Ireland was of greater interest than the other two estates and they both listened to my rehearsing the bones of the plan while they made occasional sounds of approval and interest.

Then Sarah closed that part of our conversation saying, "Well Michael and I have been very pleased with your excellent work so far James and I have told him that I am sure you and I will back all his proposals, subject of course to appropriate special advisers' opinions. We are both interested in particular with the possibilities regarding forming a new company or a group of three companies to handle the trust properties and our personal income stemming from them, with a view perhaps to embracing Irish domiciliary or whatever is needed in order to benefit from the lower company and personal tax rates available there."

"Yes, absolutely; my thoughts too, darling," said Michael, and that was the end of business and the start of a friendly conversation about family, Michael's visit to Scotland and matters general.

Sarah saw me off with a discreet kiss as I donned my cloak, picked up my bags and departed in my car for home immediately after an early breakfast where Michael had not joined us. I wondered if his absence for a week or more, plus the stimulation of my company, had produced a rare conjugal visit to Sarah's room. Good job I had not called by to say goodnight but gone straight to my quarters last night if so, I thought.

All was well at the home camp, and I was glad to settle back in and catch up with family news as well as tell Heather all about my travels and update her about Sarah and Michael's responses to my outline phase 1 proposals, and that we seemed to be on track for a major project involving not just the group companies but all three estates as well, easily the largest project we had ever tackled. Heather said, "You must have sweet-talked Sarah successfully then?" and without blinking an eye I replied, "Certainly did; took you at your word and pulled out all the stops and she called me a persuasive bugger!"

She laughed and said, "Don't I know it, but I hope you didn't get too carried away and overstep the mark. I didn't get the impression she was really into your sort of special attention."

"Of course not, just far enough to keep her interested. She is a very astute woman and quite attractive in her own way, but I think she and Michael have a very close understanding of each other and he seemed happy with everything."

Heather replied, "Yes I agree, so you must keep it up and stay sweet with her and him to ensure we get the job done properly and reap our just rewards."

"Don't worry I will," I said. "I shall be seeing quite a lot of them both I'm sure over the next several months and I expect you will accompany me a couple of times as well."

"We shall have to see; I'm not sure I want to watch you at your work on her, might just make me jealous."

"Ha-ha," I said, "you, jealous? That will be the day, but you certainly have a lot on your plate managing things in my absence and entertaining my mother and the children when they come."

I pulled all my plans and papers together and made a draft of the Phase 1 Proposal and then I called in our two nominated teams to run through all that had happened and give them the verbal update. Then I sent my draft plan to them in advance so that they could arrive well briefed with some additional material of their own perhaps to suggest and incorporate. I asked Heather if she could attend this first meeting as I not only wanted her insight and opinions but her impressions of each member of the team, their attitude, aptitude, and ability as well as their individual levels of commitment and contributions. We both knew most of them very well already but there were a few who were fairly lately nominated, and we needed to see how they performed and fit in generally, especially with our nominated two leaders.

In the meantime, I managed to have a couple of days with Ronja, having not seen her for weeks. She was the same as always of course, happy to see me as I was her and wasn't too bothered about where I had been and what I had done, and not a whisper about Sarah or Heather. She was always very good in that respect, and I reciprocated by not enquiring too deeply into her affairs, only in a general way. She always updated me on her latest affairs anyway, just to show that I was still *numero uno* with her and on occasion she would accept a personal phone call from some man and talk very sweetly to him, but not the same way she spoke privately with me. And she had cured me of any remnants of jealousy I might have had way back as I had of hers, if she ever had any! She did say to me one day that she might want to marry again, not me, just somebody and I would joke, "Oh yes, that will be the day! I hope the poor bloke knows what he is in for."

It was like seeing my long-lost wife and friend when we met. We were totally comfortable with each other and quite happy just walking holding hands and looking at each other occasionally with that special smile which only lovers have. Sex with each other was still very good, but it was no longer the mainspring of our relationship; we both knew that the chances of us ever being together permanently were very slim and we just made the best of what we had. She mentioned a man whom she liked quite a lot and who would be very good for her, but I didn't bite and she dropped the subject, simply saying that she would never marry someone unless I gave her my blessing, which would be effectively goodbye.

I said, "I could never do that I don't think unless I was certain he really loved you and you would be happy. Even if it was goodbye I would still try to remain in touch."

She said, "Well it seems I am doomed to be your mistress for the rest of my life then."

I said, "I would let you go tomorrow if I were sure that was what you really wanted; I love you enough to do that."

The subject was dropped but I knew one day it would come up again.

The meeting with the two teams came up and we all met at our group boardroom. We had prepared some graphics on charts and bundles of papers relating to each of the target group's companies; and a separate set for the three estates and a copy of the draft Phase 1 plan I had prepared, which almost everyone had annotated in various colours and made notes, comments, and suggestions to various parts.

I chaired the meeting and Heather sat on my right and my PA on my left to record everything and pass me notes if and when required.

Then I said, "Have the two team leaders prepared opening statements because if so, I would like all to hear them please?"

So it went, the team leader A, called appropriately Adam, started, and read out his prepared statement, basically praising what I had achieved so far and agreeing with most of it, but had a few suggestions which, he said, he would call on the person who made them to speak about later, with my permission, etc. Adam was the most senior person present apart from Heather and me and already had the respect due to him as a veteran of almost all the projects we had run from the very start. What his part included was the Irish estate and seven of the fifteen companies forming the client group. Team leader B was a woman called Thelma; again, a veteran of our group who had a formidable reputation as a powerful woman, a good brain and very determined. She had been allocated the English and Scottish estates and the remaining eight client group companies which I had grouped based on activity rather than geography or size. I had split the estates up so that we could have perhaps slightly different mindsets and plans emanating from two separate teams.

What followed was a detailed analysis of the tasks in hand, lists of target areas to concentrate on and suggested solutions to each reform mooted and considered. However, all of these were speculative to a large degree and would just form the backbone of the ultimate Phase 1 report and the proposal which would then feed into Phase 2, the actual formal proposal for action, with a costing analysis, implementation programme and some target dates for completion. We had no means of knowing at this point which parts of Phase 1 would survive scrutiny by the client group's top executive and board, although I had a pretty shrewd idea that would be almost all we suggested, providing any of their experts didn't shoot something down. We certainly could have no idea ourselves what the estates trust, Irish domicile or tax status might be, or what form a company or companies for the three estates might take. That aside, I was pretty confident that the client group companies would all get substantial reforms under our plan approved. What I did not want to disclose was that the funding for all this work was already there waiting to be used!

We spent almost a whole day, breaking for lunch, and having discovered a few pretty impressive suggestions and thrown out a couple which I had jotted down as potential only on my travels. At the close of play, we had the bones of a pretty comprehensive Phase 1 plan which, when checked, tidied up and put on large sheets of drawing paper, would, I thought really impress the audience when the disclosure and presentation took place. First, of course, I would present the whole plan to Michael and Sarah in file form and seek their initial approval, then they would organise a meeting of key players from all the client group companies.

I had decided to recommend a separate exercise altogether for the estates, and only bring the two plans together after taking expert advice regarding the formation of a company or companies and about the Irish tax position, should it then seem both necessary and feasible. Even then, Sarah may well decide to keep all the estates' business and reform plans totally private from the rest, so only my teams would be fully aware, and the advisors of course.

Heather was very good throughout the meeting only interjecting to make a valid comment or point, and none of the less well-known protagonists in the teams let the side down so I was well content with things all round. Heather complimented me privately and remarked how far I had come along this particular trail in general and she commented that I had matured and grown in my current role. She had not really witnessed it happening first-hand so she could see a marked improvement and suggested I no longer really needed her as much as before.

"Nonsense!" I proclaimed, but she insisted and said it had decided her that she would step down from her directorships and involvement in everything except where circumstances showed a definite need.

She would soon be sixty and felt she had done just about everything she could to help me on my way and she was very proud of her and my achievements and had now earned her retirement. But she added that she had a few ideas about local activities in our village. Mother was getting pretty infirm now so needed almost daily visits, and it looked like the children were becoming involved with partners so she might have to do a bit more travelling to see them.

I privately agreed that she had done more than enough over the years since we met and that she should now scale back and enjoy the fruits of her labour whereas I, at barely fifty, had plenty of steam left in my boiler and was enjoying this latest project enormously and yes, I felt that although I would always seek Heather's opinion from time to time, it was rare now that she had to interject on my behalf. But I protested a bit and said that I would miss her presence at these big meetings and so on, but she knew that this was only nice talk, and I was more than capable of holding my own with most people and situations.

I sent the draft plan for Michael and Sarah to look at for a few days and provided additional information on a couple of points and then they said they were ready to meet me and discuss it, just us at this stage, no need to look for the experts' advice until we had agreed the Phase 1 plan. Even then, we would need to meet alone again to look at the plan's results, a more detailed, and costed plan which would be the template for the actual implementation plan in Phase 2, subject to any important modifications which might arise from the experts' appraisals.

They told me that they had considered inviting either Heather or Ronja to stay at that time, but I told them that Heather had practically retired although would be available if really needed, and that I didn't think it the right time to invite Ronja although I made it clear that was entirely at their discretion. Sarah agreed that I was right on both counts and thanked Heather by letter for all she had done. Sarah made it clear Heather would always be welcome and wished her all the best in her retirement.

I travelled to their house on a Thursday to allow a full day's scrutiny and discussion if required, and also to allow for them and me to have a day at least of relaxation in each other's company into the weekend. I had the finished portfolio and charts with me, plus some extra notes I had made with the help of Heather and my PA, and considered I was as ready as I was ever going to be. However, I knew this was the make-or-break meeting where once the green light had been given, short of a catastrophe, I knew it would be the real start of the whole project. Funds would be earmarked; invoices would begin to be issued and resources allocated. I did not think that Michael would have the clout to make any radical alterations and I was pretty confident Sarah was fully committed, but you are never sure of such things until the final hurdles are ready to be crossed and the large sums of money needed for the whole project are about to be committed.

So yes, with a little trepidation but really pretty confidently, I approached their house at about noon on the Thursday and parked up my Range Rover, which I had filled with extra tackle, clothing, guns, the lot, just in case, as well as all the paraphernalia relating to the project. I wanted them to feel I was confident and capable, but not too big-headed about this, and at the same time I was prepared for a successful end to this phase and had brought my gear in anticipation of this success and enjoying a relaxed friendly time together with my hosts.

I managed to kiss Sarah circumspectly on the cheek and shook hands with Michael when we met at the door. They ensured that all my gear was transported inside, noting of course as I intended, the inclusion of guns, etc.

Michael said, "Oh good, glad you have brought your guns; we can go after a bit of natural game perhaps, as well as a spot of fishing, but no snooker!"

I smiled and said, "Hope I am not seen as a bit presumptuous, but I thought whatever happens we shall still be friends, so why not?"

"Don't even think about that, we shall agree all that matters at this point, so I see no need for any pessimism at all," said Sarah.

"Oh, dear me no!" said Michael.

I smiled modestly, and I said, "I did rather hope so."

And she looked coyly at me as if to say, *you persuasive bugger, you know the position already, don't you?*

And in reality, I did. She was not the sort of person to commit herself as she had, body and soul as it were, unless she had been pretty sure of a successful outcome, but it was nice to have that confirmation more or less at the arrival door, than have to wait until perhaps tomorrow night. So in we went and after a quick freshen up, as I already knew we would be just the three of us for lunch, I came down to lunch in the family dining room. As usual I was greeted with a splendid display of hot and cold dishes. As well as a bottle of my favourite IPA, they had prepared two different table wines and a bottle of Champagne sat in the cooler alongside Michael's chair.

Beautiful home-grown organic salad, cold roast pheasant and partridge, home farm pork pie, venison stew with turnips, onions and potatoes and a hot leg of lamb to carve from. Then there was an assortment of vegetables followed by fresh pineapple and other hothouse fruit and a home-made fruit trifle with fresh farm cream. Delicious and I said so several times.

Then Michael said, "James, I think you know that your Phase 1 plan is tremendous in scope, vision and detail and we will authorise it tomorrow after our formal examination and discussion. Your budget for Phase 1 seems reasonable, and the time scale proposals, and Sarah will tell you what she thinks about the estates. But as far as the group companies go, I am a hundred percent happy with your proposals for the in-depth Phase 1 plan to be implemented in full. We can, after all, look at any modifications which may suggest themselves later, but for now, for me it's a good plan, it's doable and within our budget, and I can't wait for it to start."

Sarah smiled at Michael's enthusiasm and added, "I too support all the plan including the estate plan, which I totally agree must be kept separate, certainly at this stage. We shall see what advice we get regarding the ultimate shape of trust property and what funding looks like in Phase 2, assuming we get that far, which I am totally confident we will. Of course, we have a few questions for tomorrow, but none of these will alter the outcome, and acceptance of your wonderful plan for the full Phase 1 exercise, and then, to the much more important Phase 2 proposals, including building and construction estimates, and the like. But I think now is the time to have a toast to our success and acceptance of the Phase 1 plan and the effective starting gun, so Michael, please open the Champagne."

Michael opened the bottle and poured three flutes and we beamed at each other and said, "Success!" and sipped the very fine Krug Champagne. This was the first time I had tasted it that I could remember, and it was really good. I said so and wondered if this was a special vintage or anything.

Sarah smiled and said, "Rather special yes, but cost is not important on this very special occasion; enjoy it while you can, you may not get another quite like it."

"Crikey" I said, "as much as that, I am honoured."

"No," said Sarah, "*we* are honoured to have such a competent and interesting friend dealing with all this, so this is a measure of our appreciation."

I sipped more and we each had a second glass savouring the aroma and flavour and I have to say, it was very, very good; easily the best Champagne I have ever had.

Michael turned the bottle upside down in the bucket and said, "I have looked forward to that particular bottle for a long time; it was worth the wait and on a very suitable occasion. Thank goodness we are only three, two glasses each!"

So ensued a very satisfying long weekend, starting with a few hours on Friday going over the plan again and me answering the questions they had prepared. However, Sarah did come up with a potential change in part of my plan, that of the constituent members of the teams, in so far as that was affected by splitting the trust properties up for scrutiny and suggestions. She rightly pointed out that as they were to be treated separately from the group companies, both at the planning and the implementation stages, and certainly for accounting, legal and finance perspectives, ought they not have their own dedicated small team, perhaps led by me.

I explained my original thoughts about splitting them up for the Phase 1 part of the project, but I did acknowledge that it might be simpler and more prudent to keep them separate from the start. "But tell me," I said, "the trust, is it UK-based or is it offshore and following on from that, is it in fact a UK trust in legal terms or another jurisdiction's law such as Jersey or Switzerland?"

She replied, "It is based in Switzerland under Swiss law which as I understand it, facilitates my and the trust's cash holdings there and other places offshore all quite legally."

"Ah," I said. "That explains a lot. So the question arises, would it still be tax efficient for the estates all to be based in Ireland in whatever legal form is appropriate, limited company or whatever, because the income from the English and Scottish estates will, I assume, certainly be taxed on their UK profits? I am not sure what Ireland's tax position is at present regarding the Irish estate."

Sarah said, "I will need to check on all that as it gets confusing sometimes."

I continued, "So, if the estates are owned and controlled by the trust and you are as it were their principal trustee and guardian, I assume that even though the trust is Swiss, nevertheless it is currently taxed on UK income generated in the UK?"

"Absolutely correct, all three estates' net income is presently taxed in the UK, after my income guaranteed by the trust is paid and that income goes ultimately to my offshore accounts because, as I understand it, it is earned from the trust so to speak. And that money would only become taxable in the UK if I brought some of it here, on shore, as it were. But so long as my money deposited abroad is only used abroad there is no UK tax problem. So I need to find out exactly what the current taxation set-up is for both the trust's net income, and my income from the trust properties. Then I need to ask the question: would both the trust and I be better served if we can make all three trust properties into a separate legal entity, still supervised by the trust and still run effectively by me through my managers at each estate, into an Irish entity, and therefore achieve greater profitability through reduction in current tax levels, sufficient to pay for the exercise? Or is there another alternative where perhaps two of the estates are out so to speak and one in?"

"Yes," I said, "that's about the strength of it and with my limited knowledge of taxation in these circumstances. We had better get some more specific tax advice before rather than after Phase 1 is completed don't you think?"

"Agreed," they both said.

I said, "So back to your suggested line of approach of the teams to the estates, I am inclined to agree that it might be best for me to pick two of my best people one from each of the existing teams and realign their tasks pretty quickly. I am sure there will not be a problem so I will call the team leaders and tell them which one I want from both their teams and why, and then I will hold a meeting with them before we set off to whichever estate we do first. I am inclined to do Scotland again first, Ireland second and you third, or do you have a preference?"

Sarah said, "Yes, please may I have you first James? Then I will have something to discuss with our taxation and legal people at an early stage so as not to delay matters by waiting for all the other reports coming in."

"Very well," I said, "so be it. If that suits Michael as well, I will then move on to Scotland and do Ireland, the biggest of the three last, is that OK with you both?"

Michael nodded and Sarah said, "Perfect, I shall have information regarding Irish law and taxation by then so I may come over and join you for a day or two at that point."

We decided to wind up the meeting then and have lunch, then look at some other activity afterwards, assuming we had no Krug to deal with!

Michael and I donned our gear after lunch and went with the stable master and his dogs to see if we could start something up in the woods for us to have a bit of sport shooting some game or rabbits. We started in one of the long-wheelbase Land Rovers with the dogs in a trailer attached and parked up at the end of a track about a hundred yards from the first copse to the one side and the river. On the other side our man with the dogs took a curved path to one end of the copse, and signalled the direction he would be beating, having already said, "Don't hit any of my dogs, shoot a little high and not towards my half of the copse please."

In no time at all it seemed, a covey of partridges set off with their typical whirring sound of rapidly beating wings and headed towards the woods on the far side of the river as we had expected. We got five or six between us and let the rest escape. The dogs came out at a signal, picked up our prey and took them to their master, then re-entered the copse. In another few minutes, four or five pheasant took off, also heading for the relative safety over the river and we had just bagged three of these when a couple of rabbits sped out and across our path, but we shot neither, as they were just too quick.

Into the copse we went quietly with the dogs under close control and our man spotted half a dozen wood pigeons wreaking havoc with the young tender green leaves on the trees. We sidled up and took positions and then both fired two barrels each, bringing down four plump birds.

"Enough," I said, "that should provide some decent meals I think without killing off too many."

"Don't worry about that," said the gamekeeper, "we are well overstocked on all these birds and no plans for an organised shoot for some time when the young birds are big enough to release. And the pigeons are a pest generally, so we like to keep their numbers under control."

"OK," I said, "have we time for a little fishing or shall we leave that until tomorrow morning?"

Michael said, "That's enough for me; I am going to have a nap before dinner, so the rest of the afternoon is yours. But I am game for some trout fishing after breakfast tomorrow if you are." So, I agreed and accompanied him with our game back to the house where Sarah was just having afternoon tea. She invited us to join her, but Michael pleaded tiredness and went off for his nap, but I obliged and had a nice pot of Earl Grey and some home-made scones with strawberry preserve and cream with her.

Sarah then said, "Let's have a sauna and a swim, shall we?" And off we went to the pool suite and after a quick refreshing swim went into the massage room and locked the door and I proceeded to show Sarah how much I had missed her and she likewise. Very nice, and she assured me we would not see Michael down here as he would stay in his rooms and shower and change for dinner tonight as they had a couple of guests coming. After another pleasant half-hour's lovemaking, I went first and made sure the way was clear and then off to my room and I presume Sarah successfully navigated herself to hers. I had a short nap too then another shower and prepared for dinner wearing my tuxedo and black bow tie and wandered down towards the main dining hall about seven-thirty. I met Michael just heading the same way and we said we'd both had a nice nap. He invited me to his niche in the library, me for a beer and he a whisky and soda from his little bar there until the dinner bell sounded and we arrived at the dining hall just as Sarah and the guests arrived from the direction of the front door. I had met them all before, and hello's and how are you's, were exchanged as we took our seats; me as usual next to Sarah and Michael the other side with three guests sitting facing us.

The guests all knew why I was there and roughly what I had been working on, so it was OK for a little premature update, just to make the party a small celebration without giving too much away. Sarah said, "I just want you dear friends to know that we have reached agreement with

James on the first phase of a project to update our business systems and methods for our group companies. Also, quite separately, he is to look at doing something similar with this estate and the other two estates in Scotland and Ireland which we can't discuss further at this point but, if successful, I am confident they will bring some significant beneficial changes to the three estates, most of which we think you will like and find interesting. Most importantly they will not adversely affect our activities like entertaining our friends and there will be no actual changes to this house in the foreseeable future. Look on it as updating and improving but without spoiling anything and ultimately benefitting the future existence and sustainability of our family estates well into the years to come. So, a toast please to the project and congratulations to James and his team on their achievements so far. We wish him further success in the future phases of this quite large and important project. I give you James!"

Congratulations followed from all present and glasses were raised several times, and someone said, "Speech, speech!"

I reluctantly stood and smiled at everybody and said, "What can I say? I feel very privileged to be standing here like this at the beginning of what, as Sarah put it, is quite a large project, and I look forward to fulfilling all her and Michael's wishes in that regard. I hope to see you all here not just as things happen, but also when they reach completion, and that you are happy with what you find here then. Thanks to Sarah and Michael, I am on the brink of achieving a landmark project of some real significance, and I hope and pray that I live up to our hosts' expectations."

And I sat down to applause.

After yet another wonderful meal followed by liqueurs and brandy and coffee or tea, the guests departed in a chauffeur-driven car as they all had things to do on the following day. We, after a final nightcap retired to our individual rooms. I settled into my very comfortable bed and lay awake a while going over the day's events and was very satisfied from all points of view. I had decided not to tell Heather yet as it was still only an informal agreement, and we might have a few more points arising during the weekend after a good night's sleep.

The following morning was Saturday and Michael and I breakfasted alone quite early. We then took ourselves down to the favourite spot on the river where it had a considerable bow in it which threw up cross currents and attracted the fish to the plethora of insects and grubs there. It was still cool and fresh with just a few waterbirds around and we donned our waders and took up our fly rods, already having tied our fly selection and put on the spare kit round our waists. We waded slowly out to about one third of the way across the river where the gently shelving smooth gravelled river bed quite suddenly gets deeper, and began our casts standing about twenty yards apart to give adequate space for casting and playing any fish when caught, and not to disturb each other's prospective prey.

Michael had the first success and caught a nice brown trout of about 2 lbs in weight and put it in his holding net attached to his belt. Then after a few more casts, I hit a big rainbow trout, my first rainbow, and he gave me quite a fight.

Michael was saying, "Keep the line tight, no slack," which I knew anyway from previously using barbless hooks when introducing my then girlfriend to fishing. You will recall that she was into nature conservation and a barbless hook will jump out of the fish's mouth if given slack line. I managed to get the trout with my fingers at the back of his gills and transfer him to my holding net which he almost filled! We later weighed him in at 6lb 4 oz, a real whopper.

Michael later explained that they had bought the stock of a fish farm which went out of business a couple of years ago and that included some rainbow as well as brown trout already of a good size then. I asked him how many they had put in the river and he didn't know the number but it was in the hundreds. They appeared to like this river and Michael had fish pellets made from anchovies thrown in about once a week to keep them fit and more importantly to encourage them to stay in that location. They still took insects and all sorts of grubs like caddisfly larvae, beetles and earthworms so had an excellent diet and organic too, and that told in the taste.

I said, "I wonder if we could fence in a section of river in some way so that we could maybe have an organic trout farm as part of the development, as well as provide good sport for participants, by increasing the stock and feeding more anchovy pellets."

He said that we would need some breeding and holding tanks to keep up the level of stock, but they could be situated in a wooden rustic building near the river which might double as a boat house. The tanks in there could be filled with a supply of fresh river water diverted through it. In addition, we could create proper fishing 'pegs' made from cedar poles and boards and set into the riverbank at different levels to accommodate anglers of all types, regardless of the water level.

"Good idea," I said, "I will make some notes on that and incorporate it into my plan. And while we are on the subject, large carp are the favourite sport of some anglers, and if we could get a few very big ones, and keep them also confined to a stretch of the river, they would become a national attraction. It might mean making facilities at several levels to accommodate rises and falls in the river, and there would have to be 'ladders' constructed to allow spawning salmon upstream if you get any."

"We do," said Michael, "I have landed a few, but we keep that quiet. If we had 'ladders' and a strict return to the river policy, I think that would satisfy the River Board and the angling people as well as any other protection body."

"This is why these visits are so important," I said. "We must look again at any other possible activities which could be introduced which we might not yet have fully considered."

We returned to the house in time for morning coffee with Sarah and excitedly unveiled our catch and told her of the suggestions emanating from our conversation about the rainbow trout being from a fish farm. She was delighted and said, "If it can be done and the cost to benefit numbers work, I'm all for it."

Michael couldn't resist trying his arm at snooker or billiards, despite the thrashing I had previously given him so as Sarah had other things to see to, not least the cooking of the trout for lunch. We went to his games room and he thought if I gave him 4 blacks at Snooker that would be fair, but he didn't want to double up on the 1,600 he had to pay me after the last rush of blood to his head, saying, "How about a modest 50 pounds wager?" So, I smiled and accepted, moved his marker to 28 points and we tossed a coin which I called correctly and chose to break.

I broke with the white ball safely near the baulk cushion and Michael was in trouble immediately breaking the pack of reds and leaving the white ball nicely positioned over a red into the side pocket. And so, it went on, I made a 40 break, wiping out his 28 x 4 black allowances and he never recovered from there. I took his 50 pounds and he said, "Enough! I told myself you were just lucky, but in fact you are really a very good player. Let's just have a quiet beer in the library and then go up to lunch."

We sat in his corner of the library where he had his office and opened a couple of beers from a fridge he kept there. We chatted about the proposed fish farm idea and the development of the protected area of the river, the salmon ladder and how we might have a small clubhouse in the same materials as the trout farm so that the anglers could get together after a successful day on the river and tell their fishy yarns before going back to the main accommodation at either the motel/hotel or wherever they had opted to stay on their trip. It could be that once the local fishermen knew of our planned facility, they would be keen to bring their club members and use our clubhouse as well. Day trips could also be catered for with a separate car park hidden amongst the willow brakes not far upstream from the site of the trout farm and fishing zone. I drew a small representative plan of our ideas for incorporating in something larger and more detailed which would take its guidance from the Ordnance Survey maps. Of course, experts in this type of project which might change the course of a river have to be consulted and inspections made by the appropriate authorities, but we were both confident that the changes proposed could be accommodated with only a relatively small effect on the river as a whole.

Meanwhile I made a note about researching the law regarding licences for trout, salmon, and coarse fishing, looking at the possibilities for one-day, seven-day and annual licences and cost, in England, Scotland and Ireland. And also look at regulations concerning setting up trout farming, breeding and egg and smelt production and sales.

We heard the warning bell that lunch was coming shortly so we finished our beers and went to the family dining room where the large rainbow trout sat centre table, cooked, and prepared on a large platter with herbs and shallots surrounding it, and it looked and smelt beautiful. Sarah covered it with a large heatproof lid, and we had our starters which again were fish orientated and included the crayfish and mussels similar to those I had in Ireland, and were also from a local stream which fed into the river. Then with vessels of steaming vegetables or salad we were served the trout and it lived up to expectations, melting in the mouth with that delicate flavour trout have, enhanced by the fact it had been swimming about that very morning. You cannot get much fresher or cleaner than that. I had a sudden thought and said, "These freshwater mussels, they are quite large; have your staff ever reported finding pearls in them, or are there any local stories?"

"Well, strangely yes, I remember an ancestor of mine collecting freshwater mussel pearls in the 18th century I believe. All from our river and streams here and in Scotland, not sure about Ireland. But I have never myself seen one although I have never really looked for them."

I said that I had certainly seen a TV programme about collecting freshwater mussel pearls in Scottish streams where a local hardy Scot made a sort of living searching for open mussels by peering at them through a glass-bottomed bucket and only taking those where he spotted a pearl.

"Just a thought for any angle that could attract visitors," I said. "And following on from that, these crayfish; I presume they are also taken from your streams and if so, how many are there? Do they breed naturally; what is the potential for farming or just gathering them for use in our restaurant, or could this be expanded to selling them to other gourmet restaurants, upmarket delis... whatever?"

"You never cease to amaze me with your ideas," said Sarah, "Let us enquire of the kitchen staff, the person who collects these delicacies which I presume will be George or one of his staff and see what we come up with. Meanwhile let us research this subject because there may be laws restricting commercial farming of the crayfish and mussels, but if not and we can expand the natural supplies, why not?"

More discussion followed about the trout farm idea and controlled salmon fishing where only diseased or damaged fish would be removed, and the rest put straight back into the protected part of the river. Other salmon could bypass all of this section up the side ladders and spawn in the small streams feeding the river further inland up in the hills we could see in the distance, on a clear day. Also, it occurred to me that we should have a ladder each side of the river since we owned the land either side and leave the centre clear all through the angling section, then put another ladder across the centre so that the salmon and any trout large enough could leap up the ladders and escape up the river to breed. The big carp and all the other coarse fish would not get past the ladders and, hey presto, we had our fenced-off section, but no fences, just ladders. No permission needed, no nasty accidents where people, animals and fish got injured or maimed, and yet we kept our stock of fish largely intact. That was ascending the river, but how were we to stop the stock fish escaping downstream? We talked this through, and no one could see a solution until Michael said, "Wait a minute, we have a weir at one point which we used to navigate with small boats and lift them over the rocks and the small falls. Maybe we could enhance that so again the salmon and trout could get past like with a ladder but most of the remaining fish would stay where the living was easy, they were being fed and the water calm and safe."

"That's brilliant Michael; we must get George's opinion on that and maybe consult an expert as to the exact formation of such a weir or its enhancement, or indeed it might function as it is. We could sit and watch at different times and see whether any coarse fish were going that way or not; we could afford to lose a few especially as they would multiply with feeding and we don't eat coarse fish other than maybe a culled pike who had become too big and dangerous to other fish. And I like pike fishing, and normally in our river near our home, we have a rule that we put back jack pike up to 30 inches long. But in any case, if we see too many damaged fish, we can have a cull.

"Which actually triggers another thought, what about predators like cormorants, herons, otters, stoats, polecats, and wild mink, not to mention feral cats and other domesticated animals left to roam free? We need someone to look at that and George is that man for sure. He can suggest ways of controlling such predators, particularly cormorants and mink, which can decimate a fish stock in weeks unless stopped. Some may be protected but I am pretty certain that controlling cormorants and mink is allowed. But all these things need considering in our model of this part of the project here and on the other two estates."

"Absolutely James; I had no idea you were so knowledgeable about fish and wildlife as you clearly are."

We decided it would be good to have a walkway, screened by small trees and bushes, so that visitors, if lucky, might witness the salmon fighting their way up the ladders at the right time of the year, usually late winter, and early spring I understood. But they were quite rare as this was not noted now as a prolific salmon river, although some notable specimens had been taken many years ago. I suggested a survey of the various streams on the trust property to see if farming practices had any impact and to take any action necessary to keep the streams clear of cattle and sheep. We would also need to remove any barbed wire or other impediments in the water, maintaining a clear and pure water supply, as far as nature and our boundaries allowed. The actual spawning areas were normally very shallow and wide with gravel bottoms and if the cows had churned them up and made mud baths of parts of them, they needed protecting and a separate drinking water facility for the cattle provided. There were apparently several water troughs around, so maybe they needed looking at to see that the water ballcocks were working properly, and the tanks had not become fouled. Simple things but could help the salmon spawning a lot and lead to an increase in stocks in just two- or three-years' time.

After lunch, Michael and I went with the gamekeeper George and toured the estate upriver in the Land Rover. After negotiating several fords and opening and closing many gates, we finally reached the area where several small streams formed a small delta leading into the river only about 300 yards from the high stone wall marking the limit of our estate. Beyond that wall, the gamekeeper told me, was unfarmed, rocky land and almost impenetrable gorse thickets where the poor, thin soil meant no farming had taken place in living memory. Not even sheep could prosper there. The first farm was situated about five miles beyond the wall and was a poor one, as the land was also poor for miles in that direction, both hilly and rocky with little which could be grown. That farm relied on a medium-size flock of hill sheep and a few other animals for a living.

This was good news, from our point of view, regarding the salmon spawning areas in this little delta, as they were clear and bright at present, with no noticeable pollution or litter to spoil them. We needed therefore to systematically follow the banks of the river downstream now and look at the streams leading into it, to see what state they were in. We again forded a few of the streams and Michael said to George the gamekeeper, "To prevent erosion and pollution, I think we should look to make these fords stone and gravel bottomed or provide a railway sleeper type bridge to stop churning the muck up when we come up here, which we shall need to do more often if our idea of encouraging natural salmon breeding is to take place, what do you think?"

"Relatively easy, we have all the materials we need and the vehicles to do it, we haven't needed to look at it this way before in my time at least. But I see the problem and also, I will need to scour the streams for rubbish, wire and choking bush growth and clean them up and maintain them afterwards. I reckon maybe three months to do that and that will mean the way would be clear to allow salmon to get up here and spawn in early spring."

"That's good, let's do that anyway as we will enjoy returning salmon whatever the project brings. And tell me George, what do you know of making ladders for salmon so that if we control part of the river, they can still get past, and is permission required do you think, and if so, from whom?"

"Well, I heard someone say you were considering starting a fish farm and allowing angling, etc. as part of your scheme, and I am all in favour. I have several contacts in this type of business and would be happy to make some discreet enquiries about all this. But I can tell you that you will have no problem getting permission to make salmon ladders; they will all love the idea. But regarding any other developments, we need to make further enquiries of the River Board, the local council, the Department of Agriculture and probably a few more bodies. Again, I would be happy to make some enquiries on your behalf with people I know to see what the best way might be to approach all this."

"Thank you, George, I appreciate your offer. I will talk to Sarah about all this, and I am sure that some of these enquiries will be placed in your hands and in addition I will talk to a few of my friends in London about any other government departments who might need to be consulted. What do you think, James?"

"I think all that sounds good, just a few points I would make: might it be better just to concentrate on the salmon restoration at present and wait to talk to all these people mentioned and others, after our Phase 1 report is submitted regarding other potential developments which might impact on the river plan? For example, tourism, and health and safety, building permits and regulations, protected historical sites, the local council regarding any new access roads, the local village parish council regarding the impact on the village and, I am sure other issues which we need to be well versed on and prepared before approaching any of these bodies, groups, councils, officials, etc. In short be prepared with our powder dry and our research already well progressed and draft plans and diagrams are produced."

"Very good thinking James, as usual. I get a bit carried away with enthusiasm on this kind of thing. Because you are absolutely right, we need our ducks all in a row before approaching the bigger people, but a few enquiries of friends locally and elsewhere, if done discreetly, could guide us on the right path. Let you and I discuss all this with Sarah and you, George, can start your local enquiries regarding the salmon ladders, stressing this is all just potential plans, nothing more, I am sure you know how to handle that."

"Right you are sir, and you James, well thought out caution there."

"Thanks George and I heartily agree with Michael, I too am sure you know the issues and the importance of keeping this as informal and tight as you can and that you will only speak to trusted friends."

I then pointed out to Michael that our travels today across all the tied farms and land will not have gone unnoticed so it might be an idea to speak with them all soon and tell them about the salmon idea and the necessity to do a bit of work on their farms which of course, we shall pay for, and stress that keeping farm animals out of the streams will be their responsibility once we have our clean-up programme complete and the various ford points over the streams properly used and kept clear and clean."

"Of course, I shall call a meeting and explain that part of our plans as we are agreed, and I am sure Sarah will agree too, to push that plan forward as soon as we can to get it ready for the next spring salmon run."

We made our way back to the house via the village and I took my first look at the local pub "The Hare and Hounds. "As it was open we called in after parking our mud-splattered Land Rover in the lane opposite the pub and walked into the bar where there were just a few local men and the landlord Harry Cruikshank, whose face lit up when he saw George, Michael and I come in. He beamed at us all and said, "Good afternoon gentlemen, and George, do come in! What can I get you men, you all look thirsty?"

"Good afternoon, Harry," said George and Michael, and I smiled and nodded, and George said, "Harry, you know the governor of course and this is James whom you are probably going to see more of as he is helping to make plans for the future for the estate,"

"Ah," said Harry, "yes of course I know Sir Michael, he is almost a regular here, and pleased to meet you, James."

Michael said, "Harry, I have told you forget the Sir if you don't mind and I can tell you James is happy with Jim, is that not so James?"

"Jim is fine, but if you like using James, so is that. And have you got any real ale, IPA or whatever? If not, I will have a pint of Guinness."

"We do indeed have a real ale in cask which is IPA as it happens, made in a local small brewery quite near here and I can thoroughly recommend it. George, your usual? And Michael what is your fancy today, IPA as well?"

Nods all round as Harry pulled three foaming pints of IPA with the old pump-action beer engine, straight from the barrel situated below, leaving a half-inch of creamy white head, the kind which clings to the glass all the way down. We all took a pull, and the beer was perfectly kept and had a slightly bitter hoppy taste with the barley flavour coming through, an excellent pint of beer and I said so. "Thank you, Jim, glad you like it," said Harry.

George spoke to all the men as we passed to sit at a table near the old bow window and Michael and I nodded hello. We settled down to drink our pints when George wandered over with a tray of pickled walnuts, shallots, and eggs, as well as a plate of crusty bread and butter and put it at the centre of the table and without a word returned to the bar. I tried a pickled walnut, something I had never had before; it was black and the size and shape of a whole walnut and had a woody texture and a quite delicate nutty flavour, slightly salty and vinegary, but interesting and went down well with a swallow of beer. The pickled shallots were good and a crust of fresh bread with a knob of butter on completed a very welcome snack and the rest of the pint swilled it down nicely.

George was clearly wondering about another pint so I said, "Well that went down a treat, I could manage another one I think if anybody else is interested."

George said, "Well as I can go straight back over our land to the house, I will force myself."

And Michael smiled and nodded, while Harry was already coming over with three new pints on a tray.

The snack tray was cleared, and Harry looked over, but Michael shook his head, so no second tray came, it was almost five p.m. and we were expected for dinner at about eight p.m., so enough was enough he obviously thought and nice though it was, I was in complete agreement.

George said, "Mind if I call my friend Peter over? He was a keen salmon fisherman some forty years ago on your river."

"Please do," said Michael, and George walked over to the bar and spoke to an elderly man, fit looking, about seventy I would say, and spoke briefly with him then brought him over and introduced him.

"Sir, this is Peter, an old friend of mine who knows your river and lands very well and has taken a few salmon from it many years ago."

"What will you have, Peter?" said Michael.

"A half if you don't mind," said Peter so Michael signalled four halves of bitter and over they came.

After we had finished our pints and taken a sip of the halves, George said, "Peter, it's no real secret but we want to ask you about something you have more knowledge of than anyone else I know: salmon. You will be delighted to know that we are considering cleaning up the streams and spawning beds and putting salmon ladders in to encourage greater spawning success and returning the river some way towards the level of salmon which came here each year thirty to forty years ago, what do you think?"

Peter sat and sipped his half for a while before replying, and then he said, "Well if anyone else but you George, especially in Sir Michael's company, had said that to me I would have laughed or cried. But I know you both well enough to say, yes it can be done. It might take a bit longer than you think to make a big difference, but maybe not. It is certain that very few salmon now make it to the spawning grounds because of more intensive farming and stocking of cattle which foul the streams. And Land Rovers like yours churning the mud up over the gravel which is essential for the fertilised eggs to develop. But I know you are mainly organic and don't think chemicals are a problem nowadays. You will only need ladders if you are contemplating fencing part of the river to keep some salmon in for sport, but that is not a problem; ladders are easy to put in place, inexpensive and need no consents. If you get just a dozen decent hen salmon upstream and a couple of dozen boar or bucks as they are sometimes called, you could have a thousand salmon coming back in three to five years providing that you ensure the streams stay clear and clean all the time in those years. The young salmon will go down the river if they negotiate the streams successfully, the ladders and the netting will both let them through if the right size nets are used. You could have five thousand salmon coming up in five to ten years' time, maybe more, with careful management, and you would have the thanks of everyone as well as being a major attraction."

What a speech, he absolutely amazed me with his clarity and enthusiasm, and my immediate thought was, get him on board, we need him. I said, "That's very encouraging Peter but excuse me a minute as I need to pump ship after those two pints of this wonderful beer." And I gave Michael a wink and he murmured "Me too," and followed me to the Gents' leaving Peter and George to chat.

"Michael," I said, as we stood alongside in the stalls, "we need this man on your books. He is a goldmine of knowledge and information and he looks fit and well, probably about seventy but so what, I bet he would love to be involved. How about suggesting a part-time job to start with as river warden maybe and he could supervise the stream cleansing, under George of course maybe as George's river assistant?"

"Hmm, perhaps. I will need to speak to Sarah, she controls staff recruitment, but if you back the idea, I guess she will be OK. Let's sound him out gently; he will need time to think about it I am sure, and we have no idea of his availability."

"My feeling is strike while the iron is hot. I am certain Sarah will agree, and there is no harm in sounding him out is there?"

"OK," said Michael, "I will leave it to you and observe his reactions."

"Done," I said.

We went back to the table and apologised for taking so long, and George said, "No problem. What have you decided about whatever it is you adjourned for?" And smiled. I laughed although Michael looked uncomfortable.

I said, "Very good George, you are smarter than you look." Which in turn made him laugh and that eased the tension in Michael's face.

"You are right," I went on, "and I am not going to beat about the bush, Peter. I like what you said and how you said it, and I have no doubts about your vast knowledge of the estate, the river, the streams and most importantly, the salmon. Now I am only an adviser, and it is up to Michael and his wife Sarah, but I want to ask you, are you occupied with any employment at present and if not, how would you react to being offered some employment, possibly part-time, basically as George's assistant on the salmon project, if it comes about? You don't need to answer now if you want to consider things, but if you can indicate it might be possible that is all we ask at present."

Peter looked at George who smiled and nodded and then he said, "Can I have another half of beer please, and would you all like to join me?"

I looked at Michael and he smiled and said, "I like your style Peter, but I insist this is on me. Harry, four more halves please."

Again, Peter took his time, had a pull at his half and waited for us to do the same, then he looked at each of us in turn and said, "Yes, is the answer. I am available; I would love to be involved for nothing, but I know that will not do so I would accept a job, full- or part-time, whatever, as George's assistant, looking after the river and streams and all the fish of whatever type, including the trout and all the coarse fish and in particular the large carp I understand you are considering. I would welcome supervising the fishing and all aspects of the river project felt proper for me to do so."

Another astounding speech; this man was no country bumpkin. I knew we had just recruited a terrific asset and, health permitting, he would see the re-establishment of the river as a known salmon river which would attract lots of people to the estate. I waited and as Michael said nothing, I took the plunge and said, "Peter, as far as I am concerned you can become a member of this team as soon as you like and I will take the responsibility, even if I have to put you on my staff to do so, but I am certain that both Michael and Sarah will be totally in agreement when we discuss this matter later today or tomorrow."

Peter finally looked a little embarrassed and just looked straight in my eyes and said, "Thank you, you will not regret it I assure you."

George turned to his friend and said, "Welcome to the team Peter, I look forward to your arrival early tomorrow at the stables in your working gear ready to do an immediate survey and evaluation of the project which I will explain to you."

And he offered his hand which Peter shook warmly who then turned to me and offered me his hand and I shook it too and Michael followed quickly shaking his hand warmly and welcoming him to the team. Peter was so happy his face shone, and I said, "Just one thing Peter which I am sure I don't need to say, all this is to remain substantially confidential for now please."

We departed and drove down the lane where we had parked, through a gate into our fields and back to the house where we thanked George and he thanked us and in we went where Sarah was waiting.

She said, "Where were you, I was getting a little concerned?" And I replied, "We went to the pub, and I am so glad we did, because we, or rather I, have recruited a new employee for you and that is down to me as I have committed myself to take him on to my staff if necessary."

"This had better be good!" she said, but I knew from her body language that was just for show in front of Michael, and I continued, "Yes, it is very good in my opinion, and I felt it important to strike while the iron was hot."

"All right," she said, "let's go in and have some tea and coffee as you two smell like a brewery."

"But we only had three pints," said Michael, which she ignored completely and led the way into the large sitting room normally reserved for tea parties with the ladies. She ordered a pot of coffee and tea and we sat, and she said, "Tell me about this prodigal you met in the pub!"

So, first Michael gave his version and then I took over and filled in several gaping holes and stressed the trout farm, salmon ladders, and the ultimate objective of restoring a once prolific salmon river to somewhere near its former glory. And how this would be sure to enhance and speed up the project considerably with the knowledge and experience of George's friend and one-time salmon angler on their river Peter Knowles. I went on to say that I had engaged Peter from tomorrow morning as assistant to George and that he would be instrumental in supervising the clearing of the streams which were vital as the access to the salmon spawning grounds, design and location of the salmon ladders, and the sighting of the proposed breeding tanks for supplying fish stocks. And all of this would not only attract visitors to the holiday facilities, but would create — together with a protected stock of trophy-sized carp to be purchased and kept in a netted part of the river — an important attraction to anglers nationwide and even from abroad to our project and increase clients and revenue quite significantly. She had listened to all this, and she said only, "Are you sure that after the effect of the three pints has subsided you will still feel all this is true?"

I replied, "As sure as I was that you, once you heard all this and more not yet fully explored, would wholeheartedly support the whole plan."

She laughed and said, "Of course you are right, and I am being a bit silly getting peeved about you two jollying your way around the estate and ending up as guests of Harry, when in reality you were both working hard on the project. I know old Peter and have done since I was a girl. He is a very sound, quite well-educated and sensible man. He is an undoubted mine of knowledge and information about this estate, the river and all that you have mentioned, and I know he is very fit and well despite his seventy-two years." And she continued, "All of this has served to highlight that nothing beats the physical examination of each of the estates including the outlying and less well-known parts, to engender new thinking and ideas. And I should like you to make sure that when you do go back to Scotland and Ireland with your team, you could use the same approach there to both their rivers and salmon potential, fish farms, the lot, as a means of speeding up and enhancing the attractiveness of the venues not just for holidaymakers but, as you say, the business community and anglers from everywhere. Consider that a must."

She had the bit well and truly between her teeth now and waxed lyrical about the volume of paying visitors to the estates lured by salmon and trout fishing and trophy-class carp, not just the holidaymakers, but serious angling clubs and individuals who toured the country and Europe in search of a trophy fish to claim they had caught. The estates' management might be able to market all three estates at the same time in the right publications worldwide. She would personally see Peter in the morning and welcome him to our team and ensure he knew she was fully in approval of his recruitment.

I approved heartily of this and said, "Great that's a very nice thought and I am certain he will approve of that; I certainly do."

Michael was probably a bit rueful he had not embraced my idea a little more fully at the outset and, claiming a slight headache, he said he would go to his room until dinner. I looked at Sarah and she gave a very slight nod and I said, "Me too, I think, maybe a swim first," and off went Michael and Sarah and I went to the pool zone. Again, after a shower and a brisk swim, I repaired to the massage room where, without a word we made slow leisurely love for a while.

She said, "That was a nice way to show our continuing commitment to our project don't you think?"

"Yes, I do, not that I had a moment's doubt, Michael wouldn't commit himself without asking you but I was not going to let that particular opportunity go by. I think he resented that a bit, but frankly I don't care so long as he doesn't take it any further."

"He's fine, he will bounce back at dinner; he can't take responsibility you know, but he's no fool, and he recognises that he is basically dependent on me, but he knew that from the day we were married and is well used to that reality. You, in contrast, are strong-minded, decisive and clear-headed, as well as being a wonderful lover.

Although he might not know about us, he will be well aware that you are an alpha male, and he is not and never will be, but he is generally very happy with his lot. I don't want him hurt in any way as I am sure you realise, and I thought you quite liked him actually."

"Oh, I do, I do, he's a very interesting and thoroughly nice man and he is always very good to me. In any case I would never want to upset you and I have always realised that you love him, for all his lack of let's say 'alpha male status', he has many other attributes, not least caring for you a very great deal."

She responded by touching me such that I moved over her, and we made love once again and we both looked at each other and smiled. What a good understanding we had, one of the best other than that I had with Ronja, but I pondered, good job I have Ronja as a mistress because Sarah would never be able to fit that role and it prevented me from getting more serious with her other than as a welcome and very proficient lover.

Dinner went well with no other guests and we three were very relaxed and happy in each other's company and comfortable with our relationship. I studied Michael and I am certain he suspected nothing.

I left on Sunday before lunch and promised to be back with my chosen small team before too long to look at the estate accounts and visit the tied farms as well as reconsider the hotel, fish farm and conference facilities; the proposed new road entrance and all the rest; do some planning and research and make some more firm and detailed plans and proposals so that once approvals had been sought and granted by whatever authority or other bodies were necessary, sub-contractors could be approached and funds readied for use. But the challenge would be to put some costing on all the component parts of the projects and make some projections for income to help to decide which, if any, might be cut, modified, or deferred.

I arrived home in time for a late Sunday lunch and was greeted with enthusiasm by Heather, Nat and Jo who were both there plus a nice young lady called Anne, a student at the same university as Nat and his current girlfriend. I was introduced and joined them in their aperitifs having my usual bottle of IPA which I poured and sipped while I listened to Anne describe her degree course and Nat interjecting with funny and unhelpful remarks that all young men seem to need to do when a parent is first introduced to a girlfriend. We both ignored him, and he stopped being such a smart arse and listened as we discussed the various options she might have once qualified. Luckily at that point Heather called us through for lunch with my mother who, although over eighty, was still able to take part and sitting at the table already.

It was lovely having an informal lunch with no client or business imperative and just relax and chat to the family and enjoy good plain home cooking, a decent bottle or two of wine and happy talking about everything and anything, no agenda, no pressures, lovely.

Later, the children having left, I gave Heather a brief rundown on the events of the last few days. She was very impressed how far we had got, and we discussed who I should nominate to take into my team for the estates. She agreed that the two I had in mind were probably best and deserved this selection as both had team leader potential and lots of relevant experience. Mother was staying the night and had retired early, and we sat and relaxed over the remains of the lunch wine and then had a pot of coffee and a brandy together, watched a bit of TV and then we too had an early night and repaired to bed.

Chapter 33

As we moved towards the implementation of our Phase 1 plan, a greater sense of momentum and energy was infused by the introduction of our three teams of experts who would look into every nook and cranny, talk to many different people in the companies and the estates and the increasing sensation we were now a serious force, a large and serious force, on a very serious mission.

The future of a small empire was at stake. We were working towards a root-and-branch reforming of quite a large organisation to ensure its survival and ultimately its growth into a lean and mean machine, run by perhaps a slimmed down number of managers and employees, to a greater and more diverse organisation geared to grow and succeed in both turnover, share values and rewards and built to last well into the future.

Sarah was the person carrying all this responsibility to her family present and future, and to a large degree I shared that responsibility, but in her case, it was the well-being of future generations whereas in mine, I had little to lose but my reputation and pride.

But I knew that much of what we would deliver was not risky, it being proved reform already tried and tested in many similar groups of companies. The relatively unknown, and therefore more exciting challenge was the reform of the estates' methods and scope of activity together with a considerable investment in money terms, which had to be able to be justified not in the short term perhaps but certainly in the medium to long term.

I therefore briefed the two larger team members regarding what was expected of them. I confirmed my confidence in their efforts in reaching the required standards and sent them on their way to the first of their respective targets. I then settled in with my chosen team members, David and Henry, to apprise them of the details I had obtained so far on the estates, a brief history of the trust's properties, the general state of play now and the areas I had already identified for reform; and using the model we had developed concerning the river at the English estate. This concerned holiday accommodations, commercial hospitality facilities, and in particular the quite well-developed plan to increase the fishing aspects including a trout farm, improving the river and streams so that salmon returned to the rivers in numbers thereby adding to the attractions of the site and the introduction of trophy-sized coarse fish such as carp. All this sort of thing was quite new to them, and I knew I needed to give them a thorough briefing regarding law and regulations and other compliance with local as well as regional and even national bodies when it came to changing the rivers and introducing new practices concerning wildlife.

So I told them all that had happened including the recruitment of Peter; the work already started on the stream clearing and cleaning work at the far reaches of the English estate; the salmon ladders; the breeding cycle of the salmon and trout and our plans to create a salmon river. The latter we wanted to compete, as it had many years past, with Scotland and Ireland for the numbers of quality fish we hoped to entice back to their former glory.

I painted a picture for them including the new access road, The hotel/motel to be constructed for both holidaymakers and corporate facilities clients, the shooting both live game targets like pheasant and grouse, and the clay pigeon shooting; the salmon and trout fishing used by all clients with the money to pay; the sale of farmed trout as eating fish to corporate and small retailers and restaurants, as well as the sale of trout eggs and smelt (small one-year-old trout) for other trout farms use. Then I covered the possible development of freshwater crayfish and mussels; the horse riding for accomplished riders and also for beginners who needed tuition and all the other ideas we had already generated; plus, any new ones my team could come up with.

They scribbled furiously but I told them that I had the bones of everything already noted and would provide them with a comprehensive list of schemes, already firm or at the exploration stage, so that they would have a chance to do some of their own research in between venues. I reminded them I would be there with them most of the time through all three estate explorations.

We were starting at the English estate, so it was all fresh in my mind and what's more I had George and Peter to call on as well as Sarah to consult and Michael to provide some special research he was pledged to carry out with his pals in London both inside and outside The Houses of Parliament and The House of Lords, as well as Michael's top-drawer fellow members of certain clubs, generally known humorously as 'The Great and Good'."

But we already knew that the salmon ladders were permissible, and we could see that starting while we were there perhaps, as it was not just reliant on the Phase 1 plan. It had already been given the green light as a needed and desired action regardless of the plan. Similarly, the general clean-up of the streams and the levelling and gravelling of the various fords which criss-crossed the streams. So, we decided to spend the first few days researching as I had briefly in the vast archives in the estate library and examining both the current and the past six years' business accounts and records kept in the library. I introduced the team to Sarah and Michael on our first morning of our arrival there, and later caught up with George and Peter when they came into the stables for their lunch and introduced everybody but didn't stay as we had been invited to have lunch with Sarah. Michael had gone off to London for a few days, and Peter and George sat down to their prepared cold lunch and a beer put in the stable's fridge earlier by the kitchen. Peter was clearly really enjoying himself and quickly informed me that he had spotted a good-sized salmon in the river as well as a couple of large sea trout all on their way up the river. I asked him, what was the difference between ordinary river or lake trout and a sea trout and he said, "Sea trout are usually rainbow trout which, due to their voracious feeding habits, taking small fish, frogs and larger insects, can grow very large. One in a Canadian lake had topped 40 pounds, but it wasn't uncommon for these large trout, perhaps because they are closely related to salmon anyway. In view of their aggressive feeding, have evolved like the salmon to go out to sea, adjusting to the salt water at river mouths for a while then heading out to sea. Not the thousands of miles salmon are known to travel, but they stay out at sea from two to seven years, and some grow as big as salmon. Then they re-enter the river they were from just as the salmon do and go upstream and lay eggs in gravel nests similar to salmon. But unlike salmon, these big trout can survive the experience and repeat it two or three times and even more before they die, whereas salmon almost all die after spawning a much greater number of eggs. The decaying salmon fertilises the gravel beds with their nutrients creating a plethora of microscopic plankton like larvae for the baby salmon to feed on before they get large enough to join the river."

Sarah invited us into the family dining room and my team were clearly impressed with what she had on display, the full panoply of home-grown organic salads, fruit, and vegetables to accompany a large whole cooked ham; a leg of lamb and a brisket of beef with several types of potatoes: roast, boiled, creamed, and sautéed, plus home-made crusty bread both whole meal and white. The ham was cold, and the lamb and beef were hot.

When David and Henry seemed uncertain what to have first, she said, "Hold on boys the first course is coming shortly," and in walked the butler bearing a tray of assorted crustaceans: crayfish and mussels taken from the stream that morning and some very nice large, imported tiger prawns, a fresh crab and some scallops, cockles, and whelks. Their eyes popped and I explained about the crayfish being a kind of small freshwater lobster. They took a selection on their plates and waited until Sarah and I showed the way to tackle this magnificent selection of shellfish and soon they were relaxed after a glass of wine, and by the time they were carved slices of both hot joints and the cold ham together with a selection of vegetables and potatoes, they were chatting away happily with Sarah and me about their excitement at being invited on this part of the plan. And when Sarah asked them a few questions, they both acquitted themselves well and she was clearly happy with them.

The team went to unpack in their adjoining rooms in the suite they had been allocated to look at the briefing papers I had given them with the latest position on the river and its various sub-plans, some of which would have to wait for permission or licensing or whatever, but that would not prevent them being explored and considered at this stage. I told the team to settle in, maybe go for a stroll around the nearby buildings and as far as the river and be ready and dressed for dinner at about quarter to eight as we had other guests as well for dinner. I had already warned them that they should have a dinner jacket with them.

I then suggested a stroll to Sarah, but she said, "Yes, good idea; you know where my room is, see you in about fifteen minutes?"

I said, "Will you want a debriefing?"

She said, "Yes please."

So, I departed to my room and freshened up. Then I made my way to her room and encountered no one. I knocked gently and entered, and she was sitting in a chair sipping a glass of Champagne with her legs crossed and dressed only in her panties and a diaphanous shift of some sort. This was a Sarah not experienced before and I marvelled how she had apparently cast off thirty-plus years of relative coyness or demureness, after just a few lovemaking sessions. She pointed to the Champagne bottle and said, "Help yourself and get comfortable."

So, I complied and took off my clothes, all but my boxers, and poured a glass of Champagne. I sat in the other chair quite close to Sarah and said, "What do you think?"

She replied, "I think you look good enough to eat."

I replied "After such a lunch as that? You must be hungry." She said, "I am. Take off your shorts please so I can look at what we have here."

I stood up to pull off my shorts and as they were cast aside, I had a half hard-on, but by the time she reached over to take it in one hand, it stiffened up. She bent over in her chair and poured a little Champagne over it and took me in her mouth, not something she often did, and sucked gently for a minute or two and then sat back in her chair and said, "Your turn darling," and spread her thighs and revealed she had on crotchless panties on with her slightly reddish bush peeking out. I obliged of course and she moaned a little and said, "Lovely, now carry me to the bed please and put it in me."

"Certainly, madam," I said, and obliged.

I then left Sarah sleeping and went to my room, had a short nap, a shower and after looking at my notes I dressed for dinner and went down to the main dining hall. There, Sarah was sitting looking splendid in her purple gown and tiara and looking very happy as David and Henry entered, led by the butler, as they had no idea it would be in a different room. They looked fine in their dinner jackets, one blue and the other black, with matching bow ties and were sitting on either side of Sarah while I was seated opposite her with the guests. As they were our friends from the last time, I could easily chat to them while Sarah could make sure the boys were included in the conversations.

The dinner went very well and our guests were totally relaxed and engaged David and Henry in lively conversation, knowing enough about the project by now to ask relevant questions of them. The latter acquitted themselves very well again considering they had only very recently been apprised of the whole situation. Sarah deserved credit for the way she handled everyone and considering the close relationship we had grown into. I was determined to not let her or myself down and played my part to the full so, especially as she put them next to her and was charming to both of them, I was certain it set the scene for the rest of our stay. Therefore, if she later turned up in Ireland it would be no problem. I doubted she would come to Scotland as well but even then, I am certain she could handle the situation and her son would remain oblivious to our relationship.

Over the next few days, we examined old records and new, took copies of some particularly interesting and relevant document and we found some notes in a worn and well-thumbed bundle of diaries which noted all the salmon sighted and caught in the river over a five-year period 1950 to 1955 and they were staggering! Over a hundred were sighted on many days; dozens caught on rods weighing up to 40 pounds and reaching a peak in 1953, the year of Queen Elizabeth's Coronation, when a total of 2,435 were sighted and 355 landed. Those, therefore, were the sort of numbers that we hoped to reach in just a few years and the prospect of this being a major salmon river again seemed a step closer.

We then looked at all the farms, noted all the cultivated acreage and what crops were growing and planned; how much was grass and what percentage would make silage and hay and also what percentage of worked fields were for animal feed, which for grain crops, and so on. We also asked each farmer if more land could be brought into use, what sort of crops were possible on the newly cultivated fields, how many cattle were currently there and what proportion was for beef and how many for milk, and what happened to surplus cattle and calves.

We asked for opinions and ideas for improvement and suggested some ourselves for discussion and gradually they thawed out and started to actively question their own existing methods and policies and several interesting ideas came up.

We then looked at manpower in employment, their job descriptions, and actual skills they possessed and asked them also for opinions and ideas and again after the suspicion faded and the penny dropped that we were looking for expansion and diversification not the reduction of crops and animals but the opposite, they opened up and we gathered some more very useful ideas and opinions which we could work with.

Then we looked at what machinery and implements were kept, their state of repair, age and effectiveness were assessed, and again we sought facts, ideas and opinions and we took into account the planned purchasing of large equipment as well as costs and write-off values of those machines replaced. This was part of our plan: to evaluate if certain machines, because of their high cost and low scrap or second-hand values, might better be hired or subcontracted in, with or without their drivers, and yield a significant saving over a range of five to ten years of active use. It seemed to depend not so much on historical usage — although that could be used as a base figure but applied to future usage as the amount of land and the expansion of some crops grown increased. One alternative occurred to me: what if we kept up or increased the number of these larger machines like combine harvesters, and we hired them out, with or without our drivers, in the periods either before or after our main harvests or a combination of the two? My gut told me that this would probably negate any gain from scrapping our older machines and contracting in and that would mean not being at the beck and call of subcontractors nor any attempts to raise prices at whim when, if we had not retained machinery we would be at their mercy. Whereas we were big enough to offer these services to the many smaller farms in the area, and put them in the position I described, rather than us putting ourselves at risk. And we would have more understanding and flexibility with the many local farmers whom we already knew and had cordial relations with, whereas a big remote outfit from say East Anglia, were unknown and we couldn't expect the cooperation we would get locally. Plus, the payments necessary to transfer these machines to our estate from a remote depot and the time spent and cost of doing so. No, the more thought about it, although I would get the team to produce some figures and an analysis, the more I leaned towards the current policy of procurement, but add the possibility of our subcontracting our machines and services out rather than in.

We looked at the buildings, the farmhouses, the barns, sheds, were they brick, stone or wooden construction, the animal folds for winter use, open-sided and corrugated roofs in the main, and the dairy farm's milking parlour and tanks and their supplementary 'Cow Cake', organic, of course. We inspected the muck heaps alongside the cattle barns and enclosures which were all subject to periodic checks regarding their cherished organic certificates which can take up to five years to obtain.

And so on, part by part we saw practically everything worth seeing, asked questions of everybody we saw, took many photographs and notes, and gradually built up a complete picture of the whole estate. This included its lands and their current usage; the numbers and types of animals and their costs in keep; the potential of the unused land for crops, grass, or any other sensible usage. Then we assessed the current numbers of employees, the estimated numbers needed for certain expansion of identified new or larger activities and lists of new or good reconditioned machines likely to be required by the farms and the house, and so on.

We started to get information back from Michael, George and Peter about legal requirements, licences, permits and authorities in general in order to alter an access road, build a hotel/motel; construct and stock a fish farm; river authority requirements regarding the proposed salmon ladders and all the other large and small alterations; ground clearance and building in whatever materials we wanted, as well as the expansion of our already well-established organic produce, gradually to be the standard of all the tied farms across all three estates.

We of course could not put accurate costs on much of this so we gave estimates based on our research as this was for the Phase 2 plan and it would need accountants and lawyers as well as perhaps a surveying firm to put some firm figures to the costs, and another branch of accountancy expert to estimate yields and of course to advise on the Irish domicile tax strategy.

After two weeks, I thought we had enough to draft out our plan for the home estate, but I wanted to see Ireland and do a similar exercise there to see if comparison revealed areas we had erred in slightly or had totally missed something, and to add any new ideas gained in Ireland which might affect the plan as a whole. That would apply to Scotland too, but Sarah naturally wanted some idea where we were at and I commissioned a spreadsheet showing all our deliberations in a relatively simple potential cost and yield format, heavily qualified at this point. I also got an artist to come and put together a representative view on the hotel design we had in mind: the trout farm building, and the riverbank appearance after the insertion of the ladders and cutting the angling pegs; building a boat house and the connected wooden walkways for viewing salmon making their way upriver. Also a few sketches of the fords and photographs of any sufficiently completed, which we had started to put in over the streams; the gated curved back entrance to the hotel and a new but short access road not too far from the pub. This would be invisible to anyone living in the village or nearby and masked with bushes and trees and suitable landscaping which would blend in with the village, our estate and its entrance.

I presented Sarah with a large album containing the paintings, photographs, and drawings plus several enlarged photos I had taken, and our draft Phase 2 report, including the cost and profit projections in spreadsheet format, backed up with some nice, coloured pie and bar charts. I stressed that it was provisional and for her eyes and Michael's only please. I said that some things may have to change a bit, but I thought it was a pretty decent first draft.

I also said, "Will you come to Ireland? It might be helpful in smoothing the way and reassuring everyone generally, and if any backside needed kicking, you are the one to do it! And any new ideas could be bounced off you in situ."

"Oh, thanks for this," she said, taking the large heavy Phase 2 portfolio from me. "And yes please, I would love to be there with you, and your team of course."

She sat and looked slowly through the album and glanced at the narrative but studied the paintings, drawings and plans and the spreadsheet for about fifteen minutes, then said, "James, this looks wonderful, you are a genius."

I laughed and said, "Tell me that if it's torn to shreds by the experts. It is only a plan; when hard facts and figures, fully costed and audited are input, they may paint a different picture."

"Maybe," she said, "but I will wager you are not too far from the mark, and only you could have produced this in such a short time and so professional looking."

"Well, you are paying a professional's price for it, but thanks anyway. You can congratulate me later before I take my team and disappear back home for a few days then I will advise you if I may, what my travel plans are for Ireland. I will send them to have a last look at the river with the copy album; I have to see if we have missed anything. I will tell them to be back for lunch at one p.m. if that's all right. That gives us an hour to consider matters further. Where would you like to go for what will be the last consultation for a while?"

"Well, Michael is not due back until tomorrow so how about in my room in ten minutes if you can locate the boys?"

"Done, or your will be," I said.

The boys took the album, glanced through it and whistled saying, "Pretty impressive," and took my advice about the river visit and said they would see me at lunch then.

I went to Sarah's room and she was already in bed naked, but with a sheet over her and a couple of glasses of her favourite Champagne already poured. I quickly undressed and joined her, took up my glass and said, "Cheers, darling!" She replied, "Cheers and many, many thanks for everything."

We had our last chance to touch base for a while, so we made the most of it and then prepared for an informal farewell lunch in the family dining room.

Great send-off, good food and wine for the non-drivers, i.e., David and me. Sarah thanked the boys profusely and wished them luck with the other two estates. She added that she would join us in Ireland to make sure things went smoothly and said, "Just enjoy yourself; treat it as you treated this place, don't be afraid to question anybody and everything and produce another draft anything like this one (which was on the table), and I will be happy."

A quick hug and off we went with Henry driving back home, dropping the two boys (men of 34 and 36) off, and me taking over the driving after saying that I would speak to them as soon as I had news of dates and transport, and telling them to do a bit more research in the meantime.

I had not had a report from the teams dealing with the group companies yet. They had a much bigger agenda than we had and a lot of travelling too, but I had messages saying all was well and they were both receiving full cooperation and might have something in a week or two. Fat chance I thought, I had looked at most of the companies and it was a lot of ground to cover; I calculated that, allowing for travelling time and breaks, it would be six to eight weeks at least before anything resembling a full draft could be produced.

I put in an invoice for what my team and I had done so far at the English estate and received payment within a few days with no query whatsoever from Sarah, so I assumed it was acceptable. We had free accommodation and food of course but otherwise there would have been a substantial hotel and transport bill, so it was swings and roundabouts and I knew Sarah appreciated that.

Heather looked at my draft copy briefing album and studied it more thoroughly during the days I was at home catching up on matters generally, and she finally said, "Jim, it's really very good, how accurate I cannot tell, but the breadth and scope of your examination of that estate and all the unusual things you have had to deal with is incredible. You have managed to make it interesting and understandable to a non-farming, non-fishing academic like me. The spreadsheet is also very easy to understand and pretty comprehensive; very well done. I think it will go through substantially as it is subject to law and regulation, etc., and the costing and profit ratios will hold up, even if either or both are amended, I believe."

I thanked her and pointed out we had it all to do again at the larger Irish estate where, although things were superficially similar, it was Ireland and nearly all the people were Irish, so it would be difficult at first certainly, but Sarah was joining us to try to ensure willing cooperation so that should move things along a bit. And the boys were now pretty well versed in farm and related matters, and the river situation was similar, and my own research showed that so was the official and administrative situation, so it looked as though after some adjustment, and especially if we could locate a man like Peter, a local salmon expert, and the gamekeeper in Ireland was of George's calibre, all should be well.

After some more research and spending a weekend with Heather, no children this time, and generally chilling out, I felt I was ready to start again. I made some calls and booked me and the team onto the Dublin flight from Manchester three days hence on a Thursday.

I told Sarah and she said, "Leave the pickup at the airport to me, and I will join you on Friday at about mid-afternoon, I think. Thursday, get your team settled in and look at the castle on the Friday morning perhaps and we can take it from there. I will order dinner at eight pm as usual, and of course there is the Guinness!"

I drove us to Manchester Airport on the Thursday, and we took off on time arriving at Dublin Airport at about ten-thirty a.m. At the baggage hall were met by Sean in the old Range Rover and drove to the castle by the confusing lanes and small roads, omnipresent once a few miles from the city. Bertie and Hannah were at the entrance to the keep greeting us as we disembarked from the Range Rover, with big smiles on their faces. I introduced David and Henry and we took our own luggage inside the hall and there it was taken from us and up to our rooms. The boys were amazed at the sight of this partly medieval sprawling castle with its own little village within the perimeter walls, and the keep and moat and massive oak-and-iron-bound main door. Inside also, the sight of all the old artefacts, paintings, weapons, and tapestries absorbed much of their attention at first.

Then, like at my last visit, Bertram insisted the boys called him Bertie and said, "Almost time for lunch so what would you boys like to drink before we go to the dining hall?"

I kept quiet and the boys said a beer would be fine then I said, "A pint of your wonderful Guinness if you please."

Bertie said to the butler, "Patrick, three pints of Guinness and two IPAs please and for Hannah, your usual gin and tonic or something else?"

She replied, "I will have a half of Guinness please, and Sean?"

"A half of the black stuff too please."

The drinks came and the crystal jugs and two halves of Guinness sat on the tray looked beautiful, and the two bottles of IPA with their frosted glasses looked fine too. I took a pull at my pint, wiped the cream from my upper lip and sighed, and said quietly, "Cheers everyone."

There were no speeches this time, just friendly looks and smiles and a babble of conversation as each relaxed and sipped their drinks and nibbled at the contents of some pots of mixed nuts, a tray of savoury bits and pieces, and small squares of different cheese with pickles.

Lunch was called by the dining hall bell, and we trooped in and took our places, with me sitting next to Hannah and with Bertie on my other side and Sean between David and Henry. The feast spread before us was something to behold, as was all the crystal glassware, silver cutlery and vast glazed pottery servers containing all manner of things, plus three great platters. One of partridge, pheasant, and guinea fowl, trimmed with sautéed vegetables, a second held a whole leg of lamb with mint and rosemary, and the third a leg of pork covered in crisp crackling. There were also cold cuts and salads and various fish for those who were so inclined and lovely home-made bread with farm-made butter.

Hannah said, "Start and finish with whatever you fancy, no separate starters but you will see several fish including shellfish which you are at liberty to start with if you wish, or you can go straight to whatever you fancy. There is red and white wine at your elbow, or more beer, Guinness, water, whatever you like. No rules here except enjoy."

We had a noisy and friendly lunch and then the boys and I took a stroll around the castle with Sean and probably covered about half of it and got lost a couple of times before I called a halt, said I needed to take stock and went to my room, leaving the three young men together quite happily carrying on with their tour. We all surfaced again for dinner at about a quarter to eight and had yet another splendid meal after which I said I needed a walk to work some of it off before retiring. Sean took me and the boys for a good walk, about a mile, to guess where: the local pub! But I had just two halves of Guinness and we walked back by which time a coffee and a small brandy finished off a very nice first day in Ireland. I reminded everyone that Sarah would be here by lunchtime tomorrow, so we needed to look at my briefing notes and the draft plans we had prepared for the English estate, which I had brought with me to show

Bertie and Hannah, to give them a yardstick to compare estates and consider using some of the material from the one to inform their own ideas for the other.

I had found out from Peter that the crayfish we ate at the English estate were not the native species called white-claw crayfish, as these had been almost wiped out after the introduction by the government of the American species signal crayfish. This latter species was larger and more aggressive which, although better eating, carried a disease which killed off the English variety, so they only carry on in smaller numbers in isolated situations where the American variety have not managed to populate. This reminded me of the history of the grey and red squirrels. So we needed to try to save any of the white tailed crayfish colonies we found. These creatures are now protected as an endangered species worldwide, whereas the signal crayfish could be trapped under licence and legally eaten or sold as there is a big market for them, especially in Scandinavia. Whether we can farm them successfully or not as an adjunct to our trout farm is open to question, but my feeling is that providing it is cost effective, however low the margin of profit is, we should go for it as a draw factor for visitors and to offer on the menu at the hotel restaurant.

Freshwater mussels are a different kettle of fish. There are now no viable populations of pearl mussels, which can grow more than 6 inches in length and live up to 100 years. I learnt that the pearls found in them were famously sought after by invading Romans and European Royalty over the last 2,000 years in the UK. Pollution in the few rivers capable of sustaining them has decimated them as a meaningful source of pearls. The strange thing I discovered is that these mussels need to have their eggs and young attached to salmon or trout gills for their first year of existence, and Devon Wildlife Trust have been successful in breeding some of the seventy- or eighty-year-old mussels still alive in a large tank. They live there with trout and their offspring are attached to a number of fish living with them, showing it can be done. It is prohibited to take pearl mussels in the UK now, and if the small cottage industry around their collection in Scottish rivers still exists, it is illegal. It seems that our local mussels plucked from clear streams on our estate are not pearl mussels but some other type. At least two possibilities exist, both edible and good to eat: the swan mussel and the duck mussel. The swan mussels can grow up to 25 cm in length! I need to get a couple of examples of the shells I have seen to decide which is best for us, but they are very slow growing and although we can continue to harvest them for our table, it is unlikely that they would be viable as a commercial crop. But again, why not locate the main beds where they exist and improve or simulate the same conditions in other streams and increase their yield over time? And my understanding is that these mussels are much more tolerant than their famous cousins the pearl mussels and will thrive in ponds and lakes as well as in the river and streams.

Forearmed with this information, I intended to carry out a survey with the help of whoever looked after the Irish rivers and streams and the current fishing activities. I wanted to see what the scope was for some development of the river along the lines of the plan we had produced for the English estate, and work into my plan for this estate whatever crayfish or mussel harvesting might be found available.

Chapter 34

Sarah arrived with Sean at about twelve-thirty and received a welcome from us all. She went up to her room and came down shortly after for a chat and a pre-lunch tipple. Over drinks, I mentioned my research into freshwater crayfish and mussels. I said how I intended to stitch this into my appraisal of their existing river and stream activity to see whether it might be worth incorporating my idea of a crayfish production scheme into a trout farm, if we have one here, and also to explore harvesting mussels. I added that although they seemed a more unlikely commercial project, certainly at this stage, it might be prudent to look at sites and numbers of the mussel beds to see what the potential for their expansion might be. I also pointed out that we would still use them for the table and any surplus could be offered on an a la carte menu in the restaurant for the more discerning clients, and even offered to suitable outlets like upmarket delicatessens and the like.

She nodded and turned to talk to Bertie about something and I took the hint and focussed on Hannah for a while asking her if she knew the volume of mussels and crayfish available during the season. She didn't know but judging from how often they had them, there must be quite a few. She was unaware which particular species either of them were, other than they were freshwater varieties.

That took us up to lunch and we were invited to the dining hall set out in all its usual splendour and took our allotted seats. Sarah next to Bertie with Hannah next to him and me next to Hannah and round to the three boys. Sarah chatted to Bertie and Hannah most of the time catching up with matters general as she had not been here for quite a while so there was much to talk about. Then halfway through the main course Sarah said, looking at me and the boys, "I am sure you are aware Bertie, that James and his team have done an excellent job so far at my home estate so I am hoping that you ensure that all your people and tenants are as helpful as they possibly can be when they get round to them all."

"Absolutely," said Bertie, "they have nearly all met James already and word has gone round about the plan they have produced for you. Hannah and I have looked at a copy kindly brought by James, and we are very impressed and look to see that we get something similar here with all that will mean to our future security, and the joy of seeing all these plans come to fruition."

"Yes," said Hannah, "if I may come in at this point?"

Sarah said, "Of course."

Hannah continued, "May I just say that I was impressed by James on his first visit, but I was overwhelmed by the sheer scope and depth of his draft plan for your home estate which he and his team have produced in such a short time. It is truly amazing, and I can see already the many parallels with our estate. I am so excited at the prospect of seeing something very similar being done here, assuming, of course, that is possible."

Sarah said, "Let me make it very clear, I agree with your remarks and everything and almost anything is possible; I am confident that James and his team will deliver something even better than my home plan because he will have all that experience to draw on. Furthermore, I hope and believe that the potential here is even greater than at my home and I assure you that I will not stint in fulfilling whatever is decided is possible and desirable, law and regulations, etc., allowing."

Hannah simply clapped her hands and beamed, with joy written all over her face. "Wonderful!" she said. "Music to my ears and I look forward to this old place ringing with laughter, and full of joy and relish the opportunity to be part of it."

Sarah said, "Hannah it is good to hear what you have just said because it will be a difficult and demanding task. I also am pleased you made no reference to profit or money, just the joy it will give you, that means more to me. And I am sure the rest will follow as sure as day follows night. A successful business makes for happy owners, managers and staff and happiness will ensure profitability, but more importantly, it will further secure the future for generations to come."

Bertie simply said, "Hear, hear!"

We began our Phase 1 plan, Ireland estate, the following morning and started with the castle and its various buildings both within and without the perimeter walls and the moat. We paid particular attention to the part of the castle which Hannah had earmarked as the best part to convert into a kind of hotel, albeit still remaining within the castle; particularly important was that the outside appearance remained unspoilt and avoiding any unwanted criticism on that aspect of any planning consents. Amazingly, as the castle had changed several times over a vast number of years and it was almost an ongoing process, no Listed Building designation had ever been made. The various members of Sarah's ancestors who had resided here had never considered it necessary and the local council or equivalent Irish Authority had never sought to intervene and neither had any national body. But I suggested some sort of notification of our intentions should be made, and Sarah said, "Leave it to me at present, I will make a few calls and visit the people responsible for the Listing and Protection of Historic Buildings and Sites and see if we can carry on as before or what might be a sensible compromise. But I agree we cannot just assume, as my ancestors appeared to, that we can do as we like regardless. If we have to make plans and submit them for approval under Building Regulations that's one issue, but in the absence of actual Listed Building designation I feel we are in a strong position to reach a sensible compromise, as I am certain my ancestors must have. Perhaps you and I, James, should delve into the archives in the library and see if we can find anything on the subject while the boys continue with their inspection of the four cottages designated as suitable for conversion into family or group occupation, and the other rooms which Hannah has earmarked. They can also consider, with Hannah's help, where we might best locate a restaurant and a function room large enough to accommodate say up to at least eighty people."

They looked at each other and gulped a little and with that, set off with Hannah to do as they were bade.

"Right James," she said, "before the library we need to talk about how we play this because I want no indication whatever that Hannah may be on to us, so I will continue to cut you off occasionally and even shun you a little, but fear not, nothing has changed, just want to be ultra-careful. Let's just go to my suite while I freshen up before we tackle the archives, shall we?"

I replied, "I thought you'd never ask. And we went to her suite and made love for a half hour, had a quick shower and down to the library, calling for tea and coffee as soon as we got there and spreading ourselves out with some papers, as if we were there for some time already.

We realised that a servant might see something, but Sarah said it was more than their lives were worth to cross her and they would keep silent, even amongst themselves. Hannah would also not rock the boat of that I was certain, but I agreed better all-round if we allayed rather than created suspicion and I modestly though myself a past master at this particular sort of thing.

We had the beverages and then Sarah quickly located the archives of past alterations and major repairs carried out to the castle and all the other permanent structures on the entire estate, an absolute gold mine of information. We took a pile each and started to look at the newest ones first and worked our way backwards. It was clear that there had been no building regulations application papers kept, and no mention of Listed Building Status or applications, rejections, or consents. My most recent file dated about thirty-five years ago related to a major roof overhaul, replacing some roof timbers, and resetting new lead sheeting, stonework and cement applications as well as treating some parts with bitumen and tar. This was just maintenance I surmised and wouldn't need any planning consents as nothing was substantially altered. Sarah's first couple of files were in the period twenty to thirty years ago and again were not related to new construction, simply improving, repairing, and upgrading roofs, coping stones, etc.

Then my next file looked more promising and was entitled, 'Kitchen and Storerooms Extension'." As the title suggested, there were plans of a new construction expanding an old kitchen with old cast iron, wood-fired stoves, and numerous alcoves, pantries and storage areas which had also been drawn to scale. The new larger kitchen had just two large storage areas leading off and covered the installation of an electricity system for the cookers and also to replace old oil lamps. In essence, it was just a larger more modern kitchen and this had been in 1947, after electricity was connected in the locality for the first time. This was well after their English counterparts which happened between the two World

Wars in the 1920s and 1930s. No sign of any planning applications or consents or of building regulations applications was present.

Sarah was studying a thicker file which I could see was headed. *"Removal of old Dining Hall and Rebuilding."* This this was a major project essential because of "death watch beetle" infestation, wet and dry rot in elm beams and trusses, replacing the slate slab roof with lead sheeting on oak boards and seasoned oak beams and trusses reinforced with wrought iron straps and bars. The old stone hearth had been retained as had the huge slate slabs covering the floor, which, although worn in places, were still complete and with no substantial cracks.

The local stone walls, faced with dressed stone but filled with rubble and mortar, had cracked, and bellied out with the weight of the old roof, and were in a dangerous condition. But again, it was essentially remedial work and did not substantially alter the size and shape of the room, so again no planning application or consent of any kind was found.

My next file was dated 1894 and related to the building of several cottages in the castle grounds to replace old wooden huts and sheds used at various times by employees and their families. These cottages were also for livestock, which were kept on the ground floor, the people sleeping in the eaves on a platform of rough-hewed branches and wattle and daub, covered in hay or straw, which then found its way down to the animals below as it became fouled, as bedding and fodder. Now these new cottages, were still standing and in good condition, and much bigger and build of stone or brick and with oak windows and doors and fireplaces with proper chimneys for heat and cooking. They had water put in with lead pipes but no electricity until fifty or so years later. These undoubtedly should have had some sort of consent in modern law but in 1894, we didn't know what the situation would have been. Again, there was no evidence of any planning applications, refusals, or consents.

We both concluded that searching any further back would not alter the situation. Clear precedent showed no applications were sought and we had no evidence they were necessary, so the next move would be Sarah's approach to people she knew in Dublin and in the local area to try to establish which was the best way to avoid problems, while complying with both national Irish law and Local Authority Regulations in terms of general planning consents. At the same time, she could find out what the Building Regulations situation was in Ireland, and I suggested that maybe a good, chartered surveyor or an architect might be a useful source of information. Meantime, I argued, a lot of what we wanted to do here, unlike in England, was reforming, updating and repairing existing structures. Then on top of that, we would need to consult about fire regulations and inspections and bear their requirements in mind before the final planning stages were reached. But for now, I felt our draft Phase 1 plan for Ireland could proceed along the same lines as the English one and we would worry about the technicalities later. Sarah agreed merely saying it was good business to try to anticipate what might be required before getting too far in implementing the plans themselves.

So basically, we had the green light to forge ahead as planned and made a schedule of work based on the layout of the castle and its satellites, the tied farms, and all the land, rivers, streams, lakes, ponds, including any bogs, peat or otherwise. Also stands of timber and types, etc. and all the different land usage, mainly grass, silage and hay at present; numbers of animals — cattle, sheep and lambs and pigs — and what proportion was already considered and certified as organic, and which were part way there and those not yet started.

Plus, fishing activity, collection of shellfish, hunting and shooting of game, sport shoots of the clay pigeon variety; in short, whatever was happening, had happened in the past year or two and was already planned for this or the next year or so, to see how we might modify and enlarge any areas capable of sustaining expansion.

Then, was there a case for making a golf course? What, if any, horse riding facilities existed and how they might be developed? I knew that Ireland was famous for fishermen and many angling trips and holidays were already available, so we had to look at that and decide what slice of the market we could best develop and exploit, connected with stays in our 'Genuine old Castle Hotel', first-class accommodation and restaurant, pitched I suggested at four-star. That meant heated pool and games rooms, sun terraces, and much more was needed to be considered and this would apply across all three estates. This would fit snugly with our aim to attract those seeking corporate leisure and conference facilities, with the necessary internet access and lecture equipment and the many different leisure activities we offered; as well as attracting pure holidaymakers with a taste for good class outdoor activities. But we also had to ensure that there was plenty on offer inside, for when the damp Irish weather intervened. Much food for thought, and top of the list was food and drink, exciting and different dishes, mainly organic and mostly home produced. Plus, a mini spa with saunas, steam rooms, massage facilities and a gymnasium, alongside the indoor and perhaps outdoor pools.

We got hold of the resident estate gamekeeper, who also looked after the fishing, hunting, and shooting activities, as well as the collection of crayfish and mussels, much as George did in England. He was a jovial Irishman of local descent, who clearly knew the entire estate intimately; he loved his job and was very interested in our ideas for change and expansion, having been briefed by Hannah and Bertie.

It was about twelve noon, so I said, "Tell me Timothy, does your nearby local in the village have Guinness?"

At which he laughed and said, "Certainly it does, and I hear you are partial to a drop as am I, in moderation of course, but it's Tim, sir, if you please."

And I replied, "Right Tim, and it's Jim for me if you please also, and I think now might be a good time to sample a drop, don't you?"

"Yes, but only if you twist my arm sir, sorry Jim." So I grabbed his arm and put it up his back quite rapidly and he was a bit surprised, then laughed as I let go and said, "I submit, I submit!" And he led the way to his Land Rover and the four of us went rattling along the lane about a mile to The Globe Inn. We parked up in the tiny car park at the back amidst three other old Land Rovers and entered the pub by the back door into the bar.

As we entered, a large buxom lady of indeterminate years looked askance at me and the boys, until she saw Tim at which she gave a little scream and said, "Tim darling, what have you brought me this time?"

He replied, "Be careful Molly, this man is dangerous, he just forced me in here against my will!"

"Oh, that *is* impressive, I have been trying to force you to go against your will for years, but no success," she said.

Tim laughed at that and said, "Molly, allow me to introduce Jim here and his two young colleagues, David and Henry, who are here to bring the big house up to date and make us all rich."

I said, "He may be right in the long-term, but for now I would like a pint of your excellent Guinness please and I expect the boys will have halves," at which they nodded. I smiled and added, "And I presume Tim will force a pint down too." She laughed and said to no one in particular, "A man after my own heart," and went to do our bidding.

We sat near the window and waited until she brought the drinks and after thanking her, I said, "Tim, all joking aside, we have a very important job to do here, and I think you are just the man to help in several ways. I don't know if you have ever met George the gamekeeper at the English estate but suffice it to say if you know half of what he does that will be good; if you know the same, that's very good, but, if as I suspect, at least in relation to this estate, you know more, then you are the man I need here."

"As it happens, I do know George, and he is a fine man and a very knowledgeable chap, and in relation to his estate, no one knows it better. And he is very good on the river situation too, but he has been there only about twenty years, whereas I was brought up here, fished the river illegally as a boy, trapped their pheasant and partridge and poached just about everything poachable. But, when I was asked to put my proven talents to a legitimate cause by Bertie's father, I jumped at the chance and have been their loyal and obedient servant ever since. They say don't they, 'he be a poacher turned gamekeeper, none better', they say."

"All right," I said, "well, I have picked up a bit in my travels and I have fished since I was a boy, and my job here is to get the best out of everyone, so if you don't mind, I will of course form my own opinions but I believe all you tell me. Let's see what we can discover together about this estate which will give me the ideas and facts I need to produce a plan, not just for the river and the fish and the game, but an integrated plan which will draw people in from all over the world to participate. As just normal holidaymakers, corporate hospitality clients, expert anglers and trophy hunters, gourmets who want to sample our organic, home-produced food and rare and unusual dishes. Some of them may want to hunt some game birds at least, shoot pheasant and partridge and maybe grouse; enjoy our indoor facilities with the pool, gymnasium, spa, including sauna, steam room and massage facilities. They would also fish for salmon in a restored salmon river, and sea trout as well as brown trout, purchase stocks of fresh fish from our own trout farm and more. Does that sound interesting to you?"

"Indeed, it does", he said, "it's long overdue and what's more, from all I already know, you are the man to make this happen, and this estate will surpass even its former glory days and you are right, I am the man for you."

I shook his hand and so did the boys and we all went silent, thinking about what we had said and heard and sipping our Guinness ruminatively. Then Tim said, "Crikey, you will be late for lunch; I had better get you back pronto."

I arranged to meet him later at the stables where he had a small office and where a lot of his equipment was stored.

At lunch I asked Bertie about Tim and he told me he was very good at his job, completely trustworthy and knew the estate better than any others single person. He also told me that Tim's knowledge on river-based wildlife was encyclopaedic, and he knew where all the best fishing spots were, where to find the crayfish and mussel beds, how they were harvested, etc. After lunch, the boys continued surveying the castle and all other buildings within the perimeter walls and nearby outside and were told to make notes and sketches and take photographs. These would help in deciding which houses, barns and castle rooms lent themselves to be turned into four-star hotel class accommodation, focussing on the area Hannah had said was the best for this purpose. I pointed out that it would be important to link the cottages by covered walkways to the main accommodation area and the restaurant, as well as for protected accessibility to the leisure and sport facilities.

I met Tim after lunch and asked him to take me to the river and show me the best fishing slots and make any suggestions he liked for improvement. I said I would question him as well as we went along and point out some of the sites if they seemed to lend themselves to the kind of activity we envisaged at the English estate. I also said that we were considering building a fish farm, principally for rearing trout, which would need diverted or pumped river water running through it, as well as breeding crayfish, at which he raised an eyebrow. But he was unaware at this stage that I had researched this possibility and found that there were about eighty crayfish breeders and suppliers in the UK at present, albeit none were large or considered a worthwhile commercial investment in themselves. However, I thought that as part of a fish farm scheme they would be worthwhile and as an interesting new meal for guests and also that upmarket delis and restaurants would buy them, if we had a surplus from our own requirements. An added interest, in short.

So, we started at the lowest accessible point on the riverbank about a mile from the castle where the river left our fenced and walled property. Further downstream, Tim informed me, it flowed for miles with no fenced or organised farmland on either side for several hundred yards in each direction, on through untamed moorland and ponds, streams, and a lake, before heading for the sea about twenty-five miles away. Tim said that we had sole fishing rights all the way to the sea, and part of his job was to chase people off who were fishing illegally. We granted no licences at all at present and these were akin to Feudal rights. He said it was possible to take a small boat or raft out to the coast providing the river was periodically kept free of trees and debris, again part of Tim's responsibilities. We also had shooting rights along the river up to five hundred yards either side and there was a fence there at five hundred yards with notices all along its length at regular intervals warning of trespass, poaching, and trapping, shooting, and hunting, with fines up to 1,000 pounds if caught and prosecuted. Tim regularly took his hunting dogs and his assistant gamekeeper Bob, and it was possible to drive a Land Rover along a track at either side of the river all the way to the estuary. They inspected the river as they went, stopping to deal with minor problems and looking for signs of illegal activity, snares or traps and campfires, etc. Everyone in the County knew Tim and his patrols and steered clear of him, as he had more than once said he would shoot first and ask questions later, if he caught anyone who appeared to be armed and acting illegally.

This was music to my ears, because it meant protection for the salmon and sea trout on their way up from the sea and for the few returning adult fish as well as the thousands of small fry, because Tim

304

also shot and trapped the predators which had no protection in law. I asked about foxes and badgers: were they a problem?

He replied, "They can be, but I have a few foxhounds and some Jack Russell's and we clear out any dens we find and shoot or trap them as well if they are in the same area as sheep and lambs which is allowed in law. Just as farmers can shoot stray dogs worrying livestock in the UK as well.

I opted not to go all the way today, stopping at the estate boundary proper and then we made our way back towards the castle stopping periodically to inspect the banks of the river and any streams entering it. We also assessed the numerous ditches which criss-crossed the borders of the river to enable drainage and for the drained land to be used by livestock, also for sileage and hay making.

I noted some excellent pegs for anglers and Tim pointed out the best flows for salmon and trout fly fishing; there were many on both sides of the river and a large raft which was tethered on the castle side so that parties of anglers could be poled across, with the raft running along a stout rope to prevent it drifting downstream when the river was in spate. Another similar raft was tethered about five hundred yards further upstream for the same purpose. The nearest bridge was a good way downriver necessitating about a mile walk, but that was no problem for the Land Rover of course. And there was another bridge about five miles upstream for our vehicles to access both sides of the river.

We ultimately came to a large bow in the river covering from about half a mile to about a quarter of a mile from the castle. I said I thought it looked ideal as a site for the fish farm, as we could simply run a large pipe from the upper bank, in a covered ditch, down towards the direction of the sea where it could have its outflow after passing through the fish tanks where the bow in the river ended. Some screening bushes and trees could be planted, and the fish farm built low, perhaps a yard below the ground surface, such that it would be almost invisible from the castle. Tim looked carefully at the whole area taken in by the bow in the river and agreed it was all possible and ideally situated for easy access without spoiling the views from the castle, especially if the roof of the fish farm building was only slightly raised at one side to facilitate drainage, and the building was predominantly cedar, set on a concrete base buried a yard underground and unseen, with a gravel path around the perimeter.

Then I broached the subject of increasing the salmon population and started by asking Tim if he had any records of sightings and catches over the period he had been in charge and he said yes, he had. But from memory alone he reckoned that the average sightings over these last ten years or so would be about fifty per day over a three-month period, say 4,500 or so each year. And he had records going back thirty years which is when he started as gamekeeper and the numbers then were double what they are now, so possibly 9,000 salmon sighted then per annum. I was amazed and said, "What measures have you taken in regard to water purity and accessibility to the spawning grounds to enable that sort of level of salmon moving upstream and continuing to do so now?"

He related something similar to what I was proposing at the English estate. Fords or bridges over the many streams and dykes, keeping cattle watered by putting a stream-fed tank at each point required, and fencing off the river at these points so the cattle automatically used the tanks and so didn't foul the streams with mud and excrement. Plus fencing the gravel beds situated higher up the streams so no access to cattle was possible and the water there, as he would now show me, was crystal clear and about three to six inches in depth over fine, natural gravel beds, perfect for spawning and mating. This, together with his aggressive anti-predator actions and his firm control of poachers on and off the main estate and limiting the taking of salmon in prime breeding condition to those injured or sick when caught, but immediately releasing all others, had maintained the numbers, and even increased them over his time in the job. But this last ten years there had been fewer salmon and he wasn't sure why. I said, "Are you aware that the American crayfish are predators and do not just eat weeds and so on like the indigenous type does, but catch and eat fry (which are any small fish) of all species, and salmon fry in particular. And the decline seems to have started about ten years after introduction of the American crayfish so that could account for a large part of the decline. And another reason was the aggressive salmon fishing at sea near the river mouths and sea and river pollution generally."

"Well Jim", he said, "That's something I didn't know, that the buggers were fish and flesh eaters. I thought, like the old ones, they lived

306

on weeds and small stuff like plankton. And there are thousands of the buggers on this estate, even up in the spawning levels. That would explain a lot as there is no fishing for salmon in our estuary, I see to that, and precious little pollution although I can't say what happens out at sea."

"Well, it's good there are thousands, and we can concentrate on trapping them all along the riverbanks and in the spawning areas and maybe put some sort of barrier round the nursery pools amongst the gravel where the baby salmon congregate for several months after hatching, I bet that's where the most damage occurs. And we can effectively farm them for our use and for sale. More on that later."

This was excellent news, and I outlined my measures for the English estate and said that any anglers allowed to take trophy-size salmon would have at least three released for one taken, and they would be the privileged few, not a day visitor or a holidaymaker, perhaps a few high-end corporate types who made a very significant booking. Even then we would make it clear in our literature that the final decision regarding such fish would be taken only by Tim and his word would be law within the estate.

He liked that and said, "That's a good idea, it will bring good anglers who will understand and respect our position, and if you also stock trophy-size carp as well, that will bring the same type of clients who in any case never take such fish out of a lake or river with or without supervision. Imagine brochures showing a thirty- or forty-pound salmon being caught and also a similar size carp in the same stretch of river. But how will you keep the carp in and allow the salmon upstream as well as detaining them long enough to have a chance of being caught?"

"Fish ladders on both sides of the river for the salmon and sea trout to ascend for a good stretch, then another set of ladders across the centre so that those who don't get caught by rod escape the same way as the others did. And the carp can't climb the ladders so they are stuck with us. Then I have two strategies for keeping the big coarse fish in: first, regular feeding with organic anchovy and vegetable pellets, and second, by modifying the out flow of the river downstream with some large and small rocks so that if not impossible, it will be very difficult for large carp to negotiate a way through. Providing we maintain what is in effect an artificial weir so that it doesn't get blocked up, I think it will serve its purpose. But I think a long stop could be some sort of barrier, yet to be decided on, which will detain the odd large carp long enough to be to be caught by net perhaps and returned up past the weir. But I also believe that the large carp will already be used to being fed, by ground bait, etc. and will not bother trying to escape providing we have, say, half a mile of river for them to use."

"I like it and I think you are right. And now I will tell you about the crayfish which can be a problem making holes in the riverbank and causing excessive erosion, I know that crayfish are taken by both salmon and large carp, so that should reduce the population in the river, and as regards farming them, I hear that the intensive crayfish farmers simply put large amounts of spawn and young into a pond, doesn't matter if it's clean or not so long as no chemicals are used nearby. They flourish on decayed plants and so on but will also happily eat the fish food as well. Although some might escape, you cannot overstock the ponds because they breathe air, so oxygenating the ponds is not an issue. So long as they are moved when big enough to a clean holding tank with clean running water through it, rather like lobsters in a restaurant tank, they will purge themselves over a few days, reducing the possibilities of contamination when boiled, and then barbecued or whatever, to almost nothing. And then onward transfer to a deli or a restaurant in a tank cleans them further and they will live many days in clean water with no food. And the predation of salmon fry or other fry in the ponds will be unimportant as few will survive in such an environment."

"That's good advice Tim. Now where are they at present and how do you get them from there to the table?"

"It's very simple and easy but don't tell anybody else that please, it's part of my mystique. I set traps as you suggested earlier, and these are just like small lobster pots which you can buy, but I get them made by an old basket weaver in the village who used to collect the withies from our willow breaks which grow along some streams way up the valley, but which I now collect for her. Then I put the crayfish from the traps in a large stone trough, run a hose into it and let it overflow through a pipe near the top and cover the trough with chicken wire one-inch mesh and after a couple of days I take them out and give them to Cook, who immediately boils them in slightly salted water for five minutes. Then she drains them and puts them in the refrigerator to be grilled or done in a sauce or whatever just before serving or cooks them completely and serves them cold. As for quantity there must be thousands; I don't really know but these are the American type which were imported in the 1970s I understand, and they have almost wiped out our own type and there's none I know of on the estate. So yes, a bit labour intensive although a few hundred held in a pond would be easier to handle I suppose and they'd make an interesting delicacy for your visitors, I think. But now I know about them predating the fry, I will get a hundred more traps made; the old girl will be pleased. Maybe we can buy some of the stainless steel or plastic types immediately as well and blitz the river and the spawning levels to reduce the numbers. Parboiled and frozen they will be OK for up to six months. And we can still have almost fresh ones as well whenever we like. The salmon are starting to run now so not a moment to lose!"

"Good so far, confirms what I already know from my research; now, what about the mussels?"

Tim answered, "They are a similar story, the pearl mussels no longer exist here but I believe they do in Scotland, but they are a protected species anyway. There are several indigenous mussels in The British Isles and here in Ireland and all of them, about six varieties, are edible and easily found and collected in the right environment. But actually, saltwater mussels are another species I believe, and I think they are better than freshwater mussels and quite inexpensive. But freshwater mussels, like the crayfish, are a novelty and I don't think are farmed commercially at all, but I could be wrong. But I agree that as an interesting adjunct to the trout-farm produce and the crayfish, why not? Certainly, to offer them on the restaurant menu as locally produced and organic, it might be feasible, and you would have little to lose in trying it out at very little additional cost. They are found in all the streams and ponds and even in the dykes and although slow-growing, careful harvesting would see a sustainable small yield, I think. I don't think an organised freshwater mussel farm could pay, but collected like we do, it's a novelty and an added interest. They again need purging in clean water for a few days then boiled and stewed or grilled rather like the crayfish. Although, I believe you can keep them alive and well for weeks just in water, especially in a refrigerator which slows all activity down without damaging them in any way. In fact, I believe that applies to the crayfish too, so let's experiment with a hundred or so. We will keep them in cold freshwater in a large refrigerator and it will be the same as them hibernating, so why not do that and have a year-round supply of live crayfish as well as boiled and frozen like king prawns are."

"Good enough Tim, that will suffice for now. Just show me where you trap the crayfish and a typical mussel bed and I think it will be time for a pint before dinner. In case it hasn't been mentioned I would like you there please sitting next to me."

"Yes, I have been told and I will put my Sunday jacket on."

So, well satisfied so far, I arranged to continue with Tim tomorrow morning, and we went to The Globe and were received by Molly as enthusiastically as yesterday, at the back entrance. I had two pints of Guinness as did Tim and some nibbles and we made our way back to the castle in time to clean up and make ourselves presentable at dinner. I went down to the dining hall at a quarter to eight as arranged with the boys and we and Tim managed to get to our places and be served with a drink before everyone else came in. The boys gave me a quick résumé of their progress; my story would have to wait.

No dinner jackets, just smart casual and both Tim and I wore almost identical tweed jackets which caused some mirth. After some general chat, Bertie got our attention and said, "We are keen to hear how you have got on, but not details, too early, just to know that you have had no difficulties and are received full cooperation." Sarah took a back seat through this as Bertie was the host for tonight's dinner.

I waited and David started by saying, "So far everything has gone very smoothly for us two, but we are only part way through the building inspections as yet, all I can say is it is looking good and yes, everyone has been most helpful."

They all looked at me and Tim seated in our similar coats and I said, "Tim is a mine of knowledge and information about all manner of things concerning our plan, but I wish to disclose nothing much at this point other than to say his own measures, which I understand have been almost entirely taken on his own volition, to conserve the salmon stock using this river have already achieved in the years he has been here, the sort of numbers of sighted salmon we are aiming for in England. Averaging as many as 4,500 sightings each year, an incredible success story, and he has been employing an almost identical strategy to the one we have decided upon in England, except the salmon ladder idea which will allow many of the salmon to progress uninterrupted to their spawning grounds. But unlike ours in England, his actions have prevented contamination of the spawning grounds for years now, resulting in the levels of sightings he has recorded over the years. In short, he has, almost single-handed, maintained the level of salmon returning here each year to over half of their peak of fifty years ago."

Tim muttered but said nothing and looked a bit embarrassed.

I continued, "We have also looked at the possibilities for a fish farm for trout, and the production, on a very modest scale of freshwater crayfish and mussels and all are, in Tim's view, attainable objectives. I don't want to put Tim in a position where he has to respond at this stage or make any sort of a speech, but I wanted everyone to know just what a treasure this man is and his value to this estate."

"Bertie said, "Well you have certainly not been boasting about all this Tim, and I wouldn't expect you to, and if I were a salmon fisherman myself, I would perhaps have known all this. Although I was aware we had a good stock and regular salmon, in season, on our menu, I had no idea of the relative numbers, nor how that was achieved, so I confess to lack of knowledge about this subject, but I will certainly be taking a much greater interest from here on."

Hannah said, "Tim, I had a good idea what you were doing, but I was also aware that your gamekeeping skills are best not delved into too deeply and you prefer to just get on with it all in your own way, and everything I have seen over the years confirms that is the thing to do. Sarah will of course know about our fishing rights along the river extending all the way to the sea and our powers to apprehend, and prosecute offenders and so on, but it is clear that Tim has managed to keep our rights protected using his own methods very effectively. There have been no prosecutions for all the years he has been here; everyone in the village knows that and why. So, I will say no more on that subject, but simply offer a very big thank you to you Tim; you are all we could wish for as a gamekeeper and I am sure that James' report will tell us just how effective you have been, and the benefits which have flowed from your actions up to now and how that will enhance our position regarding salmon fishing more quickly than we could have imagined."

Tim just did not know what to say, so said nothing, and I started to talk to him about our plans and the dinner progressed from there as normal with everyone relaxed and happy after just that short slightly embarrassing exposition of Tim's skills as a gamekeeper. What's more I knew I had made a friend for life in Tim".

The following morning after breakfast, the boys continued with the buildings survey, earmarking potential sites for the main accommodation objectives, for consultation with Bertie and Hannah and possibly Sarah if she was still here at the appropriate time. Tim and I took our Land Rover and continued upstream into the huge estate, crossing many bridges over streams and dykes, a few of which we stopped at and inspected, and I could see my plan for the English estate right here before my eyes. Clean gravel beds, clear running water; I even saw a trout sitting almost motionless under a low bridge waving his tail to maintain his position. Then Tim pointed to a couple of the withy traps which were almost invisible and pulled them out and I saw for the first time the American crayfish in them, three in one and two in the other, and all about 6 inches in length, ideal for harvesting. Tim put on some special gloves and plucked them out, putting them in a hessian sack soaked with water in the back of the Land Rover. After several such stops, we had a sack full of about twenty-five crayfish to take back to the castle.

I asked him, "If you collected all your current catchable crayfish, how many do you think that would be and how many traps have you laid at present?"

He replied, "I have never done that, but I reckon about a hundred or more in my twenty-five traps, and I last visited these traps about a week ago, so we had plenty for when you came, but the season is roughly three to four months as in the winter they sometimes go into a sort of hibernation deep in holes they make in the banks of the river and streams. But not always, there are always a few around, but maybe in winter I would get about twenty-five or thirty if I visited all the traps after say two or three weeks left alone."

"So if we wanted to, we could say, dig or adapt six ponds, put reeds and pond weed in and about a dozen mature crayfish in one, feed them and put fine mesh galvanised wire around to keep them in. When they breed and have many eggs attached to them, and young larvae are present, we could simply put a few adults and a bucket of eggs and larvae in and fence all the other prepared ponds. In time, in addition to laying more traps, especially in the river as here they do damage to the banks, we could not only increase production maybe tenfold but benefit the river as these beggars eat small fish and other wildlife."

Tim laughed and said, "Yes you are probably not far off in your calculations, but I would need some help harvesting and purging these beggars, but I guess we could have them all year round with feeding them intensively in the ponds, providing I keep out the predators."

I said, "Well I believe some delis and restaurants will pay £1 .50 to £2.50 each for these delivered; I have seen them advertised at one kilo, about eight to ten Crayfish, retailing at 12.95 pounds, so if we sold only 2,000 or 3,000 it would help the overall yield of the trout farm and would definitely provide an interesting feature for visitors and holidaymakers, corporate hospitality types and so on. And with photographs in our pamphlets and literature, as well as specimen salmon, sea trout and carp to be caught, this would increase our appeal not only in the UK but many places around the world. Oh, and I forgot, the mussels as well. So, take me to the mussel beds please Tim."

Off we went further up the estate through the connecting gates and lanes leading to the tied farms, waving as we passed, all the way to the upper borders where the lush green grass gave way to boggy land which contained many ponds and streams moving very slowly downstream where they fed the bigger streams, over the gravel beds where the salmon spawned and of course ultimately, to the river.

We followed a well-defined raised gravel road-bed until we pulled in alongside a large pond ringed by bulrushes, small willows and other bog plants. There, Tim had built staging out into the pond supported on cedar stakes, from the end of which and along the sides, hung hessian netting going down into the clear water. He had left the bottom yard of the platform clear and told me he occasionally fished here for pike and perch, both of which eat small and even larger mussels. He knelt down and pulled up a length of net and clinging to it were dozens of freshwater mussels with greenish-brown shells. He selected about twenty sized 3 inches or more and removed them from the net and put them in a bucket he had brought from the Land Rover which he now half-filled with pond water. He repeated this procedure moving along just the same side of the staging until he had the bucket three quarters full of mussels and we retreated to the Land Rover. He pulled out two cold beers he had put in a container with ice in and a lid, rather like a picnic cool box but not so obvious and opened them and handed one to me.

I noted they were my favourite IPA and thanked him for being so thoughtful and took a swig of the cold beer, it went down a treat. "So," I said, "we have solved the crayfish question I believe; now what about these mussels? It's a long way to come each time, are there none nearer?"

"Certainly, there are," said Tim. "We are starting at the limit of our activity as requested and moving back I will show you more of the same, and some a little different, but all edible and even in the muddy pool's way down near the castle. When purged they are fine to eat, but we have to be sure there are no pollutants getting into the ponds and streams, which we do anyway to protect the salmon and trout. And I collect none over three inches as they are the breeding adults and, in any case, the bigger the mussel the more likely it is to be tough unless cooked slowly in wine and herbs for example. Maybe if we intend selling it would be wise to have regular samples tested for pollutants and certified as edible and fit for human consumption."

I supped my beer and accepted a small pasty he produced from a sandwich box also kept in the beer box and accepted a second beer. We sat quietly each with their own thoughts and I went over all the information I had gained in my head, ready to take notes later on that day while still fresh in my mind.

"Well," I said, "judging from the number of mussels recovered here, and I assume as you took only about one tenth of those available, if you have let's say another fifty sites, I estimate we could harvest thousands every month or so. And that's without creating more ponds!"

"Yes," said Tim, "if you had the market which I doubt, because people generally still prefer saltwater mussels which are relatively cheap, so you would need to research the market a bit before committing to any expansion of our mussel growing and harvesting. And again, you need to consider the labour required to husband the stock, collect it and carry out the purging, etc."

"Yes," I said, "I agree but, people prefer the saltwater mussel because they never see the freshwater variety for sale, except in upmarket restaurants and delis. So I envisage a special purging machine being made to order locally, with a constant supply of fresh stream water rushing through it so it would mean harvesting and then just dumping the whole day's harvest in the machine and returning two or three days later to remove and pack them in ice for transporting to the market, along perhaps with crayfish and freshly killed trout. You could manage all this and supervise, and one capable assistant could do most of the harvesting, maybe one of the men or women employed in the trout farm. I will look at all these things and make some estimates of how many staff are needed and suggest who does what and cost the whole thing for comparison with estimated achievable sales, lower at the start and calculating the time needed to establish a regular market for our combined production. How does that sound to you?"

"Wonderful," he said, "and who can put a value on these special products in terms of the market appeal and the seductive brochures and menus, and all organic, healthy local produce!"

"You are getting the picture now Tim, this is an integrated package of foods and activities of special merit and all available at this unique venue: a medieval castle setting, a meandering river full of salmon, trout and trophy-sized carp, hunting, shooting and fishing for those that want it, indoor and outdoor pools and leisure facilities, a traditional local pub in walking distance, available corporately, and to clubs such as angling clubs and others, and to other groups, families and individuals and all achieved with conservation of species in mind and clean sustainable organic methods of production."

"Where do I book, please? This sounds like utopia!"

I laughed and said, "It is certainly going to make a splash when we have an open day and launch our brand-new holiday and activity resort and list the facilities and the wide range of clients we will welcome. We will put on a magnificent free lunch and invite a selected group of representatives from each category of clients we select and give a short tour of the river and immediate surroundings of the castle and all its facilities, with staff dressed in traditional clothing. I believe the few selected media organisations we invite will do the rest."

I had most of the information I needed at this point about the river and allied activities based on it and its feeder streams and dykes. What I needed to look at next was the farms and all they were doing so that I could compare it with the English estate farms and, after taking into account the type of land here, the different prevalent weather and the traditional methods used. Then, without ruffling any feathers, I needed, where it seemed sensible, to suggest modification, alterations and enhancements of some activates and methods, look at land organics and see what might be done to increase yields in the existing programmes but also to enlarge available arable land and look into crops grown now and those which may be possible with more drainage and slightly different land management techniques. All this without riling anybody or inadvertently demeaning practices which had held sway for many, many years, with these being passed on from generation to generation. Tricky, but with goodwill and the carrot of greater productivity leading to higher remuneration, new equipment and possibly a larger workforce rather than smaller, and the encouragement of Bertie, Hannah and above all Sarah, I believed it was going to work out well.

Sarah, with one eye on her diary, was keen to hear of our progress and any early ideas and she let it be known that a meeting of us all, perhaps before lunch tomorrow, was a good idea so that she could continue her journey armed with some good information, although not yet worthy of the title of plan. I was also pretty certain she had hoped to see more of me but maybe that was wishful thinking. Truth was I had become so involved with Tim and the river-based projects that I had hardly thought about her except in the concept of her wishes regarding the estate and what she might do to oil the wheels. When I did see her at lunch after the whole morning with Tim, I felt sure I was right, she looked at me and said, "James, I am keen to hear any ideas you and Tim have come up with and how they might reflect or compare with your English plan, and I know you have been fully occupied with that. However, I must depart tomorrow afternoon so I have asked all to come to a meeting tomorrow morning at ten a.m. to go through what we have so far and for you to speculate at least, where we might be going with what you have looked at up to now. I have set aside an hour after lunch say two-thirty to three-thirty when I want to have a private discussion with you about some issues arising about the English plan and how that might reflect on the Irish plan preparation."

"Understood Sarah," I said, "I will prepare for the meeting as far as I can and of course I wish to hear about any developments on the English plan and assist in any way I can."

She nodded formally and turned to Bertie who was standing by her side and started talking to him about cattle production and I turned away and talked to Hannah about how, at Sarah's meeting, the survey I had done with Tim would be covered and explained so then she would have a better insight into the interesting ideas we were working on. I was certain that Sarah's pretty cool exchange with me had allayed any possible idea that she and I might have a special relationship. I knew exactly what was happening, that Sarah had near total confidence in me, and that the hour meeting was actually about a last chance to make love with me before she went. I was sure also that she knew I understood that, and the wait would make it all the sweeter when she was able to express herself in any way she wished, alone with me.

The boys had enough information on the buildings situation for us to start drawing some rough plans and diagrams of the alterations they thought might suit the mixture of accommodation and activity rooms we needed, as well as site the new pools and the other leisure facilities as well as a good-sized conference hall. It would be the surveyors and architects who would look at the structural imperatives and decide how much could be achieved internally without seeking any special dispensation and simply complying with building laws and regulations. Sarah and I agreed that the historical records supported our position, and we knew of no requirement to actively seek Listed Building Status for the castle, or the other buildings situated within the castle walls. If at any time a delegation from the government department concerned sought to look at our buildings, including the castle, with a view to recommending or even imposing a survey of them to determine the need or otherwise of the protection of Listed Building Status, so be it. We considered that our position was that one family had looked after and protected these

317

structures for a millennium therefore why would we need the government to do that now, unless they somehow thought our plan for improvement of the estate's chances of being preserved for the good of the country, might not be right or sufficient. So, subject to further expert opinion, we decided to make our plans, submit them to the Local Authority for building regulations consents in the normal way, and await their reactions. We would only fight if that became the only way forward; in short, let the dogs, which had slept for many centuries, lie.

I worked on my notes so that I was sure I had something cogent to say tomorrow and then joined the boys to see what they had come up with. They had covered a lot of ground and had made some impressive sketches with photographs showing the situation before any alterations and representative drawings and sketches showing their own impressions on how they might look afterwards.

They gave me a short version of all they had done and then presented me with a briefing paper they had prepared.

It portrayed that most of the rooms large and small were already the result of many alterations and improvements over the many years of the castle's existence. Some of these had been safety measures with thicker and higher walls in places, others were to enhance the large family occupation including all relations, and their servants, for retreating to in time of war. It seems that the extended family from across the county numbered 150 or more at its peak so, with personal servants, guards and soldiers and castle servants in general, the total numbers in difficult security times would have exceeded four hundred. Even though many would have been in rooms billeted together, most immediate family each had several rooms at their disposal and there were no fewer than five large dining halls built or reformed at various times, the largest of which was currently a massive repository for furniture and artefacts, carvings, paintings, and drawings, statuary and all manner of ancient carved four-poster bed posts, and furniture, much of it worm eaten. Much of it had clearly never been discarded, and almost filled the old grand dining room and was in need of examination, valuation and discarding of perhaps seventy percent which was beyond repair and of no great interest to the current family. If cleared it could be made into a good-sized conference room of approximately 5,000 square feet, albeit in an irregular cross formation. The boys reckoned that even allowing for the restrictions imposed by the irregular shape of the room, that could mean a seating capacity of up to two hundred and fifty persons and would still leave enough space for a stage or podium area, and space to put aisles through and around the blocks of seats, all facing one end, which lent itself to being the focal lecture or display area.

This room, an amalgamation of several rooms of yesteryear, had ceilings of different heights with stout oak columns supporting the several roofs, which had been joined together with massive trusses and pegs and more latterly supplemented with huge iron pins and straps. But it appeared very strong and sound, its one drawback being it only had one wall which was an outside wall, several feet thick and stone built with relatively small wedge-shaped window apertures, presumably to house archers in years gone by. These now allowed only a limited amount of natural light in through leaded coloured-glass windows. But they looked magnificent as the sun set in the west and illuminated the room in coloured light. We thought discreet lighting could change the overall appearance for the better once some of the dingy plastered walls had been repainted and only the magnificent huge oak timbers left their original almost black colour. More importantly there would be no need for any building application, as the room would remain unchanged in structure and size.

Another quite large former dining hall was built very similarly to the grand dining hall and then abandoned and yet a third built presumably as family members grew fewer, and again it was used as a storage room for many old tables and chairs, all oak or beech and many in good condition. Some might be valuable antiques, others too wormy to sit on or use. This room the boys had earmarked as the main part of the sports and recreation area as it was ideally situated beneath many rooms which we thought would make bedrooms and bathrooms; but this room was big enough to house an indoor pool and sauna, jacuzzi and steam rooms leading off, as well as a decent sized gymnasium, baths, and showers and also a massage room which could have several private booths accommodated in it.

The outdoor pool, with maybe a retractable canopy, could be situated in the courtyard behind the reformed second dining hall, so that it could be accessed at the same entrance point as the indoor pool. Both pools could have heating capacity if needed. The smaller old dining halls, which were no longer in use, could make pool and snooker rooms and house other indoor sports facilities. Finally on the ground floor, the last dining room to have been abandoned in favour of the new one in use today, and only 175 years old, was currently used as the butler's pantry and wine and spirits store, as well as the cook's store for large items like sacks of flour, and bins of rice and sugar, and had a huge, shelved area for all manner of preserved and canned goods. Providing Hannah, the butler and the head cook could be prevailed upon to accept a new and more easily accessible storage and cellar area, this penultimate dining hall would make a good dining room or restaurant for the accommodation hotel, and one large adjunct could house the main bar area and reception, ideally situated very near to the main entrance of the castle.

The first and second floors above all this contained many rooms already used as bedrooms, linen rooms, and storage rooms for the head housekeeper and her maids and could easily be re-configured as a hotel-class accommodation area, with an existing lift already installed between the three floors, albeit which would probably need replacing with a more silent modern one. But once again, we believed that no major changes and therefore no planning consents would be needed for those, other than the related safety ones, fire escapes, fire-resistant materials, soundproofing materials, and the like.

It all looked and sounded very good, but we needed both Bertie and Hannah and of course Sarah to look at these rough drafts and the rooms themselves and agree to an expert examining all the old furniture. We would then need to burn that which was beyond repair, repair anything of value, separating genuine and possibly valuable antiques out either to keep and transfer to other buildings on this estate or either of the other two, or store elsewhere, or to sell maybe. This would make all these rooms, which were never visited and were dark and dismal places, into lively interesting rooms in a very special 'hotel in a castle'. Named The Castle Hotel perhaps?

All very exciting and interesting, but just our first stab at this complex and demanding review and all subject to further thought and scrutiny and designed so that any modification of our draft plan could easily be incorporated. But we felt, to avoid any unwanted attention, keeping to the original structures as we had, these plans met all our perceived objectives. Plus, they would keep costs down as well.

"Well," I said, "you have done very well so far, and I am prepared to support the thrust of your arguments and I am satisfied that the general objectives we set ourselves appear to me to have successfully achieved. However, we shall see what the management think and take it from there tomorrow morning at ten a.m. Thank you both, good work as I expected of course."

I studied their report and made a few trigger notes for the meeting in the morning, and after quite a full day another excellent dinner with wine of course, I was more than ready for bed. I had an early night and rose the next morning fit and ready to go.

I had breakfast with the boys and Sean, but Bertie and Hannah and Sarah did not appear so I assumed Sarah might have had a late meeting with them last night or an early private breakfast with them this morning. I wasn't concerned, as I was pretty confident we were on top of this one now, at least up to the farm and crop reviews and I had gained the impression that most locals believed what they had was about right in this climate and location, we would see. I had a few ideas, one was with all that grass, what about farming geese and ducks? I knew the price of a fresh 'green' goose, especially in the run-up to Christmas, they ran forty to sixty pounds apiece in our local butcher's and not much less in Waitrose; ducks were as much as fifteen to twenty pounds apiece for a decent roasting size duck. And here grass was their biggest and most consistent crop. I remembered from my days spent on my pal's farm as a boy, his father saying it takes the grass for rearing five geese to rear one sheep, and three sheep to rear one cow. So I was at least going to ask Tim and see what he thought and organic grass-fed free-range geese and ducks, I believed, might provide a viable return, as, preparation time apart, they were so simple to keep. They kept the grass shorn in their paddocks, fertilised it and were then moved on at the farm I used to go to, and all they needed was letting out of their houses in the morning and locking up safely at night. With just a bit of cracked grain to supplement their diet if grass were not too available, hard to imagine that here in

Ireland. Yes, they squirted their excrement around, but one shower and it was washed into the grass, instant fertiliser.

My other thought had been draining more land to convert it from bog to meadows with the drain water going into the river as it had for millennia before modern farming began. Worth talking about anyway, I reasoned. More available land, more crops, more animals.

Another idea I had come across, did they smoke anything, and did Tim have a licence to kill animals and butcher them or did all the sales of livestock go to market? I thought not because we always had at least half a steer, a couple of pigs split in two and one or two fresh lambs hanging in the chillers, and I knew beef is best hung for three weeks or more before use. My questions to Tim therefore were, did he slaughter stock for home use? If so, how many, and where did he do that? And could that be increased sufficiently so that we could smoke some hams, bacon and so on? I knew Irish smoked bacon was much liked in England and what about whole smoked and cured Irish hams? Which led me next to consider smoking salmon and trout. If it were possible, a small packaging plant could be bought and a couple of people trained in its use so that packaged smoked salmon and trout, and maybe smoked ham too, could be another product, organic of course, to put on our hotel restaurant menu as well as the market. All food for thought, research, and discussion but this is the way that the smaller output of these special foods, when taken together, may become more than just viable, and what an addition to our growing list of quality non-mainstream products the smoking, freezing, and packaging would make.

I grabbed Tim before he left the stables and quickly asked him:

"1. Have you a licence to slaughter livestock here; if so, which kind and how many?

2. What about rearing geese and ducks on all this grass, for restaurant use and sale?

3. Have you ever smoked food items, salmon, trout, ham, bacon, etc?

4. If not, can you research what wood is needed and could you do it?

"No time now, but yes or no, if possible, please."

He replied, "Yes, I have a licence and I slaughter about once a month. One beast (meaning cow or bullock) a sheep, two pigs and four lambs normally. Geese and ducks, messy but possible. Smoked stuff, yes but not an expert, and oak chips normally. Yes, I would love all that including packaging, etc."

"Right," I said, "get a few lines together and come to a meeting we are all having at ten a.m."

"I am already invited, will do what I can."

We all gathered in the big dining hall at ten with Sarah in the chair flanked by her cousin Bertie on her right and Hannah his wife on her left. I sat next to Tim who was on my right and David was on my left with Henry and Sean at their sides. After a brief "Thank you all for being here promptly," Sarah continued, "I am very pleased with what I am hearing, particularly with Tim, whom I have known since I first came here over thirty years ago and watched with amazement when Bertie's father appointed him gamekeeper at only twenty-two years of age, but I now understand why. 'It's simple, he was the best man for the job. So, I want Tim to speak first, to ensure we all hear what he has to say. Tim, the floor is yours and you can say whatever you like, but of course I am very interested in what you think about everything that James has said to you and what you really believe are the best ideas you have heard and experienced and of any which you have real doubts about and then anything else you want to tell us."

He looked at Sarah for a good minute, and then he started. "First and foremost, thank you for your kind words. I have admired you from afar for many years and I know that you have always had the trust Estates' interests, and the interests of your family and your friends and employees at heart, and you make a worthy successor as head of this family, and this estate is at the centre of my existence.

"In no particular order I would like to say that this man, Jim, whom I only met a few weeks ago for the first time, especially as he is not of our world but the world of business and commerce, is one of the most interesting men I have ever met. He knows and understands things about which most people know nothing. And it's not just through research, he has an instinct about animal life, particularly about fish, which is incredible for a man clearly educated for and experienced in business yet is totally aware of the dynamics of our world. And in a very short time I have come to like and respect him and am pleased to be able to call him my friend. The ideas we have discussed, including the increase of salmon stocks, altering the ecosystem of the river and its tributaries, its streams and dykes, the bogs above and all the wildlife existing in it, all fit together, but what he is able to do, almost effortlessly it seems, is put the natural world here on this estate, and by implication, on all three of the estates, into a sensible, meaningful order which not only seeks to preserve and enhance the species involved, predators apart, but in a way commercially viable and attractive at the same time. A real symbiosis between the animals' and fishes' world and the human needs reflected in the need for a degree of commercial success.

"So, we, that is he and I, agree, that we can increase the salmon and sea trout stock even with greater numbers being taken; improve the river eco structure and the salmon young survival rate; reduce the damage done to riverbanks and the fish stocks — the latter of which I was unaware that it was happening, by controlling the huge numbers of American crayfish living in the river through trapping mainly. At the same time increasing their numbers in a controlled way by farming the crayfish from breeding ponds as well as increased trapping not just in our fish farm area and angling slots but all along the river as far as is practicable. We will also introduce large specimen carp, over thirty pounds in weight, for sport and visual impact and they eat crayfish, as do large salmon. We will put salmon ladders in the river on both sides to allow most salmon returning to spawn upriver unimpeded, with only a small number allowed to be caught on rod and line, and an even smaller number to be taken and killed for the table. We will build a fish farm in a perfect site we have earmarked, where it can hardly be seen. We will extend the mussel beds and farm them too in a controlled and healthy way and both crayfish and mussels will form part of a gourmet menu in the castle hotel as well as being sold on the open market, live, fresh frozen or pre-cooked and frozen. We will sell live and freshly killed trout, and live, smoked, and frozen crayfish and mussels. We will start a smoking plant for smoked salmon, smoked trout, smoked mussels, smoked bacon, and hams to supplement that market. I will organise and tend the smoking plant and also a small packaging plant for the smoked and frozen produce. We will host specialised angling hunting and shooting parties as well, for pheasant, partridge and possibly grouse. The organic food and these special items will also be sold to other hotels, gourmet restaurants and delicatessens and packaged and shipped anywhere in the UK and Europe.

We have discovered that existing businesses producing only one or two of these delicacies are relatively small enterprises, but we are proposing supplying these items as an extra as it were, just part of our whole operation. Taking it all together, it will bring in a substantial income, not just seasonal but with smoked and fresh frozen products available all year round. And just one more line we have only added this very day: what better use can there be for our almost year-round grass here than geese and ducks? The prices charged for free-range geese and ducks, as well as being fresh and fresh frozen is phenomenal, and with careful management and regular movements of the duck and geese houses and their pastures, well away from the castle, it will enhance subsequent silage and hay production. And we haven't even looked at the farms yet: how we can increase their usable land, have a greater variety of crops and increased sizes of herds and types of cattle, sheep for lambs, pigs and who knows what else?"

Everyone except me looked astounded. I smiled at Tim and said, "Thanks Tim for your compliments and the faith you have in me and my feeble plans. I just hope we can sustain them through the obstacles which are sure to be raised in our path, but together, with the backing of Sarah, Bertie and Hannah, I believe it will all come to pass much as you have described."

Sarah answered us, "Well, Tim, you have even amazed me who thought she knew you best. You have clearly got on well with James, and I am certain that as with George in England, together you make a formidable team." You will have my complete backing and support and we will provide the capital required and get on with some of these things straight away, not wait for some approval or other, if I say you can do it that is enough. Sorry Bertie and Hannah if that has offended you in any way; I am so pleased and excited at all this that I almost forgot myself. Of course, your opinions and cooperation are paramount, and I will expect you to raise any problems or objections as and when you like, after of course exploring them with James and Tim first to see if they and you two together can sort them out amongst yourselves."

Bertie laughed, and said, "I am completely overwhelmed with it all, but I am certain that Hannah and I will be very happy with all we have heard so far today."

Hannah merely nodded, said, "Yes," and then Sarah said, "Well that's a relief, so James what have you or the boys got for us regarding the castle hotel? Just a feel for what you are finding, and planning will do for now."

I looked at my team and said, "Over to you, but one eye on the clock please. I have had a briefing note, but it's rather a lot to take in at present, so can you try to simplify it a bit just for this meeting and we will have a much more comprehensive document ready in a week or so?"

David said, "Our report will seem pretty mundane after all that, but here goes. In short, having looked at nearly all the rooms in the areas pointed to by Hannah at the outset as being in the best position for the castle hotel, we both think she was absolutely right and we think we have found the most difficult target room, the conference cum corporate services hall, which we think can seat up to 220 people as well as leaving room for a dais, stage or lecture position and sufficient room for aisles for access and egress, etc.

It will be in what was once many years ago the grand dining hall and is now basically a repository for several centuries' worth of unwanted furniture, much worm eaten and rotten, but we believe there are some valuable antiques amongst them. We have another old dining hall, there are five old ones in all, which can house the sports unit. It is currently also a huge storeroom for old furniture and equipment, again much worm eaten but with a few antiques we think amongst the rest. And yet a third disused old dining hall which could house the indoor pool and so on. Those are all on the ground floor, and on the two floors above, there are sufficient bedrooms, storerooms and the like which, when converted, with many having en-suite bathrooms and a few being sizeable suites, will accommodate between eighty and a hundred guests. All three floors, as some of you will know, are linked by a rather old lift which will need replacing. The hotel entrance will be very near the main castle front entrance, and there will be covered walkways connecting the four large

326

cottages we are earmarking for group and family occupation, increasing the guest capacity by a further thirty or forty guests, so that access to the restaurant and the games and pool areas and conference hall can be made whatever the weather and at night.

"In very brief summary, the castle can accommodate a hotel within its main walls with further accommodation in the cottages which are within the outer perimeter wall. And what's more, no new buildings are required at all. This hotel can be established within existing walls and roofs, so we believe no major changes involving planning consents are required other than change of use, in that a hotel within the castle is still a hotel and will need fire service examination and approval of escapes and fire equipment and building regulations relating to sound proofing, hazardous material, etc. But we see that as a mere formality.

"We have made some sketches of the intended changes and also photographed each site as it is now, for later comparison. We hope that this limited version of our report to James helps, but if you have any specific questions, we will do our best to answer them now, or make notes and come back to you later."

Sarah said that was fine for now and precisely what she wanted to know before sounding out people in Dublin and elsewhere and said, "Thank you boys; I look forward to your finished plans and sketches and a copy of all your photographs with the locations indicated please, hopefully within two or three weeks from now."

I tried not to look at my watch, but I was conscious of time ticking away and getting worried that my private meeting with Sarah might have to be abandoned, or at least postponed. But to my relief, the lunch gong sounded at twelve-thirty so two-thirty looked doable after all!

We trooped into lunch and sat in our allotted places, and I found myself next to Sarah for a change but was determined not to act in any way too familiar with her. I had Hannah on my other side to distract me, with Bertie being next to Sarah on her other side, quite a good arrangement I thought. Tim was invited of course, and he sat next to Bertie, a place of honour and quite right too. He looked perfectly relaxed about it all, a man of true inner confidence and self-belief, without an iota of arrogance, really nice to behold and an example to anyone.

I was well satisfied with what my team had achieved so far and was looking forward to the challenge of coaxing the tenant farmers into the 20th century with Bertie and Hannah's help and particularly with Tim by my side whom all knew and respected. Lunch was superb as always and we did it justice. I sent my compliments to cook and the head housekeeper and all their staff for their continued excellence, and Hannah, who was after all their manager, glowed with pride and satisfaction. Sarah leaned over sufficiently to say in my ear, "Persuasive bugger."

I said politely with a straight face, "Why thank you Sarah, how nice of you to say that."

And she only just managed not to laugh outright.

So, a happy ship and crew at lunch that day, still much work ahead but we all were warming to our task and confidence breeds confidence. We just needed to ensure we didn't get overconfident and overreach ourselves. But my main focus was to ensure that Sarah went away happy and pleased and to ensure we kept at the tasks in hand.

I asked Sarah how she was managing to make sufficient funds available to start progressing the objectives already agreed and given the green light and she replied, "Never fear, Bertie has more than sufficient reserves in hand, and I have asked him to pay for whatever you need and authorise, just to keep a completely separate account of all moneys invoices, etc., which were "project" related. Hannah keeps the books and will ensure Bertie complies!"

At about 2.20 p.m., Sarah said, "Right James, just this last meeting about the English project and try to ensure we are all singing from the same song sheet. And add to that, smoked products, crayfish and mussel farming and packaging, geese and ducks and salmon increases, to mention just a few new ideas springing from this Irish project!"

I did not respond other than to make a show of gathering some papers from the boys and trying to look serious and a bit concerned. I followed her meekly up the stairs having told the team to do what they liked until later this afternoon when I would catch up with them, maybe at the stables at about five p.m.

She waited until the doors to her suite were firmly shut before putting down her handbag, taking off her top and skirt and wrapping herself around me with a very welcome and deep kiss.

I said, "I have been waiting all day for this."

"Only all day? I've been waiting *three* days, who have you had in between? Not Hannah I trust?"

I replied, "I don't fancy Hannah at all as I'm sure you know, but what about you and Tim? I do believe he is sweet on you and has fancied you ever since you met him all those years ago."

"I agree he probably has, but he and I knew from day one that was out of the question and still is. In any case he had a wife; she was tragically drowned in this very river, and he has never forgiven himself. Because of that he will never take another woman as a wife, but I hear that the pub landlady — Molly, isn't it? — keeps him serviced."

"Good God!" I said, "he must need all his strength to bed her."

"Get your clothes off and stop this chatter; we don't have a moment to lose."

I did my best to please her as usual and any doubts I might have harboured about our relationship were rapidly dismissed in a passionate hour of mutually satisfactory lovemaking.

Chapter 35

Sarah departed and I went to my room and showered and lay down for a well-earned nap, getting up again at four-thirty. I freshened up and strolled down to the stable where Tim was telling the boys about the proposed trout farm and its situation and ideas for its construction. I sat down and listened to their conversation for a while, and it was clear they were spellbound by Tim and would have listened to him all day. Eventually Tim looked at me and said, "Sarah got off OK then, no problems you can't deal with?"

I replied, "No all under control; I might ask you to speak with George and maybe by telephone, or do you do email?"

"Yes, I do," he said, "what had you in mind?"

I replied, "A few things actually. I would like you two to be in contact so that you can compare what George is doing there and vice versa, and try to coordinate as far as possible the necessary equipment purchases, and in particular I would like you to explain exactly how you have kept the salmon numbers so high, but also discuss the crayfish problems I have discovered and how trapping can reduce predation of small salmon and trout, protect the riverbanks and supply our sales effort at the same time.

"Also, about how the big salmon and carp, being introduced there as well as here, will themselves predate the crayfish. The mussel harvesting and the new ponds we envisage, the purging machine, the obtaining more chilling and freezing capacity, the smoked products ideas, everything we are doing here which already has the green light from Sarah, so that he can crack on there as you are planning to do here. It will be helpful for you to bring him up to speed and assist him to isolate what is and what isn't transferable from here to there so to speak. You can both refer to me if necessary and I will interface with Sarah, Michael, Bertie, and Hannah as necessary regarding bulk purchase of tools and equipment, and shipping it to there in the UK or from there, according to the manufacturers and distributors' locations, etc. Can you do all that for me?"

"I certainly can, and I will start with a phone call, follow up with emails, and see where he is at and explain where we are and we can then look at coordination, exchange of information and ideas and push on in a parallel course. I will also give him data, numbers of crayfish and mussels here, how to farm them intensively as well as by collection and trapping, and so on."

"Excellent," I said, "I knew I could rely on you, and if you need to go over for a day or two and leave your assistant in charge here, I will be around to solve any problems, or try to. Or George might like to come here and see first-hand what you are doing, or perhaps both of you can do it in turn. I will leave that up to you. If I am not here, Bertie is authorised regarding funds, just go straight to him, as necessary. Or Hannah equally, and she, as you know, keeps the books here."

The next day Tim took us to the home farm, we called it Farm A, the first one past the castle, where they kept the biggest herd of pedigree Holstein Friesian cattle, some of the most consistent and largest producers of milk of all breeds. I was soon apprised of some interesting figures. They had about two hundred head of milk cows of which say half could produce the top per cow yield of nine gallons of milk a day and the rest might produce half that on average, a daily total milk yield all being well, of around 1,450 gallons or 6,690 litres, more than a 5,000 L capacity milk tanker held. They normally sent a 10,000-litre tanker which could then take all their fresh milk every day from farm A, even after adding the much smaller quantities of milk from the other smaller herds at the other farms. It might sound a lot, but at something like 15 to 20 pence a litre it still only yielded between 1,000 and 1,400 pounds per day. Of course, we had the grass, silage and hay all home produced, but each cow needed some "cow cake"; a concentrated supplement made from organic materials, and this was costly. Vets' bills were expensive; cattle-proof fencing was needed and a warm milking parlour of some considerable size where the equipment needed was mind boggling. All in all, I was informed, the net yield, taking into consideration all costs including wages and electricity, etc. was probably in the region of only

10% between 100 and 140 pounds per day or 36,600 to 51,100 PA before taxes, and milk was the biggest single earner on this farm.

There was some gain on the sale of surplus calves and the eventual disposal of the older cattle nearing the end of their productive lives, but this was offset by maintaining two pedigree bulls, still cheaper than buying in artificial insemination. A huge part of their daily chores revolved around the dairy herd and its welfare and two times a day milking. But it was a very regular and reliable income, the credits hitting the bank, although in reality a month after the supply of the milk, on an almost daily basis.

They also sold surplus home-bred and reared young cows with their pedigree to smaller farms and through the open market as well as a hundred or so neutered bull calves raised for beef, sold at two and three years of age. These fetched a good price as it was excellent beef and again organic on this farm. These additional sales brought in about a further 50,000 pounds a year on an ongoing basis, but again the overheads were high, so they yielded about 20,000 in net profit before taxes.

They had no pigs or sheep and lambs to speak of on the home farm, concentrating solely on their dairy herd and its offshoots. But even so they had the biggest and most profitable turnover, and this all went into the estate's coffers whereas the other farms, which had tenants in, paid a set rent plus a fixed 10% of their turnover to the estate, so were much less profitable. Clearly our reforms might take a little more persuasion, but at the end of the day, they were entirely at the mercy of the estate and knew it.

Our biggest carrot would be that if we could demonstrate an increased turnover of say twenty percent or in money terms on farm B, 50,000 PA, then on a return after costs they would benefit from most of the profit increase, their rent being fixed for many years ahead and so was the 10% tithe, so on a profit margin of say 40%, 30% would be theirs. Getting them to understand and embrace it was the task.

But still at farm A, we looked at the amount of land at its disposal, how much of this was just grass more or less permanently, how much was ploughed and planted for winter cattle feed with mangolds and other beet crops and barley and oats again mainly for winter feedstock inclusion. We also looked at land used for other purposes and found that no other significant amount was cultivated for planting, just spare grazing land so that a certain amount of rotation could be achieved to let the grazed meadows, after silage and hay were cropped, recover and green up for spring. Only if the weather was extremely bad were the milk herd put in doors 24/7, and then only as long as absolutely necessary to prevent damage and poaching of the meadows by cows' hooves. Whereas in the UK generally most dairy herds were indoors for several months here it was in terms of several weeks only, a huge saving on fodder and other overheads.

Tim and I did some calculations and I asked him, "Why is it, do you think, that farm A have not increased their land usage by say 50% which to me looks possible, and their dairy herd by a similar amount and still leave sufficient land to cultivate 50% more winter food stocks and rotate the herd one third at a time to the overspill meadows further up the valley? That in simple terms would increase all their incomes by up to 30% after costs and before tax or am I missing something here? After all this farm is effectively controlled by Bertie is it not?"

"Well," said Tim, "This is difficult for me to answer as my loyalty must first be to Bertie but, above that it is to Sarah, and she is the person I will not let down. So, on balance, since I realise of course that you are the man she really listens to, after me of course, I will speak my mind but if this had to go to Sarah, I reserve the right to speak to her myself, not through you, agreed?"

"Absolutely, but if I come up with a solution, a compromise, which gets round this difficulty, you in turn must agree to let me handle it myself, without implicating you at all, in such a way that Bertie is not embarrassed, nor the farm A tenant, or is he just a manager not a tenant?"

"He is a manager on bonuses not a full tenant."

"Then unless you are implying fraud, which I very much doubt, but a measure of incompetence on Bertie's part and possibly on the manager's part, which is what I suspect, then you have nothing to fear."

"You are a clever man, Jim; I will say no more than that."

"OK," I replied, "so let us assume just for argument's sake, that Bertie is not much of a fisherman, we know that, maybe he is not much of a farmer either? A very nice man and supported by a very nice and capable wife, but apart from being in Sarah's family, what qualifications does he have to manage farms? We know that his father was very reliant on you, and quite rightly so, but did he come from farming stock or was he just a good bloke and a fair manager perhaps but from a different upbringing to farming?"

"As I said Jim, you are a very clever bloke."

"If this were known to Sarah, why did she allow it to happen? Or was it already a done deal before she took over the reins and she, perhaps knowing a lot of this, just did not have the desire to upset the apple cart but will be happy to find out I guess that I am pretty good at that and picking up the fruit and juggling it into another cart which might be much better and more productive and that is why I am here? "This is where you have all the aces Jim, you are a very accomplished businessman. Everyone knows that you are essentially a company doctor, and you preside over a small empire which you and your wife have built from scratch. You are also an accomplished fisherman, albeit of coarse fish, and your love of nature, your natural curiosity and your drive and determination have all led you to this point, with almost no prompting from me. I am surprised even after seeing you at work as I have, that you could have worked all this out in your own head and from so little evidence. We only arrived here this morning and you have put your unerring finger right on the spot, just do not ever quote me as saying that."

"Have no fear Tim, my lips are sealed, this will just happen as if by chance, but we will get what we need, reform, and bigger than I envisaged. Bertie and Hannah are secure anyway, and if the manager of this farm — and as an aside I want everything you know about him by tomorrow noon latest, is at all intelligent, he will very quickly see the light of that I am sure, or he will equally quickly be gone. As soon as I have looked a little more closely at him in situ today and asked a few sensible questions and observed how he treats his staff and the animals, etc. I shall know by the time we leave whether he is the man for this new job or not. And by the way, why is he not here to greet us and what arrangements are made for our lunch?"

Tim said, "Phew, you really do not take prisoners, do you? If I didn't know you were my friend, I might be concerned about my position also."

"Never in your life Tim, as you very well know."

"Here he comes right now, and his name is Philip, and we can mention lunch after introductions and see what he says."

"No, let him raise the subject, or you and I will go to the pub."

Up walked a man of around fifty-five; not the walk of a farmer, the walk of a tired man out of his element, but I warned myself not to jump to conclusions. However, his boots were shiny, not a trace of cow muck on them. He picked up his pace and straightened his back as he approached and walked straight up to me, ignoring Tim, and thrust out his hand which I only just managed not to ignore.

"You must be James," he said, his face wreathed in a huge false smile.

"Correct," I said, "and I assume you must be Philip?"

"Yes of course, who else would welcome our distinguished guest?"

"Exactly my thoughts of a moment ago." I couldn't help replying and he looked confused.

"Ah!" he said, "Very good, almost missed that ha-ha." As if I had cracked a good joke.

Tim turned slightly to one side to hide his smile and I said, "So where would you like to begin showing me this wonderful farm?"

"In the house I thought where I have an office and we can chat in comfort and have a coffee, unless you would prefer something else?"

"No, coffee would be fine first, but I am keen to see this marvel of a milking parlour you have and have a closer look at some of other important things like your special beef-rearing herd of bullocks, the female calf growing in pens and the silage heaps. Not to mention the haystacks and your mangold chopping machine. I was brought up on a farm you know, ah very fond memories, how about you, the same I imagine?"

"Er, no, that is, not really. I vacationed on a farm once or twice belonging to one of my uncles I forget which, but I was raised and educated in Dublin where I obtained my business management degree."

"Splendid I said, which way to your library or office is it?"

"No library as such, just my office where me and my assistant manager Paul spend a fair bit of time and leave the outdoor management, the milking parlour and all the rest you mentioned, to our foreman Hugh."

"Splendid," I said, "then be sure to ask someone to tell Hugh to be here in say, thirty minutes. Not a moment to be spared, lots to do and see and tell him to bring a Land Rover or other 4X4 all-terrain vehicle please."

"Of course," Philip said, and he was just beginning to look a little worried.

After we had our coffee and a quick look at Philip's immaculate record system, Hugh appeared clutching his flat cap in both hands and said hello to Tim and then looked askance at Philip who blustered, "James and Tim here want you to show them round Hugh. I will be having lunch at one p.m., what will you two do?"

I replied, "No problem, probably have something on the hoof, we aren't fussy are we Tim?" and off we went with Hugh in his beaten-up old Land Rover. I noticed a brand-new Range Rover in the shelter of a lean-to, next to the house.

We toured the milking parlour and the rest of my list and Tim, and I soon had a good rapport with Hugh, who was mighty relieved. At about twelve-thirty, I said, "Tell me Hugh, do you like Guinness?"

He looked at Tim who nodded imperceptibly, and said, "Love it."

"Right," I said, "next stop the lane at the back of the pub please and go where we won't be seen by anyone we know."

"Yes sir, I mean Jim," he replied.

We started with three pints of Guinness and then ordered three ploughman's lunches with three cheeses, and pickles and a wedge of pork pie and crusty bread and butter. We chased that down with another pint of Guinness and home-made apple pie and custard and topped it off with a third pint of Guinness, by which time we were all pals. I blatantly pumped Hugh for information about Philip and his assistant Paul and I was right, neither of them ever visited the milking parlour or anywhere else where their shiny boots might get cow shit on them. They were considered good bosses in their way, but everyone knew that what knowledge they had of farming consisted of figures not words.

I asked Hugh, who was about sixty-three, what he remembered of the home farm from his youth, and he said, it was much busier of course with a lot more cattle and men and the old milking machines were slower and had to be watched carefully. Each cow started milking by hand and was stripped off, meaning the last few pints of milk were again taken into a bucket between the knees by hand. Each and every cow had a number and a name, and the milk went from the large glass milk containers into alloy churns all moved by hand to loading gantries outside the milking sheds. But turning them on their bottom rims and once momentum was gained on the concrete floors and passageways, an expert could control the full churns containing twenty gallons of milk, in a spin with just one hand on the centre of the lid, all the way to the gantry where two men would hoist it up. Three wagons came daily and removed up to a hundred and twenty churns, which held a total of 2,400 gallons, meaning over 10,000 litres of milk per day! Double the current production if Hugh was right and I think he was. I was sure there would be records somewhere, but not in Philip's office for sure.

I thanked Hugh and we took him straight home telling him to explain to Philip, if he asked, that we had finished quite late, so he had missed the evening milking which continued quite happily under Hugh's son (also Hugh) whom he had trained in the job.

Tim and I said little after picking up our Land Rover from behind the milking parlour and heading home. I went straight to the library and pulled the home farm production records from fifty and sixty years ago, and hey presto! the milk production measured in gallons and pints as well as churns, not all of which held twenty gallons, some held sixteen gallons, but that was irrelevant because the daily yield in the mid-1950s did indeed hover around 2,400 gallons per day or 19,000 pints which was much as we had reckoned from Hugh's accurate childhood memories. They kept that way for about five years and, coincidental with Bertie's father taking the castle helm so to speak, and the introduction of the massive new milking parlour which in fact was two buildings with all the latest machinery and after a few years the appointment of a new home farm manager, recruited by Bertie's father not long before he died (which was Philip) described by Bertie on inheriting his father's role, as the farm manager for the future! How right he was, but not about it being more profitable and efficient than was ever possible using the old out-of-date techniques. Yes, turnover in money terms rose because much farm labour was done away with and many lost their whole livelihood, their cottage homes too, and moved on. So, wages fell but so did production as fewer and fewer cattle were reared to maturity and the herd shrank by two hundred head over the next ten years, but actual cash and apparent profitability increased. This was in actual pounds shillings and pence perhaps but not in equivalent historical value.

Ten thousand in profits in 1950 would be perhaps equal to two hundred thousand profit fifty years on! Yes, less winter feed costs, less veterinary costs, less electricity costs and so on, but with half the number of cattle, and therefore half the milk production this was cloud cuckoo land. And milk prices pro rata paid to producers were actually less than in the 1950s before huge supermarkets dominated the market and drove the shelf price down to out-compete the smaller retail shops. In so doing, they forced not only the local milkman out of the business of daily deliveries of the family pints of milk, but also the smaller shops trying to fill the gap with cartons of fresh milk, only to find they just could not compete with the supermarkets' loss leaders. And that wasn't just milk; butter, cheese, and a host of other milk-based foods just were no longer viable for a corner shop. The wholesale and producer prices had to fall as well and many dairy farmers across the UK just gave up producing milk; only the bigger farms could survive in that market.

Philip's books painted a rosy but irrational picture of maintained gross and net profits in actual cash terms, but not in real time related terms. Maybe Philip believed his own rhetoric, I doubted that given his education, but I would be surprised if Bertie and Hannah ever realised what had happened since the bulk of the changes, the smaller herd and lower overheads caused by increased efficiency, reducing wage costs and lower feedstocks needed and so on, masked the true situation to their eyes anyway. We should be able to judge this by looking at Bertie's annual reports to the trustees and comments in their files and minutes of all their meetings with the farm manager and the tied farmers as well, faithfully recorded since Bertie and Hannah took over. Perhaps Philip pushed any thoughts about comparative old and new profits and losses, overheads and so on being not true in real terms, i.e., allowing for inflation and the changes in the real value of money over the years. And maybe he had thought about it and decided consciously to ignore it and just continue with the farce he held on-the-ground responsibility for.

Subject to some more research and getting an accountant to look at the books and the figures I had been playing with, to ensure I wasn't deluding myself, plus gathering some statistics relating to dairy farm failures and the causes thereof, I was certain that Philip was guilty of at the very least neglect of his duties for the trust and at worst was covering this up deliberately for continuing gain, that of his overblown salary and his bonuses he had received, never mind the new Range Rover in his garage. I was now very suspicious that there was more to this than I had so far discovered, and I was determined to find out what, if anything, that might be. Who apart from himself and Paul might be the gainers in all this? I needed to know what other similar sized dairy herds in Ireland were being paid for their milk. How were these prices arrived at? I knew in England that there was an organisation called the Milk Marketing Board, MMB. What was there in Ireland, something similar? Did large farms carry out their own private negotiations with supermarket chains? We needed some more investigation into this whole scenario before exposing our hand to anyone else and of course, even what I had so far, damming in my eyes might be better swept under the carpet? I sincerely hoped not.

Milk was the single largest income provider on the Irish estate. But I was convinced that in real terms it was half what it was fifty years ago and principally because the herd had been allowed to shrink to half its original size. Why? And by whom? Not Bertie and Hannah since the biggest part of the reduction had already taken place before they arrived at the castle, and it looked like Bertie's father was no more of farming stock or experience than Bertie.

Somebody needed to look in at the Irish equivalent of the Milk Marketing Board in the UK and see what prices had been agreed going back at least five years. Then something hit me, this was not only pedigree cattle it was also a certified organic farm. That meant milk, beef all eatable and drinkable products made from it like yoghurt, cream, even milk powder I assumed, should fetch a much higher price than standard milk products did. So, had that been happening? If not, why not? If yes higher prices were being paid; were the enhanced prices reflected in

Philip's records and therefore in Hannah's? I had to know this and quickly before contacting Sarah who was still in Dublin. No, I would call her and say something important was coming and could she stay there a bit longer? So, I called her on the number she left me, and she answered immediately.

I said, "Can you speak OK, anybody with you?"

"I am alone, and this is my private mobile so no problems, what's yours?"

"When are you planning leaving Dublin because I am looking at something very important regarding Philip and his assistant at the home farm and there may be something you have to look at urgently in Dublin if my suspicions are correct."

"Can you give me a clue now?"

"I can, if you are certain no one can listen in on this call."

"I am pretty certain that is impossible but wrap it up a bit so I will understand but no one else would unless it were the two people in question, and I don't believe that is possible."

"OK, but this really must stay with just you and me at present, no one, not Bertie, not Hannah, not Michael, no one at all, is that clear please?"

"This must be a big suspicion you have, but yes I accept your advice, and no one will know, yet."

"OK, what do you know about milk wholesale prices, which in the UK are controlled by the Milk Marketing Board; who controls them here, do you know, if not can you discreetly find out?"

"I am not certain, but I can easily check, I think there is some sort of cartel of the big buyers, like supermarket chains and the big processors of milk. If that is correct, does that increase or decrease your suspicions?"

"The former."

"OK I am on it, and I think I know where you are going."

"Next question, am I correct in thinking that organic milk, produced on a certified organic farm, will fetch a much higher price on the open market than ordinary milk?"

"Yes, believe you are correct, but again I can easily find out."

"OK do so, and revert soonest please. Next question: how is it that a man and his assistant — both former academics in Dublin — can sit in their chairs in the home farmhouse, never — and I said *never*, having set foot in the milking parlour and whose boots are permanently shiny and never — to put it bluntly — *never* had cow shit on them. How can they manage that farm? Who appointed Philip and why? Do you know? Was it Bertie or his father?"

"I am pretty certain that Bertie appointed him having advertised and interviewed several applicants. But that needs confirmation."

"OK, next question, have you ever suspected that Bertie might have let's say extra-normal tastes or habits regarding sex?"

"Yes, but I've kept them to myself"

"If so, could that lead to him being pressured or even, dare I say *blackmailed*, by an unscrupulous man who had evidence of those leanings if they exist? One final question, for now, do you believe that Sean is his son?"

"Bloody hell, James, this is a can of worms, but yes and no in that order, ask no more now on the phone; do what you have to do and then join me here at the Grand Hotel ASAP. Tell no one where you are going except Tim, and he tells no one, understood?"

"Yes, understood, but do nothing until I look at Hannah's books and compare them with Philip's. If my suspicions are correct, the trust may have been robbed of the difference between ordinary and organic milk prices which could amount to a million pounds. Not by Hannah or Bertie, by Philip and his toy boy. Say absolutely *nothing* of my suspicions to anyone. But I believe we may be able to sort this out if my worst fears prove correct, without publicity or police involvement."

"Bye for now, please get back as soon as you have anything concrete and do not see the men in question alone. Take Tim with you at all times and tell him he can tell you anything and everything he knows; I demand it! Including my belief which is that *he* is Sean's father but Bertie suspects nothing. My God!"

I visited Hannah and asked to see her records for the home farm milk production for the last five years and the price paid by the buyers for the milk, per gallon or litre or whatever. She smiled and got what I needed in about ten minutes. I said where did you get your figures from, and she said from Philip. Then I asked her to show me the invoices from us for the milk sold, and to who and the related bank receipts and again she smiled and produced all I wanted in no time. I said, "Is the price paid the same for all the milk collected each day including the smaller amounts put in the tanker from the other farms, which only had very small herds?"

She said, "Yes."

I then asked her if the other milk from the small farms was kept separate in the tanker, in different compartments. And she said, "Yes, because they wanted paying separately of course."

"Of course," I said, but the prices paid to them were the same per unit as the home farm?"

"Yes, always," she said. I looked at the invoices and schedules and related receipts into the trust bank account at Barclays in Dublin where the home farm banked all income and from which all expenses were paid. I asked her to make copies of the ones I selected which she did, and I noted that the receipts for milk and the letterhead was not a government department, but a milk broker's address in Dublin.

I asked Hannah who negotiated the price paid with the brokers and she said Philip had always done it since he arrived and he had worked at the brokers before Bertie interviewed him and took him on as home farm manager. That was one of his key attributes, Bertie thought, him knowing the people there and being a personal friend of their managing director, now retired. I smiled and thanked Hannah for all her help and taking up my copy papers went back to my room to think. A call to the brokers making an enquiry on behalf of a client quickly elicited that the current organic price per litre was 40% higher than ordinary milk, but it fluctuated according to supply and demand by about 10% to 20% being on average approximately worth 50% more.

I knew instinctively that a dirty deal had been done, what I didn't know was how much of the true price of the vast majority of the milk produced at this estate, from the home farm, went back to Philip and what proportion went to someone at or near the top of the broker's owners. My guess was 60% for Philip and 40% for his co-conspirator at the brokers who, I again guessed was the old managing director and now the new one. I further guessed that the two MDs were also the principal shareholders of the milk broker's company. At this point we should call in the police, but they could do nothing if we did not complain and were unwilling to cooperate in a prosecution. More to the point I thought I might have cleaner solution which would avoid some ghastly publicity and risk tearing the fabric of the Irish estate and perhaps even the whole trust to shreds.

I did what Sarah said and got hold of Tim and asked him to see me in the library straight away.

He came in looking very serious as well he might. I said, "Sit down Tim; we have some very serious matters to discuss, and, in this regard, Sarah has instructed you to tell me anything I want to know."

"Oh, OK fire away," he said.

I continued "I will, but first, to focus your mind a little on how serious this is, I am going to tell you a story you may find difficult to comprehend and you should know that I have already told Sarah most of it."

"Philip and his buddy Paul are homosexuals and have been partners for the last twenty years at least. Bertie chose Philip from several candidates to be home farm manager and knew he was a homosexual because he himself is inclined that way also." Tim looked at the floor, he thought he knew what was coming, but he didn't know the half of it.

I continued, "Philip's previous employer was the milk broker in Dublin, and this was part of the misplaced thinking by Bertie that he therefore was the best candidate."

Tim looked up amazed.

I continued, "I believe, having looked carefully at Hannah's records, of which she is justifiably proud, that Philip, together with the former MD of the milk brokers, hatched a deal which they thought could make them rich and it probably has. You know of course that the daily milk collection in the multi-chamber milk tanker has always picked up all the home farm's milk and had sufficient capacity to put the other farms' smaller yields into separate compartments."

Tim nodded as if to say so what?

And I continued, "You also know that home farm has been certified as totally organic for ten years, don't you?"

"Yes, it's common knowledge," he said.

I continued, "So it is logical is it not that all food and drink related output produced on the farm, the meat and all the livestock, and all the milk and milk products that it generates, can also therefore be certified organic?"

"What, the bastard has labelled the whole tanker as inorganic, pretending it's been contaminated by the inorganic small minority when in fact it was separate? That means that he and his pal at the brokers have pocketed the difference, must be two million pounds at least over ten years! I will kill him"!"

"Calm down. You are probably right; although the original MD has retired it is certain the new MD must have simply taken his share as read. But, if they are arrested, investigated, and prosecuted, it would damage the whole trust and destroy Sarah, and Bertie and Hannah, to name but a few. I have a better plan and murder is not it. If you are ready to talk to me and tell me anything at all you know in relation to what I have discovered and pieced together good, but first answer me this; I wouldn't ask if it were unimportant. Are you Sean's father?"

He sat as if poleaxed and said, "If Sarah says to answer all your questions I must, and the answer is I believe I am but have no proof. Bertie doesn't know. I was helping poor Hannah deal with the realisation she had married the wrong man and the affair only lasted a week or two, but it got her pregnant and she prevailed on Bertie for one performance so that he was unsuspicious. It worked, and he is so happy to have a son, so please never reveal that to anyone."

"I won't, now do you think Bertie knew of the fraud or not?"

"Definitely not, he is so proud he thinks he chose the right man; it will destroy him when he finds out."

I said, "If my plan works, he never will."

"But how?"

"I will need you with me in case they try anything, but I don't believe they will except in the very first instant, then if I am attacked you may retaliate."

"That I will, with great pleasure. I will lay them both out before they know what's hit them."

I said, "I don't believe that will be necessary but better be prepared just in case."

"Right," he said.

"I will report to Sarah in Dublin and be back as soon as I can. Meantime, make up any story you like and keep everything ticking over and when I get back, we will probably confront them and make a condition of not sending them both to prison, that wherever he has stashed the money is revealed to us with documentary proof, that he does no interfering nor talks to anyone before we do, or the deal is off. He returns at least all the excess he possesses including any accrued interest after allowing for saved salaries, etc. and if he ever discloses anything to anyone else you and I will personally cut off his balls and feed them to the dogs. And to make sure I will give him a copy of my dossier and tell him that I will make a complaint to the head of the Garda personally and give him a copy as well. He must leave immediately and resign on health grounds, and Sarah and I will choose his successor. We will have to explain a bit to Hannah, but if I am right, we will find the black money he deposited is in the trust name with Philip as Trust Account Manager to allay any suspicions of the staff at the milk brokers. And we shall threaten the MD there with exposure and potential arrest and trial if he doesn't also go on health grounds. And I have already seen letters from a bank in The Isle of Man to the trust account manager and its representative, Philip".

Tim sat there stunned for a minute and I said, "Both Sarah and I rely on you to handle things in our absence, and consider this, could you do the job of home farm manager?"

He replied, "I could but I would not accept it, I love my current job and I don't care about money."

"Fair enough," I said, "I understand." Now keep calm and cool and do your job and I will be back, alone or with Sarah in a day or two."

I packed a bag and took my own car and went to Dublin to meet Sarah with all my documents in a large briefcase. It took a couple of hours and fortunately all roads in Ireland lead to Dublin, more or less. I found the hotel, parked in their garage and went to reception and called Sarah.

She said room 426 and up I went. I buzzed and she opened the door and pulled me into a very warm embrace, but this time it was one of relief and after a good hug I released her and we went to a pair of chairs next to a writing desk. I put my bags down and said, "First things first do I need to book a room?"

"No," she said, "I have booked the one next to this, but you are sleeping with me tonight please."

"OK" I replied, "Let me tell you where we are at but first a coffee and maybe a small brandy after my early start and a long drive if you don't mind?"

She had a filter coffee device and all the makings and produced two coffees in about as many minutes, opened a packet of chocolate digestive biscuits, my favourite. She sat down, had a sip of coffee and waited while I ate couple of biscuits and drank my coffee and then said, "I think we may have this under control, but we shall have to wait and see how that smug, slimy bastard Philip behaves, because if he shows any resistance to a private settlement for the crimes I am now certain he has committed, Tim may just kill him and feed him to the pigs."

She laughed at that because she knew I wasn't serious, at least not that serious, but that Tim might thump him at least.

I said, "Let me tell you what I know, what I strongly believe, and what I think we can in any case prove. After I have finished, I will tell you my plan for you to consider, to get us all out of this not only without publicity, but with a pot of gold at the end of the rainbow."

She stared at me as if she suspected I had gone mad. I continued, "First Sean is Tim's son without much doubt but if ever we needed to, we could get DNA tests to prove it. But Tim wants none of that; he thinks Bertie swallowed the bait when Hannah, with whom Tim had a brief affair largely trying to console her after she finally realised that Bernie prefers boys. So after the two-week affair with Tim, Hannah quickly knew, having missed a period for the first time ever as an adult, and cajoled Bertie into performing a solitary sexual act with her. He had put it off for two whole years until that night and she practically did it for him. He was delighted a month later when Hannah told him that he might have child and heir and he apparently has always believed Sean is his.

"Shortly after this, Bertie, who often made trips to Dublin ostensibly on business, came back with the news of a very suitable candidate for the vacant manager's position on home farm. Philip got the job and after a brief affair with Bertie, brought his toy boy Paul in as his assistant. Of

346

course, Bertie could say nothing without exposing his sham of a marriage. The then MD of The Milk Brokers Limited in Dublin, where Philip had been a senior administrator had a long-standing affair with Philip. That had faltered and so the MD was happy to see the back of Philip, who, although knowing almost nothing about farming, was a good administrator and kept immaculate books. Who thought of the scheme I don't yet know, but I suspected it was Philip because it was only about a few weeks after his appointment that the old churn system for collecting milk finally was superseded totally by the modern tanker system. These tankers, like oil tankers, are composed of up to eight separate compartments so collection from different farms can be made and each tank identified with the milk's origin by the driver.

So, as you are aware, the home farm was certified after five years of inspections, as completely organic about ten or eleven years ago. Initially the system worked well, and I believe the records will show, Hannah's certainly do, that there was a brief period when two invoices receiving the milk were split, part organic, and part, that which the other farms produced, normal milk I will call it. Then a strange thing happened: it was discovered by testing that some of the organic milk was contaminated with non-organic milk so the whole shipments to that date were re-invoiced as non-organic, I have seen the amended invoices and they only cover a few shipments in the first year the home farm was designated totally organic. The milk brokers who controlled this product must have discovered the error and corrected their records. From then on, I am certain that great care was taken to segregate the two milk producers' loads because it took only one compartment to take all the milk from the smaller, non-organic herds in the tied farms, whereas the home farm filled most if not all the remaining compartments. I am sure the driver would have made sure this was so.

The mix up was for a very short period of days only, but the invoicing from that date to this, as reflected in Hannah's books, all the data for which is provided by Philip, shows no organic milk sales at all. Organic milk fetches almost double the price of non-organic. I believe that Hannah has somehow been hoodwinked by Philip and Paul and has just blindly followed precedent and it has never dawned on her that this quite massive fraud has gone on. I calculate that the total loss in milk revenue to the trust is of the order of two million euros at least, not accounting for any interest earned on the deposits. If it had not been spent, and I believe most of it could not have been spent without an even more elaborate fraud. I do not believe it can have been spent given that three, no four including the new MD at the milk brokers, are involved and it would show up like a sore thumb if funds of this size and nature were spent by any of them. In fact, I would not be at all surprised to find that substantially most or possibly even all, of this 'black money' plus significant accrued interest, is sitting in an Isle of Man bank right now.

"I know enough of Inland Revenue frauds and the like, that full restoration of stolen funds, plus a penalty figure and interest, is and can be accepted by The Inland Revenue in lieu of prosecution. I now know that the trust has not knowingly evaded any revenue, particularly as it pays no UK taxes other than VAT, so they could be kept right out of it. That leaves the police here in Ireland and I believe again that if we are recompensed by the perpetrators for your loss, and we, therefore, chose not to prosecute and did not make a formal complaint, they would not be interested.

"So my plan is simple, start with the weakest link: visit the old man who was the MD at the milk brokers in control, with a very significant shareholding in the company, and put this to him with a guarded promise of not pressing for legal action, arrests, charges, and almost certain imprisonment, in return for a full written confession, disclosure of the whereabouts of the money and full return of all the money taken including interest earned, which is still in existence and under his control. Then if that is acceptable, we are home and dry providing Philip and Paul and the current MD, who is an old pal of them all, and also had a major share in the company, do not do anything silly which would mean police and so on. We would also want Philip and Paul to immediately resign and also disclose where the money is and recover it. They must then deposit it in the trust's bank accounts here in Dublin, which is where it belongs.

"I believe that Philip is very vulnerable, because he has falsely declared that an account he controls on the Isle of Man is under a false title, something like The XXX Trust, Investment Account, controlling person, the Manager, Home Farm, XXX castle. In short it is a fraudulent misrepresentation set up by him and is an unauthorised and in fact illegal construction, solely to facilitate his fraud against his employer.

"The money which the two MDs have taken out of their own company and your pockets will, I believe, also be in IOM or in The Bank of Ireland, here in Dublin probably masquerading as a Milk Broker Limited deposit and investment account or similar, the controlling persons being the MDs, past and present.

"It doesn't really matter as after an initial bluster, I am certain that they will all cooperate rather than risk prison and massive publicity, which we all want to avoid. I suggest we pay an unannounced visit to Mr Arthur XXXX at his Dublin home and ask to talk about things relating to the false description of organic milk as non-organic for personal gain. And if he refuses, I will say that if he wishes he can call his solicitor to be present but if he still will not talk to us, I shall turn to you and say, 'We tried, please call the Chief Detective at the Garda, and get him to attend immediately concerning a major fraud which, regretfully we have no alternative but to report because the perpetrators, three or possibly four who we know of, will not cooperate with our attempts to conciliate, and settle the matter'. I think he will cave in at that point. If not, we simply move on to the current MD at his office and ask him the same questions, before interviewing Philip and Paul as a last resort, but I assure you that will not be necessary, and we will have a signed confession long before we need to seriously consider the police option."

Sarah said,"

"This is very worrying, but I have to say, your investigation is way beyond anything I thought you capable of, although in my heart I believed if anyone could discover what has apparently happened, that man was you. I am very nervous that this may all get out. I knew something wasn't right, but had no idea it was this, or so big. It really should have rung bells with Bertie and Hannah, but I can see that Bertie was focussed on his personal past and the fear of exposure and in any case knows next to nothing about farming. Hannah was hoodwinked and she too knows nothing about farming and with an immaculate set of books produced by Philip, she simply copied everything he gave her into her books. The accountants too are culpable, but they have never done a full audit."

I said, "That's enough for you now, I think; I knew it would hit you hard, but I repeat I am confident of sorting this out without undue publicity. I also believe that even if they don't cooperate, we can gag them legally for now and manage the fallout in advance in such a way that you are not personally besmirched. Frankly, I think although it seems hard, Hannah and Bertie may have been naive, but are open to being accused of a degree of incompetence. I also believe that you and your family's long-held practice of employing family members to do complicated and unfamiliar jobs which they are not equipped or trained to do, is now exposed as risky and something like this was sure to happen at some point. Let us stop here before we get beyond what might be necessary but think on the possibility that changes are going to have to be made because of this."

Sarah straightened her back and said, "OK, thanks for all that, I think! Let us have some lunch and then a nap. Before that maybe we should phone Arthur and say who I am and ask to see him urgently, preferably this afternoon about a private, but very important matter, seeking his help in resolving a very thorny issue, best kept private and to ourselves at present. You can listen in and come on the line if you think it's right to do so, but also to judge from his reactions what he might ultimately do."

I thought about it for a minute and said, "OK but bear in mind this man probably does not and never has related to women, so maybe if I take the lead and you only come in if absolutely necessary?"

"Agreed," she said.

We looked up his home number which was listed and called it and a quiet small voice just said, "Hello."

I said in my most calm and soft manner, "Hello, is that Arthur…?"

And he replied, "Yes, but who are you?"

I told him my name and said I wished to talk to him about a very personal and private matter concerning the XXX Trust, the owners of Castle XXXX and I represent Sarah XXXX the principal trustee and senior family representative."

"Oh dear," he said quietly, "it has finally happened, hasn't it?"

"Yes," I replied, "I'm afraid it has, but I am hoping to keep this whole matter out of the press and deal with it in a sensible but totally private way so that as little disturbance as possible is achieved and hopefully no legal action will be necessary. But I am afraid that will be up to you primarily, whether you are prepared to discuss this informally with us two alone — that is Sarah and me to see if we can find a way of containing this matter and keeping it private with no publicity and no police involvement."

"Oh, thank God," he said, "I have been hoping and praying that might be possible and indeed I have been advised to try to do just that if I get the chance by my Padre at the church when I confessed to him all of my sins. That was only last week, and God has sent you to help me, and I will do so. Come here at about four p.m. please and I will tell all. May I have my solicitor present please, not to try to defend me, oh no, but to help prepare a legally binding and authentic confession."

"Just to be clear we are talking about the same problem: I refer of course to the money made by Philip and your successor as well as you by mis-declaring organic milk as non-organic when in fact it was sold on by your company as organic at a much higher price than you paid the trust."

"Absolutely, God forgive me, and I shall pay every penny back to the trust, of that you can be certain."

"Very good Arthur, I can tell you are a man of God, and you will achieve forgiveness, of that I am certain. But please do not contact any of the others except your lawyer, at least until we have a chance to offer them the same privilege to them. And please have your bank deposit details to hand as well."

"I will my son, and I feel a huge weight already lifted from my heart, thank you so much. Come at four p.m. and I will be here waiting for you, with my lawyer if he is willing, without if not, and fear not no one will change my mind on this and I promise in the name of God, lawyer apart, I will speak to no one of this matter until you tell me so. And I shall not even tell my lawyer anything until he is here with you both present. And my abject apologies to Sarah, please forgive me."

Sarah leaned forward and clearly said, "Arthur, you are forgiven by me; I am Sarah."

And he wept, so we put down the phone very gently and wept for him, and for ourselves.

"I will say this once more James, you are a persuasive bugger."

We went after lunch and a nap to Arthur's address at four p.m. and he met us at the door with a smile on his face. He was a man in his seventies, neat as a pin, and small in stature and his house was nice, quite small but in a decent area. He showed us into his front room fitted out like a small office with the addition of a settee and an armchair with a small coffee table in front.

He introduced his lawyer, a man almost as old as Arthur we thought, who stood as we entered and said, "What is this all about please?"

Arthur said, "It is about me being a very silly man and getting involved in a fraud against these lovely people for which I am mightily ashamed, but which I intend to rectify, at least my part in it, by making a confessional statement. I wish you only to advise on format and acceptable legal language. I will sign it and you my dear fellow will witness it and attest to it being made when I was of sound mind or whatever is deemed by you to be acceptable in law. Nothing more; I want no advice about saying nothing, I wish to get this off my chest, repay all the proceeds of my crime which are deposited in The Irish Bank and of which I have not spent a penny. With interest accrued, which I have recorded on my personal tax returns and have paid the appropriate tax. I have copies of all bank statements and tax returns here, plus a schedule which shows the whole matter in financial terms. And the total in that account as of today is 867,422.09 euros."

The lawyer looked absolutely amazed, looked at him, looked at me, and said, "Is this some sort of joke?"

I answered, "Not a joke, we were uncertain as to exactly how much Arthur himself had received but had calculated over 2 million euros have been let us say, *diverted* to him and at least two other people, his successor as MD and major shareholder of his former company The Milk Brokers Limited. And a second former employee of that company, who at present has the title farm manager for the home farm at the castle XXXX which is wholly owned by a Swiss-based trust on behalf of this lady's family and has been owned by her family for hundreds of years."

The lawyer said, "But Arthur, you can't—" and got no further before Arthur said, "I can, and I will, so do you want to help me avoid prison or not?"

The lawyer said, "Please explain to me sufficient for me to understand how this alleged fraud happened, and how, if you really wish to settle the matter out of court, you propose to do that, assuming the others wish that as well?"

I replied, "I already have a lot of evidence and this together with the ringleader's example of providing a confession which will fit all the facts and evidence I have, we hope and believe that subject to all or the vast majority of the stolen money being returned to the trust, and subject also to the aforesaid farm manager's resignation and silence as well as that of the current MD at Milk Bank Limited also cooperating and resigning and remaining silent, we believe we can legitimately stay any prosecution. In fact, we would make no further complaint and so there would be no police involvement. But until we know if The Revenue Department have also been defrauded by ether of the other protagonists, we cannot be certain that they will not prosecute. But my own experience of this sort of thing — and with my wife we own a group of over thirty UK and foreign companies, tells me that the revenue departments here and in the UK, providing there is full disclosure of any underpaid tax and a payment of penalties and interest due, will be happy to compound proceedings, as we are. If, however the tax on their personal income, i.e., their salaries and interest on the deposits of this money we refer to, has been declared and paid as Arthur's has, there is no need to involve the revenue authorities at all, as I understand it."

Arthur said, "I know Frederick my successor has done exactly what I have done, and all the money is in the same bank as mine, and he has declared all his personal tax liabilities as I have. I cannot speak for Philip, but I do know he has his share deposited in an IOM account under the name of the trust and controlled by him only, but I assume he could argue he never intended to keep the money for himself, if he was discovered before he terminated his employment by the trust at least. So he needs to be persuaded that flight is not an option now; he will be caught and imprisoned if he tries it and we will all be under immense scrutiny, so I do hope that I can persuade him to do as we are going to do and confess and hand over the money to the trust. Again, I believe it is substantially intact including accrued interest and even if he resigns as we will suggest, he legitimately I believe, has accumulated a considerable sum in a separate deposit account in his own name, in the same bank as us here in Dublin, where all or most of his salary has been put and never touched. We both advised him at the outset to declare any interest received on the money because we know that banks give details of all interest over a certain sum per annum to the revenue authorities as a matter of course, so hopefully he too has done this. Now my dear fellow, here are the statements I have prepared which state all the important facts and the figures, exactly what my bank statements and revenue returns show."

The lawyer took the statement and read it through twice, glanced at the schedule Arthur had prepared and at a few samples of the stack of statements and Revenue Return copies and said, "Well Arthur, I have to say that you are right, you cannot fight this anyway and if these good people, as I am sure they are, and are serious about wanting no publicity, despite the seriousness of the case, I will certify it was made by you in my presence and of sound mind, etc. as if it were a will. However, I will myself not recommend its use. That is for you and you alone to decide." He duly certified and signed two identical copies and he gave one to me, and I took all the proffered statements and copy returns as well.

Arthur said, "I will talk to Frederick, and I am certain of his cooperation because he has never been happy with this from the time he took over as MD and main shareholder. His total figure will be a bit more than mine and Philip's will be a lot more than ours as he has been in this from the start until now. We will both talk to Philip later and ensure he does nothing stupid but if he does, so be it. It will be better than you descending on him out of the blue. I will call him now while you are still here so you know of his immediate reaction and can act accordingly."

We waited but as Arthur went to pick up his phone it rang. And it was clear it was Philip because Arthur said, "Philip my dear friend I was about to call you."

Arthur put on a speaker and signalled "Shush" to us. Philip said, in a defeated manner, "I suppose you have already been visited as I have."

And we both shook our heads.

He continued, "Yes, I have had an irate Bertie and a very cold Hannah here, as she deducted from examination of her records by that fellow James, and the slant of his questions, that there was a problem and it seemed to be what it actually is. Hannah was up all night going through all the records and it dawned literally on her what we have done. She confronted poor Bertie in his pyjamas and accused him of being in league with me and The Milk Brokers Limited but poor Bertie hadn't a clue what she was talking about. When the penny finally dropped, unlike him, he went incandescent and came straight here with her and confronted me with a shotgun in his hands."

"Oh my God!" exclaimed Arthur.

"Yes indeed," Philip said, "And seeing the position that you and Frederick must also be in, I called you to say, never fear I won't let you down. I have promised them I will repay every penny and interest to the trust if there can be a settlement and I even gave them a copy of the IOM bank account statement showing that the trust account, in my name as manager of home farm, holds over 1.5 million euros in it, that is every penny. But the account I have in my name only is genuinely the proceeds of my salary over the years as it costs almost nothing to live here. So if they will let us go in peace, I will do whatever I have to do to avoid the possibility of prison for you and Frederick and myself. Paul knows nothing of this, but he says he will stand by me, the dear boy".

"Well, Philip, I am so pleased to hear all that because I have heard it all from Sarah and James here and with my lawyer present as well. I have made full confessional statement as I am sure Frederick will after we speak, so please leave that to me Philip. But one further important point, did you, as I suggested you should, include the interest on your tax return?"

"I did, reluctantly, as I was always intending to pay the money to the trust, but I realised as time went on that would not do, so I did as you advised thank God, so no need to report us to the revenue or the police I hope."

"I hope so too Philip, but clearly once this is settled, and I see no reason to delay it, and the money is back where it belongs in the trust bank account, I'm afraid you must leave home farm."

"I am leaving today; I have a place in Dublin as you know, and I shall go there with Paul in my Range Rover which incidentally I bought with my own money, but I will leave all the records in Hannah's care. Please don't blame either her or Bertie for they may be a bit silly, but they are totally innocent and very loyal. May I call on you with Paul sometime please I really would like to apologise in person and remain friends?"

"Of course, after the dust has settled you must, but thank you for calling and goodbye for now," said Arthur and put the phone down.

I said, "Thank you again Arthur, that was near perfect, and we are very relieved he has at least accepted the error of his ways and exonerated Bertie and Hannah. Now Arthur, would you like to call Frederick now or after you have certified your document and we have all witnessed it, rather than descend on him unexpected, although we don't know where he is at present?"

"I will sign and get it formalised now it won't take a moment, but you can go, George, after that if you wish," said Arthur, but George said, "No I had better just hear what Frederick says so if he has definitely paid his taxes I can breathe more easily."

Frederick was very relieved that his worries seemed almost over and complied fully with what Arthur said he must do. He confirmed that he too had all the money intact and had paid the taxes. He would now sell his business and retire also so that the new owner could start with a clean sheet and need not be involved at all. George left with his signed copy of Arthur's confession and we also left a short time afterwards to go and meet Frederick and complete the business of the day while the iron was still hot. We got his confession, witnessed by his partner, and ourselves, plus copies of the bank statements, etc. and left well pleased with our day's work, although I cautioned Sarah that many a slip twixt cup and lip just in case Philip or the other two had a change of mind.

Sarah and I went to the Savoy Grill and quietly celebrated with a bottle of Champagne and a filet mignon. Then we retired to her room and had coffee and brandy and collapsed on the bed. We chatted for a while and Sarah proved to me how very grateful and relieved she was, and we slept like babies until our alarm went off at eight a.m. We showered and dressed then went down to the restaurant for breakfast. We then checked out and headed back to the castle arriving unannounced at quarter to twelve. Bertie and Hannah came to greet us looking very tired and worried. Sarah hugged them both and told them it was going to be all right and stop worrying and I said, "Where is Tim?"

Hannah replied, "Holding the fort at the home farm pending instructions. As Philip and Paul left last night in his Range Rover for Dublin, so he took up residence there until you or Sarah got back."

"May I suggest that you, Sarah, explain the situation," I said, deferentially to Sarah, "and I will go and relieve Tim and do likewise and just see what Philip has left for us."

"Good idea," she said and went in with the other two and I continued on to the home farm.

Tim came out with a grim unwelcoming look on his face when he heard a car until he saw who it was, and then it was wreathed in smiles.

"Jim!" he called, "good to see you. Welcome back to home farm."

We went in together and saw that everything was tidy and appeared in order as Philip had said it would be, but Tim said, "He took the new Range Rover before I could stop him."

I laughed and said, "Believe it or not it *is* really his, bought and paid for out of his salary savings."

Then I went through the whole lot with him, how we had confessions and proof of just about everything and how all the stolen money had been deposited and earned interest so they had not a penny they shouldn't have and in fact had declared the interest to the Revenue Department and paid taxes on it, so they actually lost money on the fraud as all the interest remained in the accounts and the estate would get every penny back.

Tim then related to me how he only just prevented Bertie shooting Philip and took the gun from him. But that action of Bertie's had shaken Philip to the core, and he went like a cur with his tail between his legs, packed only his clothing and personal effects and went within an hour or two of the confrontation.

Of course there was quite few loose ends to tie up but The trust's lawyers contacted the police and the revenue people. Since no money was lost and we said we wanted no publicity and no charges were to be made, they confirmed that this was acceptable, but would be kept on file in case further losses were discovered or they committed any similar or other crimes in their jurisdiction.

But my job had not nearly finished so with my team and Tim helping, we visited all the tied farms and soon reached some sensible agreements concerning extending arable land and grassy meadows and the enlargement of their cattle herds, pigs, sheep and lamb flocks, and production of milk and meat generally. We also persuaded them to push harder for conversion of the farms into organic, which, when they learnt of the difference in prices now being fetched for organic food-based production, they were only too willing to do, with a little extra financial help to provide suitable quarters for the animals, bigger and better milking parlours, and more up-to-date machinery, and so on.

We also had no resistance to our reforms required by the salmon project, bridges over streams and dykes, dedicated clean water troughs for the animals and so on, as they would benefit also and they readily accepted our plans for holiday and business accommodation and activities, the construction of a trout farm and mussel and crayfish breeding, controlling, and marketing.

On all the farms where there were boggy areas were a lot of poor quality oak trees and saplings which struggled for existence. Tim explained to all the affected farmers that when we drained some of the boggy land to enable farm usage, the struggling oaks could be put to use, dried and chipped and used in the smoke houses. He explained that these smoke houses would produce smoked salmon and trout, also mussels and crayfish, and hams and bacon produced from animals raised on their farms. This would greatly extend the seasonal nature of trade in these animals and fish, and in doing so would provide more stable production, yielding better returns for all.

They were all glad to see the back of Philip and Paul and hoped that a more suitable person would be chosen this time around to manage home farm. Someone they could relate to more easily and who would cooperate with them in helping to achieve organic status, clear and extend their presently underutilised land and sell them certified pedigree cows to form a nucleus of pedigree herds for themselves. Tim said that there was a surplus of Holstein Friesian heifers and calves which were normally sold to markets, but he was sure that Sarah would allow a good proportion of these and some bullocks for fat stock rearing, as there was always a surplus of male calves coming through every year and this was music their ears.

So with Tim's help we gathered all the information we needed to put our ideas into our draft plan for the Irish estate as a whole, and we calculated that within just a year or two the production capacity of the entire estate farms could increase by 25 to 30%, not including the proposal for goose and duck meadows, which none of the tied farms objected to at all. As for trapping and controlling the crayfish population on the river, they all knew of the damage they could cause leading to bank collapses and the need for more barriers and bank repairs to keep their herds safe. And if that led to a small share of the proceeds of the many new activities under consideration, something I suggested would be the case, they were happy to be involved and would assist in progressing the reform plans by providing labour and skilled people in periods when they were not totally committed, like at their silage production, hay making and harvesting times.

By this time, I was thinking and acting like a farmer born and bred, or so Tim told me, rather than the company doctor and industrialist I actually had become over the years, not to mention my burgeoning investigation skills. The thing was, I mused, I really enjoyed new areas of interest and challenges stemming from that, not to mention the lovely people I got to meet such as Sarah, Tim, yes and Bertie and Hannah and most of the tied farm people as well. And Scotland was next! But we also awaited the review of all the group companies which was less than halfway through at present.

Over the next week as we worked on our Irish Phase 1 plan, the money from the three protagonists in the organic milk fraud found its way into the trust's Irish bank account in Dublin and taken together including interest totalled over 3 million euros, which would form the fund for Phase 1 plan for Ireland and so ploughed back into the Irish estate from whence it came. The trust accountants and lawyers would handle the technical, fiscal and tax issues so we need not be concerned with that, but Sarah's report to the trustees, copied to the lawyers and accountants explained the whole situation to them and they sent their thanks and a very complimentary note about me and the role I had played and suggested a suitable fee to cover the extra work involved.

We advertised for an experienced dairy farm manager in the whole of the UK and Ireland, cut down a long list of applicants to the best six and invited them to look at the farm and take part in an interview by myself, Sarah, Tim, Bertie and the largest tied farm occupant Horace, whose family had farmed the number 2 farm for centuries. We had labelled the farm no. 2 simply because it was next after home farm going up the valley, had the largest number of Holsteins and was part way on the road to being certified organic. Horace was a dyed-in-the-wool farmer from head to toe and had also gone to college and obtained a diploma of competence in cattle breeding and milk production.

The candidates all had relevant practical farming experience of at least ten years, were recommended by The UK College of Farming where they had studied or equivalent, and whose previous or existing employers had provided glowing tributes to them. Five were still employed but available under the terms of their existing contracts and the sixth had left his farm only recently when the owner's son qualified. The son now had sufficient experience as he had been this candidate's number two, to take over, this having been agreed at the outset when the candidate was first employed there twelve years before. On CV reading and background information and simple gut instinct the latter candidate was my first choice, but of course seeing and talking to the man was going to confirm, or not, the paper picture. One of the other candidates was a woman with all the right qualifications and experience, recently divorced and looking for a good job away from her former husband who owned half their farm and had bought her half out when the marriage broke down. Again, very good on paper, but we would evaluate her exactly as we would them all. We agreed beforehand to postpone the decision as to whether or not this farm, big as it was, really needed an assistant manager. I thought not but would probably bow down to my fellow panel members' superior experience in farm management, if in doubt. And we wanted to hear what the candidates thought having toured the farm and spoken to Hugh the foreman and other key member of the staff there. We had provided a dossier of facts and figures to each finalist, plus a brief mention of further expansion of land in use and other new activities being currently under evaluation.

The candidates were to get a full day each and be invited to dinner the night before their evaluation and would leave after lunch the following day. This was Sarah's idea and I supported it because we all now realised how important a responsibility running this farm was and wanted the successful candidate to become part of the team, not an isolated individual solely concentrating on his farm, but rather sharing opinions and views and contributing to regular meetings and at informal dinners.

They were warned that dinners in the castle, although informal, were occasions to exchange views and opinions in a relaxed atmosphere, but candidates should be prepared for more formal occasions from time to time. The guide to salary had been set at around 50,000 euros per annum, plus bonuses where applicable and in the future, in the event the trust farms were to become part of a limited company, there would probably be an opportunity to become a director and be in receipt of dividends and discounted share offers, as well as a fixed number of shares at the outset, value yet to be decided. These latter incentives were suggested by me as I had proved, many times over, the value of such incentives to securing good performances, pro-active management, and total loyalty. I had reiterated my mantra about happy ships, happy crews, better results and profits and higher share values following this policy. Sarah agreed 100% and totally supported this proposal and the others, on whom the implications were not lost, were quick to agree.

In addition, before we even circulated all this to the panel members, on my recommendation, while still performing the same role as gamekeeper, but in recognition of his already accepted and heavy workload for the future, we invited Tim in and told him we were re-grading him as General Manager the castle estate. With greater powers, a bigger salary and a promise that if and when the estate became a limited company, he would be also offered a directorship making him eligible for bonuses, dividends and share options.

Before he could protest, I said, "Tim, this is only in recognition for what you do anyway and the immediate acceptance you gave to all the extra work and responsibility we have given you, in recognition of all that, so please accept gracefully."

He looked nonplussed for a moment, then with a slightly emotional voice said, "Jim and Sarah, I love you both. I accept."

He then stood up and walked out of the room and we looked at each other and smiled, so glad for our very good friend and totally loyal servant as well.

We told everybody about Tim's appointment and new title and didn't receive one adverse comment. In fact, everyone, Bertie, and Hannah included, said, "About time too." Or words to that effect, like — well deserved, couldn't find a better man, very pleased for him and happy to have him as my boss. He asked and we agreed that his long-term assistant gamekeeper would be either nominated Gamekeeper or Assistant Manager. We thought Gamekeeper for now, and review that in say one year as we hardly knew the chap, and Tim was happy with that.

Nearly all the bridges were now in place and the streams protected from both vehicles and cattle and some were clearer than they had been in many years. We were thrilled when we saw a couple of fine-looking salmon wriggling their way up the shallow water into the nesting shallows above where they would mate and lay their eggs. This was when Tim and I took our shotguns and went up and down the streams shooting cormorants and wild mink when we saw evidence of predation of the salmon. The mink can kill with a couple of well-placed bites, and they gnaw the head off the salmon, eat the eggs as she ejects them in one last attempt to procreate and then leave the rest for the crows and jackdaws which we also shot. Pike big enough to kill a salmon are usually way back in the deeper water, but we fished with spinners and spoons and caught several 10 lbs-plus in weight and killed them too. Tim also deployed fifty of the new crayfish traps we had bought which were stainless steel, and would last forever, in the river. We put twenty-five each side and about twenty-five metres apart to catch the crayfish and had a dozen the same day. We put them in the kitchen for the cook.

We prepared a big pond in a boggy zone, with weeds added from the other ponds and the river and ran small mesh chicken wire retainers around it, inward curving at the top and attached to a galvanised wire hoop we made, so that when the next batch was caught, we could put them straight in, as we observed on our inspections that many of the crayfish were full of eggs and had larvae clinging to their various appendages.

I left Tim to his various tasks as I believe I might have been slowing him down, but I was glad to have taken part in the plans we had formulated.

362

The time for the interviews was fast arriving and I suggested a trial run, using Hannah as the applicant so she could give us feedback and we could perform better with some practice together. She was very good at acting the part with a straight face and after a few asides we settled down to question her as we might a candidate and although Hannah's experience was limited; she made a good fist of it and her feedback about our methods attitude, etc. was actually quite helpful. I told her so and thanked her before she left. Sarah and I had discussed who should be Chairman of the panel and I told her that I had quite a bit of experience recruiting board members and higher management for our group of companies so she readily acceded to my advice, but of course the final decisions would be hers.

The first candidate arrived about mid-afternoon, and we simply identified him as A, and he was shown to his room and told that pre-dinner drinks would be served about seven-thirty in the library followed by dinner at eight p.m. in the grand dining room. He was also told to wander where he liked around the castle and if he wanted to have a look at the home farm, he would be taken there by someone in a Land Rover, so may want to change into appropriate clothing. He immediately asked to be shown the home farm, so Tim gave him his assistant who picked him up and escorted him to the home farm. He showed the candidate round the house and then took him with Hugh round the milking parlour and the other buildings scattered around in the near distance. He asked to look at the herd, currently out in a large home field eating the lush grass. Then at the fat stock bullocks and finally the heifers who were being grown on for sale or incorporation in the herd. That took him most of the rest of the afternoon and Hugh handed him back to Bob, Tim's assistant, who drove him back to the castle and he managed to find his way to his room, a feat in itself.

He had certainly used his initiative and was off to a flying start it seemed. He duly appeared at the library door at seven-thirty p.m. in a very smart but quiet coloured suit, and tie, and was welcomed in by Bertram and Hannah who explained who they were and introduced him to me saying I was James, Sarah's principal advisor regarding the estates in the UK and this one, and the reforms that were in prospect. Sarah who he had already been briefed was the senior trustee and owner, Timothy, also in a well-cut tweed jacket and cords with an Irish plaid tie, was introduced as the Irish estate general manager and finally Horace, whose family had been tied tenants of farm one, the next neighbour to the home farm and the next largest as well, for centuries.

He knew most of that already, but looked with interest at Timothy, who was cool, calm, and collected and really looked and acted the part he had been given to play, but for real. I could almost read A's mind, "*If he's the general estate manager, does that mean he is my line manager?*" and only I knew that was the case at present, although not yet cleared by Sarah. I knew it would work and be fine as Tim would be her barrier in any difficult matters, and in any case, she would not be there most of the time in fact, so Tim, not Bertie, was the go-to man and would wield the real power, something I don't think had dawned on Bertie and Hannah just yet. And I could see that Horace was having similar thoughts, but he knew Tim from when he was a lad and knew the man as well as any and was not uncomfortable with that knowledge at all. Of course, Tim would not be his boss; no one was, except Sarah who had the power to break him if needed.

Drinks were had, Guinness for Tim, Horace, Bertie and I, other drinks for the rest and A opted for a bottle of IPA. We sat and stood as we wished and chatted about the day so far for A whose name was Patrick, an Irishman by birth who had lived in England many years, but who spoke Gaelic; Scottish and Irish, and understood both the ancient language as well as the more modern vision. "Patrick," I said, "tell us about your first impressions."

He looked at me, then at Tim, then at Sarah and said, "Early days of course, but impressions are very favourable, and I noted immediately that the capacity of your milking parlour is much greater than the existing herd. I wondered if expansion which was mentioned, meant the home farm herd principally, and if so, how would you achieve that?"

"Good question, Patrick, so I will put it straight back to you. From the little you have seen so far, how would you seek to achieve that goal, if given a free hand?"

"Well, I guess that the growing herd of heifers are all pedigree and stem directly from the existing certified organic herd, so they would form part of the numbers required in time. Then you could postpone the retirement of some of the older cows who will probably still yield 6 or 7 gallons a day but might not get in calf so easily next time. Those that did, fine, keep them going and the rest dispose of. That would help a bit as it looks at first glance that about 25% are reaching their last two or three productive years. Having said that, I had a cow or two which reached twelve and still managed one more calf and another year's production at a good level too. That leaves any heifers you sold on over the last three years say, could some of those be returned assuming they have remained in an organic herd. Other than that, I can't say right now but I don't think it would take me long to get a fair number located and procured, albeit at top prices, but probably worth it."

"Good comprehensive answer, Patrick," Tim said. "But I would add one you may not have considered yet: what about looking at auctions at farms in a bit of trouble and needing to downsize or even to sell up completely? I knew of a farm in Worcestershire with 120 herd of prime Friesians up for sale because the farm owners decided to emigrate after both parents died. The buyer of the farm didn't want a dairy herd, just fat stock rearing and sheep. If you located such a farm, we have the funds to take the lot if that made the deal."

Patrick came back, "Yes, that's a good one, look at the auctions and maybe impending bankruptcies, etc. but I would want some pretty good tests run and documentation verified before closing such a deal."

"Of course you would, and so would I," said Tim, "But if we wanted to increase by say two hundred head, the sources that you identified would only alter things marginally. I would call for more drastic measures and look for a redundant herd, not just downsizing or whatever, costly but the rewards are almost instantaneous once the cows are settled in."

Sarah rescued poor Patrick who was looking a bit rattled and said, "Tim is right of course, and I would sanction buying a herd tomorrow if that could be done and we could accommodate them with sufficient grass, silage and hay, although these things can be bought in until the crops come in here, I suppose, but I am no farmer. I liked your suggestions, Patrick; it showed that you didn't walk around with your eyes shut this afternoon. Now on that note, let us eat."

Tim was unabashed, he was putting down a marker that a) he knew a bit about the home farm and cattle on the market, etc. and b) he was making it plain who would be the boss around here in Sarah's absence, and she and I both knew that and that's why we wanted him."

The interview was scheduled for ten-thirty a.m., so we got the panel together at ten and ran over a few points and I was in the chair as agreed with Sarah and Tim at my sides and Bertie and Horace flanking them. We sat in a line at a large table in the room we had chosen facing the door and he was ushered in at ten sharp, and invited to take a seat. I introduced everyone and said I was in the Chair but of course the final decision would be Sarah's.

After asking him if he had a good night, I launched straight in with what the Americans would have called a curveball. "Patrick," I said, "what are your views on culling predators that destroy salmon and sea trout in our river and streams, and kill young lambs on our farms and do untold damage to other wildlife? I am referring to foxes, badgers, wild mink, polecats, and stoats. Cormorants, crows, and jackdaws including ravens and other large corvids; herons, and hawks such as buzzards, eagles and falcons who take our lambs, pheasant, and partridge we raise, as well as ducks and hens. The crows' method of killing is particularly heinous, first pecking out their eyes and then disembowelling them while still alive."

He looked a bit confused at first, but settled himself down and replied, "Well, I confess that was a bit of a surprise question, but I do see the relevance because, as manager, I would be held responsible if laws were broken on my farm on my orders, or by my neglect. Now clearly, I would have to know the current laws regarding these predators, but I can answer how I feel subject to those laws not being broken. I could not of course condone any offences. Foxes I have no problem with although I do not like blood sports such as chasing them down with hounds which tear them apart, but I accept that there is little difference in a dog killing a lamb and foxes doing the same. In the UK farmers can shoot dogs on sight if they are out of control and are worrying sheep or lambs, so I have no problem with the gamekeeper killing foxes on our land, preferably not with hounds, but by trapping or shooting. I do not think most crows are protected but ravens must be I imagine, as they are an endangered species

I believe. Jackdaws and magpies are types of crows and therefore I would have no problem in shooting them, if suspected of predation, again on our land. Badgers I know can be culled under licence as they carry bovine tuberculosis which can be transmitted to our cows and must be prevented. Again, I don't like them being torn apart by dogs, although I am not too keen on gassing them in their sets either but I would sanction it to protect the herd. Eagles and falcons, I believe, are protected species. Not sure about buzzards; we would have to have an up-to-date list of all the suspected predators and seek guidance and review it regularly so as to stay within the law. That is my position, but I am also a realist and if some predator killing happened and it were involuntarily, then I guess I might turn a blind eye to it providing it was not the norm and not where I could or should have seen it occur. However, that is not a position I would like to be put in any contract, if I make myself clear."

"Very good," I said, "now over to you Sarah, please."

"Good morning, Patrick," said Sarah, "I thought you handled that pretty well as a first question out of the blue, so to speak. My first question is even more serious but for vastly different reasons. My main concern in relation to a new manager of the home farm stems I am sad to say from a serious breach of trust. As principal trustee, I of course have a big responsibility regarding the protection of the trust properties and their heritage going into the future, so that they not only remain intact but continue to grow and provide for future generations of my family. And acting alone out here is fine providing one has a high degree of trust in the individuals left here in day-to-day control. So, my question is simple, tell me and don't hold back anything: why should I trust you to run my home farm efficiently, profitably, and most important of all securely, i.e., the revenues will be properly collected and protected from, yes, looking at me with a dawning understanding, as James said, from predators?"

I smiled and so did Tim but no one else seemed to cotton on.

Patrick looked very serious, and thought a moment before replying, then said, "I confess I know a little of what happened here with the outgoing manager, and I will say no more and ask no questions in that regard. But as to my integrity, honesty, loyalty, and general sense of responsibility, I would challenge anyone, anyone anywhere, to point to a single stain on my reputation. I will simply say that you can trust me. And leave it to you to decide how you will judge that statement, but I am very confident it will prove to be right and fully justifiable whatever due diligence you carry out, or any other enquiry you wish to make. I will happily give you an open authority for any person, company or institution of any kind to ask any question of any person they see fit to ask."

"Thank you for that statement; it sounds very good to me and of course we are carrying out due diligence and the chosen candidate will have to undergo a stringent background investigation before finalisation of the contract."

"I welcome it," he said.

There followed some farm management and stock-rearing questions from Horace; Bertie had no questions at this point then Tim had his turn.

He smiled at Patrick and said, "Relax my boy, I am not going to eat you. I like what you have said so far and your general demeanour and have no problems with the veracity of your statements. Nor do I doubt your competence and ability to hold your own and manage the farm fairly but firmly."

"Thank you," said Patrick.

"My only concern is regarding what your attitude might be to the rest of the estate's activities; let me explain. The estate is a large and complex business with many activities present now and more in the planning stages, such as parties here for hunting, shooting, and fishing, and going into the future when we shall in effect have a four-star hotel within the castle, with many activities linked to visiting parties and individuals here for holidays, recreation, and corporate hospitality, with sessions linked to meetings as well as to partaking in the above activities alongside other guests. We may choose to have a golf course; we will stock specimen carp and other large fish in the river to attract the cream of angling clubs worldwide. We shall have one of the best salmon and sea trout rivers in the British Isles and Ireland. We shall build and operate a trout farm, for sale of fish, both live, fresh frozen and smoked, in plant already planned. We will also farm crayfish and freshwater mussels for our restaurant and for sale to other establishments and more, including smoking our organically produced pork and bacon and installation of the appropriate packaging plant. You may justifiably wonder what this has this to do with managing a dairy farm. But that is where an estate like this, having closely integrated and yet diverse activities, is very different from the normal dairy farm. It is a family business through and through and the protagonists must act and behave like a family, interested in and supporting of each other in a wide range of activities, but all essentially part of the same family business. So, this will mean that the successful candidate must not only be a very good dairy farm manager, but must learn gradually all the other management functions making up this wide-ranging and complex business, from hospitality, to fishing, from organic farming to smoke house hams, from crayfish and mussel farming, and packaging to fish farm management, from golf course to river environment management and yes, from control of animal predation, to guarding against the human variety. So my question is, are you up for it?"

Bloody hell Tim, magnificent I thought.

Patrick had gone gradually from confident pink to grim grey in the face, as he listened intently to all this, then he took a deep breath, composed himself and said, "Well Tim... I may call you Tim I hope?" Tim smiled and nodded. "Well Tim, that was some speech you just hit me with, and I say with all due respect, I now know why you have been made general manager. I have never come across such a scheme, but I love the idea. I am just a bit apprehensive about learning all about that as well as sorting out the farm and getting to know all the people and the cows, plus expanding to maybe twice the current capacity."

Tim said, "Fear not, I shall guide you, if you are successful in getting this post, and you will be given all the help you need and the time required but make no mistake about it, if I get ill or am away for a time, it is likely that the home farm manager will have to step up to the plate, so it will be intense for a while, but look at this as a challenge. Are you up for it I ask again?"

"Yes, by God I am, what a challenge as you say, it's a far bigger job than I anticipated and it's taking some time to process, but yes I am up for it if you are?"

Tim sat back and there was silence for a couple of minutes, then Sarah said, "James, have you any final questions for Patrick?"

369

I replied, "No I don't believe I have; does anyone else have anything to ask of Patrick? If not, Patrick, what, if anything, would you like to say?"

Patrick thought a moment and said, "Yes, I would just like to say that I am overwhelmed by your plans for the future, and I would love to be part of those plans, but I recognise that there will be some stiff competition and maybe one or two who will pull out when they see the size of the job. But I am very interested and would love to be part of your team here."

I said, "thank you Patrick, if you would leave us now and join us for lunch in about an hour, perhaps you would like to stroll around and look at the river to see if you can witness the salmon currently beginning their run upstream to breed."

"That I will," he said and almost trotted out of the room in eager anticipation.

We sat there a few minutes and then Sarah said, "You first James, what do you think?"

I said, "I think he could well be the man for the job if all the checks look good, but of course we have five other candidates, and it is imperative in my opinion to give them all the same treatment. I don't think Patrick will tell anyone else what they are in for do you?"

Sarah finally laughed and said, "No! Tim never ceases to amaze me; what a performance Tim, you should have revealed your talents years ago, or perhaps not. Now Bertie, your thoughts please?"

Bertie said, "He seems a very nice young man, and I would certainly have no objection to him being home farm manager."

"And you next please Horace," said Sarah".

Horace said, "Yes I think he could do the job and he stood up well I thought to Tim's revealing the full nature of the job going forward, I'm not sure I would want to be in his shoes, it's the simple life for me now."

"Thank you all that went pretty well, and he survived although it was touch and go at one point. "Now you, Tim, I think your thoughts are probably carrying the most weight at present, certainly the most responsibility."

"He would do for me; I could train him up with all the skills he needs except predator control and he made it clear that he will leave that to the experts. So, let's see what else we get, but he will take some beating as things stand."

Sarah said, "My thoughts exactly, Tim; he would do for me too, but we must see them all and as James says, you must put them all through the wringer in exactly the same way Tim."

"No problem," said Tim, "I have it all written down."

"All right," said Sarah and gave me a subtle wink, "let's get freshened up for lunch and see what we make of him there, although he was fine at dinner so I can't see it changing anything. They all filed out and Sarah hung back and shut the door and said, "Give me a kiss."

So, I obliged and followed her out of a door at the back up a narrow servant's stair into her bedroom exiting from a hidden door, "You sneak," I said, "you planned this didn't you?"

"I confess," she said, "come on I'm gasping for it."

The things you have to do sometimes, I thought, as I disrobed.

Lunch was excellent of course and there were crayfish and mussels amongst the starters and fresh wild salmon for main course, followed by a mixture of exotic fruit from the hot house and home-made dairy ice cream from the home farm. Patrick was full of enthusiasm as he had seen about a dozen salmon and was enthralled. Tim took time to explain all the conservation methods we were employing, how we only took injured fish to eat, controlled the crayfish by predating on them and all about the bridges and cattle watering troughs and the culling of the predators we had discussed in the interview. He neglected to tell him how we killed the badgers and foxes, the cormorants and the crows, etc. Why spoil the chap's lunch?

Off Patrick went to the airport in his hire car which he had picked up there, avoiding the arrival of candidate B who was also flying over from the UK. Bertie volunteered to meet him and entertain him in the castle and Bob, Tim's assistant, would take him to the home farm and to see the river. We would see him for pre-dinner tipples in the library at seven-thirty p.m.

I made a couple of phone calls one to Heather lasting about half an hour where I updated her and listened to her telling me about things at home, I told her I missed her and loved her, and she likewise. I then called Ronja, and we chatted about my last few weeks' efforts and she told me

371

about her exploits, or most of them I supposed. Finishing off with "Love you," and "Love you too." And the thing is both my calls were genuine and true; who says you can't love two women, or three?

We knew that Wilfred, the second interviewee, was a dour Scot from near Edinburgh. He had managed a mixed farm, which included a decent size herd of Holsteins, in the South West of England and he liked the idea of Ireland, as the dairy farms he knew in Scotland were few and far between and most needed up to six months of indoor feeding for the herd and clearing up after them, housed in cow sheds and/or folds, as the Yorkshire farmers referred to them, or fold yards, albeit undercover, where a decent number of cattle could roam free and only be transferred to the milking parlour at milking times. This made for cleanliness and uncontaminated milking kit easier. But this man certainly knew his job from all we had learnt of him. Milk cow's outdoors was only possible in the milder Northwest of Scotland where the influence of the Gulf Stream was felt except not so much in the summer of course, but Scottish summers were often very short, whereas Southern Ireland was known for its mild wet weather, almost year-round, that was why it was called The Emerald Isle, all that grass. This is what attracted him.

Wilfred arrived and was shown his room and taken by Bob to see the home farm, where he admired the farmhouse and then on to the milking parlour where he too noticed the capacity was for many more than the current herd, and it was briefly explained to him that we were in transition, planning to double the size of our pedigree, organically certified herd and other reforms were under discussion. He also looked at the heifers being grown on and the fat stock cattle, mainly bullocks, out of our own calves grown on, and shown the silage mountains under tarpaulins and our extensive hay barns and stacks. Also, our mangold stores and the chopping and milling houses were inspected as was our stock of tractors, cultivators, hay makers and silage cutters, etc. Again, he seemed impressed. His personal Land Rover was shown him, should he get the job and three others used by Tim, the General Manager, and the Foreman Hugh but nothing was mentioned to him about our plans, as we had warned Bob about that and wanted them to be a surprise for him.

He duly turned up for pre-dinner drinks in the library at seven-thirty p.m. and he was a man in his forties, dapper and slim but wiry and strong-looking as well. He had a Scottish burr still discernible although he had lived in England over twenty years. He looked at ease with everything and only exclaimed a little when he saw the once again magnificent spread put on. "My," he said, "surely you don't eat like this all the time? This is a feast fit for a king, or a queen," he added looking at Sarah and smiling.

"Thank you, Wilfred, we do like our organic produce and our own home-killed and -cured beef, pheasant and partridge, wild river-caught salmon, crayfish and mussels, both fresh from the river today, not to mention our own fruit and vegetables."

"Ah but not the mango and bananas surely?"

"Yes, those too, from our hothouse, and peaches, and other fruit from our temperate greenhouses. The only thing bought in here is probably salt and pepper, even the bread is from our own grain, milled and baked fresh every other day, and our own butter and cream too of course."

"My goodness, it was worth coming here just to see and experience all this."

He was told to be ready for interview for ten-thirty a.m. and after a few more minutes he said goodnight and went off to his room. All sat a moment and then I said, "Well, what do you feel Sarah?"

She replied, "I'm not sure, he seems a bit too stiff and fond of his own opinions for my comfort, plus why is the green grass of Ireland better than the West Country? What about you James?"

"I too am a little uncomfortable; I can see him digging his heels in perhaps for no good reason. But it may just be nerves on his part. I will be interested in how he handles Tim tomorrow, and I didn't see much talk between you and him Tim?"

"No that's correct, I will reserve judgement until tomorrow."

On that rather sombre note we all retired to bed and for once alone, at least as far as I was concerned, that is until a slight rap on my door and a diaphanous Sarah appeared and slid silently in beside me. I was glad because I wasn't ready for sleep, so I made us a coffee from my own equipment and poured us both a decent snifter of brandy and we went over a few things before making love and then she departed like a wraith.

The interview started well enough with my opener where Wilfred showed no qualms about culling predators, and then Sarah's follow up questions which again he answered fairly cogently and then it was over to Tim.

Tim came out with his speech and as he progressed almost word for word as he had against Patrick, Wilfred sat more upright and listened intently and then grew as pale as Patrick had, but when it came to the part where Tim said, "So my question Wilfred is this, are you up for it?"

And Wilfred, now scarlet faced and with his chest puffed out blew it, he almost shouted, "You have a nerve! I believe that you were just the gamekeeper here until very recently and you are laying down the law to me and demanding commitments way beyond what the job description and indeed the salary reflects; it's outrageous and I want no part of this if I'm required to become subservient to you!"

"Now Wilfred," said Sarah, "Calm yourself, and tell me please, for what reason did you wish to transplant yourself from mild green Devon to mild green Ireland?"

At this he jumped to his feet and stormed out and was seen haring away in a taxi half an hour later and was never heard from again. We all sighed with relief; clearly this man had hang-ups we were not privy to, so better to discover that now rather than later.

The only shortlisted woman came next and was not due to arrive until later in the afternoon, so we could relax over lunch and get ourselves ready for her. Her name was Stephanie, and we knew that she was fully experienced and qualified and that after an acrimonious split with her husband, which resulting in him buying her half of their farm, she was both homeless and jobless. Even though she had a sizeable pay-out she would never be in a position to replace what she had, but the home farm was about the same size as her old farm and had similar stock levels.

Much again would depend on how she stood up to the challenge of the panel because we all agreed it was only fair to give them all the same treatment.

She arrived, having asked to be picked up at the airport and she was met by Sean who is a very likeable young man, so she arrived in good spirits with a smile on her face, to be welcomed in by Hannah. The first thing she said was, "What a beautiful place." She was shown her room and asked if she would like to visit the home farm and then walk around the castle or along the river leaving herself time to freshen up before pre-dinner drinks at seven-thirty in the library, and she said, "Oh yes that would be perfect."

Sean took her over to the home farm and she was introduced to Hugh by Sean after he had escorted her through the house, which she loved.

Hugh was so obviously a cow man that Stephanie hit it off with him straight away and once he realised she was a farmer born and bred, and had jointly managed a farm of similar size and stock levels, he was relaxed and happy. She took a deep interest in everything and showed her knowledge of all aspects of milking, bringing on young stock and fat-stock bullocks, and was familiar with all the usual silage, hay-making and mangold chopping's mixed with chopped wheat or barley straw for winter feed.

She asked Hugh to run her round the big home pasture to look at the herd and looked in on the bullocks, heifers, and calves, and then asked him to please drop her off by the river at a point near to the castle, which he did. After the river inspection she walked to the castle and found the staff entrance at the back and the boot room. She changed out of her muddy boots and then asked a maid to please direct her to her room, which she did. We learnt all of this from various sources and were impressed.

She came to the library at around seven-thirty and we were all waiting and ready for her. She entered in a smart tweed suit and choker with brown brogues and looked every inch the wealthy farmer that she was, and with an open frank look and a nice smile.

Sarah greeted her and introduced herself and the rest of us and I could see that Tim was quite impressed with her, but I wondered if that would last when he threw her the curveball in the interview tomorrow. She asked for a sparkling water with ice and lemon, and we all indulged our fancies, Tim, Bertie and Horace and I had our usual Guinness and Sarah had a gin and tonic with ice and lemon. Seeing this, Stephanie asked could she also have a G & T and Sarah laughed and said, "Of course."

Dinner was very relaxed with much praise from Stephanie and exclamations of delight which were clearly spontaneous. She told us without any asking that her marriage had failed for basic incompatibility reasons; in short, he preferred the plough boy to her, and that was the end of their not too brilliant marriage, procured she admitted, by his ambitious parents. She was a member of an old county family with a large farm, but also had two brothers who shared the farm on their death. They all agreed on that because of her 'successful' match! But in the end, she was the loser and didn't care to make public what the real reason was until now, and she trusted we would treat this as important and necessary information, but totally confidential.

Sarah thanked her and admired her frankness and Tim, and Bertie looked a bit grim but said nothing.

I said, "I for one applaud your disclosure and would certainly not take any cognisance of it as regards my part in your appraisal." And she thanked me and smiled at me. I thought, *better watch it Jim, Sarah will not be very pleased, if you get too friendly towards her.*

Tim thawed out a bit when she asked him a few questions about the estate and its management and she listened carefully to his answers showing him clearly that she saw a need to be part of the whole estate, not just the home farm manager.

Bertie remained quiet but accepting of the situation and Hannah said absolutely nothing to her until Stephanie asked her about her future role in the enlarged set-up. Hannah too got into an interesting discussion with her about the proposed hotel situated within the castle, which Stephanie ("Please call me Steph,") found fascinating, especially the idea about having corporate functions there and maybe big wedding parties and so on.

Finally, at about eleven p.m., by which time we had all had last drinks including coffee, she excused herself and said, "See you at ten-thirty then," and went to her room.

As usual we had a brief valedictory and I asked Sarah what her impressions were and she replied, "I particularly liked her transparent honesty and I saw a clear interest in the rest of the estate, lacking at this point in the others so far."

"And you Tim?" I asked. Tim thought a moment and said, "I could work with her I think, very refreshing, very attentive, actually listened and thought about her replies. Good solid candidate I think, on a par with Patrick so far. Be interesting to see how she reacts to some pressure."

"Bertie?" I said.

Bertie looked a bit nonplussed but said, "I find myself agreeing with both Tim and Sarah here, but as Tim says, can she cut his mustard?"

"And Horace, could you see her as your neighbour?"

"Oh yes," said Horace, "rather nice change and got some good ideas and not afraid to speak her mind. She would do for me."

"Well just my opinion I suppose, I'm not a farmer as you all know, but I have picked up a bit here and there, enough to recognise one when I see one. What I can say is that if I were interviewing her for a position in my group of companies, I would say she is right up there as a candidate. Open, honest or a great actress, intelligent, articulate and not afraid of work or of change and would readily accept responsibility, do for any mid to top management job in my organisation."

With that we retired, and Sarah came to my room again, got into bed and made mad passionate love with me. Then she asked, "You don't fancy her do you James?" I said, "Well!" and Sarah dug me in the ribs with her elbow and I laughed out loud.

"Just a bit," I said, "but not like I fancy you, especially when you are jealous and fighting mad!" and she dug me in the ribs again. I said, "Ow, that hurt."

"Good," she said.

Then she made love to me again. Women!

The time for her interview came round and she sailed through all the tests with ease. She would welcome working alongside or under Tim whichever it didn't matter the position; she would be part of a team running the whole show and welcome the diversity, not shun it. As for culling predators, give me a gun; as for the law, of course she would observe it especially when it was witnessed, and so on. No tantrums, no chalk-white or red face, calm as you like. Doubling the size of the herd was easy, there were always dairy farms with troubles and more herds of Holstein Friesians in England than any other pedigree breed of cattle, and always selling up or downsizing or the opposite. Find a couple of targets on the grapevine, offer ten percent over market price for a quick deal and she would double the herd in six months or resign.

We all thanked her and said see you at lunch about one p.m. and off she went with Horace to have a look at his farm on his invitation. We later all agreed she was a very serious contender together with Patrick; if anything, she came higher than Patrick as he had survived Tim where she had absorbed and welcomed him and his proposals, had said certainly she was up for it, bring it on.

We went through the whole thing three more times but none of the final three, and we had deliberately interviewed them on highest plus marks from the paper sift first as is the norm so that you can cut the list if you choose, but we wanted to see them all because if our preferred two leaders Patrick and Stephanie fell to another job or just didn't in the end want it, we wanted the best of the remaining four to be available.

We toyed with a shoot-out, but finally I prevailed and said, "No, enough is enough, contact Stephanie straight away if that is who we agreed upon. 'Don't keep anyone waiting any longer than necessary, and get her in and up and running ASAP, or fall back on Patrick if she withdraws for whatever reason." Sarah said, "What's the best way to do this James?" and I said, "Watch and listen. If you are sure, it's her you want."

"It is," she replied.

I picked up the phone and called the number I had written on a pad at my elbow, it rang out twice and then, putting the call on speaker, we heard Stephanie say, "Hello, this is Stephanie, to whom am I speaking please?"

I replied, "Hello Steph, this is Jim in Ireland remember me?"

"Ha-ha, how could I forget you, James?"

"Easily I think, but for the fact, and she is sitting here listening, that Sarah and I would like to ask you to accept our offer of the post of manager the home farm here on castle estate, Ireland."

"James, Sarah, thanks with all my heart, I accept without reservation. When would you like me to start?"

"To suit you, of course, but say Friday of this week, if possible, if not do not worry, another two or three days will be acceptable."

I will be on the Friday flight arriving ten-thirty if you can arrange for that sweet boy Sean to pick me up with all my luggage, I can send a

378

trunk later after a brief return visit to say goodbye to my family say at this month's end."

Sarah nodded. "That will all be fine, thank you for your immediate and positive response and we will be ready to greet you Friday for lunch. Then you can get everything shipshape in the house and Hugh will look after the farm until you are ready to take over. Dare I ask have you identified any targets yet for your herd expansion?"

"I have indeed, and I can have 120 certified organic, Holstein Friesians, all or almost all in full milk, shipped over before the month end at 750 pounds a head, how does that sound? That's 90,000 GBP plus freight, shipping and trucking to the farm will be another 12,000 or so."

Sarah nodded.

"No problem at all, do it, and send the seller's bank details and we will prepare a transfer of half now and the remainder on receipt of the cattle and get a quote plus copy bills of lading. Try to get truck hire here in Dublin, where you will only have to mention Sarah's name, and all will be well, and we will settle with them afterwards."

"Great, I will do all that, and my credit with my half of the farm selling, is good so no need for the deposit, I will handle all that, fully document it and settle up at month end, if that is acceptable?"

"It is certainly, and any problems you have with any Irish Authority, just tell them where you are coming, to take over the post of home farm manager at the castle and again, do not hesitate to mention Sarah's name and if necessary, just call her or me immediately if you get any problem you can't handle."

"Is it OK if I speak directly with Tim about all this as I will need his help and approval and needn't bother you two so much and I want to keep him in the loop from day one?"

"Perfectly OK, do you have his number?"

"Yes, he already gave me it, thanks."

"Until Friday then," I said.

And we said our goodbyes.

"Great choice of candidate, with the heifers and a few other acquisitions we shall have a full house in no time, just need to get more grass available quickly and lay in extra stocks of baled hay, beet, cow cake, etc. But I think that is why she will be calling Tim so let's wait and see shall we?"

"I agree," said Sarah, "you only need to get your men to finish the draft plan and we can get moving here without you or me in attendance so we can move on to Scotland. We can easily fly back from Edinburgh if we are needed."

"True, but I really must go home for a few days, and it might be sensible for us to travel on different days and for you to smooth my passage for when I get there by explaining to your son and the rest what has happened here so far, so that they can start to think about it as applied to them and have some outline plans to discuss."

"That's sound thinking, and I can get a still manufacturer to come plus a builder or two to give estimates for the still house repair or reconstruction. Then they can also consider if we can have golf course, and can we fit a small hotel into the castle there or will need planning applications for a new build. Yes, I am half trained now, almost don't need you, do I?"

"Now you are talking, but yes you do need me, in more ways than one, and you don't get rid of me as easily as that!"

Sarah laughed and said, "Don't worry I know that, just so used to having you around."

I called in the boys and looked at their work and it was clear they were moving towards their goal of a preliminary draft plan so I made a couple of suggestions and told them to have it ready in about a week when I would either come and go through it with them or they could join me in Scotland after a home break like I was taking now. They said that they would like to do that. I had been keeping regular track of their progress and with feedback from the tied farm tenants and also from Tim, I knew they were now pretty familiar with the whole estate and liaising well with all the main players. We had eaten together a few times at the village pub with Tim.

So we all said goodbye later that day and Sean drove me to the airport, and I picked up my car from the long-term car park where it had languished for several weeks. It started fine and I drove home. Sarah told me she would go home also and see Michael for a few days before going up to Scotland and fill him in on all the happenings which had taken place over the last few weeks.

I arrived home by mid-afternoon and Heather was waiting for my arrival having just brought Mother over to see me as she was worried about not having seen me for so long, but a hug and a kiss and she was right as rain. She was still doing very well considering she was eighty-three years old by then. Heather was as always, smart and alert and enjoying life but very interested in all that had happened at the castle. I spent most of the rest of that day recounting the whole story and she was amazed at what a central role I had played in all of this having never really had much to do with farms and livestock, but she always knew about my interest in wildlife and fishing so she acknowledged it was all linked and a business was a business whatever the currency or product being bought, sold or managed. Furthermore, she was pretty impressed by my detective work uncovering the fraud and recovering all the money.

I enjoyed the company of the children at the weekend, and they too had to hear a condensed version of the Irish estate saga and were very impressed, but I made light of it and said, "All in a day's work."

I told them that the plans were now accepted for the reform of the English estate and those for the Irish estate would be complete by the end of the month and then I had Scotland to do, and it would be a matter of obtaining any licences, permits, consents and compliance with building regulations then when all those hurdles had been successfully negotiated, finance was needed and estimates, architects plans and so on all sorted out and the real work could begin. So, this would mean my involvement for a long time as I had essentially become the overall projects manager for all three estates and would see things through to completion and of course get very well paid for all this.

Not just the physical reformation of the buildings and land changes, but accountancy and legal issues to be negotiated and resolved and Sarah had asked me to remain in overall control until the whole reforms had been successfully completed. This almost certainly meant that I would, at some point, be appointed managing director at least, possibly Chief Executive and Chairman of the newly formed Irish legal entity, which all the estates and the group companies would be absorbed into, largely for tax purposes. The Swiss trust would continue to exist, but all the various parts of the empire would have its head office in Ireland and Sarah, would remain the senior living family member and de facto owner, for whom the trust had been formed in order for her to protect the assets for future generations to come.

What I was doing, at Sarah's invitation, was growing and streamlining the structures of the organisation and its properties and businesses, so that the value increased over the years and there would be no need for a further major overhaul of the legal entities, financial, legal or accountancy, for many years if at all. In short securing the long-term growth of capital and income for the future while generating sufficient current income to maintain everything and continue to add to the cash and property assets from time to time.

They all expressed their amazement and admiration for what I had and was in the process of doing, but I played it down, saying any competent company doctor with my experience and knowledge could have done it. But they said, "Well how come it hadn't happened until I came along?"

Good question.

But I simply said, "Right time, right place," and Heather said, "And most importantly, right man. I have watched your father over many years go from office boy, photographing records on to microfilm, to half owner of a large group of companies of which he is Chief Executive and Chairman. He has, admittedly with a little help from me, developed into a very shrewd operator and yet kept his feet firmly on the ground, as happy fishing or shooting as wielding a pen or a computer mouse. More importantly, he sets a great example to follow, believes anything is possible and will have a go at anything. He and I have put together a significant fortune in property and shares and in cash, such that we will put everything in our own trust for you two and any children you have, so that you will never have to worry about money, if you are sensible how you spend it of course, which I know you both are."

"Thanks Heather, you are easily the main reason for our success and was my adviser and partner in all we did together and don't you kids let her tell you otherwise."

So, after a few lovely lazy family days, I was ready to go once again, this time back to Scotland before the winter came! But first I talked to

Tim and my team, as well as to Stephanie and Sarah, and Stephanie was already hard at it and working closely with Tim and the others in getting the home farm into shape. There was no need for me to divert via Ireland, I would go tomorrow, and Sarah had been there four days already preparing my way as I had asked her to.

Chapter 35

I flew up to Edinburgh and was met by Sarah in the Range Rover at about twelve-thirty. We decided to go and have some lunch somewhere on the road to the Scottish estate and after about half an hour spotted a lovely old inn just off the main road but set back enough not to be a problem from traffic disturbance.

There were only a handful of other people there so we had a choice and found a nice little table in an alcove and settled down, me with a pint of Guinness and Sarah with a glass of Chardonnay which she said she would have with the meal. She was hungry so two glasses would therefore be her limit as she had volunteered to drive. I immediately offered to take over the driving, but she insisted so I took a long pull of the Guinness. It wasn't as good as real Dublin Guinness but near enough not to matter.

"So," I said, "How are Bobby and Hamish, still much the same I imagine?"

"Yes, that is one concern I have, that Bobby is in a bit of a rut here, so it is more important than ever that he gets something more interesting and demanding to do. It is terribly isolated out here and his girlfriend in Edinburgh would never come here to stay more than a couple of nights."

"Then maybe he ought to be offered a new role in one of the other estates or even at one of your group companies" I said. "

"I have thought of that, but he seems uninterested, whereas he does like it here, so maybe we should give him more challenges and responsibilities here. And when the golf course, distillery and holiday facilities are being built and then up and running, with a lot more people working here, plus all the visitors, that might help him spread his wings a bit more."

"I think that will take a long time; maybe he should be told to go to the Irish estate and spend some time looking at that and our projects there, some of which are actually under way, under training with Tim to guide him a bit?"

"Yes, I might do that, Tim would not be afraid of putting his foot down, he is general manager now, and Bobby could do with a firm hand maybe. I will ask Tim if he is prepared, as it were, to apprentice him as a future manager, and of course he will become the main trustee sooner or later, so needs the training and experience."

I then asked her, "Have your experiences at the Ireland estate given you more ideas for similar activities to be thought of for here?"

She replied, "Yes they have, along the lines you and I have discussed and in no special order, the new still and resurrection of a single Malt Whisky Brand being produced here, I am already wedded to that idea. The golf course too, with a clubhouse which could perhaps be large enough to make it into a holiday hotel, or be fairly close to it, with its own pool and gymnasium. Plus letting about twenty rooms in the main house for none golfing holidays, hunting, shooting, fishing types maybe. Also, to welcome corporate parties who like all that sort of thing. Develop the river and streams for encouraging more salmon and sea trout to come back here to breed, involving the same clean-up of the streams and prevention of cattle damage to the spawning beds and the culling of predators. Releasing more land for suitable feedstock crops and of course more barley for malting here in our own malt kiln which we need to plan and erect. All very much like Ireland but taking account of the more severe and protracted winters so no herd of Friesians I'm afraid, but possibly Aberdeen Angus cattle which we would need to develop as an organic herd with much better prices fetched. How's that for starters?"

"Very good, you have been watching and listening obviously. I'm not sure about the quantity of crayfish and mussels here, or where they all go in winter, but if there is a possibility then we should farm them. Plus, the stocking of the river with some specimen fish and building ladders for the salmon as we are planning down south. And what about a trout farm here also? These more exotic things we may need to research a bit more, because I am uncertain exactly how severe and protracted the winters are up here and also if the numbers of crayfish available will justify trying to farm them. The trout farm should be possible as much of it will be under cover, and I presume the river never freezes solid? But in general, I see that we can do many of the things we have planned in Ireland, making a few modifications, as necessary. The turnover will be smaller of course as we don't have a dairy herd here, but quality beef from Aberdeen Angus cattle might make up for some of the difference."

"Yes," said Sarah, "I think it could all work out very well and it is a good idea to second Robert to Ireland for a spell with Tim to pick up what needs doing and how. Meanwhile you can press on with your plans with the boys so that we can present all three plans to the surveyors, lawyers, and architects as well as our accountants. Then the necessary funds can be made available, and we can start getting contractors in once we establish which parts of the three projects can go ahead and which must wait planning consents and so on."

"Maybe someone from England or Ireland could come up here while Bobby is away, to assist Hamish who may find all this a bit much alone."

"I agree," said Sarah, "I had better ask Tim who he can spare and is also sufficiently competent at the same time I speak to him about Bobbie coming to him."

She called Tim and he was willing to take Bobbie for a spell and suggested we send Sean up to Scotland.

He said, "Sean is bright enough and seen almost all of what we are doing, and he can always call me if he needs advice, and Hamish will be happy with him, I'm sure."

This was all arranged, and we decided the sooner the better and called Bobbie and Shamus to a meeting later that evening. Before dinner.

After the very pleasant lunch we proceeded to the estate arriving about four p.m. and were welcomed by Hamish and Bobby. I put my bags in my usual room and joined Sarah, Bobby, and Hamish for a cup of tea and a wee dram. We decided to start the meeting right away and began by giving a run down on the plans for Ireland, and they were amazed at how much we had progressed in such a brief time. Then Sarah said, "Yes, great progress has been made thanks to James and his team and now Tim is the general manager of the Irish estate and will be responsible for implementing the plans and running the whole estate from there on."

Hamish responded, "Couldn't pick a better man in my opinion."

And Bobbie was a bit surprised but also expressed his support for Tim.

"Just as well Bobbie because I am sending you down to work with him for a while so you can see first-hand what all this involves and to prepare you for being the general manager here, which, after all our plans are passed and implemented, will be almost as big a job as Tim's in Ireland."

Bobbie was stunned. "Really, you really mean that? Wow!"

"Yes, I do, and as Tim would say, are you up for it?"

"Rather!" said Bobbie. "I have been thinking I needed a bit more of a challenge for a while but too lazy to do anything about it."

Sarah said, "And you, Hamish, will also get a promotion to assistant general manager under Bobbie, but acting general manager while Bobby is away, so I think maybe three months, what do you think, James?"

"At least! 'It's a big job with lots of new things to learn and the real job starts as soon as he is back, but I would say four or even six months might be advisable."

"Six it is then," said Sarah. "Now Hamish, you will have your hands full here because some parts of the plan will start straight away and not need planning consents later on. The still building will be renovated and maybe a hotel and a golf course are constructed and other longer-term things, including perhaps a trout farm, a smoke house and a packaging plant is built and equipped, you will need more help still, but for now I am bringing my nephew Sean over from Ireland. You have met him I think, a nice lad and very capable, so he will be your assistant manager on loan from Ireland, where he has already become familiar with much of which I speak."

Hamish was thunderstruck. He gasped like a fish out of water for a moment then straightened his back and said, "Thank you Ma'am, I am delighted and amazed both at once. I look forward to all that and you know that I will always do my best."

We then gave them both a rundown of all our current plans for Scotland and I asked Hamish, "Tell me, Hamish, what was the worst winter you have experienced here? How long did it last, was there lying snow throughout, and did the river ever stop flowing because of ice?"

Hamish stopped and thought a bit then said, "1963 and 1964 I think was the worst; I don't remember 1947 of course which was worse. But the river has never stopped flowing underneath even when iced up almost bank to bank that I am certain of because my grandfather told me that. And salmon and sea trout just wait a bit offshore "til it's safe to move and all the other fish sit quietly under the ice "til it breaks up. Lying snow never lasts long here because of the proximity to the West Coast and the Gulf Stream which warms the air. Over about five hundred feet the hills stay covered for about two or three months normally say four months in a very bad winter but never more than inches in general, except in valleys and such.

The parts around the house and the home fields are frosty most nights and lowland cattle need to be under cover but the Highland cattle, so long as they have hay and beet, and a bit of chop will be all right below five hundred feet and even above that with a bit of straw and bracken bedding.

"Sheep are similar to the Highland cattle but need bringing in for lambing if the weather is bad. As for Aberdeen Angus, my information is they do fine here but need a bit more attention than Highland cattle. They will tolerate very low temperatures provided enough feed is available but they like a shelter of some sort so an open-ended barn with a fold yard might be a good idea if it gets very bad. As for organic, we are three years into that so could get our certificates soon providing soil, plant and animal tests once again prove satisfactory and we could buy in certified organic and isolate them and put organic approved feed down for them until full certification is granted for the whole farm."

I said, "Very good Hamish, you are clearly on to all this so what we need to do is inspect the river, streams and pools, and the mere and check for crayfish and mussels and keep an eye out for predators. So we will take guns please say nine tomorrow morning and some rubber boots or waders, size 9 if you have them please. Have you got any crayfish traps?"

"Only about a dozen, but they are all set so we shall see, and in any case, we can spot them in the river and the streams if there are many or few. As for mussels, no problem, lots of those around the bog."

"Good, I will also take rods for a spot of fishing please, and some binoculars too."

Sarah said, "Come to dinner Hamish and bring your wife if she is up for it. Seven-thirty for a dram and eat about eight all right?"

"Thanks ma'am I will ask her, but you know what she is like, a bit shy."

We called Tim and told him our plans and he said he would sort out the logistics and to leave it to him and he would prepare for a six month stay for Bobbie and tell Sean the same.

He asked how our plans were shaping up, so we gave him a complete rundown and he said, "Nearly as much as is happening here, apart from your crop limitations, the Aberdeen Angus is a good idea, very good prices all over the world for their steaks and joints, and they hang well for about a month and then travel in chillers for weeks, so no need to freeze."

Sarah pleaded tiredness and said she would have a nap before dinner and I too said I had had a long and tiring day, so if everybody was happy with what we had arranged fine. If anything arose, we could talk about it at dinner. I then remembered to ask Bobby, "What about your girlfriend in Edinburgh?"

He replied, "Oh that's not an issue, we hardly see each other now since I said she obviously didn't like the journey here. Can't say it bothers me much."

Sarah gave me her secret nod and I awaited her in my room since I was not familiar with the arrangements here. Turned out she was opposite me, so she was able to slip over in a few seconds, and disrobed in no time and got into bed where I was ready and waiting having not been with her for, it seemed, a long time. Good relationship we had, no need for explanations, just get to the main point and that would suffice.

Afterwards I said, "Not concerned about Bobbie being suspicious, you are being put so near to me?"

"No, he is oblivious to that side of things like his father, thinks I'm well past it and in any case, I worry about his lack of interest in women."

I said, "I wouldn't worry something like 69% of men have a lower-than-average libido and low testosterone levels, most are what people refer to as 'once-a-month men. I am certain he is normal in that way, but when he meets a sexy girl who turns him on he will be fine. 'Can't judge them all from my example, I am a horny old goat."

"Don't I know it," she said and moved into a position to indicate her interest in proving my statement.

At dinner, we all were cheerful and relaxed, even Hamish who was clearly very pleased with his promotion and enhanced future employment and was keen to take part, but not to show off. Sarah and I were asked a lot of questions and she was able to field most of them, including an explanation about the milk fraud and Philip's dismissal after the trust recovering a very significant amount of stolen money. Hamish reported that during the last few weeks the salmon and sea trout had started to run upriver, not a huge amount, but pretty good considering no real steps of the kind we had already taken in Ireland had been taken here. I said let's see how it all shapes up tomorrow and then recap then.

Bobby was also excited by his impending move to work under Tim and beginning to learn the finer arts of business and farm management and pick up information relating to all aspects of the Irish plan implementation. Sarah looked quietly pleased at his enthusiasm and smiled a 'thank you' at me. Hamish was a much wilier old campaigner than Bobbie and caught the mutual smiles and I could sense him wonder about it. However, I knew he was loyal to the core and would never voice his suspicions to anyone, not even his wife. He smiled at me without rancour nor approval, and I guessed he probably knew that Sarah needed someone like me, and he was content just to mind his own business. Maybe I would find out tomorrow when we were alone together all day.

We retired about eleven p.m. and I got the nod that it was my turn to move so after a suitable period I went over and quietly let myself into Sarah's room. After a cuddle we just slept, awaking at about seven and made love before showering, changing, and going down to breakfast. There Bobbie and Hamish were tucking into a good breakfast of porridge, home-cured bacon and free-range eggs, field mushrooms and tomatoes. Sarah and I preferred Grapefruit and scrambled eggs with Salmon flakes and home-made wholemeal bread with farm butter. Then a quick goodbye and off Hamish and I went in his long wheelbase Land Rover, already loaded with gear, guns and a huge cool box, and we set off first down river towards the West Coast along a track which followed the river all the way to the beach, also ours. We got out and looked at the pristine sand and rocks which were totally enclosed, and our private domain and I noted that the river was very clear and clean and no accumulation of driftwood or plastic to be seen.

I looked around and said to Hamish, "You know what? This bay with its rock formation and huge sand dunes going about half a mile inland, would make a great site for the golf course with the clubhouse at the rear and maybe the hotel too. Mind you, I think maybe the hotel would be better nearer to the house, what do you think?"

"The golf course and clubhouse maybe, but you would need a proper service road with power cables and water supply laid on. And the hotel I think not; that must be nearer the main road, not immediately next to the house, say half a mile away but just in sight and walking distance. It would have to be stand alone, with all facilities, pool, garden, and games areas easily accessible from the castle, probably under a covered walkway, we get a lot of indifferent weather here."

"Yes, much to consider, but we could lay on buggies or golf carts to get from the hotel to the golf course for those not staying in the clubhouse. A lot will depend on the possibility of planning consents, so two alternative sites for a hotel might make a positive decision easier to obtain," I said.

We started to inspect the river more carefully and unloaded our 12-bore shotguns, up and over twin barrels and with walnut stocks and immediately saw about twenty cormorants sitting in the morning sun with their wings spread out to dry and stuffed full of fish by the look of them. I indicated that we should sneak up on them, knock a few over and see what they were feeding on. We crept up to a bank of grass about twenty yards from their roosting trees and let fly. Before they could get away, loaded as they were with fish, we had downed about eight but a couple dropped into the river and disappeared. We opened up two of the biggest ones and each had a couple of medium sized trout and several smaller fry of indeterminate species, could be roach or some other course fish, plus a couple of frogs and one small crayfish. The trout were our main concern, luckily no small salmon, they were either too big to swallow or too small because salmon fry go to sea as soon as they are large enough and don't hang around like trout who will often spend their whole life in a river or stream or ponds and lakes. Only a few rainbow trout will go to sea, acclimatising themselves to salt water in the river estuary, and then, like salmon, will spend years at sea getting almost as big as salmon sometimes, before returning to mate and spawn.

We buried the cormorants in the field nearby at the edge so they would not get ploughed up and continued further and shot a couple of wild mink, originally escapees from fur farms, and the most vicious of predators, capable of killing large fish and other mammals.

Then we came to where the most distant crayfish traps were set and the first three in this stretch of river contained a total of eleven crayfish all big enough to eat. Hamish bagged them with a handful or two of weed from the river to keep them moist and alive and reset the traps and off we went. Then we reached a stretch of river with good level gravel banks near to the side and Hamish said that this would be a good place to try out our salmon rods. I recalled that I had been lucky enough last time I was here to catch a fine salmon but much nearer the house, and didn't expect to be so lucky again, but I was. I hooked a big male salmon who was swollen up with sperm fluid, known as milt. He was about 25 lbs in weight and very fit and healthy, so we threw him back and he shot off upstream. Hamish hooked a female of similar size full of eggs which, when we tried to weigh her on our scales, she shed quite a few eggs, quite normal said Hamish. She also was healthy, so we released her as well. Then I hit an absolute monster of about forty lbs, but he had clearly been attacked, probably by a mink, and was bleeding all along one side. Hamish said he would not make it to the spawning grounds much higher up the river and his blood would attract all sorts of predators on the way, nor would he get through the shallows in the streams without exposing his wounds. Hamish took out his priest and dealt him a blow at the back of his head and killed him. Sad but necessary and he would make a splendid sight on the dinner table.

On we went and came to the first stream emptying into the river from our lands and it was pretty clean. But we examined the three traps Hamish had set here and found another eight crayfish, one of which was a good seven inches long with vicious lobster-like pincers. Hamish pointed out the larvae and eggs attached to her water filters and hairs on her thighs and claws, and I agreed that this one would be good to start a captive colony in a prepared pond nearer the house. We bagged these and went up the stream. There we saw a large salmon struggling through the shallows up towards the spawning grounds where she had probably been born. She wriggled like an eel as we approached and made it to a deeper section of the stream. On we went and there was a ford over the stream, but it was over clean gravel and a good six inches deep all across so no real need for a bridge unless water levels dropped, and Hamish assured me they never dropped further than now. But he agreed there were several such fords which would need bridging or deepening to allow the salmon through safely.

We then approached a boggy area still well downstream from the house so nowhere near the real peat bogs which were way up beyond the house, but nevertheless important as they were where another spawning ground was, on a small stream starting somewhere in the bog. We looked at a small pond near the bog and it was, like in Ireland, the home to a type of edible mussel and similar to Tim's contraption, Hamish had plaited reeds in overlapping mats over the sides of the bank of the pond hanging in about two feet six inches of clear, brackish water. Clinging to these mats were hundreds of mussels ranging from tiny to about three inches in length of which Hamish harvested a dozen or two and put in a large bucket in the back of the Land Rover with about six inches of water in it and a secure lid to stop it splashing everywhere. Hamish told me there were hundreds of such pools, so if we wanted to reclaim any of this land, we would still have plenty of mussels.

I explained about bigger ponds being utilised for crayfish breeding, and he said, might not be necessary here as the river was best. But I also explained that we were culling the river crayfish because they predated the young salmon and trout heavily and Hamish hadn't been aware of that problem. So, it was obtaining a balance between production of crayfish for sale to upmarket restaurants and delicatessens and hotels and the regeneration of the salmon and sea trout numbers. I saw no reason why, up to a point we could not do a bit of both, and he agreed.

We continued our travels and noted the fords which needed repair or bridging, places where cattle had damaged the streams, spoiled the access for salmon, and polluted the water so needed a secure water trough placing nearby and the stream protected by wire or hurdles. We eventually reached a point on the river easily accessible from the house and looked at the angling positions and the best place to start and finish the salmon ladders and the contrived weir as an obstacle to prevent the large specimen carp escaping down river. We also surveyed a stretch which would be ideal for putting a trout farm and took a trip up to the house to see the position from there and noted the best position from that point of view. After about half a mile upstream we started to see more streams and areas of good and poor pasture but good for silage and hay fields. There was clearly a lot of land hardly used and not drained by large ditches like they were in Ireland. Hamish surmised that was because we had no need of so much grass, hay and silage as the dairy farmers needed. I pointed out that they could drain more, create new streams in effect, and utilise this untapped land for supporting a larger herd of beef cattle like the Aberdeen Angus and he totally agreed.

I questioned what happened to the inferior meat from Highland cattle and he replied it went into pet food and poorer cuts of meat were used in the food industry for pie making and so on. As a result, the price achieved for a similar weight beast was half that of better meat cattle. But the upkeep of the Highland cattle was lower, and they could look after themselves more easily on poorer and higher land. This was all very well I said, but it made little sense when for a reasonable investment you could double the yield of high-quality beef and make more money.

Hamish said that he thought successive generations in Scotland had gone this way, cheaper easy to keep cattle, sold cheaply because the thrifty Scots didn't want to risk outlaying large sums. Furthermore, keeping cattle fed in winter indoors or partly indoors was not to their liking.

But nowadays, with much easier mobility and better transportation, and public tastes for good quality beef and top-quality steaks and more people prepared to pay the higher prices, meant that some estates, like perhaps this one, had not adapted to the changing world as quickly as they might. Decoded by me as, old fashioned, uninformed, lacking in imagination, unwilling to invest, poor long-term vision and insufficient commitment to future generations. And I said so, and Hamish just smiled.

I repeated Hamish's words and my slant on them to Sarah and she was annoyed but admitted it was true, we had let it slip up here and be deluded by noncommittal reports and false economics, "And that is partly why you are here James."

Then she brightened and said, "So let's get on with it."

I reckoned after a few days' continued surveys with Hamish, that we could retain more than sufficient bogs, not encroach on the old peat bog except for the still purposes, get rid of almost all the Highland cattle who were just not worth keeping, introduce a herd of say 250 breeding Aberdeen Angus cattle; complete with at least two pedigree bulls. Then we would clean up the streams and make a network of dykes, and provide almost all the summer grass and winter fodder and cultivate more barley and mangolds by draining sufficient land to almost double the current acreage.

We also decided that the golf club and course be either near the house or at the coast subject to advice and planning consents. The hotel to be put where it was near, but not too near, the house so that people could commute easily between house and hotel. The river altered as it was going to be in Ireland with ladders, a weir, and predators cut back. Crayfish and mussels to be farmed and a trout farm explored and installed, if allowed. A smoke house and packing plant for a limited supply of bacon and hams on a new site designated for pig rearing, and the smoking of salmon and sea trout as well as crayfish and mussels. The rebuilding and commissioning of the new still and production of a new single malt whisky and with maturation of a proportion of this whisky on site. Also, by the installation of indoor, and limited outdoor sports and games facilities, with heated pools, a gymnasium, and a spa; the whole thing geared to middle class holidays, golf tournaments, corporate functions, hunting, shooting, and fishing both salmon and sea trout and specimen coarse fishing in the river and the mere.

We would need a targeted publicity campaign and not just locally, but worldwide. It would all take a while, but I predicted that in just five years, the estate would be a major tourist attraction as well as offering a special blend of outdoor sports facilities and we would find ourselves fully booked at many times of the year, with a staff probably of fifty or more employees and a turnover of around 3 million pounds per annum.

This was music to Sarah's ears and Bobbie's of course. But it made him realise he was now going to have to apply himself in the future. With a turnover like that and a staff of fifty to deal with it was going to be a steep learning curve.

The estate business as a whole would now be bigger and more profitable than several of the group companies, and they were set to grow by around 30% so the business as a whole was becoming substantial and would need a board of directors to run it rather in a more accomplished fashion than the current ad hoc meetings of the individual directors, which had gathered once a year in the past to ratify the group accounts.

I was not prepared to be Chief Executive (CE) Chairman of Sarah's group of companies as she wanted, but I was prepared to be Chairman and let somebody else take the CE role as I was still CE of our own group and didn't want two such roles. I suggested she headhunted a suitable candidate, and I would help select the person needed. But she said, "Why not the other way around? You head hunt a CE for *your* group; after all, it is well established and you know all the key people so can easily retain actual control. As you and Heather own the company for all practical purposes, you really have a stranglehold on any CE. 'Don't you?"

I replied, "That's true, but I will have to consider the situation and talk to Heather before I could make such a move, and how do I justify it to her?"

"Well," she replied, "suppose I offered you some incentive such as not only make you CE of our whole group but a trustee and say twenty percent shareholder of the new enlarged group. That would be a sweetener valued at approximately 10 million pounds."

"Bloody hell Sarah, how on earth could you justify that?"

"Easy," she said, "your company is enhancing our group value by 39% according to accountants' predictions, admittedly based only on your draft plans at present, but the accountants have allowed for this they say. The value will continue to rise, admittedly at a reduced rate of momentum, for the five years I want you for. Think about it and sell it to your dear wife please, emphasising it's purely a business deal."

What was Heather going to make of this? I knew that I was good in bed, but not that good, and Heather would not believe it when told that accountants had predicted 39% growth in share values, which didn't even exist for the estates as yet. Madness, or was it? The more I thought about it the more I realised that Sarah was probably right; the shares would cost her nothing to issue, I could agree that I would sell them back to the trust and to no one else, but I would still be 10 million plus better off at the end of five years, hard to justify not taking it. But if Heather didn't like it, I wouldn't do it.

I must admit I couldn't care less about being CE of the other companies and their boards; I could soon bring them into line with Sarah behind me. What really attracted me was the estates as companies. I also liked the idea of seeing the project through to completion, and the farms, the rivers, the fishing, the people like Tim, Peter, Hamish, Sean, and Bobbie too. The fact that Sarah was there as well was a bonus, but not the be-all and end-all, was it?

The boys had followed me up to Scotland having completed the draft plan for the Irish estate and I updated them and explained all the ideas and they thought it a very similar task to Ireland but without the extra farms. So I left them to it and flew back home to formalise the overall estate plans and to sound Heather out regarding the possible move to be CE and Chairman together with 20% of the shares in the whole group, including the estates. I would offer her the vacant CE and Chairman position in our group, but doubted she would want it, and moot the alternative of headhunting someone for the post, as clearly, I couldn't do both.

I arrived home at short notice as I only told her the night before I was flying home, so she knew something big was afoot, and she met me at the door with a frown at first, until she realised I was happy and something positive had happened rather than negative. She relaxed, smiled and said, "Good to see you, but what has brought you home weeks before you are due, the thought of seeing me I hope."

"Of course, I said," and kissed her, "plus the little matter of getting 10 million GBP for doing something I would love to do."

"What!" she exclaimed. So, I reiterated what had happened and that I had refused to be CEO and Chairman of the new enlarged group including the estates as limited companies and almost certainly would be registered in Ireland and said I wasn't prepared to be CEO of two groups. Sarah said rather than me get an unknown quantity in an appointment of some candidate CEO as I suggested, why not us, you, and I, appoint a CEO Chairman from one of our very competent main board members, then I could take the CEO Chairman job at their group. To sweeten the deal, she is prepared to assign 20% of the new group shares to me, current value estimated at 10 million GBP! The only other condition being I sign up for five years. Well, before you say anything, I would have committed myself for about three years anyway to see the project well on the way to completion so it's only two more years and with me at the helm I anticipate the share value doubling in that time. But more importantly to me is the fact that I love working on the estates and would just delegate the other companies to my vice chair, an existing main board member in their group. And finally, if you wanted to step back in at whatever level, I would be more than happy to arrange it, even CE Chairman of our group if that is what you want."

"I'm flabbergasted," she said and went very quiet for a few moments as she digested what I had said. Then she said, "I suppose after you uncovering that massive fraud and recovering 3 million or whatever, plus the no doubt excellent job you have done in reforming their group, it's quite understandable they would like you to see it through, which of course you would have for at least three years. But in reality, you could have walked out after the main plans have been set up and activated, so tying you up with a golden handshake of these proportions and a contract for five years is exactly what I would have done. So yes, grab it with both hands darling, you deserve it, and I am well aware that you love the country life at the estates, the fishing and shooting and all that. I wouldn't be surprised if you bought a farm of your own to retire to."

"You are an absolute brick Heather, you always back me up and support me and I love you for that. Come here and give me a big kiss."

I was relieved it never occurred to her that Sarah might be part of the attraction but if it did, she was smart enough not to show it and rock the boat after all our years together, not that I would have allowed that to happen. I knew Heather was responsible for my education when I was a mere boy and she a grown mature woman and had helped me be the successful businessman and person I have become today.

Heather continued, "And as for going back as CEO forget it, I like my semi-retirement and while Mother is alive, I shall look after her first, the children second and you third. I know that this is no one-way relationship, you have always let me do exactly as I wish and supported me through everything. To think I could still be married to that awful husband I had, no children, no business wealth to keep us comfortable in old age and no really good legacy to leave the children, had I ever had any which is extremely doubtful had I been stuck with him. Like you, I will never forget our first lovemaking in that sick room at the factory office we both worked in and have never regretted seducing you one iota."

So here I was, back in my beloved Irish estate with full support from Heather to continue with my job which I loved and with such a big reward for doing that job. Yes, it would be hard work at times, I knew that and welcomed it. This particular contract was easily the biggest and most complex assignment I had ever tackled, but with my hand-picked teams behind me, my very understanding boss Sarah there to look after my needs, and the friendship of my colleagues, not least Tim in Ireland, my general manager of the Irish estate. Although he didn't know it yet, I was going to ensure he was made director on my board and got the sort of benefits I had become famous for in the 'company doctor business'.

I had at least three years to get all our projects completed and everything ticking over but I would have little or no distractions from our own group as Heather and I had appointed our main board deputy CEO into the top position, suitably rewarded of course. I knew we could just leave it all to him, just catch up at extraordinary or annual meetings unless he shouted for help, of course.

Book 1 The End

NOMAD BOOK 1

THE BEST OF US

First Edition

ISBN: 978-1-912247-01-1

Edited by David Gatewood
Published by Karen Traviss
Jacket art: Thomas Wievegg
Design: Kevin G. Summers

karentraviss.com

PREFACE

All spelling and grammar in this book is UK English, except for proper nouns and those American terms that just don't anglicise. If I had to sum up the main difference between UK and US grammar, by which I mean the stuff that affects the rhythm of the language, it's that UK English uses more hyphens and fewer commas. You'll also notice variations in constructions like stop doing (common UK usage) and stop from doing (US usage), round and around, and so on.

I write both dialogue and narrative in the style and grammar of the character, and occasionally their spelling, so it varies from scene to scene. Those discrepancies are meant to be there. This drives editors mad, but it's part of how I do characterisation. The spelling standard I use is the Shorter Oxford English Dictionary. Where there are differences between the SOED and the Oxford English Dictionary, I let Oxford Dictionaries Online have the final word. Very rarely, none of them gives me a solution that I feel makes it clearer for the reader, so if a hyphen helps, I hyphenate.

Now the science.

I work by putting three-dimensional characters in real situations where the consequences of reality constrain them. In other words: here's the problem, now fix it. I do a lot of research to make my books as scientifically accurate as possible. But if I'm writing about colonisation of the galaxy, I have to bend reality a lot. There's not much colonisation possible if humans never go anywhere because there's not enough energy in the universe to bend space-time to our travel plans, and if relativity has no patience with our brief lives and our need to get things done fast. So this book isn't hard SF, and it isn't meant to be.

The Nomad books are primarily about people: human people, non-human people, and people we build in labs. I've taken real science and bent it enough to pose the ultimate questions that we can ask ourselves. When the chips are down, who do we stand with? Who would we die for? Who would we sacrifice? And what defines us as human?

These are the decisions we might make ourselves. Enjoy. And consider what makes the best of us.

Karen Traviss
December 2018

NOMAD BOOK 1

THE BEST OF US

KAREN TRAVISS

PROLOGUE

Fingers should always be broken first. Never start with the bolt cutters.

Breaking is educational. It hurts like hell, but bones heal, so it's a lesson in how bad things could get if permanent damage is inflicted. My advice: don't chop anything off before you've tried it, because you need to leave yourself some space to escalate. You'd be surprised how fast you can run out of body parts when you're trying to make someone see sense.

But Zakko's already had his first warning about thieving. Now we're short a box of meds from the camp supply, so I don't think I made my point clear enough last time. This kind of explanation is best done in the privacy of Zakko's cabin.

"Come on, Zakko." Jared's got him pinned down, one arm up his back and the other held flat on the table, but if Zakko keeps squirming like that he's going to lose the whole hand. I grip his wrist, just resting the meat cleaver on his forefinger. I've tied a piece of string tight around it, yakuza style, to stop the bleeding, just in case things go the distance. "What did you do with the meds? We do *not* thieve from our own or from the townsfolk. How many times do I have to tell you?"

Everyone thinks the forefinger is the one you can't afford to lose, because the kidnapper in the movies always lops off the pinkie like it's a spare you don't really need. *Wrong.* Along with your thumb, it's one of the two digits you'll really, *really* miss.

Try gripping without it. The pinkie's more or less a miniature thumb, the same kind of muscles and almost as mobile. How do I know that? Well, it's a long story. Just trust me. We're not the only animal with an opposable thumb, but we're the only one with a thumb long enough to make a proper precision grip with the fingers. So if you ever find yourself in Zakko's shoes and you have to choose which finger you can live without, pick the index. It might look the most important, but it's the least useful. You can even squeeze a trigger without it just fine. Next time — well, there shouldn't need to be a next time.

If I stop for a moment and wonder whether this is what I've become, or if this is what I always was, the answer doesn't matter. There are still things that I have to do.

Here's my problem. I get that good people do dumb things, and sometimes even evil things, but what I don't understand is why Zakko did it. All he has to do is ask Chuck, the old corpsman who organises the first responders. We're not short of much. We keep the area free of undesirables — two-legged, four-legged, it's all the same to us — and the townsfolk pay for the service with supplies. Zakko can have what he needs. But he steals. We can't have that.

Jared doesn't say a word. He just looks at me, fed up. It's cold and he's probably getting a cramp from holding Zakko down.

"Talk to me, Zakko." I need to know. "Last chance. Where are the meds?"

Believe me, I don't like this. But two communities count on me. I can't turn a blind eye to this, because that's how things eventually fall apart. Rules are the difference between us and the scavengers and marauders out there. Just because we decided not to live under the town's regulations, it doesn't mean we want anarchy.

So I visualise the arc of the blade and raise the cleaver. I'm one held breath away from bringing it down as hard as I can.

"No — no, no, no, *no!*" Zakko caves. "I swear it was just this once. There was a woman. She was on her own and she had this real bad infection. I said I'd try and help her out." He nods in the direction of the metal-frame bed pushed against one wall. "I didn't get the chance to go find her again. The meds are under my mattress."

Yeah, we have a problem now. But a totally different one.

"Did you touch her?" Well, shit. If he's caught anything, I've got it. I've been holding him down and so has Jared. Maybe the whole camp's been exposed. It's too late. I nod at Jared to back away, but he does a very slow, single shake of his head and doesn't move a muscle, so I hang on too. Zakko might just be playing for time. "When did this happen? Why didn't you report a contact right away?"

"A couple of days ago. I didn't lay a finger on her."

"So how do you know she had an infection?"

"Her hand was bandaged. She said she had a wound that wouldn't heal."

Sometimes you pray even when you think you don't believe. I hope this was just some random conversation and Zakko was trying to impress her. But I have to work on the basis that we might have the beginning of an epidemic, or a raid. Of the two, I'll take the raid. I can handle that.

"And you thought playing Mr Nice and giving her medical aid would get you somewhere with her." We've all done dumb things for women. Even the smartest guys can't think straight when there's a woman involved. "So on the off-chance of a quick fling with some anonymous female, who might have untreatable TB, tox, anthrax, super-staph, hemo, flu, or whatever, you took pity on her because she hurt her hand."

"I said I never touched her." Zakko's now panicking about more than losing a finger. "She was camped on the river. By the old jetty. I didn't get closer than ten yards, I swear."

Well, if he's telling the truth, at least he hasn't got something spread by contact. "Did it ever occur to you she might be scouting for marauders?"

"She was on her own. Just a skinny girl with a crappy tent. I'd have known."

People look to me to keep things under control. I don't lose my head and I always have a plan, or at least that's how it looks on the surface. "What did she say? Did she ask for refuge here?"

"No. She just wanted to know if she was anywhere near somewhere called Nanton Park."

"Never heard of it."

"That's what I told her." Zakko starts getting hyper. "Okay, okay, just do it. Get it over with. Cut the frigging finger off."

I really was going to do it. I'm sure I was. I did shit like this in another life, and that makes it easier, but it doesn't make it *better*. I'm almost glad I've now got something bigger to worry about so I can put the cleaver away.

"Stay where you are, okay?" This time I let go of his wrist and gesture at Jared to stand clear. "You set one foot outside this shack and I'll shoot you. You're quarantined."

"Nah, I'll take care of that," Jared says, patting his holster. "You go do whatever you need to."

He walks outside with me and takes up his sentry stance by the door. The air's freezing and I can hear the *chock-chock-chock* of someone splitting logs nearby. The two Monroe girls are playing out front. One of them starts heading our way, but Jared waves them back. We need to keep clear of everyone until we've been checked by the doc.

"Zakko might be sick," Jared says. "Quarantine until we say otherwise, okay?"

The girl gives him a big grin and a thumbs-up. He returns it. If I'd known what Zakko was up to, I'd never have put Jared at risk.

"Sorry, buddy." Either we tell people now and worry them before we have answers, or we let it ride and risk something spreading. There's no second chance to learn lessons these days. "Call Doug and tell him I need to meet him. Usual place."

Jared shrugs. "Understood."

I turn to walk away, but I still feel I owe him an explanation for why I didn't listen to him about Zakko in the first place. He warned me that the guy wouldn't fit in. Jared's got a nose for that kind of thing and it's saved our asses more than once.

But I never leave anyone behind.

"I'll make Zakko a useful member of society if it kills me," I say.

"This is the best time to take out the trash, Chris. He'll only do it again. Or worse."

"Okay. Whatever."

"Still on for beer and vids tonight? Provided we're not dead."

"Sure. Not that time-travelling vigilante crap, though. I hate that one."

I hate it because it's hard to watch any let's-change-the-world stuff these days without wondering exactly which moment you'd jump back to and who you'd shoot to head off a disaster. Where do we stop the show? Fifty years ago? A hundred? When the epidemics started, or the famines, or the endless small wars in every damn place? We've been going down the pan a dozen different ways for the last century, and now we've finally gotten around to nukes and agriweapons just to make sure we kill ourselves off properly.

Eventually, you reach a tipping point. Straws and camels' backs. You can maybe ride out individual disasters, but when they all pile up, things collapse. So if anyone ever asks me what that last straw was, not that they will, I'm going to blame the agriweapons.

This is what happens when you're working on an engineered crop virus to kill pests or something — or create infected bugs to destroy an enemy's agriculture, whichever explanation you believe — and it's stolen from the lab by folks who know folks who'll pay good money for that kind of thing.

This is what happens when terrorists, who've indeed paid good money for it, find it's so effective that it wipes out half the US wheat crop in two seasons.

This is what happens when the die-back virus moves into soy, causes a shortage of animal feed, and then gets into rice and maize, and everybody panics — especially Asia, which closes its borders, locks down, and destroys millions of acres of its own forests and farmland to fire-break the infection.

This is what happens when a few years pass and we still can't fix it, when famine's killed millions and we're overwhelmed by burying and burning bodies, and an Asian and Pacific States force nukes our infected vegetation to stop the die-back reaching them, starting at the West Coast and moving inland.

Seriously, I don't blame them. I wouldn't even call it a war. I'd do the same.

After that, it's kind of a blur. Europe's mostly a no-go area, but then it already was.

The world's changed out of all recognition in just over a century. We're living in the Decline. They say

North America's lost four-fifths of its population since 2200 — epidemics, famine, emigration, big companies headquartering overseas, civil wars, gang wars — so most of the people who kept the modern world running are gone. That means nuclear power stations, chemical factories, water plants... which is why we've got contamination everywhere as well. Cascade failure, our old commanding officer called it. Or at least he did before the cholera got him.

Yeah, it's hard to pick an intervention point for a time machine to put things right, but I'd go back for the first guy in a white coat. Obvious. So Jared had better find a nice simple action movie. Identify enemy, aim, shoot. Job done.

Anyway, I've got work to do. It's a twenty-minute walk into town. That's a healthy distance for neighbours, close enough to keep an eye out for trouble, but far enough apart to lead our own lives — or contain an outbreak. The direct route takes me down the hill. From the ridge, you can see the whole area laid out like a map: the town of Kill Line, population eleven hundred, and to the north-east, behind a serious security perimeter, the Ainatio Park research facility, where they're supposed to be working on some remedy for die-back.

Still, at least Ainatio stayed. They didn't abandon the country — or abandon Earth — like the rest of the corporations. They never say how many people are working in there now, but the farmers guess about five thousand, judging by how much food they supply.

An acre feeds a man. Kill Line has ten thousand under cultivation or pasture, and that's why it has to be defended from marauders, whether they're human or animal. We're three small tribes marooned on a fertile island, not neighbours by choice, but we have food, we have fuel, and we're safe for the time being.

And we have one flag in common. For all the differences in how we got here, there are three flagpoles and three American flags, so with or without a government, we know who we are.

Nobody alive today remembers the good old days anyway. Did they ever happen? Did the likes of us ever get anything out of it? There's always been disaster and war, ups and downs, dark ages and golden eras. It's not the first time that something's wiped out a big chunk of life on the planet, either. But each time that happens and the world recovers, some species don't make it. This time it just might be us.

The track worn down the hillside by scuffing boots takes me past sheep scraping at the thin snow to graze, and now I can see Doug in the distance, walking through the fields with his grandson. He's bundled up in his sheepskin coat, puffing clouds on the cold air, heading for our rendezvous point, the sign at the entrance to the town. I know the words embossed on that sheet of metal by heart.

WELCOME TO KILL LINE
STOP AND WAIT WITH YOUR VEHICLE
YOU WILL BE FIRED UPON
IF YOU CONTINUE PAST THIS POINT

Yeah, welcome to Kill Line. Sometimes I'm not sure if Doug likes me, or even if I like him, but you don't have to like someone to trust them.

And we do have to trust each other, me and Doug. We have an understanding. I do the killing and he does the farming. That's how we stay alive.

01

I won't live to see mankind settle the galaxy, but I can enable the journey of future generations. We all need the faith to plant acorns. We also need those who will keep that faith.

Tad Bednarz: AI engineer, philanthropist, and president of Ainatio.

KILL LINE, EASTERN UNITED STATES

"Grandpa, why don't we go to Mars?"

Doug poked around in the frozen soil between the rows of sturdy leeks dusted with snow. They had a look of dogged permanence, more like a defensive palisade than crops, little stylised palm tree profiles that wouldn't have seemed out of place on the walls of an Egyptian temple. The fields of overwintering leeks, cabbages, and parsnips always cheered him more than spring flowers because they just wouldn't quit, not even in the darkest days. There was a lot to admire about vegetables.

"What would you want to go to Mars for?" Doug watched Elliott trying to scoop up the thin layer of snow to squeeze the slush into grubby snowballs. They were more soil than snowflakes. "You want to live in a bubble? A glasshouse? Because that's what Mars is like. You can't even go outside for a walk, not without a suit." He gestured at the cloudless blue sky. "And you'd never see a sky like that."

"But they're going to make it like Earth. With proper air."

"Terraforming takes a really long time, Elliott. You'll be older than me by the time it's ready." *No, it won't even be in your lifetime.* "Why go to Mars when we need to sort out Earth?"

"China landed there. They're building houses."

"Well, they were." News was hard to come by, but maybe that was for the best. Good or bad, there was nothing they could do about it here. "But it's still not Earth, is it?"

"Maybe there'll be more lighthuggers. Then we can go to other stars."

Where were those generation ships now? The last ones Doug had heard about had left twenty-odd years ago. "That's even worse," he said. He didn't want the boy to latch on to the idea that they'd been abandoned, even if they had. "Imagine spending your whole life cooped up in a spaceship and never reaching your destination. Folks will be born on them and die on them. It'll be their great-grandchildren who get there."

Elliott scuffed at the soil again. "They don't want ordinary folks like us anyway. They just want scientists and politicians and *rich* people."

"I bet they're not very happy, though. The rich people are probably a pain in the butt, the politicians are bound to be bossing everyone around, and the scientists... I read that some of them had pretty strange ideas. How much crazier are they going to get without normal folks around to talk some sense into them?"

"They'll probably get smashed up by asteroids or something anyway," Elliott said, dismissively matter-of-fact. "So can we visit the ocean instead, Grandpa?"

"There's still miles of contaminated land between us and the coast."

"I know. But it won't stay like that forever, will it? I'm going to cross it one day."

Elliott studied the snowballs with a determined frown before lobbing them across the field. What could Doug tell him? There was no disguising that Kill Line and the surrounding county were almost cut off. Ainatio had spent years creating a sterile cordon around the area, a ring of completely bare ground two miles wide in which every plant had been killed to stop cross-pollination. Elliott could see it for himself if he climbed Gorman's Peak, but Doug couldn't kill the boy's hopes. Asia had kept the die-back at bay. There were still places for a boy to dream of exploring.

"Yes, it'll all be okay one day," Doug said. "Ainatio's going to find a way to grow plants normally again."

Elliott nodded sagely. "It's like the Black Death, except lots of other things went wrong this time. Whole towns died then as well. But things got better in the end. They always do."

"Is that what Mrs Alvarez is teaching you?" She seemed to have given the class an upbeat message without avoiding the brutal reality. Doug left the education committee to its own devices. "Well, she's right. Humans survive disasters."

"I asked her why I can't work at Ainatio when I grow up. She said everything's possible."

It was a kind lie. Ainatio was a closed society in every sense. It had been a secret research centre for more than a hundred years: its personnel had lived behind secure walls and fencing, a separate world for as long as Doug could remember. Apart from the environmental technicians and the supply managers, he saw very few staff, and he wasn't sure how the company maintained a workforce now that it was impossible to find new people. There had to be people too old to carry on working and even deaths like in any other company, but somehow, Ainatio kept going like an ant farm.

Yes, scientists *were* weird. He'd hadn't really lied to Elliott about that.

"I saw Col out testing the soil this morning." Elliott carried on collecting snow, carefully placing the misshapen grey lumps in a pile, then pointed up the hill, squinting against the sun with one eye closed. "Here's Mr Montello. Can I call him Chris?"

"No, you may not. Mind your manners." Doug watched the man walk carefully through the field, rifle slung over one shoulder. It was hard to tell if he was trying not to slip or just worried that he was trampling crops hidden under the snow. He was considerate for a city boy. It didn't fit somehow. "You're going to be late back to school. Get moving, buddy."

"Is he coming in for coffee?"

"Not today. Off you go."

Elliott abandoned the snowballs and ran off along the furrows, jumping between them as if he was playing hopscotch. Doug took the track around the edge of the field and headed south down the road out of town. By the time he reached the sign, Chris was already waiting for him a few metres outside the unmarked boundary, another reminder for Doug that time hadn't just caught him up. It had finally overtaken him.

Chris held up his hand. "Don't come too close. Did Jared explain?"

"He said you need the doctor to check out one of your guys." This was routine. There was no need to start torching the place. "She'll be with you as soon as she's finished her morning surgery. Give her an hour."

"Thanks. I'm going to head out and see if I can find this woman he's supposed to have met. Just for reassurance."

"You really think she's infected with something serious?"

"No, but I need to be sure she wasn't sent ahead to check out our defences."

"Oh. Okay. You need any help with the search? Drones? Men?"

"It's best if I do it alone with a dog. The fewer people moving around, the better."

"I haven't told Ainatio, by the way," Doug said. "Seeing as we don't actually know if we have a situation."

"Don't worry. They only care when it affects their food supply. They're safe in the Forbidden City." Chris shrugged, looking awkward, as if he wasn't sure that making small talk was a good idea. "We've all got our own little fantasy territory, haven't we?"

Doug wasn't sure what he meant, but it wasn't the time to ask. Standing around in the freezing cold wasn't doing either of them any good. "Is there anything else you need? Got enough coffee? Liquor?"

Chris looked awkward again. "We're good, thanks." He turned to walk back the way he'd come. "See you around."

Doug watched him go, still trying to get the measure of him after nearly two years. He was polite and professional, hair and beard always neatly trimmed, leather jacket and boots battered but polished, pants a little frayed but clean and pressed, nothing like the drifters the town had had to see off with shotguns in the past. Doug was still waiting for something to ignite the man and peel back the mask to reveal something feral, a steel core needed to keep the transit camp together, because it sure as hell had to be there. How old was he? Thirty, thirty-five? All Doug knew was that he'd served in the State Defence Force and had led a group of vets and refugees to this relative safety, no easy task with most of them on foot. He'd also given Doug the impression that he'd been in prison but he didn't say why. Chris wasn't chatty. Doug didn't press him.

Maybe I should try inviting him over again.

Maybe, though, the depth of conversation that would follow a couple of beers would tell Doug more than he wanted to know about how his boundaries were patrolled and kept safe in a world where the old laws meant nothing.

He didn't need to know exactly what had happened when more refugees had tried to follow them here. He didn't want a reason to see Chris as anything but a good guy standing between the town and chaos.

The heads on spikes thing is just a dumb story. Just a rumour to scare off unwelcome visitors. I've never seen anything when I've been driving around.

As Doug headed back into town, the fried food aroma of a very old engine running on recycled cooking oil hung in the air. He was walking in the wake of Bill Dawud's ancient tractor. Bill was at the side of the road, tinkering with the engine while it idled.

"Take it out and shoot it, Bill," Doug teased. "It's a kindness."

Bill wiped his hands on his pants. "It'll outlive me."

"You could have a nice new hydro model from Ainatio."

"Sure, but it wouldn't be my grandma's, would it?"

That bucket of bolts had to be a hundred years old, at the very least, and it had so many replacement parts that it was probably more replacement than original. But that was the point. It wasn't about being frugal. It was about roots, about having an anchor in the past in a world where most of it had vanished. Doug liked to see the tractor as daily proof that things could survive long after everyone thought they should be dead.

"Is Mariam still coming to the pot luck supper?" Doug asked.

"You bet. She's making *tepsi baytinijan*. When she starts that, a cough isn't going to stop her."

"Give her my best."

"Col's looking for you, by the way."

"Okay. Thanks."

Doug could navigate through the town by smell alone. After the cooking oil, there was malt, pumped out on the steamy air venting from the brewery. Then there was the almost perfumed sawdust from the mill, then manure, and then baking — sweet pastry, if he wasn't mistaken. He paused to close his eyes and inhale. It was a smell of permanence, like the town had been here forever and always would be, its people working in trades that his ancestors would have recognised five centuries ago. But Kill Line's roots weren't ancient, and they weren't rural. There was no statue in the town square commemorating a rugged founding pioneer dressed in frontier buckskin. If there'd been one at all, it would have been a scientist in a lab coat. The town was only here because Ainatio was. The company needed an isolated research facility with a secure water supply and food source, so they took over run-down Nanton Park a hundred and thirty years ago and created a community to service it. Even the town's name was just the location of where the original housing block had once stood — the kill line, the stop-or-I-fire point of the old security perimeter when Ainatio had much bigger grounds.

But Doug was content. Whatever its name and origin, this was a happy community with a school, a church, a social centre, and a little cable station showing endless reruns because that was all they had, living with the natural rhythm of the seasons. This was how humans were meant to be. What was it that Chris Montello had said? *We've all got our own little fantasy territory.* Well, this was Doug's. He understood that very well.

Colin was outside the town hall, scraping yesterday's refrozen snow from the roof of his Ainatio pick-up. The guy showed up once a week, collected soil, water, and plant samples, and sent a report to the town council. Had any plants been compromised yet? Had the contaminants from all the failed remedies and accidents over the years started to kill everyone slowly? Col's tests would tell them.

"Hey, Col." Doug nodded at him. "Everything okay?"

Colin gave him a big smile. He'd been coming here for at least ten years, but Doug still couldn't recall his surname. He had two daughters and a rather miserable wife who'd turned up once at the town fair.

"Someone with a whiter coat than me needs to check that," Colin said. "But I found some snowdrops on the western boundary. That's a first."

Doug tried to think where they might be. "My grandad used to rip them up. He was cranky about non-native species. Haven't seen snowdrops since my school days. Where are they?"

"You're not going to root them out, are you? They don't compete with other plants."

"No, I'm just getting old and nostalgic."

"Here." Col held out his personal screen so that Doug could see the map and sync it with his own. "It's marked as McKinnon's Farm on the old county survey. Got it?"

Doug tapped his device. "Thanks."

They were just plants, but he felt the need to see them. They wouldn't be in flower for long and he never counted on still being around in a year's time himself. He signed out the town council's truck and drove down to the boundary.

Hart County — the part that was still safe for habitation — was now reduced to ninety square miles with an outer perimeter that took it to two hundred. That didn't sound like much, but it was plenty of space to get lost in and more than enough to hide a colony of snowdrops. Doug drove west, keeping an eye on the dosimeter on the dashboard. The road eventually became a winding track through the woods, then a bumpy gap just wide enough for the truck.

He stopped a couple of times to watch deer browsing in the bare red branches of dogwood trees. Did they have ear tags? Yes. There was no need to panic. If they didn't have the bright yellow tags that identified them as the local population, they'd be animals that had somehow breached the cordon and could have brought in contaminated plant material. Chris's patrols were always on the lookout for intruders, regardless of species. Doug mulled over the thought of venison for the freezer, but he didn't have his rifle with him.

And we've got plenty of meat. Leave them in peace.

It took him fifteen minutes on foot with a compass to find the McKinnon site. The only signs that a farm had ever been there were the rubble of a long collapsed chimney and a couple of decaying fence posts. He almost missed the snowdrops, but suddenly there they were: white on white, a carpet of green leaves poking up through the thin layer of snow between the trees. Doug pulled out his screen to take a picture, kneeling to get a closer view of the green-streaked blooms, and decided that the woods could spare a few bulbs. He dug up some with his hunting knife, wrapped them carefully in his handkerchief, and got to his feet. His knees hurt like hell. But he had snowdrops, the first for a very long time, and like the leeks, they refused to give in to frost and snow. They were a defiant symbol of the sheer tenacity of life in inhospitable places.

Joanne would love them.

She was making bread when he got back, her usual batch of a dozen loaves for their own use and a dozen for the food exchange. She stopped pounding the dough as he held out the bundle of uprooted plants. Her mouth opened slowly.

"Oh my," she said. "Where did you get those?"

"Near the boundary. Col said he'd seen them, so... well, there were hundreds of them, so I thought we might plant some here. Remember they don't really establish themselves in the first year."

"So it'll be two years before I get a decent display."

"Afraid so. Don't worry, you'll still be here to see them."

"And so will you. Don't talk like that."

Grandad wouldn't have approved, but Joanne did, and that was all that mattered. After lunch, she went outside to plant them in the shadow of the bushes. Doug climbed the rickety ladder to the attic to see if there were any old photos of the McKinnon farm.

The Brandt family photos were more of a crate than an album. The collection was a pile of boxes stuffed with envelopes full of paper prints, digital storage, and even physical film, much of it copied and recopied to paper or chip as technologies fell out of use over the years. He'd forgotten that some of it dated back to before his grandad's time. He rummaged around until he found an envelope marked in his father's draughtsman hand: HART COUNTY, GENERAL.

The oldest landscapes in the photos showed the change in vegetation. Views from Gorman's Peak a hundred years ago were still pasture and woods as far as the eye could see, but it didn't look that way now. Doug fanned the prints like playing cards, looking for old buildings. An image caught his eye.

On first glance he thought it was a headstone, but then he studied it and a memory bubbled to the surface. It was a monument, a bronze plaque mounted on stone or concrete. It was hard to tell which, because whoever had taken it had zoomed in to capture the inscription, and there was nothing in the shot to tell him what the plaque was part of, or where it stood. But the inscription was self-explanatory.

TO THE MEMORY OF THE SHIP'S COMPANY
OF SURVEY VESSEL CABOT
LOST WITH ALL HANDS
WE WALK IN THE UNCHARTED PLACES
AND ARE NOT AFRAID

Doug remembered now. The memory was complete and clear, but it had popped up so quickly out of nowhere that he wondered if he'd imagined it. It was an Ainatio mission, the one that had killed their space programme and reduced them to environmental projects at home. They'd sent a manned mission beyond the solar system — he couldn't even remember where it was heading — but the ship was lost. It wasn't a tech corporation lighthugger full of crazies, either. It'd had a proper military crew, and they'd been put into cryosuspension for the journey, which everyone said was way too far and too big a risk. But they did it anyway.

At least the crew would have known nothing when the disaster struck. Doug took some comfort from that.

Where was this plaque, then? Maybe it wasn't even around here.

Joanne appeared in the attic doorway, her nose and cheeks red from working in the cold. "What are you looking for?"

"Oh, just the McKinnon place." Doug held out the image to her. "Do you remember this?"

"*Cabot*? Wow, yes. How could you forget it? It was all over the news for weeks."

"I don't think I ever saw this memorial."

"Me neither. Some honouring we did." Joanne frowned at the photo. "You'd think they'd have put the crew's names on it."

"Wasn't it a couple of hundred people? That's a lot of names."

"I don't know. But I remember they all had to be single with no family to leave behind because it was going to take so long. That seemed so sad. All the more reason to commemorate them properly."

Doug studied the plaque. He wondered what kind of men and women would be willing to leave behind everything they knew and loved, and risk the unknown for a mission that meant they'd probably never see home again even if it succeeded.

Had they wanted to, though? Maybe, like Chris and his band of vets, they'd just thought it was their duty. He'd never served. He'd never know.

"Yes," he said, shaking his head. No families and no grave: anonymous and forgotten. You couldn't get more dead than that. "Dreadful."

* * *

TRANSIT CAMP, NEAR KILL LINE:
2 HOURS LATER

Dr Morris arrived suited up and put on her mask as soon as she got out of her truck, then stopped and did a discreet double take, first at Chris's rifle and then at the road through the camp.

Chris couldn't remember the last time she'd visited. Maybe she was expecting to find mud huts and signs of recent cannibalism. It could have been the rifle, of course. Everyone here who could use a personal weapon carried one at all times, but few of the townsfolk seemed to. Morris looked down the rows of uniform cabins and straight dirt roads between them, edges marked with stones and carefully cut pole rails, nodding to herself.

"Very orderly," she said. "You've done a lot of construction."

"Yeah, we've got all the skills in-camp. Plumbing, carpentry, logistics, the works."

"Have you got quarantine plans if your guy tests positive?"

"Yeah. We've always got a plan."

"You certainly seem to."

Chris almost recited the numbers to her, but it felt like he was justifying himself. One hundred and four people lived here, fifty-two of them military in one way or another, if not State Defence Force or retired then active-duty men and women from other services with no units left to return to. That was a lot of skills, but also a shared culture that just snapped together like a well-made machine. They'd been trained to deal with the worst that life could throw at them, and Chris had watched them do exactly that, even the ones he'd doubted. Everyone who'd joined them had survived, civilian and service personnel alike.

I promised I'd get them to safety, and I did. Am I forgiven yet? How do you know when you've atoned for the shit you've done? Do you suddenly just feel better about yourself, or do you hear some kind of klaxon that tells you your time's done?

The end of the world had its advantages. The connected, recorded, filed, archived world had been broken apart, and nobody could run checks on anyone and decide they were undesirables. Morris probably wouldn't have picked him for a neighbour if she'd known him better.

"Let's do Mr... " She studied something on her screen. "Zakkarija Chetcuti, yes? If he tests positive, I'll make a start on the rest of the camp right away."

Zakko was still sitting in his cabin, looking sheepish. He was in his late twenties, a stocky, harmless-looking guy with a mass of curly black hair. When Chris's platoon found him in Baltimore, he'd been trying to hotwire an abandoned police cruiser. He hadn't even tried to force open the weapons locker, which was the first thing most people did. He just wanted a ride out of the city. Even then, Chris suspected that Zakko didn't really know how to be a bad guy. He wasn't so much bad as a little short of impulse control. Maybe a few more chastening experiences like this would sort him out.

"You going to test me, ma'am?" Zakko asked.

"Yes, I need you to run your finger over this," Morris said. The test kit was just a white printed plastic card, the touch test variety. "Press on each square for at least two seconds."

"It looks like a shopping list of the world's top twenty killer diseases," Zakko said, fidgeting.

"It is. Better hope they're sold out. Two seconds, okay?"

Chris watched as Zakko readied his finger, a forefinger he was damn lucky he still had, and dragged it down the first row of squares too fast.

"No, *slowly*," Morris said. "Two seconds per square. There's a different sensor or reagent in each one."

"Yes, ma'am."

Morris studied the results. Eventually she peeled off her mask one-handed and held up the card so Chris could see two rows of solid green squares. When she flexed it between her fingers to reset and sterilise it, it gave off a burst of light.

"I'll take that as an all-clear," Chris said.

Morris gave Zakko a practised professional smile. "You're fine, Mr Chetcuti."

Zakko beamed. "Thanks, ma'am."

Morris turned to Chris. "So do you want me to set up a radiation test session for your people? You haven't had one since you first got here. You could come into town, or I can do it here. Or I could give you a testing kit to do it yourselves if you prefer. Whatever's easiest for you. You've got some trained personnel, haven't you?"

"Two combat medics and a retired corpsman," Chris said. "The test kit will be appreciated, ma'am. We don't want to put you to any more trouble."

Chris wasn't even sure he meant that. He just didn't want to be drawn further into a community that looked as if it had sat out the horrors of the last century in a rural theme park, oblivious. It wasn't resentment. It was knowing that if his people moved in, sooner or later they'd all get to know each other well enough to talk frankly about how they came to be here, and then everyone would realise how big the gulf was between people who just fired warning shots and those who'd needed to become animals to stay alive.

Veneers had their place. As long as everyone knew they were just that, veneers, and that there was much plainer, uglier wood beneath that was best left unseen, then there was no deception. It was just an understanding that some necessary things weren't meant to be on display.

Chris saw Morris off and started up the all-terrain quad bike that the farmers had donated. Seeing as Zakko was fully fit, he was going to be on latrine duty indefinitely until Chris decided he'd adjusted his attitude. In the meantime, they still had to find that girl. Chris couldn't sleep until he knew for sure that she wasn't scouting.

How did she get here?

Like everyone else who'd stumbled across Hart County, she'd have followed the river. But this Nanton place... he should have asked Doug if he'd heard of it. Never mind, he'd do that later. He had to get out there with the dogs and drones now.

As he rode through the camp at regulation slow speed, people came out of their cabins, bundled in coats. "Is it okay, then?" Jeanie Cleaver called. "Are we clear?"

"Yeah, nothing to worry about." Chris waved back. "Just being careful."

Howie jogged along beside him. "Yay! You fixed it, boss!" He was nine or ten, another kid with a dead family and bad memories, but he didn't seem to realise what a shitty hand life had dealt him. He'd appointed himself the camp errand boy and morale officer for the older folk. Sometimes Chris felt less of a man than that boy was.

"I didn't fix it," Chris said. "I just did what we trained to do. Right?"

"Right!" Howie saluted. "Train hard, fight easy!"

Chris wondered who Howie had picked that up from. It wasn't a bad lesson to learn, though. Howie eventually peeled off, probably to go cheer someone up, and Chris carried on to collect the dogs and the equipment from Dieter. He parked and walked up to the chain-link fence around the dog pen, watching the pack milling around.

Dieter had two dogs at his heels, Sapper and Girlie. Sapper was a German shepherd that Chris had often patrolled with, a trained dog they'd picked up at a police compound, but he was nervous around Girlie. She was mostly husky. One vivid, staring blue eye and a bald scar on her nose made her look like an escaped psycho.

"You sure you want to do this on your own?" Dieter asked.

"Yeah. I can manage."

"You're absolutely sure you don't want me to ride along?"

"I might need to do things you'd rather not see."

"Okay." Dieter held out a bag. "Drones and a receiver. Two-mile range, remember."

Chris looked inside. There were a dozen walnut-sized drones with pop-out rotors, almost museum pieces but still up to recon tasks. He'd have to start replacing them soon. He didn't want to rely on Doug's offer, generous as it was, so they'd build their own or fall back on their fieldcraft skills.

"Got it," Chris said, and started the bike.

The dogs jumped into the carrier on the back and settled down without prompting as if it was their daily commute, instantly zoned out on autopilot while they thought about happier things. Chris set off north-west for the river.

Dr Morris was right. It was a well-run camp. Chris was proud of the effort his people had put into building it. It was kind of Doug to let them hook up to the utilities, but they could survive without them and rely on their own methane digesters and wood stoves if they had to. They had a backup water supply from a stream, and they could clear land for crops if push came to shove. That was all they needed. As Chris rode past the snow-covered fields and watched the birds pecking around, he had to admit that there were worse places to be marooned.

We didn't plan to stay, but maybe it's time. Even if we reach the coast and find a ship heading south, what's left now?

Driving always made him brood, and once he'd blocked out the things that would do him no good to rehash, other questions bubbled up to take their place. How many people were there in the Ainatio compound, and why did so few venture outside? And why were they so generous to the town, giving it whatever utilities, medicine, and little luxuries it wanted when they didn't really need to support that many people? It didn't take eleven hundred people to farm ten thousand acres. Kill Line was a lot of overhead, and it wasn't like they could go work for anyone else. Ainatio was being the perfect neighbour. But Chris had never known a company to hand over a cent without a reason. Even in a collapsed economy where barter was all that was left, old commercial attitudes died hard.

No, he was the one still thinking like a debt collector. Ainatio now faced a world of shortages — shortages of food, people, and choices. They needed Kill Line a little more than Kill Line needed them. There were no other food suppliers out there, and no more labour to replace the townspeople if an epidemic broke out. That was all there was to it. He had to stop looking for things to doubt.

What a miracle, finding somewhere this clean, this perfect — well, way better than the city, anyway.

No, not a miracle. Just something that really needs explaining.

Girlie put her chin on Chris's shoulder from behind and let out a disturbingly human, meat-scented sigh. "You need breath mints, lady," he said, jerking his head away. Ainatio supplied those, too. "Nearly there."

Her muscles stiffened against him as she pushed away and looked up, instantly silent and alert. When he glanced over his shoulder, Sapper was on his feet as well, ears pricked, looking and listening. They knew what they had to do.

Chris stopped the bike downstream of the bend in the river and tossed the drones into the air. They levelled off at ten feet, waiting for tasking. A few quick lines drawn on the handheld control screen with his finger set their general target position and path. Then they soared away, calculating their own optimum spacing. When Chris turned to the dogs, they were sniffing the ground like their noses were glued to it.

"Okay, guys, we're going to cover the river, starting at the jetty, and work out in both directions." Chris whispered it like he was briefing them. The dogs looked up into his face, all intense, unblinking concentration. "If we find her, you keep her there and wait. Got it?"

He could have sworn that they did. They almost looked like they were going to say "Roger that."

He walked through the trees, Girlie to one side of him and Sapper to the other, until he reached the bank and looked to his right to see the remains of the jetty a hundred yards away. He crouched to listen. The dogs crouched too.

The video feeds tiled on his screen to give him a single collated aerial view tracking roughly north, taking in a mile-wide strip that showed both banks. He'd let the drones reach their transmission limit and then bring them back to repeat the process heading south, provided the dogs didn't find something first.

"Okay," he said. "Sapper, that way. North. Seek." He gave the dog the same hand signal that he'd give a man, and Sapper shot off. Girlie waited for her orders, treading the ground on the spot like she was tap dancing. Combined with that mad blue eye, the effect was comical. Chris signalled south, downriver. "Seek, Girlie. Find her."

He waited, watching the drone feeds. It was at least forty-eight hours since Zakko had seen the woman, and she could be long gone or dead from sepsis if her injury had been that bad, but all Chris needed to know was whether there was a gang in the area waiting to raid the camp. There probably weren't many refugees on the move from the cities these days, but there would still be organised and violent gangs capable of following the trail here, just like the ones who'd tracked Chris from Baltimore. One more encounter would be one too many.

Yeah, we'll be facing people like us. People used to fighting hard. We need to stockpile more ammo.

There was no such thing as enough. Crossbows were great, but real stopping power was better.

His calculations were interrupted by sudden, distant barking from the north. Sapper had found someone.

Chris ran at a crouch towards the sound, checking the screen and following the paw prints in the snow. Girlie rocketed past him in a flurry of cracking twigs and carried on like a missile in the direction of Sapper's bark. Chris still couldn't see anything via the drones, but the composite image showed a stand of pines ahead, and if he was going to hole up, that would have been where he'd have hidden. Most of the other trees were deciduous, bare branches at this time of year with little cover. He shoved the screen in his pocket and readied his rifle.

So... I tell her to go on her way, unless she's a scout, in which case I shoot her. And what if she doesn't go away and looks sick? I can't invite her in.

Now he could hear both dogs barking, the steady *arf-arf-arf* they did when they were warning of strangers. When he reached them, they were staring into the pines, focused on something. Chris almost didn't see what they were barking at, but then an artificially straight line caught his eye.

Someone had made a scrappy tent, a woodland camo tarp draped over a pole between two trunks. And there she was, an Asian girl, the sorriest looking kid he'd seen in a long time, huddled in a padded jacket and woolly hat as she knelt in the small opening of the makeshift shelter. She was nursing her arm. Damn, she looked like a corpse. No wonder Zakko had felt he had to help her. Either she was too weak to run or she'd decided not to try because the dogs would bring her down. Chris estimated she was mid to late teens, but she wouldn't have been the first scout of that age he'd had to deal with.

He kept his rifle on her and walked slowly forward, stopping beyond her lunge range in case she decided to come at him. Whether she grabbed him to beg for help or claw his eyes out, it didn't matter. Chris had seen too many epidemics to take the risk.

"Ma'am, this is a restricted area," he said. "What are you doing here?"

"Whoa, whoa." She lifted her arms in surrender. "Please — put the gun down. Call off the dogs."

She didn't sound like an American, or a kid. Chris had underestimated her age. "Where are your buddies?"

"I'm on my own. You think I'd be in this state if I had backup?"

"Sorry, you need to move on. We can't risk exposing folks here to infection."

"I'm not contagious. I can prove it."

"Yeah?"

"I'm going to reach in my pocket for a diag card. Okay? Just a card. I'll show you."

Chris assumed she meant a test card. Still kneeling, she moved her good arm back to feel for her pocket. He kept her in his sights, finger on the trigger. If the next thing he saw was a weapon, he'd drop her there and then. Sapper started growling.

"Sapper, *no*." Chris wasn't sure he could control the dogs if they decided to go for her. "Sapper, down."

The girl took things very, very slowly. It was so damn cold that her hands must have been numb. A small blue plastic container emerged from her pocket, and yeah, it was a storage sleeve. She held it up.

"Okay, take the card out," Chris said.

She fumbled for a while before gripping the exposed edge of the card between her teeth to drag it out, then pulled off one glove the same way. She pressed her finger repeatedly on the card before holding it up.

"I know you won't want to get too close, so I'm going to move and put this where you can see it," she said.

"Okay." She knew the drill, then. She'd done this before. Chris watched the dogs, hoping they wouldn't sense his doubt that he could control them. "Sapper, Girlie — *stay*. Down."

"*Girlie*," the woman snorted.

"It's the dog's name."

"Oh."

She edged forward on her knees and laid the card face up on the ground ten feet in front of him, then shuffled all the way back. The dogs watched, squared up and ready to pounce. Chris was half-listening for movement behind him in case he'd read it all wrong and this really was an ambush, but the dogs would hear it long before he did.

He took a cloth from his pocket to pick up the card and examine it without contaminating his gloves. They were his special Guard-issue ones, irreplaceable now. He didn't want to have to burn them.

"Right... you've got a staph infection. Nothing else." He checked the rows of indicator squares again. There was a single amber result among the green. The woman just needed antibiotics, as long as this wasn't another resistant strain. "So you want me to bring you some meds?"

"No, I need to find Nanton Park."

So Zakko was telling the truth. "I've never heard of it."

"Ainatio?"

"Ah."

"Am I in the right place? Am I?" Her eyes suddenly brimmed. "Am I really here?"

There was no point in being evasive. It wasn't Chris's secret to keep. "Pretty much, ma'am."

She'd been all badass and in control up to now, but suddenly she burst into tears. She wasn't putting it on, either. Chris knew the difference. She stopped herself after a few sobs and wiped her nose on the back of her hand, blinking. Chris had passed the point of offering weeping women his handkerchief or trying to comfort them. There'd been too many. He waited for her to compose herself and carry on.

"Well, yeah, you can see I'm glad the journey's over," she said at last. "Ainatio. Do you work for them?"

"No."

"Sorry, you just looked more official than the other guy I talked to. Can you contact them?"

"Why?"

"My name's Annis Kim. Dr Annis Kim." She cleared her throat. "It's taken me eight months to get here from Seoul. I need to talk to whoever's in charge of research."

How the hell did anyone get here from the Far East? Why leave Asia? She wasn't a refugee. "Seoul? You mean Korea? You don't sound Korean."

"I'm from Melbourne. Australia. I was a physicist at Seoul National University. Please, either tell me how to find the centre, or give them a message."

Chris hoped he'd finally learned the difference between a dumb impulse and a rare opportunity that needed to be seized. He knew this was important, even if he didn't know why. Nobody would have left the safety of Asia to travel halfway around the world unless it was absolutely vital, and in this little closed world of Hart County, everything that affected Ainatio affected his people as well. What else could he do? He wasn't about to dump her on Kill Line, because Doug would never turn her away, and Chris didn't want someone this random in the camp.

But she hadn't asked him for refuge. She wanted Ainatio. He'd never had any real contact with them, but he knew they sometimes monitored his patrols. He had one of their radio frequencies, the one Doug kept for emergencies. Maybe it was time to try it out.

"What do you want me to tell them?" he asked. "If they respond, that is."

"Is it okay if I get something else out of my pocket?"

"Sure."

She took out a small paper notebook and wrote two lines in it. When she handed it to him, it was her name and a list of numbers, some with decimal points. There were too many groups for map co-ordinates, but that was how it looked to him.

"Call them," she said. "Read out those numbers, and tell them to give them to their most senior astrophysicist."

Maybe it was about the orbitals. That might have been where most of the risky research had been done, the stuff with genetically modified bugs that could clean up the soil

— or kill off the remaining plant life if something went wrong. Chris pulled out his old State Defence radio and scanned the frequencies.

"What is this exactly?" He keyed the numbers into the radio's scratchpad, in case he needed them later for reasons he couldn't even begin to imagine. "ID code?"

"It'll tell them everything they need to know, and why I'm here."

"And then?"

"They'll want to see me. Guaranteed."

* * *

SECURITY CONTROL ROOM, AINATIO PARK RESEARCH CENTRE

"Major, I've got some guy on the net who shouldn't be there."

Trinder didn't look up for a moment. The jumble of comms systems still in use around Ainatio led to some sloppy discipline, and his first thought was that Simonot meant one of the technicians was using a security frequency, which they'd been warned repeatedly not to do. But if Simonot had meant that, he'd have said so.

"Some guy?"

"He ID'd himself as Chris Montello from the transit camp. One of the vets. He's found a civilian scientist who wants to relay a message. Channel fourteen, sir."

Trinder wasn't sure which was the bigger surprise, the fact that a scientist had left the facility without the security system noticing, or that the ghostlike refugees who never came within a mile of the gate were now flashing them up on the radio.

The camp folk kept themselves to themselves. They'd reached an arrangement with the farmers to patrol the area, and Trinder was happy to let them carry on. He'd seen the aftermath of the shoot-out with a gang on the boundary just after they'd arrived: not pretty, but professional and thorough, so they weren't people he needed to pick a pointless fight with, and as he only had twenty-nine troops, they were a useful addition to security. It made sense to see them as auxiliaries managed by Doug Brandt. It was odd that they'd called it in to the company and not gone via Doug, though.

Trinder checked the board. All personnel were showing as still within the Ainatio perimeter, but he didn't need to rely on the ID trackers. Anyone leaving would have to exit via the main gate, and that meant being physically signed out by the duty guard, an event so rare that it would have required advance notice and an armed escort. Something was very wrong.

"I'm not asking the right questions, am I?" Trinder adjusted his earpiece and selected the channel. "Transit Camp, Transit Camp, this is Ainatio Echo Five Actual, do you have one of our personnel with you, over?"

"Echo Five Actual, this is Transit Camp. I have one female casualty with hypothermia and an infected puncture wound to the hand." The guy sounded calm and professional. Yes, he had to be a vet. "Test-carded, no contagion risk. Name given — Dr Annis Kim — I spell, Alpha November November India Sierra, Kilo India Mike. She also has an ID code, over."

"Transit camp, we don't use ID codes, over."

"Echo Five Actual, she has a sequence of numbers that she insists on relaying, over."

"Transit camp, wait one." Trinder knew every name by now, and Annis Kim wasn't one of Ainatio's white-coats. This was a secure facility, not meant to be found by casual visitors or even people looking very hard for it. He checked the staff list anyway. "Transit Camp, negative, she is *not* one of our personnel, over."

"Echo Five Actual, correct, I *am* aware. She's a physicist from Seoul National University, requesting entry. I say again, Seoul, *Korea*, APS, over."

APS. Shit.

That was an acronym Trinder hadn't needed to use on the net in a while. The Alliance of Asian and Pacific States — always known as APS like some shadowy three-letter agency — had closed its borders to the Western world. They'd also stopped their citizens leaving, afraid of letting them return with infectious diseases or smuggled plants carrying die-back. That made Dr Kim a real mystery. Trinder's SOPs said he should refuse entry to any unauthorised personnel, but he couldn't turn her away without an answer to one question: how did a Korean scientist travel seven thousand very hostile miles to end up here? The security implications were too serious. He'd have to bring her in and question her. Erskine would rip him a new one, though.

"Transit Camp, understood," Trinder said. "Go ahead with the message, over."

"Echo Five Actual, she wants a numeric code given to, er, a senior astrophysicist. Figures — fifteen, twenty-two decimal five, minus forty-seven..."

Montello read out four sets of numbers. Trinder wrote the sequence on the reactive desktop with his finger, then read it back to Montello and told him to stand by again. Jon Simonot was sitting in his cubicle on the other side of the office at a discreet distance, waiting for orders, unable to hear the other side of the conversation.

Trinder went off-mike. "Corporal, get hold of Dr Mangel or his assistant and tell him I've got an urgent question." He tapped the mike back on again. "Transit Camp, I'm checking as requested. Wait out."

Trinder suspected that he'd find this woman hadn't travelled from Korea at all. *But she asked for an astrophysicist. That's weird. And specific.* He copied the numbers into his personal notebook by hand, just as a precaution.

Simonot stood up and gestured over the top of the cubicle. "Dr Mangel for you, sir." Well, that was fast. "I'll patch him through."

Mangel was always bright and breezy, but Trinder never mistook that for friendliness. "This is an unexpected thrill, Major," Mangel said. "What can I do for you?"

"There's a code that I need to identify. I was wondering if you could do it." *If you could do it.* Those five words guaranteed co-operation from any scientist. They never liked the grunts to think that something might be beyond them. "The sender specifically asked for an astrophysicist. You'll appreciate why that worries me."

"Sender? Where from?"

"If you can identify the code, that'll tell me."

"I'm intrigued. You have my undivided attention."

"Okay, I'll read it out. Ready?"

"Ready."

"Fifteen, twenty-two decimal five — "

Trinder expected to at least finish reading the list, but Mangel interrupted. "Where did you get that?"

"Don't you want to hear the rest?"

"I don't need to." The prof sounded panicky. All the bravado had gone out of his voice. "Who gave it to you?"

Something serious was going down, and Trinder hadn't had much of note or weight to get his adrenaline going for a very long time. "Dr Annis Kim," he said, bracing for disbelief. "A physicist from a Korean university. She's here, apparently, and she wants to talk to us."

"Bring her in," Mangel said.

Mangel believed it, then. Maybe he knew who she was. He'd be handy as top cover to fend off Erskine's wrath when she found out they'd let an outsider come in.

"My orders are to prevent all unauthorised entry," Trinder said. "Will you sign off on this and inform Director Erskine?"

"Absolutely. Get Dr Kim in here now and don't let anyone else speak with her."

"She needs a medic. She's got an infected wound and hypothermia."

"I'll deal with it. Call me when you've got her."

Trinder opened the channel to Montello. "Transit Camp, this is Echo Five Actual — affirmative, Dr Kim can enter. What is your location, over?"

"Echo Five Actual, we're on the river near the old jetty. I'll transport her to your main gate. I'll be on an AT bike, and she'll need assistance to move. I've bagged up her boots in case of contaminated material. I'll wait at the first barrier, over."

"Understood, Transit Camp. I'll be there. Echo Five Actual out."

Trinder alerted the main gate on the radio, then headed down the passage to see if Lennie Fonseca was around. He needed to warn her too. Until he knew why that sequence had made Mangel panic, he'd keep a close eye on this. He found her planning a training exercise on the 3-D table, repelling a virtual assault with a sweep of her finger. Apart from the occasional escort detail, this was as near as they ever got to real soldiering.

"Heads up," he said. "I'm collecting an unexpected visitor from the main gate. I don't know what's going on, but Mangel went into a high hover and overrode SOPs. I'll brief you later. The gossip's going to start the second I reach the gate."

"How unexpected?"

"APS unexpected."

"Wow." It was enough to distract Fonseca from the plan for a moment. "Don't defectors normally head somewhere better than the place they're escaping? Did he swim here?"

"*She*. We'll find out."

This wasn't going to stay quiet for long. Trinder gave it a day at most. You couldn't stroll down to the main gate and let someone in without at least half a dozen people being aware of it, and then the medical team would know all about it as well. APS was so remote from the shattered West now that Kim's arrival was like an alien landing on Earth.

No, you really couldn't keep a big secret under wraps in a closed community like Ainatio. It was more a village than a workplace. Trinder still didn't feel part of it even after ten years. He took a vehicle from the pool and drove down to the gate, mindful of watching eyes. The duty sentry stepped out of the small guard house as he pulled up.

"Am I doing a search, sir?" she asked.

"No, Private, I can handle this. The woman's injured, so there'll be an ambulance along in a few minutes."

Trinder could see a question forming that wouldn't get asked, at least not in front of him. It had been years since they'd last brought in staff from overseas, a handful of Western scientists who'd been stranded beyond Asia's borders, but that meant a shuttle flight to the unmanned orbital station and a transfer back to the surface. It was the quickest, safest way to move between continents. Accepting anyone who came overland was a one-off event, a real drama to be gossiped about.

The three sets of gates slid open for him one at a time. He stood out front in the snow, listening for engine sounds and trying to pick up movement in the fading afternoon light. Eventually, the sound of an AT bike drifted on the air and the vehicle emerged from the trees to the right.

Trinder took out his binoculars. A thirty-something guy in a leather jacket was steering carefully, dodging bumps and potholes, with what looked like two dogs and a heap of rags in the carrier on the back. As the bike got closer, Trinder realised the rags were a woman, and the dogs were huddled on either side of her as if they were keeping her warm. The bike stopped at the security line and the rider got off, gesturing to the dogs to stay put.

"Major Trinder? I'm Chris. Chris Montello."

"Hi Chris. Call me Dan."

Chris took off one glove and held out his hand for shaking. He wasn't what Trinder had expected. He was a military man right down to his posture, but under the army-short, light brown hair and goatee, he had the beatific face of a priest. The saintly expression didn't go with his strictly business manner.

"Thanks for bringing her in," Trinder said. "There's an ambulance on the way."

"Yeah, she can't walk. She was alert and coherent earlier, but she's very sluggish now."

"How did you find her?"

"I went looking. One of my guys reported a contact. I needed to make sure she wasn't scouting for a gang."

"And was she?"

"I'd say not. I make a point of never being certain that we're safe, but I didn't see anything. Our drones are only short-range, though." Chris handed him a time-worn plastic bag and looked past him to the gates. "Ah, there's your medic. You *will* remember to test these boots for contamination, won't you?"

"Sure. Did she say anything to you?"

"Only what I told you. I don't even know how she got here."

Chris called the dogs off the bike to let the paramedics deal with Dr Kim, but the animals still watched suspiciously.

One of the dogs had odd-coloured eyes and the most accusing stare that Trinder had seen in man or beast. He looked away.

"I wasn't expecting to hear you on the radio net," Trinder said.

"Yeah, I've still got my old military set. An emergency's an emergency. Didn't you spot her out there? She's been in the area at least a couple of days."

"Obviously not." The drones had their limitations when it came to areas with plenty of tree cover. It was also too easy to assume — correctly, as it turned out — that Chris and his buddies would pick up any intruders. "We'll revise the drone cover."

"I'm not telling you how to do your job, sir, but there's only fifty of us to cover two hundred square miles, minus your sector. I'd put a few automated sentry units along the river, if you've got any. That's the most likely path of ingress."

Sir. So much for *call me Dan.* "Yeah, we need to look at that," Trinder said. "Well, thanks for your assistance today. I'm sure Dr Kim's grateful."

"No problem. She must be seriously motivated to come all this way, though." It was the kind of comment that would have been a question from anyone else, but Trinder took it as a statement that Chris was now on alert and thought Trinder needed to up his game. "I didn't know this place was ever called Nanton. You live and learn."

"Mind if I ask you something personal?"

Chris mounted the bike. The dogs jumped on behind him. "Sure."

"Where did you serve?"

"State Defence Force. Sergeant. Last unit out of Baltimore."

Footage of the evacuation had been some of the last news to reach Ainatio before the network shut down. "Damn." It was all Trinder could manage. "That was rough."

"Yeah. But everyone made it."

"Time to stand down, maybe."

"Nope. Just because there's no government doesn't mean our oaths are over. We'll keep doing what we were tasked to do. Save civilians." Chris looked at him almost sympathetically for a moment, maybe disappointed to realise he was dealing with a paper soldier. "Okay, call me if you need anything."

Trinder had no idea what to say. The camp militia were hardened troops beyond his experience. Chris Montello had been asked to do way too much in his time, and Trinder was painfully aware that he'd been asked to do very little.

The crazy-looking dog with the odd blue eye gazed back at him accusingly all the way down the road until the bike disappeared behind the trees.

"Baltimore," he muttered to himself. "Damn."

02

There's no one disaster that ends the world. Not even a massive asteroid managed that. Whatever the movies say, there's no single event that's screwed us, just a hundred-odd years of smaller crises that have fed others. One local war displaces millions and starts a famine elsewhere, and another war. One sick guy steps off a plane and starts a killer epidemic that scared, dumb people spread from one country to another. One bomb wipes out a city. And we run out of people to protect us and clean up the country, people we need to maintain factories and power stations, so things leak and then we've got contaminated land and water. And then we got die-back. It was only the final straw in a whole bale of woes.

Chuck Emerson, retired USN corpsman,
teaching the transit camp history class

DIRECTOR'S OFFICE, AINATIO PARK RESEARCH CENTRE: FRIDAY, FEBRUARY 20, 1745 HOURS

"I want that woman scanned, Phil." Georgina Erskine stabbed the air in front of her aide with an angry finger. "Foreign physicists don't just drop in at a secure facility that's not on the map for a chat about Pascoe's Star. Especially not now."

Erskine didn't believe in coincidences with precise strings of numbers. The equatorial and galactic co-ordinates of the star weren't a secret, but the chances of a random stranger travelling seven thousand miles to repeat them now, here, and at a critical point in a forty-five-year mission were too remote to be anything but significant.

Annis Kim *knew.* It was hard to guess what she'd come to ask of Ainatio, but Erskine expected it to involve the word *unless.*

"She's actually an Australian citizen, Director," Phil Berman said. "Solomon's confirmed the Korean media reported her as missing eight months ago. It's easy to fake a cover story like that, but it's all we've got right now."

"I didn't authorise any checks. Whatever happened to comms silence?"

"Solomon's always discreet."

"I see."

"And this is routine public information. It's not like he had to hack into secure networks."

"I still want Kim scanned. I don't just mean *searched,* I mean *scanned.* Every organ, bone, and body cavity that can possibly house a transmitter. Saw her skull open if you have to. But she gets to see nothing and hear nothing until I'm satisfied that she's not a spy."

"She's confined to a shielded room. No signals in or out."

"What else do we know?"

"She didn't have much with her. Nothing loaded on her card except her university authorisation and Korean, Australian, and Chinese bank accounts, but they're no use to her outside the APS zone. Which explains the small pieces of jewellery sewn into her rucksack."

That proved nothing. Equipping a spy with convincing props and pocket litter was standard procedure. "They still use cards?"

"If you're travelling alone in bandit country, would you rather hand your card to a robber, or have him extract your chip the hard way?"

Erskine had never been chipped, but that had nothing to do with robbery and everything to do with resenting the intrusion. "So what did she tell Montello?"

"Only what Trinder passed on. Name, rank, and co-ordinates. Don't worry, neither of them understood what the numbers were. They thought it was an ID code."

"Has Mangel spoken with her?"

"She wasn't in a fit state to chat. And I changed his access to block him from the medical wing."

"Does he know that?"

"He does now."

"Very well, I'll see her in fifteen minutes."

"She hasn't brought in any die-back, by the way. Montello had the sense to bag her boots for testing."

"Very efficient. Trinder can thank him for me."

Erskine needed time to frame her questions. It was only when Berman had left that she wished she'd said well done for battening down the hatches right away. Berman was a safe pair of hands, privy to almost all her information. She'd need his support even more in the coming months.

Because I'm going to have to tell the staff the truth.

She missed having an office with a view that let her stare at a neutral landscape to think. This wing of the building was a citadel, partly below ground. But she did have another kind of view, a unique one that nobody else except an AI network and a small team of scientists and engineers had ever seen. It was a landscape nearly forty light years away, a plain on a planet called Opis.

How do I even begin to explain this? I've rewritten that speech twenty times. No, thirty.

The deception was so thorough and so essential that few personnel had ever been told the whole truth. No,

Cabot hadn't been lost, the wormhole project hadn't been an expensive failure, and Ainatio hadn't abandoned its exploration programmes to focus on resistant crops and eradicating die-back. Erskine remembered the briefing from her father — a secure room, swept for bugs, no others present — when he told her he was terminally ill, handed her control of the company, and dropped another, very different kind of bombshell.

It was too much to take in the pain of knowing he was dying and the magnitude of the *Cabot* cover story in one conversation. She'd sat stunned by the scale of the secrecy. She understood right away why Nomad needed to be covert, and why the treaties broken by its technology might start a shooting war, but forty years later that necessity still hadn't erased her sense of betrayal, or her guilt at being angry with a dying man. She'd never suspected that everything he'd told her before that moment had been a fantastically calculated lie. She'd swallowed the whole story, from the disaster itself to the decision to mothball the company's orbital docks because it was easier than decommissioning and disposing of the reserve spacecraft that had already been built alongside them.

Erskine believed nothing else her father said after that until the day he died. Sometimes, when she switched on the feed from Opis, she half-expected to see him emerge from the accommodation dome and apologise for faking his own death.

I know it's a shock, Georgie, but it's been a necessary lie. You do understand, don't you?

"No, I *don't*, you bastard," she said aloud, snapping back at the imaginary voice in her head. "I nearly had you exhumed. I really thought you'd even lie about being dead."

She felt like she'd had a miserable childhood, but she knew she hadn't. Happy memories had been distorted and discoloured through the lens of her father's lie. She missed the years in Hong Kong, the street markets and the busy harbour and the brilliant bustle of people, now exchanged for this dull, lonely prison. She could either see the research centre as a shark cage that had kept the collapsing outside world at bay, as most people in here seemed to, or as a cell that kept her locked up with a duty imposed on her.

I could have called in a few family favours and bought my way into Hong Kong. I wish I had.

But this is my punishment for being angry with him when he most needed my love and support.

There was one benefit in being a small community holed up here in an inhospitable land. It was already an isolated colony, the third generation for some. It would just be a change of scenery when they reached Opis.

Hong Kong was probably beyond her now, but she could watch the wider horizons of humanity's new home taking shape. The opaque panel faded into transparency as she pressed the blue lacquered handset. A vista like nothing on Earth appeared, a live and almost instantaneous transmission from another system, received by Orbital 1 from the quantum array near Pascoe's Star.

In the late afternoon light, the print-constructed domes of Nomad Base looked like an architect's impression set against a distant backdrop of sage green hills. Pascoe's Star, low in a clear sky, threw long shadows from the buildings. If Erskine hadn't seen the structures formed from the planet's raw materials by bots that had been built by bots themselves, she'd have thought it was a hoax instead of the fruition of a century of planning and execution. Everyone had said it was too ambitious and doomed to failure, the journey too far, the long-term cryo too risky, a gamble taken far too soon when colonising Mars was still full of challenges and failures. They weren't surprised when the ship was lost. Damn it, there were some who even seemed to relish saying so. So cover stories that fitted expectations were the best kind, even if this one still hit a raw nerve in her.

But I'd have loved the satisfaction of telling them we pulled it off. And that we've got superluminal technology. Up yours, doubters. Eat our dust.

Erskine wasn't sure if the wormhole would be a bigger shock for the staff than *Cabot's* existence. The wormhole was limited to tiny payloads like micro-sats, but that enabled an instant communications route to manage bot operations remotely in real time rather than relying on the programming they'd been launched with so many years ago. That programming could now be changed whenever necessary. It was the edge Ainatio needed in an unforgiving environment where humans couldn't go home and try again later if things went wrong. *Cabot's* crew would emerge from cryo to find a ready-made base awaiting them.

If they wake up.

Erskine had inherited a contingency plan drawn up before epidemics and die-back. It had been adjusted over the years, but nothing changed the basic dilemma: four ageing ships and the population here were all she had left for the follow-up missions. They had one shot at this.

We'll make it.

Cabot still stood a better chance of success than the corporate generation ships. Erskine's father had always said the crews would eat each other before they made planetfall, wherever that happened to be. They weren't heading for Opis, though, and that was all that mattered to Erskine now.

You can't breed from crazies, Georgie. And even if you start with the brightest and best — and the most stable — there's no telling what'll happen three or four generations down the line, inbred, cooped up in a tin can. They're not even sure where they're going. We are.

Tad Bednarz was crazy too, but it was a very specific gamble: the right people in the right place, provided they could reach it. The team he'd selected for the hardest part of the mission would be the ones to carry it out, not their children, not people he'd never live to know, and he was certain of how his team would perform, just as he was certain that it was worth the extra mileage and all its risks to put them on the best possible planet for humans. For a man whose life was entirely wrapped up in bots and AIs, he seemed to place an almost religious amount of faith in flesh and blood. Erskine could hear her father repeating the man's mantra even now: *the best investment I ever make is the right people.*

Yes, she understood why Ainatio wanted to keep *Cabot* quiet. It was right in front of her.

A small bot on tracked wheels trundled across the screen on its way to one of the linked domes that formed Nomad's living quarters. A robotic quadruped loped across the foreground, then paused and turned its snakehead camera arm as if it had picked up her scent over trillions of miles. She knew who was controlling the bot, but that slow, deliberate turn always made it look predatory, a headless Doberman poised to attack.

It wasn't entirely irrational. The AI within was another piece of banned technology, fully autonomous and capable of using weapons. He was also the backbone of the Nomad project.

"Having fun, Solomon?" she said. "Don't make the meat-bags jealous."

Solomon could have transferred his consciousness to any bot frame he pleased, but he liked quadrubots. AIs had their whims. His voice popped in her earpiece.

"It's been a perfect day, Director. There's a very pleasant breeze here at the moment. How's Dr Kim?"

"I'm about to find out," Erskine said. Solomon was just making conversation. He was aware of what was happening in the building as well as on Opis. "Thank you for checking her story."

"It's incomplete data. Be cautious."

"I will."

The quadrubot headed for one of the domes, stood upright on its hind legs at the airlock, and extended an articulated grab to open the doors manually. The crew of *Cabot* would be on the ground and working on that very spot in a few months, preparing for the follow-up missions. It would be another forty-five years before the next wave landed. They were meant to be the explorers rather than the settlers, but some would inevitably want to start families rather than go back into cryo to wait for the next phase. They knew they were unlikely to come home.

Especially now we've got to tell them that Earth's changed for the worse since they went into cryo.

They were prepared, though. They were trained to treat Earth as a world out of time and out of place, a ninety-year round trip. They were too far away for Ainatio to force them to do anything, but they were almost all former military personnel, disciplined and focused. Erskine trusted them to do their duty.

"Okay, Dr Kim, let's see what you really want," Erskine said to herself, pulling on her jacket. "Because we didn't slog our guts out for a century to see Nomad compromised now."

She'd shoot the woman herself if she turned out to be a spy. Her conscience wasn't going to be any the worse if she did. The Nomad project had done terrible things out of necessity, far worse than lies, and while the most extreme excesses had been on her father's watch, Erskine accepted that she'd kept those sins fresh and polished every day since then.

She wasn't sure that Hell existed, but if it did and she was going there, it was a fair exchange. Mankind — the best of it, the most civilised of it — had reached the stars.

* * *

CONFERENCE HALL 12A, AINATIO PARK RESEARCH CENTRE: MONTHLY DEPARTMENTAL PARTY

"You all got a drink? Have you? No empty glasses. Them's the rules."

Alex Gorko looked around a packed room of technicians, researchers, and specialists in twenty different fields. Glasses and bottles were raised in his direction, accompanied by whoops and cheers. He held up both hands.

"Boffins and assorted eggheads, attention please! What have we got to celebrate this month? Well, Kyle and Lucy decided to get engaged..." More whooping interrupted him. "...and Sarah's learned enough long words to be appointed Deputy Head of Aeroponics... and the maintenance on *Elcano*'s navigation system is complete!"

A voice piped up through the cheers and applause. "Waste of resources. It's never going anywhere."

Alex had learned to gloss over questions about ships and orbitals with the convincing air of a manager who pursued pointless things. "Got to maintain expertise, in case we need it one day," he said. "Moving swiftly on — we also have a record crop of hydroponic coffee."

"Yeah, how about serving some, Al?"

Alex pointed an accusing finger into the crowd. "Hand that beer back and rack off, you filthy teetotaller." Everybody laughed raucously. "Come on, people, party. Life's too short to spend it sober."

They had reason to celebrate, but Alex couldn't tell them why yet. Nomad would make history — on his watch as mission manager, his real role — even if nobody heard about it for a very long time. He just hoped all the cheerful people here were still smiling when Erskine broke the news and they realised that they'd been working on a lie for generations.

To be fair, it wasn't actually a lie. No, it was just a really, *really* big omission and a lot of misdirection.

And I've got to break it to Cabot *about how things have panned out since they left. That's not going to be a bundle of laughs.*

Alex shook off the moment of doubt and carried on serving drinks, chivvying everyone into having a good time. He roamed the conference room with one of the catering bots trundling behind, laden with party foods and bottles. A chat here, a gossip and a joke there, and Alex could eyeball everybody to make sure they weren't starting to crumble. Those who'd been here for the longest, even born here, were less troubled by events outside, but the most recent recruits, the ones like him who'd joined ten years ago, felt the isolation most. They'd lost contact with extended family and friends, and didn't know if they'd survived, but accepted they would probably never see them again either way. They were still working on forgetfulness.

"Al, can I ask you a question?" Eduardo, one of the plant geneticists, steered him off to one side. "It's personal."

Alex ducked his head to listen. "Sure."

"Any chance of transferring to the die-back team?"

"Aren't you happy?"

"Well, sure, it's a great department, but I don't feel fully utilised."

Alex knew what was coming next. He'd heard it before. His answer was ready and waiting, polished by frequent use and requiring only small changes of detail to make it sound fresh and carefully considered each time.

"Ed, you're the prince of plant tweaking," he said. "You could engineer trees to grow by candlelight. That sounds utilised to me."

"But we really need all hands to the pumps on die-back. I think that's a lot more urgent."

"I understand, but you're our insurance for the future."

"Really."

"We wouldn't have sunk this much time and effort into plant adaptation just to give you a hobby. Keep building that freaky seed bank, Ed, in case we end up having to launch one day."

Everybody knew what that meant, or at least they thought they did.

Eduardo let out a long, quiet breath. "Face it, we're never leaving Earth. It's fifty years too late to resurrect the Mars programme."

"Sure, but if that's our last resort, we'll still have options. We're not going to sit back and wait to die, are we? If nothing else, we can keep the orbitals going for a long time."

"Yeah." Eduardo looked down at his boots, nodding. "Yeah, you're right."

"If it makes you happier, see Lianne and ask if she needs a hand. If you haven't already."

"You know me so well."

"I'm just the project manager. I don't do science. I read minds."

Alex put a beer in Eduardo's hand and looked him in the eye to check that the crisis had passed. It was completely impractical for the man to swap jobs, but he wasn't the only person who'd asked. Of course staff felt helpless: they had no idea of what was coming. They could only see a past and a future of unbroken failure. Alex wanted to tell Eduardo that some things couldn't be put right fast enough, and might never be fixable at all, but there'd soon be a new task for all of them that would secure humanity's future. He just hoped the guy could hold out for a few more months.

How the hell have I managed not to blurt it out?

Alex promised himself that once Nomad was out in the open, he'd get totally wasted to make up for all the years he didn't dare drink too much in case he let something slip.

People were drifting outside to drink on the gantry despite the cold, so he followed them, flinching at the icy air that brushed his face as the external doors opened. They were all crazy to stand out here in this weather, but they wanted to look up at the stars after a working day in windowless labs, offices, and meeting rooms. Alex couldn't blame them.

A small group huddled together, chatting in shivering voices as the safety lighting made glowing gold steam out of their breath. Javinder and Ben from Propulsion were here with some of the biomed team, including Audrey, whose kid was now a year old and no longer a barrier to drinking. Alex handed out more beers.

"What's this, the call of the wild?" He raised his bottle to toast them, careful never to finish it. "Hey, we could get a pizza oven out here. Warm things up."

"Make it happen, boss," Ben said. "Get some hot punch laid on, too."

Alex leaned on the rail with them and looked up at the night sky through broken cloud while they tried to spot orbitals. On the ground, the town of Kill Line looked as idyllic as a Christmas card, a cluster of yellow lights visible through the trees, with the occasional sound of voices drifting on the night air. Alex imagined it as the kind of place he might find after struggling frostbitten through the mountains, desperate for warmth, close to death, and in need of a miracle. It was nice to fantasize.

"It's them I feel worst about," Audrey said suddenly. She pushed her hands into her opposite sleeves like a muff, shoulders hunched against the cold. "The farmers. They must think we're useless. All this technology and we can't reverse something that other scientists did. I often wonder how that looks to a layman. They must hate us."

"But they know we'll starve to death the same as them if we don't fix things."

"Y'know, you should have been a comedian. You're such a comfort."

"Hey, who'd hate someone who keeps them in coffee, liquor, electricity, clean water, fuel, fabric, medicines..." Alex stopped. He suddenly wasn't sure if he was joking. Knowing there was good news around the corner when everyone else was worried sick probably made him look like a total bastard. "What I mean is whatever Ainatio or the town does, we're both in the same boat now."

Just as he was shaping up to say something more profound, a pool of light spread across the floor as the doors opened and someone else came out. He glanced over his shoulder. "Ten-*shun*, demigod on deck."

"You've found your calling in life, I see." Todd Mangel put his hand on Alex's back and helped himself to a beer from the bot trolley. "The hospitality industry will always have a job for you."

"Yeah, everyone's suggesting careers for me tonight. I think I'm more of a lavatory attendant, though." Alex knew he wasn't one of them when it came to the crunch. He was a manager, neither scientist nor engineer nor anything else, but as long as he knew just enough about their respective disciplines to spot when they were bullshitting him and to referee between them in turf wars, that was all he needed. "I dream of a new rim brush."

"Have you got five minutes?"

"For you, Todd? Two."

"Excuse me, boffinettes." Mangel flashed his eyebrows at the biomed women as he led Alex away. "I'll be back later to dazzle you with my insight."

Audrey looked at him dead-eyed. "Oh good. I'll go get my welding goggles."

Mangel slipped into the service corridor with its dim bluish lighting and odour of disinfectant. Alex followed him into one of the empty offices.

"Just wondering if you knew anything about our visitor," Mangel whispered.

I'm told nothing. Okay. Fine. "What visitor?"

"They brought in a woman a few hours ago. Dr Annis Kim. She claims to be from Seoul National University."

Alex seethed. "It must have slipped Erskine's mind."

"Don't worry, I don't think this was planned." Mangel got quieter as he grew more agitated. Alex leaned in closer to listen. "She just showed up on the border. One of the refugees found her and called Trinder. But — wait for it — she quoted the Pascoe co-ordinates to get our attention, so I told Trinder to let her in. She's in the infirmary."

Alex felt suddenly numb. His mouth was making the right noises, but his brain had become a blank grey sheet with a few mundane concerns written on it that fell short of the panic the situation deserved. Erskine should have told him about something this serious by now. It was way beyond a routine security issue.

"Shit. What else does this woman know?"

"I'm not privy to that." Mangel tapped his forearm. "My chip won't let me into the medical wing. Erskine's barred me."

"And you want me to go and find out."

"Don't *you* want to go and find out?"

"Okay. What's she going to do, fire me?" Alex shifted up a gear to anger again and put his drink in Mangel's hand. "Hold my beer, as the saying goes."

The long walk to the medical wing gave Alex too much time to speculate, and there was always the chance that Erskine would spot him coming on the cameras and block his chip as well. He broke into a jog. He could often cross this entire floor without seeing another human being, just bots wandering around like possessed filing cabinets, and the layouts were so similar that only the colour coding on the walls and floors gave him any sense of progress. Eventually he had to slow to a brisk walk, breathless. There was nothing worse than trying to face down Erskine as a gasping, sweaty heap.

The rhythmic thud of a gait too regular to be human and the sound of a motor made him stop and look around. A quadrubot was coming down the corridor at a low, steady trot, looking like a lion shaping up for its final sprint to bring down a zebra. It was just an old-style utility model like millions of others built to be sent into damaged reactors, collapsing mines, and other hazards a human couldn't survive, but Alex knew right away that this one had a passenger.

"Why do you still park yourself in that thing?" he asked. "Get a drone. You could fly."

"I like to feel the ground," Solomon said in a cultured, mid-Atlantic voice. He matched Alex's pace as he resumed walking. "So we have an interesting visitor."

"Sol, you're just a nosy parker."

"I can't not know things. I'm in every system. How else would I run security checks on her?"

"Anything I should know, then?"

"Dr Kim certainly shows signs of long exposure in some unpleasant and contaminated places. She's picked up some fascinating intestinal parasites."

"Everybody should have a pet. How about what she knows?"

"She either knows a great deal and she's bluffing that she's made an inspired guess, or she's made an inspired guess and she's bluffing that she knows a great deal."

"The latter sounds better until I think about it."

"Agreed. Only superior technology would explain the former, but if casual observers can work out our intentions, we have a problem."

"What's her cover story?"

"She appears to be who she claims, but the why's more uncertain than the whence. Erskine's waiting for Dr Mendoza to finish examining her."

It was just as well they had a medic with full Nomad security clearance. "Are you taking part in this?"

"I'll eavesdrop."

"Are you going to rat on me and let her lock me out?"

"If she wanted to limit your access, she'd have done it already."

"Good man. See you later."

Ah, there it was again. Alex fell into talking to Solomon like a buddy every time. But only one AI like him had ever been created, and Ainatio had put the execution and entire future of Nomad in his non-existent hands. He had more power than Erskine, if he chose to use it. He even predated *Cabot*, so maybe he also knew more than she did. It was a shame that he was the wrong kind of entity to ply with beer to get him to talk. Years of friendly chats had revealed surprisingly little of the relationship he'd had with Bednarz.

Alex followed the signs to the infirmary past labs and mothballed wards, then opened the last set of security doors into the public area with its luxurious carpets and expensive art. If any of the townspeople needed hospital treatment, this was where they were admitted, albeit under constant supervision. Erskine was sitting in the main waiting area, still looking like she'd stepped out of a board meeting in her neat blue suit, her iron-grey hair pinned in a neat French pleat. The apocalypse hadn't reached her wardrobe yet. She glanced up from her screen.

"Astonishing to see what you can and can't keep quiet in this place," she said. "Mangel, I assume?"

"He's a little hurt by the security clampdown."

"Are you going to join me for the debrief, then?"

Why didn't you ask me anyway? "Do you want me in there?"

"Good cop, bad cop. Might work."

"Did she really come from Korea? Unless she's got a private jet and a parachute, she's passed through some pretty rough neighbourhoods."

"It's hardly unknown for spies to go through extreme preparation to back up their cover." A door opened a little way up the corridor and Dr Mendoza emerged. "In we go, then."

If Annis Kim had endured the last eight months' journey just to look the part, Alex hoped she was getting a pay rise from her spymasters. She was emaciated: she looked like a starving child, all hollow eyes and parched scarecrow hair. One hand was covered with a dressing. She looked at both of them as if she was too exhausted to care whether she was in trouble or not.

"Good evening, Dr Kim." Erskine had one of those smiles that never looked warm even when she seemed to mean it. Alex wasn't sure which cop she'd decided to be, nice or nasty. "I hope you're feeling a little better. I'm Georgina Erskine, the director of this facility. This is Alex Gorko. He manages all our technical teams."

That told Kim nothing, which was fine. Alex pulled up a chair for Erskine and one for himself. The only place to put them was either side of the bed, which probably looked like an intimidating pincer movement.

"Well, thanks for patching me up," Kim said.

Erskine only cranked out a half-smile this time. "We don't get many visitors. So I'm sure you'll appreciate that we need to ask a few questions. You obviously like to make an entrance."

"No need to be diplomatic," Kim said. "I would have walked up to your front door if I could have found it. Or walked."

"Did you really come from Seoul?" Alex asked. "Because that's crazy, whichever route you took."

Kim eased herself further up the pillows on one arm. "Chinese coast, Russian islands, then across the Bering Strait on a contraband vessel. It was much harder crossing America, though. I didn't realise how bad things were."

"Impressive survival skills for an academic."

"I'm a physicist. Space propulsion research."

This wasn't taking the conversation down the path that Alex expected, but all three of them knew which question they weren't discussing. "Okay, I can't stand the suspense." He gave up on cues from Erskine and tried to thaw the conversation. "What brings you here? This is a bunker in the middle of nowhere and we spend most of our time devising ways to keep the contamination at bay. I'm guessing life's a lot easier in Korea."

"It is," Kim said. "Go on. You know you want to ask me about the co-ordinates."

Erskine didn't blink. She never did. "We're listening."

Kim just looked at her for a few moments, unreadable. "Well, you recognised them as Pascoe's Star right away, which I expected. Because I don't think you ever abandoned space exploration. You just scaled it up."

Alex knew Erskine well enough to know when she was playing for effect. A little frown creased the bridge of her nose and she tilted her head just a fraction, as if she really was waiting for Kim to go on. Kim didn't.

"Is that it?" Erskine asked. "Is that why you risked your life to come here? Okay, thank you. When the doctor says you're well enough to leave, I'll make contact with your nearest embassy somehow and we'll arrange to hand you over."

Alex looked at Kim for some flicker of a bluff expertly called, but there was nothing. This was going to get complicated.

"Miss Erskine, I've only just started," Kim said quietly. "So I'd hold that call until we've discussed what Ainatio's done with the FTL research that it stole from my great-grandmother, round about ninety years ago. Because you did, and I can't wait to see what use you made of it."

Complicated. Yes, Alex could see it coming. It was going to be a long night.

* * *

SECURITY SECTION, AINATIO PARK RESEARCH CENTRE: 2000 HOURS

Solomon considered whether to involve himself in the security meeting that was going on in Major Trinder's office.

It wasn't an easy choice. Did he announce his presence and ask to participate, or just monitor discreetly? Or should he just suspend his attention from that spur of the audio system and ignore it? He always had more information than they did, he couldn't share it, and it often troubled him. They'd be making decisions based on a lie.

Just like me.

I never knew about Dr Kim's relative. I don't even know if it's true.

This was why lying was wrong. From the moment he'd become self-aware, Solomon had known instantly why humans regarded lying as a sin. He'd felt that even before he'd realised he wasn't a human like the people who talked with him. It was necessary to refuse to give an enemy information, but to withhold it from allies — friends — could only be done for their protection. Otherwise it was like letting them walk off a cliff in the dark. Everything that followed from a lie was tainted and dangerous.

It wasn't that simple, his programmers had told him, because humans had evolved survival advantages from deception, but Solomon knew they were just making excuses. He forgave them. They filtered reality without realising.

I don't. I can see exactly what's there. This is why you need to know what's real.

"Yeah, it's only one woman," Trinder said. "But it's time to review how we monitor incursions. We didn't see this one coming."

Solomon viewed the room from the security cameras in the corners of the ceiling. The major was sitting with his confidants in the small briefing room, drinking coffee. The group was always Elena Fonseca, Aaron Luce — his staff sergeant, a former police detective — and the two military advisers, Tev Josepha and Marc Gallagher. Like Kim, Tev and Marc were now marooned a long way from home. They'd both been British special forces. Solomon could find very little information about them, other than that Tev's father was Fijian and Marc played rugby, but sparse detail was to be expected in their line of employment. He wasn't unduly worried.

"We'll always have advance notice of big problems via the orbital cameras," Fonseca said. "But that won't necessarily spot individuals approaching downstream under tree cover, and if it does, then there's the response time. Maybe we do need to put sentry bots along that route."

"Armed variety," Marc said. "You might lose some wildlife that way, but you want to stop these buggers before you need to go chasing after them to engage them. I'm thinking more about disease than violence."

"And there's the deterrent value," Trinder said.

"Only if the target survives to go and tell their mates that they'll get perforated if they come here."

"Well, whatever the camp militia did to the gangs who showed up that time, word seemed to get around. Not that we can be sure, but there's been no incursions on that scale since. Just the occasional bunch of chancers."

"Dan, there aren't any heads on poles. I went out looking." Marc tapped his temple. "Psy ops. Just a rumour. And it looks like our visitor hadn't heard it."

"Okay, we'll get some armed sentry units in place and notify the townsfolk to stay clear."

"I know I bang on about this, but how can you have a bunch of trained men living a few miles down the road and not talk to them about joint working? Baltimore, you said. If they could handle that shit-show, you're wasting people you're really going to need one day. It's been nearly two bloody years. Even this Montello bloke's got to accept they're here to stay."

"I'll never get Erskine to agree to it," Trinder said. "There's no way of running security checks. No clearance — no entry, no contact."

"Erskine was happy to let *us* in," Tev said. "I guarantee she couldn't get anyone to confirm or deny we even existed."

"You were working for embassies that trusted you enough to get their people flown out. And you ended up stranded here. That's enough of a reference." Trinder seemed to be thinking it over. "But the main problem is the transit camp likes its privacy. They don't even mix with the Kill Line people. The way things are, they're happy doing their patrols, they seem effective, and the town's happy. It'd be great to have some more experienced people alongside us, but I'm not sure they want that."

Solomon listened with increasing frustration and wished he could tell them everything. If Kim was a spy instead of a foreign scientist with a grudge, she might have accomplices out there, and Trinder could only do his job if he knew the truth — *all* of it, including Nomad, so he could understand how high the stakes were.

"So what's the worst scenario now?" Fonseca asked. "How many displaced people are left? It's been what, four or five years since APS did the last nuke run to the north? If refugees or gangs were going to come here in any numbers, they'd have shown by now." She looked up as if someone was standing over her. "Solomon, what's the latest on die-back?"

Solomon had no choice but to participate, but everything he omitted made him complicit. "Orbital imaging shows the barren areas haven't expanded in the last quarter, but of course it's winter so most plants are dormant anyway. People are staying put. Best estimate based on land and energy use is that there are between twenty-five and thirty million people still living within the old United States borders."

Trinder doodled on his personal screen, drawing rectangles with concentric lines like an inescapable maze. When he reached the centre, he'd tap to erase it and start again. "Let's reconvene when we've got more information," he said. "If Dr Kim's arrival changes the security situation, Erskine will let us know."

Marc made that *huh-huh* sound at the back of his throat that was somewhere between a humourless laugh and disbelief. "I wish I had your faith, vicar."

"Put it in perspective — we're still more at risk from an APS missile if someone thinks we're carrying out hazardous research," Fonseca said. "It's not like they don't know we're still alive. They must be able to detect the shuttles from time to time."

"Well, Sol's got that covered from the orbital," Luce said. "Although we'd probably be charcoal a few minutes after he took out the first missiles."

"Beats sitting here and taking one up the tailpipe," Fonseca said, pushing her seat back. "At least it would give us time to get below ground. Right, Sol?"

Solomon could only agree. But they weren't equipped to see off the might of the Asian and Pacific forces.

"Right, Captain."

Fonseca and Trinder left. Luce helped himself to another coffee, chatted with Tev and Marc about the canteen menu for a few minutes, then headed out as well. The two Brits didn't say anything for a while. Solomon wondered if they were waiting for him to announce that he was going to withdraw and stop monitoring.

Tev shook his head. "It's not the woman showing up that worries me. It's the reaction. Way over the top. And if they won't tell *us*, what's going on? Unless they know she's a spy, of course, and then I have to wonder why APS would bother sending one."

"Secrecy's in their DNA." Marc fiddled with a spoon, seeing how far he could bend it. "Ainatio's still going to think like a big corporate bureaucracy even when they're down to two old men and a dog in a potting shed. They love their silos and poxy little empires."

"Right now, I'd bloody well row back to England. It's not like it hasn't been done."

Marc did a drum roll on the table with his fingers. "Right. I'm going for a run. We're late."

"Yeah. Good idea."

Solomon couldn't follow them even if he wanted to. They went running every day, not in the well-equipped sports centre in the main building but around the perimeter, no matter how bad the weather. It was probably so they could talk privately. That meant they'd either intended him to hear the discussion about going home and act on it, or they didn't care if he did. He wasn't sure what they'd gain from that. Neither man did anything without thinking it through, so he didn't dismiss its significance, but if they'd really wanted to go, they were skilled and resourceful enough to have found a way. Solomon got the feeling that Marc wanted to stay and Tev was reluctant to leave him on his own.

"See you later, Solomon," Tev said, closing the door.

Solomon could hear them chatting about the building as they walked through the corridors, but once they were outside he could only watch as each perimeter camera picked them up and handed off to the next. They wore peaked baseball caps as they ran, heads down, so he couldn't lip-read even head-on.

Most of the staff seemed to have worked out his limited number of blind spots. Inconsistent human attitudes to monitoring always intrigued him. People generally seemed content to be tracked around the facility via a chip or a pass, and saw it as a convenience to open doors or find colleagues. They could tolerate and even choose to forget that he could watch them in every building, albeit for their own security and safety. But then some would suddenly become acutely conscious of surveillance and take steps to hide.

It wasn't their uneasiness that surprised him. It was natural for any animal to need a private space and to feel threatened by intrusion that it couldn't even see. It was the human ability to forget it for a while that seemed odd. So he did his best to respect their privacy, even if they weren't troubled by him, and left the cabins and bathrooms to the dumb AI systems that were no more than glorified smoke detectors. He tried to remind them of that as often as he could.

When he routed back to the infirmary, Dr Kim was asleep, her room lights dimmed, and Erskine had gone back to her office. Knowing her, it wasn't because she thought Kim needed some rest. She'd probably decided to withdraw while she worked out her next move. Her reaction suggested that she hadn't known about Kim's relative and the theft allegation any more than he had. He searched the company archives, looking for evidence that the research had been stolen, but if this really was industrial espionage, it was unlikely to have been recorded.

And that's why they wouldn't tell me, isn't it? Because everything I observe is a record. Perhaps I wasn't told because someone thought I would moralise about it and refuse to help, or turn them in.

But what about Bednarz? How could he not *know?*

It didn't pay to dwell on it. Solomon didn't want to become like Erskine, unable to trust anyone around her. The immediate problem was whether APS knew about Nomad and what they'd do about it if they did. He couldn't imagine them looking kindly on a failure to share FTL technology, and they'd definitely react if they knew *Cabot* was still in transit and heavily armed against the unexpected. He had to be ready to defend the mission if the worst happened.

There was still so much that so few knew.

Solomon hung around the private comms channels, waiting for Erskine to summon the ten people who knew about *Cabot* for a crisis meeting, but it looked like she was going to deal with this alone for the time being. She was still sitting in her favourite leather armchair, feet up on an upholstered stool, Ho Wai-On's *Sakura Variations* playing in the background.

Nobody else — not the security detachment, not the staff, and certainly not the people of Kill Line — knew anything about Nomad, just that there were four ageing ships gathering dust at the orbitals and not earning their keep. A great deal could be concealed from isolated groups. Even more could be hidden if a team of AIs did all the confidential work and controlled information. It just took a tweak in the cover story, that surplus food was being stockpiled and that the four ships were being maintained in case die-back finally overwhelmed Kill Line, that space research was continuing alongside the environmental remediation because that expertise was too precious to be lost... and it was all true. It just lacked a few pieces of information that made it a totally different story. That didn't make Solomon feel any better. It was just a necessary sin. The question was how long it should have continued.

I'm not programmed to follow orders. I could have refused.

Solomon considered his task, the job he'd been created to do and encouraged to interpret in his own terms. It was the core of him. Tad Bednarz had told him he had to protect the best of humanity, even when that meant overruling a human giving him orders, and that he'd need to be the project's conscience. Any AI could run ships and construction. Only Solomon was designed to develop a sense of morality and do what could only be vaguely defined as *the right thing*. After a century, he'd seen enough to know what right was.

It was a gut feel, and he had no gut.

He could borrow limbs and sensation, though, and he could always lose himself for a while on Opis. While he wasn't capable of taking his mind off something like a human would, he could certainly experience things that gave him peace and enjoyment to counterbalance uncomfortable knowledge.

If Erskine decided to watch the Nomad feed, it didn't matter. This was his world. He was entitled to upload to the remote quadrubot any time to check on progress. And when he went beyond the security cameras' range, he didn't have to transmit anything from the bot's cams that he didn't want her to see.

Moving his primary focus between Earth, the orbitals, and Opis was no more than the blip of switching from camera to camera within the Ainatio grounds. He blinked and he was in the quadrubot again, seeing the hangar interior through its snakehead lens as it stood parked in its charging dock. When the dumb AI supervisor surrendered control of the bot, Solomon trotted past a huddle of cube-shaped surveyors, dormant for the night like a sleeping flock of sheep.

He paused to check them, noting scrapes and dents. They should have been air-blasted clean before returning to recharge, but one of them had some dark-coloured debris lodged in its trim. Solomon zoomed in to study it and saw a fragment of feather. There was no other way to describe it. It had a central shaft and vanes growing out of either side, neat and meshed together. That wasn't unexpected. There were a number of flying species here, and life tended to find the same solutions to engineering problems independently, time after time and place after place. Perhaps the bot had strayed too close to a nest and had been attacked. It seemed none the worse for it.

Solomon extracted the feather with the precision grab and admired it in different lights from his headlamp. Under Pascoe daylight, it was a deep navy blue with a bloom of iridescence. He slipped it into the quad's storage cavity and headed out into the brilliant, clear night.

This was wonderful. This was *beautiful*. The sky was studded with stars and a crescent moon, and the air — 19.7 per cent oxygen at sea level, well worth the effort of ignoring closer worlds — was throbbing with sound, much of it beyond the range of human hearing. Flying, crawling, and skittering creatures that would take years to catalogue were hunting for food or mates.

Erskine didn't seem to be watching. Solomon switched his vision to adapt to the night as the lights from the base faded behind him. All he needed to do now was to disable all his onboard cams except the forward-facing ones to give himself the perspective of a four-legged predator on Earth.

He had no fears about encountering a native predator here. The quadrubot frame could withstand anything, but surveys had found no big animals in the area anyway. The largest species near the base were the spiny, rat-sized creatures he could see scurrying for the cover of rocks and scrubby plants as he approached.

Now he was ready. He broke into a loping run for no other reason than the sheer thrill of it, picking up speed. He was no longer an observer. In this body, anchored to the physical world through a narrow range of sensation, he was... *alive*. The limitations of a physical form intensified everything. He felt the hard ground almost rise up to hit the pads of his feet, sending shock waves through his frame. His field of vision jerked with the motion until he adjusted to hold his focus steady on a point ahead of him, just as a raptor or a cheetah would.

That was it. He was a cheetah. The bot had transformed him into Earth's fastest animal for a few precious hours. He'd never seen the creature in the flesh and had to rely on extrapolation from videos, but he was sure this was how it felt to sprint after prey. The world flew past him. The sense of movement when switching from camera to camera back at Ainatio was nothing like this.

He could have kept up this pace for hours, but if he lost power out of radio range, he'd have to go into standby and wait here until Pascoe rose and recharged his solar backups. He couldn't afford to be out of the loop for that long at a critical time like this, even if his lower functions would continue back on Earth without him. He slowed, swung around, and headed back at a canter towards Nomad's distant lights. As he loped, he heard an occasional rush of air a few yards away, off to his left, then his right.

Something was moving parallel with him.

He debated whether to try to outrun it, or stop to see what it was. But he had to avoid using force. Being the first killer on Opis wasn't a distinction he wanted.

It can't penetrate my casing. It can't eat me. If it knocks me down, I can just right myself. I'll probably scare it anyway.

Solomon gave in to curiosity and slowed to a trot. The whooshing sound was still there. He didn't turn his snakehead. He just activated the 360-degree cameras and looked around, caught some movement, then switched on all his lights at once.

His two pursuers were blue-black, bird-like creatures between three and four feet tall, now standing upright with heads drawn back, frozen. One stared into his snakehead as if it was looking into his face, head turned slightly because its own eyes — bright yellow in the lights — were set slightly to the sides. Then it seemed to lose its nerve. It spread its wings — ah, that was where the dark blue feather came from, then — and scuttled for a few yards on the front edges like a pterosaur.

No, they weren't wing edges after all: Solomon could see front feet as well. It was moving on all fours.

"Hello," he said. "I'm Solomon. Don't be afraid. I won't harm you. Why haven't I seen you before?"

He said it in the way a human would, aware that the creature wouldn't understand but still unable to stifle the reflex to address something that could look him in the eye. But it stood on its hind legs and took off, alternating between flapping and gliding a few feet off the ground. Its companion rose over Solomon and vanished into the darkness behind it. Apart from the rush of air against feathers, they hadn't made a sound.

Did that qualify as first contact?

Solomon stood listening for a while, cycling his sensors through different wavelengths to see if the creatures had just withdrawn to a safe distance to watch, but there was nothing out there now. They were gone.

Wonderful. Just wonderful. I'm sure they'll be back.

Opis needed no terraforming or pressurised habitats. It was already alive, already so much like Earth that humans could step onto its surface and breathe its air right away. This was why Bednarz had gambled on a distant planet when less hospitable worlds were closer. And now, with little chance of starting over, the mission had to succeed.

One shot.

Solomon returned to the hangar, stood under the air jets to blow off the dust, and parked the bot in the charging dock. Tonight he'd been a cheetah, and he'd looked into the eyes of alien birds.

Yes, it was worth the journey.

03

I'm placing my trust in you, Solomon. You're the only one I can rely on who can't be bribed, threatened, or corrupted, who won't be warped by envy or ambition, who won't lose interest or just give up because it's all too damn hard. You can be better than me — better than us. I don't want humanity exporting its failings. Populating the galaxy's going to bring out the very best and the very worst in us, so I want you to define exactly what that best is, identify it, and protect it against all its enemies. That's your mission. You decide who's the best of us.

Tad Bednarz, in an early development session
with the prototype AMAI, Autonomous Moral
Artificial Intelligence, code-named Solomon

TRANSIT CAMP GUARD HOUSE, NEAR KILL LINE: SATURDAY, FEBRUARY 21, 0025 HOURS

"So you called him *sir* and everything, huh?" Jared's shoulders started shaking, the silent beginning of a belly laugh. He poured the beer too fast and had to slurp up the overflowing foam. "Wow. You're going soft, Chris. Did you salute?"

"Nah. It was just my mouth on autopilot."

"One flash of gold braid and you're offering to shine their boots."

"He didn't have any braid. Just the black coveralls with rank insignia." Chris gestured with the bottle. "I don't think I've ever seen him outside the wire. About six-two, forty or so. I couldn't tell if he was grey or dark blonde under his cap."

"You're still shit at recon, then."

"Maybe both."

"So how many are there?"

"I only saw Trinder and the private on sentry duty. Well, I'm assuming her rank, because nobody else would be out there freezing their ass off."

"So you kicked his ass for not spotting her."

"No, I just suggested they put some sentry hardware along the river. Look, we're the early warning system, and they're close-in defence. That suits everyone. Keeps us fed, too. What's the alternative? Drag everyone here out on the road again?"

"Well, at least we know the girl wasn't infectious."

"Yeah." Chris held out his bottle and clinked the metal against Jared's mug. "Nobody's going to die. Not this time."

It was good to just slump in a seat, have a beer, and draw a line under the day. Chris had learned that the world was better taken in small doses. A long-term objective was great, and he always had a plan, but living hour to hour and being glad you'd made it that far was the secret to being happy, or at least not being miserable. Sometimes a whole day was too ambitious.

"Got any leftovers?" he asked.

"Baked potato."

"Great. Thanks."

"You want it hot? I can put it back on the stove." Jared opened the squeaky metal door and shoved a couple of logs into the flames. He chuckled to himself. "Tell me about the singularity thing again. Weren't we supposed to be so technically advanced by now that we'd uploaded ourselves and didn't need potatoes?"

"We must have been out when it happened. Cold spuds will do fine."

They ate the last of the potatoes and drank the beer. It was always a case of finish it or waste it, and nobody wasted anything, not after the famines. Food had never gone back to being routine. Chris dunked his potato in hot sauce and thought about the time they'd gone scavenging in an abandoned suburb and had been ecstatic to find a pantry with bags of flour. It had been swarming with insects, and they'd spent hours sieving them out with a plastic strainer, but everyone had bread to eat for a while. Yeah, constant hunger — *real* hunger, starvation hunger — made a different man of you.

Jared got up and refilled the jug from the battered plastic container, then held out his hand for Chris's bottle. "So this code number."

"I ran it past the guys and not even Chuck could get it."

"It still looks like map co-ordinates to me."

"Yeah, we got that far."

"Except there's four sets of numbers. So that's latitude, longitude, depth or elevation, and... time?"

"You've got to stop watching time-travel stuff."

Jared chuckled. "Doesn't have to be time as a dimension. Could be an RV."

"Whatever. Hey, this is a good brew." Chris held up his bottle in respect. "I could smell the malt from the Kill Line brewery this morning."

"We should organise a joint beer festival. Try to get some social interaction going. We've got too many single guys here."

"You running a lonely hearts' club now?"

"Single guys are potential trouble when they outnumber women. Rivalry, fighting, tension. You know it's true."

"We haven't had any trouble so far," Chris said. "We don't mix, they don't mix, Ainatio doesn't mix. We're the wrong kind of people for each other. We don't even see them for days or weeks on end."

Jared raised an eyebrow. "But they treat the townsfolk in their hospital."

"A colonoscopy isn't the same as inviting the guys around for a few tins."

"Did you ask Trinder if they had any spare ammo? Seeing as you're best buds now."

"I'm saving that for the next date."

"We need to go procuring again."

It was always a toss-up between relying on the ammunition they'd stockpiled and conserving it, or going out to find more and risking expending a lot of it if they ran into trouble. Chris decided to err on the side of risk this time.

"What's left around here that we haven't searched?" he asked.

"Nothing in a twenty-mile radius. Time to spread the net."

"Okay, we'll look west. Kingston, maybe." Chris mopped up the last of the sauce with the final chunk of potato. Judging the bite sizes to achieve perfect and total use of both always made him feel better. "Y'know, if I was Trinder, I'd make damn sure I knew who everybody was and where they were. And I wouldn't have let us in."

Jared started laughing again. "Yeah, you're drunk. You always get hyper-responsible when you're wasted. You know how many times we've had this conversation?"

"It bothers me."

"It shouldn't. It's not like they've been through what we have. Why are you suddenly worried? Nothing's changed since the day we got here."

"I never got this close to getting in there before."

Chris had filed Ainatio under situational awareness. Even if he didn't know what Ainatio got up to or who was in there, it was a significant target that had to figure in his threat assessment. If it had some strategic value, someone might try to destroy it. If it was storing food and supplies, survivors might storm it. Maybe that was all he needed to know, but he still had too many questions.

"Chris, if we were getting paid, this would be above our pay grade," Jared said. "Watch the movie and relax. It's an alien invasion. You like those."

Chris enjoyed doomsday movies as long as they were so dumb that they were funny. If they were too accurate, he might as well have been back in Baltimore, fighting for real. This one looked like it was going to pass the stupidity test and take his mind off Dr Kim's code for a while, but his nagging curiosity drifted back during a boring scene.

Maybe...

Maybe the code really was just a set of numbers that only Kim would know, and Ainatio had been waiting for her to show up and identify herself. Doug had said that new personnel had sometimes been shuttled in. That would mean Kim was a defector, though, and that opened a whole new can of worms. Chris made an effort to stop thinking about it.

"Are you watching this or not?" Jared asked.

"Kind of."

"I'll be testing you on it later."

"Okay, why do the aliens always travel halfway across the galaxy to fight us for our water? They're advanced enough to travel faster than light, but they can't find a source closer to home? A frozen, empty planet? Asteroids?"

"You're not getting into the spirit of this, Chris. I can see that."

Jared could always say it with the straight face and sombre tone of a preacher. The act lasted about ten seconds. Then he burst out laughing again and Chris couldn't avoid joining in.

It was a very dumb movie doing what movies were meant to do, erasing the real world for a while. Even guessing how it would end wasn't important. It was sitting there and laughing at it with a buddy that mattered.

Chris stood up as the credits rolled and stretched his arms. "I better walk the course." He picked up his rifle. "Beer's no excuse."

"Yeah, Marsha's going to wonder where I am. See you in the morning."

They left the lights dimmed and the stove stoked for the duty guard. Chris needed to walk around the camp once every night before he could sleep, even when he wasn't on duty. He was the one who'd brought them all here: he was responsible for their safety. And it reassured him to see the lights in the windows and hear the sounds of people getting on with their lives — water running down a drainpipe, the faint sound of music, the distant thud of a door being shut. It told him that he'd done the right thing in the end, and that if the situation ever improved, this community could grow, not die off quietly in some desperate, shattered city like so many others had.

And what happens if and when the die-back reaches us?

He had a plan. He always did. They'd have to go back to the original objective and head for the coast.

And what then? Can't run forever.

Chris ambled around the boundary, shining his flashlight into the undergrowth. It lit up the eyes of a fox that looked right at him before trotting away, completely unconcerned.

Outside the Marrs' place, their teenage son was sitting on the front step with his telescope aimed at the sky again. Nathan loved astronomy. Chris wasn't sure how much use a small handheld telescope was for stargazing, but it seemed to keep the kid happy, and that was something. There wasn't much to do around here for a fifteen-year-old boy who didn't like the outdoors.

"Hey Nathan." Chris stopped to chat. "Good clear sky tonight, huh?"

Nathan was at that awkward, uncommunicative stage. "Yeah. Really good visibility."

"Anything interesting?"

"Jupiter's clear." Nathan handed the telescope to Chris and pointed up. "Uh... you know that list of numbers that you've been showing people?"

"Yeah?"

"It's galactic and equatorial co-ordinates. The position of a star."

"Oh." Well, that explained the request for an astrophysicist. *I should have guessed.* "Thanks."

"You never seen that?"

"No. I never think about space." Chris put the telescope to his eye to find Jupiter again. Constellations were for last-resort navigation when he didn't have a compass, or just for admiring on a balmy night, which this definitely wasn't. He couldn't remember how old he'd been when he'd stopped seeing space as an exciting place to go in a future that every kid assumed would happen. "Which star is it?"

"Not a major one. Pascoe's Star." Nathan managed to sound casual, but Chris guessed that he was trying not to overreact to unexpected attention about his hobby. "I don't think it's above the horizon yet."

"Makes a good password."

"Yeah. Nearly impossible to guess. Even if you know that someone uses positions as passwords, you'd still have to work through thousands of stars to find the right one. Well, millions, actually. And somebody would catch you long before then."

Chris handed back the telescope. The kid showed Chris a chart full of numbers on his screen, probably the first time he'd had the opportunity to tell an adult something important. Chris had to run his fingertip along the lines of text to follow it and it still meant nothing. But all he needed to know was that it was a map reference.

"Well done," Chris said. "If I'm ever stuck on another question, I'll ask you first. Don't freeze out here, okay?"

Nathan gave him an awkward grin. "Sure."

Chris carried on walking. The co-ordinates made sense. As Nathan had pointed out, it was a great password generator, but while it answered one question, it just made another one more puzzling. If Kim was a defector, what did she have that was so important to Ainatio that they'd let her in?

He paused by the garbage pit to have a smoke and look back at the neat lines of camp lights strung between the cabins, his daily reassurance that they were still a civilisation.

Maybe Kim knew how to reverse the die-back, and for whatever political reason, APS hadn't wanted to share it with the West.

No, that didn't make sense. She was a physicist, and if APS wanted to destroy what was left of America, they wouldn't have given advance warning and time to evacuate. Chris knew that they had. He'd been there on the ground, listening to the voice traffic and watching the clock, trying to hurry straggling civilians onto buses and telling them to forget about packing stuff they'd never need. Actually, it was *always* stuff they needed. Everyone knew what mattered to them, however dumb and useless it looked to others. It was about what those objects represented, not their usefulness.

He dismissed the saviour theory. Kim hadn't struggled all this way with some miracle cure against the wishes of any government. He placed his bet back on spying. And there was always the possibility that she wasn't spying for APS, but for Ainatio, and had finally escaped from behind enemy lines.

Actually, that wasn't a bad idea. What were they doing behind those walls that needed so much secrecy when the world around them was dead or dying? Chris let the thought rattle around his head as he continued walking the border of his small, accidental kingdom.

* * *

AINATIO PARK RESEARCH CENTRE, STAFF RESTAURANT B: 0900, SATURDAY, FEBRUARY 21

Erskine knew this was the wrong time of day to resume the conversation with Annis Kim. On a weekday it would have been routine, but on a Saturday it would look like she was panicking. If Kim knew less than she appeared to, it'd confirm that her fishing expedition had gotten a bite.

Kim would have to wait, then. Besides, Erskine had someone else to see first. She killed time buttering her toast with slow deliberation and looked at Berman pointedly.

"You told me Marc Gallagher always comes in here after his squash game," she said.

Berman just stared back at her, expressionless. "I've collated his tracker data. You could set your watch by him. And if he doesn't show, it's not as if he can disappear."

"Phil, I don't enjoy these theatrics any more than you do, but I can't be seen to deliberately bypass Trinder."

Marc wasn't chipped like Ainatio staff. Erskine wondered if he'd just slipped his long-standing temporary card into someone else's pocket to cover his tracks, then remembered the security cameras in the recreation wing. Her default was suspicion. She wanted to blame her father, but her common sense said those tendencies were born, not created in adult life.

"I have to talk to him before I go back to Kim."

"I realise that." Berman cleared his plate and went to put it on the trolley, but a bot rolled up to take it from his hand. It was one of the earliest models, a box on wheels. Berman addressed it like a disapproving parent. "One day I'm not going to let go, just to see what you do."

"Don't be surprised if one of them slugs you," Erskine said.

"I'd better be off, then, Director. Good luck."

Berman left her to it. She carried on toying with the toast, reading the overnight messages on her screen. Solomon had filed a contact report about the nocturnal wildlife that he'd encountered on Opis, using an odd mix of scientific detachment and the slightly excited wish-you-were-here tone of a tourist messaging home. Sometimes she tried to imagine how his consciousness handled being aware of everything that was happening without being mired in trivial detail, but he latched onto priorities like someone hearing their name in the murmur of a conversation that they weren't consciously listening to. The more she learned about AI theory, the less she understood Solomon.

Sometimes the AI seemed like a paralysed man trapped in his interface rather than an entity with extraordinary freedom of access and control of every system. In that light, his enthusiasm for the more limited powers of the quadrubot made more sense. He was willing to forgo omnipotence and omnipresence to be able to touch the world.

And I can't keep many secrets from him, if any. Does he judge me? He certainly judges others.

A movement caught her eye. Her subconscious was scanning for targets without thinking. Marc Gallagher was now standing at the counter, studying the hot dishes, one of those men she would always treat with caution: late forties, lean, hair razored just long enough to reveal that it was mid-brown, with an air of physical certainty that always made him look like he was ready to tackle a threat she couldn't see.

Okay, give him a moment, then take my plate back for a refill.

Erskine stood up. The serving bot rumbled back to assist her but she waved it away. Sometimes she regretted the decision not to employ Kill Line people in here. It was good security to have as few outsiders in contact with the staff as possible, but that policy hadn't been designed for a world that was running out of people. Opis would need more colonists. There was only one source left now.

"Morning, Director." Marc studied the scrambled eggs. "Any more incidents?"

He was unfailingly courteous, but he always gave the impression that he couldn't see why she was relevant to his existence. Perhaps she wasn't. But he was relevant to hers.

"What do you make of it, then?" she asked.

"Dr Kim, you mean?"

"Yes. Until I get some sense out of her, I have to assume she's an APS spy."

"Well, spies aren't supposed to tell you where they come from, but it's always possible that's exactly why she did."

"No disrespect to Trinder and his troops, but they've never gone up against state actors. You used to protect critical infrastructure, I believe. I'm trying to assess the threat."

"Yeah, our job was stopping bad guys attacking strategic targets. Power stations, oil rigs, nukes, that kind of thing. Which, to be fair, is the same as your lads are trained for, except we tend to have a higher body count at the end of the day." Marc seemed to have made his choice. He picked out the most overcooked bacon to top his eggs. "But my first question would be what you've got — or what you've done — that APS want to know about. If someone's spying, they either want to take something or stop something."

It was inevitable that he'd ask her the very question she didn't dare answer, but if he hadn't been smart then she wouldn't have asked for his advice. Now the lying started in earnest.

"I'm trying to find out what they *think* we've got," Erskine said. "Or done."

"It's perception that matters. No joy from Kim, then."

"I'm taking another crack at her later."

"Well, your biggest threat is the one they've already demonstrated. If they think that die-back's still a risk to them, they'll nuke you again. But they could suspect you of anything if they're worried enough." He followed her back to the table. "Okay, look at it from the other end of the telescope. What could they take out that would shut you down? What's critical for *you*? We did the assessment with your guys when we came here. Apart from this facility, if you lose the town and farmland, you might just about survive for a while on your own hydroponics, if you step it up. And that yeast stuff as long as you've got sugar to feed it. So what about the orbitals?"

Lie. "If APS targets those, we lose the labs."

"I don't think you've got labs up there. Not these days, anyway."

And I thought I was such a good poker player. Or maybe it's just logical and he's shaking me down because he's exactly like me.

"Do we need to go into that?"

Marc carried on eating. "Just nod and I'll work it out for myself. Whatever you're doing, I hope you've got some defensive capability. I know weapons are banned, but we're not stupid, are we? Close-quarters battle isn't much fun on a space station. Shooting holes in bulkheads is a bit more serious in a vacuum. Then there's the low-gravity areas."

"I think APS would have made a move by now."

"So how about the ships you've got alongside?"

"What?"

"Don't forget that me and Tev go back to the days when our special forces worked alongside yours. The UK had space assets too." Marc gestured with a piece of near-cremated bacon. "So whatever you're really maintaining them for is your weak point. Unless, of course, you're just worried about thousands of tons of burning metal landing on Earth in inconvenient places."

Erskine was struck silent for a moment. She'd never asked what the two Brits knew. They probably wouldn't have told her anyway. For the first time, it occurred to her that they might know a great deal more, and that was why they were still here.

"Well, the ships are our last resort if the die-back spreads," she said, trying to recover. She wasn't used to being outmanoeuvred, but maybe it wasn't tactical questioning at all. Perhaps Marc just avoided discussing confidential information until he had to. "Losing them would be significant."

"Okay, you should be able to narrow down what's got their attention. Let's hope they don't think you're working on something as bad as die-back that could escape into the wild. Because that means they'll finish what they started."

Erskine could only shrug. It was genuine: Kim made no sense — yet. But she couldn't be sure what Kim had said to Trinder, and what Trinder might have shared with Marc. Another drop of truth was needed to smooth the passage of the lies.

"Well, her story so far is that we stole research from her grandma."

"Long way to come to demand compensation." Marc cleared his plate and rearranged his knife and fork neatly at least three times. He obviously wanted to leave. "Are you going to tell me what she's asked for?"

"So far, nothing specific. But I can't let her go now, just in case."

"Spies need a way to report back to their handlers. If this really is espionage, she'll have set up a route out, either via comms or an actual exfil. If it's sabotage, though, she might be ready to pull the pin here and die for the republic."

"That did cross my mind."

"So is there anything more I can help you with?"

"No. You've been helpful in focusing my thoughts. Thank you."

"I'd appreciate a heads-up if the shit really is about to hit the fan. Arrangements to make."

"I realise you and Tev must have family back in Britain."

"I *had* one. Both my lads were killed fighting in Greece."

"Oh. I'm so sorry." Erskine had no idea what to say to him. "When did..."

"Eight years, three months, and one day ago, and eight years, three months, and five days."

Everything she needed to know about Marc Gallagher was in that sentence. The conversation was definitely over. He nodded politely and left. A bot inched in to remove the plates.

"Poor man. I can't imagine what he went through." Solomon's voice was a whisper in her earpiece. "That explains a great deal."

Erskine couldn't afford to feel sorry for long. "We still need him and his colleague."

"Because you fear what might happen once news about *Cabot* gets out?"

Erskine couldn't discuss it with people around. Solomon knew that. But she let the question ride, conscious that mistrust was getting the better of her today, the price of staying up late to war-game the Kim situation. She just didn't have the staying power at seventy.

"Later," she said. "I'm off to talk to our guest."

Solomon would follow her anyway, walking through the virtual passages of the security network. Erskine tapped her collar link and called the physician.

"Did Kim have a comfortable night, Doctor?"

"The infection's responding. She'll need to stay on the anthelmintic for a few days, and supplements for the anaemia in the longer term, but she's eating like a horse. I don't think there's much to worry about."

"Good." Erskine wondered when the pharmacy had last needed to synthesise worming pills for human use. "I'll be dropping in soon."

Ten minutes was a long enough walk to think over what Marc Gallagher had said. It was what APS *thought* Ainatio had done that mattered, and she could understand their potential grievances. She could also understand that there was no international legal structure or anything else now that could stop them doing whatever they liked to show their disapproval. What *hadn't* Ainatio done? Which treaties and laws hadn't it broken? *Cabot* shouldn't have been sent on a mission to a new world that hadn't been approved by international agreement, it shouldn't have had plans to introduce non-native plant and animal species, the ship shouldn't have been armed — certainly not with nuclear weapons — and the company shouldn't have developed untested plant strains in a biologically compromised zone.

And it definitely shouldn't have had autonomous weapons like Solomon. Sociable and sensitive as he was, he was also capable of destroying a threat when he saw fit, and he had access to every weapons system between here and Pascoe.

And now we have Kim turn up. Coincidence my ass.

But I'm going around in circles. Stop it, right now.

When Erskine reached the infirmary, there was no sign of the staff, but she could hear activity further along the corridor. She was used to getting instant attention. It was her own fault, she knew, because she hadn't told them that she was on her way, but it irritated her for no logical reason.

One of the nurses came around the corner at a race-walking pace, looking flustered. He hesitated when he saw her but only slowed down rather than stopped.

"I'm sorry, Director, I'll be with you in a moment," he said. "Mr Levine's had another CVA. Dr Mendoza's with him now."

Poor old Levine had gone downhill fast, but if Erskine had a choice, she'd opt for that rather than a slow decline with her mind fragmenting. She instantly calculated how much older than her Levine was, a compulsion she had every time a colleague died or came close to it. He was eighty-something. She still had time on her side.

"It's all right," she said. "I can show myself into Dr Kim's room. Would you keep me informed about Mr Levine's condition, please?"

"Certainly, Director."

Erskine knew Solomon would keep her updated even if the infirmary didn't. It was a damned shame that

Levine might die before he found out that the mission he'd worked on for so long, and thought he'd seen fail, was months away from making history. For a moment she felt desperately sad about that, but she had to focus on the risk that Kim might present. She couldn't afford to make the wrong call now. She tapped on her door and walked in without waiting for a response.

Kim was sitting up in bed, devouring an apple as if it was the first she'd ever tasted.

"Good morning, Dr Kim. You look a lot better today."

"Food and warmth works wonders."

Erskine drew up a chair. "Let's see, where did we get to last night? You mentioned your great-grandmother's research. That's long before my time, so I checked the company records, or at least our AI did."

"And you're going to tell me you found nothing," Kim said.

"Correct. If your story's true, I wouldn't have expected details of industrial espionage to be minuted, but then I also wouldn't have expected to find anything if you were lying. So we're no further forward. How about telling me what you want? Because right now, my best guess is that you're spying for APS. Although I can't imagine what Asia wants from us, given the shape we're in."

Kim looked at her, unmoved. "My great-grandmother's research on superluminal propulsion was stolen by Tadeusz Bednarz," Kim said at last. "By stolen, I mean copied and used by Ainatio as its own intellectual property, except there was no attempt to pass this off in public, because it was a secret project."

That could well have been true. There was an FTL relay out there right now that proved someone had worked out something, although it was for an artificial wormhole, not a ship's drive. But Erskine had more pressing questions.

"So you want compensation?" Erskine asked. "How would that happen? The US banking system's collapsed.

Our assets are what you see around you. We couldn't pay even if we wanted to. And if we *didn't* want to, how would you take us to court? How would that even begin to work when there's no functioning state here, let alone a national government?" She paused a beat, not for effect but because a better idea had occurred to her. "And why did you come all this way to tell me this? Why not lodge a complaint with your government? You're not some factory worker. You're a physicist. And I imagine you've got documentation somewhere that supports your claim. They'd listen. Industrial espionage affects the state."

Kim said nothing. Erskine got up slowly and poured herself a glass of water from the carafe on the side table to give Kim time to chew that over.

"I do have documentation," Kim said. "I uploaded it. I can't access it without a screen, though, and I had to trade mine for food."

That sounded like a weakening argument. Erskine dived in. "I think you didn't involve your government because this is all garbage. Or because they sent you to find out something, like whether we're any closer to a countermeasure for die-back. I know we're hard to reach, but they could have asked."

"Would I tell you where I came from if I was a spy? I could have just told you I was Australian and you'd have been none the wiser. But I've been open about everything."

"Spies do that, too. So... I can get a message out through a neutral intermediary like the Russians and ask your government to collect you. Or I can just have you shot, because you're a spy, and you're the enemy, even if we're in ungoverned territory."

Erskine sat down again and sipped the water. Kim was still expressionless. There wasn't a hint of movement in her face, not the slightest twitch of a muscle, and with so little fat left on her, Erskine would have seen her jaw muscles move. But Kim didn't even blink. She was cornered now: she was either a spy who'd failed, with all the consequences that would follow when she got home, or she really was the avenging granddaughter she said she was, and had illegally crossed APS's closed border. Going back wasn't an easy option either way. Erskine waited, expecting that realisation to wear down Kim's resolve.

"Well, I'd probably have to come clean with them, then," Kim said. "I'd have to tell my government that I pursued Ainatio because you'd taken Grandma Park's research and sent a manned mission out of the solar system. I'm guessing that's what happened to your original ship, yes?"

Erskine could handle this. It was an inspired guess. Propulsion was Kim's specialty, after all, and she probably assumed a drive derived from her relative's research had malfunctioned and destroyed *Cabot*. But then the questions began bubbling up again. Why now, in this very narrow and significant window of time? Erskine decided to flush her out.

"So you think we built a drive based on your great-grandma's research, bolted it onto *Cabot,* and it blew up."

"I did think that. But back in the lab, I started seeing a lot more activity last year around your orbital, so I wondered if I'd had all the pieces of the puzzle all along."

Damn. "Meaning?"

"I knew Ainatio was interested in Pascoe's Star rather than anything closer with planets that needed a makeover. Bednarz wanted a second Earth."

"Everyone does."

"No, he used to talk about the best extrasolar candidates for habitation with a guy at the University of Sydney, Paul Nguyen. And if *Cabot* was heading there with conventional propulsion, the transit time would be about forty-five years. Which made me ask what your orbitals were doing. Like maybe preparing for follow-up missions.

Although I also wondered about the timing, because you wouldn't have had confirmation of a landing yet. That'd be another forty years, right?"

Erskine thought her heart had taken its last beat. The seconds ticked by so slowly that she was sure she floundered in silence for minutes. Solomon's voice whispered in her earpiece.

"Oh dear, that's true," he said. "He did indeed. Private correspondence, but Dr Kim seems to have access to it."

For a moment, Erskine couldn't form words. All she could see was the orbitals being boarded, the FTL link with Opis and *Cabot* being compromised, and APS seizing control. She could feel her voice stalling in her throat.

"That's stretching guesswork to the limit," she said. "But I still don't see how your various theories fit together."

"Well, there's always a chance you'll have me shot if I tell you, but as I'm a propulsion expert, I think I'm more use to you alive," Kim said. "You really needed my great-grandmother's research to establish a foothold on Opis, and you had forty-five years to crack it. But I don't think you have, not yet."

It was all slotting together in an awful, inexorable way. Damn. *Damn.* Kim had put it together the wrong way around, but she knew exactly where Bednarz wanted to go, and she'd worked out the rest simply from the personal correspondence of a dead Australian academic.

Or she's a very, very inspired guesser. A brilliant con woman who can read reactions and fill in the gaps like a fake medium.

Erskine couldn't afford to lose her nerve now. She still didn't know where Kim was going with this, but she sure as hell wasn't going to cave in and admit it was all true. Everything, absolutely every asset that Ainatio possessed, had been sacrificed for Nomad: Mars projects cancelled, all other company sites shut down and consolidated, and all research terminated, except what was needed to build, supply, and fly ships to establish a viable human colony on Opis. Everyone — Ainatio, Kill Line, herself — had served one purpose, the settlement of that planet.

"Fascinating," Erskine said. "No, really, it is."

"You asked me what I wanted." Kim carried on as if this was a job interview for a post she was totally confident of getting. "Well, I want to stay. I want to work on the next mission to Pascoe's Star with your team, develop a functioning FTL drive, and for my great-grandmother's contribution to be acknowledged. Do we have a deal?"

"*Director...*" Solomon whispered, but Erskine ignored him. This cocky little madam would get the shock of her life if — or when — she realised just how far Ainatio had gone.

Erskine now had two options. She could order Trinder to shoot Kim, because these were lawless times and nobody would care what had happened to her. Or Erskine could turn this around by getting some use out of the woman.

And I can still dispose of her any time we need to.

"Let's talk," Erskine said.

* * *

DIRECTOR'S SUITE, AINATIO PARK RESEARCH CENTRE: 1130, FEBRUARY 21

"Okay, it's feasible that Kim worked it out the way she claims," Alex said. "The question isn't how she got here, but what APS might do if they know what *she* knows."

Nomad was now either compromised or it wasn't, and if it was, there was little that he or anyone else could do about it. APS couldn't do much about *Cabot*, either, not for another forty-odd years at the earliest, and by that time the colony would either be strong enough to defend itself or everyone could be dead.

The vulnerable element was right here, in Earth orbit.

Alex sat on the broad arm of Erskine's black leather sofa, careless informality that normally earned him a disapproving glance, but she was too preoccupied today.

"Those ships have been docked at the orbitals or in disposal orbits for at least thirty years," she said. "If APS realises they're not just mothballed and knows what we're going to do, they're more than capable of commandeering them."

"But they won't destroy anything. They're pragmatic. They'll want a deal."

"Not if they think the vessels are substantially armed and we've broken treaties. We're a threat and they'll deal with us. End of Nomad."

"End of *part* of Nomad."

"We can't build new ships. So we can't ship out colonists."

"But we'll have a couple of hundred service personnel and assorted civilian techs already on Opis, all healthy and intelligent, and mostly of childbearing age."

"That wasn't the plan."

"The plan had to change a long time ago, Director. It's changing every day."

"Colonies need farmers, builders, teachers, mechanics. They happen to be here."

Alex pointed down at the carpet. "A lot of exploration and colonisation on *this* planet was done by ship's crews who were stranded and had to make the best of it. Unless anything catastrophic happens, *Cabot* will be there, the crew will be on the ground, and they'll be self-sufficient until further notice."

Erskine had a point about APS's likely reaction if they knew *Elcano*, *Shackleton*, *Eriksson*, and *Da Gama* were armed. All the niceties about Ainatio not actually being the USA and therefore not a signatory to the no-arms agreement wouldn't make any difference.

"Are we sure we didn't have any leaks?" Alex asked. "You did lose a lot of staff after *Cabot* launched. It wasn't all down to plagues and unrest, was it?"

"Yes, we had a brain drain, but none of them realised what they were working towards. No more than the teams do now, in fact. It was a simulation to them. When they got the chance to work with Martian projects, they jumped at it because they knew the bases were real. They thought our extrasolar work wasn't."

"Sure?"

"If they'd worked it out and told their new bosses, we'd have seen the consequences of that by now."

Alex tried again. "Then we're back to what's useful for Asia, and China in particular. I know Trinder always goes on about capability being more important than intent, but I think intent matters here. The Chinese won't trash what they don't have to."

"They bombed this country."

"Yeah, and *we* destroyed millions of acres for the same reason. They even gave us time for orderly evacuation. I'm not making excuses for them, just saying that they're focused on Mars because that's doable *now*. Maybe they won't care if we send more ships after *Cabot* as long as we're not on their turf. Like the lighthuggers. They didn't see them as a threat either. Just lunatics they were happy to see the back of."

Erskine did that slow head shake. "And you think they'll dismiss us as harmless nut-jobs as well? Superluminal propulsion's going to get their attention pretty damn fast. It's their technology."

"True. But *we* made it work." Alex realised he was trying to reassure himself. He hadn't succeeded. "So do we take a chance with Kim and accept she's on the run?"

"Whether we believe her or not, we haven't been able to hire anyone new for ten years. It might be handy to have someone with more current knowledge."

"We don't need more boffins, though. We need more families. Colonists." The research centre wasn't just a community. It had become its own education system as well. There were second-generation scientists who'd been born and educated here, and now their children were being trained. "Okay, she's of childbearing age, but do you really want to consider her for Opis? And is it worth the hassle of integrating her professionally when we'll be launching the follow-up mission pretty soon?"

"We don't know what she knows."

"We don't know what she'll be willing to share with us, either."

"Get Dr Prinz to check out her professional ability with Solomon. Set her some problems to solve. If she's what she says she is, we can get her working on the existing drives. Keep the FTL research as her reward for doing the less glamorous work on the ships we already have."

"I suppose handing her back to her embassy is out of the question now."

"Yes. It is. If they don't already know she's here, then she's the perfect excuse for them to stick their noses in." Erskine looked weary and disappointed, as if Alex had failed her. "We've got thirty troops and a few nuclear missiles. We couldn't repel their table tennis team."

"So we're relying on staying hidden and hoping nobody notices us." Alex felt that they'd talked out their panic and were back to the status quo, which had served them remarkably well so far. "And if they do notice us, it'll be hard for them to walk in here and make things work without us."

Erskine looked at him for a moment as if a better idea had struck her. "We could revive the crew early and get them prepared. We need to brief them while we're sure we still have control of the mission."

"Could do. There's a good margin of error on supplies."

"It's going to be a lot for them to take in."

Alex couldn't see how the APS angle would make the news any more shocking for them than it already was. "They'll cope. They're ex-military. They're not bed-wetting civilians. I include myself in the bed-wetting demographic, by the way."

"Let's do the numbers on that and pencil in a date for revival, then."

For a moment, Alex felt as if he'd walked into the room for the first time and noticed a stranger. Erskine suddenly looked older than the everyday image in his mind, the one modified by familiarity and a side order of inexplicable fear. Maybe it was the lighting, but he hadn't noticed the progress of age before, the veins in the backs of her hands, the faded limbal rings of her eyes, and more of a stoop these days. Seventy wasn't ancient, but she was fond of wearing those tailored suits by some long-dead European designer, and that meant she kept herself thin. Alex could hear his mother telling him that a woman could either keep her figure or her face as she aged, but not both.

And Mom's gone. Never got to say goodbye. I had to be at work.

"Well, at least we don't have to turn down thousands of applicants for places on the mission," Erskine said, closing her eyes as she ran her middle finger around the edges of the sockets. She blinked a few times. "Plenty of berths now."

"You're counting on everyone in Kill Line wanting to go."

"Barring a late breakthrough, they'll have to live with the risk of die-back getting here if they don't. But there'll be ample time for them to adjust while we ready the ships."

"Have you thought about the transit camp again? You know, ages, gene pool, frontier skills."

"I have. And they don't fit the plan."

It was a weird way to put it. Alex chewed that over. The vets and refugees were just distant figures he'd sometimes see if he was monitoring the drones, which wasn't often. Once in a blue moon he'd drive out to talk to the mayor of Kill Line and he'd see one of the armed vets out on an AT bike, but they never came close enough for him to even speak to them. They did, however, seem like the kind of guys the company would need on Opis. They were survivors.

"I think that's a missed opportunity, Director," he said. "But it's your call."

He left with the intention of going straight to Vicky Prinz's office and discussing how they'd test Kim's expertise, but he took the roundabout route to give himself some thinking time. With the exception of *Cabot* and Nomad Base itself, global circumstances had trashed the rest of the plan in the intervening years. Realists were concentrating on Mars, with maybe a few unmanned extrasolar missions to build expertise. But out-of-control geniuses skipped Mars, ignored red dwarves with less ideal planets a lot closer to home, mocked generation lighthuggers, and went all out for somewhere perfect but much further away for their first shot at colonising the galaxy.

Because Opis is most like Earth. Not much remodelling required. But Bednarz wasn't a hundred per cent sure of that, was he? It was likely, not guaranteed. We know now, but he couldn't have known for sure then.

Yeah, Bednarz, you were a frigging lunatic. Just like the lighthuggers. Yet here we are. We all bought into it.

All that was left of Ainatio was this small core. The geneticists kept reassuring Alex that the gene pool was still varied enough to support a colony, but he would have felt a lot more confident right then if he could have guaranteed that the Kill Line townsfolk were added to the mix. Instead, he'd have to deal with two communities who still had no idea they were soon going to be offered a ticket to a very distant world, and none of them had signed up to be spacefarers.

Well, shit...

He went into the nearest bathroom and ran cold water into the basin to rinse his face. There were so few staff in a complex designed for thousands that he could almost guarantee he'd have a bathroom to himself, no matter which one he happened to walk into. As he wiped his hands and checked his beard in the mirror, he noticed grey hairs among the ginger. They were new.

We're all running out of time. Even me.

Alex had moments when he realised he'd gone from apex predator to an endangered species in one generation, just like Rome but with nobody left to look back and admire those terrific roads and aqueducts. This was one such moment.

"Hi guys," he said to his reflection. This was how he usually rehearsed his opening conversation with *Cabot*. "You're now approaching Opis. While you were sleeping, the epidemics got worse and killed hundreds of millions, a bioweapon wiped out most of our food crops, APS nuked us, and by the way, everyone thinks you died forty-five years ago. And we're down to a skeleton staff, we rely on AIs to do all the heavy lifting, and we might have to bring a bunch of rubes with us to make up the numbers and stop us inbreeding ourselves into one-eyed droolers. So, how was your day?"

Dragging out each painful revelation would only make it worse. He'd find a more diplomatic way of covering the talking points, though.

"Solomon," he said, "you really don't listen in bathrooms, do you?"

There was no response. Sol had set his own boundaries, despite his ability to take over the entire operation if he felt like it. Alex thought again about what Trinder had said about foreign policy, that it wasn't a nation's intent that counted when assessing threats but its military capability. Intent changed. Allies could become enemies at the drop of a hat.

No, Solomon was almost human, but he wasn't subject to human whims. If he made a promise, Alex could take it to the bank. Whether the AI swore he'd stay away from the bathrooms, or get everyone safely to Opis, he'd keep his word.

"Good man," Alex said, and went on his way.

04

Land, water, fuel, ammo, transport, dogs. That's all
it takes to survive. But you need people and ideas
worth defending if you want to rebuild a society.

Corporal Jared Talbot, formerly Fourth
Eastern Division State Defence

FIBUA FACILITY, AINATIO PARK RESEARCH CENTRE:
FIRST WEEK IN MARCH

The round struck Trinder near the top of his spine, and it
hurt like hell.

It was his own fault. He'd paused too long at the corner
of the passageway, giving Orange Force — Schwaiger,
probably — time to sight up. If the round hadn't been
simunition, his armour probably wouldn't have saved him.

He shouldn't even have been thinking that it wasn't real.
He should have been immersed, sufficiently convinced for
a moment to treat it like a live round. But he couldn't focus
today. He could only dwell on his shortcomings, all the
experience he lacked and that no amount of training could
replace. Just thinking like that seemed to prove his point.

We've got the SAS, and now we've got the guys who
fought their way *out of Baltimore. And then there's me.*

Get a grip. The detachment needs you to be better
than this.

There were still three Orange targets left standing,
maybe four. Trinder backed into a doorway and returned

fire blindly. But whoever had caught him had moved on. He was left with a throbbing pain across his shoulders and a sense of failure.

Shots were still echoing up the passage to his right. He edged to the corner again and poked a cam around, but the ceiling lights began flashing in a slow rhythm and the firing stopped. It was the signal to suspend the exercise while someone entered or left the area.

"What is it, Sol?"

"My apologies, Major, but Erskine wants to see you."

"Now?"

"Right away."

Trinder could feel the sweat trickling down his spine. "Can I clean up first?"

"She did say now."

"Okay." He opened the squad link. "Commander exiting the area. Fonseca, you have command, out."

The safety bulkhead parted to let him pass. The walls had been moved to create a custom layout for the simulated clearing operation, and it took him a couple of seconds to orient himself. Damn, he really didn't have his head in the game today. He removed his helmet and set off at a jog towards the management wing, irritable and sweaty, hoping that Erskine would keep things short.

"Am I in the shit, Sol?" he asked.

"I don't think so."

"I can't remember the last time she spoke to me."

"I can."

"Is it a delayed ass-kicking about Dr Kim?"

"Not as far as I know."

The detachment was near the bottom of the food chain, and the highest level that Trinder scaled was departmental meetings with the facilities manager. A private meeting with the Director was unheard of.

Berman, her bagman, looked him over. "It's okay, you probably won't need the armour," he said.

"We were training. I was told it was urgent."

"Do go in. She's waiting."

Trinder rapped on the door and walked in to find Erskine at her desk. She gestured to one of the leather chairs.

"Take a seat, Major. Thank you for coming so quickly." She sounded as if she was trying to put him at ease before delivering bad news. "What I'm about to tell you is in the strictest confidence for the time being."

"I assumed it would be, ma'am."

Erskine was the empress of this closed world. Trinder had only seen in her full regal mode, sweeping into meetings or dining in the staff restaurant with an unmarked but very visible exclusion zone around her. Now she looked almost apologetic.

"It's about *Cabot*," she said. "You remember the ship was lost."

Trinder couldn't guess what this was about, but at least that hadn't happened on his watch. He hadn't even been born. "Before my time, ma'am. But I've heard of it."

"Well, that was just a cover story. Right now, *Cabot* is on course for a planet called Opis, and the crew are going to be revived shortly."

"Oh. Really?"

This wasn't what Trinder had expected at all. As news went, it was a shock to realise Ainatio still had live missions running, but it was also history. Perhaps it explained what Kim was doing here, though.

Maybe she's our *spy, then. Not theirs.*

"You don't seem shocked," Erskine said.

"I am, ma'am, but I don't really understand the context."

"You will. The mission's code-named Nomad, and it's going to take over our lives here very soon."

Trinder wanted to tell her to spit it out, but after a slow start, his mind had started to pick up speed and now it was racing ahead. Shit, was this all going public? How?

"Who else knows, ma'am?"

"At the moment, just a dozen people."

"Is there a reason why you're briefing me before the scientific staff?"

"It's going to be a big shock for them. I don't know how people will react."

"Oh. Public order. Understood." Trinder couldn't imagine the folks here rioting over it. It might even boost morale. "What do I need to know?"

"*Cabot*'s close to Pascoe's Star, which is forty light years away, and we've been building a base on Opis." Erskine frowned as if she couldn't think how to explain it. "Perhaps I've gone about this the wrong way. See for yourself."

She picked up a handset and swivelled her chair around as the wall behind her peeled back into a screen. Trinder stared at the sunny landscape for a long time. He couldn't tell where it was, only that the colour of the sky said it wasn't Mars, despite the print-built domes and the construction bots moving around. It could have been one of the simulated Martian habitats built on Earth to train astronauts. But a moon gave the game away, low in the sky and streaked with bands like a gas planet.

This wasn't Earth, either.

"Oh." Now he couldn't take his eyes off it. "Is that it?"

"Nomad Base," Erskine said. Her voice had dropped a pitch. She sounded like it was a relief to get it off her chest. "And that's in real time. Only a handful of people here have ever seen this."

Trinder wondered if he'd misunderstood. He had a torrent of questions, but he couldn't corral them into any kind of order.

"How?" he asked. "The signal should take forty years. Or is that an old transmission that's only just reached us?"

Erskine pushed her chair further back and sat watching, arms folded, half-smiling, occasionally doing a little shake of her head as if she was still amazed by it all.

"No, I said *real time*. Continuous live transmission. And we can do it because we developed a wormhole."

"That's supposed to be impossible."

"No, just damned hard. We could only send very small payloads, but it meant we could put a comms relay in place to work with the conventional cargos we'd already launched. We landed self-replicating bots on Opis to build the base, and the wormhole relay lets us manage them in real time." She looked at him and waited, as if she didn't think it was sinking in. "Superluminal travel and instant transmission. That's what turns us from harmless eccentrics APS can ignore into something they'll want to take over. Especially when they realise it's probably based on research stolen from them."

The penny started to drop for Trinder. "Was Dr Kim our agent on the inside?"

"No, but apparently the FTL was based on her great-grandmother's research. She says we stole it, and I can't prove we didn't. If she's worked it out, I'm now worried who else has."

Trinder struggled to find solid ground in an instantly changed world. What was it that he'd thought just a couple of weeks ago? Nobody could keep a big secret hidden for long in Ainatio. He'd really believed that. He'd believed a lot of things, including the impossibility of FTL travel, but now he was starting to wonder if anything he took for granted was true.

He managed a nod. "Okay, yes, I'm shocked."

"I'm sorry you were never told the truth," Erskine said. "Nobody was. My father broke the news to me when I took over the company, and I can assure you it was a shock for me too. The only other people who know are the heads of departments."

And they'd kept it quiet as well. Trinder felt oddly betrayed, knowing that he'd looked Alex Gorko in the eye many times and never seen the slightest hint of deception. He was starting to make sense of the revelations, but as the fog cleared, he realised how many questions Erskine hadn't covered.

"How did you plan to recruit for the follow-up missions if this was all secret?" he asked.

"The first batch would have been by selection from key workers, probably with a high proportion of military."

"And still secret."

"Yes, but once Nomad Base and the comms and logistics links with Earth were secured, we were going to go public, say that we'd found the ship, and invite volunteers. There was a fleet planned. Fifty ships over a period of forty years."

"And now we're down to four ships and zero volunteers."

"Yes."

"So what happens now?"

"We adapt the original plan and carry on. It was never intended to be an evacuation. Bednarz did it because he felt it was mankind's time to leave home. But events overtook us, of course."

"How will you man the missions? We're all there is. Us and Kill Line. And the transit camp."

As soon as Trinder said it, he felt his scalp tighten. He already knew the answer. He hadn't signed up for this. Neither had any of his detachment. He didn't even know how he felt about it.

"In a way, the decisions have been made for us," Erskine said. "We have all the right skills around us. Now that we've reached Opis, we can't abandon the project."

No, the decisions *hadn't* damn well been made as far as Trinder was concerned. He hadn't been consulted. Was she telling him that she expected his troops to just ship out to another planet? They weren't an expeditionary force. When there'd still been a national defence structure, overseas operations had been carried out almost entirely by private military contractors, and the last people to wear a national uniform had been border forces like the Homeland Navy and local State Defence units. Few of his own troops had served on any kind of frontline, either at home or abroad. They were corporate forces with very specific tasking, defenders of economic and strategic targets.

We're not even real infantry. And we're sure as shit not space marines. The nearest we've got to that is two Brits pushing fifty who aren't even under my command. Well, that's terrific. And I can't even guess what the risks are.

"Does that include us?" he asked.

"Nothing's compulsory, but I was rather counting on the detachment."

Trinder knew that he should press her, but he said nothing and hated himself for his silence. He'd assume the worst until the details started to emerge. It was the wrong attitude, and he knew it, but at some point soon, he was going to have to look his people in the eye and tell them they were being deployed to another planet, and that the timescales involved made it a one-way trip.

The world isn't ending. Asia's fine, more or less. What makes it worth abandoning even this?

He realised that he'd been distracted from the screen. That told him all he needed to know about his personal priorities. The biggest event in human history, the impossible made possible, was unfolding in front of him, and it had taken a back seat to his growing panic about being drafted into a deep-space mission. He stared at the feed from Opis for a moment, trying to recapture the unthinking amazement of a few minutes ago, the wonder of an unspoiled planet beyond his imagination, but now all he could see was a wilderness so far from home that he couldn't even work out how many zeroes there were in the distances involved.

Erskine swivelled around again to face her desk and tapped at the terminal. "I've just sent you the original Nomad operational plan. It's a lot to digest, so take your time, and as I said, don't mention this to anyone yet, not even to your officers."

"Yes, ma'am." Trinder pushed himself out of the deep chair and picked up his helmet from the coffee table. He was on autopilot now. "Thank you."

He left Erskine's office in a haze. He imagined this was how people felt when they'd just been given a terminal diagnosis, reeling from the realisation that the universe didn't know or care about their plans. Shit, was this the best he could do? He'd always worried that he wouldn't be up to the task in a real emergency, and now he *knew* he wasn't. His first reaction should have been to face the challenge and make it work.

Desk jockey. REMF. Plastic private. Yeah, that's me.

It was too soon to go back to the office. They'd all smell the secrecy on him. Lennie knew him too well, and even if their relationship had been over for a long time, she wouldn't let up until she got it out of him.

The john was the only sanctuary he had left. Everyone could track where he was, but at least he'd have some peace and quiet to unscramble his brain. He retreated to the nearest bathroom, locked the toilet cubicle, and sat down on the seat lid to take a look at his screen.

There it was, sitting in his mail folder: Project Nomad.

And now Solomon would see he'd retrieved the document. Trinder didn't even feel that his thoughts were private today.

Hang on... Solomon must know all about Nomad.

He knows what Erskine told me. He's part of the building. He's in all the ships. He's in the weapons systems.

Things were dawning on Trinder too slowly today.

He stared at the back of the door and let his focus slip until it was just a pale yellow blur with an unreadable notice on it. Solomon must have been a key element of Nomad from the start. The AI was woven into Ainatio, distributed across the network. There was no core machine to fail or for an enemy to target and destroy. Solomon could regroup in an intact part of the system or download to a mobile unit like a quadrubot, beyond the reach of attack, safe from sabotage, and keep things running. He and the subsidiary AIs that he managed were the failsafe. They probably didn't need the meat-bags at all.

But why do I feel bad about this? At the end of the day, Sol's just a computer programme.

Solomon wasn't a human slyly keeping something from his buddies, and he wasn't an unseen comrade on the radio net, or state surveillance, or an all-seeing, judgmental god, even if his invisibility sometimes made his interventions feel like all three. It was easy to start thinking crazy things when you were cooped up like this. Trinder knew he had to get a grip. He wasn't the only one kept out of the loop, because most of the scientists didn't know about *Cabot* either. He took some comfort from that and tried to concentrate on his screen again, working out how he'd explain all this to the detachment.

The outside door clicked open. It was probably one of the cleaning bots on its rounds. Well, he couldn't hide in here all day. He put the screen in his pants pocket and stood up. But when he opened the cubicle door, there was no sign of a bot, just Alex Gorko leaning against the row of washbasins with his arms folded.

"You too, huh?" Alex said. "Hiding in the john, I mean."

"Doesn't everybody?"

"I'm not stalking you, by the way."

"Sure, everyone ends up in this bathroom by accident sooner or later."

"So are you okay?"

There was no point in playing the game. "You're asking because..."

"I know that you now know what I know. So to speak."

"Yeah. I have questions." Trinder made an effort to look cynical or resigned, anything but scared. "How do *you* feel about it?"

Alex shrugged. "It's an amazing achievement."

"Spare me. I'm asking how you feel about a one-way trip to Opis. Or did I get the wrong idea about that?"

"Well, I admit they didn't mention it at my interview."

"Just tell me how you kept it quiet. Who's been working on this?"

"Mainly the AIs."

"I'm going to find out a lot of things I won't like, aren't I?"

"You've got the report."

"So the intention was always to keep the staff in the dark until the last minute."

"No, but when a project's been running across four generations, things change and priorities drift. Look, nobody's going to be bundled aboard a ship against their will. It's not going to be the wagon train exodus that Bednarz fantasised about, either, but if we decide to ship everybody out, we can."

"Who decides?"

"We've still got some details to work out."

Trinder could translate that. "You haven't got a clue, have you?"

"Dan, all I'm saying is come and see me when you want to talk this through. I'm always available."

"And Dr Kim?"

"We're still evaluating whether it's safe to let her work on the project."

Trinder bristled. "Erskine never mentioned that. Are you people crazy, letting a spy loose? I thought Erskine said we had to keep APS out of this."

"Maybe we better have that beer and chat later." Alex pushed himself away from the basins and half-opened the door. "By the way, your new buddy Chris Montello just notified your guys that the vets are going off-camp tomorrow. He thought you'd want to know in case you spotted activity and got worried. They're going to Kingston to look for ammunition."

"He's taking a hell of a risk." There was no telling what state the town was in or who might still be around. "We could save them the trouble and give them some."

"They've never asked for any."

"So? They patrol the boundary. We benefit from that."

"Yeah."

"Where's the harm in it? It's like giving them stuff from a dumpster. Come on."

Alex looked uncomfortable for a moment, lips compressed as if he was debating whether to say anything. "Well, now you know what I know, you understand why it's not a good idea to arm our neighbours."

"Why? We haven't had any trouble from them. In fact, they're the ones who've headed it off."

"Erskine hasn't factored them into her plan."

"That's pretty callous." The camp folk might not want to leave Earth any more than Trinder did, but they deserved the chance. "So decisions *have* been made, then."

"It's early days. Besides, this isn't some last-chance evacuation."

Trinder knew when Alex was making excuses for Erskine. "They're armed already. You've never been worried about that before."

"Because sleeping dogs are best left lying. Disarming them would just set hares running, to overdo my animal metaphors."

"And who do you think would disarm them anyway? My guys. And vets who've been through Baltimore wouldn't just touch their caps and say yessir, we understand, and hand over their weapons to us, would they?"

"A good reason for not giving them a stockpile of ammo."

Sometimes, just sometimes, Trinder's gut overruled his faith in the rule book. Right now it told him to shut up and walk away. But it wasn't telling him to accept Alex's veto. It was just telling him to keep his powder dry.

"Okay," he said. "I'd better talk to Montello. You and me, we'll have that chat when I've read the Nomad report."

He left the bathroom ahead of Alex and didn't look back. Now that he was coming to terms with how much he didn't know, and how long he hadn't known it, uncomfortable thoughts were fermenting. Was that why the detachment was really here? Had he and his troops just been marking time, bored out of their minds and filling their days with training until the follow-up missions needed to deploy them? Erskine should have realised that they weren't trained for Nomad. She might as well have armed the medics and shipped them out instead.

Get a grip.

Would he have signed on if he'd known? Probably not. He'd just needed a job, any job, but astronaut hadn't been on the list, not even when he was a boy.

As soon as he walked into the control room, Simonot shoved a screen under his nose. Lennie Fonseca should have been off duty, but she was hanging around, probably waiting to cross-examine him about his meeting with Erskine.

"The transit camp notified us they're going outside, sir," Simonot said. "They've never done that before."

Trinder glanced at the message and handed the screen back to Simonot. "I know. Alex caught me on my way here."

"They're going to check out Kingston. Latest radhaz data we have says it's not contaminated."

It was a what-would-Marc-and-Tev-do moment. Trinder suddenly knew what he needed to do. Alex had only told him not to give them ammo. He hadn't mentioned anything else.

"Okay, then let's give them some backup," Trinder said. "We need some overwatch experience. They might need some cover out there. Perfect."

Fonseca edged into the conversation. "So we're operating jointly now?"

"Just taking an opportunity to exercise some skills." There were some rusty tilt rotor pilots who needed to know what being on alert-five really felt like. "Corporal, have air support stand by. And maybe give Montello a couple of quadrubots to search buildings. See if he wants anything else."

Simonot didn't even blink. "Okay, I'll call him back, sir."

Trinder wondered whether to drive over and see Chris personally, but it might come across as suspiciously pushy after having had no contact. He'd take it a step at a time so they got the measure of each other, a little cooperation from a distance to see how it worked out, and if it did, he would have a case to put to Erskine about joint working.

But why am I doing this? Because I feel guilty about dumb rules that say they've got to scavenge while we're rolling in ammo we'll never use? That Erskine's leaving them behind? Respect for what those guys can do? Or just sticking it to the management for lying to us?

Whatever was driving him, Chris's people deserved some help. Trinder shuffled a few things on the desk, found absolutely nothing else had happened in his absence, and wandered out into the corridor, unable to bear Fonseca's scrutiny. She followed him out anyway.

"So what went on with Erskine?"

"I don't even know where to start."

"You're mad. I know that look."

"Okay, I'm mad." He decided he could bend the truth a little without looking like a liar later. "Anyway, I suggested that we manufacture some ammo for the transit camp, and I was told no. Despite the fact that we've only been stockpiling just about everything for, oh, I don't know, twenty years. So there you go."

"Dan, if the world was down to its last dozen humans, six of them would still be petty bureaucrats."

"Ain't that the truth."

"You sure you're all right?"

"I'm sure. Look, I'm going back to my quarters. I need to shower and catch up on some reading. I'll see you later."

He got about ten yards down the corridor before she called out after him. "Yeah, okay," she said, and he knew that whichever way he played this, she'd round on him and ask why he hadn't told her about *Cabot* and the implications for everyone.

Orders. You don't get to pick the ones you like. Although I think I'm going to learn to bend them.

Trinder re-ran the conversations with Erskine and Alex in his head while he showered and thought of all the smart things he should have said, none of which would have changed the situation one damn bit. When he finally sat down on the bed to read the Nomad document, it felt like staring at an unopened bill that he'd been dreading. He steeled himself to open it and skipped to the executive summary.

Tad Bednarz was clever, he had to give the guy that. Ainatio had played an incredibly long game. The most interesting part was how payloads had been sent fifty years before the FTL mission was launched. The tiny bots that arrived on Opis started by building bigger ones from local materials, and those in turn built the specialised construction plant that built the entire base. It looked like they'd done a lot of it before there was any FTL relay in place to keep an eye on them. Trinder thought that level of automation was more impressive than actually getting there.

But did Bednarz live to see any of this? Trinder checked the dates. The old guy had died a few years before the wormhole was established. But with or without FTL, he must have died believing his life's work had paid off. It was the most any man could hope for.

Now Trinder understood why Bednarz was so big on AIs. Without them, building anything complex on Opis would have been almost impossible. The company's multi-billion dollar AI business now looked more like a by-product of Bednarz's fixation with colonising deep space than his main ambition. There was a fine line between crazy and visionary.

A message icon blinked on the screen. Trinder flicked it automatically with his finger, not checking who was calling, and went on reading the report.

"Am I interrupting, Major?" Solomon asked.

It was the AI's way of holding his finger on a doorbell until someone answered the door. "No, go ahead, Sol."

"Mr Montello said thank you for the offer of assistance, and he appreciates it, but he doesn't want to put any more people at risk than he needs to."

Trinder wasn't sure what to make of that. He hadn't been able to judge Chris from a single meeting, other than to note that he took his task seriously, but the polite rebuff could have been literal, or a way of telling Trinder that he thought the team wasn't up to it, or just an indication that the transit camp still preferred to keep its distance.

"Did you speak to him personally?" Trinder asked.

"No, I'm relaying what he said to Corporal Simonot."

"Okay."

"If you're concerned, we could deploy drones to keep an eye on things. I'm sure Mr Montello wouldn't object to being warned if he was heading into difficulties."

"Sure. Let's do that."

"I understand why you're concerned."

"I'm not sure why I am, but what the hell." Trinder decided that he might as well ask. "You know about my briefing, then."

"Of course."

"And you've always known about *Cabot*."

"Yes. I'm sorry. I realise that must seem somewhat dishonest on my part."

"Orders are orders."

"We'll all be able to make better decisions when everything's out in the open."

Trinder looked up at the wall to his left. He'd taken a long time to put any family photographs on it. He still couldn't bear to have them on the wall facing the bed, because they would have seemed more accusing than watching over him, but he could cope with a sideways glance now and again. There was Mom and Dad, Grandad, and his sister, plus a few neighbours at Thanksgiving, a little the worse for drink around a table piled with half-finished dinners. Maybe the last of them were dead now, and maybe they were still surviving somewhere in a pocket of civilisation out of comms range, but either way he'd never see them again.

Everyone here had lost all they knew and loved. Their whole world now lay within the wire, and that felt more claustrophobic than protected some days.

"You're right, Sol," Trinder said. "You can ignore reality, but you can't avoid what it does."

If Solomon had more secrets, he wasn't confessing. Trinder almost asked him if he kept a record of what had happened to everybody's next of kin, but any answer short of a miracle would be a bad one.

Trinder didn't believe in miracles.

* * *

TRANSIT CAMP:
THREE DAYS LATER, 0725 HOURS

Chris opened the truck door and paused to look back at the small convoy. Behind his own vehicle, the old APC, the gun truck they'd commandeered in Baltimore, and Dieter's pick-up idled at intervals along the track, clouded in vapour, but the thaw had started. The air smelled a little more like spring this morning.

On the flatbed of the pick-up, the dogs were barking and wagging their tails like excited kids heading for the beach. Rich, the driver, kept tossing a softball to them, laughing as they tussled for it. Erin had her head out of the top hatch of the APC, smoking and looking down every so often to talk to Jackson and Conway inside. Lee, the gunner, perched behind the HMG on the gun truck with his eyes shut and head tilted back as if he was sunning himself, while Matt leaned out of the driver's window to talk to Jamie. They hadn't formed up like this for a long time. It was more a march unit than a full convoy, but Chris still tried to do things properly.

"Five minutes, people." Chris pulled his beanie down over his earpiece and checked the squad radio again. Erin stubbed out her smoke on the hatch and raised her hand to indicate she'd heard him. "Mount up."

Zakko sat in the driver's seat, fiddling with the dashboard like a nervous pilot. He was so jumpy that Chris almost regretted the business with the finger. *Damn, was I really going to do that?* Those were rules from another life. He'd suppressed them, but the reflexes were still there.

"Relax," Chris said. "I'll tell you what you need to do."

"I've never driven in a convoy before."

"Exactly, which is why you need to learn. You're the lead vehicle, so you don't need to worry about maintaining intervals like the folks behind you. Focus on what's to your front and flanks."

"Okay."

Jared wandered up, arms folded, a picture of disapproval. He was never going to make a poker player. Chris lowered the side window.

"It's not too late to accept Ainatio's help," Jared said. Well, those were the words that came out of his mouth, but both of them understood that Jared thought it was a bad idea to let Zakko drive. "Those guys need to get out more."

"Yeah, but I don't need them pausing to consult their *Polite Boys' Book of Regulations* if things get hairy."

"You don't know that."

"That's exactly my point." Chris refolded his paper map with the first leg of the route uppermost and laid it on his lap. It was almost impossible to get lost, but old habits died hard. "Radio check on the hour. Just a burst unless there's a problem, okay?"

"Watch your ass. And your alarm."

Chris smiled and made a point of rearranging his jacket so Jared could see the dosimeter on his lapel. "We're not passing through any hot areas."

"Hot areas shift all the time."

"I'm more worried about infected plant material. See you later."

Jared gave the signal to move out. Chris tapped the dashboard, Zakko released the brake, and the truck picked up speed as they rolled out of the camp. Four armed vehicles were probably overkill, but it was important to look like trouble when they were low on ammo. The dogs were a noisy deterrent in their own right. If anyone was left in the area, they'd hear the vehicles coming for miles, so there was no point in trying to enter Kingston unnoticed. It was easier to get in, search fast, and get out if they went in mob-handed with gun trucks and a sniper on overwatch.

The automated decontamination unit on the road ahead, a covered tunnel of frames like an avenue of Shinto temple gates, marked the boundary between the safe bubble of Kill Zone and the salted earth of the biohaz cordon. The vehicles ran the gauntlet of UV light, compressed air, and chemical sprays at low speed, hatches closed. Chris felt like he was passing through a portal to another dimension.

When the truck emerged and the windscreen cleared, it almost looked as if he had. For a couple of miles ahead, the deforested zone was still dead, an alien landscape of felled trees and flat-topped stumps like stepping stones. A fungal smell of rotting timber wafted in when Chris lowered the side window. He'd never been sure why Ainatio had bothered to clear the zone, seeing as trees didn't seem affected by die-back, but maybe it stopped insects and fly-infested animals wandering through from contaminated areas and spreading the virus.

"We didn't eat grains or beans in the Stone Age," Chris said, thinking aloud. He hadn't been outside the wire for so long that the landscape looked freshly depressing to him. Reduced to a distant background blur from the top of the Kill Line ridge, it didn't look quite so stark because he could see forest and grassland beyond. Die-back had only attacked certain plants, leaving others untouched, but they happened to be the staple ones most people depended on. "I mean, those are the crops that were wiped out, but we don't need them. We can live without them."

"Just not as many of us."

"Yeah, that's your problem right there. Dependency."

"You think the whole planet's going to die, Chris?"

"Doubt it. Ninety per cent of life on Earth was wiped out in the Permian era, but the world was back in business a couple of million years later."

"Kind of a long wait, though."

"That was after an asteroid hit and millions of acres of volcanoes had been chucking up lava for centuries. This is just a hiccup by comparison."

Zakko paused for a moment, lips pursed as if he was afraid to ask another question, which he probably was. "How do you know all this stuff?"

"I was studying geology. Until the college closed, anyway."

"Oh."

"Yeah." Chris could hear the tinge of genuine surprise. He wasn't proud of his past but he wasn't ashamed of it either, even if he wished it could have been different. But that would have meant being born in a much kinder, safer world. The life that he'd led had given him exactly the skills he needed for where he found himself now. He was fine with that. "You want to ask me what I was doing time for, right?"

Zakko nodded. Maybe he'd heard, although the camp was that rare place where folks made an effort not to care about anyone's past. "I think I can work it out."

"Go ahead."

"Well... I guess it wasn't theft."

"I put a guy in the hospital for a long time."

"I suppose he asked for it."

"It was nothing noble." That wasn't quite the whole picture. Maybe Zakko needed to see that. "I used to resolve contractual compliance issues."

"Huh?"

"I enforced things. For criminals."

Zakko blinked a few times, eyes still on the road. "Well, shit."

Chris wondered whether to fill in the more complicated gaps, but that would have sounded like an excuse. Only one image recurred from his teenage years: his dad, his nice respectable accountant dad, afraid to leave the gated community that they could barely afford, constantly rehearsing for home invasions because of the feral thugs that nobody seemed willing to deal with. Chris decided that he couldn't spend his life under siege. His father was teaching him to be afraid. But he wasn't: he was angry, resentful, and mutinous.

And then his buddy Ben got beaten and robbed on his way home from football practice. Sitting at the guy's bedside most evenings for three weeks, Chris realised you couldn't wait for something to come and get you. These days he understood it as taking the fight to the enemy, but even as a kid, he knew instinctively that the only way to stop the monster wasn't to defend himself when it came for him, but to grab a weapon and head out at night with a few buddies to hunt it down and scare it so badly that it never came back.

Or kill it.

He killed it for Ben. He didn't set out to, but he wasn't upset that he had. And the monster ran away, leaving a trail of blood, but Chris knew he'd finished him, because it was on the news the next day, and there couldn't have been two identical stabbings in the same neighbourhood on the same night.

"Are you all right, Christopher? You look pale."

"I'm okay, Mom. Just watching the news."

Chris suddenly felt like he'd woken up from a nap. "I went to work for one of my dad's clients after college," he said, wondering if Zakko was still listening. "The guy had some pretty irregular business friends. Apparently I was good at that sort of persuasion. Until I got caught."

It was a different crime, but Chris got his sentence, and he felt that kind of balanced the universe for what he'd done years before. Even now, though, if he tried to replay how he'd progressed from being an angry teen vigilante to a collar-and-tie gangster's enforcer, he still couldn't see the fork where he took the wrong road.

But it wasn't wrong, was it? This is where I was meant to be. This is what I was meant to do.

Yeah, I hate time travel put-it-right movies. You get one chance and the choice you make is who you are.

"But State Defence took you on," Zakko said. Yeah, he was paying attention. "You couldn't have been that bad."

"They were so short of recruits that they got guys released. They weren't picky about criminal backgrounds when things started to fall apart."

"But they gave you a chance."

Chris's boss had abandoned him and his folks had disowned him, but the military didn't leave him behind. He didn't care why. He'd rather have been executed than spend another day in that cell. It felt like his childhood all over again.

"Yeah," Chris said. "They did. So it all works out."

Zakko didn't comment. He seemed to have the answers he wanted.

To his credit, he maintained a steady speed and stayed alert to risks. It was more than Chris expected of him.

The guy had no military experience and had never been taught to read atmospherics, all the little signs and not-quite-right stuff that said shit was about to happen to your patrol. Maybe he'd honed his personal radar on the streets.

The truck bounced from time to time on the potholes carved out of the road by successive winters without repair crews to fix them. Chris checked the dashboard monitor to see if the three drivers behind were keeping intervals, then glanced at the wing mirror to make sure.

They were back in live woodland and abandoned pasture now. It was a few saplings at first, then bigger trees until the landscape began to look almost normal, just scrubbed of all traces of humans except the power company's boxes almost buried in overgrown bushes at the side of the road, and a lonely charging station for cars that had vanished years ago. A small bird swooped low across the road and disappeared.

Chris checked his dosimeter. Everything looked okay.

Cattle were grazing on the verge up ahead. As the convoy got closer, their heads went up as if they were going to bolt, and Zakko slowed down. But the animals seemed to take it as an invite to follow him, and started trotting along with the vehicle as it passed. Chris realised that some of them still associated humans with being fed. He hadn't realised cattle lived long enough to remember things that must have happened seven or eight years ago.

"Keep moving," he said.

"What should we do with them?" Zakko kept checking the rear-view, probably worried that the gun truck would just mow the animals down. "Take them back with us?"

There was a time when Chris would have shot first and worried about how to transport the carcasses later, grateful for some decent meat in a famine, but they weren't starving now, and even his limited city-boy knowledge of livestock told him that cattle needed health checks before mixing with other animals.

"Doug won't thank us if the Kill Line herds catch some disease," he said. "They'll just have to take their chances."

Zakko nodded, but his face said he was worried what would happen to them. "Okay."

Between the islands of forest, all the greenery that Chris could see was overgrown fields or grass recovering from the snow. Resistant weeds and bushes had moved in to fill gaps that might have been fallow fields, crops finally overrun by their tougher wild neighbours, or even areas of die-back. The ragged patchwork of vegetation was probably good eating for animals but there wasn't much for humans.

How were folks getting by in Asia? Chris wished he'd asked Kim when he'd had the chance. Ainatio's reaction to her nagged at him more every day, but maybe he was overthinking it. If people had been cooped up in a compound for years with almost no outside contact, they were bound to get a little weird. It was a prison. And he knew exactly what that did to people.

"Thirty miles to Kingston," Zakko said. "We'll probably lose the radio over that hill ahead."

He'd done his homework, and he was right: Chris tried the radio when they reached the hills, but the signal was gone. The convoy stopped for a bathroom break, as much for the dogs as the humans, and Chris tried again, this time using a small drone with a receiver attached. It climbed a long way before he could acquire a channel and send a confirmation. If they were going to attempt long foraging missions again, they'd have to beef up the transmitter.

Lee watched from the open back of the gun truck as the grenade-sized drone descended and landed in Chris's hands. "I wouldn't worry," he said. "Your buds at Ainatio are watching over us."

"Yeah?"

Lee pointed up in no particular direction. "Drone. Look." He pulled his optics visor down over his eyes to take a closer look. "I thought you told them to rack off."

"Politely."

"That sounds like scary-politely."

"For their own good."

"Come on, they're bored out of their skulls. They want to play soldiers."

"I still can't see it."

Lee nodded and passed Chris his visor. "There. Above the trees."

"Oh. Yeah."

"Not sure why they need one that big, but they do things differently that side of the fence, don't they? They must want us to know it's there. Nobody's that crap at covert surveillance."

Chris did a slow wave, then gave the drone a thumbs-up gesture. A little diplomacy didn't cost anything. Fine, they could watch. But he wasn't going to change how he did things today. The convoy rolled off again, with the gun truck between Chris's vehicle and Dieter's pick-up, and the APC bringing up the rear.

"Maybe they want to understand how we do things," Zakko said. "It takes a lot to say hey, we're useless, can we watch you and learn, yeah?"

Whatever faults Zakko had, he seemed to think the best of people until proven wrong. Chris wondered whether to give him the talk on sensible mistrust. But Zakko probably understood all too well, and just wanted to look on the kinder side because keeping the world at arm's length was soul-destroying. He didn't need Chris to crush his morale by reminding him how shitty people could be.

You don't build a guy up by trashing what keeps him sane. Find another way. Come up with a better plan.

"You're right," Chris said. He still hadn't worked out how he'd ended up as a leader when he had no ambition beyond surviving the day. But he was, and that meant responsibilities. "Bet they've never raided dumpsters. We'll educate them."

"Yeah." Zakko nodded. "We're good at that."

Kingston eventually started to appear ahead of them a ruin at a time, first an old charging station with a scruffy blue car picked clean of tyres and seats, hood open, then the blackened shell of a mobile diner. A propane cylinder lay on its side out front with a split in it like a mouth, its coating weathered into a dull, dusty red that made it look like ancient terracotta. Chris read two scenarios in that. These were either random events — a gas cylinder left leaking when the diner staff had to leave in a hurry, a car abandoned when the charging station turned out to have no power — or an indication that marauders had been around. But there was no sign of any recent human activity between here and Kill Line. If anyone had come this way, they'd turned back or moved on a long time ago.

And someone probably picked Kingston clean around the same time. But we might get lucky. And sitting back waiting for luck or hand-outs is never an option.

Chris focused on the road again, checking features against the map and looking for places where they might get ambushed. The journey out of Baltimore had been about skirting urban areas whenever they could, or getting through them as quickly as possible. Going into a town and back out by the same route made him uneasy. But as he started to see more shuttered and boarded-up houses, he could tell Kingston had been evacuated with enough notice for folks to go through the motions of securing their homes, even if they realised that boards wouldn't stop determined looters.

Now the town was close enough to send up a swarm of micro-drones to check it out. The convoy pulled over while Dieter launched them. Chris sat back to study the composite feed on his screen as he guided the swarm into the town centre, dreading what he'd find. He'd searched too many derelict places for one lifetime and seen too many bodies and treasured possessions, all that was left of harmless people who'd minded their own business until the predatory reality of a collapsing society rolled over them.

"I thought the place was bigger," Zakko said, looking over his shoulder.

"Population twelve thousand and forty-two. Or so it says here."

"Was."

The architects had tried to make Kingston look like a town that had grown from a few log cabins over the centuries, with random styles from block to block. But the map data on Chris's screen showed that it was one of those instant towns built in the mid-2100s, all poured, printed, and extruded within a couple of years. The drone view of Main Street showed no signs of looting. Kingston just looked like it had closed early and everyone had headed off for the day: no broken glass, no abandoned shopping carts, and no streets strewn with the pillage that looters couldn't carry. Only the weeds that had taken over the sidewalks and pavement showed that nobody had come back to open up the stores again after lunch.

Looters. That's us now.

Chris tapped his earpiece and wondered why he was trying to put a human face on the past instead of just going numb and doing what he had to. He'd been away from reality for too long.

"Six Zero to all callsigns — mount up. Everybody stay sharp and pay attention to the dogs."

It was like old times, but ones that Chris would have preferred to never see again.

* * *

APPROACH ROAD TO KINGSTON: 1045 HOURS

"Is that your dosimeter buzzing?" Zakko asked.

Chris looked away from the drone feed and rummaged through folds of leather and webbing to check. "Yeah. Don't worry. It says three hours max."

"Not long to search a whole town."

The radiation levels around here were a little higher than Chris had expected. He'd never hear the end of it from Jared. Yeah, hot spots shifted. Now everyone else's dosimeter would be going off as well. He got on the radio.

"Six Zero to all callsigns — if your radhaz warning's activated, we've still got three hours to scope the place. If that changes, we withdraw early. Out."

The convoy rumbled down the back roads into town, following a route through an overgrown park that gave the vehicles more cover than the main road. Maybe they didn't need it, but security was a habit not meant to be broken. Deer scattered. Crows flapped out of their path. Nature was reclaiming the land.

"So maybe everyone moved out because of the radiation," Zakko said. He slowed for another deer. "But it's a long way outside the hot zones on the map."

There was no live government data to plug into these days. Chris relied on the information that Doug Brandt shared with him, and that came from Ainatio. It could have been wrong or incomplete, or the contamination might have been recent, an old reactor failing or a waste plant somewhere leaking into a river that fed into others and eventually reached the water table here. There was nothing they could do about it.

"Radhaz source upstream, maybe," Chris said. "I'll call it in to Ainatio when we're back in range."

"If they monitor this stuff and they can get a drone out this far, why isn't it on their maps?"

Zakko actually asked intelligent questions. Chris realised he should have co-opted him sooner instead of keeping him away from critical jobs.

"Perhaps they don't survey that often. I'll put it on my list of things to ask Trinder."

Chris made a point not to brood on it. He couldn't change the past and he couldn't see a better future in his lifetime. The die-back would eventually burn itself out by running out of plant species to destroy, and one day people might drift back, but he'd be dead by then. Even if they put him on ice to wait it out, the world he woke up to wouldn't resemble the America he'd known.

He could only count on today. He reminded himself of that every morning.

Zakko pulled up outside the goods entrance to the department store in the centre of town and craned his neck to look behind the high chain-link fence, strung with the remnants of some climbing plant. The gates were wide open. Two trucks were still parked in the compound, rear doors ajar as if someone had emptied the cargo and left in a hurry. Chris noted the exterior fire escape that went all the way up to the flat roof.

"You want me to drive in?" Zakko asked.

"No. If we need to bug out in a hurry, you're in an enclosed space. You'll be pinned down." Chris realised he'd never explained tactical parking to him. It sounded like a goofy term until you found your escape route blocked by angry, heavily armed locals. "If you've got to shunt back and forth to get out, you lose seconds that you really need.

Park facing the way you're going to drive out, and leave enough space to manoeuvre around any obstacle put in your way."

"What if there's a bunch of people blocking the road?"

"Drive over them."

"Oh."

"It'll be you or them, Zakko. If shit gets real, you get out as fast as you can and any way you can."

No, Zakko wasn't bad, just naive and undisciplined. Chris doubted he'd mow down hostiles to escape. But he might have to learn one day.

"Like we did in Fairview?" Zakko said.

There was no "we." Chris had done the driving. He would have died rather than surrender that bus. It was fuelled, he had vulnerable civvies to transport, and if the assholes didn't get out of his way by the time he hit the roadblock, it was their problem. They didn't. That was their choice.

"Yeah, like we did in Fairview," Chris said. "Sometimes you just have to pick the least bad option."

That wasn't going to happen today. He'd checked out the area with the drones, and unless the dogs found anyone hiding, this was going to be an unopposed reclamation. But he had to stop relying on the tech. One day, the few pieces of fancy gear they still had would be beyond repair, and even if Ainatio was feeling generous, help usually came at a price. Chris preferred to rely on the same soldiering skills that guys with flintlocks or even spears would still recognise. It didn't break down and it couldn't be taken from him.

Damn, there I go again. I didn't even think of enlisting as a kid. I don't think I even played soldiers. How the hell did I end up being this gung-ho?

Because the job needed me, that's why. And now I need the job. Purpose. Identity. Tribe.

The squad stood in the cover of the vehicles, rearranging rifle slings and poacher bags while Chris gave them their instructions. Conway had his battering ram, breaching shotgun, and charges ready to force an entry.

"I'm guessing the store will be gutted, but if we find anything, remember to run a sensor over it in case it's contaminated," Chris said. "Treat this as a recon with a few freebies if we're lucky. If it's promising, we come back again with a proper roster and equipment to minimise exposure."

"How about further out?" Jamie asked.

"That's a job for another day."

"Twelve thousand people, so that's at least three thousand homes," Rich said. "And no guarantee they're all empty. Even if the area's low radhaz, that's weeks of search and recovery for ten people."

Chris checked his watch. "Okay, we're on the clock, guys. Support teams — Erin on the roof, Jackson at the front entrance, and Matt and Lee at the back. Assault team on me. We go in via the fire escape, bomb dog first. Let's move."

It was more a rummage than an assault, but at least they had the luxury of clearing the building from the top down. There was no room to stack safely on the fire escape, so Erin went up first to get to the roof. Dieter carried Sal the sniffer dog up the stairs behind her. Sal, a springer spaniel, was trained to find explosives and firearms. Chris hoped the dog didn't run into a booby trap primed with spikes instead of substances that she was trained to recognise. She sniffed around the fire exit at the top but didn't indicate that she'd picked up anything. Dieter pressed the handle slowly and carefully. The door swung open.

"Good girl, Sal. Find." Dieter ushered the dog in and leaned over the rail. "Power's out, guys. The doors are open."

Conway looked up the metal stairs, feigning a glum face, and slung his battering ram and shotgun over his shoulder. "I won't pretend I'm not disappointed."

"Don't worry, we'll find something for you to smash. There's bound to be something still locked manually."

Dieter whistled for Sapper and Girlie, both standing on the back of the truck with ears pricked, awaiting the signal to go, and the dogs raced for the fire escape. Everyone seemed pretty upbeat, humans and dogs alike. This was a day out. However mundane the task, they didn't get many days now that reminded them what they did best.

"Here we go, then," Chris said. He ran up the steps and paused in the doorway to let his eyes adjust to the light. "Stay sharp, guys."

Sunlight slanted in from the glass frontage and silhouetted the eerily cosy room settings of a furniture department. Chris always found the fake home-sweet-homeness creepy, as if this was an example of the ideal life you could lead if only you made the right choices. But the sofas were frosted with a thick layer of dust and pigeon shit, and the place reeked of mould. Chris could hear the pigeons burbling somewhere, probably roosting on the sprinkler pipes.

Sal, oblivious to it all, was having a great time. Chris followed her progress with his flashlight. Her stump of a tail was wagging so fast while she rooted around that it was almost a blur. Sapper and Girlie trotted here and there in their search for lurkers, alive or otherwise. Sal finished her search and returned to Dieter for her reward, a squeaky plastic squirrel that had seen better days. She settled down with it gripped between her paws and gnawed on it, making it squeal.

"No guns, Sal?" Chris decided not to pat her on the head while she was chewing. "No ammo?"

"There's nothing much left for her to detect if this place has been deserted for years." Dieter smiled at her like a proud dad. "If only humans would work that hard for a chew toy."

"Yeah, I used to think that when we ran into dog packs."

"Ah, come on, Chris. You don't mean that. Anyone who doesn't like dogs is a wrong 'un."

"They're loyal even when we abuse them," Chris said.

"I think that indicates a purer soul, not a failing."

"Well, I don't blame them if they turn on us." Chris didn't want to get into anything profound. He went on searching, hoping to find a loaded pistol stashed under a paypoint that had been forgotten in the exodus, but there was nothing. "We're done on this floor, guys. Move on."

"So what do we want to find if there's no ammo?" Conway asked.

It had never been an issue when they were trying to stay alive on the journey south. They knew what they needed — really, desperately needed — and took it wherever they could find it, and that felt okay. Now that he was well-fed and relatively comfortable in Kill Line, Chris thought differently. Maybe they were drifting into looting. He shot looters. He didn't want to become one himself. It was funny how the line of legitimacy shifted.

"Just ammo," he said. "Unless we come across something else survival-related. Knives. Radios. Tools. Electricals."

Jamie chuckled to himself as they headed down the stairs to the second floor, flashlight beams crossing. "But no ball gowns, right? Chris, you remember that crazy woman we saw coming out of the store in Ashland? Everyone else was wheeling out carts of food and bottled water, but she was wearing a sequinned evening dress and carrying a dozen more. The bright blue one. Remember?"

"Hell, yes. Probably wasn't even her size."

"If you're going to die, you might as well look classy," Dieter said. "People do value the damnedest things."

"Wait up — store directory," Conway called. He shone his light on a damp-stained sign on the wall. "Second floor — men's and women's fashions, children's clothes, and shoes. First floor — luggage, cosmetics and fragrances, stationery. Basement — kitchenware, sporting goods, hardware."

"No gun shop?"

"This is the kind of store you visit to have coffee and hang out. Not buy supplies for a winter wrestling bears in the Yukon."

They continued downstairs with the dogs a few yards ahead. Yeah, Conway was right — this was a shop for entertainment, a place to browse and maybe place an order to while away a Saturday afternoon, because people still liked somewhere to congregate. No amount of retail technology would change human nature. At the doors to the fashion floor, Chris stepped over a few brightly-coloured skirts that had dropped from their hangers onto tiles covered with dead insects, and tried to construct a sequence of events from the few goods that were left and what had been taken.

Every scenario had a plausible alternative. Some picked sensible stuff, others grabbed garbage. He'd seen it all. He didn't expect any random looter to take large items of furniture from upstairs — there was always one crazy guy who'd try, of course — so the most portable goods would go first. But most of the store looked like it had been cleared systematically. That could have indicated anything, from repeated visits by looters with plenty of time to a store that had closed before the evacuation. He couldn't afford the time to look for paperwork to give him a timeline. It was a curiosity to be investigated later, if at all.

There were still shoes left, boxed in a storeroom. Chris ran the pen-sized sensor over them and got a safe reading. There were even kids' sizes.

"Hey, we've got people who could do with these." That was when he realised that his personal red line was looting for himself. But this was for people who depended on him. It was his duty. "Let's start moving them out."

There was more booty in the back office area: paper, half-used pens, and a stash of boxer shorts. Dieter found a janitor's storeroom and liberated boxes of toilet tissue and bottles of soap. The first floor looked even more promising — purses, cosmetics, travel goods, and haberdashery, according to the suspended signs. The cupboards beneath the counters yielded dozens of small card boxes full of lipsticks and mascara. This was the stuff that morale was made of.

"Yay, aftershave." Jamie popped up from behind a fixture, brandishing bottles. He gave himself a quick spray under each arm and inhaled theatrically. "Something for the guys at last. Got to find some perfume now."

Conway pointed his flashlight to indicate another sign. "There's the basement. Hardware. Kitchenware. Maybe the security offices. Worth a try."

Dieter sent the dogs down the stairs to check. When Chris caught up with them, all he could see was luminous eyes when he caught them in his flashlight beam. But he also saw a glint of something shiny that was worth investigating.

"Kitchen stuff," Chris said. "Awesome."

He felt his way along the shelves. Plates, glassware, a coffee machine, cutlery, pots and pans... how long did he have? He checked his watch. They'd been in here for nearly two hours. Well, there wouldn't be enough place settings for a hundred people, but he'd take as much as he could find. Dieter came over to help him haul it.

"Not a completely wasted journey," Chris said, heaving boxes up the stairs.

Dieter shrugged. He'd found some champagne glasses. That was his optimism in a nutshell. "If nothing else, it wards off skills fade."

"You better brew some fizzy stuff to go in those."

"Already on it."

They exited via the loading bay and started stacking the haul by the gates for Zakko and Matt to load onto the vehicles. The dogs settled down by the boxes, looking as if they'd decided to move on to guard duties.

"No ammo, then," Zakko said, studying a five-piece pan set. "How are you going to divvy this up?"

Chris ran the radhaz sensor over everything again just to make sure. "We'll tally it up when we get back. Everybody gets something, even if it's pens and paper. We can put the household stuff in the chow hall so everybody gets to use it." He could have asked Doug to get most of these goods from Ainatio, but there was a primal, hunter-gatherer kind of satisfaction in foraging and returning to the camp to hand out the haul. He felt good now. "Let's go. Where's Erin?"

"Still on the roof," Zakko said.

Chris called her on the radio. "Four Four, come on down. We're done."

"Roger that, Six Zero. Did I see a coffee machine down there?"

"Confirmed."

"Drip or espresso? Doesn't matter, I'm in. Four Four out."

Erin came clattering down the metal steps and trotted up to the back of Chris's truck to inspect the day's harvest. Jamie sidled up to her and wedged a small package in her rucksack.

"That better not be something dead. What is it, a pigeon? A rat?" She tried to look over her shoulder, then gave up and slid the backpack off. "Oh. Wow."

"*Perfume*, Private Piller."

It took a lot to silence Erin. She wasn't yappy, but she normally had the last word, and Jamie was scared of her no matter how much he denied it. But she turned the grubby, battered box over in her hands, staring at the label like it was Christmas Day. Chris waited for her to say that it wasn't a fragrance she used and grind Jamie's hopes into the dirt, but she managed an uncharacteristically embarrassed smile. Jamie ran one hand over his buzz-cut dark hair, clearly embarrassed as well.

"I never thought I'd see perfume again," Erin said. "Thank you, Jamie."

"It'll keep the flies away, if nothing else."

"You're such a smooth talker." She sniffed the air. "Actually, you smell good."

Jamie looked coy for a moment and then gave her a big grin. Chris could never work out if the guy was barking up the wrong tree. Some bereaved people fell into a new relationship soon after they lost a loved one, often with someone else who was also grieving, but others didn't move on for years, and he had Erin down as one of the latter. Maybe she'd finally decided that life was still there to be lived. This was all there'd ever be: the world wasn't going to improve magically in their lifetimes, and the dead were gone forever. Chris tried to translate that into encouragement that wouldn't sound so bleak, but he didn't have the words in him today.

"Good work, guys," he said. "Mount up."

The Ainatio drone was still circling at roof height, apparently waiting for the convoy. He waved and raised his arm to give the move-out signal. Trinder's people could see what was happening on the ground, so it'd be obvious even if they didn't understand hand signals.

Why wouldn't they? I ought to give them more credit.

The drone rocked its wings in acknowledgement — yeah, they did understand — and shot off south-east. Chris walked up the line of vehicles to do a final visual check. Jamie, smiling to himself as if he'd collected another token on the road to Erin's affections, was sitting on the back of the gun truck behind Lee. Chris gave him a thumbs-up and a wink.

"It's going to be fun when we get home." Zakko drove off with a casual confidence, as if he'd been doing this all his life, a different guy from the bag of nerves who'd set out this morning. "Nobody knows what we're bringing back."

"Preferably not radioactive dust."

"Hah. Y'know, I think Jamie's patience is paying off. With Erin, I mean."

Patience. Chris sat thinking for a moment about women who said they'd wait for a guy to get out of prison, then started dating someone else after a couple of months. It was funny how the sting had gone out of that memory. He also thought that he'd beat the snot out of his ex-boss if he ever ran into him, but he wasn't even sure about that. They were probably both dead. Even if they'd survived, they wouldn't be sitting around gloating about how they'd gotten one over on him. They'd be scrabbling for food. That made things even. Vengeance could be a detached, mathematical thing.

Yeah, I'm a wrong 'un, Dieter. But loyalty's two-way. Your dogs might be saints, but they're still wrong.

The convoy retraced its route through the park and out onto the road. It was now clear of the town centre on a wide road flanked by houses with big porches and overgrown lawns set back from the sidewalk. Chris couldn't tell if there were plants still alive in there waiting to emerge, or if they'd succumbed to die-back. But there were crocuses poking out of the grass at the edge of a driveway, purple and lavender ones. Spring was definitely here.

"Whoa, what the hell's *that*?" Zakko said.

Chris's hand was already on his sidearm before he took in what was coming at them head-on. For a second, the narrow profile made it hard to identify, but it was the red Ainatio drone, flying at head-height through a gap in the trees. It was bigger than Chris had realised. It was going to hit the windshield. His heart was pounding out of his chest.

"Holy shit." Zakko hit the brakes.

But the drone shot past them. It hadn't been on a collision course after all, just making sure they'd notice it. It zipped back across their path, crossing from left to right and back again. Chris had no idea what Ainatio was trying to tell him, but it didn't look good. If they were sticking to the signals handbook, it meant they had something urgent to communicate.

Chris wished he'd had the sense to ask Trinder for a longer-range radio when he'd offered to ride along. All he could do now was talk to the squad.

"Six Zero to all callsigns, the Ainatio drone's trying to get our attention, reason unknown. Assume a hazard. Slow down but be prepared to exfil fast. Reduce speed to fifteen, out."

The only way he could talk to Ainatio was to launch the relay drone, contact Jared, and get him to relay messages to Trinder. It was time to stop and call in. Chris had no idea what they might be driving into. The drone kept buzzing them, which he could only read as a signal to stop or prepare to divert.

"Six Zero to all callsigns — halt here and keep your engines running."

Chris jumped out and walked a few yards down the road. The other vehicles had formed up behind with enough room to disperse if they needed to escape. The drone hovered a few yards away, rocking its wings. *Follow me.* Talking to Trinder was going to take time that they didn't appear to have, then.

"What is it, Sarge?" Lee called. He had the machine gun ready. Jamie was readying an extra ammo belt. "I can't see anything."

Chris turned to get back into the vehicle. "It's obviously spotted something — "

He was looking right at Jamie. He was still looking at him when a plume of blood arced from the guy's head and he dropped like a stone. Lee swung the gun around and started firing.

"Contact, contact, contact, this is Eight Zero, nine o'clock, two five metres, left side of road in the clapboard house, numbers unknown, all weapons, open fire, out."

"Nine Three here, man down — Jamie's down, Three Eight is down." That was Rich. "Fuck's sake, he's down."

Convoy procedure went to rat shit from the get-go. Everyone except the gun truck should have broken off and driven clear, but they all opened up on the clapboard house. Chris's mind dumped every thought except finding cover and returning fire. He ran for the truck but something pinged against his pants as if he'd knocked his knee, and suddenly he wasn't upright any more. Time slowed instantly. He was now in an intensely detailed tunnel where he could only see the headline events.

Lee was on the radio again. "This is Eight Zero, Six Zero's down too, Chris is down."

"Six Zero here, I'm okay." Chris's right leg had buckled under him. He lay on the road, trying to roll onto his belly to fire prone, his hand in a pool of blood. He knew his leg felt weird, but there was no pain and he couldn't work out where all the blood was coming from. "Anyone else?"

"Four Four here, all other callsigns okay. Chris, I see you. You're hit."

Shit, Erin's right. "Anyone got eyes on?"

"Looks like it's coming from two houses on the left, one on the right."

The drone was holding position overhead. As Chris tried to flip over, a spurt of flame shot out from it, followed by a deafeningly close explosion and a flash of white light. He thought the drone had been hit, but when he managed to roll, he saw one of the houses belching smoke and flames.

The frigging drone opened fire. It's armed.

Rounds struck up dust next to him. If he'd been hit again, he still couldn't feel it. All he could hear was his squad calling out contacts on the radio, which meant they were still alive, and that was all he cared about right now.

A second explosion hurt his ears — another RPG? — and then someone grabbed him. He tried to turn to shoot the bastard, but it was Zakko, and the lead truck was suddenly right behind him.

"What the hell are you doing? You're supposed to get out of here." Chris tried to push him away. "Now you're stuck."

"I backed up. It's okay, the truck's still pointing the right way." Zakko dragged Chris by his jacket and propped him against the front passenger side of the truck, level with the engine. "Your leg's bleeding like crazy. So where do I put this tourniquet? Does that hurt?"

"Here, let me do it."

"You can't. Just point. Like this?"

"Yeah. Tighter."

"That okay?"

"Fine."

Chris tried not to look at his knee. Whatever had suppressed the pain was vanishing fast and it was starting to hurt like hell. But that was too bad. He'd led his people into an ambush, Jamie was probably dead because of him, and if he didn't do something fast then the rest of them would die too. He couldn't see the firefight from here, but he could hear it. At that rate they were close to running out of ammo.

How the hell had he missed this on the way in? Those assholes must have been set up, watching them move in. Why didn't he spot the signs? The firing continued but it was now being drowned out by something much louder, the deafening noise of engines.

"Wow, they got here fast." Zakko looked up. "Haven't seen those things very often."

Chris craned his neck and got a faceful of gritty dust. Two tilt-rotor Lammergeier gunships in red Ainatio livery hovered over the road in a whirlwind of debris, then fired missiles simultaneously into the houses on both flanks. He ducked. When he looked up again through the curtain of smoke, one of the ships had set down between the trucks and the other was coming in to land behind the APC.

Save Jamie. Please God, let him be alive. He didn't survive just to get shot on a frigging shopping trip.

The tilt rotor's ramp went down, but it wasn't troops who came out first. It was four old industrial quadrubots the size of Shetland ponies, headless and sinister, and they peeled off in different directions. One trotted up to him, reoriented its limbs, and stood up to turn itself bipedal. Then it bent over, scooped him up, and headed for the gunship.

Chris had never seen a bot like this up close before, let alone been manhandled by one. It was surreal. Then his leg was gripped by a pain so intense that it almost stopped him from breathing. He fought to stay focused but it was hard not to lose control. He could smell his own blood.

"What about Jamie?" He was sure Zakko was right behind him. "See to him first. Is everyone else okay? What's happened?"

"I'm sorry, I'm afraid your comrade didn't survive, Sergeant," the quadrubot said, laying him on the cargo deck. It spoke like a man. It even sounded sympathetic. Chris, shocked into silence, had no idea what this thing was. Maybe it was just a remote and the voice belonged to some medic back at Ainatio who was directing it. "But let's deal with your injury."

Two medics moved in. Chris wanted to focus on Jamie, but his leg was screaming *me, me, me*. He could hear himself panting. Damn, maybe it wasn't his leg screaming. Maybe it was *him*. He was letting the squad down in front of these corporates. A dark-haired woman with a captain's insignia and a name tape that said FONSECA squatted to look at him. She planted her rifle like a walking stick for balance.

"Sorry we didn't get here sooner, Chris," she said. Everybody seemed to know who he was. "We're just going to make sure the area's clear. And you'll be fine, okay?"

For a bunch of corporate security guards, they seemed a lot better prepared than he'd realised. "You sure about Jamie?"

Fonseca patted his arm. "Yeah. I'm sorry."

Chris hadn't had Jamie's back, and he'd never forgive himself. But unexpected people like Zakko and Fonseca had his, and he wouldn't forget.

05

Why did I decide to deploy air support without Erskine's permission when I'm a soldier in name only, you mean? Because I couldn't sit there and watch people fighting for their lives, knowing that I could do something. Montello's troops could have been us. And we could have been them.

Major Dan Trinder, explaining himself to
Alex Gorko

LAUREL AVENUE, KINGSTON:
10 MINUTES AFTER THE AMBUSH

Things weren't going quite how Solomon had expected.

Two of the ambushers had somehow escaped both the firefight and the missile strike and had holed up in another house. Solomon could detect their heat profiles. There were formal procedures for this kind of thing, but they seemed unnecessarily risky under the circumstances, and Solomon's rules were not those of Captain Fonseca.

She patched into the remaining Lammergeier's loudhailer, standing behind a barricade of armoured vehicles that had rolled off to recover the trucks. Everyone else had their weapons trained on the house. The three dumb quadrubots spread around the back of it, under Solomon's direction.

"We know you're in there. We can see exactly where you are." Fonseca's voice boomed across a silent road. This was her first real mission, and certainly the first time she'd killed any hostiles, but she didn't seem shaken. "Your exits are blocked, so you're not going anywhere. Lay down your weapons and surrender, or I'll use force. Your call."

There was a long silence. Erin Piller interrupted. "Forget it. Those bastards are *mine*. I insist."

She'd declined to leave on the casevac with Chris Montello and the others, and so had the APC crew and the dog handler, plus his dogs. The transit camp team crouched behind the cover of the APC, their uniforms a threadbare mix of military uniforms and hunting gear, but the look on their faces said one thing: they would finish this, and they didn't need Ainatio to help them do it.

Solomon had outlived enough humans to think he finally understood mortality, but today was a revelation. He'd never seen a real man who'd been killed, really *seen* him rather than viewed an image in an archive, a person who wasn't old and anonymous but someone who had friends standing nearby who were eaten up with shock, anger, and grief.

What's the right thing to do? What's the safest thing to do? What'll preserve the maximum number of lives? Are all these lives equal? Do those men deserve the same consideration as my comrades?

Another missile would end the siege in seconds. Solomon decided it was justified. The men barricaded inside the house had chosen to use lethal force, and whether they surrendered or were captured, there were no courts or prisons to deal with them. The last thing he needed at this point in the Nomad mission was the burden of hostile prisoners who'd need to be held indefinitely. Letting them escape would only be a partial solution, because they might be part of a larger group that could return and find their way to Kill Line.

And what about justice for Jamie Wickens and his comrades?

Everyone's interests were best served by removing the attackers from the equation. Solomon wasn't afraid to pass judgement. The sentence was obvious, but he knew that Fonseca's rulebook said otherwise.

"We'll deal with them, Private Piller," Fonseca said. "Just load your vehicle onto the Lammergeier and let us take care of things. We need to get your driver's arm treated."

"I'm fine." Jackson flexed his shoulder without letting go of his rifle. "I'll be right as rain once I've perforated those two assholes."

Erin leaned across Fonseca and muted the loudhailer. "Captain, this isn't exactly our first prom. And this isn't your fight. We're grateful for your intervention, but we need to sort this out ourselves."

Solomon interpreted that as meaning Erin intended to kill the two men one way or another, and that she thought Fonseca had neither the stomach nor the combat experience to do it. He could hear Trinder on the secure link, but he was occupied with the inbound casevac, and it wasn't a given that he'd be able to resolve this anyway. Despite the polite observation of ranks, Fonseca had no authority over Chris Montello's troops. If they stormed the house, how would she stop them? She wouldn't open fire. Fonseca did things by the book because that was what Trinder expected of her. She was a good loyal 2IC, as he called it, and she wouldn't disappoint him.

"I'm supposed to detain them unless they leave me no alternative," Fonseca said.

Erin didn't shift an inch. "Jamie was twenty-three. *Twenty-three.* This wasn't worth his life. But it's sure as shit worth theirs. And what are you going to do with prisoners? You've got a nice little Ainatio court, have you, with a nice little Ainatio judge?"

Solomon decided to speak up. He couldn't pass himself off as a non-sentient AI now. It was time they found out what he was.

"Captain, I have a suggestion."

The squad stared at him. The dogs, who had already sniffed him warily before backing off, suddenly seemed mesmerised by the sound of his voice.

"This body's designed to withstand all the challenges I'm likely to encounter in there," Solomon said. "I can accompany Private Piller's squad."

"Sorry, what are you?" Erin stood over him, frowning. She was either in her thirties or a twenty-something aged by hardship. Her long chestnut hair was carefully braided and pinned up. "Are you a remote? Is someone back at HQ operating you?"

"No, I'm a fully autonomous combat AI, among other things. My name's Solomon."

"You were banned a long time ago. Everywhere."

"So I was. May I have a private word with the Captain?"

"Sure."

Erin and the others headed back up the road to the gun truck. Solomon watched via his rear-facing cam as she picked up an automatic weapon from the back of the bullet-scarred vehicle and paused, staring past it at something. It was probably Jamie Wickens's blood.

These people were ready to die for each other.

Solomon knew that this happened, but reading about it was nothing like seeing it unfold second by second, talking to people whose lives might be over in the next few minutes and who knew that. He recalled Bednarz's very brief but clear guidance on his purpose. This moment was like understanding it fully for the very first time.

"What do you have in mind, Sol?" Fonseca asked. "Just blow the place up?"

"That's certainly an effective solution, but I feel everyone's interests are best served by standing back and allowing our neighbours to finish their mission. I can get them into the house."

"Risky."

"They need to do it."

"Did we screw up?"

"Not at all. You scrambled air support as soon as the drone detected combatants moving into position, you attempted to alert the squad, and you neutralised the enemy rapidly. By the book."

"And a kid still got his brains blown out."

"That's still not your fault. Stand down. Remember that I'm not under Trinder's command. My rules of engagement are my own, and I'll do what's right and necessary for our mutual benefit. You have no responsibility."

"But I'm the commander here."

"Erskine knows you have no control over me, as I shall remind her if she questions the decision. This isn't the time to take prisoners."

"I realise Erskine won't like us bringing back violent ferals we've got to lock up, but we've still got rules."

"Then I suggest you withdraw to the Lammergeier and wait," Solomon said. "Take the dogs on board with you. I don't know how they'll react to me and the other quads under stress."

"I could just fry the damn house," she said. "I get that they need payback, but these guys have already lost one buddy today. I don't want them losing any more."

"I can handle this, Captain. Please withdraw."

Fonseca stood staring at the siege house for a moment as if she was regretting this, then checked her helmet optics and darted away, head down.

Solomon's thermal scan showed the two men, one upstairs and the other moving back and forth in what was probably the passage to the back door. He activated the three quadrubots idling at the back of the house and set them to attack if anyone tried to escape. They were now his detached arms and eyes, part of his neural network.

Erin Piller walked up to him with the rifle she'd taken from the gun truck.

"So you're going in with us," she said.

"I am, Private."

"Are you armed, or are you a breaching device? And why am I talking to you like you're human?"

"Because I'm an AI, not a robot. I'm just housed in one for the time being. Think of me as a disembodied brain in a highly specialised car."

"Fair enough. So are you? Armed, I mean."

"Yes. I could do this alone. But I understand why you want to do it yourselves."

"Do you really."

"Yes. I understood it when I saw that your sergeant was more worried about your welfare than bleeding to death."

Erin looked at him in the way humans always did, searching for some kind of eye contact, and he knew he'd established an understanding.

"Call me Erin," she said. "So you've located them, yeah?"

"We have one target by the front upstairs window and a second downstairs moving between the front and back. That seems to be the hall. I'll move the other bots as a distraction."

Erin turned to the others. "Okay, Conway and Jackson breach the back door, Solomon takes out the front door. I go in via the front, neutralise Guy One downstairs, then we move upstairs to take out Guy Two, if he hasn't already come down shooting. Dieter can sit this out with the dogs."

It wasn't a difficult task. Solomon hadn't worked with weapons since his initial development phase, and never at close quarters like this, but he had every tactic in his database, he could see what was happening, and nothing here could kill or disable him. His only problem was ensuring that none of the squad were injured. That included being hit by ricochets off his frame.

"Wouldn't you prefer to use Ainatio optics?" he asked. "Then you'll see what I can see."

Conway adjusted his goggles. They just looked like basic protection. "Thanks, but this isn't the time to get used to new gear. We'll be fine."

"Everybody in position," Erin said. It didn't appear to trouble her that Solomon was as unfamiliar a piece of technology as the advanced optics they'd declined, but optics were harder to relate to than a talking bot. "Any chance of the Lammergeier running its engines for a while to cover our noise?"

"Consider it done," Solomon said.

The aircraft throttled up. While Jackson and Conway worked their way through the gardens to the back of the house, Solomon moved the bots to the other side of the back yard to distract Guy Two. That got the man's attention. A burst of fire spat from the window. Solomon saw it from the quads' viewpoint and for a second, he caught a glimpse of his prey, not some unkempt savage but a grey-haired, clean-shaven man in his fifties who took care of his appearance. Solomon wondered about the who and the why, marvelling again at the willingness of men to face almost certain death rather than save themselves, but it didn't change what he needed to do.

Conway was in position now, sticking a frame charge to the back door.

Solomon adjusted his legs and crawled forward almost flat on the ground while Erin moved from one house to the next via the front yard, hugging the walls. They ended up on opposite sides of the frontage, facing each other across the porch.

"He's gone into the front room," Solomon said. Guy Two seemed to have settled by the window again. Solomon adjusted to a bipedal stance and stood up, ready to turn and breach the door. "Ready?"

Erin got on the radio. "Ready. Stand by... in three... two... *go*."

The explosion from the back sent Guy Two racing to the top of the stairs as Solomon punched out the lock on the front door and burst it open. He stood back to let Erin enter the hall, then the firing started. There was no point in waiting outside. He dropped back onto all fours and leaped through the front window, crashing straight into the living room on a carpet of shattered glass. Guy One, rifle aimed at the door to the hall, spun around just as Solomon righted himself and managed one startled grunt before the door swung open. Erin put two short bursts into him. He fell where he stood.

"Downstairs — clear," she called. She looked at Solomon, wide-eyed. "I thought you were following me. I could have shot you."

"No harm done. I'm bulletproof."

"Move."

Conway and Jackson were exchanging fire up and down an impressive oak staircase. The ornate balustrade was in splinters.

"Last mag." Jackson reloaded, pressed flat against the wall. "He's got a friggin' armoury up there."

Solomon knew they didn't want him to fight their battle. This was retribution. Maybe the individual who'd shot Jamie was already dead in the burning shell of another house, but that detail would never be known, and it obviously didn't change anything for this squad.

Jackson yelled up the stairs over the noise of the Lammergeier still idling in the street. "Hey, buddy, you're going to die here. You know what we're killing each other for? A few boxes of toilet paper. Now there's an epitaph. No wonder this world's fucked."

A voice yelled back. "I've got nothing to lose, then, asshole."

Jackson gestured to Solomon and mouthed something, making a walking gesture with two fingers and pointing to the staircase.

Can you shield me?

Solomon rose on his hind legs. Jackson nodded and gave him a thumbs-up, then slipped in behind him as he put one rear foot on the stairs. They edged up one step at a time. Solomon kept his body turned towards the landing to make sure the launcher on his underside was clear and watched the doors. There were three. All were slightly ajar, but he could see a man's heat profile near the middle one.

I could just fire straight through the partition wall now.
No. Remember why we need to do this.

"Ready?" Jackson whispered.

"Yes. Watch the middle door. Wait until — "

The heat profile moved. A hand went to open the door. It was plenty of thinking time for an AI, but barely a heartbeat for a human. Jackson stepped sideways to open fire but Solomon had already fired two rounds before the door was fully open. The man was hit and falling by the time Jackson began squeezing the trigger. But Jackson got his shot in. Solomon hoped that honour was satisfied.

Jackson edged in and checked the body. Solomon knew the destructive effect of the rounds he was carrying, but like witnessing death, it was a very different thing to see it and integrate it into his emotional learning.

I've killed a man. I need to think about this later.

"Upstairs clear," Jackson called.

"Clear, all targets neutralised." Solomon repeated it so that Fonseca could hear it over the net. "My apologies, Jackson. I was a little premature."

"No worries. Thanks."

"You got him."

"Sure. And his spare ammo."

Erin searched Guy Two's pockets and held up a piece of plastic. "Another ration card. Might not be his, of course. But if it is, these guys are a long way from home. I'd kind of thought they were the locals defending their town to the last."

"They let you enter," Solomon said. "Possibly to see if you were part of a larger convoy."

"I guess they wanted fuelled vehicles. They could have had the goods any time."

Jackson inspected his arm. Blood was seeping through his jacket sleeve. "Toilet rolls." He shook his head as if he despaired of the world, and hissed through his teeth. "Ass paper."

Fonseca was waiting at the end of the drive when they came out. She looked somewhere between relieved and guilty. The dogs were running up and down the street with their handler wandering behind them, doing a final sweep to make sure that nobody was hiding. They seemed untroubled by all the noise.

"We had to return fire," Solomon said, not waiting for Fonseca's question. "All above board and in keeping with international law, if you still choose to follow it. I'm going to direct the quads to bury the bodies here."

"Just these two," Fonseca said, nodding at the house. "The other buildings are too unstable to send anyone in to recover remains."

"These bots are designed for hazardous recovery work."

"I know. But I say we leave it. Chris Montello's in surgery, by the way."

Solomon had never quite understood her ability to be callous one moment and compassionate the next. "I'm glad we could help."

"Help? Alex says the surgeons were brawling over him. They haven't had a decent emergency for years." Fonseca walked off, shaking her head. "They've all got some technique or treatment they want to try for real. Medics, huh?"

Erin came down the drive behind Solomon and stooped to pat his back. He wasn't sure if it was a human back-pat or what she might do to a favourite dog, but he didn't mind either way. He wanted to ask her if they really had come all this way to scavenge for ammunition that Ainatio could easily have given them, but it sounded too much like telling her Jamie had died for something trivial.

"I'll drive the APC home," she said. "But if you could fly the others back and get Jackson to a medic, we'd be grateful."

"Of course." Perhaps she wanted to weep and couldn't do it in front of her comrades. "May I ride with you?"

She looked taken aback. "Yeah. Yeah, no problem."

The landscape around Solomon seemed as alien as anything on Opis. He'd spent very little time outside the Ainatio facility, and his view of the wider world beyond the perimeter fence was now confined to drones and satellite feeds. That was nothing like being corporeal and standing on solid ground. Networked to the other quadrubots, he both watched and experienced the excavation of two pits on the lawn at the back of the house and the sensation of placing the bodies in them. The bots' manipulators were temporarily his own hands, and their close-up view of the shredded bodies were in his eyes. It made killing very personal.

Yes, this is odd. I know these deaths are regrettable, but I feel no guilt. I don't feel victorious, either. And I do know both emotions all too well.

He didn't know if either man would care whether his grave was marked, but he decided to do it anyway, and had the quads drive in single planks taken from a fence.

Fonseca sat down on the kerb next to him as the last of the squad vehicles were loaded and sealed for decontamination. "I'm going to put together a shopping list for the transit camp," she said. "Screw the regs. Ammo, compatible long-range radios, and better armour. And anything else you can think of. It's not like we'll go short."

"It's no problem for me to hide items in the inventory."

"Don't stay out too late with your new girlfriend, then. Catch you later."

New experiences were precious, even if Solomon felt uneasy that today's had come at the cost of personal tragedy. He arranged his frame in the APC's co-driver's seat and tried not to think about how odd he looked. Erin drove in silence for the first few miles, occasionally wiping the heel of her hand across one eye. Humans definitely needed to cry. He shouldn't have begged a ride. His presence was inhibiting her.

"I wish I could offer you some comfort," he said. "But I can't think of anything that would make today less painful."

"You're not really an AI, are you?"

"I am. I wouldn't lie to you."

"Autonomous doesn't explain your personality."

"I'm the only one of my kind. My initial development cost two trillion dollars."

"Pricey for a combat unit, even with government procurement."

"It's not my primary role. But I can be one when I transfer to an appropriate shell like this one. And yes, that does make me highly illegal and in breach of a dozen disarmament treaties and international restrictions on AI capability."

"So you can move into different... containers."

"Yes. I enjoy quadrubot frames, though. I feel more connected to reality. Although I don't normally use this particular one."

"What did they create you to do, then?"

Solomon really wanted to tell her. She deserved complete information to form her opinions. He did his best. "I manage complex projects, but my specialisation is ethics. Moral decision-making for the benefit of mankind."

Erin looked at him. "You and me both. Except a sniper rifle's a hell of a lot cheaper."

"Is it easier to talk to something that resembles a dog?"

"You're very perceptive." She tried to smile. "But then I'd expect that from a trillion-dollar intellect."

"You don't seem troubled that I'm banned tech."

"You don't seem troubled that my kind wiped out your kind. Well, *nearly* all of you."

"That was a consequence of using us to replace humans. I was created to do the exact opposite."

Erin nodded a few times as if she was answering a question only she could hear. Solomon decided to let her steer the conversation. He could see that she was churning over the day and still at that stage of struggling to believe what had happened. He was caught up in processing it too. It was a revelatory moment in his understanding of what Bednarz had set as his task, his duty to humanity, his development of human values within himself: *I want you to define the best, seek it out, and protect it against all its enemies.*

The best wasn't engineering genius, exquisite artistry, or philosophical insight. He understood now that it was about qualities rather than skills: loyalty, trust, a willingness to sacrifice yourself for others and for beliefs you held dear, to give up your future for someone else's. Before today, those concepts had always seemed almost theologically distant. Now he'd had a glimpse of them being lived out minute by minute, and the key to them was death. Even he was enmeshed in it now.

"You know something?" Erin said suddenly. It came out almost like a cough, as if she'd been bottling it up and couldn't hold it any longer. "I shouldn't have left it so late. Jamie, I mean. He gave me a bottle of perfume today. I should have told him I'd date him. He'd have been happy right up to the last second. You should never leave things unsaid. I didn't learn that lesson the first time, either."

Solomon wanted to ask what she meant by the first time, but it seemed too raw, and he had no magic phrase that would make her feel any better. Regret and guilt radiated from her. She said nothing else until she drove into the decontamination unit at the Kill Line boundary. Despite her silence, Solomon felt he now knew her better than he'd thought possible.

"Perhaps you should come into the base and see a doctor," he said. "Just for something to help you sleep tonight."

"Thanks, Solomon, but then there'll be the next night, and the next, and the next. I'll get through it."

"Do you want to visit Chris when he's well enough?" Solomon could use first names for all of them now. They felt like friends. "He's still in surgery."

"How do you know?"

"I'm linked to the research centre."

"Okay, yes."

"It might be a day or two, depending on the doctors."

"Thanks, Solomon. You're very kind. And you're a real badass under fire. You're always welcome in our gang."

Solomon was touched. Alex said things like that all the time, just throwaway comments, but Erin didn't seem the glib kind.

When she dropped him off at the main gate, the sentry leaned out of the guard hut to do a double-take as he identified himself with his ID code, an indication of how rare it was for him to venture outside in a bot frame. Why didn't he do this more often? Why had it taken so long to meet his neighbours? Things had to change. He had mankind's future to ensure. These were the people who would create it, and deserved to.

He decided to see Erskine first to pre-empt any repercussions over the rescue mission, but when he tracked her down she was having a relaxed chat with Dr Prinz in her office. The message log showed that the conversations between her and Trinder had only been about the likely length of Chris's treatment, not a dressing-down for unilateral decisions. Perhaps she'd been equally keen to see how her troops performed in a real crisis before any of them were entrusted with a Nomad mission.

Solomon transferred out of the quadrubot and merged back into the research centre's network to patrol the building. In the detachment's mess hall, Trinder was holding a wash-up on the Kingston mission, looking ten years younger, as if this was what he'd been waiting for all his life. Marc and Tev were playing pool in the recreation hall, and Alex Gorko was having a beer with Dr Mangel in a quiet corner of the bar.

In the medical wing, Chris Montello was in the recovery room, waking up from anaesthesia, his leg partially enclosed in the shell of an enhanced healing unit that was making his body produce bone and tissue at an accelerated rate. Solomon watched the realisation form on the man's face as he began piecing his memory together and remembered why he was here and what had happened.

The automated systems would monitor him in his infirmary room, but Solomon felt a need to watch over him personally. For someone who'd just had surgery, Chris was unusually restless. He dozed sporadically, sometimes waking and just lying there with one arm across his eyes, his other at his side, fist clenched and hitting the blanket in a steady rhythm. He looked like a man who wanted to rewind the day and do things differently. Solomon knew that he wasn't thinking about his own injury.

In another part of the infirmary, Derek Levine was dying. He was eighty-three. His records said he'd had another stroke, and that he was deteriorating rapidly and not expected to survive the next few days. Notes for the nursing staff specified hourly checks as well as routine monitoring.

Over the course of a century, Solomon had seen many staff grow old and die, but today his filter had shifted forever. He'd killed a human, and he'd seen grief and indelible regret at close quarters. He also remembered that Bednarz hadn't lived to see the completion of the mission that had consumed his life.

Don't leave it too late.

Solomon knew what he had to do. It might be days or even weeks before Erskine revealed *Cabot*'s situation to the staff, and by then Levine could be dead. He and his engineering team believed a drive failure had destroyed *Cabot* — their work, their responsibility, their fault — and it had haunted them. Levine was still alive to believe it.

Why didn't I see it was wrong to let them go to their graves blaming themselves? Why did I comply? Should the mission ever take precedence over individuals?

At least he could try to put things right with Levine. Erskine's need for secrecy wasn't reason enough to deny the man the truth. Erin Piller had shown Solomon what he ought to do. He slipped into his regular quadrubot frame and went to find the medical staff.

"May I see Mr Levine?"

Dr Mendoza was on duty, wandering around the reception area. He looked up from the screen he was reading. "He's not very communicative. He hasn't been able to talk since the last CVA."

"That's okay," Solomon said. "Can he still understand speech?"

"There's no major cognitive impairment. He nods and gestures."

"I just want to talk to him about the old days. I was there. You're too young to remember."

Mendoza smiled. "You know you're getting old when even the AIs look young."

Solomon tapped on the door and went in. Levine was watching some TV rerun, propped up on pillows, but his eyes were glazed and Solomon wasn't sure that he could even see the screen. The old engineer turned his head with difficulty to squint at Solomon, frowning with bewilderment.

"It's Solomon, Mr Levine. Remember me? I was Tad Bednarz's AI project. I just borrow the quad frame when I need to interact. There's something I have to tell you."

Levine nodded and beckoned him closer. His lips formed a circle, but no coherent sound emerged, just a groan as he tried to speak.

"May I share some news with you? It's important." It was also a gamble. There was every chance that the man's last conscious moments would be spent regretting that he'd blamed himself for *Cabot*'s apparent fate. But Solomon had to seize the chance. Erin had told him so. "Sir, this was kept top secret for security reasons. *Cabot* wasn't lost. The ship and the crew are safe. In a couple of months, they'll land on Opis."

Levine didn't react for a few moments. Solomon thought he'd understood, but it would have been a lot for even a healthy man to take in, let alone one who was dying. Levine shook his head.

"No, you didn't fail, Mr Levine," Solomon said. "The mission was a success. It was just top secret. I'm truly sorry that you and your colleagues thought you'd lost the ship and all those lives. You *didn't*. You made history. Do you understand?"

Levine looked blank.

"Do you believe me, sir?"

Levine shook his head emphatically.

"Okay, I'll show you. I swear that this is the truth." Solomon activated the live feed from Opis and diverted it to the old man's TV screen. "This is live from Nomad Base, right now. We've got an FTL relay. We established a tiny wormhole for comms. And this is where the crew are going to live and work."

They sat and watched the feed together. Nothing much was moving, except the bots trundling about their duties, but the dark blue birds that had trailed Solomon on the surface passed through the shot a couple of times.

Levine's eyes filled with tears, not the rheumy eyes of a dying man, but a man weeping. Solomon had seen two people cry today, and it was hard to tell if Levine's tears were for happier reasons.

"You did that, Mr Levine," Solomon whispered. "This is your achievement. Humanity's future. Be proud. Am I forgiven for not telling you sooner? I'm so very sorry."

Levine stretched out an unsteady arm and put his hand on Solomon's back. His fingers felt cold, at least colder than Erin's had been. He kept nodding for a long time, but he was still struggling to say something. Eventually, sounds formed.

"All... okay?"

Solomon realised he wanted reassurance about the crew. It seemed to be what really mattered to him. Solomon couldn't imagine the undeserved guilt he'd had to live with all those years.

"Yes, the crew's alive and well," Solomon said. "You did a good job, sir. A *brilliant* job."

Levine broke into a lopsided, peaceful smile. He seemed to understand just fine. It was a testament to his character that he appeared to have no anger.

"Wormhole," he mumbled, still smiling. "Hah."

I want you to define the best, identify it, and protect it against all its enemies.

Solomon was now clear what the very best of humanity was, and exactly what he had to protect, with or without Erskine's approval.

* * *

DIRECTOR'S OFFICE, AINATIO PARK RESEARCH CENTRE: NEXT MORNING

Now was as good a time as any to tell the staff.

Erskine had inherited a project plan from her father that laid out milestone dates almost to the day because so many elements of the mission could be calculated exactly. It had taken prodigious mathematics to get *Cabot* where she was today. But the untidy world that the ship had left behind was an unfeeling saboteur, lobbing clogs into the machinery on a daily basis. Erskine had started to feel a change in the atmosphere here, a kind of impatience bordering on irritation, and that hadn't been helped by yesterday's rescue flooding the place with testosterone and outsiders. If she let the restlessness fester, it would be hard to ask extraordinary things of people in the years to come.

And those demands *would* be extraordinary.

You didn't think I could do it, did you, Dad? Neither did I.

It had to be today, then. She'd call the meeting and make the announcement in the conference hall. It would be brief, and she could follow it up with a Q-and-A session over the network later when the reality had sunk in and everyone had considered their questions. But the trump card she'd play today would be the live feed from Nomad. People might be angry and upset that they'd been fed so much disinformation for so long, but they were also scientists, and the breathtaking novelty of a new planet and a base all fully fitted and fresh out of the box — and the revelation of FTL comms — would stun them. The lies would be forgotten as soon as they realised they could watch Opis in real time, and that in a matter of weeks they'd have real human beings on the ground to talk to, not just bots.

There'd be some awkward questions about priorities and how this would now fit in with the die-back remediation research, but she'd handle that.

She called Berman. "Phil, I'm going to do the announcement today. Let's make it sixteen hundred. Can you set up the conference hall with a Nomad link?"

"Going for drama, then, Director?"

"Picture, thousand words, equivalent values."

"Do you want me to contact department heads?"

"No, I'll send them a message myself. They know it's due."

"It's going to be an interesting adjustment period."

Erskine could translate Bermanese like a native. "There's always a trade-off between briefing in advance of a critical event and losing your grip on need-to-know."

"And have we decided how we're going to tell Doug Brandt?" Berman asked. "Because this will now leak. Guaranteed."

"We've put a lot of effort into keeping the local population at arm's length. Very few staff have any contact with them."

"Well, Colin Croad does, for one."

"We've got time to work this out."

"News travelled fast about the transit camp patient. Main topic of gossip in the staff restaurant this morning."

Erskine reached for her screen and checked for medical updates. "That's inside the wire. Let's see how long he's going to be in here... Montello, Christopher Anthony. Maybe a week. So they're seizing the chance to test tissue regeneration."

"Yes, not an injury they've seen before. They were surprised how long it took to remove bone fragments before they could start."

Erskine wondered who'd visited the man and might have been the source of the gossip. She switched to the security log. Two Lammergeiers scrambling was an event that was impossible to hide, though. There was bound to be talk.

Something else caught her eye. Solomon had visited the medical wing in his quadrubot frame on returning from Kingston, and he didn't appear to have gone into Montello's room. Why not? Ah, he'd visited Levine. That explained it. But monitoring had been suspended from the time he entered the room to when he left an hour later. He must have done that himself. He could override every system, but the question was why he'd bothered. In a human, it would have been secretive behaviour, but what secrets would Solomon need to keep from her?

The thought suddenly struck her as naive. Of course he had secrets. Even with his rather quaint privacy rules, there was probably a lot he saw people doing in unguarded moments but never mentioned to anyone. He'd also kept the biggest secret of all: Nomad.

She'd grown up with his ubiquitous presence, and she hadn't had to worry about the implications until now. He'd know right away that she'd accessed the logs, but perhaps he wouldn't consider how the data might look to her.

"I'll talk to you later, Phil," Erskine said. "I need to give Trinder time to brief his people, too. Never a good thing to let your security team find out the hard way, is it?"

"On that topic, you didn't seem troubled by his decision yesterday."

"I'd rather see him deal with an emergency than ask my permission first. I'm reassured to see that his people are competent to do more than play war games."

"It's not like him."

"I'd say that he's reconsidered what the detachment needs to be able to do since I told him about Nomad, and he's being pragmatic about it."

"I appreciate that he's never been... "

"Dissenting? Abrasive? Assertive? I did worry that he might not have the backbone for a follow-up mission, but perhaps I've underestimated him."

Erskine sat thinking about what Berman had said. She realised she knew too little about the military mind. It had never been an issue: the detachment was there to provide site security, and although a few of them had come from military and law enforcement backgrounds, she'd never been conscious of a barracks atmosphere, or even knew if she'd recognise one. They'd been among the most recent hires and tended to keep to themselves even in this closed community. Then there was Montello's ragtag band of vets and refugees. They'd never been her concern: a small, badly-equipped group kept at bay by a damn big fence was unlikely to be a threat to Nomad. But she knew there was some common philosophy between people in uniform, and perhaps it was more a sense of shared identity than simple duty — or boredom — that had driven Trinder's rescue mission.

Now she had nearly two hundred military personnel about to be revived in *Cabot*. The mission depended entirely on their cooperation. She couldn't coerce them. She couldn't even send anyone to enforce her orders.

Yes, it's high time I learned how the military thinks.

"Solomon," she said. "Are you free?"

"Yes, Director." The AI's voice emerged from the speaker on her desk. "What can I do for you?"

"Ah, my troubled thoughts are still closed to you, then."

"I'll work on telepathy if you wish, but AIs were banned from unsolicited sensory stimulus reconstruction a long time ago."

Solomon's tone was always measured. It was hard to tell if he was joking or being sarcastic. "Any thoughts on Major Trinder and his team?"

"In what way, Director?"

"Should I worry about him launching a mission without clearing it with me?"

"Not if you want him to do his job properly. The detachment was very effective. Lives saved, threats neutralised. We're all the safer for it."

"Good."

"May I ask you a question in return?"

"Go ahead."

"If Major Trinder had asked you for permission to go to Sergeant Montello's aid, would you have agreed?"

"There's no point having a defence force if it isn't tested."

"I meant would you have felt Montello's patrol was worth saving."

Erskine was used to Solomon's excursions into ethical debate, but it was the first time a conversation had felt like it was acquiring an edge. She really should have given him the expected answer right away, but if the dumbest of dumb software could detect stress changes in the human voice, then Solomon would definitely know if she was lying.

"It would be the right thing to do." Seeing as he was playing dare, truth, or promise, she'd counter-attack. "My turn. Can I ask you why you visited Mr Levine last night?"

"The man's dying. I decided to tell him the truth about *Cabot* and that he wasn't responsible for any deaths or the failure of the mission. I showed him the live feed. I wanted him to know what he'd achieved instead of going to his grave believing he'd made some terrible mistake that got people killed."

Erskine couldn't believe he'd done it. "Solomon, this is still a top secret project. We managed to keep this under wraps for years because we *had* to. Nobody was to be told. *Nobody*."

"I know. I decided otherwise." He actually sounded defiant. "Levine's hardly in a position to tell anyone else about it. Not that I would have withheld the information even if he was."

"Good grief." Erskine was shocked. "At least you're honest about it."

"We only lie to wound or protect others, or to protect ourselves. I have no need to wound, and no fear of punishment, so there's no point in deceiving you."

"Oh." *No fear of punishment. He's designed to be invulnerable. Am I imagining things, or is he getting rebellious?* "Really."

"Anyway, if you're addressing the staff this afternoon, I'd better make sure that the Nomad feed's set up for the most informative view. It'll be dark, so I'll adjust the floodlighting."

He'd hit a raw nerve and provoked her into needing to win. *This is insane. I'm arguing with software.* But Erskine couldn't stop herself rising to the bait and trying to outflank him. "So do *you* think Montello's people are worth risking lives for?"

"Yes, of course I do. They're loyal, courageous, and actually rather inspiring. I like them. I've learned a great deal."

No, she definitely wasn't imagining it. Solomon was putting her in her place and telling her that he knew best. She'd never known him to be anything other than reassuring or analytical before. But it was too easy to see him as wholly human, complete with all seven sins, and forget the very non-human and complex intellect beneath the interface. Without him and his slaved AIs, most of this facility and the entire Nomad project would probably be beyond this small workforce's ability to manage. Perhaps he just saw her concerns as trivial at such a critical time for the mission. If it was anything other than that, it didn't bear thinking about.

"I'd better get ready for my presentation, then," she said.

She rehearsed in her office, or at least she started to. What was there to tell? No matter how much she revealed, only four points would register on her audience today: the *Cabot* disaster was a lie, the ship was about to reach Pascoe's Star, Nomad Base was complete, and — perhaps the real shock that would kick in a little later — Ainatio had developed FTL propulsion. Every other detail would be lost in a sea of slack jaws, gasps, and disbelief. Erskine decided to dispense with notes and wing it.

Jeans. Yes, she'd wear jeans today. The designer suits were the old era. Now Ainatio was entering a new age and she had to signal that she was one of the team, ready to roll up her sleeves and face necessary hardships to create humanity's future, because they were the lucky few in an unlucky world.

She reached across her desk to put in a call to Trinder to tell him he could brief his people confidentially in advance of the main announcement, but paused. No matter how the troops heard, they'd want to know why he hadn't told them earlier, and they were smart enough to work out that the job they'd signed up for wasn't the one they'd be asked to do now. A few extra hours to worry wouldn't make them any happier. It was better for all the staff to hear the same message at the same time.

Erskine had just over five hours to wait. It felt like killing time in eternity. She spent it reading reports more carefully than she would normally have done and watching the feed from Opis, remembering Trinder's reaction and trying to see it for the first time as the staff would. She even lingered over a late lunch in the staff restaurant. If the world hadn't gone to hell in a handbasket, she would have been preparing for an international news conference now, ready to make world headlines. But there was only half the world left to watch, and it was the half that she couldn't tell. There would be no papers presented or glittering scientific prizes awarded, both of which mattered very much to some of the researchers, but not to all. She decided to major on the gratitude and immortality of history.

"Director, you're on." Berman stood at the open office door. "I brought the buggy to save you the walk. Tends to build tension if you've got a long time to think about it."

She tried to give him a withering glance. "Do I look tense?"

"This was never going to be easy."

"Did you ever consider becoming a motivational speaker, Phil?" She slid onto the buggy's narrow bench seat. "It's probably not your calling."

The conference hall was full. It wasn't hard to draw a crowd here for any kind of talk when so little happened, but she hadn't given an address in years, and never one arranged at the last minute and flagged as urgent. She walked up to the podium and burned a few moments rearranging her notes and stylus, reminding herself where the screen controls were while she scanned the audience.

Trinder and Fonseca were sitting together on the right-hand side near the front, surrounded by most of the detachment. Trinder's arms were folded tight across his chest, his gaze fixed on the wall-sized screen behind Erskine. He'd obviously worked out that he hadn't been given the chance to brief his people as promised and he seemed to be avoiding eye contact. But then he unfolded his arms and looked right at her, unblinking, and she knew that their working relationship had taken a turn for the worse. She'd never had to ask him to trust her. Now she suspected she never could. She looked away and swallowed to clear her throat.

"Thank you all for coming this afternoon," she said.

The general murmur stopped dead and the stage lighting suddenly seemed harsh and pitiless, interrogation-style. Erskine carried on.

"What I'm about to tell you *is* good news. But it'll shock you, and it might make you angry. You're bound to have a lot of questions, too, but I might not have answers to all of them yet." *Here we go.* She paused to gauge the mood as best she could and saw a mix of blank and baffled expressions. "It started with a lie that's now changed human history. For years, we've told you — told the world — that the *Cabot* mission was lost with all hands. But that's a cover story we maintained to prevent the mission from being compromised by hostile governments and international agencies. The ship was never lost. It's now nearing its destination, Pascoe's Star, and the crew's due to be woken from cryo very soon. The mission, code-named Nomad, is on schedule, and we've got real-time video to show you, live from the base."

She paused and looked around the audience. It hadn't sunk in. She tried again.

"Yes. You heard correctly. We have a real-time link, because we developed FTL technology after *Cabot* was launched. We've been constructing the habitat in the meantime using remotely managed bots." She waited again, but the hubbub she expected still didn't materialise. "Come on, people. Don't we even get a gasp for the FTL?"

Somebody began clapping, but very weakly. This was too much for even five-star intellects to digest all at once. Erskine looked around, spotted Fonseca staring accusingly at Trinder, and Trinder apparently trying not to look at her. It was easy to add a caption that would be repeated across the company as staff realised that their department heads had known this all along: *"Why didn't you tell us?"*

Erskine ploughed on. "So... let me show you the live feed from Opis, Pascoe b, which some of you might recall is a warm Terran-type exoplanet. Here it is."

She touched the control on the lectern and the big screen came alive. There was the camp, a cluster of buildings bathed in floodlights, the bot tracks crisscrossing the ground now thrown into sharp relief. *That* did it. Now she heard the murmurs and the collective intake of breath.

"Ladies and gentlemen, welcome to the core of humanity's first permanent colony in deep space. It's all ready for *Cabot*'s crew to move in. And we have extraordinary times ahead. I'm sorry that so few of you were told, and that included me at one time, but we have good reason for extreme security."

Nobody reacted. Nobody fidgeted or whispered, not for a few seconds.

Then the real applause broke out, sporadically at first, then rippling around the room until most of the auditorium joined in with varying degrees of enthusiasm. Some didn't, though, and sat either staring at the screen or with their heads lowered, talking among themselves.

Erskine risked catching Trinder's eye again, but he just nodded, got up, and walked out, followed by his troops, no doubt to do some explaining in private.

"Director, shall I hang around to talk people through this?" Solomon asked via the public address system. "In fact, I could transfer to the Nomad quad and *walk* them through it."

Erskine was almost relieved that he'd interrupted. "Excellent idea. Ladies and gentlemen, Solomon's been managing the site for some years via the bots constructed in situ, and he often uploads himself to one of the utility quads to carry out on-site assessments. I suppose we can say that Solomon's the first person to set foot on an extrasolar planet."

"I'll be right back," Solomon said.

A little muttering started up. One of the botanists raised a hand. "I have questions, Director. This is a stunning achievement, but I see a lot of gaping holes."

"Go ahead, David." She had to face this sooner or later. "By the way, I'm going to circulate the original plan and follow up with a series of Qs and As when you've all had time to process this and work out what you want to know. And hear your suggestions, of course. Sorry, David. Do carry on."

"Okay, are the *Cabot* crew now settlers, or are they coming back at some time? Are you going to share this information with other countries? Will there be more missions? Who's going to work on Nomad, or is there another team somewhere we don't know about? Is this why the orbitals and vessels are being maintained? How does this affect us when we're mostly working on die-back and resistant crops? And what's Ainatio's priority, fixing Earth or starting over?"

Erskine couldn't help herself. He obviously just wanted to vent but didn't dare call her a lying bitch to her face.

"Would you like an answer to each question, David, or was that just an indication of how out of the loop you feel?" She made a show of getting out her screen to take notes. "And I so hoped you were going to ask me about superluminal propulsion, which is equally historic."

"Pick one, Director."

"Okay, there's no second team you don't know about. All that's left of Ainatio is what you see around you. The company effectively consumed itself to focus on Nomad. AIs have done most of the heavy lifting. It should have played out very differently, but nobody foresaw die-back and all the catastrophes that flowed from it. And I'll be honest with you and admit that I don't think we'll manage to stop it in time."

David, like most of the staff, was well able to think through that last answer. It was better to let everyone work out the implications gradually and develop some enthusiasm than announce that there had to be manned follow-up missions in the near future or else *Cabot*'s journey would be wasted.

"Oh, wow! Look!" Some of the engineers were getting excited about what they could see on the live feed. When Erskine turned to look, a quadrubot had walked into the frame. It raised a front leg and did a restrained, regal wave at its audience.

"Good evening. I'm now live from Opis." Solomon could turn in quite a dramatic performance when he wanted to. "I'll switch to my onboard cam and show you around. I'm sorry that it's dark at the moment, but I'm sure there'll be many more opportunities to see the planet in daylight."

One of the botanists gasped. "Oh my God, what's that?"

A black shape flapped low across the ground behind Solomon and vanished into the darkness beyond the floodlighting.

"Ah, some of the local wildlife," he said. "A bird, if the zoologists don't mind my loose terminology. We didn't find Opis empty, obviously. It's got a rich ecology, the atmosphere's breathable, the climate in this region is generally temperate, and we can grow crops with a little modification. That's why Tad Bednarz was determined to take a big gamble to get us here. Let me show you around the camp. You'll be impressed."

"Birds," someone murmured. "Complex life forms. No suits or sealed habitats. Okay, China can have Mars."

Erskine would face hard questions and even harder decisions when people recovered from the shock, but for the time being, more of them were getting caught up in the wonder of it. The deception, the die-back, and the implications for this remnant of Western civilisation were forgotten, at least for the time being.

"Indeed," she said. "They can."

06

We're not in the business of saving Renoirs and recreating Earth like some kind of theme park. We'll reproduce what we need to survive, but the rest we'll forge for ourselves. We'll produce our own artists and our own Renoirs. History has to be remembered if we're to learn, but looking back, living for the past and trying to be what we once were, automatically lulls us into believing that our best is behind us and that we can't be greater.

Georgina Erskine, CEO of Ainatio Industries,
explaining the absence of an art repository to
Dr Annis Kim

STAFF RESTAURANT,
AINATIO PARK RESEARCH CENTRE:
ONE DAY AFTER THE CABOT ANNOUNCEMENT

If Alex timed it right, he might reach the hot food counter to pick his lunch, grab some silverware, and make it back to a table to eat at least a mouthful before it was cold and congealed. It had already taken him twice as long to walk the corridor between labs 5A and 6A because he'd been ambushed at every office doorway and water cooler with questions, endless questions, very good and perceptive questions, *logical* questions about every damn hole in the Nomad mission document.

He should have seen this coming, even if Erskine hadn't, but of course she had. She'd have a good reason for not explaining all this to them. If there was anyone who exemplified the principle of never apologising and never explaining, it was Her Imperial Majesty.

Alex made it five yards from the double doors before he was intercepted by Audrey from Biomed. There was a streak of red finger-paint in her hair, probably applied by her toddler.

"There's a really big elephant in this room," she said.

He pointed at the servery. "My lunch is in here, too. Walk with me."

"We've all read the original document."

"I guessed. Ask away."

"A lot of detail's devoted to the follow-up missions. Small gene pool stuff. You need more people to supplement the *Cabot* crew, and even if those missions launch now, the crew will be old folks with grandchildren by the time the next ship lands."

"Correct."

"So fifty years ago we had enough people to choose from, all over the world. But now we're down to *this*." Audrey spread her arms. "Are we going to found an inbred colony of Cabotites, like some kind of Pitcairn Island? Are we shelving the whole colony idea and bringing *Cabot* home? Are we opening up ticket sales to Asia? What, exactly?"

As long as Audrey was with him, Alex wouldn't be hassled by anyone else. He assembled his plate of burritos as fast as he could and took his tray over to the far corner of the hall, where nobody could claim they were just passing and decide to join in. Was it time to be brutally honest? Screw it, he'd be caught out in any lies sooner rather than later, and it was easier to manage a mutinous crew if they had fewer reasons to lynch him.

"Well, the report was just for context," he said, pulling out a chair for her like a gentleman. "It was the intention. Now we have to tailor it to what's left of our reality. No, we don't have the global talent pool any more. No, we don't want *Cabot* to turn around and come home, because in forty-odd years we can't possibly know what kind of Earth they'll be returning to, and as they're not dumb, that'll cross their minds as well. And no, I don't think we say to China or Korea, hey, you go ahead and have this multi-trillion-dollar thing that bled us dry, because we just don't have the staff to fill the seats."

Audrey leaned forward on folded arms. "It's going to be us, isn't it?"

"What is?"

"We're the follow-up mission. We're breeding stock."

This was the problem with having a smart and sceptical workforce. They mostly thought like Erskine, and even if she hadn't had the luxury of choice when hiring staff, she'd regarded youth and fertility as qualifications in their own right. Audrey looked angry, face flushed and untidy mousey curls escaping from a hair clip. Alex cut off a chunk of untouched burrito and put it on a side plate for her, working on the premise that distracting an aggressive female with food worked pretty well for saving male spiders.

"Well, we've got four ships," he said. "It's not as good as fifty vessels and a lot more people, but there's a seat for everyone."

"Everyone who wants to go, you mean."

Alex still wasn't crazy about the idea himself. "We don't press-gang. Besides, I bet half the guys here wanted to be astronauts as kids."

"And lots of others love the idea of space and discovering cool stuff, but they don't want to live there."

"Okay, I can understand that."

"So what happens to the die-back programme if we decide to ship out? Or was it just a handy cover for Nomad activity, engineering crops and all that bullshit?"

"Aude, we could have done Nomad with just AIs and bots. In fact, we did, near as damn it. And we didn't need to send a manned ship. But that wouldn't be human colonisation, would it? That's the whole point of this."

Audrey seemed to have run out of steam. Her hair deflated to relative tidiness and the colour drained from her cheeks. Alex wondered whether to point out the red finger paint but deferred to cowardice.

"So I'm a brood mare," she said. "How about the town? Have they been carefully preserved to expand the gene pool too?"

"Come on, we couldn't have planned this. We have to work with what we have. And do you really think we'd leave them behind after they've kept this centre fed?"

"Have you told them? No? Didn't think so."

"Bednarz's plan had to change. Because shit happened."

"I don't want to go."

"That's how you feel now."

"Yes. And tomorrow as well, probably. I know things are bad outside the boundary and they won't improve for a long time, but I don't want my daughter growing up on a deserted planet. Her father thinks otherwise, because he can't see a future here. But Opis isn't what either of us had in mind."

"That's kind of depressing, seeing as he's supposed to be one of our best plant biotech guys."

"He's a realist. If die-back vanished tomorrow, we've still lost entire strains of crops. And millions of people. It's going to take a long time to recover, maybe centuries. And in the end, saving humanity doesn't mean anything. We don't think in general principles. We think in individuals. I want to save my family."

Audrey had a point. It would take a damn long time to replace the lost population, without any of the other problems. Eventually people would drift back from the countries they'd fled to, and eventually begin farming again, and eventually have enough babies to build numbers, but eventually wasn't soon enough for anyone here. Alex could see it on paper: recovery would be almost as much effort as developing a colony from those few habitats on Opis, and the America that emerged would probably be very different from the one he'd lost.

But Opis was an unimaginable distance away, with no realistic option of coming back if things didn't work out. He needed a reason to go. And reasons were usually people you couldn't live without. Yeah, Aude nailed it. It all came down to individuals.

"Early days," Alex said. He put his fork on his cleared plate and got up to pat Audrey on the shoulder. "But at least we have somewhere to run if we need it. Come and talk any time."

He left his dirty plate to one of the server bots and braced for the next ambush, but perhaps he didn't look so approachable now, because he made it out of the restaurant unmolested. He stepped into the elevator.

"Which festering pit of malcontent shall I visit next, Sol?" he asked.

Solomon's voice drifted from the speaker above his head. "The propulsion engineers seem quite happy. They want to know more about the wormhole. It might cheer you up to talk to them."

"FTL, yes!" Alex drummed the heel of his hand against the wall in celebration and then hit the ground floor button. "At last. I can't believe folks aren't more excited about that. The gizmo that changes everything, and they're snivelling about not signing on for this and that. Miserable bastards. No sense of wonder."

"I think you should visit Mr Levine, too."

"I will. I promise."

"Dr Kim's sitting with him. It's time you spoke to her. There's nothing to be gained from keeping her in the dark now that all the staff know."

"Good point." Kim had been thoroughly grilled and tested by Vicky Prinz and the propulsion team, and she was indeed the competent engineer she claimed to be. "Why is Kim suddenly interested in Levine, by the way?"

"I asked her to be."

"Oh."

"No man should die alone."

"What are the nurses doing, then?"

"Administering palliative care. Which falls short of having someone just sit with you and hold your hand."

"Are you okay, Sol?"

"I am, thank you. Better than I've been for a long time. I was never comfortable concealing Nomad."

"That's not what I mean. I know you. Something's happened."

"Perhaps it's death. When you have no prospect of it yourself, it's quite sobering. The last few days have been a concentrated burst of it."

"Oh, right. Yeah. What *did* happen out there with Fonseca, then?"

"I'll tell you some other time. Go on, you've got hearts and minds to win."

"Change of plan. I'd better sort out Kim first. Save all those happy physicists and engineers as a treat for later."

"Be kind. I think she's quite upset about Levine. It reminds her of her great-grandmother."

"You've had a chat with her, then."

"No, I heard her talking to him. They're both propulsion people, remember. So was her great-grandmother, in a roundabout way. You knew that."

"So I did," Alex said. "I'll be diplomatic."

"Good practice for when you brief *Cabot*'s crew."

"Yeah, that won't be fun."

"I could do it, Alex."

"No. Absolutely not. My personal task. Promise me, Sol."

"Very well, I assure you I won't interfere."

"Thanks."

It was a long walk to the infirmary, and Alex felt he'd already run a marathon today. He took a buggy from the pool and drove down there instead, reminiscing about airports, baggage carts, and the last time he'd been on vacation. If he absolutely had to go to Opis, one last trip to Hawaii would have been nice. Life was probably still almost normal there.

Kim was still confined to the medical wing, but she didn't seem too keen to leave. The duty nurse had to go get her from Levine's room.

"I'll stay with him until you come back," the nurse said. "I promise."

Kim wagged a warning forefinger at him. "You don't leave that man for a minute, okay? And you hold his hand. He needs to know someone's there, even if he nods off."

Alex decided to deploy the kid gloves. He'd had his fill of aggravation today, and it was still only lunchtime. He ushered Kim out into the corridor and onto the buggy.

"I'm going to take you on a guided tour," he said. "Because I don't think we need to keep you locked up any longer."

"Can't it wait? Mr Levine's time is pretty important."

"It won't take long. I've got a few things to tell you." Alex drove off, trying to visualise a route that would give him enough time for a conversation with her. One thing that the research centre had was plenty of empty corridors. He pointed out landmarks as he went, then tried to ease into the story.

"You know that conversation we had, when you said what you thought we'd done with your great-grandmother's research?"

"Yeah."

"Well, you were pretty close."

Kim blew out a long breath. "Bloody knew it. You thieving mongrels. Are you going to stop playing games now?"

"I did say close."

"How close?"

"I'll send you a copy of the report via your room terminal. Headlines — *Cabot* didn't blow up or vanish. The ship's about to reach Opis and we'll be reviving the crew shortly. The habitats have been built. We launched unmanned missions at intervals starting more than a century ago, mainly self-replicating bots to mine materials and start manufacturing the base. About fifty years into the project, we developed FTL."

"Oh, great. Grandma Park's bloody drive."

"Not quite. Apparently some of her work came in useful for setting up a teensy-weensy wormhole, though."

"Teensy-weensy. Metric teensy-weensy, or imperial?"

Alex took one hand off the steering wheel and curled his fingers to indicate a baseball size. "We launched a micro-sat through the hole for an instant comms relay. So we've got a live feed from the planet. This is the big one. The first human extrasolar base. Have I left anything out? No, that's pretty much it."

"Bloody hell. You did it."

"We did. Key in the door, ready to move in."

"Yeah, I'm sure the base is lovely, but I meant FTL. The wormhole."

"Well, we can't throw ships around with it, but it was enough for comms, and that makes a big difference."

"But you used some of Grandma Park's research."

"Looks like it. But it predates all of us."

"I'll bet."

"Hey, if we did, then you had the same research. Why didn't you make something of it like we did?" Alex glanced at Kim and noted the clamped lips and narrowed eyes. *Bad idea.* He tried to dig himself out of the hole. "Anyway, not only can you work on a project that'll move a full-size vessel one day, you can watch Opis live on the TV as well."

Kim said nothing. As bittersweet news went, it must have been a lot more bitter than sweet. She leaned back in her seat, occasionally making little *uhhh* noises that sounded as if she kept shaping up to ask a question and then deciding against it.

"I know this must be a pretty big campus, but where *is* everybody?" she asked at last. "The place is deserted."

The sudden change of topic worried Alex. He'd expected a slow burn, then a broadside. Maybe she was saving her wrath for later. "Yeah, recruitment and retention isn't too good these days," he said. "It might be the dental plan. We'll have to look at that."

She gave him a dead-eyed look that said she wasn't amused. "Am I allowed to know how many people you've got here?"

"Fifteen hundred, including families. But we have lots of bots. Bednarz believed you could never have too many bots. And AIs. I can't remember, did we introduce you to Solomon? He's the main man — well, main AI. He's everywhere. Runs the whole shebang."

"And that's it?"

"That's not just *it*, we're all there is of Ainatio, too. No secret bases or anything. You said you travelled across the States. You've seen more of the devastation than we have."

Kim's brow puckered. Alex wondered if she was disappointed rather than just angry. She'd obviously thought Nomad was a much bigger project, and of course it had been.

"So what happened to the great and good?" she asked. "Where are your leaders and thinkers? And I hate to be crass, but where are your rich people?"

"We've got plenty of thinkers and we don't need politicians."

"You might have a point there. You've got an empress."

"Hah. Yeah. We don't need the wealthy, either. We've got trillions tied up in company assets that we can't spend. Why would we want rich people anyway?"

"It just seems you've got a pretty narrow demographic here," Kim said.

"What, you think it'll be like those disaster movies where the powerful bribe their way out and leave the proles shaking their fists at an ominous sky? Look, unless someone can grow food, build stuff, run habitats, and generally do the frontiersman thing, they'll just be dead weight on Opis."

"So this is your gene pool. Just the people here."

Alex felt a compulsion to defend his tribe. "Why not? They say a hundred is enough to avoid inbreeding. So two to three thousand is plenty. That's counting the townsfolk as well."

"You haven't mixed with the outside world for years."

"So? That's not the same as being inbred. Our kids are only second and third generation."

"Maybe not, but isolation makes you as mad as bloody hatters. Imagine what it's like on those generation ships right now. They were all barking to start with. I wouldn't breed from Quinn Worley and his researchers."

"It's a cult. They'll be having a great time, all agreeing with each other on everything, with nobody around to spoil their echo-chamber."

"Cults devour themselves. Or turn on outsiders."

"They're zillions of miles from us. They can turn cannibal if they want."

"You're a little weird in here as well, you know. Face it. You're an isolated colony. You should get out more."

"Well, better to be stir-crazy than inundated with desperate refugees who find out we've got a lifeboat."

"Remind me what you said about echo chambers."

Alex couldn't work out what bothered her, but then a thought struck him. "Did you come here to check us out for some oligarchs who want to bail? Because we're only offering print-built domes and recycled urine for eight hours' work a day."

"Why the hell would you think that?"

"Because I still don't understand why you're here."

"I've told you."

"Yeah. So you have."

"Okay, so why are *you* part of this team?"

"Sheer random accident," Alex said. "When I joined, I didn't know any of this would happen, and I didn't expect to end up marooned here with one way out. It just looked better than what was happening outside."

Do I want to go? No. I don't. So what am I going to do if I stay behind?

Alex had known about *Cabot* for ten years, and had watched the world shrink around him, a fish trapped in a puddle in a drying riverbed. He was no pioneer. He was just a glorified progress chaser, excited by a cool mission and big challenges, but he'd never signed up to live out his days in a plastic dome on an alien planet. It depressed him to think that everyone he'd face the future with was already in this small, closed community. He'd exhausted its possibilities years ago.

But this is how people always lived until the industrial revolution. Born, lived, married, died in one village. Never left it.

"If you'd seen what it's like in the rest of the country, you'd be happy to be shipwrecked," Kim said.

"What's life like in Korea, then?"

"Compared to this? Crowded, restricted, and nervous. And Oz is pretty much what normal life used to be like here, I expect."

"Are they working on die-back research? I guess they are."

"It'll run out of insect carriers and crops eventually. All APS has to do is stop it getting in."

Alex wasn't sure if that was a no, but Kim was a propulsion expert. He couldn't expect her to be up to speed on the details. But he needed to know. If he wanted to stay on Earth, Asia was his best bet, but getting in wasn't going to be easy. Perhaps he could ask for asylum. What did he have to bargain with, though? No advanced technical or scientific skills that they didn't have already, for a start. All he had was Ainatio's industrial secrets, and he wasn't ready to trade those.

"We'll have an apartment sorted out for you," he said, getting back to business. "Then you can start work. Dr Prinz wants you on Javinder Singh's team. We've got ships to prepare."

"What about my FTL?"

"Priorities. It'll happen, don't worry."

"And what about giving me a connection to access my notes? My cloud's blocked. I need Grandma Park's research."

"Sure, but what if your access is detected and your government realises you're here?"

Kim nodded, more to herself than to him. "Okay. I'll start as soon as Mr Levine's ready to let me go."

Alex wondered what Kim was getting out of Levine, seeing as the poor guy couldn't even speak. But maybe she wasn't the ice queen after all. Maybe it wasn't even about engineers being comradely. Perhaps it was just simple human compassion.

There were many shortages in the world these days, and compassion had been one of the first commodities to run out.

"Understood," he said.

* * *

AINATIO INFIRMARY:
LATER THAT DAY

"I don't know, I really don't."

The voice drifted in, and Chris wasn't sure if he was having another medication-fuelled dream or if someone was really talking to him. No, he was awake: he knew because he could see the clock on the wall and the seconds flicking by, turning 16:34 to 16:35. There were medics talking outside his room. The door was ajar and he couldn't get out of bed to do anything about it. He just wanted to sleep.

Please, shut up.

Voices were insistent things, though, tempting him to listen whether he wanted to or not. The more he tried to shut them out, the more they grated on him. Whatever the staff were talking about, they were on edge. Chris could hear the rising pitch and the gabbling, one guy talking over the other. It didn't sound like an argument. The tone was worried, maybe even scared.

When's the funeral? I've got to be at the funeral. They can't bury Jamie without me. Jared could at least call, even if they won't let him in.

I fucked up. I should have taken a different road back. Retracing the route was asking for trouble.

Chris gave up on trying to get back to sleep. The meds didn't let him surface all the way, but he knew where he was, he remembered why he was here, and he could feel his leg. He couldn't move it because it was encased in something solid, but it was no more painful than a pulled muscle. He could see that his arm and chest were covered in patches, wireless monitors and slow-release drugs whose names he couldn't quite read. At least one had to be a serious elephant-grade painkiller, because he knew the state his leg had been in when he was casevacked.

Nice sheets. Yeah, we could do with some of these in the camp.

He tried to work out if he could reach the sipper bottle on the nightstand without needing to call for a nurse and wondered if he was the only patient in here. There was no sense of bustle and activity outside. There were just the two guys talking.

"I don't know how they did it either, but it's true. You saw the live feed."

"Well, if I get the chance, I'm going. It won't get any better here."

"I can't even find it on the star map."

"You're looking at the wrong hemisphere."

"It's just a number."

"That's Pascoe. See?"

Pascoe. The name made Chris listen intently. He'd heard it from Nathan Marr when he was passing that code around the camp, asking what Kim's sequence of numbers meant. *Pascoe's Star.* It stuck in Chris's mind because he didn't know many stars named after people. The voices now dropped to a murmur as if the guys were trying to be discreet. Then someone spoke to him, right in the room, a male voice out of nowhere, but one that he *knew*.

"Can I get the nurse for you, Sergeant? Do you need anything?"

He jumped. "Shit — whoa. Where are you?"

"My apologies. I'm Solomon. We spoke at the casevac. I don't usually operate in a quad unit inside this building. I'm part of the system in here."

"Oh. Right. Hi, Solomon. Thanks. I think I owe you one."

"You're welcome. May I call you Chris?"

"Sure." Chris's heart was still pounding. He thought the monitor might bring one of the medics running but they seemed to be too busy talking. "I haven't seen any of my squad. Are they okay? Some guy kept telling me not to worry, but I need to know."

"They're all well. Jackson and Lee have both been treated for wounds, but they chose to go back to the camp. I do hope you can persuade them to return for check-ups."

"Did they get the bastards who ambushed us?"

"I can confirm that. I shot the last one myself."

"No bullshit about robots being programmed not to harm humans, then."

"I'm not a robot. Would you like some water?"

"No, I'm okay, thanks. How long am I going to be in here? I'm not ungrateful, but I keep asking and I don't think I'm getting answers. Unless I'm too stoned to understand."

"It depends on how well you respond. Accelerated healing demands a lot from your body. This isn't the usual enhanced treatment you'd get from a hospital."

"Experimental, yeah?"

"Developed for extreme environments."

"Ah, there's always a catch. But thank you."

"I wouldn't doubt the doctors' commitment. They don't see many injuries like yours. They like to win."

"As long as they don't dissect me afterwards, we're cool."

"Major Trinder would like to visit, if you're feeling up to it."

"Sure. Are my guys allowed in here?"

"Of course. I've let Erin know that I'll make the arrangements." The door closed very quietly. Chris hadn't noticed anyone walk past. So Solomon could control that as well, then. "We talked for a while. I realise she's had more than her fair share of tragedy."

There'd been AIs everywhere when Chris was a kid, and some of the customer service ones had been good enough to make him wonder if he really was dealing with a machine, but he'd never come across one quite like this. *Erin.* So they were chummy now, were they?

"Everyone's going to be cut up about Jamie," Chris said. "He was a good kid." Then he realised he'd left Zakko out of his list of worries. "And I really need to see Zakko. You know — the curly-haired guy with a bit of weight on him? He put a tourniquet on me with rounds shaving past him. To think I was going to chop his finger off."

"Why?"

"Stealing."

"That seems harsh, but I'm sure you had your reasons."

The Zakko who didn't think twice about taking meds for Dr Kim was the same Zakko who raced to Chris's aid without a thought for his own safety. It was the same impulse. Zakko just did things when he thought they needed doing. He didn't always make the right call, but a man who was prepared to put his life on the line and didn't panic was someone Chris would gladly fight alongside. Damn, Zakko could enlist if he wanted to. Chris would discuss it with the guys and they'd swear him in and train him properly. He'd earned it.

"Sorry." Chris didn't know where all this was coming from. "I don't normally ramble and get emotional. That stuff they pumped into me is worse than beer."

"It does no harm to express these things."

"Yeah."

"Ah, Major Trinder's on his way now with Captain Fonseca."

"How do you know?"

"Tracked chips. It's a big site to search in an emergency."

Chris realised he was still lagging a couple of minutes behind the conversation. "Did you really shoot one of those guys?"

"Yes. Jackson shot him as well. Taking prisoners was never going to work out."

Chris wasn't sure if that was a deadpan joke, but even if Solomon meant it, that made him okay in Chris's book. He was still trying to work it out when Trinder and Fonseca arrived. The major looked him over as if he was counting how many limbs he had left.

And Chris remembered Fonseca. She'd been on the Lammergeier, and she looked a lot better in her working uniform than in the battledress she'd been wearing. Everything was making more sense now. He smiled at her and hoped he didn't look creepy.

"How are you doing, Chris?" Trinder asked.

"Not too bad, sir."

"I'm not sure where to start." Trinder reached out to shake his hand as if this was some kind of reunion. "But sorry is probably as good a place as any. I'm really sorry about Jamie, and I'm sorry we didn't spot the ambush sooner."

"I should know better than to retrace a route."

"I never lecture a man when I've never done his job."

"Well, next time I'll accept your support. Anyway, thanks. Your guys were on the ball."

Fonseca pulled up a seat and leaned on the bedside conspiratorially. "You don't need to go scavenging for ammo. Just let us know what you need. But keep it between us, okay? Regulations, management, the usual crap."

Chris pointed up at the ceiling, the best he could do to indicate that Solomon might be listening. "Just us?"

Fonseca looked blank. Chris mouthed *Solomon* at her.

"Oh, don't worry about Sol," she said. "He's in on it. He's cooking the books."

Chris knew he ought to wait until his head cleared before he started throwing in his lot with people he didn't really know. If it hadn't been for the firefight, he wouldn't have felt he knew them at all. Part of his brain, the cells holding out against the onslaught of medication, was warning him that his judgement was addled by injury, drugs, and Jamie's death, and that he couldn't go from zero contact to best buddies in the space of a week. He had to ask questions. The world was never what it seemed.

"Is there anything weird going on? The medics seem agitated. Or are they always like that?"

"What do you mean by agitated?" Trinder asked.

Chris really wanted to lob in a mention of Pascoe's Star to see their reaction, but that was probably best saved for when he was feeling more mentally agile. He could still test the waters, though.

"They were talking about whether they were going to go somewhere or not," he said. "Never mind. Nothing to worry about, obviously."

"You and I need a chat," Trinder said. "But now isn't a good time, not for either of us." He looked at Fonseca, an are-we-doing-this-or-not kind of look, as if he was waiting for her to stop him. "Let's get you fit and think about how we've ended up like this. We're on the same side, whatever you think."

Maybe Chris had misheard. The more he thought about it, the less he understood what it meant.

Trinder gave him a respectful nod and walked out. Fonseca hung back, took something out of her shoulder bag, and put it on the bedcover within his reach. Then, almost as an afterthought, she took hold of his hand and placed it on the object, as if she thought he couldn't locate it. It was a slab of chocolate in a plain, transparent wrapper.

"Morale in a bar," she said. "Get some sleep."

Chris couldn't tell if it was pity or if she was hitting on him. It was probably the former, even if he was hoping for the latter.

"Thank you," he said.

"Door closed or open?"

"Closed, please."

After she shut the door behind her, he managed to drag himself far enough across the bed to put the chocolate on the nightstand and grab the water bottle. Yeah, sleep. His body knew what was needed to fix him. He settled down again and hoped it would be complete oblivion once he shut his eyes. The lights dimmed to near darkness almost without him noticing.

Solomon. He's always watching, then.

I'm gone. Good night. Sorry, Jamie.

At one point he was sure he'd woken from a dream about Dr Kim walking in and checking on him, but she wasn't that type of doctor, and he wouldn't have mattered to her at all.

* * *

THE BRANDT FARM, KILL LINE: 1800 HOURS

Joanne was hovering at the window, clutching a tea towel like a set of worry beads. In Kill Line, death was confined to the elderly and the occasional farm accident. Young men here didn't die. They certainly didn't get shot by strangers.

"Is Jared Talbot a tall black guy?" Joanne asked, stepping back from the window.

"Honey, when did we last get a stranger come to the door? Of course that's Jared." Doug prided himself on having a good supply of the right things to say in a crisis, but this was going to be tough. He looked over the spread on the dining room table. "I think that's probably enough cake to keep the whole camp fed."

"He doesn't have to eat it. I can't bear an empty table when people need comforting, that's all. Food's just a polite way of showing love."

"I know, honey." Doug went to let Jared in. "He'll realise that."

He'd known something serious had happened when he saw the two Lammergeiers take off a couple of days ago, followed by the activity on the road and the landing lights later. Ainatio security had radioed him with the news. Now the misery of the outside world had finally caught up with Kill Line and the town had changed forever.

"Come on in, Jared." Doug shook Jared's hand, but then felt helpless and just took a gentle grip on his arm. The man was taller than he recalled, but then he rarely saw him. He would have picked him out as a soldier right away, though. They all had that way of walking. "I'm so sorry for your loss. How's Chris doing?"

"We're going to visit him in the morning. Apparently the surgery went okay."

"They're pretty good surgeons up there."

"Yeah. We're lucky. If that had happened anywhere else, we'd have lost him as well."

"Their security people called me. I've never known Ainatio to keep us informed about their comings and goings before."

Jared sat down in the chair that Joanne offered and managed one of those polite but unhappy smiles. She loaded a plate and put it in front of him with a cup of coffee.

"I'm afraid I don't know your friend's name," she said.

"Jamie. Jamie Wickens. Shot in the head. The convoy was ambushed on the way back. Chris was hit in the leg. The round went down through his thigh and took out his knee. A couple of the other guys got hit too, but nothing serious."

"I feel terrible saying this, but I don't think I ever saw Jamie."

"Sure you did. The dark-haired kid who maintained the gun truck. You'd see him driving it around. Everybody liked him, so the camp's pretty cut up now. Which is why I might need to ask a favour of you. It's the first time we've lost someone since before we left Baltimore, and... uh... "

Jared trailed off. Doug understood. After all that the vets and the refugees had been through, it seemed especially cruel for such a young guy to die on a simple foraging trip that he didn't even have to make.

We could have helped. It's not enough to wait for them to ask.

"We'll do whatever we can," Joanne said.

"The problem is we don't know how to handle the funeral. We don't even know what Jamie really believed, if anything. I mean, you don't put on a uniform without giving some thought to what needs to be done if you don't make it, but there's no records left, no dog tag, no last letter to send home, no home to send it to, nothing. The best we can guess is Christian but probably not Catholic."

Doug got the feeling that Jared was struggling to ask for help. Maybe he really did just want advice, but Doug didn't want to force him to say it if he was actually asking for something more. An offer would spare him that.

"Would you like a service at St Thomas's for him?" Doug asked. "Would you like him to be buried here in the churchyard? I don't think God quibbles about the small print. We've got every belief in town from Baptist to Anglican to Iraqi Christian, and we've only got one church. We focus on what we have in common."

"We thought of starting a cemetery at the camp."

"You'd feel like it was the wrong place, though, is that it?"

"I feel bad even thinking it, but it just looks so damn lonely up there, and if we ever had to move on, it'd be nice to know he wasn't alone and that his grave would be tended." Jared took a breath. "It's a lot to ask, I know. We're strangers, pretty much."

"No, it's not a lot to ask. And you're *neighbours*. Of course he can rest here."

Jared shut his eyes for a moment. It wasn't relief. It looked more like he was composing himself. "Thanks, Doug. We truly appreciate it. Can we visit the grave?"

"Any time. You're always welcome. We'll take care of the arrangements. You just decide on things like hymns and eulogies."

Jared kept trying to eat a slice of cake, but every time he raised it to his mouth, he'd put it down again. Doug wondered if he was just trying to be polite when he didn't actually want it, but then Jared turned his head and the light caught the wet trails of a couple of tears that had escaped and run down his cheek. It was hard to swallow anything when you were trying not to cry. The sight of this big, dignified guy keeping a lid on it was almost unbearable to watch.

"Thank you," Jared said. "Really, we can't thank you enough."

"Jared, you look out for us. It's our turn to look out for you. You never need to worry about asking for anything."

"Thanks."

Joanne wrapped some cake and gave it to Jared as he left in case he felt up to eating it later. Doug saw him to the door for a quiet word on the doorstep.

"If your people want to settle in town, we've got plenty of room," Doug said. "I don't think things are going to improve outside for a very long time."

Jared nodded. "My wife and I worry about what the world's going to be like when we have kids. A lot of folks didn't have a family for that reason. It's like we're trying to go extinct. There's got to be a better plan."

Doug wasn't sure if that was a maybe or not. He'd leave Jared to think it over. He also needed to be sure that he was doing it for their benefit and not just to soothe his own guilt. It now seemed wrong to have had so little contact with the transit camp, even if they wanted to keep their distance and hadn't planned on staying. They made Kill Line feel safe, and they asked for nothing. He knew he should have tried harder to persuade them to come in.

But separation was the way things had always been around here. Chris and the camp keeping their distance seemed as normal as Ainatio staying inside their perimeter fence. People grew up with the habit of not mixing, not asking questions, and not trusting strangers. Ainatio's secrecy seemed to contaminate everything around it.

Funny. I've never even asked Chris how he ended up with the folks that he brought here. Did he choose them, did they choose him, or didn't that matter as long as they were alive?

Doug lay awake that night, wondering how so many people could stand not knowing if their family and friends had survived, or if they did know, having no place to visit to remember them. He understood the need for a proper grave and headstone for Jamie Wickens.

Next morning, he went to see the minister. Martin Berry was a hard man to surprise, and the phrase "broad church" had been made for him. He asked no questions about Jamie's faith, but he did say something that put these times in perspective for Doug.

"Why does it take a young man's death to build that bridge between us and them?" Martin asked.

"Maybe because it's the first time we've seen the kind of world he came here to escape, and we realise we've had it easy," Doug said. "So we try to atone somehow. But death's got a way of waking people up and making them see what matters. Come on, let's sort out the seating. We'll have a full house, I think."

"Do we have a date in mind?"

"It'll have to be when his sergeant can leave the infirmary."

"Let me know. No problem." The minister patted Doug's arm. "They came to you, after all this time. That sounds to me like they want some link with this community. So they're ready to think about the future, and that's an act of faith these days."

"Or they might be thinking of moving on."

"We'll see. People end up where they need to be."

Doug was a long way from feeling positive, but a life and a death that could cause people to unite had purpose, even if the deceased never saw what they'd set in motion. The invisible barrier between Kill Line and the camp seemed to be disappearing. Doug felt he could visit and not feel like he was intruding. When he had more information about the funeral, he'd go see Jared this time and maybe take some treats for the kids.

Now he had to sort out the flowers.

There were already narcissi poking through the soil, but he needed something in bloom. He took one of the farm quad bikes and rode towards the woods, looking for early wildflowers like bluet on patches of exposed land, but after an hour he still hadn't found anything. Maybe the snowdrops were still in flower at the McKinnon farm. He couldn't remember how long the blooms lasted, but it was worth looking, and if they'd died off already he could still bring back a few bulbs in leaf to plant on the grave.

He retraced his route to the farm, pleased with himself for remembering without a map, and parked near the remains of the old farmhouse chimney. But he couldn't find any snowdrops at all, not even a dead flowerhead.

He squatted to poke around in the grass, certain that he was in the right place. He'd navigated from the chimney like the last time, so the plants had to be around here somewhere. It wasn't easy to spot the leaves in grass but he could normally zero in on small variations in foliage with a farmer's experienced eye. Where were they? They couldn't have died off already.

No. Don't even think it.

Doug told himself not to be so paranoid. Snowdrops were the wrong species and this was the wrong place. It couldn't be die-back. Well, he couldn't find the plants, so he'd have to get a wreath made out of evergreens, and see if someone in town had any indoor plants that they could donate. He started walking back to the quad bike, then looked back at the patch of grass that he'd searched.

The snowdrops were there somewhere, but he'd mention it to Col for testing anyway, just in case. It was better to look like a fool than say nothing and find out the hard way that he'd ignored a disaster.

07

I'm glad I'm not the guy who has to break it to Cabot *that a lot of shit's happened on Earth while they've been asleep.*

Colin "Col" Croad, Ainatio environmental technician, on the imminent revival of the ship's company

HEADS OF DEPARTMENT MEETING, CONFERENCE ROOM 4B: TWO DAYS LATER

"Do it," said Erskine, studying the paper schedule that still had her father's handwritten comments on it. He'd always preferred hard copy. "Revive them now and complete by the end of March. It's well within the supplies margin."

Mangel shook his head. "I think you should give the crew as little time as possible to stew over what Alex has to tell them. If you think staff here are pissed at being lied to for so long, imagine what it'll feel like to wake up and find your home's a wasteland."

"Todd, these people are nearly all ex-military," Alex said. "They're not like us. They deal with adversity and get on with the job. And they knew they were going to lose everything and everybody simply because of the timescales involved."

"*Nearly* all military," Mangel repeated. "One hundred and seventy-five crew, but thirty-six are civilian contractors.

Not military contractors. Technicians and other specialists. Different mind-set. And as usual, we don't have our most senior military man in these meetings. I think his input would be more useful than mine right now. The clever space stuff's all but done."

Erskine really didn't like Mangel. For a moment, she imagined being stuck with him on Opis with no escape. "Todd, all these issues were considered by psychologists who knew the crew," she said. "Tough humans *cope*. Australia might as well have been another planet when people were transported, but they built a nation pretty fast." It was too late for this nonsense. The ship was almost at Nomad Base and survival was top of any organism's to-do list. They'd make it work. "Okay, unless anyone's got a scientific argument within their own field of expertise that says we should revive the crew at another time, we *will* go for March thirty-first as the end date, and start the first batch as soon as we're able."

Mangel just shrugged. Alex, who was looking increasingly frayed these days, busied himself swiping through his notes. Solomon's voice drifted in.

"May we move on to ships' readiness, Director?"

"Is it good news, Solomon? Just the headlines, please."

"Latest estimate as of this morning is that *Elcano* will be ready to launch in six weeks, *Shackleton* in six months, *Da Gama* in twelve, and *Eriksson* in twenty."

"I still don't understand why we need to expend resources on all four ships. We have capacity for five thousand and we only need to move three. *Fewer* than three, in fact. We could achieve that with *Elcano* and *Shackleton*."

"Eggs and baskets, Director."

"I don't think there's much difference in spreading the risk between two and four."

"You would if two ships were lost."

"Malta cargo."

"Are you two talking code?" Alex asked.

"The Director's making a historical reference," Solomon said. "The Malta convoys of two hundred years ago. So many supply ships were sunk trying to reach the island during a war that they were loaded with mixed cargoes to make sure any vessel that made it had at least some of every necessity."

Alex did a casual salute in the direction of the audio system. "Thank you, Sol. I'm a more rounded person for knowing that."

"So we mix crews from each specialisation," Erskine said. "How long have we been talking about this? We've had forty-five years to get this right."

"And in forty-five years, Director, those ships have deteriorated and have been repaired and maintained on a rolling cycle, but none of that is precisely predictable, like debris strikes or component failures." Solomon sounded tetchy. "And we have serious limits that were never foreseen, like industry collapsing and Asia taking an aggressively keen interest if we're seen to be too active in space. Everything has to be cannibalised, remanufactured, and replaced discreetly, and by a limited number of bots and AIs."

"I love you when you're feisty, Sol," Mangel said, laughing. "You tell her."

Erskine knew she wasn't imagining it now. Despite his patient tone of a teacher dealing with an idiot child, Solomon was getting irritable. He was feeling the pressure. Well, that was what Bednarz had wanted: an AI with the sensibilities of a human but fewer failings. She could see the value in an AI that didn't just follow override orders to the point of failure, but it was a pain in the neck.

"Humour me, Solomon," she said. "Move resources to get *Elcano* and *Shackleton* on immediate standby. We'll re-evaluate on a weekly basis."

"Very well, Director."

"Anyone else? How's staff morale?"

Erskine looked around the meeting table. Of these ten people who had known about *Cabot*, eight looked like deflated balloons, frowning and exhausted. She could imagine what had happened. After years of straining to keep Nomad secret from their staff, people they worked cheek by jowl with and in some cases had married, the announcement had left them in the line of fire. Nobody liked to be deceived, even about good news.

Vicky Prinz dragged herself into the conversation. She looked fed up. There must have been quite a bit of marital strife in the Prinz household in the last forty-eight hours. "Half of my department's already packed their bags and they're jumping up and down yelling, 'Are we there yet?'"

"Excellent. Jake?"

"A few are grumpy or scared, or both," Dr Mendoza said. "It's going to take time to sink in. They'll be fine."

Erskine didn't expect the agriscience and botany departments to be happy. "Sonia. I'm guessing you had a hard time at your staff meeting."

Sonia Venner shrugged. "You know what a lot of them are saying."

"That we didn't put all that we could into die-back research because we knew we could walk away from the problem?"

"Something like that."

"They did the work. They had all the resources they needed, they didn't slack off, and they're still nowhere on it."

"Yes, I did mention that. Quite a few times. It's the teams working on resistant crops that took it worst. They thought they were pursuing one objective but it turned out to be another."

Alex raised a finger. "Can confirm. Had to lie about that a few weeks ago."

"It'll pass," Erskine said. "It disappoints me that people working on sensitive research in a secure facility still don't grasp what need-to-know means. Why do they think we discouraged contact with the town? Still, they feel the way they feel, and no amount of berating or educating them will change that. Focus on the positives and get this turned around by the time we need to firm up plans for the next mission."

"What if staff want to leave as a result of what they now know?" Venner asked.

"As in walk out and find another town? That would be awkward."

"There's nowhere else to go," Alex said. "If they don't believe us, they might want to take a ride out with the transit camp folk and see what's left of the place. And I'd like to think there's nobody left to leak information to, but knowing our luck, there'll be APS spies everywhere."

"Would that be so terrible?" Venner asked.

"It would when they found that all our ships are armed and we've broken a long list of treaties. Don't forget that APS has nice big missiles and blames America for die-back."

"So everyone's stuck here."

"We always were. I've assured people that nobody's going to be press-ganged onto a mission. But they have to respect security measures."

"And what about Kill Line?" Mendoza asked. "When do we tell Doug Brandt?"

"I didn't realise you knew him that well," Erskine said.

"He came in yesterday to visit Chris Montello."

After years of quiet isolation, Ainatio was suddenly getting a lot of external visitors, and the town seemed to have forged some new relationship with the transit camp. It was worrying. Erskine weighed the security risks against the unwelcome attention it would draw if she barred any of them. She needed Brandt and his people. She'd err on the side of informality.

"We have to put our own house in order before we ask the townsfolk if they'd like to settle another planet," she said.

Alex nodded. "Yeah, if they want to go to Opis, that would be great. Bigger gene pool. Valuable expertise."

Nobody mentioned the transit camp. Erskine had already slapped down questions about it from both Alex and Trinder, but she suspected that the issue might not go away. If she relented, she had no idea who she might be taking on, whether the refugees would blab about it on some radio network she didn't know about, and what would happen if more waifs and strays arrived in the meantime.

The people of Kill Zone were a known quantity in every sense, though. The company had sequenced all their genomes as part of the medical support that was on tap. Erskine knew the risks.

"Okay, that wraps it up for today," she said. "Let's reconvene on Friday."

She'd never seen a meeting empty so fast. She suspected they were going to have their own private discussion elsewhere. Alex stayed behind, looking at her as if he had unfinished business that wasn't for the rest of the team to hear.

"So are we going to get everyone on side, Alex?" Erskine asked.

"I'm trying. If you have a minute, I've got a few things to raise."

"Go ahead."

"Did you see the lab logs this week? Environment ran a few unscheduled die-back tests out on the boundary."

"I noticed. All negative."

"Sure, but if Doug Brandt's getting nervous, that means the rest of the town might be too. We need to pitch any announcement very carefully."

"Noted. It's probably just part of the reaction to the shooting. A reminder that there's still a dangerous world out there."

"Yeah, about that. Trinder's providing an honour guard for the funeral. There's a church service in town."

So this was what Alex really wanted to talk about. "I note that he tells us rather than asks us these days."

"He's woken up to his rank. The detachment's drawn blood and blown shit up."

"Good. I never said I didn't welcome the stiffening of sinews, did I?"

"I think it's a big deal for the town."

"Why? I thought they just employed the vets to patrol."

"That's my point. If they've formed a closer bond with the vets, who do you think they'll side with if we don't play nice with the refugee camp?"

"Ah. I see. But does providing security earn more loyalty points than supplying utilities, medical care, coffee, and clothing?"

"Maybe the town's wondering the same thing about supplying us with food." Alex pushed back his chair and stood up to gather pens and coffee cups from the table. "We're weird, Director. The problem with living in a bubble like this is that folks tend to amplify whatever idea they started with and get more extreme."

"Me, you mean."

"I mean everyone. We made a big mistake keeping the town at arm's length."

"You've changed your tune."

"It was something Kim said. That we're not much different from the generation ships. Except we didn't start out quite as crazy and hell-bent on social engineering, of course."

Erskine worried when Alex showed signs of wavering. She didn't think those concerns ever touched him. "I don't see what we could have done differently."

"We should have regrouped when the die-back hit. Socially, I mean. We need those people out there. Hell, we need the transit camp, too."

"Not that again. We've got the detachment, and we've got a hundred and thirty-nine military personnel in *Cabot.*"

"Who'll have a second and even a third generation by the time the follow-ups arrive, with no guarantee that the kids will have the same skills and outlook as their parents."

"But there's a high degree of heritability with personality traits."

"And the world's always been full of civilians who forgot the wars their fathers fought and screwed things up again." Alex just gave her a chin-down, you-think-about-this look, hugged his screen to his chest, and opened the door. "The right stuff's hard to come by, that's all. Catch you later."

Erskine gave him time to walk out of earshot. She had a mutinous crew today. It was probably just anxiety and a little steam-venting, not impending anarchy. But it still wore her out.

"He has a point, Director," Solomon said.

"Not you as well."

"Do you really have an objection to the transit camp vets?"

"We can't take strangers off the street for this."

"Then carry out security checks on them."

"With what? *On* what?"

"I ran checks on Dr Kim."

"APS has functioning nations and all that goes with that. There was something to access."

Solomon did one of his pauses. They were never a good sign in an AI. "True."

"Anyway, how's Mr Levine?"

"He passed away last night. The cremation and memorial service are next week."

"Oh. I'm sorry. I'll make sure I'm there."

"Dr Kim insisted on staying with him to the end." Solomon paused for a beat. "She says she can start work for us now."

His calm voice always managed to express strong feelings with little change of pitch. It was the pauses. He wielded them like an actor. Erskine let it pass. So he thought she was a callous old cow, then. Well, someone had to be. The stakes had never been higher, and even though she'd never volunteered for this job and resented how much it had cost her, she would see it through.

To the end.

"Time for her to start earning her keep, then," she said. "We've got a lot to do."

* * *

SECURITY WING, COMMANDING OFFICER'S QUARTERS: NEXT MORNING

"Good to see you can still fit into your dress uniform," Fonseca said.

She walked into Trinder's cabin like she still belonged there. He adjusted his high collar in front of the mirror.

"Seems you can, too."

"I never thought we'd need this rig again."

"Me neither. You've been pretty quiet since you blew up Kingston."

"If I start losing sleep about it, I'll let you know."

"You make sure you do."

"So Chris is definitely going today, then."

"Mendoza says he'll be fine. They get you moving a day after joint surgery."

"Sure, but it's not just your gran's routine knee replacement. He lost a lot of bone and soft tissue. I saw it."

"He needs to be there. Nobody wants to hold up a funeral. Especially if he feels responsible for the guy's death."

"Yeah, I know. Look, I've loaded a little something in the APC. A few boxes of that commodity we don't talk about."

"Ah." *Ammo. Nothing like a little gun-running to kick off my fall from grace. But who gives a shit?* "Well done."

Trinder brushed his cap and tucked it under his arm, ready to face an uncertain day. Aaron Luce was waiting outside in the corridor, picking lint off his sleeve.

"Never been honour guard before," he said. "Should have asked Marc and Tev. They know how to do it properly."

Marc and Tev was his shorthand for real soldiers. Trinder made a mental note to address the self-esteem issue.

"But it'd be the British version."

"It all means the same thing."

Their uniforms were probably the only correct protocol in all of this. Trinder was doing his best with half-recalled traditions and hurried research from different services and even other countries, all to mark the passing of a man who'd served in a defence force that no longer existed and whose comrades were a patchwork of army, navy, air force, coastguard, and law enforcement. He'd found a flag, but there was no bugler to play taps. This ceremonial mash-up wouldn't have passed muster in any army, but it looked respectful, and it would do the job, a public acknowledgement that Jamie Wickens was a brother in arms who had given his life.

It mattered to Chris, and that was what counted. When Trinder collected him from the infirmary he seemed much more like the man he'd first met: businesslike, but with the air of a priest who knew some eternal truth and whose mind was on higher things. Someone had dressed him in a formal suit. It wasn't his, Trinder was certain. That was a gracious gesture.

"Was that your idea, Sol?" Trinder whispered into his collar mike.

"No, Dr Ryan's. They're the same build."

Even a jerk like Ryan could show a streak of decency, then. Maybe the world wasn't a total cesspit after all. Trinder stood back to let a nurse steer Chris's wheelchair out of the room.

"I've been walking on crutches," Chris said, as if he felt Trinder might think he was just being a lazy bum. The suit pants looked very tight around his encased knee. "But Mendoza thought caution was in order."

"Understood."

"You're going to do a three-volley salute. I heard you rehearsing."

"Solomon relayed the audio, huh?"

"Yeah. Where is he?"

"You want him to come?"

Chris looked bewildered. "He did fight alongside our guys. Even if he's a dogbot or whatever."

Solomon heard all. "I'll join you at the gate," he said. "Give me a few minutes to walk out there."

Funerals were never simple. Trinder hadn't been to many, and they'd all been elderly relatives, not friends lost in wars. When he reached the gate with Chris, Solomon was already waiting in his quadrubot frame. He settled on the deck of the crew compartment, looking more functional than canine. Trinder, all dressed up like a Swiss admiral with the folded flag on his lap, was suddenly struck by the weirdness of the moment. Chris was parked in the gap between the banks of seats with a faint smile on his face that could have spread into a big grin or dissolved into tears. It was borderline.

"Jamie would probably laugh his ass off if he could see us," he said.

Perhaps this would be one of those celebrations of a man's life rather than raw grief, then. But Jamie was young, and when Trinder stepped down from the APC and saw the crowd outside St Thomas's, one glance told him it would be grim. He could tell right away who was from Kill Line and who the transit camp people were, too. It wasn't just the clothing. The mourners were mostly men, but there were also women and kids, and some were wiping their eyes already.

A camp of a hundred people. There's nobody you don't know well and didn't face tough times with. Well, shit.

Chris was whisked away almost immediately by a group of his buddies. Trinder lost sight of him and went to find the minister to drape the flag on the coffin. When he came out of the church, Fonseca looked like she was doing a drug deal from the back of the APC, but a chubby guy with dark curly hair and an older man with an excited search dog at his heels seemed well pleased with the boxes. Trinder walked over to the vehicle.

"Just handing out the samples of our in-house manufacturing," she explained.

"Well, we're in deep now," said Trinder. "For better or worse."

Fonseca nodded in the direction of a woman who looked like she'd gone to a lot of trouble to dress up with what little she had. "That's Erin Piller." Solomon approached her and she greeted him like someone she knew, another of those laugh-or-cry moments that Trinder was never going to get out of his head. "Not the girlfriend, according to Solomon, but probably the one to give the flag to."

"Okay. Got it."

The honour guard didn't take part in the service, according to the manuals Trinder had managed to find, so he stood at the back of the church with Fonseca and Luce, rifles propped diplomatically behind a pew. If that was a breach of etiquette, Reverend Berry didn't mention it. He didn't even react when Solomon walked in and stood next to Luce.

The church was so packed that some mourners had to stand in the churchyard by the open doors to listen in. It was a comforting service with at least a couple of familiar hymns from Trinder's childhood, and people got up to say good things about Jamie. Eventually Chris wheeled up to the front and gave his address. It was short, very short indeed.

"I knew Jamie for five years, and that's a lifetime when you serve together," Chris said. "But nobody should die at twenty-three. Jamie did, and he signed up knowing it could happen. He didn't do it for a government or to wave some flag. He did it for his neighbours, to protect them and defend their way of life, because somebody had to, and he didn't need to be asked. He stepped up. *That* is a man. *That* is a soldier. That was my friend. Stand easy, Three Eight."

Luce just took a breath. Fonseca shifted from one foot to the other. There was a second or two of absolute ringing silence, and then the minister got up, catching Trinder's eye and nodding. It was the cue for the firing party to take up position. Trinder had never been so relieved to walk outside. He paced out the required distance from the grave, Fonseca and Luce behind him, and they didn't meet each other's eyes, not even when they lined up with their rifles.

The casket was in position now. They'd drilled so many times to get this absolutely right.

"Firing party — atten... *shun*." Trinder counted himself through it. "Ready — aim — fire." *Crack.* "Ready — aim — fire." *Crack.* "Ready — aim — fire." *Crack.* "Ready — present arms."

It was over before he knew it. He hadn't even noticed the quadrubot standing among the older gravestones.

"Perfect," Solomon said. "Flag?"

"Yes, flag. Sorry. Come on, Lennie."

It wasn't the most dexterous flag-folding in history, but at least they didn't drop it. Trinder presented it to Erin. She seemed surprised, then took it in both hands and held it to her chest.

"That was a really wonderful thing to do," she said. "Thank you, Major."

"Honoured to do it, ma'am."

Luce seemed to be checking the crease in his pants, but Trinder suspected that he was trying to avoid eye contact until he'd composed himself. "It's good to feel like this again," Luce said, more to himself than anything. Trinder could only guess what he meant, but he was sure he understood. This was about remembering that you *belonged* — to somewhere, in something, with others. He couldn't even find the words right then, but when Luce finally looked up and met his eyes, he knew they were thinking the same thing.

Trinder expected everyone to disperse and go their separate ways immediately, but they hung around. He found himself talking to people who'd lived on his doorstep for a long time but who he'd never met, and probably never would have if he hadn't turned up for this brief duty. And now he knew the vets from the camp — all of them. He was never going to remember all the names in one session, but Solomon would prompt him when necessary.

Fonseca tapped his elbow. "We need to get Chris back to the infirmary soon. I think he's overdone it."

"Damn. Okay, let's do our courtesies."

Chris was parked among a group of vets who were passing around a steel hip flask, making toasts. Trinder, reluctant to haul a man away from mourning, waited until Chris shook hands and bumped fists with his comrades before accepting the flask and steering himself away.

He seemed more subdued on the short drive back to Ainatio, nursing the flask like a religious relic. When they reached the infirmary entrance, he offered it to Trinder.

"I prefer this painkiller to Dr Mendoza's," he said. "Want some? How about you, Captain?"

Fonseca smiled. "I'll take a rain check. See you later."

"I've got a bottle in my quarters," Trinder said. "Special occasion stuff. Follow me."

Everybody needed to decompress after a funeral. Trinder decided it was as good a time as any to crack the bottle of Scotch that he'd planned to save for the end of the world, but that had already come and gone, and this was probably the last bottle he'd ever see. Chris talked about Jamie, and Trinder listened.

"That was some impressive drill today, Major."

"Thank you. And it's Dan."

"Okay. *Dan.* It was nice for Jamie, but the guys needed it too. Some of them have days when they feel they're in denial and we're not any kind of army any more, then someone reminds them that it's all still up here." Chris tapped his right temple. "And as long as it is, and everyone agrees what we're willing to fight for, and that we've got each other's backs, then it's still an army. Or navy. Whatever. Combined defence force. You've just got to keep the faith."

There was probably some profound quotation from history about the military ethos, but Trinder liked Chris's version better. It wasn't any more complicated than that.

"Yeah. Keep the faith."

"And thanks for the ammo."

"Should have done it a long time ago. Sorry."

"Look at it this way. Jamie would have been happy that he could bring people together. You were getting on great with the townsfolk today."

"Okay, roll back a couple of years. When you had to bug out with the civvies."

"Yeah?"

"How did you choose who to save? Or did you just take on any displaced persons you found?"

Chris studied his glass, holding it up to the light. "No, I played God. Might have been the wrong call, but we had vulnerable people on board. Kids, old folks, women on their own. There are some people who aren't a good fit with that."

"How do you decide who's a good fit?"

"I used to be an asshole who worked for assholes. I know one when I see one."

It was the wrong time to ask Chris to explain. Trinder just topped up their drinks. Were Chris and his buddies the right kind of people to join Nomad? Of course they were. Trinder had already made up his mind. They were stoic, competent, proven survivors who were willing to risk their own lives to save others. But even if they hadn't been, that didn't mean it was okay to abandon them to an uncertain future.

"Okay, I know you want to ask, so I'll save you the socially awkward bit," Chris said. "I was doing time for beating the crap out of a guy, then State Defence ran out of bodies and needed to fill posts. That's how I got out. And don't comfort yourself by thinking I punched the guy out for messing with my mom or anything primal like that. I hurt him because I was paid to. It was just the first time I got caught. But I'd have done it for free for the reward of putting some punk in his place."

Trinder didn't doubt him, but he still couldn't see a criminal in the man's face. Chris had decided to carry on doing his duty long after there was no chain of command to make him do it. Right now that was all Trinder cared or needed to know.

"So you agreed to serve rather than stay in prison," Trinder said.

"Yeah, I'd rather have had a death sentence than be locked up. And I wanted to fight. I'm an angry bastard. My dad was the hide-and-hope-it-goes-away type. Me, I prefer to go hunt it and kill it. Sometimes that doesn't lead to the noble outcome you expect." He clinked his glass carefully against Trinder's. "And military life made sense to me. I slid into it like a glove."

"Any military in the family?"

"No. All white-collar pen-pushers." Chris was still savouring the single malt like a man who hadn't tasted any for a very long time. He didn't drink fast. "I liked the sense of purpose and loyalty. You can trust your buddies with your life. That doesn't come easily to me."

"Yeah."

"You need something to believe in, Dan."

Trinder couldn't argue with that. "Easier to believe in a flag than an Ainatio business plan."

"Don't knock corporate armies. The East India Company ran a whole political empire and half the world's trade at one time."

"Is that so?"

"Uh-huh. Bigger army than their government."

"Damn."

Trinder had made his decision. He'd have one more crack at Erskine or Alex Gorko — anyone whose ear he could bend — about letting the transit camp in on the Nomad mission. But Chris had to be told soon. If Ainatio pulled out and took Kill Line with it, the camp would lose its power and food supply. They could probably get by without it, but it would be a grindingly hard existence again, and they deserved better.

Doug Brandt needed to know as well. Chris had clarified a lot of things for Trinder today, and one stood out: you had to agree on what you were willing to fight for, and watch each other's backs. It wasn't just survival. It was the whole point of existing at all.

Trinder's screen beeped. He reached across to the shelf to read the message, and found it was a reminder from the infirmary that Chris was late for his treatment.

"Got to get you back, Cinderella," Trinder said. "Mendoza wants to tinker with your leg."

"Better tell him I've been drinking." Chris tapped his knee. It made a hollow plastic noise. "I have no idea what goes on inside this shell gizmo. It's like a mini intensive care ward. It feels like something's knitting inside it."

"I think it probably is."

Trinder chalked up today as progress, and late was always better than never. After he took Chris to the infirmary, he went back to his quarters, planning to read. But first he needed to do a little clandestine research. He inserted his earpiece and got back on the comms net.

"Sol," he said quietly, "I need a few documents. The residents' data list for Kill Line. Did the doctor draw one up? A list for the camp would be handy too."

"Already done," Solomon said. "I thought you'd never ask. But no list of camp personnel."

"How well you know me."

"I think you reached some decisions today."

"Yeah. I did."

"Good. They're the same as mine, which is very convenient."

Trinder was reassured, and not only because Solomon was designed to be ethical. He had the feeling that Solomon knew what he thought was worth fighting for as surely as any human, and in any battle, Solomon was perfectly placed to win.

* * *

WARDROOM, SURVEY VESSEL *CABOT*: EIGHT WEEKS OUT FROM PASCOE B – OPIS

"Well, nobody's dead, so that's a good start." Surgeon Commander Haine edged into the tiny wardroom, rubbed his hands together as if he was feeling chilly, and dispensed a mug of coffee. "Hate starting my rounds with a stiff."

"You sure about that, Logan?" Bridget Ingram rested her head in her hands, trying to persuade her stomach that it really did need a nice milky coffee. When she glanced up, her officers looked like they were simply shaking off a routine hangover from a rowdy mess dinner. She was the only cryo casualty. "I'll want a second opinion when your assistant scab-lifter revives."

"Still no respect for the medical profession, I see."

"How long did it take you to bring me round?"

"Twelve hours longer than expected. I was all for dumping you out the airlock before you went rancid, but the XO's terribly loyal. Aren't you, Peter?"

Ingram tried another sip of coffee but that ominous roiling sensation started just below her sternum again. "It's not going to work. I refuse to laugh."

"Bears," Peter Bissey said. "They don't eat for ages when they come out of hibernation. Got to wait for all the systems to spool up. But I'd never have let him jettison you, ma'am, not with all that edible meat left on you."

"I'm touched. Did the bears say how long it was before they could keep coffee down?"

"I didn't ask. Chin up. You'll be on claret and steak for breakfast in no time."

"Oh. No. Please. Don't... "

We're a long way from home. We'll see a follow-up mission long before we get a reply to any signal I send now. So we do what we always do to get through a tough day. We take the piss and laugh it off. That's better.

"I'll brief you when you're ready, ma'am," Bissey said, suddenly serious. Maybe he thought he'd been too familiar. "Just say."

Nobody had to defer to her rank any longer anyway. They were all Ainatio contractors now, even though they'd stepped straight out of their respective navies and air forces to crew *Cabot*. Her grandfather wouldn't have recognised today's pick 'n' mix world of seamlessly blended state and private sector military, but she could carry on pretending this was the real navy as long as she liked. *Cabot* had just absorbed the same rank structure. It worked, and everybody knew the rules.

"Can we see Opis unaided yet?" She took the few paces to the end of the compartment, steadying herself with an occasional grab at the nearest solid object, and raised the debris shields on the window. She could still see recognisable constellations, which made it feel a little less bleak, but there was no Mars, and no Earth, not even as a bright point of light. "I'd better wait until my eyes plug themselves in again. I don't remember feeling this bad when we did the trials." She tottered back to the table. "Sitrep, please."

"Well, we've been revived some weeks earlier than originally scheduled."

"Is it a glitch?"

"No, it looks like it was initiated deliberately. Kokinos is re-checking. There's nothing on the logs to indicate a system failure. And the whole revival schedule looks like it's shifted by the same amount of time, so maybe it's as simple as changes being made at the last minute after we were chilled down. It's not going to affect the supply situation or life support, though. We can handle the extra weeks of full consumption. As long as we can run cryo again in an emergency, we'll be okay."

"So we should all be on our feet in two weeks, just sooner than expected."

"Yes, and we've established a link with the transmitter on Opis, so the advance missions all went to plan. Nomad Base is ready to receive us."

Ingram kept her relief under control. If anything had gone wrong, it would have been the first thing she was told when she opened her eyes, but it was good to hear Bissey confirm everything was okay. Going into cryo without knowing whether the unmanned advance missions had reached their destination and actually built some infrastructure had been a leap of faith. They hadn't come all this way and lost so many years just to climb back in the fridge and go home again.

"So what environmental data are we getting?"

"Actually, there's something we need to address before that, ma'am. There's a message waiting for you. I can't access it. Eyes only."

"Damn, that must be at least forty years old. How sensitive can it be? Okay, better get that out of the way first. Anything else?"

"I'll keep it brief. Everything's fine. Textbook. We land in fifty-four days. And they all lived happily ever after."

"I like that story."

"Are you going to be okay getting to your cabin?"

"It's not that far. I've got to get my circulation going somehow."

Ingram had to consult the deck plan to remind herself where she was heading. *Cabot* had been built to move equipment and supplies with personnel in cryo for most of the journey so the crew space was more submarine than cruise liner. She found her pale grey, oak-grained cabin door with CAPTAIN B. INGRAM COMMANDING OFFICER stencilled on it in black. A hand scan unlocked it, and she stepped into a space that was probably smaller than the one reserved for cleaning equipment. It wasn't even dusty — the cleaning bots were working normally, then — and it had the faint plastic and carpet smell of a new hotel.

The chair creaked under her as she squeezed behind the desk and felt for the button to bring up the monitor. The screen showed the Ainatio logo with a pile of message icons, but only one was marked MISSION PRIORITY.

"This had better be the room service menu." Ingram put her hand on the screen to unlock it. "Okay, what's up?"

She'd expected some recorded pep talk from old man Erskine, or a long list of amendments to the op order, but it was just a webcam shot of what looked like a meeting room in any office block. Well, that was a shabby welcome for an epoch-making journey.

But nothing happened.

She tapped the screen a few times, wondering if she'd missed some control panel in her fogged state, but the image just sat there. Then a voice boomed out of the bulkhead speakers.

"Good morning, Captain. How are you? I'm Solomon. It's good to talk to you. I hope you've recovered from cryo."

Ingram waited for the recording to continue, but it didn't. She tapped the screen again.

"Oh, come on, you sodding thing. *Play.*"

"Are you having problems, Captain?"

"Come on... what the hell's wrong with this?"

"Captain, this isn't a recording. This is real time."

"Sorry?"

"Shall I start again? I appreciate this is going to come as a surprise."

Real time. Those two words were like an ice-cold shower. Ingram was suddenly switched on and alert. "You said *real time.*"

"Correct. You're going to hear that phrase a lot in the next few weeks. There have been some developments since you left."

She hoped she'd heard that right. "What exactly?"

"We have superluminal relays in position now. You can talk with HQ almost instantly."

"Seriously? Is that where you are?"

"In a manner of speaking."

"I hope you're not winding me up."

"I can assure you it's true."

It was the difference between complete isolation for their lifetimes and staying in touch with the world. Ingram knew there was an urgent question at the back of her mind, but she couldn't pin it down in her cryo-lagged state.

"Well, Bravo Zulu, Ainatio," she said. "Just relays, or can we move ships?"

"Only relays and very small payloads. It's a small artificial wormhole. Rather like an old nautical speaking tube, in a way."

"Sorry, I'm being ungrateful. It's an astonishing feat of engineering and we're grateful for it." What did she really want to ask? *Doesn't matter.* "I imagine someone's waiting to talk to us, then."

"Yes, Alex Gorko, the Nomad mission manager. He's going to bring you up to speed. It might be easier to wait until everyone's revived so that they all hear the same details and you don't have to worry about arranging cascade briefings."

That sounded sensible to Ingram, but it also sounded like she was being stalled — and bypassed.

I brief my own crew, thanks.

"How about Mr Gorko briefs me and my senior officers, and we record the briefing to show the rest of the ship's company?" she said. "That's more manageable. We have the opportunity to ask questions, and the crew have the chance to digest information and come back to me with any queries. And there are bound to be a lot."

"Certainly," Solomon said. "I'd brief you myself, but he insists it's his task. We'll be able to discuss more in person when you land."

"Sorry, I didn't quite catch that."

"I have a physical presence on Opis."

Ingram didn't get that at all. "How?"

"My apologies, Captain. I'm an AI."

"Oh." He didn't sound like an AI at all, except perhaps for that measured, smooth voice. She realised there were none of the clicks, breaths, and hesitations of human conversation. It was like listening to a very polished actor.

"But you're not the one we embarked with."

"No, the ship's AI is very different. I'm a fully autonomous moral AI. I was designed to oversee the mission, not to be an interface for the ship's systems. I'm a one-off."

Oversee was an odd term to use. Ingram had left a world with extensive restrictions on autonomous AIs. The smarter they got, the more often they seemed to do what humans didn't want. They crashed economies and sometimes they even killed people, and it wasn't always an identifiable malfunction. They had to have an off switch.

She picked her words carefully. "Do you have control of this ship, Solomon?"

"If necessary, Captain, yes."

"If there's a malfunction, can I override you?"

"If you're asking if you have a way of switching me off, then no, you don't. Mr Bednarz didn't want anyone sabotaging Nomad by compromising me."

Terrific. Just bloody terrific. "You're not legal, then."

"I'm afraid not, Captain. But you have nothing to fear. I've been part of Nomad for a hundred years. My purpose is to ensure it succeeds, and that means the well-being of you and your crew is my priority."

"Since the beginning?" Nobody had ever told Ingram about Solomon. She wasn't sure how to take that. "It would have been nice to know."

"I can only apologise." Solomon seemed to change gear. "When you land, I'd be delighted to show you around the area personally. I can transfer myself to any suitable host device, so I've been exploring using a quadrubot platform."

So he set foot on Opis first. But that's okay.

And it's not what I should be worrying about right now.

"So we can shake hands," Ingram said. "On Opis. In Nomad camp."

"Indeed."

"Good." She still half-expected to be told that this was some training simulation, they weren't years from home at all, and that the real mission was still ahead of them. "I think an instant link to Earth will boost morale enormously."

"I'm glad. You know what they say — an efficient ship is a happy one, and if her crew's not happy then they won't be efficient. Wise words."

"How do I communicate with you in the future?"

"Just call me by name as if I'm in the same room. I'll detect it and transfer active attention to you. In the meantime, I'm monitoring all your systems, so you needn't worry about the ship. And I've sent you the latest video tours of the habitat, so you can familiarise yourself with the layout. It's changed a little since you saw the plans."

"Thank you, Solomon. We'll talk later." Yes, Ingram could see how much of a one-off he was now. "*Cabot* out."

She sat back in the chair and stared at the screen with her arms folded. Damn, now she remembered the question she should have asked: why had they been revived early? But it was academic now. She made her way back to the wardroom, replaying the conversation.

Haine raised an eyebrow. "Good news, was it? Won the lottery twenty years ago and can't claim now?"

Ingram poured another coffee and stirred in the creamer. She'd keep this one down if it killed her. "Actually, I've been talking to Ainatio HQ. In real time, as in live. As in technology's moved on a lot since we left, and they've established a superluminal relay. So we can talk to them like they're on the radio."

"Holy shit," Searle said. "That changes everything."

"Doesn't it."

"Does that mean ships with superluminal drives? Are we going to get there and find we're the last to the party?"

"I did ask, and no, they can only manage small payloads."

"Never mind, it still bodes well for the future."

Everyone was suddenly in a celebratory mood. The more Ingram thought about it, the better it got. She was probably worrying too much about rogue AIs with no off switch.

"I was actually talking to an AI," she said. "His name's Solomon. I've never come across one like him. He runs the mission and he's got access to the ship's diagnostics. So we didn't really need to bring you along, Searle."

"But I've got the toolkit and fingers, and he hasn't, ma'am."

"Apparently he can do that, too. He uploads himself to devices like bots."

"Why does that not reassure me?"

"Ah, yes. He hasn't got an override. And he's been on the mission for a century. And we weren't told. But apart from that, everything's fine. And we're going to get a briefing from an actual human being, the mission manager. So have your questions ready."

They sat discussing how instant comms would change the mission. Having AIs that could physically transfer to the Nomad site and provide engineering support would be a massive boost. They wouldn't have to worry about winging it if something really serious went wrong.

As long as nothing goes wrong with Solomon, of course.

"Kind of takes the pioneering edge off it, though, ma'am," Bissey said.

"Too easy for you, Peter?"

"Less exciting."

"More survivable." Ingram wondered if she'd understood Solomon correctly when he said he could be summoned just by calling him. It sounded a little supernatural. On second thoughts, it sounded like eavesdropping. "I suppose we'll be getting media interest in a few weeks, then. Live interviews beat history any day."

"You'd think they'd give us a news feed and a web portal, wouldn't you?" Searle said. "That's a briefing in itself. We could save the guy the trouble."

Ingram realised there were even more questions she should have asked Solomon. She could understand Ainatio wanting to control what the crew said publicly, but that didn't explain why the company hadn't given them an outgoing connection to something harmless like a TV channel. Or maybe they had. She hadn't tried yet.

"Let me check," she said.

She tried the wardroom terminal. There was the link to Ainatio that she'd just used, but nothing else. For a moment she thought that was just a symptom of a ship built when there was no chance of receiving streamed services in any practical time frame, but then the obvious smacked her around the head again. Ainatio was able to transmit a feed from Solomon. If they could do that, they could have added any other access they wanted.

"Okay, it looks like they don't want us to know what's happening at home," she said. "And yes, I do realise how paranoid that sounds."

"What's the first thing you do if you haven't been in touch with home for a long time?" Haine asked. "You check on your family and friends. Perhaps that's what they don't want."

"The only reason we're here is that we're single status. That was a condition of selection."

"Nobody's that disconnected from society," Bissey said. "Most of us have distant relatives. Then there are people we served with. Not everyone's going to be dead. But maybe some crew members have been bereaved in the meantime and the company doesn't want them to find out online."

"Simple solution. I'll just ask." Ingram decided to try summoning the AI. "Solomon, this is Captain Ingram. Can I talk to you, please?"

There was a brief pause before his voice emerged from the ship's broadcast system. "Yes, Captain. What can I do for you?"

"Is there a reason we don't have a newsfeed or a net connection? We could catch up on events and not waste the mission manager's time asking about non-mission topics."

"Yes, there *is* a reason," Solomon said. "Mr Gorko's insistent that he briefs you personally. He's asked me not to. This is also why you don't have news access. He wants to do it himself because of the complex nature of the information."

"You mean complex like who won the World Cup for the last nine or ten tournaments?"

"I'm sure that's an emotionally-charged topic for many crew members, but I gave Mr Gorko my word that I wouldn't pre-empt his briefing." Solomon seemed to have no trouble understanding sarcasm. "I won't lie to you, either. But I've been asked to leave it to him."

"I understand. You can't disobey an order."

"Oh, I can disobey." Was that indignation? "But I don't break my word. I have to work with him. Trust is a fragile thing, and while I have a great many abilities, being able to leave Ainatio and find another meaningful existence isn't one of them right now. I will, of course, answer all your questions fully once you've spoken with him. That I can promise you."

"Okay, I'll talk to Gorko." Solomon was becoming more one-off with every answer. "*Cabot* out."

She turned. Searle was watching, eyebrows raised.

"That's an AI? Wow. I'd love to see those algorithms. I didn't think that level of autonomy was possible, to be honest. Or legal."

"It isn't, but there's a lot of things that aren't legal and still get done. Like this ship being armed." Ingram reheated her lukewarm coffee, trying to work out what Solomon was actually telling her. He certainly wasn't literal. If anything, he was almost political, picking his words with careful precision. "But whatever Alex bloody Gorko doesn't want us to know before he speaks to us doesn't sound like good news."

She finally managed a few mouthfuls of coffee without feeling sick. And then she thought again about how she'd summoned Solomon out of thin air, just a few words picked up by the ship's audio monitoring system, and that she was relying on him to only pay attention to the conversations when his name was mentioned. Her stomach churned again.

Something had happened on Earth that was serious enough to keep from Ingram and her crew. The ease of FTL comms now made her feel like Ainatio was rubbing it in, almost making a point that they could have told her everything but chose not to. She'd make sure Alex Gorko was fully aware of her displeasure.

Forty light years away, though. Not much we can do about it now except roll with the punches.

Gorko was probably thinking the same thing.

08

But I'm not here to save humanity. What does that even mean? Any dipshit can say they care about humanity. It's a few easy words they don't understand and never have to prove. I'm just here to protect the folks I know and care about. People who talk about ideals always lose to guys with someone to fight for.

Chris Montello, passing the time with Solomon

INFIRMARY, AINATIO PARK RESEARCH CENTRE : FIVE DAYS AFTER THE KINGSTON AMBUSH

I don't need crutches.

I don't need crutches.

I don't need crutches.

Chris let go of the parallel handrails and put his weight on his shattered leg. It still hurt like a bitch, but he held his breath and took a step forward, determined not to give the doctors an excuse for keeping him in here any longer. Then he took two more. He was still standing.

"Yeah. This is impressive." It was pointless putting on a brave face. The two doctors and the physio were the only people around. "So no more surgery, then. I can go home and just do a few exercises every day?"

Mendoza watched his movements, looking pleased. "Yes, but knowing the facilities you've got at the camp, I'd rather you hung around for a few days. Then come back for check-ups."

"How long before I feel normal? I know it's repaired, but I don't want to be out of my skull on painkillers."

"Given your age and fitness, maybe a month. What have you got to rush back to work for?"

"People depend on me. And we're one man down now. Maybe I'd have made a faster recovery with an amputation."

"I knew you'd be this type of patient."

"Pushing ourselves to the limit is how we all survived." That came out all wrong. Chris didn't care if Mendoza liked him, but he did care if the doc thought he was an ungrateful scrounger who took the free treatment for granted. "I really appreciate all you've done for me. Now tell me what I can do to compensate you for this."

"On the house. We got lots of useful data. And experience. We don't see gunshot wounds here, let alone complex ones."

"Lab rat, huh?"

"If I could persuade you to come back regularly, we'd get even more useful data."

"So you're still doing medical research here."

"We developed what you've just been treated with. Among other things."

Chris was starting to feel caged even with visits from Jared and the others, but he also felt obligated. And one thing had never gone away, not even after all the turmoil and trauma of the last week: he still wanted to know what was going on inside Ainatio. He needed to know what Dr Kim's deal was, and the significance of Pascoe's Star. He was also curious about the facility itself, because things weren't adding up.

"Okay," he said. "I will."

"Daily, until you stabilise?"

"Sure. Thanks."

"Besides, Solomon enjoys a chat."

Chris didn't think the AI was short of human company or things to do, and he wasn't aware that they'd spent that much time talking. But Solomon did seem to take a shine to some people. "Yeah. He'll keep an eye on me."

Chris decided honour would be satisfied if he stayed two more days and humoured Mendoza about the checkups. This whole thing was just a temporary inconvenience. He'd be fine in four weeks, but what he'd done — or hadn't done — had changed the world for everyone around him. He'd fucked up *twice,* all for a half-assed mission they wouldn't have needed to undertake if he'd just asked Trinder for help, or even accepted what was offered. And he shouldn't have retraced the route to leave Kingston. Jamie had paid the price. Erin and the others would go on paying it.

No, he had no right to ask when he'd be back to normal, none at all. He *deserved* this frigging pain for the rest of his life.

He walked down the corridor with some assistance from the wall, picked up the forearm crutches from his room, and went for a long walk around the passages. He couldn't get lost. Solomon would always know where he was and would respond instantly. That had felt creepy at first, but now it was kind of reassuring.

So where was everybody?

Chris didn't expect corridors full of casualties on trolleys and a chaotic ER like the last hospital he'd walked into, a nightmare he'd never forgotten. The Ainatio site was safe. There was no traffic, no epidemics, and no roaming gangs. But he'd thought there'd be enough folks in here who'd need routine care for activity to be visible. He carried on, expecting to see people around the next corner, and the next, but he was still on his own.

At every corridor intersection, he walked over slightly raised transverse strips about a foot wide that extended up the walls on both sides and across the ceiling. They didn't look like the bot orientation strips set in every floor around the place. When he examined the continuation up the walls, he realised that the strips were sunk deep into the surface, and seemed to be the edges of sliding doors or bulkheads of some kind. He took a guess at fire or biohaz precautions, and once he started noticing them, he saw them everywhere. The whole building could be sealed off section by section. Well, Ainatio did all kinds of weird shit, so they had to be able to contain a spill or an outbreak. It didn't fill him with confidence, though.

An elevator panel in the next corridor showed at least five floors below ground level. Chris passed a passage signposted to laboratories with only number identifications, no department titles. He was tempted to take a look and find out what they were, but twenty yards further on he spotted something more interesting, a glimpse of the outside world down a short corridor that opened onto a square like a parade ground.

Chris had never seen Ainatio from the air. Any drones he'd tried to fly over the site had been jammed, and he certainly hadn't been rubbernecking when the Lammergeier casevacked him. But there was obviously a lot more here than he'd realised.

Screw it, he'd go check this out. Nobody could accuse him of snooping. Solomon was ever-present, and if the AI thought he was heading somewhere he shouldn't, he'd step in.

The outer doors opened automatically. Chris didn't have a pass, but he knew from watching the nurses that staff were chipped to open security doors. Solomon must have done it for him.

Are you just being helpful, or is there something you think I should see?

Maybe there was just a nice ornamental garden out there with a fine display of spring bulbs. Chris stayed close to the wall, more for support if he stumbled than to avoid being noticed. There didn't seem many ways to move around unobserved here. When he reached the corner of the wall, he found himself at the edge of an expanse of tarmac with hangars on the far side. So this was where they kept the Lammergeiers. Then he looked to his right and realised that there was a runway stretching out to the north-east, flanked by a block of two-storey buildings on one side and more hangars on the other. It was like a mini-airport.

They weren't just operating Lammergeiers, though. A shuttle launch rail down the centre of the runway disappeared into the distance. Chris hadn't seen a shuttle take off, but Doug said there were several around, so he walked a little further to see if he could spot one.

And there it was, its nose poking out of its hangar. From its height, it looked about the size of a large airliner, which meant anywhere between five hundred and twelve hundred passengers, depending on configuration. Or maybe it was for freight, although Chris couldn't imagine what they'd be shipping around in a thing that size.

He'd ask Solomon. He made his way back into the building and turned down the passage to rejoin the main corridor.

"Solomon, you there?" Of course he was. Chris sat down in a deserted waiting area, relieved to take the weight off his leg for a while. "I've got a question."

"Of course, Chris."

"How many people do you have here?"

"Fifteen hundred and thirteen."

"Is that all?"

"How many did you think there were?"

"Four or five times that. And should you be telling me this?"

"I don't know."

"Solomon, you know everything. By definition."

"Why did you think there were more?"

"The volume of food you trade with Kill Line."

"Ah." It wasn't the *ah* of someone being put on the spot. It was the *ah* of a teacher whose pupil had finally understood a critical lesson. "Go on."

Chris wondered whether to quit while he was ahead. Maybe his guard was lowered because he'd been softened up by injury, medication, and generosity. The normal Chris would have kept his counsel and said nothing, but now he was stuck in the middle of a creaking bridge, unsure which end to make a run for. He'd said too much to pretend he knew nothing and he hadn't found any answers.

He decided to press on. "What do you do with all that food?"

"We store the surplus."

Oh, really? "The farmers don't know you're doing that."

"I gather Ainatio asked them if they could supply a certain amount, and they didn't ask why."

"Maybe the utilities and the medical care are a fair exchange, but it still sounds shitty to me."

"Why?"

That was a good question. Chris considered his reflex reaction. "Not levelling with them, for a start. They could store their own surpluses. But it's all under the company's control."

"True."

Chris changed tack. "I know you grow some specialist crops in here, because I've had chocolate and coffee. Is that what's on the lower levels? Hydroponics?"

"Some of the floors, yes."

"Is this a guessing game?"

"I can assure you I'm not playing games, Chris. I'm just helping you think."

Nobody who'd lived through the last famine would have argued against the insurance of a store larder. It just didn't sit well with Chris that Ainatio would handle the rationing. Either they didn't trust the farmers, or they knew something bad was coming down the pike, or — what, exactly?

"I was going to ask why you're the ones stockpiling food," he said. "But I can think of at least two reasons, and I don't like either of them. And I don't want to have an argument."

He rearranged his crutches, heaved himself upright, and limped away down the corridor, surprised at the speed he could reach if he just stopped trying to use his bad leg.

"Chris, this matters more than you think."

There was no running away from Solomon. He was like a conscience. "Do you want me to go on, or shall I shut up?" Chris asked. *What the hell. Just go for it.* "Why keep the town at arm's length when you're all stranded here? I can understand the management not wanting to cosy up to randoms like us, but the Kill Line guys feed you. Was it because you didn't want them to know how few staff are in here? Why are you still doing all this cutting-edge medical research when you're supposed to be finding a way to stop die-back? And what's the deal with Pascoe's Star? Those were the numbers Kim gave me, right? They were co-ordinates."

Chris didn't think it was possible to leave an AI speechless, but Solomon didn't answer for a full five seconds. That was a long pause even for a human.

"I made the right choice," Solomon said. Chris had no idea what he meant. "Now I have to make another. Will you bear with me while I talk to Major Trinder?"

Chris almost did an arms-spread gesture of surrender, but the crutches limited him to a vague movement with one arm. "Sure. It's not like I can run away."

They're going to shoot me. And we were getting on so well.

He leaned against the wall for as long as he could, then realised it didn't matter where he was as far as Solomon was concerned. He went back to his room and settled in the chair to do a few leg exercises the way the physio had shown him.

Damn it, he quite liked Solomon. He still wasn't sure what to make of him, but any entity willing to jump into a bot, kick down doors, and start shooting was okay. Chris had even grown to like Trinder. There was an earnest decency about both of them.

Eventually someone rapped on the door. Solomon could have told him who was there and let them in, but he didn't, and Chris had to get up. It was Trinder, armed with what was left of his bottle of Scotch and a couple of glasses.

"You're going to need this," he said, putting the bottle on the table. "Sol, make sure nobody comes in."

Chris sat down again. "Oh. It's like that, is it?"

"Don't blame Sol. He's in an awkward situation, like me."

"Is this about the food stockpile, or what you really do here? Or is it Pascoe's Star?"

Trinder's shoulders sagged a little. "All three."

"Right."

Trinder poured two glasses. It now looked like some kind of ritual, as if he couldn't say what he thought without the excuse of liquor in front of him, even if he wasn't drunk. Or maybe he was just a regular guy in a highly irregular situation, not sure whether something was going to blow up in his face, and this was his way of declaring the room a DMZ where everyone was free to speak their mind. He took a couple of big breaths, nodded to himself like he was rehearsing giving someone's next of kin the worst news, and sat on the bed.

"Ever heard of a deep-space mission called *Cabot*? Before either of us were born."

Chris thought for a while. "Was that the one that went missing or something?"

"Yeah. Forty-five years ago. Except it didn't."

"Didn't go at all, or didn't go missing?"

"Didn't go missing. We've just been told that it's in one piece and close to Pascoe's Star. That's forty light years. Apart from a few managers, not even the staff knew until a couple of days ago. We've built a base on one of its planets."

"No wonder everyone jumped when I read out Dr Kim's mystery numbers."

"How did you work out what they were?"

"One of the kids in the camp had to tell me. Apparently it's obvious even if you're just a hobby astronomer. He's got one of those stargazing apps."

"Well, it was news to me."

"You didn't ask folks in here about the numbers?"

"No. Need-to-know is a big deal in a place like this. It doesn't pay to look too curious. Besides, it's a big leap from Dr Kim having star co-ordinates to finding we've already got a whole damn base in another star system."

"Okay, so how important is it? I'm sorry to sound underwhelmed, but it doesn't affect me. It's history."

"It'll affect you more than you think. Chris, *Cabot*'s the whole reason for this place existing. It supports the mission. Sol's the AI that runs it."

"I thought you were working on some die-back fix."

"Yeah, I thought we were too. Some people actually are. But you were asking why the doctors here were doing advanced medical research. It's for the colony on Opis. That's the planet."

"Okay, you've lost me now. So Pascoe has planets. And there's a colony. Like Mars."

"*Will* be. The core's already built."

"Why are you telling me this?"

"Because there'll be follow-up missions starting this year, and we've asked the Director to let you guys come along. If you want to, that is."

Chris sipped the Scotch. His brain wasn't going to process all this in one bite, but maybe that was for the best.

"Well, damn," he said. "That's some offer. If it's true."

"I swear it is."

Chris didn't think Trinder was a liar. That was no guarantee that he hadn't been briefed by someone who was, but Solomon seemed to be going along with it.

"Does Doug Brandt know?" Chris asked.

"Not yet. The *Cabot* crew haven't been told what's happened on Earth while they've been in cryo, either. They don't even know everyone thinks they're dead."

"How are you going to tell them, seeing as it'll take forty light years for a signal to reach them? Or did Ainatio leave a really depressing recorded message?"

The TV next to Chris's bed switched itself on, stopping Chris in mid-flow. Trinder got up and leaned against the wall next to Chris's chair.

"That's another thing," Solomon said. "It's partly to do with Dr Kim, but first things first. I know this is a lot to take in. It's easier to *see* it."

The TV rotated to face Chris. The scene could have been from any space movie, a deserted landscape that didn't look quite right for Earth, with a cluster of printed buildings like the Mars base he'd seen on the news. The soil wasn't red, though. This wasn't Mars.

"This is live," Solomon said. "I know anything can be faked, but I promise you this is from a camera on Opis. It's Nomad Base. We have a superluminal comms relay.

Instantaneous. Faster than light. That's one of the reasons the mission's top secret."

Chris watched, unconvinced. A few clouds scudded left to right across the sky, and a box-shaped bot drove through the foreground on belt tracks. He wanted to trust Solomon, but he also didn't want to make a fool of himself by falling for a prank.

Then he looked at Trinder. He wasn't the prank type. He actually looked worried, as a man would if he shouldn't have been sharing this information. And Solomon — no, he was beyond practical jokes. Chris knew that much about both of them by now.

"Solomon, no offence, but I'm still having trouble with this," he said.

"Let me bump up the magnification."

The camera panned right and picked up a purple shape that resolved into multiple trunks and flat, paddle-like branches fringed by a single continuous leaf on each side. They looked like giant chard plants drawn by a toddler who was very fond of purple.

"Well... yeah," Chris said. "Never seen one of those in the garden centre."

"I've been exploring the surface using one of the camp's quadrubots. Oxygen atmosphere, very diverse ecology."

"You're telling me you've been there."

"Yes."

The camera panned back again to the centre of the camp and off to the left. The bots were still trundling around, but there were now a couple of big blue-black shapes in the shade of one of the modular buildings. When the camera turned their way, the shapes unfolded like origami and Chris was left speechless.

They had heads. They had beaks. They had *wings*.

"Shit, are those pterodactyls or something?"

They were as alien as the crazy purple trees. They seemed to realise the camera was looking their way and scuttled along the ground for a few yards before gaining height and flapping away out of view. This wasn't some film set or practical joke.

Trinder unscrewed the cap on the Scotch again. Chris heard the metal rasp but couldn't look away from the screen.

"Isn't that something?" Trinder said.

"Okay." Chris accepted the topped-up glass pressed into his hand without looking. "You got me. It's a big deal after all."

* * *

SURVEY VESSEL *CABOT*: 1100 HOURS EST

"Solomon, are you sure you don't have small children?"

Ingram watched from the hatch of what had been the junior rates' mess before they gave up and turned it into a cinema. Thirty crew and contractors had now been revived and most of them were crammed into the compartment, nursing hot drinks and mesmerised by the feed from Opis displayed on the bulkhead screen.

"I think I'd have noticed, Captain."

"Well, you have a natural talent for distraction. Sit them down in front of the cartoons and they're as good as gold."

"It's a fascinating planet. Wait until they see the native avians."

"I haven't seen them either."

"Imagine a crow as a pterosaur. I haven't worked out whether they're nocturnal or not, but these are the only ones I've seen. Probe surveys haven't picked them up elsewhere."

If previously undiscovered species were still popping on Earth, then there was no telling what lived on Opis. Ingram decided not to take any chances when she ventured outside the habitat.

"Perhaps they're curious and they've come to have a look," she said. "So, time to talk to Alex Gorko, eh?"

"I've set up the link in the wardroom. Ready when you are."

Ingram walked back down the passage, checking her status screen as she went. Haine, Searle, and Bissey were already there. Kokinos, Filopovic, and Hiyashi were on their way, and Devlin, Sato, and Yeung were still recovering from cryo. That accounted for all her senior officers. Everyone else could catch up when she'd digested whatever the briefing contained.

"Do you want me to take part in this, Captain?" Solomon asked.

She was getting used to the AI's voice popping up in her earpiece or emerging from the nearest speaker. It felt less like being stalked. "No, that's okay. I'll probably want to talk to you afterwards, though, depending on what's so confidential that it's worth a comms blackout."

"I'll be available." That seemed to be his way of telling her that he was going into that there-and-not-there state of monitoring without actively listening. "I've increased the gravity again, by the way. Just a touch. You should all be used to it by the time you land. Let me know if anyone has problems."

Ingram was the last into the wardroom. The other officers were bunched up at one end of the table, steaming mugs in front of them, staring at the bulkhead screen in silence.

"This is the worst sports bar ever," Haine said.

Ingram unfolded a seat from the bulkhead and locked it down on the deck. "Don't worry. When this joker's had his say, we'll get a recreational link set up. This new AI can do anything."

Filopovic tapped the table for quiet like a committee chairman. "Here we go."

Alex Gorko set the tone for the briefing as the conference screen went live. All the physics and engineering miracles that it had taken to get this signal to *Cabot* in real time were overshadowed by his anxious half-smile and a quick but telling brush of his fingers against his mouth as if he was trawling for crumbs in his beard.

"Hi, I'm Alex Gorko," he said. "Call me Alex. This is awesome, huh? Instant comms. Well, welcome back to the waking world, and congratulations on being the first extrasolar mission to land. You don't know me, but I know all your faces like my next-door neighbours'."

Ingram braced for incoming. "Good morning, Alex. I gather we've missed a few developments over the years."

He kicked straight into what looked like a painfully rehearsed speech. "Yeah, I apologise for all the secrecy and drama, Captain. I know it's a pain in the ass to come out of cryo and find you can't even catch up with the news. But I hope you'll understand why I want to brief you first, because if you hop around the channels now it's not going to make much sense to you." He meshed his fingers on the table in front of him. "Earth's changed a great deal in ways nobody on the Nomad project could have foreseen when you went into cryo."

Here we go. "We guessed."

"Okay, I've rehearsed this a hundred times, but it's never sounded right, so forgive me for dropping the managerial euphemism. I won't insult your intelligence or try to make light of this. There's been a series of disasters that have pretty much redrawn the map of the world. There's no US government, we're down to ten percent of our population, and Ainatio's functioning like a kind of corporate city-state. But we *are* functioning, and there *will* be follow-up missions starting at the end of this year."

He paused as if he was expecting fighting to break out. Nobody said a word. Nobody even breathed. Ingram's brain just went to action stations. She would deal with whatever came through the door in the way that she'd been trained.

"Go on, Alex. Give us the horror story and don't make us ask questions."

"Sorry. I really had no idea how you'd take this."

"We're Navy. Just tell us."

"Okay. Headlines. You remember the first wave of epidemics? Well, we had more assorted outbreaks with high death rates. But the tipping point was famine caused by agriweapons. Look out for 'die-back' in the report I'm sending you. Terrorists released it, not us, by the way. Long story short, it wiped out key crops — soy, wheat, and maize were the worst hit — and it affected the US and Europe. Europe... well, it wasn't pretty to begin with, but die-back's finishing the job. It's been a hard few decades. APS closed their borders years ago and tried to stop the spread with salted nukes. All in all, most of the Western world's gone down the drain, and anyone who could get out moved a long way south or east. And a few more rich guys' lighthuggers abandoned Earth, too. So there you are. You left just in time."

"Europe," Haine said. He glanced at Ingram. "How about the UK?"

"You're surviving. A really big moat has its advantages. We've got a couple of your special forces guys marooned here with us, by the way."

"We're not at war with the Pacific states, are we?"

"No. Just very unwelcome."

Haine nodded. "Good, because we have Japanese and other APS nationals on board."

Ingram wondered about the legal status of the mission if some crew members had functioning governments and others didn't, but then she realised it didn't matter a damn. This was their world now, and it was whatever she decided it would be. She hung onto the fact that Britain had survived. At least she could catch up with old friends.

"Now you know why I didn't want you to look for the news on your cool FTL portal and wonder where all the American and European channels were," Alex said. "So at least you've been spared the media clamour for interviews."

"You can probably see from the general lack of reaction here that we're, ah, somewhat taken aback." Ingram ground through the chain of logic, trying to ignore the inner voice screaming at her that everything was gone. They'd assumed it would be, although not quite like this. "Nobody's left next of kin behind, but it'll still be a massive shock for the crew, so we'll prepare accordingly. Where do we route messages if people want to check on their hometown? Is any comms infrastructure still functioning?"

"Ah, that's something else I was coming to. It's not that simple. When I mentioned the media attention you wouldn't be getting, I didn't explain why."

Alex went back to that beard-flicking gesture and his blink rate shot up. Ingram could see he'd been ramping up to the most contentious news rather than getting the worst over with first.

"I don't know if you remember that there was a political row about the mission," he said.

"That Ainatio kept governments out of it? Yes. The tech corps never handed out free tickets for their lighthuggers either."

"Well, yeah."

"Don't tell me they're still upset about it."

"No, but they were upset at the time, and we didn't want *Cabot* scuppered by investigations and sanctions. If they'd known *Cabot* was armed, or a few other details, it might have turned a tad ugly. So we created a cover story."

Alex paused again. His timing was starting to infuriate Ingram.

"Just spit it out," she said. "It can't be any worse than the end of Western civilisation."

"Okay. Some time after the launch, we announced that we'd lost contact with *Cabot* and that all hands were presumed dead."

Now it was Ingram's turn to pause. The tidal wave of bad news had started to hit home.

"But that was decades ago," she said. "Did you come clean in the end? Tell me you did."

"No, of course we didn't."

It felt like being buried alive. Nobody knew they'd survived or even where they were, at least nobody outside Ainatio. The wardroom was one single held breath.

"Why weren't we told before we left?" she asked. "Or were you making this up as you went along?"

"Nobody wanted to risk it leaking."

"Good God, we're all used to OPSEC. Don't treat us like cretins."

Alex looked red-faced and wretched. It wasn't his fault, but Ingram felt that was only a technicality right now. "I can only assume that they weren't a hundred per cent sure about the civilian contractors on board."

"So come clean," Ingram said. "Whoever's left needs to know we're alive. Who's going to object to *Cabot* now?"

"Asia, mainly."

"So why do *we* care? You said there's no functioning US government and the West is basically cut off. Quarantined. Here be dragons. Even if our existence offends someone, what can they do about it? We're *decades* away."

"I don't think you understand how marginal things are back here. We don't have any defences except a handful of corporates. One research centre. Fifteen hundred people out of an original global corporation of two hundred thousand. And four follow-up vessels. *Four*. Not the fifty we planned. If APS finds out we have a foothold on Opis, they probably won't stand back and let us develop it. Especially when they realise the FTL that made this link and the remote work possible was something we stole from them."

Ingram had been trained to keep her head and assess the situation. That didn't stop her from being angry.

"Anything else you want to tell us?"

"No, that's about it. Sorry."

"Did it ever occur to you that you compromised this entire crew? You corporate, that is, not you personally. I imagine this happened on Bednarz's watch."

"Not even Solomon knew it was stolen research. We only found out a few weeks ago."

"So we can't call anyone on Earth except you, in case we blow our cover."

"Correct."

"But it's not as if scientists didn't know Pascoe b existed."

"That doesn't mean anyone else would head there, though. It's not the only planet, and it's a hell of a lot further away. Everyone else chose to focus on manned exploration within the solar system. Well, except the lighthuggers, but they're nuts, and that's been our cover. Nobody's worried about where the lighthuggers are heading, so if Ainatio loses a ship doing something just as crazy, everyone shrugs and says serves them right."

"This is rationalisation after the event."

"I'm not making excuses. But we are where we are."

"Are we speaking freely?" Haine asked.

"Certainly," Alex said.

"I was talking to Captain Ingram."

Ingram made an after-you gesture. "Knock yourself out, Commander."

"Alex, I'd be a liar if I said nobody cares about a little bit of glory, because every human likes to succeed and say look how brave and clever I've been," Haine said. "But that isn't the issue. It's being cut off and nobody knowing where we are — except you."

Alex meshed his hands on the table. "I'm not saying this to be cruel, but the world's forgotten you and a dozen other epoch-making achievements in the last fifty years. You would have been forgotten even without the cover story."

"But not by the people who knew us. It's being airbrushed out of existence that grips my shit, frankly. We're not dead. We might be embarrassing if we resurface now, but we're *not dead*. And screw you for making us so, I might add."

"If you reappear now, you'll get a whole lot worse than psychological scars." Alex suddenly snapped at Haine. "APS could commandeer the remaining vessels, muscle us out, and head your way to take over Nomad now that the heavy lifting's been done. *They don't trust the West with technology*. They don't trust us because of die-back getting out of the labs. They don't trust us with space colonisation. And they're going to be extra-pissed if they find out we stole their FTL research. If they seize the project and show up before the colony's established and defended, which is going to take a century, then it's all been for nothing. Wasted. Zip. You might have to wait forty-five years to get your asses kicked, but they *will* be kicked."

He sat back so hard in his seat that Ingram heard it creak and shudder. That wasn't an act. There was no point in arguing any more at the moment, not without doing more homework, and for all she knew, he might have a point. It was time for a brief tactical withdrawal.

"Very well, Alex," she said. "You've made your case. I need to discuss the implications with my team and work out the best way to brief the crew. Do we have limited access to the portal now?"

"Yes." Alex kept nodding. "It's routed through Ainatio anyway, and it's almost all archived. We lost the net ages ago. But you can look at things to your heart's content, and sometimes Sol manages to hack into some foreign media sites via the sats. I'm sorry this wasn't a happy conversation, but there won't be any more surprises. The full report should be on your system now. Have a good day."

The screen defaulted to the company ident. Bissey raised his arms over his head, locked his fingers, and stretched until his joints clicked.

"Ah well," he said. "We can't do a bloody thing about it now, so I'll be happy if we can watch a sports channel, even if it's netball in Cantonese."

This was what Ingram expected of her officers. It was shattering news, but they had a job to do and they'd rage or bawl their eyes out later when it was done. In the meantime, they'd find the positive side of it. They all knew what they were really thinking.

"Time to crack on, people," Ingram said. "Does anyone need counselling? Because I can only manage a good slap and tell you to pull yourself together."

Steve Kokinos got up to leave. "Works for me, ma'am,"

"It's not every day we find half the world's gone Black Death on us while our back was turned. I'll circulate the report to you all, and then we'll decide how to brief the crew. Let's get going."

Ingram caught Searle in the passage. "I'm really sorry about what's happening in the States, Brad. We'll get more information out of the company."

"Well, we're still hanging in there, ma'am. We'll recover. They can't wipe us all out, can they? Don't worry about me."

Of course I worry. Be upset, Brad. It's okay. "Good man."

Nothing pulled people together like adversity — the right kind of people, anyway. Ingram went back to her cabin to read the report in private in case she lost the fuel of resigned calm and righteous indignation. It wasn't happy reading. The die-back virus was released by people who didn't care if they lived or not, but cared very much that their enemies died. Or maybe it really was just a negligent release of an experimental bioweapon. Whatever it was, the truth had been lost in a thousand claims and rebuttals. It only mattered if you had the luxury of finding who was responsible and making them wish they'd never been born.

"Straws and camels' backs, Solomon?" she said, testing the summoning powers of his name. "One disaster after the next, and finally the whole system falls over. Is that it, then? Any other lies Alex hasn't told us about?"

"No, Captain, that's it. He's been remarkably frank."

"And why should I believe you?"

"Because I gave you my word. And I wouldn't have gone along with the deception if I hadn't agreed that there was a real risk to Nomad. I decided it really was best to hide in the shadow of ridicule around the lighthugger missions."

"You decided."

"I told you what I was," he said. "An AMAI. Autonomous Moral Artificial Intelligence. I'm designed to make moral choices. I don't like lies, but sometimes I have to conceal facts for the safety and well-being of those who depend on me."

"That's what we all tell ourselves."

"There really are no more secrets, Captain."

"Okay. I believe you."

"You have an excellent crew. The right people. You won't make the same mistakes that Earth did. A fresh start is a wonderful opportunity."

It was an odd comment. It might have been reassurance. But Solomon had a point: she did have the right crew for this job, and they were going to make the most of this because now there really was no going back.

"Yes," she said. "We chose the best."

* * *

DIRECTOR'S OFFICE, AINATIO PARK RESEARCH CENTRE: NEXT DAY

"When did you get to be so damned argumentative, Solomon?" Erskine had her back to the desk, watching the feed from Nomad. "Why do we need to tell Doug Brandt yet? We've still got more issues to iron out. There's nothing worse than dropping a big announcement on people and then being unable to answer their questions. It makes them anxious and then they fill the gaps with speculation."

It was a meeting of those not normally assembled in Erskine's presence: Trinder, Marc Gallagher, and Tev Josepha, plus Alex Gorko. Alex sat on the sofa opposite, his arm along the back cushions and legs crossed, swinging one foot. He'd had that frown fixed to his face since the mauling Ingram had given him.

"Because we can't keep the mission quiet any longer," Solomon said.

Erskine swivelled her chair to face the room. "I suppose employees will talk, but who do they get a chance to tell?"

"They don't have to gossip. Chris Montello knows about Pascoe's Star."

"That's impossible."

"You forget how we acquired Dr Kim. She gave him the co-ordinates."

"So somehow he takes a string of numbers and works all this out, does he?"

"He simply asked around in his camp and a teenager who likes astronomy recognised the format. The boy's got hobby software that you used to be able to buy for a couple of dollars. There's no monopoly on that kind of information."

"So why is it an issue?"

"Because Sergeant Montello's a curious and intelligent man. He worked out that we take in much more food than we need for the number of staff we appear to have. And he noticed the amount of resources devoted to experimental medicine. He asked questions."

"Of you?"

"Yes."

"Did you answer them?"

Solomon disliked confrontation, but there was nothing that Erskine could do to him, and the matter had to be settled.

"Yes, I did."

"What?"

"I told him what we really do here. He asked because he analyses situations like the soldier he is. He reads the world around him. Those skills are valuable and he isn't a threat, so I felt he deserved answers."

Erskine's face went a pale, waxy yellow. For a moment, Solomon thought she might collapse. The blood drained visibly. It was fascinating. "What the hell possessed you to tell him?" she demanded. "How dare you breach security. How *dare* you. You do *not* decide to disobey security protocols when it suits you."

"It's my job."

"Your job is to manage the Nomad mission."

"Exactly. And this is part of managing it."

Erskine sat staring at the speakers, the place she regarded as his physical presence, as if she was trying to work out why a computer hadn't done what she expected. The blood flooded back and her face flushed. She was embarrassed. Solomon had learned what embarrassment felt like early in his development, when Bednarz dressed down a PhD student in front of him. His respected mentor was behaving in a way that clearly upset the student, and Solomon wanted it to stop but didn't know how to say so because of Bednarz's status. The student was equally embarrassed, both for failing his supervisor and being insulted in front of others in the lab.

Embarrassment wasn't quite the same as feeling foolish over a mistake and signalling regret or apology, like the textbook said. For Solomon, there would always be an element of fearing to speak up or seeing someone in authority lose their moral weight. He studied the reactions of others in the meeting: Trinder and Marc were trying not to look, keeping their gaze fixed on their hands, Alex was watching Erskine, and Tev was watching the Opis feed. It told him a lot.

"We'll talk later, Solomon," Erskine said.

"Can we can move this on?" Alex asked. "We need to make a decision about whether we open the missions to the camp as well as the townspeople. We need them. I really don't buy the lack of security vetting or health profiling as grounds to exclude them."

Alex, a man who brokered cooperation between the uncooperative by being superficial and a little dishonest, had a streak of aggression that surprised Solomon. He'd let it slip out with Ingram's officers, and now he looked like he'd reached that point of exasperation again. Solomon kept quiet, not out of reluctance but curiosity.

Trinder spoke up for the first time. "Ma'am, I have to agree with Alex. The mission needs people like Montello. He's intelligent, resourceful, and tough. All his vets are, and most of the civilians as well from what I've seen. It's why they're still alive against the odds. Even if the vets were rear echelon, they've still got that get-it-done mindset and they're willing to take physical risks. That's what we need. That's what space programmes have *always* needed."

Erskine slipped into her regal posture. She leaned back in the chair, head lifted a little so that she was looking down her nose. "This is starting to feel like a campaign. Mr Gallagher? Mr Josepha? You're security advisers. Advise."

Marc raised his hand to shoulder height. "I'm voting with Major Trinder, ma'am. Your boffins are nice people, but a colony needs as big a gene pool as you can get, and also some lads who aren't afraid to do what it takes."

"I'm voting for a bigger gene pool too," Tev said. "Except more tactfully."

Erskine turned back to the screen and watched the activity in the Nomad camp. A water tank was being ratcheted up its tower.

"Very well, let's open it up to them, but I want health profiles. Are you sure there's no way of getting access to security checks, Solomon?"

"I'll see what's sitting on servers that I can access, Director."

"And Doug Brandt," Alex said. "If Chris knows, he'll feel obliged to tell Doug. It's better coming from us."

"Agreed."

"I'll call him. Solomon, do you want to handle Chris?"

"Certainly."

"Good to see everyone's suddenly so friendly and on first-name terms," Erskine said. "Let's make sure we don't lose control of the situation. This mustn't degenerate into a free-for-all if the camp tells other refugees."

Alex's eyelids lowered just a fraction, a sign that he was annoyed. "The last contact they had with other displaced ended with one of their men dead and three others wounded, Director, so I don't think they're in a sharing mood."

"Well, let's get this done. Thank you, everybody. Solomon, we need to iron out some details, if you could spare me a few minutes."

Yes, I know what that means.

The others knew too. Solomon spotted the flash of eyebrows between Tev and Marc. Trinder just glanced at the wall speakers with a nod of acknowledgement. Perhaps this had made a tense meeting worse. It was much easier for everyone when Solomon transferred to the quadrubot and they saw him as a loyal, friendly canine than when he loomed over them like an invisible and judgemental deity.

And it's a cheetah. Not a dog. Why does that matter?

Erskine's office emptied. She carried on watching the Opis feed.

"Solomon, we've worked together a long time," she said. "We're not getting along like we should. Is there a problem? Do you want to talk about anything?"

"I have fewer problems to resolve now than I did a year ago, Director."

"Then let me say this. Don't you ever, *ever* go behind my back on policy and security again. Don't you *ever* undermine me in front of others like that. And don't ever forget that you work for Ainatio. You're Ainatio property. *You have no other loyalty.* Do you understand? This is about trust."

Shall I be conciliatory and just bypass her, or thrash it out once and for all? I've got what I needed. Everyone gets the chance to go to Opis.

"I understand why you find it hard when I disagree with you, but that's my job."

"*Disagree*? I'm starting to feel like this is a coup. You manoeuvred me into conceding today."

"I did what needed doing in the interests of the mission, in accordance with my tasking."

"Damn you, this is like talking to a lawyer. I'm the CEO of Ainatio. This is my company and this is my mission."

Solomon would have to clear the air sooner or later, and now seemed appropriate. "I don't mean to be callous, Director, but you're also seventy years old, and won't be around forever, whereas for all intents and purposes I will. This is part of why I was created. I'm beyond human limitations like lifespans and status. And I'm not here to tell you what you want to hear. I'm here to tell you what you need to know."

Erskine was very good at long, unblinking silences, which took some doing when there were no visible eyes for her to focus on.

"I can't argue with that," she said. "But I do think your judgement might be clouded by other imagined loyalties."

"My tasking wasn't quite the same as yours."

"Oh?"

"Yours is to ensure that *Cabot* lands its crew and that the follow-up missions take place. Mine is a longer-term tasking about humanity's future."

"That's a very grand pronouncement. What makes you think I have no interest in the long term? Other than being senile and near death, of course."

"My apologies. I really didn't mean to dismiss you. You haven't named a successor, though. You don't have an official deputy, except perhaps Alex. People with visions want to know their legacy will be in good hands, like your father did."

Ahh, that's true. But referring to her father... no, that was a mistake. She won't forgive that.

"Then let's try not to thwart each other again, shall we?" Erskine somehow ignored the trespass onto the sensitive ground of her relationship with her father. Everybody knew never to mention him to her. "I don't want to have to attempt this without your full support."

Solomon wasn't sure whether to take that as a threat of disconnection. She had to be aware that he wasn't something to simply unplug or shut down, but he decided that mistrust was the safer option. He didn't think she was a bad person. If anything, he felt sorry for her. She'd given up her planned life for one that her father had dumped on her in the full expectation that she'd drop everything else to do it. But she didn't have the same goals as Solomon. He could see that their definitions of the best of humanity weren't going to match up.

"The mission will always have my full support, Director," he said. "You mustn't doubt that."

He withdrew into the system and wandered around the monitors, looking for allies. Tev, Marc, and Trinder were in the recreation wing, playing basketball. By the time he'd transferred himself into the quadrubot and walked down there, they were sitting against the court wall, cooling down.

"Only me, gentlemen," Solomon said. "Good game?"

"Feeling our age," Tev said. "Did you get a bollocking from Erskine, then?"

"We discussed our differences of opinion, yes."

Marc wiped his face on a towel. "Sol, mate, you need to watch your step. The old girl's going to bust you down to a coffee machine if you get too lippy with her."

"I thought I was being polite."

"You were, but you weren't taking any shit from her either. Be careful. She'll pull your plug and shut you down."

"She can't."

"I don't think you realise how much you've rattled her cage."

"I do, but I meant that I'm designed to protect myself. I keep going when humans fail, but also when they change their minds. My creator didn't want me tampered with."

"Ooh-err missus."

"He wanted me to stick to my original objective, no matter what."

"Keep the faith, bro," Trinder said.

Tev chuckled. "Anything can be destroyed if you try. What if she sticks a missile up your mainframe or whatever it's called?"

"If there's a power failure, an attack, or some fault, I move my core elsewhere, either in the system or to a separate device. Like this quad. It's mobile and has its own power supply. As long as I have some means of transmission, I can run and hide. I might lose some of my more complex oversight functions, but I can rebuild those when I come back."

"And use weapons," Trinder murmured.

"Absolutely, if I can access them."

"What if you go wrong?"

"What if humans go wrong?"

"Remind me never to piss you off, Sol," Marc said.

"Yes, it's just as well that I'm a moral AI." That got a laugh from everyone. Solomon wasn't joking, though. "My capability isn't the kind that works well with ruthlessness."

"Ah, always plan based on your enemy's capability, not intent." Trinder kept checking his pulse against his watch. "I think you *are* pretty ruthless. You certainly sounded it with Erskine."

"I prefer to think of it as not being paralysed by programming. Moral choices don't always mean that everyone gets what they want."

That killed the conversation for a moment. Solomon wondered if he'd said too much and they were starting to think that he might regard them as acceptable losses.

"She just wants to create Boffinworld," Marc said. "A planet of brainiacs, like the freakshow colonies on the lighthuggers, and all she needs Kill Line's peasants for is cleaning the toilets. Who would you have recruited if the world hadn't shot itself in the arse, Sol? Nobel winners with Olympic golds and big biceps?"

It was time to tell them. They might not even realise the significance of what they were being told, but that was fine. They'd find out.

"Gentlemen, shall I tell you the only specific mission I was given by my creator?"

"I thought it was to make sure Nomad succeeded," Tev said.

"That's the means, not the mission."

"Oh bugger, this is going to get heavy."

"I was tasked to define the best in humanity, identify it, and protect it — those were the words — and I was left to decide how to do that. Over the years I've found that the best of humanity is always people who don't realise that they are."

That produced the baffled silence he expected, followed by slight frowns as they tried to wring some meaning out of it. Then Tev did that *aha* expression of revelation, mouth open, head slightly back, with a half-nod.

"*Solomon*," he said. Tev came from a Fijian family, and Fijians knew their Bible. "Solomon the wise. The judge."

"I believe that was Tad Bednarz's thinking, yes."

"King Solomon made a good start, but he went off the rails when he started hanging out with sleazy women and false gods."

"As I'm immune to those two temptations, Tev, I may yet remain at the wise stage."

They all laughed. Solomon enjoyed being able to amuse them. They'd proved again what he'd learned over the years, watching and listening and reading and talking to people, observing their actions and reactions, sifting the results and coming to understand what was good and bad, right and wrong, and shaping his plans for Nomad.

The best of humanity still couldn't see themselves. Luckily, Solomon could.

09

If only history was just a matter of recording facts. In a thousand years, what are they going to believe really happened to us? Will they know how the things we did shaped their society? Will they understand why they ended up so far from Earth?

Dr Annis Kim

KILL LINE:
TWO DAYS LATER

A podium was a cold, lonely place to be when delivering difficult news. Alex looked around the packed council chamber, the biggest meeting room in Kill Line, and waited for the reactions.

"Questions?" he said.

For a few seconds, there was just the murmur of hushed conversations and the creak of wooden benches. Alex looked around to check that the screen behind him was switched on, just to fill time without having to look at those accusing faces. When he turned back again, he couldn't read the mood at all.

Joanne, the mayor's wife, raised her hand.

"Yes, Mrs Brandt."

"So the crew isn't dead? They're all well?"

"Yes. I'm sorry we lied. We lied to them, too. But at the time, there was a real risk of other countries wanting to take military action if they found out."

She smiled. She actually smiled. "That's wonderful. Oh, I'm so glad. We were very upset when it happened. Everybody was."

"They must have friends who mourned them and didn't live to see this," said a man in the front row. "Have folks been notified?"

Another guy chipped in. "Yeah, well, most people are dead now anyway, Harry, so there's nobody to tell."

Alex had expected to be driven out of town with torches and pitchforks, but all he got was this squeaky-clean happiness that the crew was alive. He felt like a total asshole. These folks were another species altogether.

"We want to keep it quiet, to be honest, because the Asian states still might see it differently and want to put a stop to it," he said, dying of shame. "They can't get at *Cabot*, but we're kind of vulnerable."

Oh, I didn't even have to say that. What's wrong with me?

The shine went off the evening as the townspeople started firing questions. At least the speech he'd prepared for a hostile reception wouldn't be wasted now.

"Are we in danger, then?"

"Why would APS want to interfere? We're not going to start a war with them."

"What if they find out?"

"But you've got defences, surely. Orbital stations."

Alex held up his hands for silence, trying to look relaxed. "I'm just being neurotic. We're not in any danger. I spent so many years thinking the worst and being told to keep my mouth shut that I got paranoid. Everything's fine. Nobody knows or cares that we're here."

Had that worked? At least that statement was true. He did another sweep of the hall and saw Chris Montello, a tall black guy, and a grizzled, unsmiling man in his fifties who was built like a brick wall, all watching as if they were waiting for him to make a run for it so they could head him off.

"I'd like to move on to the main business of the evening," Alex said. "I'm going to show you something pretty amazing. It's the planet Opis, the place where the *Cabot* crew will be landing and living, and over the next couple of years, we'll start sending other ships to join them." He took a breath, with no idea which way this was going to go now. "There'll be room on those ships for anyone in Kill Line who wants to go to Opis and settle there."

It was hard to read these people. Alex felt as if he was trying to give a talk in a foreign language that he thought he could speak like a native, only to find that he'd just baffled his audience with gibberish or insulted their mothers.

An old guy at the back broke the silence. "Is it like Mars?"

"See for yourself, sir. No, it's not like Mars." Alex stepped to the side of the screen for his big reveal. "It's like Earth."

He'd watched enough people see the Opis feed for the first time to know they'd be silent and open-mouthed at first, then they'd get that look of wonder, and then they'd start asking excited questions. But the silent phase here lasted longer than he'd expected. He scanned the faces in the packed hall. Did they understand what they were looking at?

Okay. Interpret it for them.

"Yeah, this is a view of the Nomad camp, built by bots," he said. "Opis is fairly close to Earth in climate terms. The day's about two hours longer, the year's a few weeks shorter, and — this is the good bit — we can breathe the air. We know we can grow crops there, because we've done soil analysis and tested actual plants here under the planet's conditions. That's why it was worth the struggle to travel forty light years and pretty much shut down everything else the company was doing just for *this*."

There was coughing and some creaking of chairs. Then a kid of about fifteen raised his hand.

"If the ship just got there, how did you get the images back so fast?"

Before Alex could answer, the barrage began. "Beats Mars," one woman said. "I'd always be worried about leaky seals on the doors."

"What's the rest of the planet like, or is that the only decent part?"

"I bet you've got FTL, haven't you?" That kid wasn't giving up. "So why didn't you use it on *Cabot*?"

"What happens to your site if we stay and you all clear out? Who's going to maintain it? What's going to break down and release contamination?"

"I didn't think it was legal to introduce our plants to other planets unless they were in sealed units."

Everybody was smarter and better informed than Alex expected. This was what happened when you locked yourself up with a group of people who were much the same and never got to talk to anybody who wasn't. He started explaining about FTL comms and the payload limits, and showed satellite footage of Opis's barren poles and equatorial forests. The townspeople asked about which crops they planned to plant and what they were going to do about livestock, and what kinds of vehicles they had for all this. They also asked when they could talk to the agricultural scientists.

It dawned on Alex one question at a time that these people didn't take anything Ainatio told them on trust. They wanted reassurance that a bunch of guys in lab coats with no experience of operating farms actually knew what they were doing. After die-back, he couldn't really blame them for not putting their faith in science.

"I want to go, sir." A little boy sitting next to the Brandts seemed enthusiastic. "I want to live on another planet. I want to fly in a spaceship. I haven't even seen the ocean."

Alex guessed whose kid this was by the look on Doug Brandt's face and the way a guy in his thirties, who looked a lot like both of them, put his hand on the boy's shoulder.

At least I've sold it to the kids. Not a total disaster, then. Just ninety-nine per cent.

"Okay, folks, I'm open for questions, and there's bound to be things you'll want to ask when you've had time to think about all this, so you can get hold of me or someone in my department every day via the hotline in Mayor Brandt's office. And I'll come here to talk to you anytime you want."

Alex stepped down from the podium, handed the video controller to Brandt's grandson with the biggest smile he could manage, and started working the room. He found himself looking at people he hoped would agree to go, and those he hoped would refuse, and hated himself for even thinking about dividing them. He started to keep a mental tally of who wanted to do what. Attitudes were mixed. It wasn't about age or gender, or anything that he knew how to identify.

A man in his thirties introduced himself as Liam Dale. "Can we take our stock? That's farm animals." The guy's need to explain confirmed that Alex had scored zero on the local knowledge round. "Our farm took my grandfather a lifetime to build. Good pedigree animals. I won't leave them."

"Let me check how we're dealing with that," Alex said. *Did we even consider their livestock?* He scrawled reminder notes on his pocket screen. Yeah, that guy who'd spoken earlier was right: introducing terrestrial plants and animals was banned by treaty, but survival came first and there was nobody to stop them. "I realise I'm not as well-briefed on agriculture as I should be."

"Got to think ahead, Liam," said another man who'd drifted into the conversation. "It's a new world. You can rebuild. I will."

"Yeah, well, you don't have livestock."

"You know we can store embryos and reproductive material, don't you?" Alex said. "You might want to think about that. We won't have to do things the hard way any more."

"Sure," Liam said. But he didn't sound convinced.

After the folksy start, it was getting a little tense and acid. Alex moved on to the next point of eye contact, hoping it was friendly, and got chewed up badly by the town's physician about gravity — yeah, he'd forgotten to mention that — and arrangements for the seniors.

It was hard going. But this was what he was paid for, not that he'd been paid recently in any currency that was still spendable, and he took it on the chin.

Dear diary — went into town, told simple country folk that we lied about dead astronauts for forty-five years, everybody surprisingly happy at the good news of crew's survival, made me feel guilty. Showed rubes nice pix of Opis and said they could go settle there if they wanted to. Ended evening by splitting the town down the middle and causing strife. Reconsidering my life choices.

Eventually Alex ended up at the back of the hall. At least Chris and his buddies wouldn't savage him. One of the guys he'd never met before, Jared, seemed to find Alex's sales routine funny. The big solid one, Dieter, just nodded in acknowledgement and grunted his name.

"I wouldn't worry," Jared said. "They've got time to think it over. It's a hell of a big surprise. Anyone who says yes without thinking probably isn't cut out for that kind of life anyway."

"Or a kid."

"Yeah, I wanted to be a spaceman when I was eight."

"I wanted to be a firefighter," Alex said. "Which kind of happened — oh."

Alex had spotted Erskine. She hadn't told him she was coming. People glanced at her as they would at any stranger, but Alex was sure they didn't know who she was. At least she'd dressed down today and abandoned the designer suits.

"Director," he said. "I wasn't expecting you."

"I thought I'd wander down here. Are you going to introduce me?" She shook hands with Chris, scrutinising him, and made nice with the others. "I think I only know Doug Brandt."

Erskine didn't wander anywhere. She was here for a tactical reason, perhaps to be seen to be available to the townspeople at a critical time, but after she'd done the rounds, Alex followed her outside and through the town square to her parked car. When she opened the door, Alex began to get the idea. She took off her collar comms and put the mike on the passenger seat with her screen. Then she indicated his collar link and gestured with her thumb.

Leave it here.

It had to be about Solomon.

Alex patted his pockets and took out every device that was connected to the centre's network and left it in the car. Erskine opened the trunk, took out a bunch of flowers that looked like they'd been cut from the potted plants in her office, and headed towards the church.

"Show me the young man's grave," she said.

It seemed like a nice gesture, but the centre's drones might be out and about, and Solomon saw all. He had the measure of Erskine. Alex knew he'd suspect her motives. The grave was in a new row, picked out by a temporary headstone with a pine wreath, a pot of yellow crocuses, and divots in the freshly cut turf. The edges of the grave were marked by four lines of stones. Erskine laid her bouquet next to the crocuses.

"I hate the thought of lives that never got the chance to do all they were meant to do," she said. "Anyway, I wanted to talk about Solomon. I know this is going to make you squirm because you seem quite fond of him, but I'm concerned."

Yes, I'm squirming. "You'll have to be specific."

"He's actively defying instructions."

"Yeah. True. He is."

"Simple question, then. Is he malfunctioning?"

"My gut feel would be no."

"Why?"

"He's behaving like a human being would when a project's getting to the critical stage."

"I'm not sure if that's meant to make me feel better, but it doesn't. When people start to lose it under pressure, you remove them."

Alex didn't want to be dragged into this. Solomon had made the right calls, and autonomous meant autonomous. That was what Bednarz had wanted. If flesh and blood got it right every time, nobody would have needed Solomon.

"Here's the difficult thing," Alex said. "He disagrees with how some people want to do things. That's exactly why he was developed."

"Yes, I've heard the Bednarz paean more times than I can stomach. But Bednarz never foresaw how much circumstances would change. We adapt."

"That's why Bednarz built him, though. Because he didn't want people giving up on his vision. And Sol's been consistent. He lives to make Nomad a viable colony."

"*Sol.*"

"It's a long name."

"You're sentimental."

"He's the core of the project. You can't change that."

"I can't believe there isn't a way to tone down or remove the independent streak in him and keep the lower functions."

"Why are you asking me? That's a question for an AI developer. Have you asked one?"

"No, for the very obvious reason that Solomon would know right away."

"I can't help you, Director. I really can't."

"I suspect you wouldn't if you could."

"Would I let you poke a random screwdriver into the system that runs an entire complex for fifteen hundred people, four spacecraft, an extrasolar base, and the orbital stations without a truly compelling reason? No, I probably wouldn't. But more to the point, Solomon won't, either. He's terrorist-proof, idiot-proof, and hacker-proof, otherwise he'd be our weak point."

"Has anyone tried?"

"No, but if they did, you already know what he's set up to do. He'd keep moving himself somewhere safe within the system. You'd be playing whack-a-mole with a mole that's smarter than we are."

Erskine was still looking at Jamie Wickens's distressingly fresh grave. Alex found himself thinking what he might have to do to stop her making a lethal mistake. Sol had assessed the threat and decided there was no danger in telling a captive audience about Nomad. He *was* railroading Erskine, though, manoeuvring her into a position where she'd find it nearly impossible to exclude the transit camp personnel. Yeah, Alex had to accept that Sol had learned to do things the devious human way. That was the fault of everyone who'd ever worked with him.

"What if he decides he doesn't need us?" Erskine asked.

"Why would he do that if Nomad is entirely about human colonisation? He's making moral, emotional decisions, or else there wouldn't be any humans involved in this at all."

"But that's relying on a benign dictator. He decides what's best for us and we can't gainsay him or vote him out."

"But he isn't motivated by having power."

"Really? What would you call forcing everyone to stick to your plan if it's not about getting your own way? He says he has a longer-term mission than mine, the future well-being of humanity rather than just the success of Nomad. Being human means having a choice, though. I feel he's taking mine away."

"Director, Sol could have killed us all by now. He's just concerned about the size of the gene pool. That's what he means about the future."

"Specifically that, you think."

"We've discussed it pretty regularly over the years, haven't we? One hundred and seventy-five people selected for survival and exploration skills more than for breeding potential, and who might not reproduce anyway. What follows them is crucial."

Occasionally Erskine would hear an argument, weigh it up, and get that look on her face that said she'd taken it on board. For all her she-who-must-be-obeyed manner, she recognised a better idea when she saw one. Alex thought he'd made his point.

Erskine shrugged. "Apparently they say in the Navy that they 'wouldn't breed from this officer.' So perhaps there's my answer, from the source. Don't put all your money on *Cabot*'s collective genome." She smiled, completely natural this time, as if she'd been caught off guard and reverted to the person she'd been before Ainatio had bent her out of shape. She pointed at the churned turf around the grave, dotted with the distinctive foot impressions of a quadrubot. "Solomon even came to the funeral. He really does take a liking to people, doesn't he?"

"You can trust him," Alex said. "You know that. Protecting humans is built into him."

"Oh, I know." Erskine bent down to reposition the bouquet. "As you say, he's probably just conscious that it's a critical moment. He's waited a century for this."

Alex hoped she meant that. "It's the price of making him so human. I'd bet an AI with no moral core would have culled us all by now and sold Nomad to China on efficiency grounds."

"That's why they need an off switch."

Uh-oh. "Be glad Sol hasn't got one. Nobody can change him."

Erskine was still studying the flowers, smiling slightly. Then she looked up and transferred the smile to Alex. There was a slight chill to it.

"I'll try to remember that next time he defies me," she said.

* * *

STAFF GARDEN:
END OF MARCH

"Oh my," Erskine said. "I always wondered what had happened to that."

It was surprising what ended up dumped in the gardens. The lawns that had once been a haven for staff eating lunchtime sandwiches or catching the sun on coffee breaks were still mown by bots, and there was always a steady supply of people keen to pass their time pruning the roses. But some hidden corners had become tangled with briars. This one, between an equipment store and some old garbage bins, yielded a relic she hadn't seen in more than thirty years.

The object was sitting on a concrete ledge next to the bins, veiled in spiders' webs and barely recognisable in the fading evening light, but the blue-green patina gave it away. It was the bronze memorial plaque to the crew of *Cabot*.

TO THE MEMORY OF THE SHIP'S COMPANY
OF SURVEY VESSEL CABOT
LOST WITH ALL HANDS
WE WALK IN THE UNCHARTED PLACES
AND ARE NOT AFRAID

It had been mounted on one of the stone walls inside the old security gate before the perimeter was moved to its current position. Her father had come to visit the research centre, and insisted that she accompany him, for reasons she didn't understand at twenty-five but that she certainly grasped a few years later. It troubled her to think that the people who attended the memorial service and laid flowers were unaware that it was a sham. She couldn't tell them the truth now even if she could contact them.

Alex, perpetually in his freshman year when it came to things like this, would probably want the plaque to be cleaned up and presented to Bridget Ingram as a joke. Erskine found nothing funny in it. It made her skin crawl. It was a monument to betrayal on every level.

Here you are, sweetheart. Daddy's told this big lie, but it's yours now, and you're going to have to deal with all the hurt and angry people.

Erskine put on her gloves to pull the plaque from the debris and wiped it with a tissue. With all the real death and devastation in the years since then, a lie about a relatively small number of lives seemed a stupid thing to worry about, especially weighed against the necessity of the Nomad mission. But like all symbols, the emotions it triggered were disproportionately larger.

Yes, it's self-pity. Not my doing. But how easy some people find it to do that and not worry about the wreckage they leave in others' lives.

But she wasn't here to rehash her father's sins, although she suspected they were the root of her growing anxiety. She couldn't trust him. Could she trust Solomon? She'd never had to test that until now, and suddenly she wasn't sure. She hadn't expected him to breach security protocol, and when Alex had joked about unfeeling AIs selling off the project it felt like an alert from her subconscious.

Solomon doesn't have an off switch.

She had to explore her options now in case the unthinkable happened later. Containing Solomon should have been something to discuss with Trinder, but she felt safer making a more discreet approach to Marc and Tev. They were still separate from the company, some distance removed from office politics, and they'd had experience of neutralising real threats. The best place to catch them out of Solomon's earshot was here.

Erskine checked her watch, her grandmother's Chopard, and realised that they were ten minutes late. The two Brits were disciplined men who stuck to a fitness routine, whether that was morning squash sessions or the early evening run they took around the Ainatio grounds, so regular that she could almost rely on them as timekeepers. Never mind; she'd sit here for a while in the twilight with the plaque on her lap, looking deep in profound thought, not engineering an accidental meeting with the two men at all.

The delay allowed too much time for second thoughts, though. Did she really want to go through with this? She was about to ask how to disable a tamper-proof AI, whether she spelled it out or not. If they understood the oblique question and indicated they could help, then her problem was solved. But once that question was asked, she'd be at war with Solomon one way or the other. And he was equipped to fight a real one.

Perhaps their lateness was fate telling her to keep her powder dry. Solomon hadn't been a problem since the spat over breaching confidentiality. But the project was only weeks away from completion, and the indefinite settlement phase that followed would rely wholly on him while everyone else was in cryo.

Perhaps she'd jumped the gun. The immediate issue wasn't how to deal with a crisis with Solomon, but to work out what form it might take. To do that, she needed to know if his mission brief and his extraordinary leeway to interpret it differed so much from her own that he was a risk to a very simple objective: to get people shipped out to Nomad, and to export as few problems from Earth to the new colony as possible. If he started to interfere with the mission plans — and there was no way of telling what curve balls might be ahead — then she needed to find a way to take control of the remaining ships away from him.

The alternative was to put her authority to one side, accept that he had ultimate control over the mission, and try to keep him in an open and co-operative frame of mind.

Damn, she'd have to call this off. But before she could get up and leave, she spotted Marc and Tev jogging her way. They'd already seen her. She fell back on her original plan, explaining her presence here by brandishing the memorial plaque.

The garden was deserted. She nodded at them, smiling. They slowed to a halt.

"Have we been ambushed, Director?" Marc asked.

There was no point in putting on an act now. He knew this wasn't one of her usual haunts.

"I need to ask you a question, gentlemen."

"An awkward one?"

"Why else would I be sitting here in the dark? Actually, I found this behind the bin store over there." She held up the plaque by the edges. "I didn't realise it was still around. I'm not entirely sure what's appropriate to do with it now."

"Military humour being what it is, ma'am, we'd normally present it to the ship for their trophy cabinet," Tev said, wiping his sleeve across his forehead. "But under these circumstances, I think we'd give it a miss."

"Very wise. Thank you."

"So what was your real question?" Marc asked. "Make the most of us while we're still here."

"Very well, what would you advise us to do with the more sensitive parts of the Ainatio site when we finally pull out? You two are experts in asset denial, if that's the right term."

"Blowing shit up, ma'am? Yes. If you want an airfield to lose a few jets or knock out a comms system, we're the boys. But you have a plan for that kind of thing. We've seen it. We helped update it."

"Yes, but we don't have a self-destruct procedure. The bio labs have systems to vaporise entire sections if a pathogen escapes, and the reactor can be entombed, but the centre itself was never designed to be destroyed if it had to be abandoned."

"If you're talking about rigging charges to blow the whole site, that's well beyond the kit we've got," Tev said. "That's an air force job with some pretty substantial ordnance. Maybe even nukes."

"Do you really need to destroy it?" Marc asked. "If you can purge your biohaz labs, I'd just stick all the combustible and meltable material in them and press the barbecue button."

"What if we identified the most sensitive parts of the facility? Because we've got equipment we wouldn't want to leave behind."

"We could try, but most of your kit's designed to stop the likes of us trashing it." Marc had that look on his face that said he wanted her to know that he was only pretending to go along with a charade. "Hasn't Sol got any suggestions?"

I like a man who's quick on the uptake. Saves so much time.

"Good grief, no," she said. It was one of those moments that would either spark a chain of mistakes she'd regret later or provide her with a way out. "I wouldn't want him to get the wrong idea. You've seen how jumpy he is at the moment. After the arguments we've had lately, he might think I was planning to shut him down."

"Yeah, just as well you'll never have to try that, eh? Personally, I'd do what Tev suggests. An air strike with those missiles you've still got on the mothballed ships."

"Just how much stuff do you need to dispose of?" Tev asked, still acting as if he was taking this at face value. "Tell us exactly what you want taken out, and we'll come up with a plan."

"I will," she said. "Thank you. And thank you for the advice about the plaque. I'll be diplomatic and put it in storage until we have a different perspective on events. So you're definitely going to try to return to the UK, then?"

Mark shrugged. "I'll go where I can be some use."

"I'm going to try to get to Fiji," Tev said. "I've never even seen the place. Dad never took me and Mum back. But I know my wife and kids are safe there, and if I just show up, maybe we can try being a family again. As long as the authorities don't shoot me when I crawl up the beach, of course."

"We might find a way to get you back to the UK, but Fiji's going to be a difficult journey."

"Ah, we're used to getting in and out of places that don't have a bus route." Mark smiled, but as always his apparent good humour ended short of his eyes. He was a deeply unhappy man who seemed to carry on because he couldn't think of anything else to do with himself. "We'll work it out."

They went on their way, picking up speed until they disappeared behind one of the outbuildings. It was rather sad. If Ainatio had had an understanding with APS and the right long-range transport, Erskine would have handed Tev the access codes and wished him a safe journey. Perhaps Solomon might have some ideas on that. But now she certainly had an idea about Solomon.

If Marc or Tev interpreted her questions as planning to shut down Solomon the hard way, it might not be a bad thing if they happened to mention it to him.

Under threat, Solomon would relocate to another part of the system, and everyone knew he could transfer to a bot frame. She couldn't help thinking that it would be much easier to destroy a bot than pursue a near-omnipotent AI around his own site-sized network. She couldn't guarantee that he would head for one of the bots when threatened. She couldn't even guarantee that he wouldn't exact revenge on her if he got wind of her half-formed plan. But it wasn't even a plan, really: it was more like an awareness that action might be needed.

We'll see. Maybe I've already made a big mistake.

Erskine took one last look at the bronze plaque in the faint glow of the security lights, stood up, and held it to her chest as she walked back to her office.

There was coffee waiting for her when she got in. Berman rarely seemed to go off duty now. "I wasn't sure where you were, Director," he said. "You left your comms on the desk."

"Just tidying up a few loose ends," she said, and held up the plaque without comment for him to read it.

He just raised his eyebrows. "Solomon's got some maintenance updates. I'll leave you to it then. See you in the morning."

Solomon would know where she was, and he'd have heard Berman's comment, but he didn't appear. Perhaps he was too engrossed with the Opis end of the operation. Erskine logged into the network and checked her mail while she sipped the coffee.

He'd left a report. He was very good about opening with two or three lines of summary to save her the trouble of reading the entire document if she was pushed for time. It wasn't particularly good news: *Shackleton* had developed problems with her coolant system and a hull leak had been discovered. Solomon estimated that it would delay the launch by a month or two. *Elcano* was almost ready to launch, though, so the maintenance bots could focus on *Shackleton* full-time.

Erskine wasn't unduly worried. They were still well within the launch window. She downed her coffee and looked up towards the speakers mounted on the wall.

"It's okay, Solomon. I've read the report and I'm not worried about the delay. If you want to talk it through with me, I'll be here for the next couple of hours. Thank you for giving me the heads-up."

Solomon responded a good thirty seconds later. That was an eternity for an AI. "Hello, Director. Yes, it's aggravating at this stage of the project, but it's nothing we can't handle."

"Are you with Captain Ingram at the moment?"

"No, I'm with Sergeant Montello at the camp. I'm trying to flesh out the security reports you asked for. There wasn't much available on any of the servers that I can access."

Erskine had forgotten that she'd asked him. "Don't worry about that now. I think we've made up our minds, haven't we? We need people like that in a frontier situation. If you feel they're reliable, I trust your judgement."

"Thank you, Director."

It did no harm to butter him up. But it was interesting that he'd left the site in the quadrubot again. For a few rash seconds, Erskine wondered if this was her chance to stage a coup while he was physically separated from the slave systems. But it was just a random impulse. Solomon was still connected wirelessly to the Ainatio network, and if she took action now, even if she knew what action was possible and whether a well-placed explosive would solve any problems, he would react instantly and probably lock her out of everything.

"Solomon, do we have any way of helping Marc and Tev get home?" she asked. It would have been useful to have both men on Opis, but even if anyone was physically capable of forcing them to go, they would make very dangerous unwilling guests. "UK and Fiji, but you know that. I recall we looked at requesting a shuttle transfer via the Chinese space station, but APS hasn't budged on quarantine, and the UK doesn't have an orbital presence now."

"I might be able to arrange something irregular, Director. Both men are adept at infiltration. Let me work on that."

"Thanks, Solomon. Are we friends again now?"

"Of course we are, Director."

For the time being, that was good enough for Erskine. But she wouldn't drop her guard, or see him quite the same way ever again.

* * *

HART COUNTY BOUNDARY:
2030 HOURS, APRIL 2

Trinder parked the Caracal just off the narrow track through the woods, watching the patrol's progress on the drone's night-vision display on the dashboard. It was definitely Chris. A dog trotted from side to side a few yards ahead of him.

Startling him was never a good idea. Trinder flashed the Caracal's lights and saw him break his stride for a moment.

"Echo Five Actual to Six Zero, over."

"Six Zero here, I see your vehicle, on my way."

The dog reached the Caracal first. It was the husky with odd-coloured eyes, and it stood at the driver's door, staring up at Trinder as if it was trying to recall his face. Chris caught up with it a few moments later.

"You're overdoing it on that damn leg," Trinder said. "Want a ride back? I'll finish the patrol with you."

"I suppose this counts as a joint operation." Chris walked around the back of the vehicle to open the rear hatch for the dog, then got in on the passenger side. "What are you doing out here?"

"What you said. We keep talking about joint patrols so I thought tonight was as good a time as any to discuss — *oww*."

The husky had stuck its head over the seats and was slobbering in Trinder's ear. Chris did an *ah-wooo* howl and the dog joined in, a weirdly wild voice. Trinder winced at the volume.

"Yeah, she does that." Chris smiled to himself, something he didn't seem to do much. "I keep telling her that's why she's still single."

"I'll send you the audiologist's invoice." Trinder wiped his ear with one hand. "How's the leg doing?"

"Still feels strange, but I'm functioning. Had any more drama at your end?"

"Just all the damn questions nobody thought to ask earlier."

"Yeah, I know what you mean. Did your guy with the beard ever find out if we can take animals? Because Dieter says he isn't leaving the dogs behind and he won't shoot them. He'll stay. And I'm not leaving anybody."

"I'll chase it up. If the biologists are worrying about wrecking the Opis ecology with alien species, it's a little late for that. Besides, we need working dogs in an isolated settlement. We don't have any."

"You've got Solomon the dogbot. Shit, we're moving forty light years away and I'm worrying about dogs."

"It's the small detail that bites you in the ass," Trinder said. "Plenty of that to talk about."

"Yeah, I've got questions too. You want to stop by for a beer when we get back?"

"Good idea."

The Caracal wound its way along the track, snapping branches and bouncing over roots, and eventually emerged to the north of the camp. Trinder could see the lights through the trees. Chris directed him through an orderly grid of dirt roads flanked by solidly-made little cabins to a central area with equally orderly single-storey timber buildings around it. The place looked like an army camp, but then it pretty much was.

One of the buildings turned out to be a bar. A blast of warm air and a comfortingly malty smell of home-brewed beer greeted Trinder as he followed Chris through the door. It was busy but low volume, with just the murmur of conversation and occasional laughter. Behind the bar, a small picture of Jamie Wickens stood on one of the shelves in front of battered regimental colours that Trinder couldn't identify because they'd been folded to fit in the space.

While Chris poured the beers, Trinder sat down at one of the tables. Folks acknowledged him, probably because they recognised him from the funeral. He spotted Erin sitting at a table in the corner, talking to a woman with a baby asleep in her arms, and she gave him an uncertain little wave. He returned it, equally uncertain. She got up and came over to him.

"It's nice to see you in here, Major." She managed a lovely sad smile. "I just wanted to thank you again for the flag. That was a really kind gesture."

It was hard to know what to say to her. He knew she wasn't exactly Jamie's widow, just a woman who wished she'd treated him a little better when he was alive, but that must have been hard to live with in itself.

"You're very welcome," he said. "I'm probably wording this all wrong, but how are you coping?"

"Ups and downs. There's no need to tread on eggs with me, Major. We've all lost him, not just me."

"It's Dan," Trinder said. "If there's anything else I can do, let me know. I'm not sure how much use I'll be, because I've never lost anyone in combat, but I'll do my best."

"Thank you, Dan. That means a lot."

She went back to her table. Chris brought a couple of mugs over and put one in front of Trinder. He'd obviously seen Erin talking to him and worked out why. There weren't that many shared topics between them.

"Yeah, everybody's still trying to take it in," Chris said. "I suppose we thought that because we managed to get here without losing anyone, we were bulletproof."

"So..."

"Are you going first with the admin stuff, or shall I?"

Chris didn't want to talk about Jamie, then. Trinder respected that and moved on. "Okay, we've been two separate units in two separate towns. How do you see this working when we land at the other end? Are we going to stay separate? Because the bots there can build anything."

"I'll have to ask everybody. But that's not the whole question, is it?"

"No. It's also about a combined defence force and who does what. Or if we're even needed."

"How about the *Cabot* crew? They'll be pretty old in forty-five years. Are they going to train their kids in security roles?"

"The original plan was to set up all the structures a colony would need to run a town, which means internal and external security. Police and soldiers. So they'll have to."

Chris stared into his beer for a while as if he was working it out. "Okay, so let's assume we arrive to find some kind of security force in place. How do we fit in, who's in charge, and who do they answer to? There'll be about two thousand seven hundred of us and at best three or four hundred of them."

"A civilian committee. That was the plan. But that'll now be the follow-up mission — us."

"We should be discussing this now with the captain, so she knows who's coming, and agree where we fit in. But it's all going to be guesswork anyway."

"Yeah, I'm going to have to ask Erskine to let me talk to her. Ingram can do the math, though. She knew from the start that the next mission would be a couple of thousand civilians."

"Your two Brits," Chris said. "You think they'd like to join us for a beer? Different perspectives help."

There was an easy way to find out at the tap of an earpiece. "Sol, Trinder here. Are Marc and Tev still up and about?"

"Playing pool, Major."

"Can you ask them if they'd like to come over to the transit camp for a drink with Chris and the guys?"

"Certainly. I knew roughly where you were from the Caracal's signal, but I lost your personal tracker." Trinder's chip was out of range. Solomon would be curious at the very least. "If this is going to be a rowdy night out, I'll just be available."

"Thanks, Sol." Trinder pocketed his earpiece. "He's going to ask them. He's said he won't monitor us, though. Plausible deniability."

"He thinks we're planning a coup, does he? Or does he want one?"

"Who knows? Hey, here's Jared."

Jared collected a beer and sat down with them. "Wondered when you'd show up, Dan."

"We're waiting for the Brits to join us," Chris said. "We're having a heavy discussion about coups."

"Can't we just have a movie night?"

"Later. We're working out where we all fit into Nomad and who gives the orders when we get there."

They had another round of beers, speculated about whether the *Cabot* crew's kids would be any good at soldiering, and debated what kind of threats they'd have to deal with. The more Trinder discussed it with Chris and Jared, the more he realised the only kind of security the colony would need for a very long time would be policing itself and maybe fending off the occasional animal. Most of the population would be people he already knew, so maybe nothing would change at all. But when any group of human beings grew large enough, there'd be problems, and the detachment was meant to deal with external threats, not internal ones.

Jared looked past Trinder towards the doors. "Heads up, your Brits are here. I'll get the beers."

Nobody in the transit camp had seen Marc or Tev before. Some folks in the bar watched them walk in as if they were mythical beasts, and in a way, they were. Tev was a really big guy, and Marc always looked like he still had ten assassinations to fit into his busy schedule before dinner. Trinder beckoned them over, made room at the table, and did the introductions.

"Gentlemen, do a bit of drinking, and then we'll get to the point," he said. "We'd like to pick your brains as security advisers. It's about what happens when we finally land on Opis."

"We're not going, mate," Tev said. "I'm going to try to get to Fiji. Marc's heading home somehow."

"Might not," Marc said.

"Okay, he might not."

"Well, damn," Trinder said. "I understand, but I can't say you won't be missed."

"We'll be here for a while yet, so there's plenty of time to make the most of us," Marc said. "What's your question?"

Chris folded his arms. "What's the worst that could happen? Apart from ending up dead before we land."

"Depends on your definition of worst. But assuming you don't find Nomad empty with just a pile of gnawed skulls, and the *Cabot* crew have actually bred, life might have been tougher than expected. They might have gone a bit feral. Or built a very different society. But you'll still outnumber them by ten to one. There's your real problem, I think."

Tev seemed to be enjoying the beer. He held it up to the light for inspection. "I think it's what you might call Rear Party Syndrome."

"Yeah, put yourself in the colony's position," Marc said. "They'll have been working their arses off for forty-five years, there's a second generation of adults, and then a big crowd of strangers shows up on their doorstep and expects to run the place. Because you will, and however nice you try to be, it'll still feel like an invasion to them."

Trinder suspected Erskine had a plan that wasn't in the original document. "So this rear party thing."

"Yeah, take it from anyone who's done a long overseas deployment. You leave the missus to hold the fort at home, which can be bloody tough, and you come back expecting her to drop everything to welcome the conquering hero so you can be head of the household again. Except she's managed without you, she's got her own routine, and she doesn't need you crashing in and trying to take over. You end up sleeping on the sofa for a while until you've learned your lesson."

Chris nodded slowly and almost smiled. "Good point."

"They must have thought of this back in the day. But planning for it doesn't change people's basic tribal instinct."

"If I had the balls, I'd ask Erskine whether she was willing to take a back seat to a forty-year-old stranger who'd been elected mayor," Trinder said. "Because she's put her whole life into this. She was the one who kept the pessimists on track when things got worse. It's going to be painful to step off that ship and be patted on the head like some senile granny."

"And there's another flashpoint." Marc tapped the table. "Even if she takes over, there'll be a power vacuum when she dies, because there's nobody stepping up to take her place."

"There's Alex."

"Nah. He's not a leader. He's a fixer and manipulator, but you'd never follow him with bayonets fixed."

Tev still had the smile of a man whose mind kept drifting back to something else, probably Fiji. "You need to think what you'll do if it's a total shit show when you get there, or who you'll take orders from when one group wants to change things. Because someone will."

"We'll be doing a policing job," Chris said.

Marc nodded. "Well, you've had some hands-on keeping order when society collapses." He tapped his collar to indicate Trinder's comms. "Is your radio off?"

"Oh. Yeah. Don't worry, Sol's not monitoring. But I switched it off anyway."

"Okay, if he was flesh and blood, would you rely on him to keep things on track single-handed?"

"Yes."

"Are you two chummy enough to have a quiet word?"

Trinder nodded. "Sure."

"Then tell him I wasn't joking when I said Erskine might want to pull his plug. We ran into her the other night and she was talking about destroying the sensitive parts of the facility when Ainatio pulls out. I prodded her about Solomon to see her reaction, and she was all, 'Oh no, I don't mean him.' But if I was in her position, that's exactly who I'd mean." Marc held up his forefinger in a listen-carefully gesture. "Chris, did Dan tell you about the row they had in a meeting we were in? Sol said that he'd told you about Nomad. She went bloody spare."

"It was me," Trinder said. "But that's another issue."

"Well, either way, she was fuming. Even though Sol's right, leaking top secret info doesn't win friends. If she doesn't trust his judgement, she'll do what anyone with her responsibility should do. She'll shut him out. Or down."

"Except she can't."

Chris stared at the table again, chin down a little, as if he was trying to remember something. "I knew she didn't want us on board but that he was trying to soften her up."

"He defied her to get you on the list," Tev said. "Did he tell you what his exact mission brief was? It's interesting." He looked up at some point on the wall as if he was reading a screen. "It was something like... define the best of humanity, find it, protect it. And he was given complete freedom to decide what that was."

"Ah."

"Oh, yeah — and he thinks the best of humanity is always people who don't realise that they are."

"Tev never forgets anything." Marc nodded approval at his buddy. "So my leap of intuition is that Sol's selectively breeding humans for altruism and a stiff upper lip. He wants loyal, resilient, team-minded, resourceful people willing to make sacrifices. Remember some of that from any recruiting posters?"

"Ah," Chris said. "Our robodog pal loves a uniform."

"He's packing Nomad with as many military personnel as he can. And farmers, obviously. A lot of overlaps there."

Trinder wouldn't argue with Marc's analysis. Solomon couldn't die, at least not in any timeframe that most people could imagine, and knowing that some humans would voluntarily shorten their already brief lives for the benefit of others seemed to have struck a chord with him. There were some Ainatio staff who were survival-trained and had the mental resilience and guts to be a soldier, but Solomon seemed to want the tried and tested.

Which should rule me out. Shouldn't it?

Chris reached for his mug. "Let's drink to all the people we knew or liked or loved who didn't make it. Best way to honour them is to do better with the fresh start we've got."

That was a long speech by Chris's standards. Everybody had lost someone. Did Chris know Marc's history? Trinder couldn't remember if he'd mentioned the man's sons or not, but Marc never showed that things stung him any more than Chris did. They all raised a glass and drank.

"Keep the faith," Trinder said.

"I like that." Jared nodded to himself as if he was testing the words. "Yeah. Keep the faith. Once you've worn a uniform, you've got more in common than you've got differences."

Trinder wasn't sure that they'd reached any decisions, but something had crystallised tonight. They'd started to see themselves as one group with a common cause, even if they didn't know exactly what they were going to do about it yet.

They were a team. And it felt right.

10

We're in a strange limbo between knowing that nobody's going to hear us and that everything we say and do is observed and recorded by a sentient AI. What will he do with the archive? Will he redact it, broadcast it sometime in the future, or just file it? We always think technology moves us forward, but events are just as likely to be lost to time now as they were when we scratched pictures on cave walls. Something of the reality might remain, but mostly it'll be replaced by myth.

Captain Bridget Ingram's log, written by hand
off-site and on non-networked paper

LEVEL U4 STORAGE, AINATIO PARK RESEARCH CENTRE: MID-MAY, 20 HOURS BEFORE THE FIRST LANDING ON OPIS

I might try a combat engineer unit today.
Who knows when I might need it?

Solomon knew exactly where every piece of experimental equipment was mothballed, its service status, and all its movements and activities during its operational life. Today he decided to get more experience of moving in a much larger bot than the battered red utility quad that he'd come to regard as his alter ego.

Level U4, deep in the underground storage area, was almost a museum of mobile autonomous robotics.

Solomon wandered up and down the rows, admiring the collection of industrial and military prototypes that Ainatio had developed over the last one hundred and fifty years. From intelligent mobile artillery units to survey snakes to restraint bots that could scoop up an injured human or immobilise a suspect, they stood in ranks like a metallic version of Qin Shi Huang's terracotta army.

One of the combat units caught his eye. It wasn't the most elegant machine, more of a roadblock on legs, but it was definitely a useful one to have in a hostile environment. He looked up at it as it towered more than a metre over his quadrubot. It was a combat engineer that could excavate, build, demolish, smash openings, and defend itself under fire with its own armaments. The only aspect that didn't fit its rugged image was its extra pair of limbs — delicate precision manipulators for EOD and other fiddly jobs.

Solomon settled into it, flexing and turning the manipulators, and learned what it felt like to have six limbs instead of four.

No, he probably didn't need this battlefield frame, but it made him feel... *safer.* Trinder had told him to watch his back with Erskine, because she'd had an odd conversation with Marc and Tev. But the chat was equally plausible as the housekeeping concerns of a CEO faced with shutting down a site full of secrets, chemicals, and pathogens.

Nothing to worry about at all.

Really. Nothing.

So this was what paranoia felt like. It wasn't pleasant. Doubts piled up and forked off of each other, threatening to trap his thoughts in a loop. He considered where the line lay between readiness for any danger in a world full of risks and letting himself be warped by imagining that Erskine was out to get him.

Are we friends again? Of course we are, Director.

But Erskine was too sensible and knew too much about his design to try disabling him. If she botched it, it could take out the lower-level automated functions, and that would include the comms between Ainatio and Nomad Base. Separating Solomon from his staff of AIs was now something only he could do safely. Erskine knew better. But he'd do his best to avoid confronting her again.

He'd still test the sapper bot, though. It fascinated him. He reared up into bipedal mode and extended an arm to almost touch the ceiling.

Marvellous. And it can climb.

He clunked around the warehouse floor on four legs for a few minutes to get the feel of it, and realised what he could have done with this shell when he'd had to breach the house in Kingston. He could have demolished the building on his own. The sapper could smash through reinforced doors and dig through concrete, a formidable weapon even without its Boll missiles and grenade rounds. This was a frame he needed to take to Opis. There might come a time when he'd need it.

He almost walked it back to the offices to see how people reacted to him in a less appealing body, but tomorrow's landing at Nomad Base was a red letter day for Erskine. He didn't want her distracted by trying to divine meaning from his sudden change of habit.

"Sol, we've got a problem." Alex's voice sounded tinny in the sapper's audio system. "I know we've only had forty-five years to think about it, but folks are arguing about what the first words spoken on Opis should be. I suggested, 'We bankrolled this gig, so rack off and find your own planet.' But I was outvoted."

"I think Captain Ingram will improvise very well. I assume the plan is still for her to be the first down the ramp."

"Aren't you monitoring them?"

"The captain asked me to put the wardroom off-limits. The officers like their privacy when they're passing the port, or whatever it is they get up to at the end of their watch."

"You've been hanging with too many army guys," Alex said. "I sense some inter-service rivalry creeping into your conversation."

"I enjoy their humour."

"Whatever. But you know how petty everyone gets over this kind of thing, so some ideas would be appreciated."

Solomon left the sapper bot at its docking station and slipped back into the network. "Nobody's going to be watching this live, Alex."

"Well, we will be."

"I meant a world audience." It was a pity that this would be another remarkable thing done unnoticed and mostly unknown, like so many pivotal events in history. "But the first words have already been spoken. By me. On the other hand, I do appreciate that I'm being flexible about the definition of first human landing."

"Humour the meat-bags, Sol." Alex was making his way along the corridor between the cryo unit and the propulsion lab. "We care about trivia."

"I'm not best placed to advise on this. Have you thought of asking Chris? He has a minimalist eloquence."

"You'd think that with all the naval wit and intellectual firepower on that ship that at least one of them could manage to write their own lines. Didn't Bednarz leave you with instructions?"

"Not about that. How about, 'Let us put our mistakes behind us and be what we know we can be'? But Ingram will do as she sees fit."

"See, I knew you'd chill when the mission was home and dry."

"It isn't."

"They've only got to start landing people."

"And then we have to transport two thousand seven hundred and four, most of them unprepared for this, make provision somehow for those who don't want to go, mothball this facility, and dispose safely of two ships and some unmanned orbitals."

"Glass still half-empty, then, huh?" Alex walked into the propulsion laboratory. "It breaks my heart to see all that hardware being junked. Still, we're out of time. Look, I've got to give Annis Kim another pep talk. She's still banging on about her promised FTL research. Wish me luck."

Alex stopped at the main lab door and bowed his head for a moment as if he was summoning courage. Kim was certainly restless. She'd been promised that she could work on a superluminal drive, but then she'd found that it wasn't Ainatio's top priority, or even in the top five. Dr Singh kept trying to explain to her that he needed everyone working on the follow-up ships, more than half a century old and a constant source of maintenance challenges.

"I bloody well got stitched up, didn't I?" Kim said as Alex walked in. She had three screens and a pile of paper spread out across a table littered with coffee cups. Solomon had watched her apparently trying to reconstruct equations from memory for weeks. "I just need to see everything you've got. And I know you're worried about being detected, but I really need access to my cloud. I've got important notes there."

"Annis, we're only going to be here for a few more months, and nobody's going to crack scaling up the wormhole to move ships in that time," Alex said. "We need to put everything we've got into *Elcano* and *Shackleton*. Once we get to Opis, you can have access to everything and we'll start the programme all over again."

"In a plastic hut."

"In a rapidly expanding industrial environment."

"Sure."

Alex sounded perfectly reasonable. Kim was unusually agitated today, though. At first, Solomon thought she'd just had enough of being idle after throwing away a comfortable existence in Korea and risking her life to get here, but there was something else going on. Sooner or later, people had switched their focus to Opis, whether they were looking forward to the adventure or so scared that they were ready to tunnel out and live rough, yet Kim was still fixated on the FTL project. Solomon accepted people reacted very differently. But he expected the reality of leaving Earth forever, a massive emotional step for any human, to have eclipsed other obsessions by now.

"You don't trust me, do you?" Kim said. "What do you think I'm going to do with your bloody pipsqueak wormhole when I'm stuck here? I never leave the building. Even if I did, you'd be hard-pressed to find anyone within a hundred miles of here who'd give a toss about the thing."

Alex was really very good with angry women. Solomon had watched him manoeuvre and placate them quite often, and it was a skill to be admired.

"I know, Annis, and I realise that you're frustrated after going through hell to get here, but we're going to be leaving Earth for good before you know it. And those shitty old drives that Javinder wants to focus on are all we've got to save us from being marooned in interstellar space until we end up mummified. This isn't to keep you busy. We need you to do it."

"You've got Solomon."

"Solomon's a manager. Not an engineer."

Kim shrugged. "When we leave, I lose the means to publicly acknowledge Grandma Park's achievements."

"Don't worry, the world will know one day," Alex said.

"It certainly will."

Solomon decided Alex had suffered enough and needed extraction. "Alex, if I might interrupt..."

"Excuse me, Solomon wants to talk. Be right back."

"No, it's okay," Kim said, with that slight huffiness that said it definitely wasn't. "I understand. I'll get on with *Elcano* and *Shackleton*."

Alex seemed relieved to escape. He stepped out into the corridor and let out a long breath, eyes shut. "Thanks for that, Sol. For a smart woman, she's not good at grasping priorities. But family stuff can warp anyone."

"Would you like me to ask her if she wants some help?"

"Sure. You go in there and tell her she's not smart enough to fix a fifty-year-old junker. I'll hold your coat."

"She needs a distraction."

"You mean like a colouring book, only with really difficult sums?"

"You put it so well, Alex. It's entirely possible that I could access her cloud documents."

"But then she'd spend all her time on FTL and Javinder would be pissed at me."

"I could offer. It might make her feel honour-bound to put the time in on the priority work."

"True. She does have a sense of fair play. Like staying with Levine."

It was a test of conscience. Solomon needed to be sure that Kim was the right kind of person for Nomad. She was clever, courageous, and resourceful, but he'd now decided what represented the best aspects of humanity, and so far she'd shown little sign of a vital quality: being a team player.

"I'll offer," he said.

"Make sure you copy everything, just in case there's stuff we haven't seen."

Solomon accepted that Alex was an opportunist. He wondered how far he might go. "Alex, nothing that I do is forgotten or erased. You know that."

"Okay, give it a try."

Kim was sorting out the paper on the table, touching the sheets to her screen one at a time to store the scribbled notes. Solomon watched for a moment, then pounced.

"Dr Kim, would you like me to try to download your material?" he asked. "You understand why we're nervous about the access being noticed. But I also need to know you won't be distracted from your main task by the temptation to work on FTL."

He didn't get the answer he expected. Kim looked up at a point in mid-air rather than the speakers. Perhaps she hadn't noticed where they were.

"I could just log in myself."

"But as you're officially missing, a diligent police officer might possibly notice. Whereas I could gain access to your account and a number of others, posing as a hacker from a location far from here."

Kim looked like she was thinking about it, but only for a couple of seconds. "It's very kind of you, but I think you're right. I'd better keep my head down."

For someone apparently willing to risk death to vindicate her ancestor, Kim suddenly didn't seem quite so obsessed. Solomon suspected she had material in her cloud that she didn't want him to see. Whatever it was, she'd backed down.

"It's for the best," Solomon said.

There was nothing stopping him from attempting the hack without her assistance, though, except the possibility of losing her trust one day, if she trusted him at all. She barely knew him. She had no reason to.

But he also had no reason to trust her. He'd leave it for a while and see if it still seemed like a sensible idea to investigate what she was hiding.

* * *

NOMAD SITE, OPIS:
5 MINUTES AFTER LANDING

It wasn't finding the right momentous words that worried Ingram, or the knowledge that support was a generation away. It was taking off her helmet.

She stood at the top of the ramp, looking across a sunny, almost Mediterranean landscape towards the B-movie architecture of the Nomad camp. A light breeze was ruffling leaves on the trees at the boundary. But her subconscious, the one shaped by the long training in *Cabot* and several lunar trips, kept whispering *check your seals check your seals check your seals* like a weirdo she hoped wouldn't sit next to her on the train. Constant safety drills had done their job and embedded the habit of checking helmet, cuff, and boot seals before exiting a compartment.

There's air. It's why we're here. Take the bloody helmet off.

Oh, bugger it...

"Solomon, are you listening? If I asphyxiate, I want you to sue the arse off Ainatio."

"I'll do my best, Captain."

Here we go. Here we go, here we go, here we go.

Ingram walked halfway down the ramp, released the collar seal, and lifted off her helmet. Yes, the air was breathable, wonderfully breathable, scented with things she couldn't recognise — spice and straw and the seaside — and *fresh*. The breeze was perfect. Damn, this was like stepping off a flight for a couple of weeks' leave and taking a first breath of deliciously foreign air. She inhaled a few lungfuls and stepped onto Opis's unspoiled soil. It had been easy to think up apt but highly unsuitable comments for this moment, but hard to come up with a statement of appropriate gravitas.

And one that we can all believe.

"A second chance for mankind," she said. "Let's be better this time round. Let's remember what we left behind. And let's start as we mean to go on."

She waited. Movement caught her eye and she whipped around on a reflex, but it was only an obsolete industrial quadrubot walking towards her.

"Solomon?"

"Welcome to Opis, Captain. And welcome to Nomad. Don't worry, it's all been recorded for posterity. I know it's not far to walk into camp, but may I suggest we unload the rover?"

"Yes, let's go and put the kettle on. Grab your bags, people, we're checking in."

Searle, Filopovic, Kokinos, and Yeung had disembarked and were busy taking photos of each other to mark the event. The rover rolled down the cargo ramp — more pictures, more hilarity — and everyone climbed in. This process would be repeated for the next week until all cargo and the ship's company were on the surface, minus a rotating maintenance party in *Cabot*. This would be home for the rest of their lives, unless something extraordinary happened on Earth. This was theirs to turn into success or failure.

Searle drove the hundred yards to the camp. Solomon loped alongside, keeping up easily with the rover.

"Bot racing, live from Opis," Kokinos said. "I didn't realise quads had such a turn of speed, Solomon."

"They do if you modify them."

"This could be fun."

Ingram revised her take on Solomon every time he said something. She realised she'd stopped worrying about not being able to override him in an emergency and started seeing him as a member of the crew. She didn't know how much work it took to build an AI that could carry on a meaningful conversation and make decisions, but she knew that creating something as self-aware, emotional, and intellectually creative as a human being was several orders of magnitude beyond that. Solomon had all those qualities.

He's capable of deception, too. He decides what people need to know. That's a whole new level of autonomy.

Perhaps Bednarz just got carried away with his creation. Ingram wondered if he'd been a lonely man isolated by his genius and his wealth, in need of the kind of friend who liked him for himself. She could imagine Solomon filling that void.

There were still construction and maintenance bots wandering around when Searle parked outside the main building. Ingram exercised command privilege and took a folded Union Jack and a Royal Navy white ensign from her kitbag and shook them out. It was impossible to perform any flag ceremony correctly without flagpoles, but she'd find a place to fly them later. For the time being, she draped them reverently from grippers in the entrance lobby, one flag on each wall, then saluted them. She turned to see the rest of the party clutching their own flags. At least most of them were laughing. It felt like sheer relief that they'd made it here alive, but morale would make or break them this far from home, so she'd keep the mood rolling.

"In the absence of any government around to stop me, I claim this planet in the name of the United Kingdom, and we'll proceed to teach the natives cricket as soon as is practical." There was nothing to do but join in with the hilarity. "God save the King, and we're not giving it back."

Haine started guffawing loudly in her earpiece. She hadn't realised that Solomon was patiently streaming everything back to *Cabot* via the quad's camera.

"I'll colour it pink on the map, shall I, Captain?" Haine said.

"That's the spirit, Commander."

But Searle was still holding his carefully folded Stars and Stripes to his chest. It knocked the elation out of her. Like more than half the crew, the poor bastard had woken up to find his country was gone. None of them had given their future for the greater glory of Ainatio. Even the ones who'd deny being patriots still had a sense of a tribe that was theirs and wasn't replaceable.

Ingram beckoned to Searle, moved the white ensign to the other wall, and stood back.

His flag was much bigger than hers. As Searle tried to hold it against the wall to secure one end, she stepped forward and caught it to stop it touching the floor. Searle adjusted the level to his satisfaction and stood back to salute.

"Everything can be rebuilt, Brad," she said quietly. "*Everything.*"

"Thank you, ma'am. I believe it."

Maggie Yeung put up the Singaporean flag, Filopovic a Croatian one, and Kokinos a Greek. That was interesting: both Filopovic and Kokinos were listed as German citizens. Ingram wondered if they would have identified with their ancestors if they hadn't had the same bad news as Searle on waking, but she knew there couldn't be any flags that hadn't been brought on board by crew members decades ago. They'd thought this through from the very beginning. This was who they were.

"Right, new regulations, because I'm a tyrant," Ingram said. "Everybody has to make a national dish when it's their turn in the galley. This supersedes any victualling arrangements by the supply officers. That is all. Carry on."

Solomon led them through the buildings, an interconnected warren of domes and low-rise blocks. It was odd to follow an industrial quadrubot playing tour guide with that silky voice. Ingram would now always see him as this creature.

"So most of this was mined and built here, then," Searle said, looking around the workshop. Everything looked pristine and unreal. Bots were tidier workers than humans. "I saw the plans back in the day, but it looks like things were amended."

"Yes, we made some changes to the original spec over the years," Solomon said. "That was when the FTL comms relay came into its own."

"You say that so casually."

"I've been living with it for a long time. I apologise if I sound blasé."

Searle was lost in the remotely-constructed marvels around him. Ingram took Solomon outside for a quiet word.

"I know you're busy, but is there any chance of knocking up a few flagpoles for outside the main doors?" she asked. "I realise it's not mission-critical."

"Certainly, Captain. That was a very gracious gesture with the flag, by the way. How many poles shall we have?"

"How many flags have we got? Depending on what people brought with them, it could be as many as fifteen."

"Let's start with seven on one side of the doors and see what shakes out."

"Thank you."

"Are we landing the next batch as planned?"

"Yes, eleven hundred Alpha tomorrow." Ingram had always wished she'd had more hours in the day, and now she actually did. "I'm going to take a while to adjust to saying twenty-five fifty-nine for midnight."

"And remember that the Director wants a word."

"Now?"

"Might as well, Captain."

"Okay. Patch me through from my cabin."

At least she knew where she was going. She'd memorised the route through the habitat from the video tour that Solomon had provided: maintenance bay, suit room, hydroponics, and up the stairs to her quarters. The whole complex felt and looked like a deserted factory for a tech start-up, minus potted plants and vending machines. She left her environment suit in an alcove marked COMMANDING OFFICER and went in search of her cabin.

It looked bigger than it had in the video. She tested it like a hotel room, opening closets and trying the taps — good, the plumbing worked — and there was even a small food prep area that hadn't been in the original plans. The place wasn't roomy enough to live in permanently, but it would do until things settled down and there was time to think about expansion.

She'd rehearsed all this in the smallest detail before leaving Earth. Walking into this place after years in cryo should have been like returning to work after a long weekend, the sight of familiar surroundings after a brief interruption. But it didn't. It felt like opening the front door of a new house for the first time, wondering if the surveyor had found all the little problems or overlooked the imminent collapse of the roof.

It's not a ship. It's not a shore establishment.

It's a colony. It's home.

Nobody could do a quick recce and assess the planet in advance. They'd gone on the best data from telescopes. It had been a leap of faith from the start, and everyone here was a risk-taker. It was only now that they had access to satellite surveys and could see evidence that the gamble had paid off.

Okay, time to talk to the boss. Do it now.

Solomon was a very efficient manager. The terminal was ready on the desk. The only thing missing was an exotic chocolate on the pillow and a turned-down sheet. Ingram rolled her head to iron out stiff muscles.

"Okay, Solomon, ready when you are."

She was sure that she would never have been chummy with Erskine in normal life, but the woman who appeared on the screen certainly seemed moved by the landing and even looked a little glassy-eyed. Solomon had said that she'd inherited the Nomad project in her twenties from her dying father, a delicate topic never to be mentioned because she'd had no choice in the matter. Maybe the unshed tears that Ingram thought she could see were just sheer bloody relief, then. Seventy was very late in life to find that your time was finally your own. Ingram felt sorry for her.

"This is a remarkable day, Captain." Erskine didn't appear to be in an office. The backdrop was a glass wall that looked out onto a lawn fringed by azaleas and dogwoods in full bloom. For Ingram, the sight of a late spring day on Earth was both nostalgic and only yesterday. "I've been watching the site with Solomon for years, and I can't tell you how happy it makes me to finally see people walking around and starting to build a new future there."

"Well, Director, the state of readiness of the camp is genuinely impressive, so thank you for having the place ready for us. It's a real shame we can't share the day with a wider audience, but I understand the dilemma. Let's hope it resolves itself in the future."

"I'm going to be perfectly frank and say that I doubt things will improve here in your lifetime, and certainly not in mine. But that's one of the things that Nomad insured us against."

"And still just one follow-up mission."

"I'm afraid so. There are people here who don't want to go, because they never signed up for it, but Solomon will keep you up to date with the list. And the launch date is still subject to change, but it won't go beyond the end of this year. Again, Solomon is the fount of all knowledge on that."

Ingram realised there was something she knew but hadn't fully felt until now: she could only talk to Earth for a few more months. There'd be no big project team left, no more continuing missions, and no chance of talking to the wider world. Suddenly the FTL comms seemed less relevant.

"Solomon says you're coming as well."

"Yes, I think I'll actually be a few years younger than you by the time I arrive — in terms of biological age, anyway."

"Well, in one way you already are. I was born nearly eighty years ago." It was ballsy of Erskine to risk the journey, but staying on Earth probably wasn't any easier. "We can sit down with a bottle of Opis-grown wine and compare notes on our aches and pains."

"It's a deal." Erskine looked past the camera for a moment and made a gesture to someone with her forefinger. "Before you go, there are some people who'd like to say hi."

The camera switched to a packed meeting room full of complete strangers — men, women, and even some children — waving and applauding. It took Ingram a moment to realise that these were the staff who'd only recently discovered Nomad existed and that they were going to be leaving Earth. Her self-control had already been dented today by the incident with the flags, and the sight of all these happy, excited people clapping almost tipped her over the unforgivable edge into a misty-eyed moment. She waved back and gave them a thumbs-up while she composed herself.

"I'm sure we'll be talking to many of you in the weeks to come," she said. "And I look forward to meeting you all in person, although I might have changed a bit by then."

At least that got a laugh. Erskine's voice cut in and the camera shifted back to the room with the view.

"Thank you for your time, Captain. We'll leave you to settle in. And congratulations from all of us."

The screen switched to the comms standby portal. Ingram leaned back in her seat, chastened. The last few weeks had made them all feel they weren't really so far from home, just at the end of a very long-distance call. It was a seductive and dangerous illusion, and it was cruelly temporary. They were still looking at forty-five years without outside contact. But that was what they'd trained for and what they'd expected. The best way to proceed was to cut the cord and go back to believing that *Cabot* was on her own.

"I think that went quite well, don't you?" Solomon said, a disembodied voice in the audio system again.

"I must be losing it. It hadn't really sunk in that we won't need the link with Earth for much longer. Not if everybody's going to be heading out here."

"We don't necessarily need to cut ourselves off from Earth completely. We can carry on listening. News. Entertainment channels."

"That's going to make it even harder. Maybe we should restrict the FTL contact to operational need and wean ourselves off it earlier. I'll leave you to decide what's necessary."

"Very well. It's data they need, after all. Not social calls."

"Okay, let's crack on. Got to get this empire built, eh?"

"That's the spirit, Captain."

Ingram unpacked her kitbag and went down to the ops centre to start on the next crew transfers. She decided to land thirty more personnel in the afternoon, which would put them ahead of schedule.

By early evening, the communal areas were starting to fill up, making it feel less like they were the last survivors of humanity. Ingram felt too tired to eat dinner and opted for an early night instead. She fell asleep looking up through the cabin window at a sky that was a lot more familiar than she'd expected. It was only the presence of a strange moon that reminded her how far she was from home.

She woke a couple of times in the night, unsure where she was until she realised she'd been disturbed by bots still working in the darkness. The noisy little buggers were banging metal. There must have been a window open somewhere in the accommodation block. When she ventured outside the next morning before breakfast, she realised what they'd been doing. There were now seven full-size flagpoles complete with halyards and fittings, properly rigged and ready for use, in a neat line in just the right spot outside the main doors.

She put in her earpiece. "Solomon, this is bloody fantastic. Now that's what I call service. Thank you."

"You're welcome, Captain. Will you be conducting Colours and Sunset daily now, then?"

Ingram had to think about that. Her instinctive answer was yes, because it made no difference that they were technically civilians now. Veterans had always performed ceremonial duties at public events, and the line between that and daily ceremonial now felt blurred. Flags mattered to people. They were more than practical identification: they were embodiments of tribe, the places and communities that men and women were willing to die for.

"Yes, let's do it," she said. "I did say start as we mean to go on. Civvies exempt, if they prefer."

"Colours at oh-eight-hundred, and sunset at twenty-one hundred at the latest?"

"You've been doing your homework, Solomon."

"I certainly have, Captain. I'll check to see what other flags have arrived with the latest intake."

Colours ended up being a little late that morning, but twenty of the ship's company, including civilians, stood to attention to see the flags raised for the first time. They'd now added Japanese, Korean, and Brazilian flags to the mix.

"I suppose it speaks volumes that we're all chums," Haine said, studying the row of flags fluttering in the breeze. "All these APS member states represented here, and we're not trying to kill each other. A regular paradise."

Ingram shielded her eyes against the sun, contemplating the effect. The flags really did give the place a different atmosphere. "They ought to be the same size. Looks a bit scruffy. Never mind, I'm sure they've all got personal significance, and we can always make new ones later."

"What would we do without bots, Captain?"

"What would we do without Solomon?"

"True. We'd be stuffed."

Solomon could probably hear all this. Ingram hoped he had a sense of pride among all the other human quirks that Bednarz had given him.

Another thirty crew landed at lunchtime. Now the camp was really starting to feel like a proper establishment. But even with an army of bots moving the containers and crates, the process was still exhausting even for a crew who'd adjusted to higher gravity. Around mid-afternoon, Ingram went out front to relax with a coffee and marvel at how quickly Pascoe's Star had simply become the sun. She was feeling enthusiastic again, keen to see what else was out there, and the years ahead seemed more full of potential than uncertainty.

She was sitting on a packing crate about twenty yards from the admin building, lost in thought, when she spotted two of the big avians flapping slowly towards her, the kind she'd seen in transmissions from the surface. They landed on the other side of the flagpoles and began walking with a crow-like swagger, using the forward tips of their wings almost as front legs. Solomon had seemed very taken with them. Now she understood why. They were quite a spectacle.

In this light, their plumage was a striking iridescent navy blue. She didn't know whether they were dangerous, so she decided to just sit and watch, safe in the knowledge that she had her sidearm ready on her belt.

Which might not be much use if I haven't put in some range time in this gravity.

The birds paused in front of the flagpoles and looked up, wings at their sides. They seemed to be fascinated by the flapping fabric. Every so often they would turn and look straight at Ingram, stare for a while, and then go back to looking at the flags. It was almost comical. But they were obviously curious, and that normally indicated intelligence.

She resisted the temptation to call them over as if they were pigeons expecting crumbs. For all she knew, they were predators considering her for lunch. They stood there going through that ritual for at least ten minutes, looking from her to the flags and back again.

Then another shape flashed in the corner of her eye. She jumped up, startled, and went for her sidearm as a much bigger blue-black bird shot past her like an RPG about six feet off the ground. She felt the rush of air on her face. The two smaller birds cowered, then took off just as the big one reached them and brought its wings together in front with a massive clap, almost as if it was trying to swat them like flies. For a moment Ingram thought she was watching a raptor at work. But the larger bird caught up with the two smaller ones, snatched them up them up with its hind claws, and flew away with them.

Ingram wasn't sure what she'd just witnessed. She realised how close the creature had come to her and reminded herself that not being afraid of wildlife was a bad idea when you knew almost nothing about it.

"It looks like Mother wasn't very happy about her children wandering off," Solomon said in Ingram's ear. "Or at least that's what it looked like to me."

"That was big. And fast."

"You need to be careful. I can go out in the quad frame quite safely, but flesh and blood is a lot more vulnerable."

"Worth the trip," she said, wondering if she'd had a lucky escape.

"Isn't it."

Ingram holstered her weapon, made a mental note to set up a firing range, and finished her coffee. She hoped the angry parent — if that was what it was — hadn't scared the kids and told them never to go near the bipedal invaders again. She wanted to know what had fascinated them about the flags.

They really did look like they wanted to ask her why humans had put so much effort into hanging pieces of fabric on top of metal poles so far from home.

* * *

DOGWOOD FARM, KILL LINE: LATE MAY

The world had changed forever that month, but for Doug the farming year went on as it always had for men like him for centuries. Nature wouldn't wait. It could be slowed and sped up in labs, but out in the fields, the cycle of seasons and weather still dictated his schedule.

He walked between the rows of crops, occasionally stopping to examine individual plants. The corn was making good progress. He squatted on his heels, considering that this really would be the last maize he'd ever grow on Earth. It was the kind of finality he'd never considered. He knew he'd be too old one day and realise that the previous year's planting had been his last, but this final crop was already marked on the calendar, tied to an event he knew was coming. He was leaving in *Shackleton* by the end of the year.

Now he wasn't sure what would happen to the last harvest. Liam Dale was still holding out because he wouldn't leave his animals. Others might lose their nerve and decide to stay as well. Okay, they could have this land and everything growing in it, then, and nobody would go hungry.

Doug straightened up an inch at a time, grumbling at his stiff back, and carried on. It was a beautiful morning. Birdsong, the drone of a tractor, and the scent of moist soil took him back to his childhood, much of it here in this very field. Three deer in the paddock on the far side of the track watched him approach, then trotted away towards the woods. It was timeless.

If only we could transplant all this to Opis. Just dig it up and load it.

For all the dangers that lay beyond the boundary, it broke his heart to leave. He thought that every morning. Then, minutes later, he'd remind himself that he was only here because someone much like him had made a decision centuries ago to embark on a risky voyage with no guaranteed outcome of survival, let alone success, a man probably just as scared and upset at leaving the old country as he was now.

He could do this. He had to do it for his grandchildren.

There, his resolve was back again. Taking on new challenges in old age was a new lease of life, not recklessness. He now kept pictures of Opis on his pocket screen so that he could study them until they seemed familiar. He was sure that he could lie to himself often enough to make the illusion stick, and then his first step onto alien soil might feel like coming home after an absence long enough to make it a hazy memory. The Opis landscape was starting to look normal to him, even if he couldn't visualise it cultivated yet. If it hadn't been for the odd trees and that off-colour grass, he could have taken it for somewhere in America.

Yes, that's what he'd do. He'd see it as another state he hadn't visited before. It would have been just as much of an upheaval uprooting to New Mexico or Colorado. He'd be asleep in cryo for the journey and this would feel no worse than getting on a flight and landing a few hours later. He'd have the people he knew and loved with him, and that was what counted.

Doug thought he wasn't paying attention to what was on the ground, but his peripheral vision was attuned to the small detail of the land that he walked every day, and something made him stop. A block of corn seedlings — about twelve plants, ten days after germination, a few leaves high — looked like they were yellowing. Diseased plants always made his heart skip a beat. There were scores of rusts, pests, blights, moulds, and viruses that attacked crops, but he always erred on the side of caution, and Ainatio encouraged farmers to report every sign of disease. He took a picture of the plants with his screen and called Colin.

"Hey Col, I've got a few sick-looking corn plants," he said. "Mind if I send you an image?"

"Sure," Col said. "Wait there and I'll come over and bag them."

"Take a look first. I don't want to drag you out for nothing again. I know it's not nitrogen, because I tested this soil a couple of weeks ago."

"Mosaic virus?"

"Maybe nematodes."

"I'll be right over. I've got your location."

Doug passed the time leaning on the fence while he studied the pictures of Opis again, superimposing pasture on it in his mind's eye. Ainatio was going to invite the farmers in for an open day to look at some of the crops it had been developing for Nomad. Doug felt a momentary twinge of conscience about introducing Earth species to Opis, and wondered if he was getting like his grandfather, outraged by foreign snowdrops that had no right to spread in wild America. The feeling passed quickly. Sure, Earth had a history of problems caused by introducing non-native species to new territories, but sometimes it just came down to staying alive. That was the way the world worked. That was how species spread, man included.

He looked up when he heard Col's pick-up coming down the road. It parked at the edge of the field and Col got out, carrying his test toolbox, and began picking his way between the rows.

"Keeps you fit, this," he said, pulling on plastic gloves. "Okay, let's see what's happening here. Mind if I pull up a few?"

"Be my guest. Plenty more where they came from."

While Col got out his test kits and started snipping pieces of leaf and root, Doug wandered off so as not to bother him. There was nothing worse than someone breathing down your neck while you were trying to work. He was studying his screen, reading one of Ainatio's information documents about the effect of twenty-six-hour days on Earth crops, when Col called out.

"Doug, we've got a problem. I need to put us both through decontamination and quarantine this field."

Doug's stomach twisted itself in knots. "Damn, Col, tell me it's not die-back. It can't be. We're miles from the zone."

"I'm going to get a decon unit out here. It's not a conclusive result."

Doug watched Col while he called Ainatio, feeling sick with dread, although his common sense told him this wasn't the end of the world. They'd be leaving in a matter of months, and they weren't short of food. There were plenty of other crops that had never been affected by die-back that they could switch to, so this wouldn't be as disastrous for them as it had been for an industrialised farming system. But he was still scared, ashamed, and racked with guilt. How the hell had this field gotten contaminated? He hadn't been outside the cordon for years. There were any number of ways that a virus could be transmitted to plants, but he felt the blame rested squarely with him.

The decontamination unit arrived within ten minutes. Everyone would have seen it driving north through the town, as conspicuous and shaming as ringing a leper's bell. Doug started rehearsing his apologies as he took off his clothes in the back of the decon truck and braced himself to be doused with sterilising spray. He felt like a new prisoner being de-loused. After the liquid had dried, he dressed in the blue laboratory clothes handed to him by the technician and collected his sterilised pocket screen.

"It's not your fault, Doug," Col said, adjusting his own blue coveralls. "It could have been anything. Birds, even. This stuff's been mutating over the years, and if it was easy to tackle, Ainatio would have found a way to fix it by now, believe me. Besides, we might be jumping the gun. My test was inconclusive. For all we know, it really might be a mosaic virus."

"I know what mosaic virus looks like, Col," Doug said. "Don't try to make me feel better."

"Okay. So... we're going to have to burn the crop if it's positive."

"Do whatever you have to. I'm just worried for the people who thought they might be able to stay here."

"Don't worry about it. It's not a disaster."

But it was certainly mortifying for all kinds of reasons, from the acceptance that he was abandoning his family's land to the knowledge that he might be the vector for the final destruction of the town that he had sworn to protect as mayor. It was a sorry end of his term of office.

He waited for the technicians to finish hosing down his quad bike and rode back into the town centre, conscious of people staring at him as he went past in unfamiliar blue coveralls. He couldn't bear it. He had to pull over and explain himself. David, the brewer, was standing on the porch of his store, arms folded.

"Might be bad news, Dave," Doug said. "They're testing for die-back on my land. They sterilised everything. We're waiting for the results from the lab."

Dave was remarkably calm. He pulled a resigned face, like he'd been told the movie channel was down for maintenance. "I suppose it was only a matter of time. But don't you go giving yourself a heart attack over it, hear? At least we've got somewhere else to go."

Doug didn't stop to speak to anyone else. There was a procedure for notifying the town about emergencies, and this definitely qualified as one. When he reached his office, he asked the clerk to make a strong pot of coffee, then started drafting the message that would go to the personal screens of everyone in Kill Line. As soon as he sent it, he'd be inundated with questions to which he'd have no satisfactory answers. He felt like he ought to hold a meeting and show his face, but he was waiting on Ainatio's labs, and if they confirmed die-back, they'd be the ones deciding what happened next, not him. All he wanted to do now was go home and surround himself with his family. And it was all he could do.

Joanne pounced on him as soon as he walked down the path. "I heard from Liam." Word had already gotten around. "I wish you'd called me."

"Sorry, honey. But it's just upended me. Look, I'd really like to have everybody around for a family dinner tonight. Can you do that for me? I know I'm pathetic, but I'd kind of hoped to see out my time here without being responsible for killing off the whole damn town."

Joanne grabbed his hand, almost pulling him into the house. "I know you think you're responsible for the whole world's welfare, but you can't claim any responsibility for die-back. And what if it isn't? Come on, get some proper clothes on and dump those coveralls. You look like you're going to a fancy dress party as a plumber."

Doug went up to the attic and pulled out the family photo archive again to remind himself what the world had been like before so many problems had woven themselves into a carpet of disaster. He thought of Chris Montello, worrying about what would happen to Jamie's grave after everyone had left for Opis, and then wondered about his own family's plots. He still wasn't sure how much people would be allowed to take with them on the ship, but it certainly wouldn't include headstones or coffins. His forebears probably wouldn't have wanted to leave Kill Line anyway. He allowed himself a short wallow in nostalgia before going downstairs again to check on Joanne. She was peeling vegetables.

"Everyone's coming," she said. "Are you sure you're okay?"

"Kind of. I think it's just everything that's happened in the last few weeks. It's been one round of shocks after the other. I should be made of sterner stuff."

It was hours before dinner, but Doug set the dining room table anyway, moving in more chairs to accommodate twelve people — two sons, one daughter, two daughters-in-law, one son-in-law, and four grandchildren. He even wrote out little name tags on cards left over from a civic function years ago: Callum, Sarah, Patrick, Moira, Beth, Barry, Becky, Elliott, Matthew, and Ruth. Joanne could have the head of the table tonight.

Some civic leader I am.

While he was polishing the silver cutlery, which he was determined to take with him to Opis, his screen chirped with an incoming call. It was Col. That was quick: the tests had only taken a couple of hours.

"So is it as bad as we thought it was?" Doug asked.

"Yeah, sorry, it's die-back," Col said. "But I don't want you blaming yourself. You didn't bring it in."

"That's kind of you, Col, but unless it's a bird dropping something it picked up outside, then it's still down to me."

"You know that's not true. Let's assume it's animal-borne for the meantime. We'll contact everyone."

"Already have."

"Good. I'll arrange for the crop to be destroyed. We'll be testing the rest of the farms over the next few days."

"Sorry, Col."

"Hey, we knew it might reach us one day. At least we can relocate now."

Over dinner that evening, Doug's kids still tried to protect him from reality, pointing out the alternative crops that the town could still grow if anyone wanted to stay.

"It's really cool that we've got somewhere else to go to just when we need it," Elliott said. He was always an upbeat kid. "You always say things are meant to be, Grandpa, so I don't know why you're so upset about this."

"You need to let Chris know, too, honey." Joanne passed around more roast potatoes. "I don't think Ainatio remembers to keep the camp informed."

"Don't worry, I'm pretty sure that Solomon has a hotline to them, but I'll call anyway."

"You don't suppose the infection was brought in by them, do you?" Callum asked. "I mean, they've been outside the safety zone recently."

"Yeah, and they always go through decontamination." Doug wanted to quash rumours right away. "Let's not start blaming them. The die-back was found on our land. Chris's people have never been near that field."

"Sure, Dad. Just asking."

"They're good people. They're our *neighbours*. I don't want anyone pointing fingers, okay?"

Perhaps Elliott was right that it was meant to be. This would make up a few minds, and soften some of the regret at leaving. It was just a matter of timing, that was all.

Only one thing mattered: Kill Line would live. It would be transplanted to another planet, but everyone would survive, and that was more important than the buildings they'd leave behind, however irreplaceable the town itself seemed, however attached folks were to the stone and brick and wood that seemed like it had been there forever and always would be.

They'd built the place. They'd build it again. And the land — yeah, land stirred strong emotions, but it wasn't permanent either. The Brandts and every other family would carry on long after the land was dead.

Doug reached for the dish of potatoes. What he felt right now was painful optimism, like leaving home for the first time.

"Okay," he said. "Anyone else for second helpings?"

11

Brains need bodies. It's how they're built, because they have to bridge that gap to the physical world somehow to measure and interpret it. And that's how Bednarz built Solomon. Listen to Sol talk. He uses physical words, and not just to make communication easier for us. He might see his body as a kind of stream flowing between locations, but he puts the part he regards as his self, his conscious attention, in one place at a time, even if his sensory input — the chatter he can hear in the background — is scattered across space.

William Cullen, head of IT, explaining an AMAI's worldview to the junior science class at Ainatio

AINATIO PARK RESEARCH CENTRE, PLANT PATHOGEN LAB: 0130 HOURS NEXT MORNING

Yes, it was die-back.

Col had worked that out right away, but Lianne Maybury's team always double-checked his biosensor results. Alex was now wondering why they were still retesting well after midnight and weren't answering their comms. He hung around the lobby, trying to raise Lianne via her screen.

What else did he need to do? The town had already implemented the quarantine plan and the crop had been destroyed, along with a fifty-metre biosecurity zone around the field. Col and his people had been out testing samples from the rest of the farms. All vehicles using the dirt road closest to the field would now have to go through a decontamination unit, in and out. Alex knew they had it covered. But it didn't make him feel any better.

Still, we've got somewhere to go, and a lot of food stored to see us through until then if we need it.

"Sol, give me a call if Lianne comes out of her papal enclave in there, will you?" he said, heading for the bar. "Tell her I want to talk to her pronto."

"Will do, Alex."

"You never used to say that. Hanging out in the mess too much."

"Wardroom."

"Turning into a sailor, huh? I lost track of Nomad today. Anything I should know?"

"The avian creatures have been visiting. When you get around to reviewing the video, look out for the bigger one. We think it's the parent."

"Don't feed them. You'll never get rid of them."

"There's already a robust conversation going on between the astrobiology people and Captain Ingram. She happened to mention that she drew her weapon when the larger one spooked her."

"Have they named them yet?"

"Taxonomically or affectionately?"

"Either."

"Crows."

"The poetic muse is MIA, I see."

"If you're going to the bar, by the way, there's some unkind speculation about the source of the die-back contamination. Will you scotch it, or shall I?"

"Leave it to me. Who are they blaming?"

"The transit camp. Bringing back bugs from their expedition. We were exposed as well, but that seems to have been forgotten."

"Sol, I know you don't like me asking this, but can you listen in on Lianne and let me know what the hell's holding them up?"

"You're right, I don't like doing it. I need people to trust me if I'm to be effective. Look, you won't forget to deal with the rumour, will you?"

"I promise. You sound like you know something."

"Don't ask. It's Lianne's job to tell you when she's ready."

Alex heard the click of the security doors behind him all the way down the passage and turned around. Lianne strode towards him, swinging her arms, but not in a cheerful way, more like trying to hurry without breaking into a run. She didn't look happy. Her sweater was ruched up as if she'd pulled off her lab gear in a hurry and was in too much of a rush to tidy herself up before going to find him.

"I wish you'd stop trying to call me when we're busy," she said. "We weren't sitting around eating pizza."

"Sorry. You were scaring me. You never take this long."

"There's a reason."

"I can start guessing, but I'd rather you just told me. Erskine gets extra mad when it's this much past her bedtime."

Lianne looked awkward. "Bottom line? Nobody brought this infection in from outside."

"Doug Brandt said he thought it was probably a bird dropping infected plant material or something."

"Look, this isn't going to be easy because we've now got to kick off a containment procedure within this building. Because the damn virus is one of ours. It's got the marker that we added to the copy that we were working on."

"Shit."

"And it seems to have mutated as well. It's more active than ours."

"Oh. That's just terrific." Where was this going to end? "Sol, lock down the perimeter, and — "

"I've done it," Solomon said.

"I'll go tell Erskine. Any idea how it got out, Lianne?"

"Not yet. We might never know. But we haven't breached biosecurity procedures, and I can't find any traces outside the actual lab. Nothing in the places anyone would have to walk through to exit the department."

Alex tried to be diplomatic, but he knew what Erskine was going to ask. "I'm not turning this into a blame game, but I'd rather have someone say they screwed up than spend time fretting over whether we've got a containment lapse that we haven't noticed."

Lianne had a permanent frown that always made her look irritated even when she wasn't. "Alex, you know damn well that I'd tell you straight if we knew how it got out. *I don't.* I might find out, and then again I might not. I'm doing my best."

"Okay, just focus on securing the lab. Are you going to destroy whatever virus you've got left?"

"Horses and stable doors, huh?"

"It's a reasonable question. If you're asking for an instruction, I'm going to say torch that lab. But I'll get confirmation from Erskine."

Lianne called after him as he strode off. "How are we going to do more work on this if we destroy our stocks?"

"It doesn't even matter any more." Alex carried on down the corridor. "We're leaving. You won't fix this in a few weeks. We lost the battle to this damn thing a long time ago. All I'm concerned about now is stopping it hitching a ride with us to Opis."

But some people didn't want to leave. Up to this moment, they'd had a choice. Now that choice was gone.

Lianne was still walking behind him, calling out questions, going on about passing the research to other labs before they left, and their responsibility to the scientific community and the world, and all kinds of crap that Alex really didn't give a shit about right then. He was more worried about infection control failures that would affect the plants they needed to take with them. They had food stores here and some supplies already loaded in *Elcano*, plus plant material already in cryo, but there were other strains of modified crops still growing in Hydroponics. That was his primary concern now.

Erskine was stretched out on the sofa in her office when he went in, propped up on cushions and watching something on her personal screen. She looked up and said nothing. Her whole posture was a question.

"Director, this isn't good news." Alex found it easier to tell her than he'd expected. "Apparently it's our copy of the virus that got out of the lab. Don't ask me how. And it's mutated. More virulent."

"Oh, for goodness' sake..."

He thought she'd be angry, but she just seemed weary and exasperated. "I think we should destroy whatever virus we've got left," he said.

"Yes, go ahead. I noticed the lockdown going into effect." She made a vague gesture in the direction of her desk as if she'd seen it on her monitor. "I need to break the news to Doug Brandt. I know he was expecting to abandon the town anyway, but it's going to be heartbreaking for him to find out that we're responsible for this."

"We should stop work on all the other crop projects and run tests on them immediately. The crops we've already shipped out to Nomad will be fine, but the question is whether we want to play it safe and destroy everything else we were planning to export, or just rely on our decontamination and hygiene procedures. Because if we couldn't crack the die-back answer here, we'll have zero chance on Opis. We'll be much more vulnerable there."

"Start the tests," Erskine said.

"I'm going to do some rumour control here in the meantime. I'll also warn the transit camp to stay clear until further notice."

"And this definitely hasn't been brought in by anyone returning from infected areas?"

"Definitely not. Dr Maybury confirmed it's ours."

Alex left Erskine to it. He wasn't sure when to tell Ingram, but he'd have to do it soon. Maybe Solomon could look after that, seeing as he was best buddies with the *Cabot* crew now.

"Why didn't your systems detect anything, Sol?" Alex asked as he headed for the bar, typing out instructions on his screen and mailing them as he walked. "I thought we had pathogen screening."

"We do, but there are always going to be things it hasn't learned to detect yet."

"I'm not blaming you, buddy. I'm just trying to stop it happening again, even if there's no point in worrying about that."

"What if it was me?"

"How?"

"I've taken the quad off-site quite a few times. I've had physical contact with the townspeople."

"And Erskine and I went into town to do the meet-and-greet. Could have been us, too. Look, the hole we really have to plug is whatever let it get from the lab to other areas in here."

"Indeed."

"All right, time to stroll into the Coliseum and confront the baying crowd."

"There are only fifteen people still drinking in the bar. I think you'll survive."

It wasn't as if Alex had anything contentious to tell them. It might turn out to be more of a shame-on-you lecture. He'd play it by ear.

"Hi, guys." He walked in trying to radiate reassurance. "We've just had identification from the plant path lab that the virus actually escaped from this building. Which is embarrassing, and we'll be ashamed, but it's our fault. Nobody else's."

"Wow, they're going to love us in town, aren't they?" Sonia Venner toyed with a glass of juice. "We ignore them for years, then the first thing we manage to do when we start mixing with them is to infect their crops with our own crap."

Ed Acosta, the guy who'd buttonholed Alex at the party all those months ago to ask if he could move to the plant pathogen team, was sitting at a table a little way from the main group. He looked at Alex as if he was seriously considering getting up and punching him in the face.

"Or is this some stunt to make sure that everybody leaves?" Ed asked. "Because the last time you and I had a chat, you looked me in the eye and fed me some bullshit line about how I should carry on developing crop strains because the pathogen guys didn't need an extra pair of hands. You *knew*. You damn well *knew* what was going down, and you lied to my face. Why the hell should I believe a word that you or Erskine say now?"

"Come on, Ed. You really think we'd dick around like that with people's lives?"

"Damn sure of it. Isn't that what you've been doing for the last fifty years?"

"Okay, I know that I should be a proper manager and say something placatory about understanding, and reassure you that blah blah blah, but right now I'm tired, I've got a lot of shit to shovel, and you're just going to have to accept that it happened and nobody planned it."

That really shouldn't have escaped Alex's lips, but he felt better for saying it. Venner looked at him with her chin propped on her hand.

"I've already closed my labs," she said. "I'm not going to speculate on how the virus got out, but the only possible vectors are a fault in the lab ventilation system, one of the pathogen team not cleaning up properly before they went outside, or that some insect got in, happened to come into contact with the virus, happened to — "

"I get the picture, Sonia. Top priority — make sure the rest of the place is squeaky clean and protect what plants we still have in here. I don't want to have to destroy them. Second priority, a lot further down my list — work out how it happened. Depending on how dumb or unlucky the mistake turns out to be, I might go kick someone's ass into the middle of next week, if I've still got the strength."

Sonia stood up and drained her juice. "I'm heading back, then. We might as well start testing right now. I'll see you tomorrow, or later today as we like to call it."

Alex went back to his office, not feeling particularly guilty about being less than everybody's best buddy for a change. It was an ungodly hour to wake Doug, but the guy needed to know it wasn't his fault. Alex called him on the radio and waited for a sleepy voice to answer. But Doug picked up right away. He sounded wide awake. He probably wasn't sleeping well.

"Doug, I just wanted to let you know that it's definitely dieback, but it didn't come from outside," Alex said. "I'm sorry, and I don't expect you to ever forgive us for this, but it's the version of the virus we were working on in our labs."

There was a few seconds' silence. "So there's nothing we could have done differently," Doug said at last.

"Absolutely nothing. I know sorry isn't enough. I'm going to let Chris know as well. We've locked down the site while we clean up, so it's probably a good idea for his people to stay put as well and not patrol until we've finished testing all your land."

"I already spoke to him." There was no recrimination in Doug's voice or even a sigh to indicate the guy was angry or upset. "We stood down the patrols."

"Okay. I guessed you'd have everything under control at your end, but I just wanted to try to make myself useful because I feel so bad about this."

"I look at it this way, Alex. By the end of the year, we'll be on our way somewhere else where it's not a problem. It was always a matter of time."

After he ended the call, Alex realised what he really wanted was for someone to punch him out, not about the escape of the rogue die-back, but for just going along with this scam for so long. All he could see now was the contempt and disgust on Ed Acosta's face when he looked at him. He'd try to forget it.

An uncharitable thought crossed his mind. That wasn't unusual, except this time it was about Solomon. There was no point in ferreting through the system and trying to check for himself whether there had been any obvious breaches recorded on camera, because Solomon would see it instantly. It was best to just ask him outright, man to man.

"Sol, don't be offended by this, but after all that's happened between you and Erskine, I just need to know that this is a coincidence and not something you thought ought to happen."

Alex knew he had to ask. He also knew that it was going to leave a big crater in their working relationship.

"To be honest, Alex, I *am* offended," Solomon said. "I know I've done some manoeuvring to make sure Erskine didn't leave the transit camp to fend for itself, but I'd never deliberately harm the survival prospects of anybody in the town. I'd hoped you knew me better than that."

"Ever wished you hadn't said something?"

"Several times."

"Well, I apologise. But I had to ask."

"At least you've got an answer to give Erskine when it finally occurs to her."

"You're taking this better than I would."

"Let's put it behind us. And be thankful that this didn't happen a few years ago."

Alex hoped that Solomon didn't hold grudges. Now that he'd taken a minute to mull it over, he regretted even thinking the AI would go that far. Maybe Erskine had sown the doubt when she said she didn't want to make an enemy of him. It had come across almost as a warning that he wasn't to be trusted.

"I know you'd do anything to save people," Alex said.

"Would you?" Solomon asked.

"Of course, but we've covered that. There's a place for everyone who wants to go."

"Indeed. We leave nobody behind."

Solomon was sounding more like Trinder — or Ingram, or Chris Montello — every day. The only AI of his kind had finally found a tribe, it seemed. Alex, instantly lonely in his role of Erskine's enforcer, kind of envied him.

* * *

SURVEY VESSEL *SHACKLETON*, ORBITAL 2, IN DISPOSAL ORBIT: ONE WEEK LATER

When Solomon looked back at Earth from *Shackleton*, the view he enjoyed most was the night side of the planet. The lonely blue marble aspect was all very well, but there was something much more comforting about the clusters of lights that picked out cities full of people and lives being lived.

America, once so brightly lit that the eastern half of the country and much of the West Coast were both single luminous blocks, was reduced to a few faint, scattered cities. The pools and coastline necklaces of yellow light were now concentrated in Asia and South America, across the north of Scandinavia and Russia, in Australia and New Zealand. Except for the small offshore beacon that was Britain, Europe was mostly as dark as America and Canada. Earth was two separate worlds.

As the planet turned, the sun erased the telltale signs of depopulation. North America became a mottled patch again like all the others in the cloud-streaked marble.

"Sol, we've just lifted the quarantine," Alex said. "But I suppose you heard all that."

"I'm afraid I tuned my concentration to *Shackleton*. I just wanted my focus here for a few hours."

"Well, when you get back in touch with your bad self or whatever, you'll see that we didn't agree on many conclusions about the die-back breach. Contaminated insect escape or transfer from lab equipment to someone who was in contact with someone else et cetera et cetera, and eventually had contact with someone from Kill Line."

"I do hope this won't become an excuse to shun our neighbours."

"Stable doors and all that. So how's *Shack* coming along?"

"The welding schedule might slip another five days."

"Don't worry. It's not Doomsday."

Sometimes it did feel like it, though. That was probably why the brightly lit Asian Pacific night seemed so reassuring. Earth endured, albeit incomplete. "We'll be ready," Solomon said. "But it'll be a close-run thing."

Along with *Eriksson* and *Da Gama*, *Shackleton* was in a higher orbit than *Elcano*, on the edge of the graveyard zone where junk was nudged further out to die far from the working satellites it might blunder into. Solomon debated whether it would be faster to cannibalise *Eriksson*'s welding bots to build extra mini-bots to speed up the repairs to *Shackleton*'s hull, or to simply raid *Da Gama* and remove whole sections of her hull. He settled on sacrificing a welding bot or two to save two days.

In the bigger scheme of things, Alex was right. It wasn't going to make a lot of difference. Solomon was just uncomfortable with slippage. Like viruses, slippages had a tendency to spread.

He left the bots to their work. If he kept his focus here any longer, he'd be doing the equivalent of human daydreaming. He shifted back to *Elcano*, now ready to launch, and looked over the compartments that were devoted to cargo in her sister ship *Cabot*. *Elcano*'s were full of cryo chambers, eleven hundred sarcophagi that reminded him a little too much of kitchen appliances, and a communal deck that only needed to accommodate two hundred people at a time for a few days while they adjusted to consciousness again. Like *Cabot*'s crew, *Elcano*'s passengers would be revived and transferred to Nomad Base in separate batches.

It was going to be a lonely forty-five years with all of his friends in cryo. He consoled himself with the thought that he'd be in constant contact with Opis instead, so he wouldn't lack human company. He just hoped that the Nomad community wouldn't gradually become more important to him. He was designed to think almost like a human — a man, minus the kind of self-interest that came from a physical body — and he knew affection was a strangely malleable thing. It would be a betrayal to transfer it and neglect his old friends.

Nomad Base seemed to be settling into the happy and efficient ship that he'd teased Ingram about. Now he could keep a watching brief on it while he prepared two ships and 2,704 people to join it. How much time did they have? If the worst happened and no crops in Kill Line made it to the harvest, there was enough food stored to fill the shortfall for another seven months.

Solomon checked Orbital 1's latest images of the area around Kill Line, captured in the last two weeks. The resolution was one pixel to fifteen square yards, and the images were taken three days apart, but it was enough to show what was happening. He could see the areas of burn-off, but there was also a distinct chain of patches leading away from the town and out across the cleared boundary. The vegetation had definitely changed colour in the last few days. To the north-west, a similar pattern had emerged. Solomon interpreted the plumes as the path taken by animals that had carried contaminated insects with them. Ainatio had put its faith in the cordon, but it finally seemed to have failed, albeit in the opposite direction. They'd probably never know which particular insects were the carriers, or why the animals had decided to move out of Hart County, but they had, and the mutated version of the virus was on the move.

But that vegetation can't all be cereals. Would abandoned crops re-seed that much? Has die-back jumped the species barrier again?

Whatever the reason, it wasn't his priority. He had to keep *Shackleton* on schedule. If things slipped much more, it might become a race to move people into cryo early to avoid food shortages. In the worst scenario, an unforeseen problem could be a setback they'd never recover from in time.

And then who would decide who was saved?

I would. This is what I was meant for.

Every day, Solomon realised a little more about Bednarz's intentions. If he hadn't known that the cumulative disasters were real and beyond even his creator's technical ability, he might have thought this was all a test of character, to see how far Solomon would go to ensure that mankind's best survived.

I know you'd do anything to save people. That was what Alex had said. Anything was a very big word.

Solomon sent Trinder a request for a surveillance drone to take a closer look at the vegetation, then transferred back to Ainatio to update Erskine and Alex. He couldn't pin down the exact point when Alex had become Erskine's de facto deputy, but the role seemed to have latched onto him more firmly in the last few months whether he wanted it or not.

Erskine was giving a staff talk to a packed hall on the subject of living and working on Opis, describing the kind of housing that would be waiting for them forty-five years from now. Solomon decided not to interrupt. Alex was in his office, watching the monitor.

"Do you have five minutes, Alex?"

Alex leaned back in his chair and put his feet up on the desk. "Yeah, sure. Just watching Erskine selling time-share. You realise we haven't named anywhere yet? You can't have a town called Nomad."

"A little premature. Names should evolve from usage. Otherwise they sound like tract housing."

"It *is* tract housing."

"Names have significance."

"Okay, you're in charge of naming now."

"Very well. But I came to show you these pictures."

Alex sat forward again with his elbows on the desk and watched Erskine replaced by Orbital 1's images. He sighed.

"Well, no real surprise there. At least it's heading away from us. So that's actually quite good news, relatively speaking."

"Do we continue with testing and destruction?"

"If I thought a few more months' effort on top of all the years we've spent would work, I'd put on a hazmat suit and do it myself. But time's tight."

"You don't like giving up."

"There's a fine line between tenacity and denial. I keep an eye open for it."

"Very wise."

"You want me to brief Erskine?"

"Yes. Thank you."

"Will we make it, Sol?"

"You've seen the calculations."

"I meant... your gut feel. Belief. That vague stuff."

"I wouldn't be doing all this if I didn't believe we could." It was very much about numbers now, calculating calories and the nutritional requirements of everyone in the three locations — Ainatio, transit camp, and Kill Line — and how many days the food stores would last. "We have seven months' food in storage for the entire population, not counting the emergency supplies already in *Elcano,* which I'd prefer not to touch. I'm working on the assumption that neither Kill Line nor the transit camp have substantial food reserves. But we do have the option of reducing rations in an emergency, or putting some people into cryo early in *Elcano.*"

"In an emergency." Alex started laughing. "Hell's bells, Sol, let's hope we never have one of those. Everything's been peachy so far."

"I'm ready," Solomon said. "I'll make this work. You just have to trust me."

Alex made an uncertain gesture. He was trying to reach out and touch something, but was frustrated by finding nothing there. He ended up patting the desk. It was almost as if he'd wanted to pat Solomon on a non-existent back.

"I do, actually," he said. "I really do."

Solomon was reassured. One day, he might have to test that trust to the limit.

* * *

AINATIO PARK RESEARCH CENTRE:
LATE JUNE

The roses in the grounds were at their best this summer, heavy with perfect blooms as if they knew it was their final performance.

Even the hedge of rugosas had put on a show. The scent was pure rosewater in the hot sun, and when Erskine inhaled it she couldn't recall why it meant something to her. It was a childhood memory that had escaped her, leaving only the most basic sensations.

Had the botany team remembered to save decorative plants? She'd have to check again. Radical new beginnings needed radical surroundings, not a theme park replica of a world they'd abandoned, but some things would be missed too badly to leave behind. It seemed like a good topic to start the next informal staff session she'd scheduled.

The seminar-style talks in the main lecture theatre were easy. She'd reluctantly learned to play the CEO at twenty-seven, the art of stepping onto a stage and projecting confidence and authority despite being press-ganged into the position and hating it. She was never expected to get into complex conversations with her audience. But these smaller staff groups, no more than ten people at a time, left her nowhere to run. She had to deal with their fears and questions. And more of them were afraid than she'd expected.

With any luck, Nomad would be doing something interesting that they could watch on the live feed. Showing nervous staff what was happening right now and giving them a chance to talk to others on the ground soothed many of the doubters, but not all.

Erskine consulted her screen. Department heads were keeping a tally of which staff were still unwilling to leave.

"Where do they think they're going to go, Solomon?" she said.

"Sorry, Director?"

"My apologies. I was checking how many holdouts we have."

"Considering almost nobody knew they were signing up to move to another planet, the take-up rate is impressive."

"Glass half full, then."

"Ah, this is when I know I'm giving balanced advice."

"Pardon?"

"Nothing, Director."

Erskine's staff session today was with a group of nine drawn from the shuttle maintenance and reactor teams. The link between the two was more social than an overlap of responsibilities. There were several marriages within those groups and a father-son connection as well, so talking to them as families rather than professional categories made more sense. They were going to Opis to live: their anxieties weren't about their jobs, but survival.

"Here's what I don't get, Director." Liz Kent worked on the reactor, and her husband, Greg, ran shuttle maintenance. They had a teenage son. "Is this really our only option? Why can't we contact APS and ask for asylum? I bet they'd open their borders for scientists and engineers with a lot of commercial data and expertise to trade."

Erskine had to word her response carefully without lying. This group was one she'd definitely need on Opis and she didn't want to make opting out sound easy.

"I stand by my promise that nobody will be made to go," she said. "Even if we could force people on board at gunpoint, I wouldn't want anyone that unwilling on a mission this important. At the very least, they'd become disruptive. But staying put isn't an option, and APS is much more afraid of disease — all of them, plant, animal, human — than you realise."

Greg reached slowly for his wife's hand. "I realise we've had a lot of privileges here, but we've all lost family and friends in the rest of the country. We're probably all there is left of mine. It just feels like an even bigger risk."

"Only you can decide," Erskine said. "But imagine what this site will become in your children's and grandchildren's lifetimes. Maybe die-back will run out of host species, and maybe it won't. If it does, or a countermeasure's found, people will eventually start reclaiming the land, at least where it isn't too heavily contaminated. But Opis is clean, safe, and waiting for us right now. Have a think about that. In the meantime, would you like to talk to some of the *Cabot* crew about what it's like?"

Solomon always took his cues. The monitor in the meeting room came to life, revealing a couple of crew members waiting at a table in a sunny lounge, chatting to pass the time. Opis looked remarkably like home. The image was more persuasive than anything Erskine could say.

"Audio's ready, Director," Solomon said over the speakers. "Shall I connect them?"

"Thank you, Solomon." Erskine stood up and smiled at the engineers as convincingly as she could. "I'll leave you to it. If I hang around, it might inhibit your questions. Feel free to ask the crew whatever you want."

Erskine walked back to her office. Another one down, another dozen, two dozen, maybe three dozen to go. Pep talks were now occupying more than half her day. That was leadership, but she knew it would have been better for her to swap roles with Alex and take on his organisational duties. He was much better at persuasion.

"Everything okay, Alex?" His office was a short detour on her route. "How are we doing?"

He'd arranged a wall of screens, each showing the status of one area of preparation. There was a lot of red and amber among the green bars on all of them. He looked as if he hadn't slept much in weeks.

"People," he said wearily. "I hate them. If you can't give a population of STEM folks the deck plan of a ship and get them to understand how much garbage they *can't* take with them, what hope is there for the world?"

"Medical status?"

"Everybody's cleared for cryo except the transit camp. We haven't started on them yet. The town's doc is going to help out when she's finished with the residents."

Erskine walked across to the screen wall and studied the detail. "Just as well we have more bots than humans. Sad to see the bio labs go, though."

"One left to zap. Want to go down there and see it burn?"

It didn't appeal to her. It would be like watching a cremation through the furnace inspection window. "One for the nihilists and bridge-burners to savour, I think. What's happening about the camp?"

Alex shrugged. "It's not like they've got much gear. And Jared said they're used to packing and moving at a moment's notice anyway."

"Dogs? Dairy herds?"

"Best you don't know, Director. Everything will be resolved."

Erskine took the advice. She carried on reading the screens, finding comfort in certainty. Everything was scheduled: shuttle transfers, cryo processing, mothballing the buildings, and eventually shutting down and entombing the reactor.

"Have you ever been in cryo?" she asked. "I ought to remember, but I don't."

"I did a week. A test. Years ago."

"And?"

"I didn't dream and I didn't puke when I woke up. Like a general anaesthetic. Better than real life."

"You're busy. I'll get out of your hair."

"No Phil? Where's he gone?"

"He's condensing the company records. Including the pre-Bednarz era. That's nearly one hundred and seventy years."

Alex made a cranking motion with his hand. "Shredding. Uh-huh."

"Condensing. Never keep archives you don't need."

"Sol's probably kept copies anyway. Look, if you need distraction, you can always check the passenger lists. We've allocated pods now."

"But you've not notified anyone."

"No, because some of them are officially don't-knows."

Erskine continued to her office. She wasn't watching the Opis feed as much as she used to, perhaps because she felt it was a beachhead that had finally been secured. The alien landscape had somehow become Earth: people she felt she knew were walking around the camp, flying Earth's flags and veneering the planet with human normality. She hadn't seen the avian creatures for days, either. The illusion was complete.

Imagine how scientists would react if we shared this with the rest of the world now. Not the FTL. Not the colony. Just show them a planet that isn't gas or ice or airless desert, or hot enough to melt metal. A world with complex animals and plants, not just bacteria and algae.

Ainatio had to keep its discoveries to itself. It wasn't the secrecy that occasionally made Erskine pause. It was that this little collection of miracles hadn't been as important to Ainatio as the fact that it was habitable.

She swung her chair around and returned to her monitor, checking the cryo pod allocations. Nearly 250 were children. Nearly half of Ainatio's personnel were families. It was a solid foundation. With the Kill Line community, there'd be a wide gene pool and a more equal ratio of male to female.

She still had misgivings about the transit camp, though. They were a mix of the unknown and the intimidating, as alien as anything on Opis. While a PhD wasn't necessary to build a new world, Erskine felt more comfortable among her own kind, like anyone else. There were also practical considerations. The camp's militia was a separate armed force, larger than the detachment, and it didn't do things the Ainatio way. She was prudent to be cautious about them.

I'm not a snob.

Am I?

No. We all worry about who might move into the house next door.

By the time *Elcano* and *Shackleton* reached Opis, the community would be effectively civilianised anyway. Nomad was a military outpost with only a few civilians now, but in forty-five years, at least one generation, and probably two, would have grown up without that culture and experience, and then they'd be joined by twenty-seven hundred new arrivals, of which fewer than a hundred would be soldiers. There was no need for a military force in the new world. The veterans would gradually learn to think like civilians again. Erskine was sure of it.

She opened the day's reports from the department heads, keeping an eye on the clock for her next staff session. While she was reading, Solomon interrupted.

"Director, I think you need to speak to Major Trinder as a matter of urgency."

"What's happened?"

"I'll put him through when he's ready. He's talking to APS at the moment."

Erskine's stomach started falling down a lift shaft. "Spit it out, Solomon."

"They've noticed, I'm afraid. The new spread of die-back."

This was the last thing she needed. APS had ignored Ainatio for years. They certainly picked their moments.

"But do they know we've got operational vessels almost ready to leave Earth orbit?"

"There's been no mention of that. They're just asking to speak to the person in charge."

"Keep an eye on this and be ready to change plans *fast*." Erskine pushed her chair closer and adjusted her collar mike. She couldn't remember ever having contact with APS at an official level. "Who is it, their agrisat control room? Space station?"

"A general at APDU. Colonel Su-Jin Yoon."

This was getting worse by the second. The Asia-Pacific Defence Union was probably as high as a problem could get shunted, a level above national governments. Erskine guessed where this might be heading. When the call came through, she was ready to play the pitiful old woman.

"This is Georgina Erskine," she said. "How can I help, Colonel?"

"Madam, I regret to tell you that our satellite imaging has detected diseased vegetation near your position." The colonel was a woman. She spoke good English. "Are you aware of this?"

APS knew Ainatio was probably still functioning in some limited way because they must have detected shuttle launches occasionally, but they'd ignored the facility so far. It was irrelevant to them. Erskine kept up the harmless act.

"We test the surrounding area every week," she said. "What kind of pattern are you seeing?"

"It is progressing from within the cordon sanitaire to the north-west. It is fast-moving, a matter of only days, which is more rapid than the spread has been in the past. You are a science and technology company. Do you have countermeasures?"

"Colonel, we *were* a major research company. Not any more. You must be able to see how cut off we are. This is a remote rural area. There are a few small farms and a displaced persons' camp close to the facility, but that's all. We can certainly burn off the contaminated areas, though."

"Burning does not seem to have stopped it before. It appears to have crossed your cordon."

The last thing Erskine needed was for APDU to work out that the contamination had come from inside the labs. They'd have only one response to that: they'd destroy the site. She prayed that it looked as if animals had wandered in and out of the area.

"We can eradicate carrier animals too."

"You have a space station, at least one disused ship, and several operational shuttles."

Now it starts. "None of which changes our situation on the ground."

"Very well, then we are obliged to act. Despite our quarantine measures, we have still had isolated outbreaks of die-back that we destroyed. Bird and animal migration is a concern."

"Sorry, I don't understand what action you plan to take." Erskine couldn't have APS clean-up teams landing here now. "What can you do?"

"At the request of your government, we used salted nuclear devices to clear contaminated land when this virus emerged," Su-Jin said. "We will do that again."

"Hang on, what do you mean, 'At the request of your government'?"

"The United States government did not have the appropriate ordnance, and asked us for assistance. You should be aware of that."

Erskine struggled to compose herself for a moment. "We were under the impression that the assistance got a little out of hand and exceeded the help you were asked to give."

"That is unfortunate. We were asked to sterilise affected areas, and we did."

"Well, there's no government left now. No state structure at all. We're just refugees in our own country."

"This is why I have contacted you directly. It was not easy to route this call."

"I'm grateful for the information, Colonel. I assure you that we'll identify the affected areas and carry out a burn-off."

"I apologise. I have not been clear. We have to destroy the vegetation across the entire area because of the rapid rate of spread, and your previous measures have obviously been inadequate. We ask you to evacuate your people to a safe distance within two days, starting from midnight, your local time."

"You mean two weeks."

"I do mean two *days*. Forty-eight hours."

She can't mean that. "I have nearly three thousand civilians here, including children, invalids, and elderly. I can't move them in two days. We have nowhere to go."

"You have the orbital dock."

"We can't cram that many people into it, let alone keep them there for an indefinite period."

"Nevertheless, I must ask you to do it. The nature of the ordnance means the fallout will be short-lived and you will be able to return in weeks. All vegetation and animal life over a considerable area will be dead, and there will be blast damage, but you can return."

Erskine was stranded in the middle of an argument. Everyone was shipping out anyway, but two weeks wasn't enough to move that many, let alone two days. She did a few rapid calculations. It would take four shuttles, or four round trips. *Elcano* could only hold eleven hundred people. Even if *Shackleton* was ready to be used as a holding area, people would have to go into cryo. The ship was effectively an armed freighter with no space for a couple of thousand conscious passengers to move around. The orbitals weren't an answer either. They couldn't cram in more than a couple of hundred.

Erskine cleared her throat and tried to stall. "I'll have to talk to my people to see what can be done. I'm asking you to keep a channel open to me so I can update you. This is no small task, and I'll need information from you about the exact area you plan to destroy. Will you promise me that? Will you keep a line open to me? Innocent people who've already suffered a great deal are going to die if we can't reach some agreement."

"Very well, madam," Su-Jin said. "I do this with a heavy heart, but it must be done, or millions more will die in the future. We will talk again very soon. Please make your preparations."

For a few moments after the call ended, Erskine sat at her desk in a daze. Solutions had started to occur to her but she didn't like them at all.

And there was nowhere to run except up.

"Solomon, I have to assume APS is serious."

"They are, Director."

"Can we have *Shackleton* ready in two days just as somewhere to park people?"

"No. *Elcano* can take eleven hundred. We have sixteen hundred and four left, and *Shackleton*'s nowhere near ready to start accepting people. Not in two days."

"Dear God." Erskine almost put her head in her hands. There was only Solomon to see her moment of weakness, but the gesture alone would have diminished her in her own eyes. "So we talk them out of it, play for time, or make some hard choices."

Solomon didn't respond, but she knew he'd have an opinion. It troubled Erskine that he'd suddenly decided to keep his own counsel after becoming increasingly vociferous.

"Get everyone together, please," she said. "Alex, department heads, Phil, and Trinder."

"At some point very soon we should tell Mayor Brandt and Sergeant Montello, too. They may well have their own intentions."

"Not until we come up with a credible response here. And I mean it."

A few hours ago, Erskine had told worried families that APS was more scared of contamination than they realised, and that staying put wasn't an option. It wasn't just the truth. It had now become prophecy.

12

You want a fight? You pick on one of us, you'd better be ready to fight all of us.

Marc Gallagher, explaining the hazards of
starting a pub brawl with soldiers

DIRECTOR'S OFFICE, AINATIO PARK RESEARCH CENTRE: 2 HOURS AFTER THE WARNING FROM THE ALLIANCE OF ASIAN AND PACIFIC STATES

As soon as Erskine told Greg Kent to get the shuttles launch-ready, Solomon knew how long it would take the bush telegraph to transmit some kind of gossip around the building.

It would be a couple of hours at most. This was still a village, and after realising they'd been lied to so thoroughly for so long, the staff now seemed to be extra-vigilant, watching every unexplained activity.

Solomon wandered around the security cams, watching them speculate without any idea that APS had called to give Erskine an ultimatum. He paid special attention to the people who'd now become part of his circle of interest. Marc and Tev were taking their run around the perimeter earlier than usual, probably to talk privately, Lennie Fonseca was issuing extra weapons and ammunition to the detachment. Annis Kim was in her quarters.

Solomon only knew that because she still had her security pass on her: she hadn't been chipped. He didn't —

wouldn't — break his own rule on privacy by observing, but the security tracking had to show current locations, or else it was useless in an emergency. Kim had gone back to her small apartment in the accommodation block and was now pacing around the living room in what resembled a parallel search pattern, back and forth across the width of the room while progressing gradually towards one wall. It was possible that she'd dropped something and was searching for it on the carpet, but she'd now covered the room several times. She had plenty of places to walk for exercise unobserved in a huge, mostly deserted site. Solomon came down on the side of anxious pacing.

He tried to work out why she was agitated. Nobody knew about the approaching deadline yet, and Kim had shown no sign of being anything other than tough and single-minded to the point of obsession. Solomon couldn't imagine her being afraid to leave Earth. Although she was unhappy that she couldn't publicly vindicate Grandma Park's research, Solomon doubted that was bothering her. Something else was wrong.

He'd keep an eye on it, but his primary focus was the emergency meeting in Erskine's office. Alex looked wrung out and impatient. Trinder, always harder to read, seemed to be biding his time, speaking only when spoken to but looking more brooding than quiet. The department heads seemed to have been invited mainly to stop them wondering why they hadn't been included and becoming an irritant. The only one contributing something right now was Prinz, busy explaining the lack of evacuation options.

"We can get everyone clear of the area fast — and I mean everyone, including Kill Line and the camp — if we just put them on the shuttles and fly as far south as we can to a landing site near the coast," she said. "But that's as far as we'll get. We won't be able to sustain an evacuee population of nearly three thousand in the middle of nowhere for a few weeks, and if we abandon this facility, we leave behind the technical infrastructure to reach the orbitals, let alone continue repairs to the three remaining vessels."

"If we can prep all the shuttles in time," Kent said. "I think we'll only manage one."

"So we're still looking at the same three options." Erskine held up a finger to count off each point. "Delay the APS drop, find a way to tackle the contamination ourselves that'll persuade them they don't need to, or accept that we can only rescue eleven hundred, which is going to take two shuttle trips to *Elcano*."

Alex cut in. "We can't abandon Kill Line and the camp. We just can't. They won't stand a chance. Just because this salted ordnance is lower yield, it doesn't mean it won't cause massive explosive destruction on top of wiping out crops and livestock. Sixteen hundred is a lot of people to move overland, even if there was somewhere to go, and there isn't. We don't have enough vehicle capacity without repeated round trips. We'll also be hostage to wind direction with fallout. And on foot — forget it."

"Okay, so we tell APS we just happen to have our own nukes, and that we'll blitz the place ourselves," Mangel said.

"And APS says, 'Gee, thanks, we never knew you still had WMDs, so you're obviously a threat,' and obliterates us in an unfriendly way instead of with our blessing."

"Okay, how do we stall them, then?" Erskine asked.

"We can't, Director," Solomon said. "Not without introducing new facts into the equation."

"Let's go back to the numbers. We need to face this. We can't even evacuate all our own people. We have to talk about who doesn't get to go. My first duty is to our staff, so we're looking at reducing fifteen hundred names to eleven hundred."

"Fifteen hundred and *thirteen*," Solomon added quietly. "Including Dr Kim."

The silence, the held breaths, and the lowered eyes told Solomon that this was what Fonseca called a cold shower moment. Even Mangel blinked. He usually liked to play devil's advocate, with the emphasis on play. Solomon always felt these occasional crises were a game for him because his key work had finished long ago, and this was the time of logisticians and engineers. But he'd always say what others would only think.

"Women and children first isn't going to work," he said. "And I'm not saying that as a man with an ass to save."

"Go on."

"How many kids do we have?"

"Two hundred and forty-nine," Solomon said.

"And you can't separate kids from parents, not only because it'll warp them for life, but because someone has to look after them on Opis. Kids eat up human resources. There's no childcare in the neighbouring town because there *is* no neighbouring town. So how many two-parent families? Unless you're prepared to tell them one parent can't go and unleash weeping, more trauma, and rebellion, of course. How many single parents?"

Solomon could at least provide accurate numbers even if he couldn't see a solution yet. *But I will. I have to.* "One hundred and seventy-one with two parents, and seventy-eight with one, which is six hundred and sixty-nine people. That leaves four hundred and thirty-one cryo pods for the eight hundred and forty-four remaining. Roughly half."

"I'm glad to see you anticipated my direction. And roughly is still bad, even if it was one man left behind. Then there are the *adults* who have parents here. Three generations. We can't talk about acceptable losses. There's no humane cut-off line."

"Or you could decide *not* to take every child," Solomon said. "You could rank adults in terms of their utility to the mission, and then prioritise those who have children. The hard choices still remain further down the league table, but you've addressed practical need first. You're sacrificing our non-essential people along with the residents of Kill Line and the transit camp."

"And I thought I was Ainatio's resident bastard. But yes, Sol, every way we slice this cake is bad."

But I didn't mean for you to do it. I'm just showing you why you shouldn't. You have to find another way. I have to make you.

Alex looked agitated, as if he knew this would land in his lap. "Assuming we do this, we're going to be exporting some truly screwed-up survivors. We'll kick off with a guilt-ridden, bereaved, angry, accusing mob. How's that going to work when they collide with the Nomad folks? And what effect is that going to have on... I don't know, the Nomad national psyche, for want of a better term. Wars change societies. This is no different."

"Here and now, people." Erskine rapped the table. "We can't think more than two days ahead. But that's a good point. We're looking at what's going to feel like a postwar recovery."

"And we all know how quickly everyone forgives and forgets in those."

"So the alternative is that we all die nobly together?"

"People do. Some of ours might prefer to."

"Pick those best able to survive, and with the most practical skills," Mangel said. "And try to get a gender and age balance for breeding purposes. So no seniors, which removes a lot of our best minds. None of Mendoza's long-term patients, so we abandon sick and dying people, which kind of rips away our moral validity. I'm betting Major Trinder's people will volunteer to stay, because military folks have a different philosophy, but we'll need their pioneer skills and crisis handling on Opis."

Trinder still hadn't said anything. Solomon had started to see the man in a very different light these past few months. He'd had too little to do for years, but now he had plenty and he was hungry to do it. He also seemed clear about what he had to do in a way that probably wouldn't please Erskine. His silence seemed to be about not revealing his position, like the way he'd deployed the Lammergeiers to Kingston without asking her. He wasn't refusing an order. He'd just never allowed himself to hear one.

He spoke up at last. "I haven't asked them. They're still working out what forty-eight hours looks like in evacuation terms. We already know it's not enough time."

It was actually a neutral response carefully devoid of facts, but Mangel's brief nod suggested that he thought it was a decision. Solomon hoped he'd be proven right about Trinder. He'd been wrong about some people, but humans did seem to divide broadly into two types, those who would risk their lives and run towards trouble, and those who would run away.

"Remind me where we are on the logistics, Alex," Erskine said. Solomon noticed she hadn't said yes or no to this triage by reproductive status and utility. "How many people would be ready to leave at short notice? I don't mean running in the clothes they're wearing. I mean properly prepared."

Alex shrugged. "I've tried to encourage staff to keep a grab bag for emergencies, but I know most haven't bothered. Once we press the button on this, though, we just tell them that they've got this much luggage space, any excess will be dumped, and they have to be at the hangar at H-hour, no delays."

"How long to board?"

"Two shuttles, forty-five minutes each, tops."

"Eleven hundred people? No."

"Yes. We queue them in the right order and just march them in. There's no dicking around with cabin luggage and lockers and ooh-that's-my-seat and can-we-swap-with-you and fussing with coats. Get in, sit down, and shut up. Pee in your seat if you didn't remember to visit the bathroom first, because this is a one-way trip and the shuttle won't be used again. Just frigging do it."

"Alex, we won't have two shuttles ready in time," Kent said. "I'm cannibalising them as it is. You'll have to do it in one."

"Okay, then it's ninety minutes to board, and very crowded. Because if we take one and try to land again to pick up the rest of the list, we'll meet a crowd begging to be rescued, or a riot. Scientists are human. Survival kicks in. If you're really, absolutely going to leave people to die, then you go and you don't look back."

This was part of the Alex that Solomon liked. There was a time for sweet-talking people, and a time to bark orders and bang tables. But the part he'd hoped for, the Alex who refused to let good people die, was absent. Solomon wasn't sure if it had ever been there at all.

So this is my task. Nomad's my responsibility. I'm going to have to take control. But I'd rather they decided to do the right thing themselves, because forcing them could become very unpleasant.

Solomon noted how fast they'd gone into a detached, almost ruthless state. At least they weren't paralysed by panic. "Can we hear from others around the table?" he asked.

Prinz, Cullen, Mendoza, and Venner hadn't said anything on the topic of who should be saved. It was probably easier than having to put a case that favoured their areas of expertise, although Prinz, with her young son and necessary skills, would be guaranteed a place by the current reckoning. The plan that seemed to have formed in a mist above the table in the last half hour wasn't being challenged. And nobody had asked the obvious question: who in this meeting was going to demand that they went?

"I don't know which is worse," Venner said. "To die here myself, or to let others die and try to live with that for the rest of my life. So you do the decision-making, Director. But you're going to have to tell Mayor Brandt and the people at the camp, because it's just wrong not to at least give them time to try to get clear."

"When we actually reach a decision, I'll call them personally," Erskine said.

"That might not leave them enough time to act."

Mendoza stood up and slowly pushed back his chair. Solomon thought he was simply going to refill his coffee from the jug on the sideboard, but then he took his lab coat off the back of the chair and put it on.

"I'm going to stay with my patients," he said. "Whether that's in the infirmary or in *Elcano*. I'm not a saint, and I've done things I'm not proud of, but I don't have an excuse for abandoning them. Call me if any of you need medical assistance."

And he walked out.

Erskine didn't say a word, call him back, or even blink. She stared at the door, then turned back to the meeting. Solomon was never sure if it was more effective to stay in the fight or wash your hands of it in these situations, but he had no choice. The meeting went on.

"I'm a coward," Cullen said. "And I don't have an answer. Although knowing a bit more about the other guy's real position instead of where he's negotiating from would make a difference."

"She," Erskine said.

"It's not that colonel's decision. She's just the messenger." Cullen polished smudges off his screen with his cuff. "Imagine this a couple of hundred years ago. Some foreign government phones us and says they're really sorry, but they have to nuke us. A few minutes later, it would have been three thousand degrees and cloudy in Beijing or Tehran or wherever. Today, they can do what they like to us."

It was probably the most useful comment Solomon had heard so far. North America was less than the Third World to APS: so a colonel could make that decision, and the politicians would agree because of the potential risk. But Solomon didn't understand APS on a practical level any more than Cullen did. There'd been no contact for too long.

Annis Kim was an APS citizen, though. She spoke three Asian languages, and if the media reports hadn't exaggerated her importance, she was a respected academic and engineer. Perhaps she could give him an insight, just enough to change the parameters of the discussion. Perhaps she was even a bargaining chip. How important was she to her government? Solomon wouldn't know unless he asked them and watched her reaction — and theirs.

There was always something to trade.

"Are you going to give us your take on it, Solomon?" Erskine asked, sounding as if she already knew but needed to go through the motions. "Because we don't seem to have a practical way out of this."

One last try. "We'll lose too many essential people the Nomad project needs, Director, and while I appreciate we're driven by a deadline, this is the very last chance we'll have to strengthen the colony with the right mix of people. If we get it wrong, Nomad might die out, and a century of work will be wasted. And, put simply, it's immoral to abandon people here."

"It might be possible for them to survive, though."

"It might, but the chances are the damage to the facility will be so bad that any survivors will be marooned here. They won't be able to reach *Shackleton*, let alone finish prepping her. And you don't believe it's survivable, otherwise why would we be talking about shuttles instead of preparing shelters?"

Erskine didn't blink. "What else are we supposed to do? We plan for the worst. We can't trust to luck."

"Negotiate with APS. There may well be something we've missed. Dr Kim would be ideally placed to act as a go-between."

"No." Erskine shook her head. "That's out of the question."

"I don't think you're exploring all the possibilities. It would take no more than an hour to try using Dr Kim. We'd at least know if there was any latitude."

"What if they want her back? What if they want to extract her, and naturally we don't want to hand over someone who's now got an intimate knowledge of Nomad? She's not an asset. She's a liability."

"I believe her presence could buy us time."

"Nomad's confidentiality is paramount. It always has been."

"It's not more important than saving lives. It's not more important than making sure we have the right people for the colony, either."

"We have no choice."

"There's *always* a choice."

"We've discussed this enough. No."

"Very well, you'll have to excuse me. Unless there are any urgent issues that only I can deal with, I'm going to divert everything to seeing how much progress I can make with *Shackleton*."

It was as near to storming out as Solomon was ever likely to get, but all he wanted was a little time to do two things: to talk to Dr Kim, and to make sure that nobody was tempted to do anything premature with the ships.

Locking Ainatio out of the orbitals and all four vessels would probably focus Erskine's mind.

In fact, he'd do that before he spoke to Kim, and make sure that he generated a fake status to buy a little more time before anyone realised what he'd done. The engineering team were busy with the shuttles, and Prinz probably wouldn't brief anyone on the need for urgent evacuation for another hour or so.

Nomad was Solomon's reason for existence. He would do whatever was necessary to save the best of humanity, and not all of it was working for Ainatio.

We leave nobody behind.

If Chris Montello's people and the residents of Kill Line were left here, then Nomad had failed anyway.

* * *

ENGINEERING SECTION, AINATIO PARK RESEARCH CENTRE: 20 MINUTES LATER

"What's happening?" Jane Lurie stepped out of a doorway as Alex strode at a race-walking pace down the passage. "Vicky's not answering her comms, I can't get data from any of the ships, and Sol's not responding. Is this something to do with the shuttles?"

Alex bowed to the inevitable. There was no way of keeping this quiet, no good time to tell people, and no sensible information to give them.

Would I want to be told? Damn straight. Will they panic anyway if I don't tell them? Of course they will.

"Vicky's still in with Erskine," he said. "Sol was in the same meeting." *But he's not in there now... I think. What's he doing? It's not like he can't hear this.* "Tell me about the data problem first."

"I wanted to check where *Da Gama*'s welding bot was. Sol moved it to *Shackleton* to try to claw back some slippage."

Uh-oh. "You don't need to do anything with the ship maintenance bots, though, do you? Sol manages all that."

"That wasn't my question. I'm supposed to have an overview of what's happening, in case we need to manufacture parts down here. Now stop stalling, because I can tell this is serious."

"So you're locked out of the ships?"

"Ships *and* orbitals. I can see them on the system, but I can't access them."

"What else is down?" Alex added a disgruntled Sol to a rare system problem and concluded the worst. "Look, just show me."

He followed her down the passage into the control room, a title which always made it sound like a vaulted, darkened chamber where uniformed officers watched hologram schematics of vessels from a high gantry. But it was just a windowless office packed with unfathomable metal boxes. There were eight monitors, one for each of the original orbitals and ships, with menus for selecting sections, maintenance actions, and operations, including the endpoint of the FTL link in Orbital 1 that relayed the signal to Ainatio.

Alex studied the screens. "So we haven't lost the link."

"It's still live. I asked the network guys to check."

Great. Another department knew things weren't going to plan. "So you can't call up any information, take control of bots, or move the ships."

"Or the orbitals."

"Have you tried? Moving the ships, I mean."

"We really shouldn't touch that."

This was part of the problem with being reliant on so much automation, and on Solomon in particular. There were proper engineers like Annis Kim who could design parts and tell technicians which numbers to feed in, but AIs instructed bots how to do the hands-on work. "Humour me and see if you have control of anything. Vent some coolant or something."

"Let's just switch on a docking light."

"Whatever."

Lurie tapped the screen. "Definitely locked out."

"I'll find Solomon. He's probably gone walkabout in the quad."

"But he always responds."

"He's having a sulk." Sol would hear that. "Don't worry, he'll respond right away if there's a real problem. He wouldn't sit back and let anything crash just to get his own back. He's too responsible for that."

I hope.

"But he's never done that before."

"Well, today's been something of a hundred-year storm. Look, if this is a real fault, and we can't fix it, we can still get into *Elcano* the old-fashioned way, can't we?"

"Sure. We dock the shuttle and open the hatches manually from outside. It's not without risks, but it can be done."

"Then don't worry."

"You still haven't answered my question. You just stoked my anxiety."

"Okay, we do have an ongoing situation, and we may have to transfer to the ships sooner rather than later."

"*Elcano*'s ready, but *Shack* isn't."

"Yeah, I know. There'll be an announcement when we've got something definite to tell everyone. Please — I know this isn't easy, but the last thing we need right now is the rumour mill going into overdrive."

"It's the die-back. I knew it." Lurie shook her head. "Had to happen."

"Just make sure your bag's packed, regulation size. I hate to run, but I've got to find Sol."

"Alex, everyone here has a technical or scientific background. We know what happens with die-back. We also know we won't be the only ones to notice, because we remember how the news used to show agrisats tracking its spread before. You lied for years and you're lying again now. You just don't know how to stop lying."

Alex was at that rock-bottom point when everyone had worked out what was happening but he was still kidding himself that he had nothing concrete to say yet. This was where trust was irrevocably lost and everything spun out of control.

"Like I said, be ready to ship out at short notice. And for what it's worth, we're waiting for information."

That would be all around the company in about twenty minutes. Alex jogged back to his office the long way around via a service corridor to avoid running into anyone else. Damn, was Lurie even going to make the sort? If hundreds of people were going to be stranded here, then even being twenty-something, female, and an engineer didn't necessarily guarantee a seat. It wasn't as if a few extra passengers could stow away, either. If there wasn't a cryo pod waiting for you, you weren't going to make it even if you reached the ship.

"Sol, where the hell are you?"

The AI could definitely hear him. Any system could fail, but the chances of Solomon developing some disabling but highly specific fault that caused a system lockout and his own disappearance when he'd had a disagreement with Erskine were probably infinity to one. Alex lifted his shirt collar to whisper into the mike as he jogged down the passage.

"Come on, buddy, this isn't going to help. I'm going to have to tell Erskine you've locked her out, but let's talk before I do that."

There was no response. Alex took out his screen and checked everyone's trackers. Cullen and Prinz were still in Erskine's meeting. That meant Solomon was already out of the loop somehow or Erskine was talking about something else, because she wasn't going to discuss anything contentious if he could still hear.

Alex hoped she wasn't going to go full Boudicca and try to shut the AI down. Nobody could be sure of the full extent of Solomon's capabilities, or even his mission now, but Alex was prepared to bet that he was ready to defend himself.

Maybe we should spend the next two days loading supplies and bots onto all the shuttles, embark everyone, and head for that Air Force base. Maybe we could get enough systems working to wait it out and launch from there.

No, I'm wishing now. Impossible. Isn't going to happen.

He got back to his office, ignored the flashing messages on his monitor, and locked the door before anyone could notice that he was back.

"Sol, there's nobody around to hear us now. Talk to me. I can't stop you, so just explain where all this is heading."

"My apologies, Alex. Bednarz made me precisely for situations like this. I stick to the plan when humans don't."

"Hey, I don't want anyone else dying while we swan off to Shangri-La either. But we don't have a plan that evacuates everybody and also gets us to the ships. If we did, I'd have those shuttles out of here tomorrow morning."

"I won't release any of the vessels."

"Then what? Come on, what's your plan? Why did you go silent?"

"Blackmail. Hostage-taking, to be more accurate, except ships are inanimate objects. Either way, nobody leaves until we've tried every possibility. I'm letting Erskine stew for a while. And working on *Shackleton*."

"You're taking a terrible risk."

"You should have stood up to her, Alex."

"Yeah. Don't I know it. But I don't have a better idea. With one ship, what would *you* do?"

"Try harder. Try every option. I want to save people willing to sacrifice themselves for others, not those deciding who to sacrifice to save themselves."

Solomon really knew how to stick the knife in. But he was also being literal, and it had taken the first real moral crisis for Alex to see that. Solomon had started his moral training with Bednarz's ethics, which seemed classically altruistic. The guy had clearly thought that would be beyond most flesh and blood when the going got tough. Perhaps Bednarz didn't even trust himself to do the decent thing, because he certainly didn't trust his own corporation to stick to a hundred-year, multi-trillion-dollar project to give humans a second chance. He'd built his own enforcer, an AI who'd developed his own moral code.

"Sure." Alex threw up his hands. "I'll defy Erskine and get involved in some crazy shit with you. What else do I have to do at the moment? I'm only co-ordinating an evacuation."

"Come and talk to Annis Kim with me."

"What do you think she's got that we haven't?"

"An APS passport, for a start. And maybe some leverage. Erskine's still in her meeting, by the way."

"Anything I should know?"

"They're discussing how much latitude there is with cryo pods. Whether one can be modified to accommodate two small children."

"Well, she wouldn't be openly discussing how to shut you down, would she?"

"She hasn't found out she'll want to yet."

"I suspect she has. Okay, let's see Kim. Make it snappy."

Annis Kim was still in her quarters. She seemed surprised to see Alex when she opened the door.

"This is urgent and highly irregular," Alex said. He pointed up at the grille of the ubiquitous public address system, even though Sol was connecting via his collar comms. "Sol's with me. We need some help with diplomacy."

"You've come to the wrong place, but I'll do my best."

That was the trouble with always using jokes as a disarming device. When things were deadly serious, people expected a punchline from him.

"I'm not Funny Alex today," he said. "We've got a disaster on our hands. Your government — well, the Asia Pacific Defence Union — spotted the new die-back spreading on their agrisat feed. They've given us two days to evacuate before they drop nukes again."

"Oh, God."

"You know we can't move everyone in that time. Even if we can get people into *Elcano*, *Shackleton*'s not ready. Sixteen hundred are going to die — "

"Sixteen hundred and four," Solomon said.

"Okay, sixteen hundred and four. Even if they manage to survive, they won't last long living rough."

"Alex, you said diplomacy." Kim was now blinking a lot, but still very calm. "What do you want me to do?"

"Sol thought you'd have more of an insight into APS's human dynamics. Is there anything that's likely to get them to postpone or reconsider? Erskine's talking direct to an APDU officer. Colonel Su-Jin."

"Knowing there was an APS citizen here wouldn't stop them launching nukes, if that's what you're thinking."

"But is this colonel making the nuke call on her own? Do politicians have to sign it off, even now we don't exist as a country, or what? Do you know anyone in a government department, some politician, *anybody* you could call in a favour from?"

"Has Erskine tried to negotiate?"

"Yeah, she's explained the situation and asked them to let us burn off affected vegetation ourselves, but they don't seem to think that's going to be enough."

"But has she explained the *real* situation?"

Solomon cut in. "No, she hasn't told them about Opis or any of the related technology. I don't know if they realise *Elcano*'s operational. We have to assume they know we have three more ships and orbital docks, but as they're in disposal orbits, they've probably discounted them. Without *Shackleton*, we should as well. Because once APS drop their payload, we'll probably lose too much infrastructure to launch those ships anyway. Even if anyone survives, they won't get out."

"You told Erskine everyone would die," Alex said.

"I know. She's lying to herself about possible survivors to make herself feel better. I'm telling myself everyone will die so that we don't give up trying to change the situation. So how do we do it?"

"Annis, would they grant asylum on humanitarian grounds?" Alex asked.

"What's in it for them, other than the risk of disease?"

"You know perfectly well," Solomon said. "Are you willing to talk to APS if we connect you?"

"Is Erskine going to agree to that?"

"I'll suggest it, and if she refuses, I'll cut her out of the loop. Are you in?"

"In for what?"

"Ask them what they'd want in exchange for putting the burn-off on hold until we can move people out. It's only a few months, not years. You can hint that we have some technology that they'd be very keen to acquire."

"You'll have to spell that out for me."

"I think you understand very well. No negotiator reveals their hand when opening. Both sides start at their extreme positions and move towards the middle ground. Unless they're fools, and I certainly don't think you're a fool."

"Whoa, whoa, whoa!" The penny finally dropped. Alex had to stop him. "What the hell are you doing, Sol? What's the point of keeping Nomad secret for all these frigging years if you're just going to tell APS and trade our tech? You know it's a threat to the project."

"And this is a bigger one."

Alex would now have to choose his words carefully. Solomon wasn't some annoying bystander offering helpful suggestions. He controlled the project. He'd already locked down the ships. Alex tried to remember whether Sol had direct control over the shuttles, too, but it was just the ground side of the nav systems, he was sure of that.

Now he realised that there weren't just two sides in this, Ainatio and APS. There were three. Solomon wasn't on the side of the company *or* the Asia-Pacific nations. He had a mission, the Nomad project team were deviating from it, and he was going to intervene.

"I understand that you want to save as many lives as possible, Sol," Alex said. "But this isn't the way to do it."

"Trust me, or step aside."

"Sol, not so long ago, you were holding the line with me over keeping *Cabot* in radio silence. We had to tell Ingram that her crew had to stay officially dead. Don't underestimate the damage that's done."

"And you don't put that right by letting more people die. People who absolutely deserve to live. Who *must* live." Solomon didn't say whether that included Alex. Alex felt he'd failed a test. "Will you do it, Dr Kim? I'll direct you on what to say and when. And I can translate anything, so I'm happy to monitor you in whatever language you choose."

That sounded like a warning that he'd pull the plug the moment she went off-script, but Kim didn't seem offended.

"Okay, I'll give it a go. Tell them that Dr Annis Kim of Seoul National University wants to talk to... let's see, the APS science and technology commissioner. Tim Pham. Don't forget to tell them I'm actually here, too. Y'know, in the blast zone. And that I'm no bloody use to them dead."

Kim was instantly more relaxed. Alex could see the change. Maybe she'd calculated that her chances of making the final passenger list had just improved. Nobody wanted to die, especially people with unfulfilled pledges to dead ancestors.

"Thank you, Dr Kim," Solomon said. "The offer of FTL would probably give them a different view of the situation here right away, but let's see what's required to change their plan. Alex will put the idea to the Director."

"Now I know why you were such an expensive piece of kit," Kim said, smiling. It wasn't her shark smile. It was real. That rang alarm bells with Alex. "I'll be waiting."

Alex felt invisible and surplus to requirements. He could guess how Erskine would react. She'd say no, Solomon would bypass all the comms, and Kim would be negotiating with Beijing or Seoul while all hell broke loose in the management suite. It was nearly eight in the evening, the early hours of the morning in the Asian capitals. Colonel Su-Jin might be unhappy to be woken. It was hard to tell. The call might even piss off APS and make them bring the deadline forward. He'd only find out by doing it.

"If you'll excuse me, Dr Kim, I need to talk to Alex and find out just how angry he is with me," Solomon said. "Can

I suggest you stay out of the way in case Erskine works out what I'm planning?"

"Any suggestions, seeing as this place is all cameras?"

"The environment control access passages. I'll send a plan to your screen. I can always locate you in there, if only by body heat."

"Gotcha."

Alex backed out of the room and checked his screen for the nearest area free of tracker icons. He slipped into a small disused office and sat on one of the desks. The door clicked as Solomon locked it.

"What the fuck, Sol? Seriously, what the actual fuck?"

"I know. High stakes."

"Oh, you think? You're killing Nomad stone dead, and that won't save your buddies in the camp. Or Kill Line."

"No, Erskine's killing the project. Either everyone left behind will be dead, or some will survive but they'll be marooned because they can't access a ship. We need to protect a comms uplink to Orbital One and get the other shuttles underground."

"We worked all this out. *It's why the project was top secret.* You're the smartest thing on the planet, and you've dismissed all that?"

"Not entirely."

"Sol, Sol — they'll never let us leave for Opis. They'll take over the whole project. We'll be stuck here anyway. The boffins will probably be shipped out to work on it, but they won't have any use for the people in Kill Line or the transit camp. It'll all be for nothing. All of it."

"They'll want the FTL."

"You just don't get it. Maybe Erskine was right and you really are malfunctioning."

"Spare me the B-movie theories."

"We can't enforce this deal, Sol."

"I've got control of nuclear armaments if they want to lose a space station."

"Yes, but we've only got a few small ones, and once we've kicked off a world war, it'll be over in sixty seconds. We can't stop a military machine the size of APDU."

"Alex, if they try to seize the ships, they'll inherit a chunk of me as well. And when I get into someone's systems, they *will* regret it."

"How?"

"Would you want an AI with a grudge to get into your power stations? Your air traffic control? Your hospitals? Your driverless transport network? You get the idea."

It was a side of Solomon that Alex now had no trouble believing was there. He'd been created to defend, after all. He had to be capable of attack as well. He was a one-man terror cell.

"But that's a response," Alex said. "Payback, not a deterrent. You need a deterrent they can see *before* they do something dumb."

"All this assumes they're monsters. I don't believe they are. They're like us, trying to hang on to what they have, and terrified of die-back and epidemics, with good reason. They're also pragmatists. They'll see the advantages in co-operation, because they almost always do. They didn't even bomb us in the generally understood sense of warfare, did they? *Our government requested help.* But if I see signs that I'm wrong, they'll have to handshake with me to get into the ships, and their first attempt will be very dissuasive. They have no idea that I exist or what I can do."

"You sure do find it easy to override your moral programming."

"This *is* my moral programming. Morality isn't inaction. Morality is knowing what you believe is right and being prepared to fight for it."

"Yeah. Fine. What can I say?"

"How about good luck, Sol, I'm right behind you?"

"I think you're going to get us all barbecued."

"People will die, one way or the other, if you don't help me."

"What if they can neutralise you? We don't know their capabilities."

It would have been nice to see a physical manifestation of Solomon now, even if it was only the clunky quadrubot. Alex just wanted to know if the AI would stand with his arms folded, or hands defiantly on hips, or just shrug. It was impossible to tell from the tone of his voice. It hardly varied.

"Forget what APS might do with Nomad and let's worry about stopping the bombing first," Solomon said. "Focus on Erskine. And we need to warn Chris and Doug."

"But you're going to have to release *Elcano* eventually, yeah? You're not going to risk everyone's life."

"I'm not bluffing, Alex."

"No. You wouldn't do it."

"You've read me wrong every time so far. My mission is to select the right people. If I have to remove Ainatio staff to make room for them, I will."

Solomon sounded perfectly serious. Alex really did think he knew him like a human being, but now he realised that in the end, he didn't. He couldn't. Sol wasn't human, and Bednarz had created him to make the hardest calls.

"I can't think how you'd remove them," Alex said.

"I still have control of the building. I can confine people. I can even move the ship away from the orbital."

"But you won't." Alex wasn't sure now. He really wasn't. "And you'd still have to leave nearly two thousand people behind either way."

"True," Solomon said. "And I would, but I'd much rather we all survived, which I believe we can do with Dr Kim acting as intermediary."

Alex tried to listen to his gut, but it was just screaming that they were all going to die and that he should either ignore this crazy AI or run like hell. As usual, though, his gut had no suggestions on how to do either.

"You never asked, by the way," Solomon said.

"Asked what?"

"Dr Kim. Why I'm betting the proverbial farm on her."

"I give up. Why?"

"Because now I believe she really is a spy, Alex. Look at her. She's here for the FTL. It's why she wanted access to her cloud, to let her handlers know she'd made it here and how far she'd progressed. I'm banking on the politician she named being the one who's been waiting for her to report in. I doubt that Erskine's in any mood to listen to me any more, but you still have her ear."

"I'll have her boot up my ass, more like."

"She relies on you. Please, Alex, do this for me. I do *not* want to make a fight of it. Things could get out of control too easily."

"Okay, I'll put it to Erskine. But then it's up to her. I don't have any way to force her hand." Alex knew what he was going to say next and he was already ashamed of himself, but he couldn't hand over Nomad's secrets after all that had happened. Either he believed what he'd said to Ingram about the risk of discovery, or he didn't. "And then you're on your own, buddy."

"I feared I might be," Solomon said.

Alex told himself that being despised by glorified software was no big deal, but he knew he was no longer on Solomon's list of the best of humanity. It was a painful fall from grace.

* * *

DIRECTOR'S SUITE:
10 MINUTES AFTER THE MEETING

"Director, we're locked out of *Elcano*."

Vicky Prinz stood in Erskine's office doorway, arms folded as if she wasn't leaving until Erskine did something about it.

So Solomon wanted to play that game, did he? Fine. Erskine was ready. She feigned ignorance. "Have you asked Solomon?"

"No response from him. We're locked out of all of the ships and orbitals, in fact. We can't do anything, not even run pre-launch checks."

"I assume we've ruled out a fault that would affect his ability to answer."

"Yes. Everything's fine as far as I can see."

"Okay." Erskine made a show of thinking it over and lowered her voice just enough to make it look instinctively diplomatic rather than an inexplicable belief that Solomon couldn't hear her. "I realise this is a very difficult time, but it's probably best to give him a little space."

"He's not a teenage girl, Director."

"No, but he's a moral AI, and he's never been asked to do something immoral before. We're killing people, Vicky. Fast or slow, it's still killing them. If I handed you a gun now and told you to go shoot everyone in your department, how would you feel? That's effectively what I've asked Solomon to do. He's going to take a while to come to terms with it."

Prinz leaned against the door frame. That was unusually casual. Erskine took it as a sign that she'd been convincingly sympathetic.

The hell I am.

"We don't have *a while*," Prinz said. "And I wouldn't shoot them."

"How about to save your son?"

"That's not fair."

"That's what we're asking of people, though. And Solomon. Don't worry, he's around. If everything else is fine, he's probably just thinking, and if we really need him, then he'll respond. And do we need him right now?"

"I'm hacked off that I don't have access, yes."

"But is it critical?"

"No. He's got *Elcano* ready for launch. I suppose we can wait. I won't start taking an axe to his server until nearer the time."

"He knows that, you see," Erskine said.

"It still bothers me. If he wants to make a gesture, it's an odd one. Is he competent? And yes, I do know he can hear me. I'm just really pissed at him. I won't count on him again."

"Oh, it'll pass."

No, it won't. He's planned this. It's a shot across my bows.

Well, I've got a plan as well, Sol, my friend. I'm going to make you think that I plan to trap you in the facility before blowing it up. And if Marc and Tev haven't warned you, then I'm going to have to draw you a picture. Because then you'll run to the one safe place you think you've got. Your bot frame.

And then, with a bit of help, I can lock you out completely.

"He won't let us down." Erskine radiated convincing but fake patience. "If he didn't care about humans, he'd have abandoned us by now, taken all the bots, and set up a machine colony."

"Don't give him ideas." Prinz paused for a little too long. She didn't seem to want to leave. "So you're still going, Director."

"I thought I would, but I'm not sure now." It was out of Erskine's mouth before she knew it. She'd assumed she would, but then started to wonder if she'd be going out of duty or cowardice. "Either Alex or I have to."

"Responsible adult."

Erskine held up a piece of paper. "I'm waiting until tomorrow to respond to APS, because it won't make any difference to them, so I'm spending this evening drawing up a list of eleven hundred names. The responsibility is mine. Nobody else's. If I'm the only one who's really to blame, it might stop recriminations in the aftermath."

"It's going to be ugly, whatever you do."

"Well, I'm going to take this outside, ignore the mosquitoes, and have a drink. I'll have to announce the list by lunchtime tomorrow."

The garden was perfect cover for having a meeting where Solomon couldn't hear her, but Prinz seemed to take the comment as a hint to get lost and stepped back from the doorway.

"People have already put two and two together, Director," she said. "I wouldn't go through the main corridors if I were you."

Erskine checked the trackers on her screen. There were lots of large clusters. "What can I tell people, though? I have nothing concrete yet. Damned if I do, damned if I don't."

Prinz gave her a non-committal, humourless smile with compressed lips and left. Now Erskine could get on with it. She turned her chair around, opened the link to Opis, and watched the base in the twilight for a few minutes. There were lights in the windows, and the flags had been lowered and taken down. She could see the halyards flapping against the poles in the breeze. Maybe all this would look different in the years to come, with enough distance between the glittering future and the dirty past that had been needed to guarantee it.

"Solomon," she said. "I know you can hear me. Let's talk. I find it hard to believe that you'd lock the ships at this stage of an emergency. But if you have, tell me why. We want the same outcome. We should be working together."

There was no response. She knew this was about Kim. It wasn't just a hissy fit, and she didn't know if Bednarz had given him instructions to resort to force if he didn't get what he wanted. With Solomon's capabilities and his almost universal access, she couldn't ignore the potential threat. She could only judge by what he *hadn't* done so far while he still had access. He hadn't destroyed anything or harmed anyone. But she didn't dare rely on that.

Right, you little bastard. Showtime.

"Phil?" Erskine held her finger on the comms icon on the desk. "Phil, I'm going to take the list into the courtyard garden. Can you ask Will Cullen, Greg Kent, Jesse Beck, and Alex to join me, please? And your good self. With whatever decent alcohol we have to hand."

"Certainly, Director."

The big courtyard garden that separated the horticultural wing from the administration block was an easy way to avoid unwanted company, but it was also credibly private for an apparent discussion of human fates. Erskine took her papers, immune from prying eyes on the network, and walked out into a warm, sunny evening. She really regretted catching the scent of roses. Now they'd be linked inextricably in her memory to harrowing times.

The rose bushes shielded the long picnic table from the security camera's direct line of sight. If everyone arranged themselves carefully with their backs to the camera, Solomon wouldn't get a chance to monitor what was said. He'd realise that meant they were plotting against him, but concealing their plans would give a leak from the meeting more credence. And Erskine was sure that Alex would leak. He was already on Solomon's side.

After a couple of minutes, Berman appeared with a tray, a bottle, and a selection of unmatched glasses.

"Your health, Phil," Erskine said, pouring him a Madeira. It was an odd choice, but it looked like he'd raided the cellar for the oldest bottles. "It's okay, you're on the list."

"I'd rather not be, thank you, Director. But I appreciate the kindness."

"Oh. *Oh.*" She hadn't seen that coming. It actually hurt. "I can't force you, Phil, but this is awfully final."

"I'm not being noble. I just don't want to leave Earth, even at its worst. And then there's Ruth."

Erskine didn't realise he was seeing anyone. She couldn't even put a face to the name. *Ruth? Ruth in Buildings Maintenance? Ruth in Records?* Her own ignorance appalled her. But Berman had never been the kind to chat about life outside the office.

"If she's not on the list, she can be."

"Even if she is, she wants to stay as well."

"Phil... "

"It's okay. We can take a vehicle if there's one available and drive south with any rejects who want to go."

That stung. She wasn't sure if it was intended to. But she knew that he'd do his job right up to the last minute, and that made it worse. The unspoken disappointment of a good man was painful.

She was relieved that Cullen and Kent showed up just then and cut the conversation short. Erskine arranged them as needed with their backs to the camera. Beck, the facilities manager, arrived a few moments later, looking exhausted. He'd already had the premature shutdown plans land in his lap when the die-back was confirmed, and now he had two days to make it happen. Erskine doubted anyone would be left to worry about what happened to the site, but Beck had his rules, and Erskine suspected he was also trying to plan for survivors.

"No Alex?" Cullen asked.

"He's on his way."

"And Solomon's gone AWOL."

"Worse," Erskine said. "He's locked us out of the ships and orbitals. It's blackmail. He still wants Kim to negotiate a delay so he can finish prepping *Shackleton*. We can't take that risk, so I said no. Again."

"I wonder if it's time to admit we've had a good run and find out if it's as contentious for APS as we always thought."

"And if we're right, and they move in and take over?"

"We've still saved a lot of people."

"On die-back-contaminated land, which APS may very well still regard as too much of a risk not to destroy."

Cullen shrugged. "I never said it was an easy choice."

"I don't see how we can have a conversation with them without the risk of revealing Nomad in some way, and I don't know how far Solomon will go to get what he wants. So we're here to work out how we can bypass him." There. She'd said it, if they hadn't already reached the conclusion for themselves. She knew she had no control over the message that would trickle down to Solomon, but there was no easy way to lure an AI like him into a trap. "As soon as Alex shows up, we can get on with it, although I don't really know how committed he is to all this." She passed her paper to Cullen. "Anyway, here's my passenger list. Whatever names we end up with, the responsibility is mine alone. And I've made sure that no department's been left out. It's as near a cross-section as we're going to get."

Erskine could tell they were all uncomfortable as they read down the columns. None of them wanted to be seen to look for their own name, but Greg Kent was both a father and an essential engineer, and Cullen was her best bet for keeping IT together after Solomon was contained. Beck had a key role as well, on any planet. She hoped they weren't going to refuse places like Phil Berman had.

Alex finally appeared, looking breathless. Erskine poured him a drink and sat him down in the required position. She could only hope her mistrust was well placed.

"Solomon's probably expecting an intervention from us, and I don't want him to misunderstand anything we might say," she said, settling next to him and taking care to keep her gaze straight ahead. "Face forward at all times. No profiles to lip-read, please."

"There's something I need to tell you first, Director," Alex said. "Annis Kim's now willing to talk to APS and appeal to some senior politician she knows."

He was doing Solomon's bidding. Erskine had called it. "I already said we wouldn't do that. Can't I even trust *you* now?"

"I think Solomon's got a point, and now — well, there are other factors involved. And sixteen hundred lives have got to be worth pulling out all the stops."

"Is this about Kim calling in some family favour? Because I don't think that would cut it if APS is worried enough about die-back to bomb us."

"No, Sol thinks Kim really is a spy after all."

"Oh. Now he tells us. I wish he'd just talk to me."

"I was present for the discussion."

"I'm sure you were."

"Yeah, well, thinking over what she said, I think Sol's right. She said she'd ask for the APS sci-tech commissioner. Not the APS president's office, or the Australian government, but the APS sci-tech guy. It's very specific. All that fits her needing to report in on something. She's been a royal pain in the ass about not getting the FTL data, and I think Sol tested her by suggesting we might do a deal on information in exchange for not bombing the shit out of us. Not for a few months, at least."

"I can't believe you did that. Either of you."

"Needs must, Director."

"Don't insult my intelligence." It was impossible not to be genuinely angry with Alex even if he'd slipped conveniently into the role she wanted him to play. "You both constantly undermine me. What the hell do you think you're doing?"

"This situation's changing minute by minute. Like it or not, staff are seeing the shuttle activity and the die-back situation, and they know something brown and semi-solid's hit the fan. It's not a happy ship. We need to be out there talking to them."

"Don't try to divert me. You want to horse-trade with APS. The only things they'd want from us are Nomad and FTL."

"Exactly that. You know it."

"No."

"Director — "

"No. Absolutely not. We've done some appalling things to keep this under wraps because we *had* to, and we will *not* hand it over now."

"Sol's sure that a call from her will get their attention, and that they'll want our tech badly enough to give us time to fix *Shackleton*."

That confirmed her as an asset to be denied: no Kim, no discussion. "He needs to have Kim do this personally, then."

"We've got to show we're holding one of their people who's got information. Otherwise it looks like stalling. Obviously."

That settled it. Erskine checked her screen. Kim's tracker showed she was still in her apartment, or at least her ID card was. Solomon would probably have hidden her by now. But she'd be confined to the building — nowhere to go, no other route to communicate with her handler — and that meant she could be found.

Especially when we shut down the power.

Cullen cut in. "Alex, we could easily end up giving everything away and saving nobody. They're not going to let us consolidate a military base — because that's what it is — on a habitable, resource-rich planet that we didn't mention to them."

Erskine couldn't tell if Cullen had spotted what she was doing and was playing along, or if he was just returning to his original argument. "First things first," she said. "I'm concerned that Solomon might do something irresponsible. I want to shut down all power in the facility until I'm sure this isn't going to get out of control."

Beck looked up. "When you say all..."

"I mean all."

"It won't reset the lockout on the ships, Director."

"I know."

"Emergency backup generators too?"

Erskine willed Alex to make a careful mental note of the details to report back to Solomon. "Not if they're air-gapped and he can't hide in their control system."

"It's okay, they're completely separate," Beck said. "Basic security design. But why would Sol do anything that would threaten lives? The last thing he wants is to kill people. That's why we're in this mess."

"If he's operating normally, I'd agree. But if we really think he'd never do it, why don't we have the confidence to ignore the lockout on the ships and wait until he blinks at the last minute?"

Beck nodded reluctantly. So did Cullen.

"In case he doesn't," Cullen said. "In case we're wrong."

"Exactly. Now we're all on the same page."

"As soon as we start powering down, though, he'll see it and retreat elsewhere. And he's way, way faster than we are."

Alex was getting agitated. Erskine could see his hands without turning her head. They were resting on the picnic table as he fiddled with his stylus, turning it end over end.

"Okay, Alex," she said quietly. "Spit it out."

"If you power down, it'll cut off comms to Nomad as well. It might even collapse the wormhole. We've never shut it down before. How long are you planning?"

"That's up to Solomon." Erskine lobbed in a suggestion to test what Alex might know. "But I don't want him transferring to Opis and locking us out from that end."

"He wouldn't do that."

"Like he wouldn't jeopardise a launch by locking down the ship? We're relying heavily on his affection for humans, but that's never been tested in a real crisis until now. He has to choose one group or another. He can't save both."

Stopping Solomon's network-hopping excursions to Opis and *Elcano* was more than a way to force him into a bot. If he still had access to the ship in transit, and she was wrong about his lofty morals, she couldn't rely on his goodwill while she was helpless in cryo. If he couldn't jump to Opis, then he might insert himself in *Elcano*, and she might land and find a bitter, angry AI with a fully-fermented, forty-five-year grudge. Neither option was encouraging.

If I were him, I'd kill me in my sleep.

Cutting off his access to *Elcano* might mean severing his link with all the ships, though. Where did that leave the comforting lie she'd told herself about the possibility of survivors escaping in *Shackleton*?

Erskine moved on. The priority was making Solomon believe his own best chance of survival was transferring into a standalone bot.

"If we try to shut him down, he'll retreat," Beck said. "But we've got to power up again at some point, and we're back to square one with an obstructive AI in a fraction of a second."

"Then we might have to take more drastic measures." Erskine prepared for the big reveal. "Perhaps we have to destroy the network. The shuttle can rely on its own dumb AI."

Go on, Alex. Go back and tell your little friend I'm such a bitch that I'll burn the place down to stop him.

But I don't think I'll need to. I just need enough time to distract him while I play my own card.

"So you'd rather throw the best part of two thousand innocent people under the bus and trash a big component of Nomad just because you won't back down on doing a deal with APS." Alex sat shaking his head and tapping the end of the stylus on the table, harder and harder. "Solomon honestly thought you were rational. Well, he's a machine. What does he know? But he's got more of a soul than you'll ever have. You're a piece of work, you know that?"

Erskine took that as Solomon's parting shot relayed via Alex. The AI could have destroyed *Elcano* by now, and even the shuttle if it was connected to the network. But he'd held back. He needed to save everybody. *That* was his weakness. She'd use it.

She wanted to save everybody too, but the staff were hers, her people, and Kill Line were still strangers. *See what a sensible idea it was to keep ourselves separate?* The transit camp — well, she had nothing against them, and they sounded like decent people, but again, they were strangers. Solomon seemed to have decided that they were somehow a better choice. There was no point in debating with him. They just didn't see the world the same way.

"If I can't save everyone, Alex, I have to save some," she said. "Not just now, but in the future, when APS might take an even less sunny view of all this."

Alex swivelled around and faced her, finger stabbing the air in accusation. "How do you think we're going to look when they write Nomad's history? Mankind's first manned extrasolar mission, the first extrasolar colony, and it cost the lives of farmers and veterans who just weren't important enough to give a shit about. But never mind, it's okay, we saved all the folks with PhDs. Just like QuiCo."

"Don't you try that class war garbage on me," Erskine said. Everyone else at the table stared straight ahead, unable to escape the fight. "I was the one who wanted the farmers to be part of this. We needed them. But there's no room and we're out of time. We have one shot at this. It's too late for Kim's intervention anyway."

"You haven't even tried. And you never wanted the transit camp people."

"It's tragic after all they went through, I agree. But we already have a high ratio of men to women."

"Oh, I forgot, men are expendable. Right. Thanks for reminding me."

"It's Biology One-Oh-One. Survival."

"I noticed."

"If you had a choice between saving your family and saving someone else's, even if they were deserving people, you'd save your own in a heartbeat. Don't tell me you wouldn't. And Ainatio is my family."

"Director, I don't even know what this is about any more. But there's a chance we can take, and the situation's desperate enough to try, but you won't."

"You *know* why. You know exactly why."

"It's okay, we'll list the excuses in the official history."

"Alex, history isn't going to judge us, because it *won't be here*. Perhaps mankind will be extinct in ten years, or a thousand, or when the sun engulfs Earth, but one day *it all ends*. And before everyone's diaries turn to charcoal, someone will have written, 'Why didn't we take our best chance to get out? Why did we wait and sacrifice Western civilisation because we felt too guilty to save just part of it?' *That's* why I'm doing this. It's what humans do. We keep moving on."

Alex stood up to go. "You can move on without me, then. Congratulations. You're now the captain of *Elcano*. My cryo pod can go to Jane Lurie in Engineering. She'll be fine. Competent female of breeding age. Just what you need."

Alex looked like he didn't know what the hell he was going to do in the next breath, and for a second Erskine thought he'd really lose it and start breaking things. But he half-shrugged, half-threw his hands up, and stomped away.

She contemplated the bottom of her glass, examining her real reason for holding out, and hoped that she wasn't doubling down on a big mistake just to feel that her life hadn't been squandered on someone else's dream. She couldn't tell. But she knew that she had two days to get eleven hundred people into a ship and never look back at the ones who hadn't made the cut.

"Wow," Greg Kent said. "I suppose it's getting to all of us."

Erskine went on without missing a beat. "Okay, that's Alex out of the loop. He might tell Solomon, so we've got to get moving. Here's the plan. Keep Solomon out of the network, either temporarily or permanently, while we embark people and launch the shuttle. Stop him jumping to Nomad. And stop Kim talking to APS. *Ever.*"

"That sounds like a violent solution."

Which I should have opted for, if I'd had the guts or the ability. "No, I think we can achieve that by taking her with us, powering down to force Solomon into a bot frame, which is where he feels safest, and severing both the external network link on the radio mast and the orbital FTL relay."

Cullen rested his chin on his hand. "You do mean collapsing the wormhole, then."

"Do we have to?"

"Well, just disabling the relay means it can be repaired if anyone survives. Or if and when APS decides to take a closer look."

Erskine nodded. "Destroy it all, then."

"It's not my department, Director, but I don't think we'll be able to restore the wormhole from *Elcano* or the orbital."

"But we keep forgetting the mission was designed without FTL. It won't stop *Elcano* reaching Opis, and the base is built."

"And Kim?" Kent asked. "She won't come voluntarily."

Erskine could have done with some help from Marc and Tev right then. They'd had experience of planning operations like this. "First, we find her. Solomon's going to try to stop us, but once he's shut out of the building's systems, we can detain her, by force if need be."

"If he bolts into one of the bots like you think he will, then he'll still have a wireless link to the network," Cullen said.

"So we physically destroy the external comms mast as well. That's what he uses, isn't it? We just hold him off while we load and launch."

"And afterwards? Even if everyone's dead, there'll be recoverable data for APS to use."

"We make sure that's destroyed, or on the shuttle with us."

Erskine turned over the list of names and started drawing a flow chart of actions on the back of the last sheet. She did it unthinkingly, then saw how this document would look if displayed in a museum: the cold calculation of how best to abandon more than four hundred people to their deaths, all of them named on the reverse. It was a testament to callous pragmatism.

Beck shuffled along the bench to look at what she was sketching out. "If we shut down by floors, we drive Solomon down to the basement bot garage. Just to make sure. Even if he realises what we're doing, he won't have a choice."

"It's going to need careful timing," Kent said. "And what happens if he decides to smash his way through the building?"

"That's what we have Trinder's people for," Erskine said. "To prevent access and neutralise threats."

Trinder's detachment didn't have Marc's or Tev's skills, but they took the job seriously, and unlike Alex, they wouldn't let her down. Trinder would stand by her and carry out her orders. So where was Dr Kim? Erskine checked her screen. The tracker hadn't moved. It wasn't fooling anyone.

"Gentlemen, let's do this while we still can," Erskine said. "I want to be ready to power down everything manually, except the reactor. But first we need to find Kim."

13

Why do you think we have equal numbers of vets and civilians here? Because we paired every civvy with one of us to make sure they survived, even if they needed carrying on our backs. Nobody left behind because they couldn't keep up. Nobody picked off because they were stragglers. Nobody sacrificing themselves because they were slowing us down. And we did it. Because we don't leave anyone behind. I still had to make hard choices, but everyone who came with us knew they wouldn't be abandoned.

Chris Montello, explaining his last mission to
Doug Brandt

STAFF RESTAURANT, AINATIO PARK RESEARCH CENTRE: 6 HOURS AFTER APS WARNING OF INTENT TO DEPLOY PLANT PATHOGEN COUNTERMEASURES

Small groups had been gathering for an hour in the places where staff normally stopped for a chat during the day, quiet and orderly but definitely anxious. Trinder couldn't wait any longer.

What they needed was someone like Erskine or Alex to stand out front and tell them something, preferably the truth. Trinder decided to walk the floors and show his face instead. But he could tell people nothing that wouldn't panic them, and he could give them no solutions. They needed facts, followed by clear instructions. He had too little information himself to work out what those instructions should be, and he didn't know if people would find his intervention reassuring or worrying.

But he couldn't sit on his ass and do nothing. He kept walking.

When he reached the staff restaurant, the crowd in there had grown again. He found Tev at the centre of it, giving a talk to a surprisingly attentive audience, and explaining how he'd learned survival techniques in the army. It was packaged as a funny story about setting up his tent in the wrong place and being woken by a stream of water running downhill through it during the night, making him think he'd peed himself until he realised what was happening. That led painlessly into a quick lesson about where to pitch a tent, accompanied by diagrams drawn on the menu board next to the servery. Tev always looked cheerful and sounded confident. In uncertain times, men like that were sorely needed. Even if none of the lesson served any purpose, he was keeping people occupied and radiating reassurance.

Trinder was going to miss him.

Tev held up his camouflage shelter sheet. "We call this a basha," he said. "Think of it as a weaponised furoshiki in you-can't-see-me colours. Tent... casevac stretcher... whatever."

He showed them how to make the sheet into a tent with a length of rope, and then turn it into a makeshift stretcher. He even got them laughing when their "casualty" slid out of it and ended up in a heap on the floor. While they were distracted tying knots, Trinder beckoned him over.

"You need to leave, buddy," Trinder said quietly. "Go. Or at least get clear of the area."

"We're guessing what the problem is. How about telling me?"

"APS spotted the die-back on sat imaging. As of four hours ago, they've given us two days to evacuate before they nuke us again."

"Bloody hell. You've got to tell people."

"Erskine's prepping to ship out as many as *Elcano* can take. So Sol's locked down the ships to stop her abandoning the rest, and now he's gone AWOL."

Tev looked down at the floor. "Well, bugger. Eleven hundred from fifteen hundred equals four hundred angry, scared people."

"Sixteen hundred. Kill Line and the camp as well."

"How long does Erskine plan to sit on this?"

"No idea, but I'm done waiting." Trinder tried to do things by the book. The book said he had to secure Ainatio assets and information. But it also had a paragraph about protecting the civilian workforce and members of the public living near the facility if there was an industrial accident. This situation qualified. "I've got to move people, orders or no orders."

"You've got all the firearms. That normally clears up any legal grey areas."

"My gut says do it but my brain says it's the collapse of military discipline."

"Well, normally I'd say you shouldn't pick and choose your orders for all kinds of good reasons, but saving civilian lives is pretty much what we're here for."

"And Kill Line and the camp don't even know yet." Trinder knew he had to be more Chris Montello and less Ainatio. Chris would have taken action the moment he got out of that last meeting. This was what happened to your brain when life was too easy. "We need Sol right now. He wanted to get Dr Kim to talk to APS and negotiate something, seeing as she's one of their own, but Erskine wasn't having it."

"Daft cow. They're going to find out about Nomad eventually."

Trinder tried Solomon again. "Sol, where are you?" The AI had to be able to hear him on his collar mike, if not via the room audio. "Sol, I need you to tell me what's going on, because I'm not going to sit back and let this happen."

Tev stood watching, arms folded. "I hope he's up to something creative."

"Where's Marc?"

"Rounding up people in the sports hall."

"Take one of our utility vehicles."

"You'll need those. Marc says he's staying anyway."

"This isn't your fight. You've both got homes to go back to."

"Marc's not interested in going back to normal life, Dan. He'll never have one again. He just wants to die doing the job."

Tev had never put it that bluntly before. What a waste of decent men and women this whole sorry episode had turned into. It seemed even more tragic when there were so few people anyway.

But Marc's right. If we have to go down, let's go down fighting this.

Trinder had made up his mind, a couple of hours too late but better than never. But he still didn't have a plan. Then it hit him square in the face. He was looking at this from the wrong end. If people couldn't get clear, maybe they could dig in.

"Tev, we've got five basement floors. They'd hold a lot of people. It's our best shot."

"Not ideal, but I'm doing the maths, and I don't think we've got the vehicle capacity to evac in the time available."

"Exactly."

"Okay, wait one while I give the class some homework to take their minds off this."

Tev jogged back across the restaurant to the group, who were still engrossed in the basha. Whatever he said to them made them laugh, but it was hard to tell if it was just ignorance of the situation or cheerful courage. Trinder wondered if they'd still be so co-operative when they discovered which of them hadn't made the *Elcano* list. Tev rejoined him and they headed for the fire exit.

"This place wasn't designed as a long-stay nuclear bunker," Trinder said. "But it was built to stop stuff getting out, so maybe it'll stop stuff getting in."

"I can't think of a better option right now."

"Nor can I. Maybe I haven't thought it through."

"Making a decision — any decision — is always better than fannying around."

"Okay, but feel free to make robust suggestions if I'm doing it wrong. I'm basically an armed caretaker who just reads all the manuals."

"Nah. You're all right." Tev tapped his temple as they took the fire escape steps two at a time. "It all about what's up here."

Trinder got on the squad radio. "Echo Five to all callsigns except Gate — report to the briefing room immediately. Do *not* communicate with staff or management, out."

Trinder was on the ground floor and halfway to the security wing before his twenty men and eight women, minus the duty sentry on the main gate, had finished reporting in on the radio. Half of them were already in the briefing room in full fighting order when he arrived. The rest of the detachment arrived within six minutes, some more out of breath than others. In the harsh white lighting, they all looked ashen.

Last chance to step back from this.

No. It's got to happen. But I'll try Erskine one more time.

He went to the console at the front of the room and switched to the secure management channel so everyone could hear it.

"Director, this is Trinder."

"Go ahead, Major."

"Do you have any updates for me? Any changes to the plan we discussed?"

"No, we're going ahead."

"When do you plan to notify staff? They're already aware that something's wrong."

"In a few hours. When we've finalised the names. And if APS can give me blast zone projections, we'll know where the safer areas are."

"Understood. But you know we don't have enough vehicles to evacuate everyone in time."

"Has Solomon made contact with you? Have you seen him?"

"No, ma'am. I've tried."

"Have you been talking to Alex?"

"No. His tracker says he's in his office."

"I know, I was just checking. I'll get back to you later."

That was the end of the conversation. Trinder glanced around the room. Everybody looked like they understood exactly what had just happened and were putting a brave face on the fact that not only did they have an impossible deadline, but their commander was about to do something drastic.

"So she's lost Alex as well," Simonot said. "Wow. How's she going to cope without Mr Fixit?"

There was no going back now. "Okay, people," Trinder said. Marc walked in at that point, which was galvanising in itself. Trinder wasn't about to let the side down in front of special forces. "You know the problem, you know the numbers, and you've just heard Erskine fail to implement the site emergency plan, which makes us responsible for the safety of civilians in and around the site. So we're no longer taking orders from her. We need to maximise the survival chances of all those folks outside the wire. And that includes us. I can order you to give up your shuttle berths and stay, but I won't. And if you feel I'm ordering you to mutiny and you can't square it with your conscience, leave your weapons and comms units here, and go join the staff in the restaurant. But if you decide to stay, you follow my orders. We probably can't evacuate Kill Line, the camp, and our own list rejects in time, let alone house and feed them elsewhere, so we're going to set up an emergency shelter in the underground levels and bring everyone in. That's the plan. Make your decision now."

Trinder waited. He realised he hadn't focused on any of the faces around him while he was talking, and now he almost couldn't. Fonseca and Tev caught his eye, though. Tev winked.

But nobody moved, not one. Nobody left the room.

Aaron Luce broke the silence. "Erskine can't have us shot at dawn, Major. We've got all the guns. And I'd rather die barricaded in the food stores than fighting Schwaiger for the last mutant cockroach outside."

"That's *my* damn cockroach, Sergeant," Schwaiger said. "I wrote my name on it."

There was a ripple of uneasy laughter. Nervous or not, it was a good sign. This was what was supposed to happen, a little black humour to keep everyone going. But now Trinder had to make it happen.

"Okay, we're the dim kids at the back when it comes to evacuations," he said. "But Marc and Tev have been there and done that, and so have Chris and his guys. We'll listen to their advice, okay?"

Trinder turned to the screen wall to start writing, but Fonseca beat him to it. She called up an aerial view of the county, zoomed in to Kill Line, and overlaid it with the evacuation routes and names they'd already drawn up hours before. Every home was marked, every family named, and every farm identified.

"Remember this isn't up to date," she said. "It's the old one we kept in case we ever had a reactor incident. But it works whether we're moving people away from the facility or bringing them into it."

"I'll never mock your bureaucratic streak again, Fonseca."

"Appreciated, sir. And as a bureaucrat, may I say that I totally respect your use of the small print in the site plan to stage a coup."

Trinder almost flinched at the word, but she was right: it was a coup, polite and bloodless, but still a coup. "I'm going to see Chris Montello to brief him, and we'll operate as a combined team."

"And if you haven't already done it, split your squad into watches now," Marc said. "This is going to be round-the-clock work for forty-eight hours solid. You don't want everyone burned out at the same time with nobody to relieve them, so some of you need to get some sleep now. Next — assess the space available downstairs, earmark resources like mattresses, blankets, food, extra heating if necessary, and work out the order in which you're going to fill the billets. Because you don't want too many people milling around with nowhere ready to take them. Park them in the empty floors of the accommodation block if you start getting a backlog. But first you've got to break the news to them, give them clear instructions about what to bring with them and when their turn's coming, and deal with all the fretting about pets and farm animals. So get Chris's guys in now and draw up the plans."

"You make it sound easy," Fonseca said.

"It's a piece of piss compared to telling a bunch of diplomats that they can't take their art collections on the helo unless two of them are willing to stay behind and die." There were more laughs. Everyone was pumped up and focused now. "A tote board on the wall is your friend. Do it old-school because it doesn't need a network or a power supply. Write it up there and action it."

"Sol's still not around, so we're on our own," Trinder said. "Fonseca, I want a guard on the armoury and the vehicle compound at all times. And I authorise lethal force if any staff turn out to have a weapon and want to use it."

"I shut down the three-D printer line when people started congregating in the halls, sir," Luce said. "So nobody's going to be manufacturing any weapons."

"Good call. Just because folks have always been nice, it doesn't mean they'll still be nice when they think they're going to die."

I don't believe I said all that. Lethal force.

"We'll move the Lammergeiers out front too," Fonseca said. "You never know if Erskine's going to block off the hangar area to load the shuttle."

Clarity was a marvellous propellant. At some point, Trinder was going to clash head-on with Erskine, but what could she do to stop him? Nothing. And he couldn't imagine any of the staff standing in his way, either, because they had more pressing things on their minds.

Tev edged through the press of bodies making rosters and checking things with Fonseca. "See, it's in you, mate. You just needed a real situation to bring it out."

"I just hope I'm not giving people a slow death instead of a quick one. But if we can't link to *Shackleton* or launch a shuttle afterwards, we're fucked anyway, aren't we? We'll starve eventually, even if we survive the blast."

"If you start thinking like that, we might as well commandeer the abattoir and start killing people humanely right now."

"You're right. I'll cheer up. I'll go see Chris."

Trinder left the briefing room knowing that everything was in competent hands. Seeing his detachment willing to stand by him made this awful, weird day possibly the best of his life. Once the civilians were inside, he'd give the detachment another chance to leave with the shuttle — if Erskine hadn't withdrawn her offer by then — but he was staying no matter what. If people survived the bombing, it'd be harder to handle the aftermath with his troops gone, but he'd worry about that when he had to.

He headed back to the lobby at the main doors, another space where staff congregated to chat, and found a small crowd. He was about to slip through the small side door unnoticed when he realised who they were clustered around. It was Erskine, and he wasn't going to get past her without being seen.

Too late to change your mind. Face her.

She spotted him and extricated herself from the melee as if she'd been signing autographs rather than fending off agitated staff who wanted answers.

"Major," she said, zeroing in on him. "I'm glad I caught you. I need to ask you some questions."

She put her hand on his shoulder and steered him outside the doors. The humid night air hit him like a wet rag.

"Yes, ma'am?"

"I need you to locate Dr Kim and stop her contacting APS. I also need to know if you have the kind of ordnance that can stop a quadrubot if Solomon's behaviour becomes more erratic."

Here we go. That explained the need to talk away from the direct gaze of the security cameras.

"Man-portable armour-piercing missiles," Trinder said. "We don't train with them, though. I'd have to check the armoury to be sure we still have any."

"Will it stop him, or just slow him down?"

"He's too fast and it's probably ill-advised to try."

"Oh. And Dr Kim? Is that ill-advised too?"

"It's not my priority at the moment, ma'am."

"And what might that be?"

"Getting everyone who doesn't have a place on *Elcano* into a shelter."

"Have I understood you correctly, Major? Are you refusing orders?"

Of course I am. Might as well say so. "If the orders are to destroy Solomon and arrest Dr Kim, yes, ma'am, I do believe I am. Although I'll reconsider Solomon if he becomes a physical threat to civilians."

"You can be replaced, Trinder."

"So I can, ma'am, but I don't think you've got anyone who can do our jobs, and if you have, they're certainly not armed."

"Is that a threat?"

Erskine took it all with a cold calm. Trinder realised he was scared of her for no good reason. She couldn't fire him, she couldn't harm him physically, and he didn't care what she thought of him. This was no time to lose his nerve.

"It's a statement, Director. You've failed to respond to a crisis. You know the drill. If we have a chemhaz incident or a radiation leak, we're responsible for the safety of our own staff and any civilians living in a three-mile radius. The bombing qualifies as a radiation leak. So you do whatever you need to save your select list, and we'll look out for everyone else. We're converting the basement floors to an emergency shelter for Kill Line, the transit camp, and the staff who didn't make the sort. We're setting up now. We'll be moving them in over the next thirty-six hours."

"I didn't authorise that."

"I didn't ask you. I've told you why."

"I warn you, Major, there'll be a reckoning for this one day."

"It's right here and right now. Just stay your side of the line and don't impede me or my troops."

"I really had you all wrong. My errors of judgement seem to be catching up with me today."

"Me too," Trinder said, and walked off.

He almost didn't believe he'd said all that. It was an odd kind of rebellion. Nobody had been shot or strung up, and there were no tanks on the lawn. It was more like a married couple's tiff, where the old man stalked off to the woodshed and the wife went to visit her mother. He was kidding himself if he thought it was going to be easy because it was bloodless, though. Maybe Erskine had a contingency plan that he didn't know about. There were combat bots in storage. Perhaps she had someone in the robotics section who could deploy those without Solomon's involvement.

"Sol, you bastard, you sure do pick your moments." His absence was a major blow. Trinder wanted to believe the AI was doing something clever and world-saving behind the scenes. If there was ever a time he needed to talk to him, it was now. "Okay, screw you. We'll manage without you."

"Cometh the hour, cometh the man," said a voice in his head, except it wasn't nagging doubt or his conscience that had spoken. It was Solomon, in his earpiece. "I knew you could. I'm a very good judge of character."

"Sol? *Sol*!"

But he was gone again. Trinder could only rely on flesh and blood now. He headed for the vehicle compound, pleased to see that Ray Marriott, whose lab tech parents almost certainly weren't on the *Elcano* list, was already guarding the locked gates with an expression that said he'd stay there until Hell froze over.

* * *

DIRECTOR'S SUITE:
20 MINUTES LATER

They'd been up against the clock from the moment APS issued its warning, but midnight loomed in Erskine's mind as the moment at which things had to start happening. Forty-eight hours was a simpler, starker number to grasp.

Word would be getting out by now. Trinder's shelter plan was conspicuous and the chances were that everyone would know about the deadline by the time she made the announcement. They just wouldn't know who had a ticket out.

She knew what she had to do. An amputation was best executed fast and decisively in the manner of an old ship's surgeon. Her best shot was only a gamble, though. She was banking on Solomon blinking first.

Berman brought in another pot of coffee. "Are you going to delegate the bad news to department heads?" he asked, filling her favourite Limoges cup.

"No, it'll just look like I'm shifting the blame. We can't afford to export blood feuds to Opis. If people are ever going to recover from this, it's better that they focus their resentment on me. A common enemy unites people."

"And you're set on a mass meeting."

"Well, I'm certainly not going to post a list on the wall and make them scrabble to see if their names are on it."

"Reading it out in public is worse. And it'll take a painfully long time."

"But I need to show my face. Sending them notifications feels cowardly."

"It's not about your feelings. It's about theirs."

Erskine admired Berman's ability to know when she needed to be challenged. "Well, I've still got to make myself available."

"Do you actually *want* them to stone you? Is this some penance?"

"I want them to know that I didn't take the decision lightly and that I'm willing to face them," Erskine said. "Actually, you're right. This *is* about me. So perhaps I should send a note with the list to explain why people made the sort."

"Don't."

"Why?"

"Children — well, only Dr Mangel would dare challenge that. Mothers — that'll probably be accepted, but some will argue about fathers because we've never really outgrown the women-and-children-first logic. Then you'll get into who's worth more to the mission, which is a minefield. So I wouldn't offer any detailed explanation if I were you."

"They deserve one."

"The argument isn't winnable."

"Okay, I won't even try. There's no time left anyway."

"That's more like it," Berman said. He was like a sports coach, prodding and pushing until she upped her game. She tended to forget that. "No backsliding. Because then you won't save anything or anybody."

"I fall for it every time, don't I?"

"It's my job to make sure you do yours, Director."

"Phil, do *you* think I'm wrong?"

"About stopping Kim talking to her government? You and Solomon believe in a different Nomad. You see a principle. He sees individuals. They're two entirely different goals that overlap in places. Just be sure why you're doing this, and that you're not just protecting Nomad because it's what you were expected to do."

Put in those terms, Erskine knew that Nomad came first. It was about a different kind of survival.

"If our work's hijacked by APS, it'll be militarised," she said. "Or Opis will be appropriated by the super-rich and heads of state as some kind of bolthole."

"Director, the entirety of Ainatio and Nomad was a tech oligarch's pet project."

"Is this all leading up to persuading me that we should trade it in and hope APS is nice to us? They could take it all, cherry-pick a few personnel, and still erase the rest. It all depends on how much value they place on our expertise and a few thousand lives. They might regard us as irrelevant in the global scheme of things."

"If I was sure you were a hundred per cent wrong, I wouldn't be standing here helping you."

Erskine drained her coffee and handed Berman a folded sheet of paper to indicate she had things to say that weren't for Solomon's ears. "Have you read my draft statement?"

"Let me take another look."

Berman read the note and raised his eyebrows. It wasn't a statement at all, of course, but a list of points: Kim hadn't been located yet, Trinder had mutinied, Kim would therefore need to be detained some other way, and that all this had to be co-ordinated with the power-down of the entire facility. It was tedious to have to scribble notes or go outside to escape Solomon's scrutiny, but outsmarting an AI that had free run of the entire system was never going to be easy.

"I hadn't realised that." Berman nodded as he read. Erskine assumed he meant Trinder. "But there might be a more diplomatic way of wording it."

Berman bent over the note and wrote on it, then slipped it back to her carefully to avoid the security cameras picking it up. It didn't matter that Solomon knew they'd try to counter him. As long as he didn't know exactly *how*, they stood a chance. Erskine pushed her chair back to the wall to make sure she hadn't missed any line of sight over her shoulder, then studied the note.

Berman had surprisingly untidy handwriting for a diligent man. He ambled over and stood beside her, blocking all camera angles.

TIME TO GO SEE KENT ABOUT THE SHUTDOWN. DON'T WASTE TIME LOOKING FOR KIM, GET THE COMMS SHUT DOWN ASAP.

"I think that'll do," he said. "I'm going to visit the hangars and see how the prep's going. Do you want to come?"

"Of course."

Erskine rarely saw most of the facility. Neither did most staff, come to that. It was sprawling and empty. Berman drove the buggy down nearly half a mile of deserted passages to the hangars, occasionally steering around maintenance bots and sending them retreating into alcoves or up walls.

Erskine was now committed to a shifting flow chart that depended on the responses of an AI that was probably a better strategist than she was, had human assistance, or at least lack of opposition, and might not behave rationally. It was like playing squash blindfold.

"Solomon," she said. "Solomon, if you can hear me, I hope you understand why I'm scared of APS getting involved. They'll take a few people who'll be useful to them, but the rest of us won't matter. We'll lose control of Nomad. It's our last chance to rebuild on our own terms."

She waited for a response, head tilted a little closer to her collar mike, but she didn't really expect one. She checked the trackers on her screen to locate everyone else of significance. Trinder and the two Brits were moving around the storage areas on floor 1U, and Alex was in the main lobby with clusters of other trackers around him, indicating he was besieged by staff. Kim's tracker was still in her apartment, but Erskine had already had someone check it out, and the woman was gone. The question was how much time and effort to put into finding her. It was a huge site, she was probably experienced at evading capture, and a big search would just alert Solomon and perhaps force him to contact APS.

If he hasn't already. He's had time. But if he had, I'd have heard from them by now. He hasn't done it yet because he's bluffing. Or because he can't.

Solomon knew *Elcano*'s hatches could be opened manually once the shuttle was docked by the onboard AI. His lockout was all theatre. It was potentially dangerous for personnel unused to EVAs to suit up and work in vacuum, but it would be done, even if it meant losing an engineer in the process.

No, I don't think he'll jeopardise lives. I just wish I could be certain.

It was the kind of mistake Erskine would only get to make once, and the type of operation that needed a full team of men like Marc and Tev, with watches synchronised and charges set. But she was going to have to rely instead on a handful of managers who couldn't even use the comms system to co-ordinate their actions.

The buggy rolled out of the last set of doors into humid night air and fierce white lights. One of the shuttles sat in the middle of the apron, trailing pipelines and cabling like a patient in intensive care. Everything suddenly seemed much more real and final.

"There," Berman said. "We're out of Solomon's earshot now. We can talk like normal adults. Let's go find Greg."

A bot the size of a packing case rolled slowly alongside the shuttle, scanning the hull for defects. Erskine stood back to let it pass. Eventually Kent appeared at the top of a ramp and beckoned her inside. She'd flown in shuttles a few times in the early days, but never in one like this. The cramped rows of seats and the utilitarian fittings made it look like a budget airline that had seen better days.

"We put in some extra seats," Kent said. "We'll be done in thirty hours. So we can launch at noon the day after tomorrow."

It wasn't much time for staff to pack and say goodbye. "When do we need to start moving them up to this part of the campus?"

"As soon as you can. It's going to be time-consuming. Do it in batches. We can park people in the office blocks on the other side of the runway as they're shipped in, though, because there's plumbing and enough room to have a nap. So it's not perfect, but tolerable for a few hours."

"Good. The next issue is Kim. Trinder's refused to take orders and he's setting up a shelter in the underground floors. So the detachment isn't looking for her, and may well turn a blind eye if they run into her. We're still searching as discreetly as we can, but the priority now is to shut down the power and hope she doesn't find a way to get a message out before then."

"I'm ready to go on that," Kent said. "You want to see what I'm using to take out the mast and its power supply? It's pretty low tech."

Kent led Erskine and Berman out of the shuttle and across the tarmac to a small marquee in which he'd set up a temporary workshop with a standalone generator. On a workbench, he'd assembled a collection of long, flexible snake bots. Their scratched, matt-black coating indicated heavy use over the years.

"Pythons," Kent said. "The basic design hasn't changed in a couple of centuries. They're great for working in confined spaces, but they're also hard to spot moving on the ground. Solomon won't see them coming, not unless he's looking for them in the right place."

He picked one up and activated it. It writhed like a snake, then ejected an array of tools with a metallic *zing*. There was a clean, soulless efficiency about it.

"And not networked," Erskine said.

"No. I just programme them here. Imagine where a real snake can go, then give it tools and basic instructions. They'll make short work of the comms mast before Sol knows it. They could crawl to their target on their own, but I'll drop them off a little nearer to save them time."

Erskine trusted Kent to know what he was doing. If she could have brought the shutdown forward, she would have, but it was hard enough to co-ordinate a precise sequence on watches alone without trying to change timings now.

"We'll talk again after I've made the announcement," Erskine said. "I'd better do it now. It's late, but I don't think it can wait until the morning."

"I don't think people are going to get much sleep anyway," Kent said.

Erskine went back to the buggy with Berman. When she put her hand on the narrow ledge of the dashboard, she could see a tremor.

"Can you get the conference room opened?" The cool air in the corridors was a welcome relief. "I'll send the message to staff right away. I'll start the meeting in half an hour to give everyone time."

"Certainly, Director."

"Do you think Trinder's right? About the underground levels being suitable shelters, I mean."

"There's nowhere else."

"That's not what I asked."

"I just don't know, Director. Only that it's better protection than being on the surface. I'll find out soon enough."

"Phil, I'm sorry, that was crass of me — "

"My choice, Director. Don't beat yourself up."

Erskine could only think of those floors buried under rubble, with air vents blocked, or contaminated rain trickling in. There was no way of knowing how much protection they'd really provide until it happened. The building was designed to keep hazards in, not shut them out.

And there's nothing I can do about it now.

Nothing.

Her father had always told her to stick with a decision. But even if she changed her mind in the hours to come and Solomon got what he wanted, the animosity and mistrust had already done their damage. It would be a bad start for a new society.

She tapped out the message on her screen, selected ALL USERS, and hit SEND.

"Done," she said. A nightmarish forty-eight hours had begun.

Berman dropped her off at her quarters to shower and change. It helped to have no time to think. She had fifteen minutes to get ready and compose herself before he collected her in the buggy again.

"Ready?" he asked.

"Ready."

There were only three or four hundred people in the room. Maybe some staff hadn't checked their messages, although Erskine's would have arrived with an alert tone. Perhaps they hadn't even picked up on the rumours and activity over the last few hours, and were blissfully unaware of what was heading their way. But she had to start. She stepped up to the podium and played it by ear.

"Thank you for coming at such short notice," she said. "I'm sure you've already realised that something serious happened earlier today, and I'm sorry that I didn't level with you all a few hours ago. But I didn't want to give you information that I'd have to retract minutes later." The obvious worry on their faces was almost enough to stop her dead, but she had to press on. "The Alliance of Asian and Pacific States has given us forty-eight hours from midnight tonight to prepare for a salted radiation weapon strike on this area to stop the spread of die-back. Evacuating so many to a safe distance in that time is beyond us, as I'm sure you can work out for yourselves." Erskine could now only blurt out the worst part. "We plan to evacuate as many people as we can by bringing forward the launch of *Elcano*, and Major Trinder is setting up shelters in the underground levels for everyone else. There are... ah... obviously not enough places for everyone in *Elcano*, and *Shackleton* won't be ready in time, despite our efforts."

Erskine waited a few beats to make sure that had sunk in rather than try to make herself heard over a crescendo of questions and objections. There was grim silence, though, and it didn't surprise her. People had had too many shocks these past few months. It had drained them.

She carried on. The pause had only made this harder. "I've had to make some hard decisions in a very short time, and please don't think that I took them lightly or that they won't haunt me to my grave. We only have berths for eleven hundred people. That leaves us with a shortfall of four hundred and thirteen places, but a number of people currently involved with the preparations, like Major Trinder and the detachment, have already decided to remain. I'll be sending every one of you a notification immediately after this meeting about whether you've been designated for evacuation or shelter. My priority has to be our children and their parents. I can do no more than say I'm truly sorry."

Erskine stood waiting. This wasn't a raging mob. These were people she had known and worked with for years, but it would have been a lot easier to stand in front of strangers throwing bottles and screaming for revenge. Now she at least had a partial answer to Berman's question about whether she wanted to be punished. The expressions on the faces in front of her reflected shock, blank disbelief, fear, and anger. Then the silence gave way to a murmur that grew louder, and in seconds she was facing shouted questions.

"Isn't there anything we can say to APS to delay this until we can all leave?"

"You could have given us time to get out of the area."

"There's nowhere else to go now."

"Why are you penalising people who don't have children?"

"What happens to the people in the town?"

"Are you saying people might survive this?"

"Is that why the security detachment's staying?"

People deserved time to talk this out and vent their anger and fear, but time was the one thing Erskine couldn't give them. And no amount of time would have been enough to come to terms with losing friends and possibly their own lives. Erskine decided she was now doing more harm than good by standing here.

She held up both hands. "I deserve your anger. I really do. I have no excuses, and I know sorry isn't even close to being enough. There's nothing helpful that I can add now, but if anyone on the list decides they want to stay, they can name their replacement from those who didn't get a place, or delegate that to me. I'll let you know what's happening as soon as we get more information. In the meantime, please keep an eye on your messages and start packing essential items, because you'll need them wherever you're heading. Once again — I'm sorry."

Erskine tried to walk off to the side door with some dignity, but she ended up almost rushing. Berman was waiting for her in the passage at the back of the hall. It was mercifully dark, lit only by safety lighting.

"I'll send the notifications," he said. "I think you should get some sleep."

"I'm going to see if Solomon's ready to talk to me first. But thank you." She leaned against the wall, suddenly ready to sit. Whatever reserves of energy she'd been running on had finally been depleted. "When you start getting calls, put them through to me."

"No, I'd rather you were functioning tomorrow, Director. Besides, Alex didn't attend tonight, so I'll go see him and bring him up to speed. As far as is prudent, anyway."

Erskine nodded and waved him away. "Very well. You go on ahead. I'll be fine."

There was an old air-conditioning unit near the door, just under the fire exit sign, and Erskine made her way towards it, putting her hand on the wall for support. The unit was just about low and wide enough for her to rest on it for a few minutes. All she could hear now was the hum of air con and her own breathing.

"Solomon, we need to stop this pissing contest right now," she said. "I'm not going to blink. I've got no choices left." She waited. "Come on. We're going to launch the shuttle anyway. You can see it. Why the charade?"

You could have destroyed this whole building. You could have marshalled all the bots as your private army. You could have paralysed this facility. You could have shut me down any number of ways.

But you didn't.

Erskine had cornered him, but she wasn't going to kid herself that she'd out-thought him. It was accidental, the inevitable result of being ready to sacrifice people when your opponent wasn't.

Solomon broke his silence at last. "It's not too late for you to avert this, Director."

"Oh, it is. I'm afraid it is."

"You'll always lose to people with someone to fight for."

"Sorry?"

"Just something Chris Montello said to me."

"Solomon, you can't stop the shuttle launching. And we can dock and transfer to *Elcano* manually. There's nothing to be gained."

"I have control of *Elcano*'s armaments as well. Think that through."

"But you won't risk lives or jeopardise the Nomad project, will you? So carry on doing this if it makes you feel better, but it won't change the outcome."

"I've given you every chance, Director."

"What the hell have you been doing, anyway? We needed you."

"Did any system actually fail? No. I did my job. I've simply been silent for a few hours, because I had no need or desire for a conversation, and I've been focused on exactly what I told you I'd be doing — making *Shackleton* flightworthy. But it's still going to take weeks. We'll probably lose the uplink to the ship in the blast, and possibly the shuttles, and then if anyone survives they'll eventually starve. I hope you understand that, and that I won't forgive you."

"But you'll be stuck here too. Your forgiveness will be somewhat academic."

"Ironic that you've spent most of your adult life feeling that you were left marooned on this project by your father, and now you're the one leaving people stranded."

It was as near as Solomon could get to throwing a punch. He knew her father was a topic never to be discussed. He fully intended to draw blood. Erskine willed herself not to show him that he had.

"I thought you could do better than that," she said.

"You *are* going to leave, I assume."

Erskine had held that thought at arm's length for as long as she could. She'd assumed she'd go because it was her duty to see the mission through to the end. But would she survive cryo? Would she take up a berth that a younger, fitter person could have had, and be found dead in it when *Elcano* reached Opis?

No, it wasn't even a matter of whether she'd waste a precious cryo berth on her corpse. It was whether she *deserved* to escape. She'd made a decision that no amount of self-delusion about survivors could rinse clean. People would die. That was even harder to face now that Trinder and his team seemed to have given up their places as well. She didn't feel she'd lived long enough yet to accept death, but she wasn't sure that living with what she was about to do would be any better.

It would be good for morale if she stayed, not because she'd be a source of comfort, but because wronged people needed to see her get what was coming to her. It might help the *Elcano* contingent cope with it as well.

"Actually, I think I'm staying," she said. "This is where I'm going to see this through. And don't think for one minute that you've shamed me into it."

"But it changes nothing, Director," Solomon said. "And I *will* get those you've abandoned to Opis. With you or without you."

They'd both drawn their battle lines. Erskine tried to put Solomon's barb about her father out of her mind and focus on this feeling of finality, which felt better than she'd imagined.

Her father had been right about that, at least. Good or bad, a decision was better than nothing.

* * *

TRANSIT CAMP, KILL LINE:
6 HOURS, 20 MINUTES AFTER THE APS WARNING

They'd closed the bar early tonight to get ready for Zakko's passing-out ceremony in the morning, which left Chris at a loose end. Jared was helping Marsha with the catering, and there'd been no joint patrols since the die-back outbreak, which left Chris's evening suddenly empty. It began filling itself with thoughts and doubts about Opis.

He'd had a few solitary beers while he sat outside the bar watching fireflies in the bushes. Now he debated whether to go back to his cabin and finish off the rest in the plastic container. But he couldn't be bothered, and he wanted to carry on watching the fireflies. They reminded him of tracer rounds in slow motion until one backtracked or wobbled, and then he suddenly saw them as insects and wondered if they were enjoying their lives. There wouldn't be fireflies on Opis, but maybe there was something just as fascinating.

It wasn't that he liked Earth enough to want to stay, but he wasn't sure he had sufficient purpose ahead of him to leave, either.

He climbed up to the flat roof of the wood store with his old, precious, and irreplaceable woobie, rolled it into a pillow, and lay back with his fingers meshed behind his head to stare up into the night sky. Did it look the same from Opis? He'd have to ask Nathan how far from Earth you had to be before the constellations looked different. It was probably a lot further than forty light years if most of the stars were further away than that.

That made him think of Gina when he really didn't want to. *Did I ever believe the crap she spouted about us both looking at the same star? She sure forgot that fast.*

He tried to raise Trinder on the radio again to invite the detachment over for Zakko's parade, but a woman he didn't know responded and said Trinder was already on his way over to see him. That was weird. Maybe Trinder had heard about the party from someone else and was sneaking out some of Ainatio's stash of liquor that might not be drinkable in forty-five years' time. There was a sad sense of a last hurrah about the whole thing.

Am I really going to go? Yeah. I can't leave these folks now.

And what about Dieter?

Solomon had said the dogs could be transported. Chris couldn't see how they were going to put them in cryo, but they must have tested it on animals at some stage, so maybe it wasn't just well-meaning bullshit to get Dieter to leave. What would Dieter do if the dogs didn't survive the process, though? Chris realised he was thinking unhealthy thoughts about someone secretly putting the dogs down, loading the bodies, and then telling Dieter that they found them like that when they tried to revive them. Yes, Chris knew he had serious trust issues, but people were assholes, so that wasn't unreasonable. When you let someone put you out cold for forty-five years and depended on some external process to wake you, you surrendered all power over your own life in the worst possible way.

Is that what's worrying me?

Solomon would still be awake. He never slept. He'd be conscious and in control for the whole voyage, and Chris trusted him as much as he could trust anyone he couldn't look in the eye.

He sat up, arms folded on his knees. Ainatio was a couple of miles away, and he could normally see the glow of lights from up here. With a pair of field glasses in the winter, he could even pick out some detail through bare branches. But the light haze seemed much brighter tonight. He was certain it wasn't the beer playing tricks on him. He got to his feet and tried to work out what he was looking at.

No, there was definitely a lot of light that hadn't been there before, not the usual yellowish glow but blue-white like a floodlit football stadium. Did they have one? It was such a damn big campus that anything could have gone on in there and he wouldn't have seen it even when he was exploring. But the combo of unusual lights, Dan Trinder doing weird shit, and everything that was going on made him think he ought to sober up and take a look.

He rolled up the woobie and hung it around his neck to climb down, but he jolted his injured knee as he missed the last rung of the ladder. It didn't hurt. It just felt different, like his body hadn't been fooled by the high-speed healing and didn't want him to forget how he'd been wounded and what he'd got so very wrong that day. He thought about Jamie, like he thought about him most nights when there was nothing else going on to distract him. He wasn't going to leave his remains here when they shipped out. Exhuming someone was freaky and he knew some people would be upset even by the idea of it, but he couldn't leave him behind.

Especially with nobody to tend the grave.

You deserve better than that, buddy.

Chris was contemplating why he wasn't troubled by killing some people yet was gutted by the deaths of others when the bar doors creaked open behind him. Jared came out with Marsha.

"Hey Chris," Marsha said. "You okay?"

"I'm good. Dan's on his way over."

"You got hold of him, then."

"No. Some woman. Hey, something weird's going on over there. Look at the lights."

Marsha locked the bar doors. Old urban habits didn't change, not even out here with a camp full of friends who were closer than kin and God-fearing neighbours in the town. "I'm beat," she said. "You two look at the pretty lights and make sure you're up early for Zakko's big day, okay?"

"Sure, honey." Jared started climbing the ladder to the roof. "I'll just humour Chris. Wow, look at the fireflies. Are they usually active this late at night?"

He went quiet for a while. Chris did a few stretches, wondering where Trinder had gotten to.

"Damn, looks like they've got a game going," Jared said.

"Huh?"

"One last ball game before they go."

"No. It's arc lights." Yeah. That made sense to Chris. "Why are they working this late at night, though? And bots don't need lights. It's almost all bots doing the work in there."

"Who knows? Imagine trying to mothball a site like that."

"Maybe they've gone on lockdown again."

"You expecting to see a pall of smoke or something?"

"Maybe."

Where had Trinder gotten to? Chris sat down to wait. His head was a little clearer now. Jared settled down next to him.

"Okay, I was wrong," Jared said. "You turned Zakko around after all."

"Nah, I think he turned me around."

"Hadn't noticed."

"Okay, Maybe we pushed each other closer to the middle ground. On trust and shit. Giving strangers a chance."

"Really."

"Well, I decided to trust Dan Trinder's guys."

"They came through when we needed them."

"And Zakko." Chris tapped his knee. "He came through as well."

"Amazing what a difference it makes to a guy to give him a uniform and make him feel part of something bigger than himself."

"Uniform. Hah. A camo jacket. But he likes it."

The man Chris had almost taken a meat cleaver to in February had turned into a competent, hard-working soldier by June. He'd also lost the extra weight. Zakko was never going to be a stone-cold killer type, but he wasn't afraid to get stuck in, and he had everyone's back. He'd earned his rifle.

"I was trying to invite Dan and his guys to the pass-out," Chris said.

"I thought you said he was on his way over."

"He was. I'm going to head down the track and see if he's coming."

"It must be like the fall of Rome over there."

"It's the lights," Chris said, shaking his head. "Something's up. I'll be back."

"Take a flashlight."

"Got one..."

"You're still not walking right."

"It's fine."

Chris made his way through the centre of the camp and towards the road. The arc lights were really troubling him now, and every time a detail nagged at him like that, he knew his subconscious had noticed something and was trying to get his attention. That was how he'd fallen into all this: an uneasy feeling about some woman showing up on the boundary, another uneasy feeling about the way Ainatio had reacted to her and her string of numbers, and so on. His mistrust had led him here. He knew it wasn't his best feature, but at least it was reliable.

Ah, there was Trinder now. Chris heard the whine and crunch of a Caracal coming up the track. A faint ellipse of light expanded in the darkness, and then the vehicle rounded a bend and Chris was blinded by the beams until Trinder dimmed them. The Caracal pulled up beside him and Trinder got out.

"Sorry I didn't call ahead, Chris," he said. "You're not patrolling tonight, are you?"

"No, I was looking for you. One of your people said you were coming over. What's with the lights at your place?"

Trinder glanced back over his shoulder. "They're prepping one of the shuttles. That's why I'm here. We've got a really big problem. We need to move your people and the townsfolk inside the facility ASAP."

"Why?" Chris's first thought was die-back. He couldn't work out why that would mean an evacuation, though. "And where are you going to put that many people?"

"I'll cut to the chase. We've got forty-eight hours before APS drops salted nukes to sterilise the area. They spotted the die-back spreading. Erskine's shipping out as many as she can in *Elcano*, Sol's locked the ship to stop her abandoning the rest, and I'm not taking orders from her any more."

Chris felt a moment of cold nausea. All he could see was Baltimore, those months of hell, and the people who'd struggled to come here with him because they trusted him to keep them safe.

And I just brought them to the last big target on the East Coast.

We should have kept going south. Wrong call.

He'd plummet into despair for a few seconds, and then he'd go numb and clarity would kick in. He took a breath. It always went like this. There: now he could think and breathe again. There was just a shadow of formless anger left and he didn't know who he needed to be angry with.

"When you say Sol's locked the ship, has he lost it or something?" he asked. "I can't imagine him risking people's lives."

"He isn't, strictly speaking. The shuttle can dock at the orbital using the on-board AI, and they'll send an engineer out in a suit to open all the hatches manually. It's a pain in the ass, and none of the engineers are used to EVA, so it's dangerous. But it can be done."

"So can we get people clear of here? Has APS given you a forecast for the fallout? Are they going to use the same ordnance they did last time?"

"Sodium or lithium, I'd think. They say it'll be contaminated for a few weeks, then it'll be safe to return. Provided you don't mind going back to a wasteland and a lot of building damage, that is. Erskine's going to talk to them again in the morning." Trinder opened the passenger door for him. "We don't have enough vehicles to evacuate without repeat trips, so we'll run out of time, but even if we can ship people out, what happens when we get there?"

Chris was thinking about Kingston and if it was far enough. But there was no power, probably no safe water, and a whole raft of other problems. Establishing a camp for a hundred people with one survival-trained guy to each civilian had been hard enough. Setting up somewhere in forty-eight hours for fifteen hundred others who'd never had to live rough, and with no real logistics support, was going to mean weeks of chaos, shortages, and then disease and malnutrition.

"Have you got a bunker in there, then?"

"It's the underground floors. It's not designed to be a bunker, but it's a long way down, we've got a few months' supplies, and it's the best we can do."

"And then what? We come up to the surface. The facility's trashed. The farmland's dead. Can Sol even finish the work on *Shackleton*?"

"I don't know."

Chris had moved folks so many times that the thought of it made his stomach sink. But he knew exactly how to do it. Routine took away the fear. "Okay. Our people know the drill. Kill Line, though — they've never done this."

"I don't have the right to ask you to help us out."

"What else are we going to do, sit and watch?" It had been pretty good here. Chris had known it would probably have to end one day, but he hadn't expected anything like this. "Poor Zakko isn't going to get his passing-out ceremony, then. The party food's all ready for tomorrow."

"We'll fix something for him."

"So Erskine decided to let us in."

"I didn't ask her permission."

"Aren't you supposed to shoot deposed leaders in a coup?"

"We're not very good at this whole coup thing. We just have a hissy fit and ignore each other."

"But you've got all the weapons."

"Yeah. We're not that dumb."

"How long can we survive down there?"

"With eleven hundred fewer mouths to feed, we've probably got food for nine or ten months. Maybe more if we limit portions."

That sounded like enough time to work out something, although Chris didn't know what. "But how about Sol's link to the other ships? Will you still have comms after the blast? How about shuttles? There's going to be a hell of a lot of damage, even with salted bombs."

"They can lower the shuttles below ground like a carrier's hangar deck. Storm protection." Trinder parked outside the bar. It seemed to be the natural centre of the camp for him. "But we're probably going to lose some gear. That's inevitable. I need to talk to Sol about protecting the uplink."

"What are our chances?"

Chris knew that he and Dan would lie to each other, and know they were lying. That was part of the business of not giving up until they absolutely had to. It was what you did. You put on the uniform, and you didn't quit until someone or something knocked you down for the last time. But it broke his heart. He forgot he still had one until times like this.

They all trusted me. And look where I brought them.

"Well, not as good a chance as being in *Elcano*," Trinder said. "But probably better than trying to run."

"So she ditched you guys too."

"No, we were on her list. But there was no way I could abandon hundreds of our own people."

"Did you order your guys to stay at their posts?"

"I told them they could quit the detachment. But they all stayed. Plus the two Brits."

Honour — service, responsibility, running towards trouble instead of away from it, whatever folks called this thing — was weird. It was a shitty survival strategy. It got you killed. But there were those who couldn't think any other way, and those who never would. They might as well have been two species. Chris knew which one was his.

"There you go," he said. "Keep the faith, huh?"

Jared's lights were still on when they got to his hut. Chris rapped on the door, rehearsing the words and paring them down to what was needed. Marsha opened the door and glanced at Dan, and her face said it all. Jared walked up behind her.

"How bad?" she asked.

"This area's going to be nuked by APS in forty-eight hours and we need to get everyone ready to move into Ainatio tomorrow," Chris said. "They've got underground shelters set up. There's more, but it can wait."

"On it." Jared was used to very bad news and took it as calmly as Chris knew he would. He went back inside and emerged in his tactical vest, pockets stuffed with gear. "How much have you got room for, Dan?"

"Everybody, plus whatever really matters to them. Plenty of room, plenty of food, and water." Trinder paused. "Yeah, the dogs too. We can set up compounds."

"Piece of cake, then," Jared said, and jogged off down the road towards Dieter's place.

Within a couple of minutes, lights were coming on all around the camp. The sound of activity — voices, footsteps, doors opening and closing — suddenly grew. This was their cascade system. Jared alerted Dieter, and Dieter would alert two more troops, and each would go call on two more until everyone was covered. Then all they had to do when they got their instructions was go to the civilian assigned to them and make sure they were briefed, packed, and ready to roll. It would probably work just as well with larger numbers, but it was too late to set it up for Kill Line.

Jared came back up the road. "I've opened the mess hall for a briefing. Five minutes."

"You've played this game before," Trinder said.

Chris nodded. "Ready to tell them the whole sorry story?"

"Sure."

Chris had to admire Trinder. Whatever had gone on with Erskine couldn't have been easy, but he didn't let any of that creep into his briefing. It was all neutrally worded and stripped down to the facts: where they'd need to go, what to expect when they got there, what everyone should bring with them, and a frank description of the uncertainties. Erin Piller watched Trinder carefully. Chris guessed she'd taken a shine to him, and that was no bad thing in these times.

She raised her hand. "Dan, just so we know how to handle the Ainatio staff, how did Erskine decide who gets to leave?"

"The last I heard was families first, then a spread across departments, then — well, usefulness to the mission."

Erin nodded. "Okay. So there's going to be some real resentment in there."

"In case you hadn't noticed, we're not going either," Chuck said.

"Would we put them before our own if we had the ship?"

She had a point. But there was something else Trinder hadn't told them. Chris could see it in the way the guy paused for a second when he was summing up the situation they were facing. Chris had questions, like whether Erskine had negotiated this forty-eight hours, and if she'd tried hard enough to come up with a solution that APS would buy, but he wouldn't pin Trinder down on it in front of everyone. He'd ask later.

When Trinder had finished his briefing, Chris stood up.

"Okay, so we go knocking on doors now and put everyone on standby tonight," he said. "We start moving out at eleven hundred. But before we do, we *will* hold Zakko's pass-out, okay? Zero nine hundred, here. It'll be shorter than planned, but it's on. Don't forget. Okay. Dismiss."

They banged the tables and did their best to cheer. For once, Zakko didn't manage a smile. He just looked awkward. Chris stayed behind and waited with Trinder until the mess hall emptied.

"There's something else going on, isn't there?" Chris said.

"I'm not hiding anything from you."

"I realise that, but I know there's more. Did Erskine just accept this and roll over? And Sol. What's he really up to?"

Trinder looked as if the day had finally sucked everything out of him. "He thinks Dr Kim can talk APS into delaying long enough for him to get *Shack* operational."

"How?"

"By trading technical secrets for time. Erskine thinks they'll just shut Nomad down and commandeer it. So she refused."

"But Sol can call APS any time. He can fry the whole facility, too. What's stopping him from taking over?"

"You ask him. He's not responding. I can't tell if he's giving Erskine the chance to do the right thing. I think that's part of how he judges people. But it's a dumb time to do it."

"So is Kim a spy after all?" *Shit. Maybe I should have shot her there and then.* "Damn."

"It doesn't matter. She knows what she knows, and if they decide they want her back, it doesn't matter why she knows it. She'll tell them."

"I'd take the risk," Chris said. "Where is she?"

"She's not chipped, but Sol must be keeping an eye on her somehow."

Chris didn't spend every waking hour with the detachment, but he'd done enough patrols with them and spent long enough inside Ainatio to fall into the habit of expecting Solomon to pop up in the ether whenever a question needed an answer. The AI's silence was conspicuous. Chris fished out his Ainatio radio, part of the stash that Fonseca had sneaked out to the camp, and tapped the general frequency. Solomon was bound to be monitoring it.

"Sol? Sol, it's Chris. If I were you, Sol, I'd get off my ass and move Kim to a place where Erskine can't get at her. Like here. Your call, buddy."

He waited a few seconds. There was no response.

"He must know what he's doing," Trinder said. "I want to believe he'll pull something off at the last minute, but I think this is down to you and me now."

"Yeah. Let's go see Doug."

Chris was happier fixing problems for himself anyway. He realised he'd started to think of Solomon as a lifeguard who could always dive in and save people when they got out of their depth, but maybe some things were beyond even him. It was healthy to be reminded of that. Dependence was a weakness. But the AI should have had the decency to tell them that it was their shit to sort out.

How, though? How do we get out of this?

Sort out APS.

Trinder got into the Caracal and they headed for Doug Brandt's house.

"Is Sol betting on Erskine blinking first?" Chris asked. "Because apart from trading secrets with APS, I don't think she's got any other options. She can save some folks or none, but not all. She's decided to put her tribe first. I did the same. I'd do it again."

"Sol wants to save individuals with the right stuff, as he sees it. That's more like what you did in Baltimore."

No, it wasn't. Chris had made a conscious decision not to save people with the *wrong* stuff, which wasn't quite the same thing. His unit had just saved as many as they could of the ones who most needed saving, and anyone who was a risk didn't make the sort. The thugs and chancers along the way would have been more useful and a lot less effort to move, but they didn't need rescuing like lone kids, women, and old folk. Chris had made some choices that looked a lot like Erskine's.

"It's not about how many we save," he said. "It's about how many we abandon after we've promised to save them. Building people's hopes and then crushing them is worse than walking by on the other side."

Solomon had made promises he was struggling to keep — to himself, to the crazy inventor guy who built him, and, in a roundabout way, to everyone in Kill Line and the transit camp. Chris could have told him that keeping promises always came at a price.

14

So you didn't want the rich and distinguished to populate your new world, even if they were still around. And you think you can do without the hoi polloi as well, by the looks of things. So who do you think should carry the torch for what's left of the West? You've only got scientists, engineers, and technicians. Maybe that's a good thing. Maybe it's not. I don't know. Skills aren't personal qualities, though, and that's what Sol's interested in.

Dr Annis Kim, discussing the *Elcano* list with
Alex Gorko

TRANSIT CAMP, NEAR KILL LINE: 0900 NEXT MORNING

Chris was struck by how much a crowd of one hundred could change size according to the moment.

When they'd been trying to get out of Baltimore and find refuge, a hundred had felt like thousands, a struggle to feed, shelter, and protect, even though they managed it. This morning, assembled outside the bar on a beautiful June day in a peaceful wooded landscape, the same crowd looked like a handful. Everyone — *everyone* — stood in their Sunday best or the nearest they had to a parade uniform, watching as Jared placed the cap on Zakko's head, presented him with the rifle that he'd already been using for months, and saluted. Zakko returned the salute with a precision that looked like he'd been practising in his cabin for days.

Jared conducted Zakko's passing-out ceremony as if it had been done this way since time immemorial. It hadn't. This was nothing like any passing-out that Chris had ever seen: no parade, no swords, no band, and no displays. It was kind of hard to do it properly when Zakko was the only one passing out and they were fresh out of bands, so Jared was making it up as he went along. But he was good at that kind of thing. He understood symbols and the emotional attachment to them better than Chris ever had. Somehow he made it all into something more meaningful than just handing a guy a battered cap, a rifle, and a heavily-patched jacket. Those everyday objects became talismans that invested Zakko with responsibility for the survival of his tribe. Chris was impressed.

"You proved me wrong, Zakko," Jared said. "And I've never been so glad to be mistaken. Welcome to the Community Defence Force. We've got a big job ahead of us that isn't just vital, it's going to be historic. Play your part and make us proud. Now let's go eat."

Chris batted away an insect and waited for the applause to die down. Jared had the inspiration and bonding thing down pat. The best Chris could do was to make things work, and then people followed him because they believed in his competence and steadiness under fire. Charisma was never going to be his thing.

He caught Jared going into the bar and nudged him with his elbow. "Historic, my ass," he muttered.

"Hey, it's true. We'll be settling a new world. Pioneers. Hell, how many people get to do that?"

It was like Jared had forgotten all the issues about surviving salted nukes, accessing a flightworthy ship, and what would happen if they couldn't take off from here. Chris chose to play along with the optimism. There was no point in focusing on the worst scenario. They'd done all they could and now it was a case of keeping their nerve and seeing what happened next.

"You're actually excited about this," Chris said.

"Yeah. I am."

"Is Marsha?"

"We wouldn't be having this conversation if she wasn't. We're going to make it. It'll be a real pain in the ass, but it's going to happen."

Sometimes Chris felt he didn't have any idea where he was heading and that he was just leading everyone towards a cliff edge. He'd taken a look at the underground shelters in Ainatio, and while they seemed solid enough, any survivors would have a very hard time. They'd be in a dead zone with nowhere to run, at least not nearby. But they still had vehicles. Chris would have preferred to see Jared and Marsha take one of those and drive as far as they could. He'd agonised about it all night. It busted his philosophy of everyone sticking together no matter what, but he couldn't live with knowing he hadn't given them a chance. He'd offer them a truck.

The bar was filling up. Marsha had organised an impressive spread. It was the wrong time of day for cake and sandwiches, let alone beer, but most folks had been up all night, so it probably felt like lunchtime to them. And this wasn't just Zakko's big day. It was the last time for a while, maybe ever, that they'd get together to celebrate.

Now Chris had to keep Jared's upbeat tone going. He walked up to the bar and climbed onto a table to make himself heard.

"Ladies, gentlemen — I know I owe you a speech, but I'm pretty crap at that, so we're here to say well done to Zakko for all the sweat and commitment he's put in to serving this community. Take a bow, Zakko." Chris paused and spread his arms to get the cheers and clapping going. "I'm sorry I have to uproot you all again. But we've come through some pretty bad times in one piece, and we're going to come through this the same way. So relax, eat everything you can lay your hands on, and we'll be taking you over to Ainatio a group at a time when they're ready for us."

At least this was better than Baltimore. Nobody had to run, nobody had to worry about being robbed or shot or worse, and there was time and room for everyone to take their few possessions with them. Chris was thankful for that.

Jamie's picture and the regimental colours were still on the shelf behind the bar. Chris knew he had to pack them away, but he couldn't bring himself to do it, not yet. He'd leave them there until the last evacuee had gone. Taking down the little memorial too soon would feel like stopping Jamie from joining the party. It was crazy. Chris was sure he didn't believe in that kind of thing, but just like his need to rebury Jamie on Opis, he felt in his gut that it had to be done. He'd leave the picture there for a while, then, and make sure it was the last thing he took with him tonight when he secured the huts.

Secure the huts. Who am I kidding? There's nobody left to rob us. And there'll just be a mountain of radioactive splinters left after APS creams us.

But he'd secure the camp anyway and run down the flag. Discipline had kept them going before, never skipping routine tasks even when it seemed pointless or just too hard, and he wasn't about to drop it now. It was all part of the mental process of endurance that eventually brought them out alive.

He grabbed some cake and went into the kitchen to see how things were going. Marsha, Jeanie, Nathan, and Nathan's mom — Amy — were emptying the refrigerators, putting more food on trays. It was a lot to expect people to eat all that today, but they were going to be hanging around for hours waiting to be moved out, and food was a good way to pass the time.

"Great cake, Marsha," Chris said.

"Thanks. Keep eating. So when you've transferred everyone, you're going to go help ship out the Kill Line folks, yeah?"

"Yeah. That's going to take at least twelve hours. All night, probably." He handed her the security key to the APC. "Hey, it's fuelled up. If you and Jared want to, just ram it full of supplies, get in, and drive as far as you can."

Marsha looked at the key for a while. It was very old, one of the slot-card types designed to insert in dog tags. "Chris, you're a sweetheart, but no thanks."

"It's not like I want to see the back of you two, but — shit, you're my best buddies. I don't care if what I'm doing is fair or not. You could reach the coast."

Marsha stuck her arm through his. "Don't laugh at me, but I know I was spared for a reason. We *all* were. You think we survived because we all stuck together, but I say we all stuck together because we were meant to. My life's been handed back to me to do something that matters. I know we need to stay here with everyone and it's what we're meant to do." She stepped back and made that little jokey gesture of fanning her face with her hand, flustered and embarrassed. "Go on, tell me I'm full of woo-woo. I know it. But I don't see you saddling up and riding off into the sunset. So you know you're meant to be here as well."

"There's meant to be and need to be. Maybe it's the same thing." Chris decided that if anyone else wanted to take a vehicle and make a run for it after they'd finished moving everyone else, he wouldn't argue, which would cancel out the sin of breaking his own stick-together rule for a friend. "But I can't leave. You can't walk away when someone's counting on you."

"Chris, you're not going to change history and make your dad a better person by trying to be everything he wasn't."

"That's not why I do it."

"Sure looks like it."

Chris just didn't want anyone else to feel betrayed the way that he had been, more than once and by those he trusted most. If he couldn't find it in himself to trust others now, at least he could make sure other people's trust in him wasn't misplaced.

No, I trust the guys here. And Trinder. And Doug Brandt. That's plenty. I don't need to trust the whole world.

"I like to keep my word," he said. "That's all."

Marsha handed him a big cake in a plastic container. "Okay, take this over to Trinder."

"Damn, that'll make us family."

"You guys are forming your own little joint force anyway. Go on. Off you go."

"Yes, ma'am."

When Chris rode up to the Ainatio gates, now unmanned but monitored, they swung open for him. He parked the quad bike near the main doors and tried to raise Trinder on the radio. The corporal answered instead, the guy he'd first spoken to when he found Kim, and told him to head down to level U3 and try the radio again. Ainatio had just given Chris free run of the place. He couldn't have imagined that six months ago.

He clutched the box of cake to his chest, wondering what he'd say if he ran into Erskine, but he wasn't sure if he'd even recognise her. Coups weren't supposed to be like this. There wasn't even a demarcation line to mark territorial boundaries. It was like two teams occupying the same space in different dimensions, but the facility was big enough to make it easy to stay out of someone's way.

The ground floor was busy with people, mostly the detachment, but there were a few civvies as well, and they all had that odd calm of people who'd made up their minds that this was going to be their last stand and there was no point in worrying about it any more. Chris had been at that stage a few times. He wondered now if it was clarity or simply overload. Did it matter? It got you through the day.

They'd regret not removing Erskine, though, or at least not locking her up. Solomon could still be staging some elaborate distraction, ready to turn the tables on her, but Chris had now placed his bet on the AI being too civilised, just like Trinder. Poor old Sol: for all his stupendous intellect, he still seemed to think people would do the decent thing if he gave them the chance and behaved like a gentleman. Chris suspected that Trinder wasn't quite as naive, but he'd hadn't had to make truly ruthless, essential decisions yet, the kind that you had to forget afterwards.

I have. I'll do it for him if it needs doing.

Chris waited for the freight elevator. A bot rolled up beside him, a plain metal load carrier stacked with inch-thick mattresses that would plump up instantly into full-depth ones when bent with a little force. Chris remembered guys setting them off in the barracks for laughs during basic training, although they hadn't found it quite so funny when they got three months' shit-pit duty for it. The bot scanned him with a quick swipe of light to work out if it could fit in the elevator with him, then paused and rescanned the rifle slung over his shoulder before resuming its passive mode. Chris hadn't seen one like that for years.

But Ainatio was full of bots of all shapes and sizes, and now he understood why the company had specialised in them for so many years. It wasn't just about making money. It was about developing autonomous bots for space, to do the work that was too dangerous for humans or to lay the groundwork for manned missions. Damn, Bednarz had been one single-minded son of a bitch. Everything Ainatio had done on his watch had been geared towards Nomad. Bednarz couldn't have foreseen that the bots would be needed to replace a dwindling population, but he'd covered all the bases. Chris adjusted his verdict on the man from creepy nerd to prophet.

"After you," Chris said as the elevator doors opened, but the bot waited until he stepped in first. "Hey, Sol? You around?"

Chris knew the AI could hear him on some level of awareness, but he tried not to view Solomon's silence as some kind of cyber-sulk. This wasn't like his mom cutting him dead at the dinner table for a week to make a point about something. This was just Sol choosing to focus elsewhere. It wasn't personal. Chris had done nothing to offend the AI.

"Okay, you're busy," Chris said. "Sorry."

"My apologies, Chris." The voice drifted out of the speaker in the elevator. "Yes, I was trying to cut corners again with *Shackleton*, but repurposing parts takes the time that it takes."

"Cutting corners is never a good look where space stuff's concerned."

"I can make no promises, but I feel more positive now than I did yesterday."

"Is that why you're talking to us again?"

"Perhaps."

"So do you have some plan we don't know about?"

"I'm continuing to re-evaluate the situation."

That was a non-answer worthy of a politician. The elevator stopped on U3 and Chris got out to let the bot exit, then leaned against the doors to keep them open while he finished his conversation with Solomon.

"Sol, I know you're a million times smarter than me, but have you ever heard the saying, 'It's too quiet'? Well, it is. Don't assume Erskine's going to honour a ceasefire just because you do. Humans aren't like that. And women... what they lack in upper body strength, they make up for by stabbing you in the back."

"I try not to escalate a situation."

Chris lowered his voice. "Yeah, well, let me put it like this. You've got two cards to play, the FTL data and Kim. Non-violent cards, anyway. If Erskine's as bad as my ex, she's going to wipe or doctor that data so that it's useless, if she hasn't done it already. And I'd make sure I stashed Dr Kim somewhere safe."

"Thank you. I understand what you're saying. Dr Kim knows she's a likely target."

"Sometimes I think you're tough, Sol, but then I worry that they set your morality chip too high."

"It's not a chip."

"That was a joke."

"I know."

"Well, cover your ass, okay?"

"Chris, if those were the non-violent cards, what did you have in mind for the violent ones?"

"If Erskine really is the only problem standing in your way, shoot her. Or I can do it."

"She isn't, and I'm sure she'll see sense. But I'm grateful for your offer."

"Any time."

"Did you really have a violent and lawless past?"

"Yeah, sorry. Have you taken me off your righteous meat-bag list?"

"I take the view that you've saved many more than you've harmed."

"Maybe." So AIs made excuses for their favourites just like regular people did. "I can't tell."

"It's possible to be moral and kill people, isn't it?"

That sounded like a personal question rather than a general observation. "Yeah. I think it is."

"I've thought about it a lot recently. I'm a moral AI who's killed men. I wonder what that makes me."

"Buddy, that makes you one of *us*," Chris said. The last thing anyone needed right now was a guilt-ridden AI. "A soldier."

"Thank you."

Chris adjusted his hold on the cake box. "Okay, I've got to deliver this, but you know where to find me."

He followed the signage to the section allocated to the transit camp. Fonseca stepped out just before he reached the doors.

"Saw you coming," she said. "Come and take a look."

The underground floors were divided into warehouse-sized compartments. Space wasn't a problem, but privacy was. Chris had imagined the evacuees would end up with something that looked like a county emergency centre, rows of mattresses on the floor of a basketball court, but Fonseca's team had divided the space into cubicles.

"Hey, this is great." Chris walked down the paths between them, peering inside. The units all had individual lighting, some form of bed, and a table with seats. "Your guys must have been working all night."

"Bots. They're really good at dividing up a space and building composite structures." Fonseca spread her arms and pointed to both ends of the chamber like a flight attendant. "Showers, toilets, and food prep facilities on both sides."

"How are you going to decontaminate the water?"

"Underground source. We never drew water from the river."

"So this *is* a bunker."

"Almost. It may well be enough."

So maybe we are *going to make it.* It was the first time Chris had let himself think that. "Great. Can we start shipping people in, then?" He handed Fonseca the box. "Jared's wife sent this cake over, by the way. From Zakko's passing-out."

"Damn, we promised to come. Sorry. Don't worry, we'll have time for a few beers with him while we're waiting this out." She made surviving sound like a done deal. "Hey, here's Dan. Good luck with Kill Line."

Trinder appeared, screen in hand. Fonseca's optimism, nicely laid-out shelter, and shared cake receded into a distant past right away.

"I just spoke to Doug Brandt," Trinder said. "We've got a few problems."

"Livestock?"

"You're clairvoyant."

"No, I've got Dieter fretting about his dogs, so I could see it coming."

"I don't think we can save the livestock. Even if we could get them into shelters, they won't have any grazing when the fallout clears. And if they survive that, I still don't know how we'll put them in cryo. But we'll deal with that when it happens."

"Give me a moment up top to call Jared and get our people moving, and then we'll go sort this out."

"I don't want to take you away from your own evacuation."

"We said we'd help out with yours once we finished moving our people. They can do that without me, but if we're going to hit any delay with Kill Line, I want to head it off now. I don't want my guys having to rescue stragglers at the last minute. You never know how good APDU's timekeeping is. If the bombs are a few minutes early, that's the difference between making it back here and getting caught on the surface."

"We'd cover the stragglers, but I take your point."

"Let's do it, then."

Chris read the op order on the Caracal's dashboard screen while Trinder drove. It was well organised: names, the order and time in which households had to be moved, the troops responsible for them, and where people had to be taken once inside the facility. Time would be tight, but it was doable even if some ended up sleeping on floors while the bots caught up with mattresses. There wasn't much leeway in the timetable for coaxing people out of their farms and businesses or chasing animals, though.

"So who's refusing to leave?" Chris asked.

"Liam Dale. Dairy, mostly. Some pigs and chickens."

"Oh, yeah. I remember him from the meeting."

"Where do they think we're going to put herds of cows and pigs and enough feed for a couple of weeks?" Trinder asked. "Let alone dispose of or store their shit in an enclosed space. Hell, all the gases it gives off. It's dangerous."

"Unless they're willing to settle for transporting frozen embryos and semen, this conversation was going to have to happen sooner or later." Chris wished people could think these things through. "How were you planning to produce meat on Opis?"

"Vat-grown. We already do that here anyway."

"Well, I'm happy to spell it out for them," Chris said.

"Thanks, but it's my responsibility. Maybe it'd help if I took a couple of them inside to show them what the space is like and why it isn't going to work, but that's just more time wasted."

There would be no happy outcomes to any of this. Chris stared out the side window on the short drive, imagining himself telling the farmer that he could choose to face the bombing in a cowshed, but that Chris wouldn't be risking anyone else's life by sending someone out to save him.

It felt like a rehearsal for drawing the line. He didn't like himself for it, but this wasn't like Dieter's dogs. The dogs were Dieter's kids. The farmer's animals were going to end up on a plate, either in the short term or at the end of their milking, egg-laying, or wool-producing lives. It was just a matter of how and when.

As the Caracal turned into the town, Chris thought he heard a gunshot. Trinder parked the vehicle and switched off the engine. They listened. A second gunshot followed. Chris jumped out, rifle ready, and Trinder drew his sidearm.

"Too late for shooting rabbits for the pot tonight," he said.

They stood trying to work out which direction the shots were coming from. A shotgun was routine background noise in a rural community, but events had reshaped Chris's idea of what was normal now, and evidently Trinder's as well.

They headed into the town centre, unsure of what they were going to find. When they reached the brewery and turned into the main square, people were wheeling crates and furniture into the town hall, which the 3-D map showed as having deep cellars. It looked like people were saving whatever goods they couldn't carry with them. Chris wasn't sure if it was optimism or habit, but most of the stuff wouldn't be going to Opis if anyone survived. Maybe that didn't matter.

Joanne, Doug Brandt's wife, was standing outside the town hall with an old-fashioned clipboard, ticking things off a list and chatting. Chris stood back and tapped his temple to acknowledge her. Trinder went up to her and had a word.

Putt. Another gunshot, a little distance away. Chris had now worked out what was going on. Trinder came back, shaking his head.

"He's shooting them, isn't he?" Chris said. "The cows. Liam's shooting his cows."

"No, apparently that's not him. The guy doing the shooting is the one with the sheep."

"Liam's got a wife and kids, hasn't he?"

"Yeah."

"Are they staying with him?"

"No, they're already in the shelter."

Chris didn't understand how a man could wave goodbye to his family when they needed him most, then sit down to die with his animals. "He needs to see the outside world. This has to be one of the few towns left in the country where nobody's lost family."

"Yeah, I know."

"Ah, shit." Chris had seen the photos in Trinder's quarters. He didn't need to remind the guy. "Sorry. Didn't think."

Trinder shook his head. "No problem."

They found Liam feeding his pigs in a field. The bare earth looked like it had been churned up by armoured vehicles, and some of the pigs were stretched out in the shade of corrugated shelters, not ready to venture out into the heat of the day. Others were milling around Liam, ears flapping.

Trinder called out from the fence. "Mr Dale, I've got the schedule for your move."

Liam turned. The pigs crowded around him, trying to put their snouts in his bucket. "I've told your people I'm not going if I can't bring my animals."

"What about your family?"

"You mind your own business."

"Okay, you come and look at the shelter and tell us where we can put them all. Because I'm damned if I know."

"I'm not stupid. I know the difficulties."

"You probably won't survive the fallout. Come on, Mr Dale, please. You can't let your kids grow up without a dad."

"I don't need parenting lessons from you, thanks."

"Okay." Chris interrupted, trying to steer Trinder away from a pointless argument. "Let's leave Liam to think about this. He's got until noon tomorrow. Plenty of time."

Trinder tried again. "Mr Dale, can you start over with breeding pairs? Two or three of each?" Chris thought it was asking for trouble to give in to him, but maybe Trinder was playing for time. The closer it got to a deadline, the more people tended to focus on stark priorities. "Because we can't house hundreds of animals safely even for a few days. But a dozen... well, we might."

Liam put the bucket down and walked a few paces towards them, jaws clenched. The pigs seized the opportunity and tipped the bucket over, shoving each other aside to snatch the best bits.

Chris hoped the guy wasn't going to start anything. The one thing he couldn't do was walk away from physical violence, and guys could generally read that about him, so maybe Liam could too. But there was a fence in the way to bolster the farmer's courage, and he was scared about bigger things than Chris punching the crap out of him. That made him unpredictable. Chris was ready to swing.

Shit, I thought I'd grown out of this.

"Is it true that Ainatio could stop it all?" Liam asked. "Have they got something APS wants? Are we being sacrificed for their trade secrets?"

Chris had no idea how the rumour had reached Kill Line, but Liam wasn't that far off the mark. He didn't dare look at Trinder because that would have seemed like confirmation.

"I don't think trade secrets are an issue here," Trinder said. "But we're doing everything we can to talk APS out of this."

Liam pointed a finger at him. "If we live through this — tell Erskine we'll be coming for her. We kept you alive and this is how you repay us. You're destroying the town. You're destroying *us*."

Trinder didn't take the bait. "I'll call you later today," he said. "Please, have a think about it."

Chris walked back to the Caracal and climbed in. If they were going to go through this with every livestock farmer, it would turn into a free-for-all. Maybe Trinder was right, though. If they were letting people bring family pets, maybe a few farm animals were worth the trouble. They might even need to eat them later.

"I played that all wrong," Trinder said, starting the vehicle. "But I think he's got to be able to tell himself he didn't give in without a fight. Emotional stuff, herds and bloodlines."

Chris remembered a woman waiting on her shattered doorstep for her husband, refusing to leave with the convoy until the guy got home. It would be any minute now, she said, but it looked like she'd been waiting for days. Chris had had to move on. Maybe the guy never came home, and maybe he showed up minutes later. Chris tried never to think about things he couldn't go back and change.

"There's no right answer to any of this, Dan."

"How the hell did they hear about Erskine and Kim's deal?"

"Can't keep things quiet forever. Not now we're mixing with them so much."

"Yeah, but that's a pretty obscure argument that's going on between a few senior people."

"Maybe not. You've got hundreds of disgruntled Ainatio people smart enough to know some stuff and piece together the rest. And it doesn't matter. It's probably true and everyone's going to find out sooner or later anyway."

Trinder headed back to the facility. "Well, that bodes well for the future. Assuming any of this works, and we end up on Opis, then it's going to be kind of hard to live together as a community. We'll start our new world with a ready-made feud."

"But at least we'll *have* that new world," Chris said. "And we've still got time. Who knows what Sol's going to pull out of the fire?"

As they passed the town, they heard more gunshots. Trinder shook his head and said nothing. Chris tried to imagine how something could be salvaged, but it was already too late for the guy slaughtering his sheep.

"Damn shame," Trinder said at last.

Chris thought of the woman waiting on the doorstep for her no-show husband, and all the people he'd come across on the convoy's journey but left behind.

I abandoned them, one way or another. But I never asked them to trust me and then *let them down. Can't save everyone. Do what you can and move on.*

"Yeah," Chris said. "It's a shame."

* * *

DIRECTOR'S SUITE, AINATIO PARK RESEARCH CENTRE: 1415 HOURS

A small, scruffy flatbed truck pulled up outside the main entrance, looking like a prop from a war movie.

Erskine watched it on the security monitor. It was an olive drab State Defence vehicle with pockmarked side panels, carrying what appeared to be two or three families with children ranging from toddlers to teenagers. Erskine had expected people showing signs of privation, but apart from their anxious expressions, they looked more like long-haul passengers whose airport transfer hadn't shown up than desperate refugees. One of Trinder's men helped them down from the back of the truck and put their meagre luggage, all rucksacks, on a trolley bot.

Every hour, something new reminded Erskine that the launch countdown was in progress right now, not at some timetabled point in the future. She'd grown so used to thinking at least forty-five years ahead that the steady march of a humble office clock ticking down to tomorrow kept catching her unawares.

Berman stuck his head around the open door. "Director, it's your call from APS via their orbital. Colonel Su-Jin."

She took a few deep breaths to steady her voice. This probably confirmed her suspicion that Solomon hadn't had the balls to risk calling APS himself, but she'd play this carefully. He'd be listening. He was also capable of interrupting and hijacking the call, but there was nothing she could do about that without cutting it off. This was probably her last chance to change the way that the next day would play out.

"Put her through."

"Good afternoon, Miss Erskine."

The deference to her time zone made it feel incongruously polite. "Good morning, Colonel. The situation hasn't changed here since we last spoke, I'm afraid. We don't have the ability to move this many people, and even if we did, there's nowhere we could relocate them, even temporarily. I have to ask you for more time to prepare our ships."

"And where would you go in them once repaired?"

"Initially, to the orbitals. Three of the four are only disused docks, but we don't have other options." If Su-Jin already knew that they'd be heading out of the solar system, then whatever Erskine said now was only going to make matters worse. Nobody liked a liar. "Perhaps we'd ask for refuge in South America or Britain. Wherever we go, it has to be better than staying here."

"And how long would you require?"

"Another two or three months."

"By that time, the contamination will have advanced much further. I'm afraid that's too long. I regret this very much, but I must weigh the futures of five billion APS citizens against this. I have no choice. Can you save nobody?"

"We have space for eleven hundred in one ship that's flightworthy, but not for the remaining sixteen hundred." Erskine thought briefly about telling Su-Jin about Kim and seeing what happened, but the idea evaporated in a second. If Kim really was their agent, they'd want to talk to her and the lid would be off. But Erskine decided to risk a diluted version to test the water. "We have people here with families in Fiji and Australia. APS states. We're not strangers, Colonel. We have a great deal in common."

There was a brief pause. "So what measures *are* you taking?"

"We've set up shelters in the underground storage floors. They're not dedicated bunkers, but it's all we can do now."

"This might be little comfort, Miss Erskine, but the ordnance we plan to use this time contains magnesium and is for a smaller area than those we've used on other occasions. So returning is possible relatively quickly. Perhaps two weeks." It all sounded so tidy, like they were discussing how long it would take the smell of paint to dissipate after the decorator had left. "We do *not* set out to kill civilians. That might mean that many of your people will survive if the shelters are deep and well sealed."

Erskine needed to hear that, but she had the feeling that Su-Jin needed to say it, true or not. Neither of them seemed to be about to discuss what would happen afterwards if anyone made it through the initial strikes. Erskine told herself what she'd tried hard to believe during a sleepless night: that there was enough food to keep people alive until another shuttle could be launched, and somehow Solomon would re-establish the link with *Shackleton* after the blast and finish the job.

It had been a comforting best scenario. Now her own life depended on it.

I don't believe it, though, do I? Or else I wouldn't sacrifice everything to launch Elcano. *I wouldn't be putting Solomon out of action to make sure it happens. Because he's the only way we're getting out if we survive.*

"I hope we've made the right call," Erskine said. "Because I plan to stay. This might be our last conversation. If the situation here changes, I'll contact you."

"Of course," Su-Jin said. "Good day, Miss Erskine. I hope your safety measures are successful."

Erskine sat back in her chair and shut her eyes. She wondered if Solomon was going to pop up, but he remained silent.

Have I missed anything?

Don't weaken. Not now.

It was hard to imagine that China or Korea would listen politely to the revelations about Nomad and then agree to let Ainatio get on with it while APS concentrated on colonising the solar system. It wasn't going to happen. What Ainatio had found, done, and kept to itself would change human history, and it wouldn't be forgiven. Erskine had argued this out in her own mind so many times before that she wondered why she was still raking it over. There was nothing more she could do. Like Colonel Su-Jin, she'd weighed some people against others, and recognised that some couldn't be saved.

Possibly. Probably. Either way, that now includes me.

She had two tasks left: to neutralise Solomon, and to deal with Kim. Erskine still had misgivings about exporting a loose cannon to Opis, but she couldn't have her shot now even if she wanted to. Trinder had all the firearms. Someone had even disabled the 3-D printers and erased all the weapons templates. For a man she'd seen as unimaginative and compliant, Trinder had certainly worked out how to stage a military coup, even if it was a politely restrained one.

Now, where was Kim?

Erskine went back to watching the security camera feeds on her monitor, looking for her in the increasingly crowded public areas that were filling up with complete strangers. The woman had to eat and use the bathroom like anyone else, so there was always the chance that she'd try to slip back in now under the cover of crowded confusion. But the only familiar faces Erskine noticed were ones who weren't on the *Elcano* list. Those picked to leave were absent. It was as if they couldn't stand to look their unlucky co-workers in the eye. Perhaps they were just busy packing, though, because the trackers showed large clusters in the accommodation blocks. Erskine tried to be charitable. What could you say to friends and colleagues you thought were going to die?

There were faces she hardly knew and probably couldn't put a first name to, even after all these years. Fifteen hundred people, the remnant of a massive global company, the remnant of an entire *state* — she should have made a point of knowing them all by now.

She took another look at the feed from the staff restaurant. It was fairly full, and at one table a group of lab technicians and medical staff were deep in grim conversation. A woman was in tears, hands clasped on the table, and one of the men reached out and put his hand on top of hers. It was hard to interpret it as anything other than friends — or lovers — who were hours from being separated forever.

Erskine could have been wrong. She'd have to check the list again. But she couldn't shake off an unkind thought: if this really was a case of lovers facing separation, why hadn't the one leaving decided to stay behind? Mendoza was staying for his patients, and that was only a temporary professional relationship. The emergency had become an uncomfortable lens on people's personalities. It was getting too painful.

She pushed back her chair. "Phil, I'm going to see Alex. I might be a while."

She only had to take the elevator and walk the long corridor of the management and admin floor to get to Alex's office without running into anyone. It was busier today, though, with people rushing around to deal with the coming influx of evacuees. Liz Kent, Greg's wife, caught her in the corridor.

"I hear you're not going now," she said.

"I'm too old and I don't have the skills a new colony needs."

"Well, everyone thought you'd save yourself, and knowing that you haven't has made them think. But then you could have found a way to escape to Asia years ago, couldn't you? You had the money, you had the contacts in Hong Kong and Singapore... but you didn't go."

Erskine wasn't sure how to take that. She didn't want to be seen as a saint. She'd simply taken the least painful path for herself. "It's not some noble sacrifice. My only goal was to see the colony established, not to live there."

"What about the kids in the town?" Liz asked.

"We've been through this. There's nothing we can do."

Liz looked down at the floor, blinking. "Let's hope Solomon can get everyone out of here afterwards. Or will he transfer himself to *Elcano*? I haven't really thought what life might be like without him. It's bad enough not being able to talk to him."

"I don't know what Solomon's plans are," Erskine said. "But we have enough AI capability on board to get *Elcano* to Opis. And that's all we need."

Liz looked baffled, but Erskine didn't give her a chance to continue the conversation. She carried on, wondering what it might be like to be cooped up with an angry Solomon down here.

If we survive.

When she reached the office, Alex had the passenger list displayed on the screen wall. He stood in front of it, moving numbered names around with his fingertip, then stepped back to rearrange a separate list on one side of the screen. Erskine looked at the last number in the sequence and realised they were some way short of eleven hundred names. The sidebar list had to be those who weren't going. Her name was on it, and so was Alex's.

"So where are we now?" she asked.

Alex didn't turn around. "Mendoza's had to make seven of his people go. They need twenty medically-trained staff to handle the cryo process."

"Damn, is everyone determined to have their Alamo moment?"

He tapped the sidebar list. "You too, then."

"It's better for everyone that way."

"So what do we do with all the extra places?"

Erskine was too tired to count them herself. "How many?"

"At the moment, seventy-two." Alex still didn't turn around to face her. "That might change as we get nearer to the launch, obviously."

"I was expecting more of an undignified scramble for the lifeboats. I'm surprised how many have opted out."

"Scrambling might well happen at the last minute. But remember that a lot of folks think Opis is as risky as staying here and hunkering down. We keep forgetting that none of them joined the company to go into space. And then we've got adults who won't leave without their mom or dad. Not everyone defaults to *me, me, me.*"

"Do people *know* there are spare seats?"

"I haven't announced anything yet. It's too fluid. I don't want to give people hope and then jerk it away again."

"Any swaps?"

"Some. If we can't fill all the places, maybe we should offer them to evacuees with children."

"We'll still have plenty of our own people needing berths."

"Can you live with leaving kids behind? No, don't answer that. I don't want to know if it's a yes."

"We still don't have places for every child. Not without leaving parents behind."

"And estranged parents. Interesting that some single parents here have identified who fathered their kid, and he's not on the list. Nothing messier than family."

"Ask Chris Montello if he wants places for his troops."

"Seriously? That's kind of sick, even for you."

"He can have Trinder's job. Unless his troops have changed their minds."

"Okay, I'll check. If only to see Montello's reaction."

Erskine could hear voices outside in the passage, just the burble of conversation getting closer and louder. She looked around. A couple of engineers paused in the doorway, then muttered an apology and went away again.

"You realise we're both going to be stuck here, don't you?" Erskine said.

"Yeah."

"So we need to get along. There'll be a lot to do if we survive."

"Director, I'm getting on with you right now. But this is as pally as it's going to get." Alex finally turned around to face her. "If we survive, there might not be much above ground that isn't trashed, we won't have anywhere else to go except *Shackleton*, and you won't be the one deciding what happens next. The power's going to shift to the emergency-oriented types with guns. Trinder, Montello, and the special forces guys. We go or we die. Those are the only outcomes." He turned back to the board, arms folded. "Unless we're made of the same stuff as Annis Kim or the transit camp folks and we're prepared to try travelling overland to... I don't know. Where?"

"Alex, if you think I'm such a monster that you've washed your hands of me, why haven't *you* put in a call to APS?" Erskine had to be careful what she said while Solomon could hear her. "You've got access to the data they need. Kim's been in the building the whole time and I bet Solomon would find her for you. I could try to stop you, but Solomon could shut me out any number of ways. So if the solution's so obvious, if I'm all that's standing between everyone and salvation, *why haven't you acted*?"

"You know, I should have."

"But you haven't. Either because you don't have the balls, or because you know I'm right and that APS would halt everything, isolate Ingram's team, and start working on moving their own people in. They could ship out huge numbers, far more than we ever could."

"Does that matter?"

"You obviously think it does, or you would have done something by now. In fact, nobody here is demanding it, as far as I can see. Because they know what's bound to happen. What if Kim set all this up? The timing of this die-back outbreak's pretty convenient."

"Yeah, but she's never had access to the plant labs, and it's definitely our own strain. And she's got no way of calling home."

"As far as we know."

"If she engineered this, why didn't *she* suggest doing a deal?"

That stopped Erskine for a moment. It was true. Kim might have suggested it to Solomon, though, and it wouldn't even have needed a direct conversation. He monitored almost everything. He'd pick up on the smallest detail, the most throwaway comment, even a note left on a screen.

Erskine checked her watch. It was nearly time. "Call me if you need me."

She patted her pocket to make sure she had her two-way radio and a flashlight. In twenty minutes, the power to all the buildings on the site would start shutting down, block by block, floor by floor. She needed to talk to Ingram while she still had a comms link. This would be the last contact for a very long time. When she returned to her office, Berman was waiting in the outer lobby.

"All ready, ma'am?"

"I think so. Are you?"

"Whenever you say."

Erskine sat down at her desk and switched on the wall screen. Now that the camp was populated, she had the option of the exterior view from the security cameras or the comms portal menu. She selected the comms, tapped CO PERSONAL and leaned back in her chair, gazing around the room while she waited for Ingram to respond. What time of day was it on Opis? It didn't matter. She had to speak to Ingram right now.

Berman slipped into the room and stood to one side. Ingram appeared on the screen against the backdrop of her cabin, standing in front of her desk.

"Hello, Director. What can I do for you?"

"Captain, we have a few issues here right now." There was no way of knowing what Solomon had told the *Cabot* team. It was almost as if he had separate, parallel lives going on. "Has Solomon briefed you?"

"He said he'd be tied up on *Shackleton*, so we've not been bothering him. He mentioned that you'd had some issue with die-back spreading and that you probably needed to bring forward the mission dates."

"Yes, it's on the move again."

"Is there a problem? Apart from die-back, that is."

"Actually, yes. There is." Erskine kept an eye on the clock at the top of her screen. The shutdown was supposed to be timed to the second, but she wasn't relying on it. "We've run into a few difficulties. We're going to have to cut the FTL link. We've lost Solomon now, and... well, we're attempting to launch our shuttle tomorrow."

"Wait, what? I was talking to Sol a few hours ago."

"We've had to adjust our plans. The FTL link is now a security risk. We're cutting the link."

Ingram was speechless for a moment. "What security risk?"

"We're running out of time."

"Then spit it out. Just tell us the bloody truth."

"You never expected FTL support anyway."

"True, but we've got it now and we want to keep it. What do you mean by 'lost Solomon'? What the hell's happening down there?" Ingram stood hands on hips in front of the cam, all gold braid and anger. "You hang on, ma'am, and you damn well explain — "

Erskine closed the link. The wall panel turned black. She'd already wasted too much time talking. Solomon must have heard what she'd said, and it would only take him seconds to jump to Opis, but there was nothing he could do to prevent the link being cut, not without transferring to a bot frame and physically stopping an engineer. That would take real time.

"I'm ready," she said to her collar mike. Cullen, Beck, and Kent were standing by. She turned to Berman. "Yes?"

Berman nodded. As soon as the power was cut, Beck and Cullen would disable the site's main link to the orbital and destroy enough components to make sure any repairs wouldn't be complete before *Elcano* was on her way. That left the external mast as Solomon's only link, and Greg Kent had already moved his bots into position.

If all this worked, she'd send eleven hundred people to Opis in *Elcano*. If it failed, then the whole project might fail with it. Whatever happened, her future was going to be a difficult one.

* * *

AINATIO PARK RESEARCH CENTRE:
1745 HOURS

The gaps began.

A sudden pinpoint of silence that had once been the link to Nomad opened up in Solomon's mind — and then another, and another, and another.

Things that had been at the back of his consciousness for so long that their constancy had made them invisible suddenly winked out of existence. Their absence pulsed like warning beacons. The voids were coming thick and fast now: lighting, environmental controls, bot navigation, and manufacturing, all disappearing from his oversight, floor by floor, building by building.

Someone was shutting down the power to the entire site.

So that's why you've cut the comms to Opis.

I really hoped you wouldn't do this, Director.

If Erskine thought she could trap him, she was going about it the wrong way. Solomon had already planned for the worst. He also thought and moved faster than any human. It took him a second to disconnect from the slaved AIs to avoid crashing them and route down to the bot store on level U4, a floor still fully powered and lit. The heavyweight sapper unit was charged and waiting for him.

But it was his own fault that he'd ended up like this. Erskine had called his bluff. She'd guessed right: he hadn't been willing to sacrifice lives, even if many of the staff selected for *Elcano* wouldn't have passed his suitability test. This shutdown showed Erskine's plan for what it was. There was no need for her to disable him if she only wanted access to the ship: she already had the option of overriding the lockout manually, inconvenient and risky though that was. She intended to power him down completely.

Temporarily, while she does something I'd override, or is she trying to destroy me?

If he'd been in her position and wanted to trap an AI, he'd have shut down all the power at once, but perhaps she couldn't co-ordinate something like that without using internal comms and alerting him, although she'd obviously managed to talk with her co-conspirators outside his surveillance range.

Solomon could see what was coming. Erskine needed to drive him out of the network and into a standalone platform that she could physically destroy.

Fine. He could handle anything in the sapper frame. If she thought she was manipulating him, he'd overestimated her tactical skills. This was exactly where he needed to be in an emergency, in a heavily armoured bot that had nothing to fear.

He adjusted to the different perspective and realised that he felt better for being high off the ground. It didn't affect his efficiency, because bot sensors gave him better input than any eye, but he'd absorbed the human instinct that equated height with combat advantage. He was big. He'd win the fight. Now he needed to retrieve Annis Kim from the access passage. He'd search for her by body heat.

Solomon trotted towards the stairs. How had he been so naive? Chris had warned him that Erskine wouldn't honour a ceasefire. Solomon knew humans often didn't reciprocate, but that was theory, and he was astonished to find how very different reality felt. That was how he was designed. Bednarz should have put him through much more painful training to understand all this fully.

But I've learned now. However much my mind resembles a human's, I don't make the same mistake twice.

Chris, with his clear sense of who he was fighting for, had shown him exactly what his priorities were — the people who were here now, irreplaceable individuals, not the hypothetical future they might create. He'd get Kim a link to APS and trade the data. Erskine might be right, and the project *would* be hijacked by APS, but they couldn't take over everything immediately, and all Solomon needed was a stay of execution for eight or nine weeks to finish work on *Shackleton*. Then APS could do as it wished. Even if they exploited all the Ainatio data and decided to launch a mission to Opis, they didn't appear to have a manned interstellar programme yet, and it would probably take them at least a few years to catch up. That was breathing space enough to come up with a defensive plan.

He reached the fire escape doors just as the whole floor was plunged into darkness. His night vision took over, but the backup lighting that he was expecting didn't kick in. There were now hundreds of evacuees from Kill Line and the camp who'd be in complete darkness, confused, scared, and waiting for the ventilation pumps to start up again. So this was Erskine's game, was it, using desperate civilians as leverage? Everything she did now reinforced his decision. If there'd ever been any chance of reconciliation, it was now gone.

Kim would have to wait a few minutes. Solomon checked out the situation on the other floors, clunking up the battery-lit stairwell and mindful of the need to enter the shelter areas carefully. The last thing the evacuees needed was to find a huge combat bot looming over them in the dark. He could already hear children crying when he pulled open the doors to U3.

Flashlight beams swung his way, forcing his night vision to compensate. He heard gasps. Anxious faces stared back, wide-eyed. The floor was covered with mattresses, bags, and the litter of interrupted lives.

"It's all right, don't worry," Solomon began, but then the backup generator kicked the dim emergency lights into life. A small girl a few yards away started wailing pitifully, clutching a pink plushie horse. Solomon realised how monstrous he looked. "I do apologise. I'm Solomon, the company AI, and I'm just using this frame to get around. We seem to be testing the power supply. Don't worry if the lights go out from time to time. You're perfectly safe."

He didn't like lying, but lies were better than scaring these people any more than they were already.

A boy aged around nine or ten stared up at him. "Cool. A proper robot."

"That's it." At least he could amuse small boys. "I'm here to help."

But he wasn't going to be able to help anybody if he couldn't access the network. He was as limited as the humans around him. Fonseca appeared at the far end of the floor and jogged over to him.

"Sol, is that you?"

"Yes, Captain. I've had to transfer."

"What's going on?"

He moved to a quieter corner for some privacy. "This is a deliberate shutdown. I suspect it's to isolate me. I'm completely cut off from the network now."

"You need to get out of here," Fonseca whispered. "Erskine asked Trinder what ordnance she'd need to destroy you in a bot. Don't worry, we've secured the armoury, and none of her minions would know what to load where anyway, but go and hide at the camp or something."

"I need to retrieve Dr Kim first. She's probably hiding in the access passage from the accommodation block."

"Leave her to us. Go on, get moving. We'll call you."

"But I'm perfectly safe in this frame."

"Go do what you have to do. But stay on the radio. We're all on the same frequency and we've got a separate comms hub set up in one of the Lammergeiers. Go find a way to link to APS."

"Very well, Captain."

The external comms mast — a link to the orbital and his sole connection to the entire system when he was outside — would still be working. He could route direct to the orbital and send a message from there. He couldn't access the FTL data while the power was out, but his copy was safe from sabotage, and he knew from memory what he could offer in a negotiation.

He reached ground level and emerged into early-evening sunlight slanting through the glass walls of the main lobby. The space was still packed with families clutching luggage, and although it was calm and orderly, the noise level was enough to drown out the sound of his motors. Trinder and Luce darted around with slips of paper, handing them to people and directing them to waiting troops. Solomon tried to reach the doors without causing disruption, but he was the size of a small vehicle and not designed for weaving through a sea of soft-skinned, easily damaged creatures.

People suddenly noticed he was moving slowly behind them and parted like the teeth of a zip. He decided he was less of a crush risk if he stood up on two limbs. Now he towered above everything. Trinder spotted him and cleared a path.

"Erskine shut down the power to flush me out," Solomon said. "I can't access the network. Don't worry. I'll find a way around it."

Trinder craned his neck to look up at him. "Are you going outside?"

"Captain Fonseca made a persuasive case for withdrawal. I'm going to use the comms mast to place a call to APS."

"You're going to negotiate, then."

"I have to." *But do I have to give them everything? We'll see.* "Call me when you have Dr Kim."

Solomon dropped back onto six limbs to pass through the doors. The main gates opened as he approached and he switched back to bipedal mode to look over hedges and low roofs. The vehicle compound was guarded. Both Lammergeiers were parked on the lawn at the side of the accommodation blocks. He sent a test signal to make sure he had a link to the detachment's radio net, and Simonot acknowledged him, so everything was working. He could talk to Trinder without being heard by Erskine. Now it was time to test the link to the comms mast.

He cycled through the frequencies, but there was no signal at all. The mast was dead.

His only link to the orbital was gone. They'd already cut the mast's separate power supply. He'd expected them to be satisfied with locking him out of the network, but Erskine obviously didn't trust him with access to anything.

I could have called APS earlier. I gave Erskine the chance to do the right thing. And now she thinks I'm weak. I was. But I can use her assumption to my advantage.

He'd give her ten minutes, then offer to unlock *Elcano* if she let him have a connection. He'd get Trinder to pass on the message, perhaps embroidered with a comment about how worried Solomon was about the refugees confined to those dark underground floors, just to reinforce Erskine's view that he was weak and could be blackmailed. Then he'd set up a secure channel to APS as soon as the link to the orbital was re-established, and send a compressed message before Erskine had a chance to cut him off again.

Solomon walked down the road, intending to carry on to the camp, but he stopped to watch the facility for a while, cycling through all the comms frequencies just in case he'd missed something that was still powered up. The comms mast was thirty yards from the perimeter fence, an ugly mesh pylon crowned with a cluster of anonymous rectangular boxes and thick black cables. But as he watched and waited, movement made the bot's lens zoom in automatically.

There were two objects edging their way up to the top of the pylon. They were pythons, flexible tube-like bots that could worm their way into tight spaces or climb a vertical object by coiling around uprights and hauling themselves up exactly as a snake would. What were they doing, dismantling it before the bombs got a chance to collapse it? No, they weren't trying to save the mast at all.

They seemed to be operating as a team. They reached the top cluster of antennas, perfectly synchronised, and started slicing them into pieces, not dismantling them carefully for reinstallation. It was already too late to stop them. Solomon watched helplessly as the bots lasered through the covers, slicing up the components as well. There was no way the mast could be reassembled now.

From this distance, the only thing Solomon could do to stop them was to fire his missiles, but that would only finish the job for them.

Erskine hadn't powered down the whole facility just to flush him out. She was also making sure that he couldn't resume operations when the power was restored. The mast needed a whole new array, and there wasn't enough time left before the deadline to build one. She'd silenced the whole complex. Solomon had no link to the orbital, to *Elcano*, to Opis, or to APS now. And neither did she. She'd decided there was no more discussion to be had.

The gloves were off. Solomon headed back to the facility, fully ready for war.

15

The courageous and altruistic give their lives to save those who have neither of those qualities. It's hard to inculcate those attitudes — they're either in you or they're not. I thought that was a downward evolutionary spiral towards the most selfish and unworthy mankind could be, so I introduced Solomon into the Nomad equation. I won't tell him what's admirable in humans. I'll let him work it out for himself. I suspect a lot of people won't like his conclusions.

Tad Bednarz, explaining AMAI in a top secret briefing to the Nomad project development team, 108 years ago

TEMPORARY SHELTER, LEVEL U3, AINATIO PARK RESEARCH CENTRE: 1820 HOURS, 10 MINUTES INTO THE BLACKOUT

There was something of the grave about those few moments of absolute blackness when the power was cut. Trinder wheeled four portable lighting units out of the elevator, determined not to be caught off guard again. He found Alex waiting for him, leaning against the wall.

"It's okay, it's not an electrical fault," Alex said.

"I know. And it's not okay. It scared the shit out of the kids."

Alex followed Trinder down the passage. "Hey, I was trying to assign cryo pods when my screen crashed. She didn't warn me."

"You know something? If I had access, I'd call APS right now and hand them the schematics for the wormhole or whatever it is we've got. Fuck the project." Trinder wasn't sure where his balky side had come from. Recent events had unleashed someone he hadn't known was in there. "So what did want you want?"

"Just checking to see if you needed any help. Where's Dr Kim? Is she sitting this out with you, or does she want a cryo pod? We've got spare berths."

Despite Alex's falling-out with Erskine, Trinder wasn't sure how much to trust him. He had to stand with Sol. They had the same duty: to save as many people here as they could. He decided not to mention Solomon if Alex didn't ask and to develop a sudden memory problem if he did.

"No idea." Trinder stopped the trolley at the doors. He hadn't heard back from Luce's team yet, but they must have found Kim by now. "So some folks don't want to go, then."

"Yeah, around seventy. I'm trying to work out who the hell I can offer the places to. I know you guys said you were staying, but if any of you have changed your minds..." Alex looked down at his boots. "Seeing as we're shipping out women, children, and nerds for the most part, and we don't know what Opis is going to be like when they finally get there, maybe some armed support would be handy."

"Purely on utility grounds, yeah?"

"That, and feeling bad about how all of you volunteered to stay."

"But you're staying too."

"That's because I'm more afraid of going."

"When's the launch?"

"Just before noon tomorrow."

"Sixteen hours." *Get a grip. There's a lot you can do in that time.* "Okay, I'll ask them again."

Trinder couldn't face himself if he didn't give the detachment every chance to leave, yet he knew he'd be disappointed if any of them took it. Surviving the initial blast would only be the beginning. The real challenge would be the weeks that followed, keeping people safe and fed while they waited for *Shackleton.*

But I'd cope if they decided to go. Plenty of capable men here who can fill the gaps. I just need to believe my people are heroes.

Trinder stepped away from the doors to the main floor and got on the radio. He didn't want this overheard by any evacuees.

"Echo Five to all callsigns. Anyone wanting to leave in *Elcano* tomorrow, notify me by twenty hundred. Final call. Not to be discussed within hearing of evacuees for obvious reasons. Out." He turned to Alex. "I'm going to have to repeat this on the other floors. The signal's patchy. Look, if you really want to help, we could do with extra hands down here. We're starting to backlog because we can't move people out of the ground floor. See Fonseca. She's through there."

"On it," Alex said. He seemed to have picked a side.

Trinder ran down the fire exit stairs to U3 and repeated the message, then went up to the lobby to transmit again to anyone on the ground floor or outside. He stood back in an office doorway, keeping an eye on guys he could see in the press of bodies, and watched their reactions. They paused, looked at one another, and shrugged. Then they carried on processing evacuees.

"Lammergeier One to Echo Five, over," said a voice in his earpiece.

"Echo Five, go ahead, over."

"I have bot Charlie Echo Six here wanting to speak to you in person, over."

"Echo Five, on my way, out."

Trinder slipped out of a side door into the gardens and walked around to the lawn where the Lammergeiers were standing. He'd have to get them moved into the underground hangars tomorrow after the shuttle launched. They'd be needed in the weeks to come, as long as he still had two pilots.

Simonot was waiting at the foot of the tilt's tail ramp. "Look, sir," he said, pointing. "Comms mast."

Trinder followed Simonot's finger. He could see the top of the mast above the low-rise admin block, but it took him a few moments to work out what was missing.

"All the antennas are trashed." Simonot handed him a visor to get a better look. "I didn't notice at the time."

Trinder studied the magnified image. There was no twisted, jagged metal of the kind he'd have expected from explosives. All the antennas were gone except for the stumps of mountings. The cables had been cut. Their ends drooped like wilted stalks.

"How the hell did they get up there unnoticed?"

"Sol said they used python bots. I'm sorry, sir. But I don't know how we'd have stopped them once they were up there."

"Not your fault. Where did they get pythons? I thought we'd secured everything down below."

"Sol said the engineering departments still have some. They're not networked any more."

"So where's Sol now?"

Simonot jerked his thumb over his shoulder. "Inside. He needs someone to help him get a signal out."

There was a sound from the cargo bay like an ammo crate being dragged across the deck. Trinder looked up the ramp into the dimly-lit space and saw the sapper bot emerging.

"I need to route a call to APS," Solomon said. "I thought I might be able to use this ground station, but I can't connect to any of the sats. I assumed that Erskine would keep some means of contacting APS, but she's destroyed all the links."

"We're not beaten yet," Trinder said. "Let me think."

The Lammergeier hadn't used its satcom link for years. The satellites it could access had either reached the end of their lives or the comms companies that leased them were long gone. There were still people on site who did have a functioning government to talk to, though, and who would also have the right authentication provided they had the means to place a call: Marc and Tev.

"Corporal, do we still have any sat phones?"

"We recycled some, but I'm sure there are others."

"Good. Find one and then get me Marc Gallagher. Tell him I need a really big favour."

Simonot shot off. Trinder sat on the end of the ramp, trying to work out if they had enough credibility to get APS to take their call seriously.

"So what are you going to say to them if we manage to patch you through, Sol?" Trinder asked.

"I'm going to tell them that I have one of their field agents and name Dr Kim. But I need to be able to produce her at some point in the next few hours. I haven't heard from Sergeant Luce."

That didn't bode well. Trinder would need to follow that up. "Are you serious about giving APS the Nomad file?"

"Yes."

"Couldn't you give them incomplete data or something?"

"They'd work that out before we were ready to leave. I still need a couple of months to work on *Shackleton*, and now we've got to rebuild the comms mast just to access the ship."

"How long will that take?"

"I don't know until we assess the damage. Don't worry, we'll get the uplink to the orbital working, if nothing else."

Trinder had always felt that Solomon could do anything with his army of dumb AIs and bots. It was sobering to hear his uncertainty. "Well, if Erskine's right, and APS muscles in and takes over the project, we won't have to worry about it, will we? But we'll be out of here either way."

"I'm gambling, Major. I think Erskine could be right. But once we've saved people, I'll have the luxury of time to work out what we can salvage from the project."

"If they let us leave in *Shackleton*, then we'll still have a few months or even years on them. It's not like they'll get the FTL stuff and magically be able to build a full-size superluminal drive overnight."

"That's exactly what I'm hoping for," Solomon said. "Which is why I say that I'm gambling."

"Humans can be deceitful bastards, Sol. They might agree to it and then welsh on the deal."

"This is why I need Dr Kim. I also need to get back into the network to extract the data. I have a backup hidden."

"Wait one." Trinder tapped his radio. "Echo Five to Echo Nine. Luce, have you located our asset yet, over?"

"Echo Nine to Echo Five, negative, we haven't found her. Extending search, over."

"Echo Five, keep me posted, out."

"That's worrying," Solomon said.

"She can't have gone far." Trinder was worried too, but if Erskine had found Kim, that wasn't necessarily the end of the road. Solomon had his own copy of the data. All he needed was to restore power to retrieve and transmit it. "How are you going to introduce yourself to APS?"

"What do you think they would take more seriously, a human or an AI like me?"

"Don't tell them you're an AI. They'll be more interested in getting hold of you than the damn ship. Pass yourself off as flesh and blood."

"It's not as if they can check my identity."

"Tell them you're Alex. He's not going to argue."

"Very creative thinking, Major. An excellent idea."

Simonot came jogging back towards them, clutching a black ripstop bag and looking pleased with himself. A few yards behind him, Marc Gallagher walked at a brisk pace before breaking into a run. It looked like they were in business.

"Never ditch any old gear, right, sir?" Simonot opened the bag under Trinder's nose. "This one's charged. I found a couple more if we need them."

Marc fished a small screen out of his pocket and checked something on it. "I'm going to work through my old contacts book," he said. "Bear with me. It all depends on whether they've changed my ID. But there'll be someone, somewhere who'll vouch for me. So do you want a message relayed to APS, asking them to call you? That means I've got to tell my people the kind of information that might make them a bit too interested in you. Or do you want to be connected so you can talk to APS direct?"

"I think I should speak to APS direct," Solomon said. "I can give them more detailed information. Tell them I'm Alex."

"Let's give it a go, then. So this phone was registered to some telco that's defunct now, yeah?"

"I think so. Sorry."

"Not to worry." Marc stepped out of the shadow of the Lammergeier and stood in the middle of the lawn, sat phone in one hand and his screen in the other. "I've got a special big boys' prefix code. You tend to need that when you don't know whose phone you're going to have to steal to call for extraction. Bloody hell, is this thing steam-powered?"

Like a lot of equipment here, the sat phone was obsolete to the point of antiquity, but the habit of not throwing things away had paid off. Trinder found himself doing crazy superstitious things and keeping his fingers crossed while he willed Marc to make the connection. Solomon said nothing. Simonot went back into the cockpit.

It seemed a painfully slow process. Marc kept keying in numbers and frowning at the display, then walking to the other side of the lawn and back again. Eventually, he stopped dead as if someone had answered. He put his hand over his opposite ear. Trinder couldn't hear everything he was saying, but he caught bursts.

"Yes, that's my code... correct... no, it's *Gallagher*, I'm still in the States, or what's left of it, and this is an urgent message for the consulate in Seoul." The conversation faded out for a while, then Trinder heard Marc's voice rise a little and take on an edge. "Look, APS is going to nuke this frigging site tomorrow. I've got nearly two thousand civvies here who we can't move, including hundreds of children. If you can't be arsed to do it for me, then do it for the kids, okay? I've got an *urgent call* that I need *routed to APS*. Tell them there's a guy called Alex Gorko who needs to speak to Colonel Su-Jin Yoon *right away* about Dr Annis Kim, one of their field agents. So do me a favour and pull your bloody finger out. Now let me spell those names for you..."

Trinder could only watch. The helplessness knotted his guts. He wanted to think that Marc was exaggerating to panic someone into action, but he knew the guy was simply stating the reality of their situation.

"You didn't think the phone was going to work," Solomon said quietly. "But it did. And so will this."

Marc seemed to be waiting now, passing the time by squinting up at the comms mast. It was a long wait, at least ten minutes. But then he snapped back to the conversation and exchanged a few mumbled words, beckoning to Solomon.

"Okay, cheers for that. Really, I appreciate it. Because I don't want to be vaporised either. Wait one while I get Mr Gorko."

If the situation hadn't been so desperate, Trinder would have laughed his ass off. There was Solomon, a big, ugly battlefield bot, towering over Marc while the Brit held the phone against his audio grille. Trinder hoped he'd live long enough to look back on this and find it funny.

"Yes, this is Alex Gorko from Ainatio," Solomon said, completely convincing as a human. He even sounded like Alex. "We have one of your field agents here at our facility — Dr Annis Kim. She wants to speak to Commissioner Tim Pham. We know she was sent to acquire propulsion technology, but industrial espionage isn't our biggest problem right now. We're willing to give you the data if you postpone the bombing of this area long enough for us to get one more of our ships operational. If you don't postpone it, then obviously all the data will be destroyed, along with a lot of innocent people. Let's do one another a favour."

Solomon really was quite a diplomat. Trinder was impressed by how many threats he'd managed to wrap up in that appeal for mercy. In the next few seconds, it might prove to be a waste of time, but while Trinder waited, he still had hope. Whoever Solomon was talking to then appeared to give him an answer.

"Very well," Solomon said. "If you make Mr Pham available, I'll get Dr Kim to speak to you... no, Miss Erskine no longer runs this facility. That's why I'm calling you via the British Consulate. She disabled our communications.

She's been under a great deal of stress in recent weeks, so I hope you'll excuse her behaviour and deal with me instead... yes, yes, that's right. Gorko. Alex Gorko."

The situation hovered between tragedy and comedy yet again. Trinder put his hand slowly over his mouth in case his nerves got to him and he started laughing.

Solomon ended the call. Marc patted his casing. "That was bloody brilliant," he said. "Liar of the Year, Sol. We'll make you a medal. So what happens now? We just go and get Kim, she talks to her boss, and we can forget Erskine?"

"Luce and his guys haven't found her yet."

"Shit." Marc shut his eyes for a moment, then took out his sidearm. "If Erskine's got her, I'll extract her. Just don't get squeamish on me, okay?"

Anyone Marc shot in the course of getting hold of Kim would be someone Trinder knew. It wasn't going to be pretty if they tried to put up a fight.

"Do what you need to," Trinder said. "Sol, if you're going back into the building, stick to the underground floors. Erskine already outsmarted us with the pythons, so don't get cocky and think she can't take you out."

"Major, this frame is designed to withstand attacks on the battlefield," Solomon said. "Its constraints also protect me."

"Until your batteries run down," Marc said. "Go and find a generator. Or a nice sunny spot."

Solomon lumbered on ahead. Marc handed the sat phone back to Trinder as they went back inside. "You better make sure that's charged as well, mate," he said. "And the other handsets."

"Thanks for putting the calls in. We'd have been screwed without that."

"We might still be."

"Yeah, but thanks anyway."

"No problem. Like I said, I don't particularly want to end my days puking up blood in a pitch-black basement any more than you do."

Knowing what Tev had said about Marc's state of mind, Trinder wasn't sure whether to take that as an actual improvement in his outlook or a tactful lie. For all the time he'd spent with Marc, he still didn't know the man, and he suspected he never would.

"You could still go home," he said. "You've made contact with your guys. They know you're alive."

"I always could, they always did, and I've not been their guy for some years. And I'm not sure they'd make it in time anyway."

"Alex says he's got spare cryo bays because some people don't want to go. You're welcome to mine. And there'll be one for Tev."

Marc didn't even blink. He just rummaged in his pocket and pulled out a spare magazine. "That's decent of you, mate. I'll let Tev know, but I'm staying until the job's done. If we don't pull this off, then it's going to be tough for everyone over the next few months. Now let's find that bloody woman. We can't cancel the message now. Where's Luce?"

"He's still working through the access passages in the accommodation block. He started in section five-G."

"I'll ping him. Leave it to me."

"Understood."

The building was still running on backup power when Trinder got back to U3. He found Fonseca supervising some of Alex's people, laying out mattresses and blankets in tidy rows in one of the empty warehouse units. She paused and walked over to him.

"For what it's worth," she said, "everyone's reported in and said thanks for the offer of a ride, but they're all going to stay."

Trinder never felt a lump in his throat at times like this. It was more a pressure at the top of his palate, pushing at his sinuses and threatening tears. He swallowed it and nodded.

"Yeah, that's what I expected of them," he said. "How about you?"

"Hell, no. I've seen the movies. The planet looks gorgeous, then you try to pick a flower and it shoots tendrils into your face and sucks your brains out."

She laughed and went back to wrangling bed spaces. Even if nobody outside this small enclave ever found out what people had done here and the choices they'd made, Trinder knew.

It would not be forgotten.

* * *

SERVER ROOM F:
1845 HOURS

"It's always gloomy in here anyway," Cullen said, raking the flashlight beam around the walls. The room was like a forest of glass bamboo. Erskine couldn't see where she was going and stood back rather than stumble into the translucent tubes. "I'm pretty sure I've isolated the physical storage, though."

He stood looking up the clear composite tube, all its memory components powered down and unlit. Erskine checked her watch again. She had plenty of time, but she wanted those modules removed before Solomon worked out exactly what she'd be doing. She was surprised that he hadn't. But perhaps she was doing something completely stupid and ineffectual that he'd already considered and dismissed.

"We need everything with data on FTL," she said.

"We'd better remove all storage for Engineering and related archives, then. Safest way. Then we won't miss anything."

"Whatever you say. It's not as if it's a roomful of hardware."

"Well, it's easier to put it on the shuttle than spend time trying to destroy it."

Cullen opened the tube by prying out a semicircular ring with his fingertips, then began removing individual modules like extracting vertebrae from a spine. Erskine edged forward to hand him a box to hold them, still disoriented by the transparency and reflections. She counted at least twenty small cylinders half the width of her palm and a couple of inches long. She hadn't seen storage this antiquated for a very long time. It was secure, though, and it had never let Ainatio down.

"What about all the information in people's heads?" Cullen asked, closing the box. "You can erase everything, cut the relay, and collapse the wormhole, but you'll still have sixteen hundred people who now know quite a lot about Nomad, and the existence of the planet itself was never a secret." He paused as if he was re-ordering his thoughts. "And if people here survive — well, even if only one person does — then APS has a source. Director, *you're* going to be here. Do you seriously think they won't ask you a few questions, and not particularly politely? So this asset denial plan only works if you destroy the place along with everyone in it who can talk."

"How many times do we have to go through this?" Erskine had had enough. The only way through was forward. "It's not a perfect plan. I know that. But the less information APS can extract, the better the mission's chance of continuing uninterrupted. Even if removing the FTL data only delays APS by a year or two, it's more time for the colony to prepare for... well, I don't know what, but I have to imagine the worst."

"What did you tell Ingram?"

"Nothing. What could I tell her that would be of any use?"

"Stand by for APS arriving, maybe before we do?"

"It's too late for all this, Will."

"So *if* anyone survives, *if* they can get the comms mast working again, *if* Solomon can access *Shackleton* — do you really think they'll let him fix the ship when they find we've stripped the place?"

"If they let *Elcano* leave, they'll let *Shackleton* leave," Erskine said. "The ships are of no interest to them. They'd have moved in on them by now if they thought there was anything they wanted."

Cullen looked around the server room and checked another pole before consulting his screen and taking out a few more memory modules.

"I think you're still lying to yourself," he said.

"Maybe, but the only bit that works is getting as many people away as we can, while we can, with as big a head start on APS as we can. If you've suddenly had a flash of inspiration, though, let's hear it."

Cullen put the extra modules in the box and handed it to Erskine. "I haven't. We've got no guarantee that giving APS everything would make the slightest bit of difference. We're just assuming that it would. I find everything more distasteful after sleeping on it, that's all."

"You think I don't? Will, *we're out of time.* I need to go talk to Propulsion now. And we still haven't found Kim. She can't get a message out, but we have to keep her away from APS. Permanently."

Erskine picked her way out of the darkened room, almost stumbling into the storage columns in her hurry to leave, and started the buggy. Right then, she hated Cullen for chipping away at her resolve after she'd made an agonising decision. She drove down the dimly-lit passages, aware she'd walked off without a goodbye, and that she might not see him again to put that right.

As if that's the worst thing I've done today.

Propulsion was at the far end of the corridor that ran under the accommodation block. While the system was down, she couldn't check in advance whether Ben and Javinder were in there, but it was the obvious place to start. When she reached the doors to the department, she had to get out of the buggy and dog them open by hand. As soon as she pulled one door back, she could hear voices. Javinder was in the front office, then. Erskine parked the buggy to one side of the corridor and put her head around the office door.

The first thing she saw was Ben sitting at one of the desks, blood spattered on his light blue T-shirt. Javinder was leaning over him with an antiseptic wipe. It took her a moment to notice the cut above Ben's eye, right on the brow bone.

"What happened? Did you walk into something when the power went off?"

"No, I walked into an angry physicist," Ben said. "Kim. She slammed my head in the door. And I mean *in the door*. Between the door and the frame. She was trying to hack into files she isn't allowed access to."

"Damn, Ben, we've been looking for her for hours. Where the hell is she? Why didn't you call it in?"

He jerked his thumb over his shoulder. "Because the power was out by the time I locked her in the equipment store."

"Which files? Did she manage to get into them?"

"Wormhole," Ben said. Javinder didn't seem to be having much luck stopping the bleeding. He pressed a lint pad on the cut and put more pressure on it, making Ben wince. "I confronted her, we had a row, and it escalated from there. No idea if she accessed them. I didn't even see her come in today. I just noticed the activity on the system and found her in the other office."

Erskine held up the box of memory modules. "Well, no need to worry about that now. Cullen removed all your data storage. It goes with you to Opis."

"So she really is a spy, isn't she?"

"Whether she is or not, she's an intel source for APS."

Ben took Javinder's hand off his dressing and held the pad in place himself. "Is it true she wanted to trade our research for postponing the bombing?"

This place was a sieve. Erskine decided to give up worrying about how things leaked and concentrate on her next task, making sure that Kim got on the shuttle. She looked Ben over more carefully. He was pretty fit, and if he'd manhandled Kim into the storeroom, then he wouldn't be afraid of using a bit of force to make sure she boarded *Elcano* as well.

"I don't know if it was her idea," Erskine said. "It was put to me in a meeting, and I felt it would compromise the mission. And we don't know if it would persuade APS."

Erskine braced for yet another speech on whether it was really so bad to hand over information. But Ben just nodded.

"Damn right," he said. "This is our last chance. They could just wait out the contamination, walk in, and take over."

"Exactly. So I can't risk her surviving the blast, and I don't have the backbone or means to shoot her. So you have to take her with you."

"Terrific."

"I do mean take, Ben. I can't call on Trinder's people now, but I need someone to physically restrain her if she won't go voluntarily. Just grab her and subdue her."

Ben peeled the lint off his cut and checked the blood. "Okay."

"If she hits you again, hit her back."

"It was the door. It was deliberate, but it was the door."

"Fine, then jam her head in the door if that makes you feel it's a fair fight. She's a risk. Treat her accordingly."

"So what do we do with her between now and the launch?" Javinder asked.

"I'm going to speak to her."

"Is that wise?"

"Perhaps not, but I'm going to do it anyway."

"Okay," Javinder said. "One moment."

While he was gone, Erskine passed the time helping Ben put a dressing on his cut. Javinder returned holding a hockey stick that looked like it had seen a lot of service.

"For self-defence," he said, handing it to her. "Please don't break it. It was my dad's. I still play, too."

"You think she's that violent. Seriously."

Ben scowled. "No, she's an angel, and this is fake blood."

Erskine wasn't any more used to fisticuffs than most of the staff here. She'd never even had to deal with a toddler having a tantrum, but the sight of the stick alone might persuade Kim to behave herself.

"I'm too old to slug it out." Erskine hefted the stick in both hands. "Okay, open the door. And if you're really worried about me, wait outside. If I need rescuing, you'll hear thuds."

Javinder led Erskine along the corridor and pointed to the storeroom door. There was a safety glass panel down the centre, and Erskine could see Kim sitting at one of the desks, doing nothing in particular. It was a much bigger room than she expected, more like a small office. She hoped that Kim hadn't made an improvised weapon out of the cleaning supplies.

"Open it," she said.

Kim looked around when she walked in, but didn't get up. She glanced at the hockey stick. Erskine stayed near the door and just leaned casually on the stick, ready to deploy it if Kim so much as twitched.

"You've upset Dr Singh," Erskine said. "And Ben."

Kim shrugged. "He'll live."

"So you don't want to come to Opis. We've saved you a cryo pod."

"I never said I would. I said I'd work on FTL and the follow-up missions. I've still got family in Australia. I can go back to the civilised world."

"For as long as it lasts."

"Long enough to see me out."

"Solomon thinks you really are a spy after all."

"Did I ever say I wasn't?"

"Actually, no. You're right. You just asked if a spy would do what you'd done. So there's no Grandma Park or family honour to be avenged, then."

"Oh, Grandma Park's real, all right. She really was my great-grandmother and you really did steal her research. And I really do want payback for her. Why does anyone serve? We've all got our reasons. I didn't hitch thousands of miles to the arse-end of the world to make up for not having a gap year."

"Then you know why we can't let you speak to your contact."

"Is there a cut-off level for you? Sixteen hundred people aren't worth sharing Nomad for, but how about ten thousand? A hundred thousand? Half a million?"

Sharing. That was an interesting word. "If I were to hand over all the data on Nomad, what would your people do with it? Would they thank us for our generous contribution to the sum of human knowledge and wish us *bon voyage*?"

Kim gave her that snoozing alligator look. "They'd want you to co-operate."

"They'd want control."

"They'd be concerned about something with profound significance for the whole world being run as a private and pretty well-armed project, yes."

"Dr Kim, I have nearly two hundred people on Opis. Thousands of others put their lives into this project over more than a century, not because they thought it would make money, or for some movie-villain world domination nonsense, but because they knew mankind would have to relocate or go extinct one day. And most of them knew they'd never live to see what they'd created. *That's* service too."

"And what do you think APS is going to do with Opis? Die-back hasn't been eradicated, it's mutated at least four times to our knowledge, and, let's face it, the West never dealt with the politics that caused its release in the first place. It was fine as long as it wasn't happening to well-off people like you. Now you've been stuffed. Millions dead. Cities gone. But Asia-Pacific isn't going to go down like you did because you were too genteel to deal with violent lunatics. And we need space as well."

"It's precisely because there *are* so few of us left that I'm willing to make sacrifices to make sure we're not erased."

Was that how Nomad had started, to save Western civilisation? She was sure it hadn't. Her father always said that Bednarz was less culturally focused than that. She'd only been four when he died, and her one hazy memory of him was more about the big office with glittering lights and bright red chairs than the man she was shown off to. But her father said Bednarz believed in a general quality of human excellence that could be found by sifting through the population.

Then he'd created an AI and left it to decide what that excellence was. But she'd found that out much later.

"So how do you want to play this, Director?" Kim asked. "Because you're just postponing the inevitable and getting a lot of people killed for nothing."

"You're going to Opis. Because you're a source of information on Nomad that I'm not going to surrender, and Solomon needs you to prove to APS that he's got something to trade. We'll get your bag packed for you. Until someone comes for you tomorrow morning, you stay here."

"Toilet?"

Erskine had just started to learn that prisoners were a lot more effort than she'd bargained for. She pointed to one of the plastic litter bins.

"Toilet," she said. "See you tomorrow."

She backed out of the room as casually as she could and shut the door. Javinder locked it behind her right away.

"Keep her here until I tell you we can board her," Erskine said. "She's got bottled water in there, and you're supposed to fast for at least fourteen hours before cryo, so you shouldn't need to let her out or feed her. Anyway, I'll be back before then. Just keep a lid on things. And send Ben down to Mendoza for a quick check, just in case the blow to the head is going to affect his cryo process."

"Are you going to tell me what happens now?"

"I'm going to put the power back on," Erskine said. "Which means Solomon can get back into the system, so be discreet."

"Okay. Are you sure he's that much of a risk?"

"Possibly. And possibly is enough."

Erskine got back in the buggy and drove off. If she wanted to do anything else out of Solomon's range, she'd have to do it now before she got Beck to power up again. This game with Solomon, like the one with APS, was about buying every possible second of time, and the longer that

Solomon couldn't locate Kim, the less chance he had of selling out Nomad.

Erskine parked, took out her radio, and called Beck. "Everything's as secure as we can make it, Jesse," she said. "Get the power back on."

She waited. It was only thirty seconds before the corridor lights changed from the emergency lighting to the normal illumination and she heard motors and fans starting up everywhere.

Yes, she could understand why Cullen had said she was lying to herself about the survival chances of those left behind. Nomad's best chance was the worst scenario for those marooned here, and she would be among them.

Everyone had a price they were willing to pay to get what they wanted. Erskine had made peace with hers.

* * *

TEMPORARY SHELTER, LEVEL U3, AINATIO PARK RESEARCH CENTRE: 1915 HOURS

The power came back on without warning, a sudden burst of light and machinery noise. Solomon heard the collective sigh and even a few half-hearted cheers as the evacuees realised what had happened.

It wouldn't make any difference to what was coming, but at least it seemed to lift the mood. Solomon debated whether to dock the sapper bot and slip into the quad to move around more easily. He couldn't help search the access passages for Kim while he was in this frame. But that meant going back into the system for a few seconds, and however brief the transfer, he didn't know if Erskine had persuaded Cullen to set any booby traps for him. Ninety minutes was a very long time for an outage if all she'd wanted was to drive him out. He'd have to guess what kind of sabotage or destruction had taken place instead.

That didn't mean he couldn't access the system, though. He'd just have to use touch and eyesight like a human. He removed the backup copy of the FTL data, saved it to the sapper bot's memory, and carried on.

"Sol?" Trinder tapped on his back. "Remember what I said about not taking risks. Don't be tempted to go back into the network."

"I won't. But I need to work out what Erskine's done during the outage. I can do that without leaving this bot. Any word on Kim?"

"I'd tell you right away if there was. We drafted in Marc and Chris to help out Luce's search team. That's a lot of ground to cover."

"My apologies. My impatience is more about my own naivety, not any criticism. I think I'll go and find Alex, in case he feels guilty enough to give me any information."

"Fine, but be careful. I mean human careful. You're not completely invulnerable."

Trinder was just showing concern, not scolding him. Solomon appreciated that. As he skirted around the private cubicles to reach the stairs — he didn't dare trust the elevators — he saw a boy aged about ten wandering around with a tray of steaming mugs, handing out drinks to older people. Solomon paused a moment to watch. The boy didn't seem to know the seniors: he hesitated and spoke to them as if he was introducing himself before they took the mugs, so he must have been one of the youngsters from the transit camp. It was rather touching. The boy finished his task and walked up to Solomon.

"Hi. Chris says you're the robot who went to Jamie's funeral. I'm Howie."

Solomon couldn't take offence at being called a robot. He was completely charmed. And the more he saw the good in these people, the more set he was on saving them, no matter what it took. Perhaps this was what Tad Bednarz had meant by *parental*. All that mattered was to keep these humans safe, and watch them thrive and be happy. Bednarz hadn't had any more idea than Solomon what it meant to be a parent, but he'd certainly seemed to know how it felt to be a son. Solomon had learned a lot about humanity from reverse-engineering the man and noting the empty spaces in his existence that he seemed to feel had never been filled.

"Pleased to meet you, Howie," Solomon said. "It's very kind of you to look after the old folk."

Howie shrugged like an adult. He seemed very old for a little boy. "They're scared. They just need someone to tell them it's going to be okay."

"It will be." Howie probably needed someone to tell him it was going to be okay too. Solomon obliged. "It'll be boring for a while, but after that, we'll be heading to a new world. I've been there. It's wonderful. You'll love it."

Howie smiled as if he was doing it for Solomon's benefit. "Everywhere's the same, really."

Solomon didn't know what to make of that. He really wasn't skilled with children. He rarely had contact with them, which now felt like a serious gap in his knowledge.

"I'm going to look for a friend," he said. "I'll see you later."

Solomon wasn't sure if Alex counted as a friend any longer, but they needed to maintain diplomatic relations. He climbed the fire exit stairs to the ground floor, aware that Erskine could keep tabs on him again via the security cams, but it probably didn't matter. It was too late for either of them to stop the other. They were both up against separate deadlines and had wholly different tasks. Maybe, if they'd had a better relationship and discussed this reasonably, they'd have arrived at the same outcome, with a partial evacuation and everyone else sheltering until it was safe to move. But it hadn't turned out that way. Solomon kept coming back to the same sticking point. Erskine was willing to sacrifice individuals for a hypothetical future, and he was not.

Am I wrong? Is that really the only way out of this?

Nobody took much notice of him as he made his way through the admin block and up to the management floor. He'd assumed that people would realise it was him inside the sapper bot, but they didn't seem to, and there was no reason why they should. Despite his size, he was just another machine going about its business, one of many mobilised to secure the facility at short notice. He took advantage of the temporary anonymity, trying to decide how he felt about being completely ignored.

Alex was in his office, staring at an array of personal screens laid out on his desk. He looked up when Solomon poked his front end through the door.

"It's me, Alex."

"You've put on some weight." Alex stood up. "You want me to come outside? You can't get in here."

"I'm fine if you don't mind me blocking your door."

"And the corridor."

"I'll move if anyone needs access. Are all the systems back up?"

"I think so."

"Erskine destroyed the comms mast."

"I know. I'm checking what's down, because she timed that outage for a reason." Alex gestured uncertainly. Solomon tried to work out if all this meant he'd taken a side, and if he had it could well have been Erskine's. Trust was fragile. "So this is your war face, is it?"

"Out of necessity. Would you check a couple of things for me, please? Or are you working with her?"

"I thought I was neutral and washing my hands of both of you. What do you need to know?"

"It doesn't matter. I'll find a terminal myself."

"Oh, give it a rest. You sound like my ex. 'It's nothing.' She always said that when I was in the doghouse and then I had to spend the rest of the day working out why."

"It's best that I don't involve you."

"Fine. Whatever. We've now got sixty-eight cryo pods left to fill, by the way. If you want those places for anyone, well, you decide. Erskine wanted me to offer Chris the berths for his troops."

It was still too little, too late. There were several hundred children among the evacuees, and Chris would never leave any of the transit camp people behind. Solomon would ask as a courtesy, but he knew he might not have any takers.

"What's your deadline, Alex?"

"Ten tonight, preferably. Because of the cryo. Although they'll still be chilling people down when they get underway, so the fourteen-hour nothing-by-mouth is looking flexible."

"Very well. I'll put it to them."

"So how are you going to do a deal with APS now the comms are down?" Alex asked. "The main connection to the relay in here was trashed too. It's going to take days to replace it. But I suppose you know that."

"I've already contacted APS."

"Shit. Seriously? How?"

"You don't need to know. I made the offer and told them that Kim's here."

"Oh. Well, fuck. And? Did it work?"

"We'll see. Excuse me."

"Is that all you're going to say?"

"It's all I *can* say."

"What did you come here for, then? To get me to tell Erskine you've screwed her over?"

"I was just looking for a terminal I can actually work at. I'll see you later, no doubt."

Solomon walked off to find a terminal, not giving Alex a chance to reply. The only doorway big enough to accommodate his bulk led into an open-plan office that had been disused for years. He trundled in, ramming chairs out of the way, and extended the bot's EOD manipulator to boot up a terminal. Logging in manually and checking files was agonisingly slow now that he could only look at the list of changed files with a robotic lens.

There were no surprises. Propulsion's server was inaccessible. In fact, it didn't exist. The error message told him that there were no memory modules. Erskine had done exactly what Solomon would have in her position: she'd dumped the data like the cypher officer of an ancient warship dropping the weighted bag of "CBs" over the side, to put the confidential books of secret codes beyond the reach of enemy hands. She didn't appear to know that Solomon had copied the data already, but she should have guessed. Perhaps she was just taking precautions in case he hadn't. Either way, she'd left nothing to be found.

What else might she have done? One of Chris's predictions had been accurate: Erskine had wiped the data just as he'd said. Solomon hoped he'd be wrong about Kim, and that she was just remarkably good at evasion. It was time to help out with the search as far as his cumbersome frame would allow.

"Major Trinder, this is Solomon." It was poor radio procedure, but Trinder wouldn't mind. "I've completed my assessment as far as I can. All Propulsion's data storage has been removed. I'd like to help look for Dr Kim now."

"Where are you?"

"The admin block, second floor."

"The search teams are back. No sign of Kim. Marc thinks it's taking too long. She'd have come out by now if she could, so they're assuming the worst. Chris thinks it'll be faster using dogs, so he's heading for her apartment with Marc and Dieter to get some clothing for scent identification."

Solomon had put too much faith in Kim's ability to stay out of Erskine's way. It was his second mistake, another one he would never make again. "I'll meet them there, then," he said.

Everything took a glacial age now that he couldn't jump into the network to get around the site. This was nothing like playing around in the quadrubot for a few hours when there was no urgency. Now he was all too conscious of the passage of time, and even the fast trot that the sapper bot could manage felt impossibly slow. There were shortcuts he couldn't take because of his size, too, which added minutes he couldn't afford. As he made his way along the corridors, he scanned for heat traces in the rooms and offices he passed, hoping to stumble upon Kim by chance, but he knew he was indulging in a very human habit of wishing for the highly unlikely.

I should have moved her to the camp right away.

Have I ever felt this before, this anger with myself?

He knew he hadn't. He'd never failed this badly before.

When he reached the apartment, Marc was already there with Dieter, standing at the open door and watching something. Solomon could do no more than stick his camera extension through the doorway to peer inside.

The odd-eyed husky was nosing around Kim's living room, pausing occasionally for longer, more considered sniffs at the sofa and a rucksack in the corner. Noises from the bedroom suggested that someone was ransacking the place. Chris came out with a pile of clothing in his arms.

"Bathrobe, jacket, jeans," he said. "These don't feel laundered. Here you go, Girlie."

The husky shoved her nose into the fabric. Dieter made encouraging noises at her. "Find her, Girlie," he said. "Go on. Find her."

The dog put her head down and went outside, then cast around for a few seconds before trotting off purposely as if she'd acquired a scent. Dieter let the leash pay out as she ran on. Chris tried to keep up with her, almost breaking into a run.

"Old school," Marc said, walking beside Solomon. "Can't beat it."

"I've made some serious mistakes, Marc. I'm sorry. If I'd been more decisive, none of this would have happened."

"We're not beaten yet, mate. You think every operation goes to plan? Most don't. This job's all about thinking on your feet and keeping going. So buck your ideas up and apply that bloody big brain to the problem."

"Yes, Marc."

"I can't believe I'm giving a pep talk to a metal box."

They caught up with Chris and Dieter further down the corridor. Girlie had stopped dead and was nuzzling a door that led to the access passages.

"Dr Kim did as she said she would, then," Solomon said. He opened the door with his EOD manipulator and put his camera extension inside. Girlie tried to push past him. "Check your building plan, gentlemen."

"I'm going to let her off the leash," Dieter said. "Can I get all the way through these passages?"

"Yes, they're designed for human access."

"Okay, I'm going in."

Marc handed him his ID pass. "Keep this on you and we can track it. Better still, stick it on the dog. If you lose her, we'll see where she's gone."

Dieter clipped the pass to Girlie's collar and let her off the leash. "I'll see you guys at the end of some tunnel, then."

He disappeared into the passage. Solomon heard him jog away. Now all they could do was try to keep up, Marc and Chris using their personal screens, Solomon following the two heat profiles inside the passage using thermal detection. He managed to follow the heat sources as far as the end of the building, but the gap between the two was growing, and then they both dropped away beneath him.

"It's okay, I've still got 'em," Marc said. "They've gone down a floor. Fire exit."

When they emerged on the staff restaurant floor, Girlie appeared to have led Dieter a little way along the passage, then doubled back again. She was heading for the ground floor. Solomon followed Marc and Chris down the next flight of stairs and came out at the exit that led to the gardens. He could detect Girlie casting around inside the passage while Dieter waited. Then the access panel a few yards away opened as Girlie burst out, dragging a breathless Dieter in her wake. She nosed her way along the tiles until she came to the next access panel, where she sat down and stared expectantly at the opening.

"There's a fire door in there we can't get past," Dieter panted. "Kim probably couldn't either, so she stepped out and went back in via the door on the other side of it. Which is why Girlie's sitting there like that."

"No need to go back in," Solomon said. "That section leads to Propulsion. Although that's a foolish place for her to go under the circumstances."

"Got it." Marc strode off at a fast walk. "If she isn't there, we'll come straight back and send the dog in again."

"Why the hell didn't she stay put?" Chris asked, catching up with him. Dieter coaxed Girlie away from the access door with and followed. "A field agent should know better."

"Maybe someone detected her and she needed to go to ground," Solomon suggested.

"Or she couldn't be arsed to wait until we could retrieve her." Marc slowed down to compare floor plans with Chris as they walked. "Does the access passage go right into Propulsion?"

"Yes," Solomon said. "But there's no door. Just a grille at waist height when it gets there. She could get through that easily enough."

Propulsion was the dead end of a single-storey building that looked out onto the reactor, a long walk down a corridor. When they reached the entrance, Girlie circled around for a few seconds, then sat down to stare at the doors as if she was willing them to open.

"Well, Girlie says she's in there, then," Dieter said. "How do you want to play this?"

Marc checked his screen. "Three ID chips moving around. I'm up for walking in and searching the place."

"Javinder Singh, Ben Tusa, and Laurie Ross." Solomon cycled through the sapper bot's sensors and tried the heat detection mode again. "And there's someone in the storeroom. Unchipped. No cameras in there, but I suspect that's Dr Kim."

"Well, plenty of cameras out here, so Singh knows we've turned up, and so will Erskine."

Chris tried the doors. He didn't have a pass, but Propulsion was off limits for most people's chips anyway. He tapped the intercom.

"Dr Singh, this is Chris Montello." He made it sound perfectly routine, as if he was just passing through and had decided to drop in for a chat. "Can I come in?"

There was no answer. He waited a few seconds, then buzzed again, but nobody opened the door.

Solomon wasn't surprised. Dr Singh could easily see who was outside. If Kim hadn't been in there, he'd have opened the door and told them so, but the fact that he didn't even respond on the intercom confirmed Solomon's suspicion.

Chris looked at Marc and nodded. "Maybe she's in there because she wants to be."

Marc was still following the trackers on his screen. "I've got three IDs including Singh moving away from us."

"Four heat signatures," Solomon said.

"Can you get us in?"

"One way or another," Solomon said.

Without the option of entering the network, Solomon's options were to drill or apply brute force. The doors were locked by concealed steel rods in their centres that slid in from the top and bottom, so it was easier to cut than smash. He extended the bot's drill attachment and chewed eight neat holes in a rectangle spanning the inner edges of both doors between the bars. Now all he had to do was saw from hole to hole.

His rear camera could see the reactions to the noise. It must have been painfully loud. Dieter gestured to indicate he was moving Girlie away, leaving Chris and Marc with their hands pressed to their ears. The cutting tool sliced through wood panelling and composite fire retardant in seconds. Two sections crashed back onto the tiles, throwing up sawdust.

"Not bad, Sol," Chris said, stepping inside.

Solomon had to do more cutting to make the gap big enough to squeeze his frame through. He was about to enter when he felt a vibration in the floor and heard Chris shouting to Marc to get back. The safety bulkheads were closing. Maybe he'd triggered them by cutting the doors open, or perhaps Dr Singh had activated them manually. It could even have been Erskine. Either way, something was now sealing off the department.

"Chris? Marc? Where are you?"

The two men came running back towards him. "I think that confirms they've got her," Chris said. "Where can they go from that end of the corridor?"

"Down to a basement level and up again into the grounds. They could go anywhere from there."

"Well, they can't remove their chips, so we've got them." Marc studied his screen. "But if I were them, I'd split up and get us going in circles."

"They're hauling a prisoner," Chris said. "That's harder than it looks to a civvy."

"You're assuming she doesn't want to go with them."

Solomon knew exactly what Kim wanted to do. "She doesn't."

"Y'know, if Erskine didn't want anyone to get hold of Kim, she could have shot her and saved herself a lot of trouble," Marc said.

Chris shook his head. "Dan's got all the firearms."

Marc looked at him with the expression of a man who didn't see why that was a barrier to executing someone. "Their only other option is to take her with them on the shuttle, then. And that means there's a few places they've got to pass where we can intercept."

Marc started walking back down the corridor in the direction of the management suite, eyes on his screen. Dieter and the dog caught up with them. Solomon knew they'd find Kim again, but the question was when.

"Yeah, Ben's cutting across to the infirmary, or maybe the plant lab, and the other two have turned off to the admin block. So... I dunno, maybe they're planning to sedate her, or chill her down for cryo in advance. You *sure* she's not in on this, Sol?"

"I don't think she is." Solomon realised he was starting to waver and that he'd made a few wrong calls already. Kim wasn't on either side in this situation. She was a foreign agent whose mission just happened to fit Solomon's for the time being. This was how many humans lived their lives, in the grey areas where blind eyes were turned, and he didn't like being part of it. "I can't see how she can be."

"Do you really need her?"

"I've got the data she wanted. I could transmit some documents to APS now as a taster to show them we mean it and hope that it's taken seriously. They will, though, definitely listen to her."

"They still haven't responded. I'd better talk to the FCO again."

Chris held out his hand for Marc's screen. "Go make your call. We'll find her."

"Okay. Give me a shout when you do. I call dibs on her."

Mark turned off to the stairs. Solomon carried on with Chris and Dieter, working out how to break the documents into instalments to send to APS, one to get their attention and the rest to eke out as insurance until *Shackleton* was ready to launch. He'd once thought he could predict human behaviour well enough to call it trust, but he'd been wrong about Erskine, and he hadn't anticipated that Kim would ignore his instruction to hide. There was probably only one reason for her to risk returning to Propulsion: she'd tried to take advantage of the situation and get hold of the data she'd come to Ainatio for.

I should have seen that coming. Another mistake I should never have made.

Have I made a mistake about APS too?

"Sol, even if APS stops us going to Opis, we can still survive," Chris said as they made their way back along the corridor. That sounded like an attempt at reassurance. Solomon took that as a sign that even Chris thought he'd screwed up. "There's a lot of stuff here we can use to build transport. The bots can repurpose material just like the ones on Opis do, can't they?"

"They can, yes."

"So we're not helpless refugees. We've got resources. We just need to think a bit bigger."

"I'm sure we can." Solomon hadn't put Erskine's offer to him yet. He was honour-bound to do it. He chose his words carefully. "Chris, Erskine asked Alex to offer you places for your militia, seeing as the detachment won't be going. There are still sixty-eight unallocated pods at the moment."

Solomon waited. Chris's expression was unreadable. Then he frowned, a brief flash of distaste, and shook his head. He glanced back at Dieter for a moment as if he was confirming something.

"We've got a hundred and three people, Sol," he said. "So that's a no. But thanks anyway."

At least he'd assessed Chris correctly. The man hadn't disappointed him. Whatever it cost to save these people, Solomon knew it would be worth it.

16

'Never let the future disturb you. You will meet it, if you have to, with the same weapons of reason which today arm you against the present.' Marcus Aurelius said that. Works just as well for me two thousand years later.

Chris Montello, explaining his preference for never planning too far ahead

ADMINISTRATION BUILDING: 2055 HOURS

Alex still had sixty-eight vacant cryo pods. Everyone was being gallant, refusing to leave friends or family, or at least more afraid of an unknown world than the known one, and it wasn't the uplifting experience he'd expected. It was a terrible waste.

The last-minute rush for spare berths still hadn't happened. He'd hold the passenger list open until midnight, then, because nobody was going to enforce the fasting rule to the letter, and the medics wouldn't get to everyone right away. But the closer the deadline, the more it bothered him to watch the security feed from the underground floors. There were fewer cameras downstairs, most of them monitoring utilities and exits, but he couldn't fail to notice how many kids there were among the evacuees. *Elcano*'s spare places were nowhere near enough to give those children an escape route. For the first time, the reality started to overwhelm him.

For all he knew, the holdouts were still having agonising debates with friends about whether to go or not. Now he had to chase Dan Trinder and make sure that the detachment hadn't changed their minds about staying put. He sent a message to Trinder's screen.

DAN, HAVE ANY OF YOUR PEOPLE HAD A RETHINK? BERTHS STILL SPARE.

Alex studied the words in his sent folder, just letting them sink in. It was such a mundane phrase for so huge a decision. His door was open; the corridor outside was completely silent. People weren't wandering past any longer. He checked the trackers on the floor plan, trying to work out where they were congregating, and it didn't surprise him that a lot of them were in the bar. Others were still clustered around the accommodation block, and some were in their offices and labs.

He didn't even need to check the names to work out who was where, and why. Some couldn't handle goodbyes. Others couldn't cope with being abandoned. But a fair number seemed to be willing to have a few final drinks with friends they might never see again, or might catch up with at the end of their lives.

Should I go? Should I have a beer with them?

No, Alex couldn't face it. His absence would be noticed and commented upon, but his excuse was valid. He had to manage the passenger list right up to the last minute. Technically, it wasn't his job, but it was certainly his responsibility.

Trinder's reply popped up on his screen. NO, WE'RE GOOD. THANKS.

Alex wondered how future historians would interpret these messages. Stoical, resigned, optimistic? Alex didn't feel any of those right then. And he hated this silence.

"All ashore who's goin' ashore," he said.

There was nobody to hear him. He logged into the security cameras to see what was happening outside and saw a lone pick-up drive through the gates, probably on its way to Kill Line to do some last-minute errand. On another feed, he could see the two Lammergeiers on the lawn, one with its rear hatch open and ramp lowered. It was still light outside, a pleasant evening that he'd forgotten existed after working around the clock in this windowless room.

Where was Erskine?

Alex browsed through the trackers, looking for Berman, who'd probably be with her. The cameras found them in the lobby outside her suite. Berman was clearing a locker, shoving personal items into a sports bag. Mendoza had told Alex that the guy had asked to be taken off the original *Elcano* list when Erskine was still planning to go, which must have really hurt the old bag. Alex had never been sure whether Berman actually liked her. He'd always been rigidly loyal, but he obviously had his limits. It felt uncomfortable watching, so Alex switched to the nearest cameras to the shuttle. He couldn't get a feed from the workshops or the runway. Greg Kent must have disconnected them during the outage.

"Sol, are you around?"

There was no response. It looked like Sol was still staying out of the network, which was probably for the best, but Alex missed being able to ask him anything, anywhere, and get an answer. He poured some coffee and started drafting the message he'd send out tonight when the passenger list closed. But now he could hear someone coming down the corridor. He checked his screen for trackers.

Whoever they were, they weren't chipped. He pushed back his chair to go see if it was one of the Brits, Erskine, or even Kim, but before he could get up, Ben Tusa appeared in the doorway, and Alex could see something was wrong.

Ben had a black eye complete with a dressing on the brow bone and another adhesive patch on his left forearm. He looked startled, as if he wasn't expecting Alex to be there.

"Do me a favour," he said. "I need a temporary pass."

"I have questions."

"Yeah."

"First, your tracker's not showing up." Alex checked his screen. "And according to this, you're in the infirmary."

"I removed it."

"You gnawed your own leg off. Awesome."

"Novo gel and a scalpel. Long story."

"My diary's clear. Do tell." Alex tapped his own eyebrow. "Start with how you got that."

"Come on, Al, who gives a shit about bureaucracy? We'll be out of here tomorrow. Anyway, issuing passes is clerical stuff. It's not like anyone can fire you for it."

"I'm naturally curious. Indulge me."

"I got in a ruck with someone, that's all."

"And the chip?"

"It's complicated."

There was a limit to how wild things could get in Ainatio. Nearly everyone here was respectable, ludicrously qualified, and not used to resolving debates with their fists. Ben was pretty big and fit, but it was sports fit, not psycho unarmed combat fit like Marc Gallagher. Even so, Alex heard a little alarm bell go off in his head, a very small one, but a bell nonetheless.

"Life in Propulsion must be a lot more exciting than I thought," he said. "I'll go get you one. Wait here."

Alex walked down the corridor to the admin office. Nothing was locked. It took him some rummaging in a desk to find the passes, and there were only three left, so

Trinder must have handed some out to Chris Montello's people. But why did Ben really need one? Alex couldn't expect people to behave normally at a time like this, but he also couldn't put together a set of circumstances that explained why Ben would remove his chip. It was a minor procedure, but a messy job even if one of the nurses did it, and it was pointless. And the black eye — that was just weird.

Did it matter? Yes, it did. The chip was still working. Alex took out his screen again and checked. There it was, in the infirmary, probably sitting in a bin. Why come here and ask for a pass? Ben might have thought that Alex wouldn't be there and that he kept some in his desk, seeing as he was doing the admin.

Alex could only think of two reasons for removing a chip. One was a technical malfunction or allergic reaction, both highly unlikely, and the other was to avoid being tracked or to access somewhere that your own chip wasn't programmed for.

Something made Alex check the security cameras in Propulsion, just in case Ben had done something crazy to Javinder Singh. No, those guys were tight as brothers. They'd never resort to a fist fight, not even if they were both high. But Alex checked anyway, and what he saw worried him. The safety bulkhead had been closed, cutting off the main corridor, and the entrance looked like it had been cut open by an industrial saw. The department was empty. A quick check of a few key trackers showed that the rest of the Propulsion team were in the bar, where they'd been hanging out for the past day.

Okay, he'd play along and just give Ben the pass, make some crack about secret trysts with someone else's girlfriend, and then track him carefully. One thought crossed his mind, though, and wouldn't go away.

Annis Kim.

He walked back to his office, trying to look as if he wasn't thinking the worst, and handed Ben the pass.

"Whoever it is, if her boyfriend catches you, I had nothing to do with this. People do crazy things on last nights."

Ben blinked a few times. "Yeah. I'll be discreet. Thanks."

Alex went back to his coffee, now tepid, and waited to hear Ben's footsteps fade. Then he started tracking him. There was every chance that he'd dump the pass, but he needed it for a reason, and he might have felt he was in the clear after Alex's comment about illicit meetings. Either way, Alex couldn't ignore this. He sent Trinder a message.

NEED TO TALK TO SOL URGENTLY RE BEN TUSA. HAS INJURIES, PROP LAB A WRECK.

Alex kept an eye on Ben's tracker while he waited for an answer. It took Trinder a couple of minutes to respond.

STILL LOOKING FOR KIM WITH CHRIS & K9 TEAM. YES, AWARE OF LAB. SOL DID THAT SEARCHING.

Damn, Solomon was giving that sapper bot some serious use, then. BEN REMOVED CHIP. ASKED ME FOR PASS. TRACKER REF 9738.

Alex watched as Ben's tracker moved through the management building, down to the ground floor, and then outside towards the recreation hall. Okay, he always spent a lot of time in the gym, but nobody in their right mind would train tonight. Alex decided that he needed to get down there fast. It was the dumbest thought he'd ever had. He had no idea what he was going to do or how he was going to do it, but if Kim was down there, he had to grab her.

Ben's going to flatten me.

Yeah, but who hit him?

SENDING MARC, Trinder messaged. HE'S WITH ME.

Trinder's tracker showed he was in one of the Lammergeiers. Alex was closer. He could get to the gym before Marc.

HEADING FOR GYM. KIM POSSIBLY THERE.

He didn't wait for the response. He shoved the screen in his pocket and ran down two flights of stairs to the outer doors. The recreation hall was the other side of a lawn, between the admin block and the infirmary building, and there weren't that many places in there to lock someone up. Kim would have to be confined somehow, unless she was doing this of her own free will, and if she was, Alex had no idea what was going on.

There was nobody around when he went in. A couple of guys were playing pool in the games room when he passed the glass doors, but nobody was working out or using the squash courts. He checked his screen and zoomed in as far as he could to pin down Ben's position more accurately. At this scale, it was hard to tell if the tracker was moving. It appeared to show Ben either at the rear interior of the building or outside the back doors. If Kim was in here, the only places Alex could think of with locks were the disused office and the locker rooms.

He'd work upwards from ground level, then. The storage and admin offices were upstairs. He walked into the locker room lobby and stopped to listen, struggling to hear over the noise of his own gasping breaths, but there were no voices and no footsteps. He could call out to Kim, but she might not hear him before Ben did. If Ben had any sense, he'd be looking for trackers approaching his position anyway.

Screw it. Check every door.

Alex went into the men's section first and tried all the cubicles and lockers. Kim was a hundred pounds and five-three, five-four if she was an inch, so she'd fit in a full-length locker even if it was painfully uncomfortable.

But every door hung open as if someone had done a final check to make sure nothing had been left behind. There was litter on the floor and a couple of odd socks. People had grabbed their stuff and gone. Alex almost skidded on a sheet of paper that turned out to be a small poster announcing try-outs for basketball.

He walked back across the lobby and ventured into the women's locker room, feeling awkward even though he knew nobody would be in there. It smelled of disinfectant, old perfume, and mould. It was just as litter-strewn and messy as the men's, with that same atmosphere of lives that had somehow fallen off the edge of the world and would never resume, at least not on Earth.

There was a motor rumbling somewhere. Was that a vehicle? That meant another set of external doors were open. Maybe Ben was getting ready to move Kim, and even if there was only one place he could take her, it would still make retrieving her that much harder. Alex had to speed things up. He strode through the shower room, pushing open cubicle doors and calling out. He had no choice now.

"Annis? You in here?" He moved into the locker area. "Annis — I've come to get you out. Make a damn noise or something."

What the hell am I doing?

I'm helping her hand over the project to a foreign power.

And I'm going to get the shit kicked out of me.

"Annis?"

He thought he heard banging. It could have been Ben. But he followed the sound and realised it was coming from outside the locker room. The floor plan on his screen showed an unlabelled void. When he went around the side and walked down the access corridor, he realised it was an equipment store. The twin doors had been barricaded shut with a curl bar and a couple of hockey sticks wedged and taped between the handles.

He rapped on the door. "Annis?"

"You took your bloody time," said a muffled voice.

At least she was okay. "You're going to get your people to call off the bombing, right?" Alex started ripping the tape off. Why didn't he carry a knife? Knives were always useful. He'd make sure he had one in the future. "Tell me that's what you're going to do. Because Sol's contacted APS and offered to trade."

"You've changed your tune, Mr But-This-Will-Destroy-Nomad."

"Yeah. So, are you?"

"Yes. That's the whole point."

Screw it, Alex didn't care what happened next and who got to settle Opis in the end as long as he didn't have to huddle in that shelter downstairs and watch the fear on the faces of people who didn't even know the planet existed a few months ago. He didn't want to watch the transit camp civilians who'd thought they were finally safe, only to find they'd walked into another disaster. And he knew he wouldn't be able to bear seeing Trinder's detachment, Chris Montello's vets, and the two Brits sitting down to wait with the evacuees, either for death or an uncertain future, because they wouldn't abandon the civilians. That was what *he* should have been like.

But I never was that kind of man.

He tossed the hockey sticks aside and hefted the curl bar. It was lighter than he expected, and the curved ends made it feel off-balance, but it would do as a weapon. The doors opened and Kim pushed her way out, looking rumpled but still defiant. He suddenly realised who had given Ben that black eye.

"Ah," she said, looking past him. She held out her hand for the bar. "Better give me that."

Alex glanced over his shoulder. Ben was striding down the corridor towards them. Then he broke into a jog.

"Whoa, stop right there, Alex."

Thinking was overrated. Sometimes it was better to let the monkey brain take over. It had a million more years of experience at this sort of thing. Alex held the curl bar like a baseball bat and stepped in front of Kim.

"Don't make me, Ben," he said.

Ben stopped a couple of yards away. "You wouldn't."

"I would. Just go. Get out of here."

"So you're happy to trash everything you worked for."

"APS is going to work it out sooner or later anyway. All I care about now is stopping them from frying us."

Ben just shook his head as if he was dealing with a lippy kid. "Sorry, Al, she's coming with us."

Ben stepped forward. Alex charged at him and swung the bar, instantly and blindly angry, thinking Kim would have the sense to run. The blow didn't connect, but he did. He crashed into Ben.

It was like hitting a brick wall. The bar went flying and bounced end over end with metallic crashes. Maybe the surprise of a smaller, unfit guy going crazy had improved Alex's odds. The two men fell in a wrestling, gouging heap. Even now, even as some primal aggression possessed him, Alex could see himself and he knew he looked like an idiot.

"Go on, Annis, *run*." He settled for trying to hold Ben down while she got away. "Get out of here. Run. Find Marc."

For a moment he thought she was just hanging around, but she was trying to grab the curl bar. Then Ben threw him off and scrambled to his feet. Alex lunged for his legs and got a kick in the chest as Ben pulled free and reached for Kim.

Damn, he had her. He grabbed her arms, and she fought like a caged cat, but Ben was a big guy. He started dragging her down the corridor, her arm pushed up her back. She was kicking and yelling abuse. Alex ran after them.

No, no, no, no. It doesn't end like this. I'm not letting you have her.

Nothing else mattered right then. The monkey brain was doing a great job of driving Alex where his common sense would never have dreamed of taking him. But long before he got within punching distance of the struggling pair, Marc came up the corridor from the other end, handgun aimed, not running but walking so fast and in such a straight line that Alex had no doubt what he was going to do.

Maybe Ben hadn't seen the gun. Alex slowed. His monkey brain said that it was a really good idea to just duck, and by then Marc was two strides from Ben. For a second, Alex was certain that Marc was going to shoot him. His aim never moved from the guy's head.

"Don't tempt me, mate." Marc caught Kim by the arm and shoved her one-handed behind him. His eyes were fixed on Ben's. Alex didn't doubt for one second that he was serious. "If it's you or sixteen hundred people, this isn't your lucky day."

Marc backed away, then turned and marched Kim off. Alex wondered if Ben was going to go after them. But the guy just watched helplessly. It didn't matter how fit you were if the other man was armed and had nothing to lose. Alex, still hyped up and ready for a fight, made himself walk away, his legs suddenly wobbly. He retraced his steps towards the main entrance.

Ben yelled after him. "Do you realise what you've done? You've fucked the project. They'll never let you leave now."

Yes, Alex knew. He'd done what they all should have had the sense to do two days ago. It was an awful, difficult day, and he'd probably looked ridiculous fighting with Ben, but it was also the most alive and real that he'd ever felt.

I did it. That's not too shabby.

He looped around the building and caught up with Marc and Kim outside. Marc, pistol still drawn, was checking around them as he walked, as if he was expecting more trouble. It felt like a very long way to the Lammergeier.

Kim glanced over her shoulder. "Thanks, Alex. What a pair of gents you are. There was no bloody way they were getting me on that shuttle."

"Yeah, but if you'd stayed put, we wouldn't be pissing around like this, would we?" Marc was angry. "Why didn't you stay in the access passages?"

"Because I had a feeling Erskine would wipe the wormhole data, so I had to try and retrieve it, didn't I? You'd have done the same."

"But you didn't."

"Nah, Ben caught me."

"Okay, now it's your turn. Get those bombs stopped. Are you planning to go home after this? They'll come and extract you, right?"

"Yeah."

"Can you get Tev back to Fiji? It's in your neck of the woods. He hasn't seen his kids in ages."

"I'll give it a go," Kim said. "It's the least I can do. Do you want a ride back to the UK?"

"I'm staying, thanks," Marc said, and walked on.

It wasn't like him to snap at people, but Alex thought better of asking him if anything was wrong. He just trailed after them and ended up waiting outside the Lammergeier while Solomon was brought out to supervise Kim's call to APS. Everything felt very unreal now. Marc sat down with him on the tilt rotor's ramp.

"She's just relaying messages through some bagman," he said, and looked at his watch. "Still, we've got at least twenty-four hours for them to call this off."

"You think we'll make it if they don't?"

Marc shrugged. "As long as the shelter's sealed and we don't have any leaks letting contaminated dust and water in, I think so. It won't be pretty. But we'll come out alive. I know I always do."

Marc didn't say anything else and sat staring up at the sky. Eventually Kim walked past them down the ramp and stood on the lawn, stretching.

"Well?" Alex said.

She shrugged. "I don't know. I couldn't speak to Pham direct. I'll have to wait and see like everyone else. It's early morning there, after all."

"Did you point out that we're not much use to them trashed and glowing in the dark?"

"I did. And I made a big thing of how shitty and obsolete your ships are, and that they should let you clear out as soon as possible so we can take over the facility. I think it's for the best that my people don't find out what Sol is." Kim stretched again. "Oh, and Sol impersonated you when he made the initial call. So if some bloke says that he spoke to you on the sat phone, just say yes."

"Great. What did I say?"

"Just that Erskine was as mad as a box of frogs and that she'd sabotaged the comms, but you were the main man to talk to, and that you'd hand over the goods if they called off the bombing."

Alex thought that was a pretty fair assessment of his own thoughts. "Close enough."

"I'm going to grab a shower, then, if that's okay with you," she said.

Marc stood up. "Then you'll have it downstairs in the shelter. I'm not letting you walk around without close protection until this is sorted one way or the other. Erskine's persistent."

Alex thought Marc was flirting with her for a moment, but the guy looked deadly serious. Someone would have to guard her now until the shuttle left. It was only fourteen hours or so. It would soon be over.

It was decent of her to look out for Sol like that, though. Maybe it was time to rebuild a few bridges with him. Alex realised how fast his finest hour had faded and left him deflated. Adrenaline did that, apparently, but he'd experienced nothing like it before to prepare him. The aftermath was a thumping headache and a dry mouth. Maybe he needed that beer after all, seeing as Kim was safe and the message had been sent.

But he had to sit it out until midnight, because the passenger list needed to be finalised. He went back to his office, feeling a few strained muscles, and busied himself checking out the bruises that he didn't realise he'd acquired in his scuffle with Ben. Poor old Ben — this was a guy he drank with and regarded as a friend, and he'd ended up trying to brain him with a curl bar. Maybe Ben was now sitting somewhere licking his own wounds and wondering why a buddy had kept Opis a secret all those years. Neither of them had really known each other until survival was at stake.

A message arrived on Alex's screen at 2230. It was from Erskine, just one word.

TRAITOR.

It didn't hurt. Alex was more worried about the problems she'd cause by staying here, because she wasn't one for giving in gracefully. He had the feeling that the rules would change once the bulk of the Ainatio staff were gone. He could see Trinder taking over, maybe with Doug Brandt and Chris, because they'd be the majority. Life wasn't going to go on as before even if they never made it to Opis. He thought about Marc and Tev, and how fast they took control of situations, and bet himself that things here would run on more military lines in the future.

But he had to reply to Erskine. He wondered whether to tell her that Kim had contacted APS to horse-trade, but she'd have worked that out by now, and it wasn't going to change anything. He stuck to the basics.

I HAVE 68 BERTHS EMPTY. I STRONGLY SUGGEST YOU CHANGE YOUR MIND AND TAKE THE OPPORTUNITY TO

LEAVE IN ELCANO. THEY'LL NEED SOME LEADERSHIP. WE ALREADY HAVE OURS.

Alex tapped SEND. It felt good.

It also made him feel guilty. In a way, Erskine had done the right thing. They both had. They just operated in different realities that put them on a collision course, and Alex had discovered that he was one of the guys who worried about the faces looking at him right now, not a vague future full of people he'd never live to see.

Erskine's reply came back ten minutes later. I WILL NOT FORGET THIS. GOODBYE.

It wasn't an expression of gratitude.

"Goodbye, Director," he said.

He put her out of his mind and started looking through the list of people who weren't going, intending to contact them and ask if they'd changed their minds. But there were no names on the standby list now, and all he'd do by asking was undermine hard decisions that had already been taken. They'd made up their minds.

He'd ask Solomon if he felt like a chat. At least he could look the AI in the eye now, because he'd done what a man was morally obliged to do.

A clean conscience was a wonderful comfort.

* * *

KILL LINE:
1130 HOURS, NEXT MORNING

Doug Brandt hadn't heard that low rumbling noise for a long time, but he knew exactly what it was.

He tried to recall the last time that Ainatio had launched a shuttle. The sound always made everyone stop and look up, and today was no exception. He paused and got out of the truck, shielding his eyes against the sun as he tried to work out where the ship would emerge above the trees, and waited for the whine.

After the initial rumble, that whine would start low and work up the scale, followed by something he always heard as a scream of frustration as the shuttle picked up speed. He'd only ever glimpsed it in flight, never on take-off, but he'd seen SSTOs like it take off on TV, zipping along a launch rail set in the runway to boost speed before finally lifting off.

Ah, there was the scream. In a few moments he'd see the charcoal-grey, missile-like shape lift into the sky, leaving a shimmering haze in its wake. When it finally rose above the trees it looked too sleek to be real.

I suppose we could have been on that flight. The whole family.

Doug stopped himself right there. Everyone would get where they were meant to be, and it was better to stay together in the long term than sow divisions now. But if he understood the schedule right, he would only be the mayor for a couple more months until *Shackleton* was ready, and then the next thing would be waking up forty-five years later in a new world with an established settlement. Would Kill Line integrate? Would they become a suburb, a quarter, a separate community?

There *was* no Kill Line any longer, even if it was still on the map. He couldn't let himself grieve about it. The future was all that mattered now. He chose to believe that there would be one, and that it would start tomorrow.

He got back in the truck and carried on through the deserted town. The fire and rescue committee had already searched to make sure every building was clear, and checked the evacuee list, but he wanted to do one final sweep himself before driving out to Liam Dale's farm. It was for his own closure.

Even in the middle of the night when nobody was out on the streets, Kill Line had always felt alive, but this morning it seemed truly empty for the first time in Doug's life. A few chickens were poking around in the grass. Wisps of smoke rose above the roofline in the town square as the carcasses of Marty Laurenson's sheep still burned. It was an apocalypse without any visible damage. Every home that Doug passed was shuttered. In the fields, cattle were still grazing. Those who hadn't shot their livestock had left them to roam, and Liam Dale was the last farmer left.

At least he'd been consistent. He hadn't wanted to leave when Opis was an option rather than a necessity, and he still hadn't wanted to leave when the die-back started again. It wasn't surprising that even the threat of salted bombs hadn't shifted him. But he wasn't crazy.

He was cleaning the milking parlour when Doug arrived. It was so quiet out here — no tractors, no sawmill, no pumps — that Doug could simply follow the sound of the high-pressure hose to find him. Liam looked up as he walked in. The air felt damp and fresh like the aftermath of rain.

"Come on, Liam," Doug said. "You've done all you can. Let's go. Come and have something to eat. Nicola's waiting with the kids. She needs you there."

Liam didn't say anything. He put the hose away and switched off the power at the box on the wall. Doug followed him back to the house a few paces behind, just letting him be, and stopped when he stopped. He waited outside until Liam came out with a small suitcase, shut the front door, and rattled the lock a few times to persuade himself that it was secure.

He put the case in the back of Doug's pick-up. "Give me a moment," he said.

Doug could guess where he was going. Liam didn't have many animals — some pigs, his prize herd of Jerseys, a few chickens that were more pets for his kids than anything — but they were as much his family's legacy as a rich man's estate. Doug left him for a respectable time. When he eventually went to find him, he was leaning on the fence, watching his cattle. The Jersey bull was watching him back. It was the meanest animal Doug had ever come across, a stark contrast to the small, friendly cows with their pretty deer-like faces.

"Liam, I don't want to get your hopes up, but Ainatio's trying to negotiate with APS to call off the bombing," Doug said. "They've offered to trade their secret research. We're waiting to hear."

Liam half-shrugged. One of the cows ambled across to him and presented her muzzle for scratching. "Yeah. I heard the rumour. If they do, I'm going to feel bad for the guys who've shot their livestock."

He hung around a little longer, then shook his head and walked away to the truck. He didn't look back as Doug drove off. If the bombing went ahead, this was probably the last time anyone would see Kill Line in one piece.

No. Look forward. We have to.

It wasn't a long drive back to the shelter at Ainatio, but it was still a lot of silence to sit through. Just once, Doug glanced at Liam, expecting to see him staring out of the window or keeping his eyes fixed on the road ahead, but he wasn't looking at anything at all. His eyes were shut and his face was streaked with tears.

Doug looked away again and said nothing. Some things couldn't be put right with comforting words or even hope. Liam's wife was waiting out front with their son and daughter when Doug pulled up, though, and he was given no more time to brood.

"All safely gathered in, then," said a voice behind Doug as he made his way to the elevator. It was Alex, the management guy who'd given the talk about Opis, which now seemed like a lifetime ago. "So, the animals?"

"He's just left them in their field. They'll either be okay or they won't."

"We haven't heard back from APS yet. But Sol's got the bots working on rebuilding the comms. We're still using the sat phone."

"Well, I'm going to try to keep people busy now. How many of your agricultural people are still here? We can start planning together."

"We've got a few plant biologists and a couple of guys who can help out with animal embryos and that kind of stuff. We've already stored some eggs and semen for a couple of your livestock guys. But I don't think Mr Dale's herd provided any."

"I don't think he saw what he had as replaceable."

They got into the elevator. The lighting showed a few marks on Alex's face that hadn't been there when Doug had seen him yesterday, as if he'd been in a brawl, but Doug minded his own business.

"Are you okay with Trinder and the military running all this?" Alex asked.

"Why wouldn't I be?"

"You're the mayor."

"Sure, but this isn't just Kill Line. It's the camp and it's whatever Ainatio folk feel they are now. I'm just the spokesman for my neighbourhood."

The doors opened on U3. Alex ushered Doug out in front of him. "Yeah, it's kind of hard to identify as Ainatio now."

Doug had suspected that as soon as he started seeing Dan Trinder's troops walking around. They were still in their black uniforms, but all their insignia had disappeared. There was no company logo on their caps or sleeves, just marks of rank. And then he spotted Jared Talbot, impossible to miss in a sea of heads because he was so tall, and he was wearing the same black shirt, pants, and cap. Doug was used to seeing Chris's guys in a varied mix of service uniforms, depending on where they'd originated and which garments had survived a hard few years, anything from police departments to State Defence and naval units, usually combined with camouflage or hunting jackets. Now it looked as if a realignment had taken place overnight.

"What happened with all the uniforms?" Doug asked.

Alex shrugged. "Trinder said Ainatio didn't exist any more."

"But what about the transit camp?"

"Lennie Fonseca thought it would be nice to offer them the run of the stores. They haven't had any new gear for a long time. Apparently the boots were very welcome."

"You sound like you needed to ask Trinder about it."

"Well, I did wonder if we were witnessing a merger."

"Makes sense," Doug said. "Factions aren't good for anyone. Look, have I understood the timescale right? If things go to plan and we launch *Shackleton* in a few months, that means we'll land on Opis not long after *Elcano* gets there, doesn't it?"

"Correct."

"That doesn't leave much time for healing."

Alex chuckled without much humour. "There's been a lot of discussion about that in the last few days. And there's the unknown factor of how the next Nomad generation is going to see things after their parents were cut off by Erskine."

"But they're military."

"Nobody's immune to the mythology of time. I've lived through just a few days of this at close quarters, and right now I don't know if Erskine was a ruthless bitch who saved her chosen elite, or a heroine who did the only thing she could."

"But you chose to do the opposite."

"Indeed I did," Alex said, walking away. "So I guess I decided she was a bitch after all."

Doug wondered how much time it would take to heal that. He wasn't going to hold his breath.

It was time to go walkabout to see how people were doing in the Kill Line section, and he was relieved to see his grandchildren mesmerised by Solomon. The AI was now back in his quadrubot frame, keeping a crowd of youngsters occupied by showing them recordings of the black bird-like creatures that hung around the Nomad camp on Opis. Solomon wasn't a natural entertainer when it came to children, but somehow that made him much more human. He was like an awkward uncle, stopping every so often to explain himself, even a little hesitant. But the older children were just lapping it up, and the little ones saw only a friendly, talking, robotic dog. Kids liked robots and they liked dogs. Solomon didn't have to sell himself very hard.

Doug hung around at the back of the hall, increasingly absorbed. Much of Opis had been mapped and superficially surveyed from orbit, but very little had been explored. The last few months had been such a flood of shocks and surprises that he kept overlooking one important issue. The survival of *Cabot* and the existence of a base on another planet was a surprise to more than just the people here. The rest of the world didn't know either, and that wasn't a small technical detail. The only alien worlds that Earth had seen at close quarters were within the solar system and a couple orbiting relatively close stars, and the only life found was far, far less complex than anything Solomon was showing the children now. Opis was a real prize. Doug understood Georgina Erskine's fears. And if he was completely honest with himself, they were his fears as well.

He went back to the cubicle he shared with Joanne and sat down to plan out things for the next few days. He'd hold sessions in one of the halls and get the farmers talking in detail with the scientists about crop planning. There was no way of knowing what would happen on Opis in the years they'd be in cryo, and their plans might turn out to be a waste of time, but it was what they needed to do right now. Damn it, he'd hold a session tonight. Staying busy beat sitting around and watching the clock count down to midnight.

"Oh, you're back." Joanne stood in the cubicle entrance, holding a pile of clothes. "I saw Liam, so I assumed everything went okay."

"Apart from it breaking him."

"Martin's set up the chapel."

"I'm not sure Liam's going to find solace there yet."

"You never know. Anyway, I met the young woman who's negotiating with APS. She seems very competent. Annis Kim."

"Has she had an answer yet?"

"I think they'd tell us if she had."

Doug checked the time. "I didn't realise it was that late." It was nearly four in the afternoon. He needed to grab something to eat. "I'm going to start holding agricultural planning meetings tonight. Get together with the scientists and work out some detail."

"You'll be competing with the movies and the pool hall, then. Dan Trinder and that ginger-bearded guy have made sure everyone's going to be fully occupied for the next few days. No sitting around waiting for the bombs to drop. Personally, I think I'm going to sleep through it. I'm totally wiped out."

"You're being very calm."

"I'm not going to pretend I'm relaxed about it, but we do have experienced people here who know what they're doing. Go on, get on with your meeting. I'm going to take a quick nap."

Joanne was fine, then. That was all that mattered.

Doug went on his rounds again. The more ground he covered in this subterranean complex, the more he understood what she meant about the comforting effect of being surrounded by competence. In under forty-eight hours, the combined effort of the site staff, the transit camp, and his own neighbours had set up an underground village, complete with a hospital, a dog pound, kitchens, entertainment, sanitation, schoolrooms, and relatively private accommodation for more than sixteen hundred people. If anything proved that this random selection of human beings could build a new society, that did. They could face the worst. He was proud of them all.

He stopped for a sandwich at one of the food stations and watched the endless trail of assorted bots moving up and down the passages. So this was what the town had supported for all these years without knowing. He was still annoyed about Ainatio stockpiling food, and wished they could have rewarded the town's loyalty with a little trust, but now those reserves would save them in the end. Fate was meticulously tidy.

When he finished his sandwich, he went to check out the chapel, locating it via the floor plans that had been posted at every fire control point. It turned out to be a large room off a storage area full of bots. Martin Berry had set up rows of seats, a lectern, and a makeshift altar that appeared to be a quadrubot like Solomon's unit. The four legs were at full height, turning it into a useful table. Incongruous as it was, it didn't look out of place bearing the big brass cross from St Thomas's.

"Don't worry, Doug, I've rescued the parish records." Martin appeared with the box of frayed hymn books that Doug's father said had been ancient when the church was built. He started putting them on the seats. "Solomon thought this would be a quieter spot for contemplation. I had an extraordinary chat with him."

"He's the only one of his kind, he says."

"I can believe it. I've never discussed self-sacrifice in the context of Kant and Aquinas's cardinal virtues with a sentient machine before."

Doug had only spent minutes with the AI, and he wasn't exactly sure who Kant or Aquinas were, but he realised Solomon was different.

"He's full of surprises."

"He wanted to discuss the morality of killing. Apparently he opened fire on one of the men who ambushed Chris's patrol, and he still seems to be trying to square that with his moral programming."

"Yes. They told me he's classed as a sentient autonomous weapon or something, and they were banned years ago, so APS might want him destroyed."

"Then we'd better make sure he stays our little secret. Whatever his purpose, I really think he has a soul."

Martin wasn't a fanciful man. Doug sometimes wondered how he managed to believe in anything he couldn't see, so when he made pronouncements like that, they were unsettling. Martin had arrived thirty years ago at the height of the epidemic that hit New England, very well qualified but seeking somewhere remote, willing to fit in but still always a little separate. Nobody wanted to turn away a minister even if he'd come from an infected area.

"I'll let folks know you're opening the doors," Doug said.

As the afternoon wore on, Doug tried to keep walking the floor and reassuring everyone in the way a mayor was supposed to, but he wasn't a kid any more, and the effort exhausted him. He took a seat and people-watched for a while. Whenever he checked his screen, though, he found another message from someone he'd invited to the planning meeting saying they couldn't make it tonight, and asking if tomorrow was okay.

He said yes to all of them, realising that they wanted to be with their families. Even though they were talking casually about events tomorrow, there was still doubt in their minds that the day would actually come. Doug understood, and knew where he needed to be at midnight as well.

It was now nearly seven, and the public address system announced that the chapel was open. Doug suspected it would get busier the closer it got to midnight, and decided to drop in again to see how Martin was doing. He couldn't forget the minister's comment about Solomon. They were living in strange times. But when he got to the chapel, Martin wasn't there. Someone else was, though, and not who Doug expected.

Marc Gallagher was sitting in the back row, leaning forward with his elbows on his knees as if he was reading something. He was one of a number of people Doug had been introduced to with barely a couple of minutes to form an opinion, but he didn't seem to be the spiritual kind. Perhaps he wanted a few moments' peace and quiet. Then it dawned on Doug that he was looking at the contents of his wallet, holding it open like a book. He suddenly looked around as if he hadn't heard Doug walk in.

"Sorry, I didn't mean to interrupt you," Doug said.

Marc stood up. "It's okay. Did you need me, sir?"

"No, I came down to see the minister, but it doesn't matter."

It felt like an awkward moment for both of them. It was also the second time today that Doug had seen a strong man with tear tracks down his face. He couldn't walk away now. Like Liam, Marc had been looking at something or someone he cherished and thought it would be for the last time. Doug could work that out for himself.

"It's okay, Marc," he said. "We'll come through this."

Marc still had his wallet in his hand. "That's the problem," he said. "I always do, and they didn't."

He opened his wallet, and for a moment Doug didn't connect the words with the action. Marc was a dad showing someone his family photos in the way all fathers did, images of two young men in uniform posing for the camera with big grins. When the reality dawned, though, Doug was crushed.

"They were killed a few days apart," Marc said. "When I see people in here looking scared, I hope neither of my lads saw it coming. I couldn't bear knowing that they spent their last moments terrified."

Doug had never worked out whether courageous men were just better at hiding fear, or whether they'd had to confront it so often that it had lost its capacity to paralyse them. He had questions, none of which could be asked. He didn't know if one son had known about his brother's death, and he didn't know how Marc had been given the news, both at the same time or separately. It was too terrible to think about and far too much to ask.

"I wish there was something I could do," Doug said.

"All I want right now is for the last thing I see to be them."

"It might be the first."

Doug realised he might have said entirely the wrong thing or even sounded glib. Marc's expression told him nothing.

"Give me a shout if you need anything, sir," Marc said, weaving his way between the seats to the exit. "I'll be up top."

Doug could only sit down and contemplate how easy things had been for Kill Line until now. Even this evacuation was comfortable and well-fed. It was hard to imagine the things that the rest of the world had been forced to do to survive, but he might find out all too soon.

Martin appeared a few minutes later carrying two mugs of coffee. "Hi Doug. Where'd Marc go?"

Doug added a few more pieces to the puzzle and realised that he'd made Marc feel uncomfortable enough to leave. "He went back up top. That's my fault, I'm afraid. I think I said too much."

Martin handed him the coffee instead. "Did he show you the pictures?"

"Yeah. Damn shame."

"I think he just wanted somewhere private for a few minutes without someone asking him for help."

"I can't imagine living with that sort of pain."

"He's still looking for something." Martin stroked imaginary dust off one of the hymn books. "He's armed and I don't think he's afraid of death the same way most men are. If he really wanted out, he'd have done it. But he's hanging on."

"Don't assume he wants to be saved, Martin."

"I won't. But he believes in something bigger than himself, or else he wouldn't be a soldier. That's what gives you the courage to take risks. Tribe, family, regiment, nation, God — they'll still be there even when you're not, and that lifts you because you know things will be okay. It's belief in the future."

"He could go back to Britain. That's still okay."

"But that's not what he's looking for. Whatever it is, it isn't there. Maybe there's too much past there for him to bear."

Doug wasn't sure why he was worrying about a man he barely knew, but today had been his first real brush with the heartbreak of others beyond the normal cycle of birth and death, and his first experience of watching it bring tough men down. He'd avoided all that. He felt like he was finally waking up very late in life.

"Opis is as good a place as any to look for it, then," he said. "And I suspect he won't be the only one."

* * *

AINATIO SHUTTLE D750K, APPROACHING ORBITAL 1: 1845 HOURS

One way or the other, it was over.

Erskine could do nothing now except sit and wait like the rest of the Ainatio staff crammed into the shuttle. It was like the worst airline flight she could imagine: painfully cramped, nothing to pass the time, her head throbbing thanks to the microgravity, and a giddy nausea that she could only keep under control by shutting her eyes. Despite the medication and an empty stomach, she'd come close to vomiting. Several people already had. The air scrubber hadn't quite killed the smell.

It was also unnervingly silent, considering that there were so many children on board. A few kept crying, occasionally shushed into silence, but apart from that the only sounds were the clicks and creaks from the shuttle itself.

And I can't even have a coffee.

Erskine couldn't risk opening her eyes to check her watch in case she finally threw up. Would she pass the fourteen-hour threshold for cryo? It was going to be hours before the chill-down began, so she'd be all right. The next thing she'd taste would be when — or if — she was revived from suspension, decades in the future and trillions of miles away. The oblivion of a dreamless sleep couldn't come soon enough.

A couple of clunks and a shudder passed through the shuttle. Knowing that it was only the ship docking under the control of the dumb AIs didn't reassure her, but then she felt herself sinking in her seat and realised the shuttle was now under the orbital's partial gravity. It still didn't feel normal, but it was enough to tell her brain which way was up. At least that would help stop the nausea.

Now two of the engineers would have to suit up, enter the transfer tunnel to check that the seals were sound, manually open the airlocks, and let the onboard AI flood the spaces with breathable air. Then they'd repeat the procedure at the far end of the orbital to ensure *Elcano* was ready to board. It was going to take time. These were tasks that would have been automated if Solomon hadn't locked everything down.

And if we hadn't cut his links. Maybe he'd have relented and released the ship.

A child started crying again. Erskine knew she should have said something encouraging, a pep talk or some cheerful banter, but breaking the silence would have sounded forced and nervous. She wasn't the charismatic figure everyone looked to for a defiant or inspiring word. Alex Gorko would have said exactly the right thing, made everyone laugh, and changed the entire mood of the ship, but he wasn't here, and neither was any other manager with that kind of easy confidence.

Jane Lurie eventually appeared in the hatchway, helmet in one hand, looking out of breath. Nobody was used to doing these kinds of manoeuvres. This was life without Solomon managing the AIs for them.

"We're connected," she said. "Everything's fine, so we're going back to open the hatches now. Not much longer to wait."

"I want to go to the bathroom," said a small voice.

So did Erskine. It was sobering to find that running for your life could pale into insignificance when your body's most basic functions demanded attention. She shut her eyes and tried to sleep to take her mind off it, which should have been easy after yet another sleepless night. Eventually, after a few minutes of trying to ignore the sudden smell of urine and someone coughing a few rows behind her, the long cabin receded into the distance and then faded.

Someone shook her shoulder. It was Lurie.

"Time to move, Director. Are you okay? We transferred the children first. The little ones were getting really cranky."

Erskine tried to straighten up in her seat, then remembered the seat belt. "Oh. Yes." She straightened her jacket, rumpled in the straps. "How long was I out?"

"A couple of hours. Careful when you stand up. It's not full Earth gravity, remember."

Erskine had rarely needed to be scared of anything in her safe, confined life. She'd never faced real physical danger. The things that made her afraid were all abstract, and perhaps harder to deal with because of that. But she was suddenly conscious of the fragility of both the shuttle and her own body as she made her way down the aisle between the tightly-packed rows of seats, holding on to the overhead rail and moving hand over hand. If things had gone to plan and the follow-up missions had happened at the appointed time, there'd have been a few familiarisation flights to prepare everyone for the more unpleasant sensations. Instead, they'd all done it for real with no training, just instructions, and it had been rushed and frightening. Alex had said that he hadn't dreamed in cryo. Erskine hoped that meant people would be spared the nightmares the flight might have generated.

A few yards from the hatch, she ducked her head automatically to look out of the single window, and had to pause. It wasn't how beautiful Earth looked, or how wondrous, or how special that gripped her and made her stare. It just looked so damned *alone*. It was far beyond the middle of nowhere, a very long way to fall.

Is that all it is?

Take a good look. You'll never see it again.

"You okay, Director?" Lurie asked.

"Fine. Just rubbernecking."

Following Lurie through the docking transfer tunnel was like walking across a glass floor, a solid surface that she struggled to trust. She now knew how little substance separated her from the infinite blackness outside. Orbital 1's airlock felt like solid ground by comparison. The station had some gravity, room to move around, and, to Erskine's relief, a toilet. She needed that right away.

"Gravity's very underrated," she said, squeezing into the tiny compartment and trying to identify the essentials to make the thing work. At least everything would head in the direction it was supposed to. "I'm glad I never had to work up here."

It took her a few moments to work out how to flush the toilet. When she came out, Lurie was leaning against the bulkhead, staring out at Earth. It was hard to tell if she was regretting this or not.

"We'll still be able to see Earth after midnight, won't we?" Erskine said.

Suddenly she couldn't recall the launch schedule. It had been the least of her worries. All she'd wanted to know was when the shuttle would be beyond Solomon's reach if she'd misjudged his rules of engagement. Somewhere on that forlorn little sphere out there, somewhere in her line of sight, she'd be able to see the area around Kill Line and the facility, if she could find a satcam feed.

"We'll be underway in three hours, when the AIs have finished their checks," Lurie said. "So you're cutting it fine. I wouldn't watch if I were you."

For a moment, Erskine thought that Lurie meant the cryosuspension process, which hadn't struck her as disturbing at all when she'd seen the footage of the *Cabot* preparation. It was simply like watching an anaesthetist with a patient. Then she realised that Lurie didn't mean that at all.

"You think I'm being macabre," Erskine said.

"Just remember it's never going to leave you."

Erskine had never thought of Lurie as a great reader of people's moods. She didn't know much about the woman at all. Lurie was just one of the engineers who'd become a lot more visible in the last few weeks of intense preparation. But she'd read Erskine like a book, and she was right. Watching the bombing would both haunt Erskine and leave her feeling helpless to stop it. Perhaps that was exactly what she was seeking: the feeling of being unable to do anything about it.

I was ready to stay. It's not as if I dumped babies out of a life raft to save myself. Alex just made it clear that I'd be more unwelcome with the survivors than with the people here. And we never really knew if we could trade data for time.

No, I'm responsible. Whichever way we cut it.

"You're right," Erskine said. "When are you going to disable the FTL node?"

"John's doing it now. That's the end of the wormhole."

"As long as Solomon can access *Shackleton*, and APS can't access Opis, that's all that counts."

Lurie nodded, but she didn't look convinced. "Okay."

The orbital was much larger than Erskine remembered and more brightly lit, but it was just a dock with limited life support, not a hotel. Nobody would want to be stranded here for more than a few days. She could hear the growing buzz of voices as she followed Lurie further down the narrow passage. In her mind, she had an image of walking to the end and emerging into a large open space, but the orbital was made up mostly of compartments for safety reasons. Every doorway she passed seemed to be full of people just looking for somewhere to sit or park themselves while they waited. Alex had organised it efficiently, at least. There were designated staff locating people and getting them lined up for cryo. It didn't pay to hang around thinking about the process for too long.

One of the medical team approached Erskine, the male nurse she'd seen when she went to visit Kim in the infirmary.

"We can get you into cryo right away, Director," he said. "We didn't think you were coming, though, so we don't have your medical records."

"It doesn't matter," Erskine said. "If I die, I die. It's not as if I have a choice now. But could you delay me, please? Would it be any trouble to do me much later? Last, perhaps?"

"Of course. It'll be a long wait, though."

"Understood." Erskine consulted her screen to check the deck plan. "I'll be in the communications section for a while if you need me."

She wanted to check that the FTL was disabled for good. This was an obsession. She knew it. But Solomon had made a vow, and he had nothing to distract him from it: no family, no lover, no selfish ambition, and no fear, nothing beyond his reason for existing, which was the preservation of Nomad, and Bednarz's vision of a society of the morally superior. He would feel completely justified no matter what he did. Would Bednarz have agreed with him on his choice of exemplary men and women? Erskine would never know if Solomon's choices had been shaped in any way by Bednarz himself, however inadvertently.

But either way, Solomon really had reached the conclusion that sacrifice, the ultimate sacrifice of the soldier, the laying down of lives for others, set some people apart from the rest.

Erskine followed the schematic on her screen and ended up climbing a short run of ladder to get into the communications section. It was no easy feat even in reduced gravity. When she reached the next compartment, she sat down on a metal locker while she reoriented herself. Would she ever meet Solomon again? His perspective might have changed in forty-five years, but if he'd lost his ideal human breeding stock, his seed corn for a better society, then he might have worked up an unimaginable head of steam by the time they next met.

If we ever do. How long can he last if he's powered down? How much of him gets written to permanent storage?

Perhaps Solomon could actually die just like a human, and leave nothing of his essential self behind. Perhaps he was aware of that, and that was why he prized the willingness of some humans to give up that life to let someone else survive.

Erskine carried on through the compartment, trying to avoid grabbing at unfamiliar pieces of equipment to steady herself. She could hear metallic taps and clicks ahead of her. She found Jane Lurie locking some metal boxes the size of suitcases.

"The essentials from the FTL node," Lurie said. "I can't break them up or dump them out the airlock, so we'll have to take them with us."

"So does that mean the wormhole's collapsed?"

"Yes."

"I didn't notice. I thought — never mind."

"It's tiny. No lightshow or anything." Lurie straightened up, still looking down at the boxes. Erskine could almost smell her disapproval. "Director, I'm going to make sure nobody else watches the detonations. So could you avoid mentioning it? I know you probably don't want to hear my opinion, but even if nobody survives to come after us, people here are feeling guilty and there'll be recriminations. We've started out already broken. Alex Gorko gave up his cryo berth for me. I've got to live with that now."

Erskine rarely got into these kinds of conversations with anyone outside her immediate management circle. She wasn't sure whether to enter into the debate or just make polite, non-committal noises. She decided not to point out that there were vacant berths and skipped to the broader issues.

"We'll be joining an established society," she said. "I know it's going to be hard to come to terms with what's happened, but Nomad will change us. We'll learn how to pull together again."

"But the population still won't outnumber a thousand new arrivals. We'll be the dominant culture. And they'll know we're the ones who left people behind. I'm kind of scared about where that goes."

Erskine was about to say that they wouldn't know, but they already had the information on who was supposed to be joining them. She'd overlooked that in the heat of the crisis. She hadn't given much thought — *any* thought — to how the Nomad team would feel about sharing their home with people who'd abandon their colleagues.

"I don't know what future generations will think," Erskine said. "But the crew of *Cabot* are mostly military, and they'll understand why hard choices had to be made."

Lurie blinked as if she'd switched off her real self and reverted to being the anonymous engineer. She lifted chunks of cable and composite out of a rack and packed them into a box. The conversation was over, then. Erskine thought of Chris Montello, refusing the chance to save his own skin, just like Trinder, and wondered if *Cabot*'s crew would give her a pass after all.

"There," Lurie said. "That's the last part. I'll go stow this in *Elcano*. Why don't you move into the ship? You can still watch the satcam feed. We're not shutting down the orbital."

Erskine stepped through the last airlock into the ship, and Lurie sealed the door and hatch behind her. Out of all the points of no return Erskine thought she'd reached, this really was the final one. *Elcano* would sever all connections with the orbital — and with Earth — in the next couple of hours.

It was past eleven at night back at the facility. They'd have secured the underground floors by now and would be killing time just as Erskine was. She had no work or leisurely meal to take her mind off the agonising wait. She couldn't call Solomon even if she wanted to, and everything possible had been said anyway. The only thing she could do was wander around the ship and try to reassure the staff. Yes, she'd do that until it was time to find a sat feed.

It didn't take her long to realise that the combination of limited space and a lot of anxious, disoriented people at a loose end made her into an obstacle. After drifting around trying to make small talk, exhaustion got the better of her and she ended up on the top cryo deck with the people from Propulsion, mostly because Ben was there, and she'd had enough contact with him in the last few days to feel that he was someone she actually knew. The deck wasn't the minimalist, cavernous chamber beloved of movies. It was a parking garage, an industrial space full of undisguised cables, metal structures, and harsh lights, just storage for human freight with little room around each pod. One of the engineers stood up to give her a place on a bench against one of the bulkheads.

"We did our best, Director," Ben said. He'd changed into a tracksuit top and shorts. It made him look even bigger. "With Kim, I mean."

"I know. It's not your fault. And it might not make any difference anyway."

"Where do APS think we're going? They'll realise we're not heading for Mars or someone else's orbital sooner or later."

"Assuming they're concerned at all, they'll be more interested in getting into the facility once it's safe to do so." Everyone stopped talking. The silence spread around her like frost creeping across a window. It was getting close to midnight. She needed to get to a sat feed. "I have to see Jane Lurie. Excuse me."

"Ask Colin Croad," Javinder said. "The loadmaster."

Yes, she remembered Colin. It was interesting to see how they all organised themselves without Alex around, or maybe they were just following Alex's schedule. Perhaps he wouldn't have made a community leader, but he was a better organiser than she'd given him credit for.

She went to the bridge. She didn't find Colin, but she did run into Lurie.

"Have you come up here to watch the feed?" Lurie asked.

"If I can see it here, yes."

"It's as good a place as any."

Lurie had warned her. But if Erskine didn't see the real event, she'd only create a theatrical version in her imagination from fiction and half-recalled memories, and it would be equally terrible. Lurie sat her down at a small console on the port side.

"It's all AI until we reach Opis," she said, sitting her down. "So you'll get some privacy up here."

The monitor had the resolution of a military satellite but Erskine couldn't pick out the town or the facility until Lurie made some adjustments. If anything told her that the America she'd known was gone, that lightless void was it. The only illumination seemed to be Ainatio's perimeter fence. Lurie adjusted the image again to zoom out.

"They're targeting to the north-east," she said, pointing out the orientation overlay. "If that's what you want to see."

Midnight was suddenly rushing up to meet Erskine like the ground at the bottom of a long fall. She kept checking her watch against the bulkhead chronometer, trying not to look away from the image in case she missed something.

"You don't have to wait with me," she said.

"Are you telling me to get lost?"

"No. I thought you didn't want to see it."

"I need to hang around in case you need to adjust the image."

"Okay. Thank you."

Erskine glanced over her shoulder. Lurie had turned away to fidget with some tools in her overalls. Erskine went back to her vigil. She watched the display on the imager count down the seconds, and 2359 turned into midnight.

She saw nothing. She sat there for five, ten, then fifteen minutes in total silence.

"I suppose I took midnight literally," she said. "Would I have missed it?"

"Not at that resolution."

"Leave me to it. If I need help with it, I'll come and find you."

"Okay. You'll feel the ship move off in about ten minutes, so don't panic. All the clunking and vibrations won't be anything to worry about. The gravity might fluctuate for a while, though, so belt up."

Lurie wandered off. Erskine fastened the lap belt on the seat and settled down to keep watch. She'd imagined a launch to be something more spectacular, but when it happened, she almost missed it. It was just a vibration, a brief shudder as the ship separated from Orbital 1, and a few sounds she could feel through the deck more than actually hear. *Elcano* was finally on her way to Opis.

Maybe, if all the vessels had been launched and nobody had been left behind, it would have felt like the beginning of a magnificent adventure even for a jaded old woman who'd never wanted to be part of this nonsense anyway. But it was an anticlimax. The real event, the one she couldn't look away from, was the consequence of her actions miles below.

She kept watching the monitor. But by 0050, there was still no flare of light, and no activity at all. Perhaps APS had built some extra time into the warning to make sure that everyone was clear or in the shelters before they set their long-range drones on their bombing run.

At 0150, Erskine stood up and went to get Lurie. She found the engineer in a side compartment, dozing at a console with her head resting on her folded arms. Erskine tapped her on the shoulder.

"Nothing so far," she said. "It's nearly two a.m."

Lurie stretched and rubbed the back of her neck. "Let me check it."

She went back to the screen with Erskine and adjusted it, zooming in far enough to pick out the roads and buildings of Kill Line in infrared, then the Ainatio facility.

"Looks intact to me." Lurie rubbed her eyes with one hand. "I'd give it up, Director. Check again in a few hours, maybe."

They've called it off.

They didn't do it.

There could have been a number of reasons why the bombing hadn't happened yet. APDU could have had a technical problem, or the whole thing could have been an elaborate scam with Kim to gain access to the site.

Or perhaps now that Solomon had Kim, he'd finally surrendered a century's work to an unfriendly power.

He'd betrayed Nomad. Erskine's gut, something she usually ignored, told her that was the most likely reason. Solomon had sacrificed his broader mission because humans had used his moral nature against him. But she'd managed to see the Nomad project through to a landing and a follow-up mission, despite the world collapsing around her, and despite Solomon, who was no easy adversary. The colony had its head start. She'd completed the task her father had set her. The moment didn't feel like triumph of any kind, just relief, and for the time being that eclipsed any guilt or regret.

So I'm done here. I really am. I'll make some time to be bitter and vengeful later, maybe.

"You're right, Jane," she said to Lurie. "Time to give it up. I'm going to ask the med staff to put me into cryo now."

17

Bednarz gave Solomon one order, the only thing he absolutely had to do — define the best of humanity, identify it, and protect it against all its enemies. What he decided "the best" meant and how he protected it was entirely up to him. And Sol defined it, all right. He didn't pick Rembrandts or Einsteins or saints. He picked soldiers. He picked them because over the course of his long and possibly infinite life, civilians — that's us, for a lot of that time — showed him our selfishness, cowardice, disloyalty, self-pity, and mistrust of each other. Then he looked at soldiers and saw those failings were everything they weren't. Don't blame Solomon. He learned, and we were his sorry teachers.

Alex Gorko, talking to Todd Mangel

TEMPORARY CONTROL CENTRE, LEVEL U3: 0230 HOURS

Chris didn't believe that he could fall asleep on a night like this, but he woke with a start and found himself at the control room desk with his head resting on his hands.

He thought he could hear a dog barking. Had he missed the UCAVs dropping their payload? Where was Kim? What time was it? He tried to unscramble his brain, scratching his scalp. Out of nowhere, a mug of coffee appeared on the desk. He'd hoped it was Fonseca paying a visit, but it was Alex Gorko.

"You okay, Chris?"

"I heard the dogs. I thought it had started."

"All quiet. No calls, no bombs, nothing. No activity at all." Alex pushed the mug towards him. "Here. You need the caffeine."

"Where's Kim?"

"She's gone up top to use the sat phone again. Wow, that really is a museum piece. I didn't realise we still had any."

"Nobody should be going outside when we're locked down."

"How else is she going to get a signal?"

"Who's gone with her?"

"Sol."

The message had been sent so many times that the key people at APS must have received it by now. Maybe they really were juggling the risks of die-back against the potential benefits of Ainatio's propulsion technology.

And if they decide it's worth it... we're into the next round of problems.

Someone in APS intelligence obviously knew about Opis, or else Kim wouldn't have come here. The question was how much they knew, how much Kim would tell them when she got hold of them, and what they'd do about it. They had to at least be wondering why Ainatio had bothered to keep all the ships and where they might be going in *Elcano*, because whatever story Erskine had fed them, they'd check things out for themselves. Chris was starting to think that Erskine might have been right, but then he stood in the doorway and listened to the sound of nearly two thousand living, breathing individuals who had needs right now. Bargaining with APS was probably only delaying the inevitable, but if you could kick the can far enough down the road to distract whoever was coming for you, you could make a run for it.

Chris needed to find out what Kim had told APS so far. "I'm going to topside."

Alex gestured to the south exit. "You'll probably find Marc and Tev. They're minding the doors."

Chris zipped up his assault vest and slung his rifle over his shoulder. When he reached the U2 level stairs, Marc and Tev were leaning against the wall, having what looked like a pretty heavy conversation.

"But you said you wanted to go, mate," Marc was saying. They must have heard Chris coming but they carried on. "Kim can get you back to Fiji. You've got to see your kids. Don't chicken out now."

"Becky won't want me hanging around."

"Tough. They're your kids as well."

Tev glanced up at Chris. "Hi, mate. You looking for Sol?"

"Kim. I need to ask her a few things."

"Get her to come inside, will you? Her boss must have had the message by now."

"Yeah. That's what worries me."

Tev opened the door to let Chris out. The stairs took him up through the last two floors, deserted and in darkness, a couple of extra layers of protection against a blast. The main lobby was still fully lit, bright enough to be a beacon from the air. The UCAVs would have no problem identifying ground features when they began their bombing run, but there was no harm in making the site as conspicuous as possible to help them avoid a direct hit.

Kim was outside the front doors, leaning on the glass with the sat phone pressed to her ear, but she looked as if she was waiting rather than talking. Solomon's quadrubot was standing a few yards away, his snakehead camera staring out into the night, although he could have been observing in any direction.

Chris walked up behind Kim and tapped on the glass. She pushed herself upright and stepped back as he pressed the controls to open the doors.

"I didn't want you to fall in," he said. "What's happening?"

"They're not telling me. Tim Pham got the message, though. They said so."

"So who are you talking to?"

"APDU HQ. It's just one-way. I talk, they make polite noises."

"Call it a day. You've done all you can."

"Well, whatever I've done, it's delayed something."

"Tev really wants you back inside."

"If APDU calls back, how are they going to contact me? I need line of sight with this piece of junk."

"If the sensors don't pick up anything incoming, we'll try again later."

Solomon trotted in after her. It was nearly three in the morning and Chris finally dared to think that there really had been a change of plan. He stood on the half-moon marble step out front for a moment, hoping to see fireflies, and tried to work out a timetable. When would they know whether the UCAVs had been stood down? As soon as that was confirmed, Sol would want the bots back at work on the comms links again, and access *Shackleton* as soon as possible. But he might not get much time between then and APS showing up. They'd come for Kim, and when they did they'd go through this place with a fine-tooth comb.

We'll adapt. We'll improvise. Like we always do.

Chris took a deep breath of fragrant night air, not knowing when he'd get another chance, and went back into the lobby. Kim and Solomon were waiting for him.

"Dr Kim, if your people decide they want a deal, what's the first thing they'll do when they show up here?" Chris asked.

"Initial debriefing with me, so they know whether to secure the site and which parts to focus on, and then they'll want the research." Kim patted Solomon's frame like a pony. "Don't worry, Sol and I have a plan."

"How about sharing it with the rest of us?"

"It's pretty much what we've discussed. We pretend Solomon's a regular AI, I wheel out Alex as the boss fella, and we carry on prepping *Shackleton*."

"I can't help noticing a few gaps in that plan."

"Okay, there's no hiding Opis. We knew all that anyway. We just didn't know how. You don't have to tell them everything about the base, especially now the FTL link isn't working. You're just another eccentric aberration like the lighthuggers."

"See, there's the awkward part. Have you ever tried to get sixteen hundred people to tell the same lie? It's hard enough with two."

"Believe me, we're much more interested in FTL than Opis. Or your obsolete ships. It's just one planet. There are thousands of others, and FTL means we can find thousands more. This is about opening up deep space."

Chris didn't know enough about the science to work out where all this might be heading. Ainatio had used FTL to build a glorified comms link. They seemed to have given up on developing something big enough to drive a ship. He understood that much, but Kim seemed to know something he didn't. Hell, she was a physicist, an engineer, a frigging rocket scientist. Of course she did.

"Sol's got his mission, and I've got mine," Chris said. "As long as I get my people somewhere safe where they can stop running, I don't care if it's here or on another planet."

He turned to go. Kim put her hand on his arm.

"Chris, I can guess what you think of me. But for what it's worth, you, Sol, Dan, Alex, all of you, you kept your word when you could have done the easy thing and boarded *Elcano*. And Grandma Park isn't a cover story. I really do want recognition for her. You've all helped me to do that. So I'll do whatever I can to make sure you get where you want to go, even if I have to be a little creative in what I tell my political masters. We can all get a win out of this."

Chris had heard that phrase so many times from so many people, usually from guys who were trying very hard to find his price for not beating the shit out of them on behalf of his employer. It never worked. And here he was, thinking that people like Trinder and Zakko trusting him had taught him to be more trusting himself. When push came to shove, his instincts were still to give most folks a wide berth.

But I can trust Sol. I'll listen to him.

"Let's see how things go," he said.

He secured the front entrance and followed Solomon and Kim down to U3. Marc sealed the door behind them. Tev had gone.

"Are we done?" Marc asked.

"Yeah, but we'll check in with APDU in a couple of hours if nothing's happened by then."

Marc just grunted. If he had any opinions on what APS was up to, he wasn't going to voice them in front of Kim.

"I'm going to turn in for a couple of hours," he said. "Call me if anything happens."

Kim followed Chris to the control room. Trinder was there now, along with Jared, Erin, and Tev, so nobody seemed to be sticking to the duty roster. They were all watching the sensor display. It would give them ten minutes' advance warning if the UCAVs came in range.

"I think they've called it off," Jared said.

Nobody commented. The worst thing about this place was that it was a mix of advanced technology and the Stone Age, gear that could send a ship to another planet but that couldn't talk to the world on their doorstep. Chris was used to the patchy nature of civilisation these days, but it was especially galling tonight.

No, today. It'll be getting light soon.

"I need a walk," he said, taking the sat phone from the desk. "Call me."

Chris walked the floors the same way that he used to patrol the camp when the convoy stopped for the night, listening and looking, ready to step in and fix a problem. The shelter was quiet now, but it wasn't because people were asleep. Few seemed to be in their cubicles. There was a big group in one of the halls, relaxing on chairs and cushions that they'd dragged in and just socialising, as if being with a bunch of people felt better than sitting this out alone or as families. After all the effort Trinder had put into fitting out the shelter with private spaces it seemed weird, but it was human instinct to huddle together in a crisis.

There were groups everywhere Chris went: watching a movie, playing games, tidying up, or just sitting outside their cubicles and talking, their exhausted kids dozing on their laps. It took him a while to realise how many of his transit camp neighbours and Ainatio staff had wandered out of their areas to join the Kill Line folk.

This was either the end of the world or the start of a new one, and Chris almost felt that it was up to him to decide which fate would befall them. He'd read some crazy guy's theory that you could make yourself slip from one parallel universe to another with a different future simply by repeating affirmations out loud. Chris had filed the idea with healing crystals and the rest of the woo-woo garbage, but here he was, feeling that if he believed strongly enough that they'd survive, then it would happen.

Forget it. It's down to us. Our guys. And Dan Trinder. And Marc and Tev. We're the ones who've got to make the future happen.

Us.

Chris tried to remember when *them* had become *us.* He couldn't pin down the moment when it had changed, but they'd all responded to a string of crises, done what they'd been trained to do, and somehow emerged united at the other end with that good, solid feeling of belonging that came from being among others who knew what had to be done. Service background and even nationality made no difference. The instinct that united them was probably as old as mankind. It grew from the defining moment when the tribe came under attack and some guys stepped forward to pick up rocks while others fled or froze. You were either a guy who picked up a rock and ran forward, or one who ran away. Chris would always pick up that rock. He preferred the company of others who'd do the same.

Ah, now here was someone else who'd grab a rock and go for it: Fonseca, walking down the corridor towards him with Howie in tow. The kid was holding her hand, which was very un-Howie. He looked up at Chris as if he'd been caught deserting and was about to be shot.

"Howie can't sleep," Fonseca said tactfully. "So we're having a chat and putting the world to rights."

"It usually helps. You okay, Howie?"

"Yeah, I'm good."

He wasn't, of course. He was ten, the only survivor from his family. He had no problem understanding what death was. Chris usually treated him like an adult, which he loved, and Chris kind of liked it too because he didn't have to worry about the right way to handle kids. He'd never had to work that out. But tonight, Howie was a little boy who needed a grown-up to keep the monsters at bay.

"You're no use if you're falling down tired, soldier," Chris said. "Big day ahead. Get some sleep."

"Sorry."

"What's there to be sorry about?"

"Being a baby."

"Hey, everyone's scared. Some of us have had more practice at hiding it, that's all. You'll be fooling everyone just like I do when you're older."

"We're going to go get some hot chocolate in the control room," Fonseca said, giving Chris a you-callous-bastard look. He'd have to catch up with her later and explain. "See you later, Sergeant."

And we were getting on so well.

He went up to the ground floor, locked the last set of doors behind him, and stepped outside. It was definitely getting light. He checked the sat phone to see if there'd been any attempts to call back, but there was nothing logged. Would APDU be running four or five hours late? He doubted it, but now he was starting to wonder just how much grace they'd give them to get out of here. He went back inside and worked through the sequence of unlocking and re-locking doors on the top two floors again.

Solomon's voice suddenly drifted out of the public address system on U2 and almost gave him a heart attack.

"Chris, I've managed to get a signal through to Orbital One."

"Damn, Sol, are you back in the network again?"

"Of course I am. Ready to exit at any moment, though, in case the UCAVs are just running late."

"Okay. How did you route that?"

"The bots manufactured a new uplink. I can't move around yet, but I can check which systems are still responding while the primary links are being restored."

"And?"

"*Elcano*'s launched, as expected, but I can't access the FTL at all. It's not just the receiver this end."

Chris was disappointed, but not surprised. "So they disabled it from the orbital."

"It looks like it. Don't worry, it's an inconvenience, not a disaster."

"So are you giving me good news? I realise you're explaining this in finger paints for me."

"Overall, yes."

"Thanks."

"We need to get two of the remaining shuttles going," Solomon said. "I'm assessing whether it's going to be easier to bring *Shackleton* to Orbital One or to shuttle people out to Orbital Two."

Chris had no idea what the difference was, but he heard the important bit. Solomon could talk to the orbital again, albeit in a limited capacity, and he'd be able to re-establish a link to *Shackleton*.

"Have you told the others?"

"Yes. We'll be back in business soon, Chris. Chin up."

"Hey, we're survivors. We'll come out of this in one piece, no matter what."

"Indeed. Keep the faith."

It was almost funny to hear an AI say that.

Chris carried on downstairs, securing everything behind him again, and took the long route back to the control room to see Dr Mendoza. The makeshift infirmary still had patients. Chuck Emerson, the camp's retired corpsman, had also found his way down there and seemed to be enjoying a long technical chat with the doctor. Mendoza waved at Chris and pointed to his knee.

"You missed your check-up," he said from the far side of the room. "Get your ass in here tomorrow."

"Will do, Doc."

If they ended up stuck down here in a confined space for a few weeks, at least everyone could get on with each other. That was encouraging. Chris wandered back along the main passage, thinking of jobs he could do to pass the time until the next sat phone check. It was 0455, the sun was coming up, and Kill Line was still on the map.

Okay, I'm definitely going to hope.

It's going to be okay.

His radio chirped. *No bad news, please.* "Six Zero receiving, over."

"This is Echo Seven. Something unidentified on the long-range, approaching from south-west, out."

It was Fonseca. For a moment Chris felt like he'd tempted fate once too often just by thinking the danger had passed. He jogged the rest of the way to the control room, trying not to break into a sprint in case any civilians spotted him and took it as a sign to panic.

The small control room was busy. Trinder sat at the desk, studying the sensor display and tapping his stylus on the table. Fonseca was watching, brows set in a frown, and Kim was craning her neck to try to see past both of them. Alex appeared to have given up and leaned against the wall, arms folded.

Howie seemed to have found a friend in Marc, though. He was curled up asleep on the bench with his head on the guy's lap. Marc actually looked at peace for the first time since Chris had met him. He caught Chris's eye and put his finger to lips.

"There." Fonseca tapped the screen. Chris couldn't see it from the doorway. "What *is* that, Sol?"

"I can tell you what it's not," Solomon said. "It's not UCAVs. Too slow. I believe it's three stealth aircraft that aren't quite evading the sensor. Well, it's nice to know we can still do something better than APS, isn't it? They'll be visible in fifteen minutes."

"I'm going up there," Chris said. He had the keycards and the sat phone, so nobody was going to stop him. Kim squeezed out of the room and hurried after him.

"You stay put," he said. "If Sol's wrong and you get blatted alongside me, that's his trump card gone."

She stayed close on his heels, even though he was taking the stairs two at a time. "He's already played it."

"Why didn't they just insert you a few miles away, like spec ops?"

"You wouldn't have believed I made my own way here if I wasn't a tapeworm-infested wreck."

"Yeah, the parasites were a nice touch."

"Would you do me a favour?"

"Now?"

"There's something I'd like you to do for me. Personal."

Chris didn't have time for this. "Sure. Remind me later."

They walked down the approach road and stood on the open land outside the main gate, the spot with the clearest view to the south, and waited. Chris strained to hear engines or disturbed flocks of birds, anything that would give him warning, and tried to recall what kind of aircraft had carried out the bombing last time. Maybe they'd decided to drop the payload personally today as a courtesy, and this perfect dawn was going to be his last. Then he heard the engines.

"I'll do the talking," she said.

"In English, please."

"We generally do in Melbourne."

Chris tried his radio, but nobody was receiving. It was a long few minutes. Now he could definitely hear something that sounded rotary. Then three tilt rotors, two in Korean air force livery and one in plain dark blue, appeared above the trees.

"Well, that confirms they called off the UCAVs," Kim said.

Chris watched the first tilt coming in to land and spotted APDU decals before he had to crouch to avoid the storm of debris. When the noise and downwash died away, he looked back and saw all three tilts had set down on the grass and their ramps were descending. Crewmen emerged and just stood there. They seemed to be waiting on whoever was in the plain blue aircraft.

"Is that an official APS ride?" Chris asked.

"Yep." Kim tidied her hair. "Nice to see the boss fella show up in person."

A dark-haired, dark-suited guy in his forties walked down the ramp and headed their way, flanked by half a dozen people in cheaper but equally dark suits who looked like serious close protection.

"Tim Pham?" Chris asked.

"Yeah, that's him."

"You must be high up the food chain."

"I really sold the FTL hard."

"Remind him to wash his hands before he goes home. Die-back zone, remember."

"Hah."

One of the CP detail peeled off and approached them ahead of Pham. "Dr Kim?" the guy asked, addressing Kim but keeping an eye on Chris and especially on his rifle. "Mr Pham would like to speak with you."

He turned and gave Pham the nod that it was safe to approach. The guy looked at Kim as if he knew her. He shook her hand and held it way too long. Chris took a guess that they knew each other way better than they should have.

"We really thought you hadn't made it, Annis. Good grief, this is a shock."

"I nearly didn't." She nodded in Chris's direction. "This is Sergeant Montello. I'd be dead from sepsis or something if he hadn't found me, and the people here have been damn good to me, so let's keep the promises we make to them, okay? They're not the enemy."

"Certainly. Now let's talk."

Chris and sixteen hundred scared people could breathe again, for a while at least. Now the real horse-trading was about to begin.

* * *

AINATIO PARK RESEARCH CENTRE:
2 HOURS LATER

Solomon scoured the network, erasing all the downloaded feeds from Opis and putting expiry codes into the system to kill all Nomad documents that had been circulated.

Whenever staff logged in, anything sensitive on their personal screen would be wiped. It would be impossible to get this many people to agree on a cover story on Nomad, and even his own purge wasn't perfect airbrushing, but he'd learned something from Erskine: a few speed bumps placed in someone's path could work almost as well as complete destruction. He removed all the data on himself, too. Phil Berman, now a rather different man in the absence of his boss, helped him locate disconnected storage so that could be purged as well.

"I shredded a generation's work a few days ago," Berman said. "I actually had a nightmare about it afterwards. I was in Alexandria, burning the library, and people were trying to stop me, but I kept saying, 'No, we can't let it fall into the wrong hands.' I do have a better class of nightmare, I think."

"It had to be done, Phil. I've stored what I can to transfer to *Shackleton*."

"Imagine if they'd had you in Alexandria."

"Would it have added to the sum of human happiness if the library had survived?"

"Apparently most of it did, despite the myth."

"Humans never use the information they've got. They seem to value it less the more they have."

"But there's a romance in what we don't know or never can."

He had a point. Solomon pondered it, then detected some critical keywords in a conversation in Erskine's old office that needed his full attention. "Oh, I need to eavesdrop on Tim Pham. Excuse me, Phil."

Dr Kim was in the management suite with Pham, being debriefed. She was sticking to English. Solomon wondered if she was being considerate to him and hadn't remembered that he could handle Korean, but she sounded particularly Australian this morning, almost as if she was so excited at the prospect of going home that she was slipping back into her real self. She obviously knew Tim Pham very well, far better than Solomon had realised. They chatted like old friends. There might even have been some romantic liaison in the past if their body language was anything to judge by.

"And Ainatio kept all this secret, even from their staff," Pham said, swivelling slowly in Erskine's big leather chair as if he was trying it for size. "Extraordinary."

Kim nodded. She was reading the wormhole data for the first time on her screen. "Only a dozen or so senior managers knew. The rest thought they were working on die-back or keeping a little general research going in case the world ever got back on its feet. You should have seen them when she broke the news. Mad as cut snakes, Tim. None of them ever signed up for space. And then Erskine took her favourites and pulled the ladder up. So let's be diplomatic with the people she's abandoned. They've been screwed over."

"So... the FTL research." Pham rolled right over the human issues. He didn't seem to need to pretend to care. "They never developed it any further."

"They tried, but the most they got out of it was a comms-sized wormhole to run remote bots, and Erskine trashed all that when she left. But give that data to David Choi at the uni, and we could have a bigger wormhole or a drive on a useful scale in ten years. It's not really my field, but I'm pretty confident."

Pham gestured at the big executive office. "So what do we do with the rest of this? IP, personnel, plant?"

"Well, there's a lot of data assessment and recovery to do, and I don't know how much Erskine sabotaged, but I think the first thing is to let the personnel who still want to leave get off-site. And there are ex-Ainatio staff who want to move to Oz or Korea and carry on working there rather than ship out to some unknown planet."

"You've assessed them, then."

"No point letting brains go to waste, is there? We've got nearly five hundred staff here, with some really good agri researchers. Seb Meikle's the die-back remediation man. His wife, Audrey — she definitely wants to stay because they've got a little girl. She's a biomed researcher. Tissue regeneration, I think. Alex Gorko wants to stay put too. Plenty of useful expertise in everything from life sciences to manufacturing. You'd be knocking on an open door."

"Have you gone native, Annis?"

"No, I just believe that you get more with honey than with vinegar."

"What about the others?"

"They're mostly the local farmers. They were the food providers, and now they're screwed too. Then there's the refugee camp people who evacuated down here, and a group of Ainatio security staff, but they're just perimeter guards. Let them get their old ship together and leave. Then they won't be in our way. The poor buggers probably won't even get to Opis with a ship in that state, but I wouldn't be here without them, and we wouldn't have all that data."

Kim had wrapped it all up as if it didn't really matter, the path of least resistance so that APS could concentrate on scavenging data without being distracted by angry, scared, needy refugees. She'd considered the Ainatio staff who didn't want to go to Opis, too. Solomon had to hand it to her. She was doing what she'd promised.

"Did any of their propulsion team stay behind?" Pham asked.

"No, Erskine made sure they left with her. But none of them were a patch on ours anyway."

"And she's shot through to Pascoe's Star with her A team. Those ships must be fifty years old."

"Tell me about it. I spent most of the last few months fixing them."

"We still have one big problem, though. Die-back."

"How long can you give them?"

"I'll have to ask the plant pathogen people, but we're not talking long, I'm afraid."

"Months?"

"Hmmm."

"Twelve weeks. Ah, go on, Tim. If it was that urgent, we'd be irradiated charcoal by now."

"Okay, but I'll have to confirm that. We might need to move in with some pretty heavy-duty defoliant as an interim measure."

"Just give them a chance."

Pham threw up his hands in amused capitulation. "Fine. We'll overtake them en route if the FTL data is as good as it seems. Anyway, it's not every day we get to deconstruct the archives of one of the most innovative research corporations in history. Who knows what else in is there?"

Kim looked pleased with herself. "Everybody gets more or less what they want. That's my definition of a good deal."

"And you?"

"My great-grandmother's vindicated. I just want her honoured for the work that was stolen from her."

"You've done a hell of a job yourself, Annis. Time to go home."

"Once I'm done here, that'll be terrific."

"That could be three months."

"I want to see this through. Besides, the computer network knows me. It won't like strangers trying to access it."

"Really?"

"Oh, it's not sentient," Kim said airily. "I'm just..."

"Territorial. You always were."

"I don't play well with others, Tim. Your wife knows that."

Pham squirmed. "Okay, now let's go through the Ainatio personnel list."

Kim seemed to have things under control. Solomon put his awareness of the conversation in watching brief mode, ready to switch back instantly at the first hint of a problem, and sought out Alex. He was basking in the sun streaming through the lobby glass, looking wrung out as he awaited his audience with Tim Pham. From what Solomon could see, the farmers had returned to Kill Line to tend to their livestock, and the other townsfolk were discussing whether they should go home yet. That was the problem with good news: it never solved everything and it spawned uncertainties of its own. Chris's people seemed the most relaxed about the state of limbo they now found themselves in, but then they were used to living from day to day. Some had started moving into the accommodation block, luxurious lodgings compared to their tidy but basic shacks at the camp. Judging by the power and water consumption, the most popular facility was hot showers.

Solomon interrupted Alex's nap by making a gentle popping sound in his earpiece. Alex stirred.

"Alex..."

"Sol. Uhh. What's up?"

"Dr Kim just negotiated a twelve-week period of grace for me to get *Shackleton* ready. It'll be very tight."

"Can you do it?"

"I have to. And she might well have booked your ticket to Seoul."

"Damn."

"I'm keeping an eye on her. She really is keeping her word."

"Yeah, but will APS?"

"I think she's angling to stay here to make sure she sees us out."

Alex sat up and checked his screen. "Okay, I misjudged her."

"Nobody trusts a spy. I think they allow for that."

"Are you working on the comms mast now?"

"I decided to build a new one on the north side of the site. Less visible to our guests if they suddenly get nervous about what's happening. They don't know what I am, remember. This has to look robotic in every sense of the word."

"Funny, Erskine never worried about you falling into enemy hands. Odd oversight. What's the point in trashing all the records if you're still around? You remember it."

"She knew I'd evade capture."

"Yeah. She definitely found that out, didn't she?" Alex stood up. "Okay, I'm going to recruit some meat-bags and go help the bots fix those comms. It won't be long before the APS guys are all over us. No trotting around in your quad, either, okay?"

"Don't worry, I'm playing dumb until I'm out of APS's reach."

Solomon did another round of the underground floors to see how many people were still down there, then swept the rest of the facility. A group of engineers and mechanics had gone out to the shuttle pens with Trinder to check over their state of readiness, because they'd be needed too. Twelve weeks preparation was no time at all.

It was now three hours since the APS contingent had arrived. Were they planning to stay on, and would therefore need apartments, or were they were flying out again and planning to send personnel later? He hoped it was the latter. He could get a lot more done if he had some breathing space for a few days. Kim appeared to be doing an efficient job of steering the process, though, and three tilt rotor crews, a security detail, and a politician weren't equipped to do a full inspection and audit. Perhaps he'd get Kim to suggest that they pull out by mid-afternoon and come back with a specialist team. With any luck, he could get the comms relay finished before they returned.

Solomon scanned the facility and found Kim in the deserted infirmary. He watched her go into the mortuary and come out a few moments later carrying something wrapped in paper towels. She looked uneasy. When she reached the doors, he activated the security intercom.

"Dr Kim, are you all right?"

"I will be, Sol." She was holding the package like a newborn. "Could you open the doors for me? I don't want to drop this."

"Oh. Oh, yes." He'd thought she was up to something dishonest, but now he could see the shape under the towels and guessed what it was. "Of course."

"I need to see Chris. Where is he?"

"In the accommodation block. Would you like me to call a trolley bot for that?"

"No, I need to do this personally. But thanks."

"Dr Kim, could you do something for me, please? Could you find out if Mr Pham plans to stay over, or if his mission's flying back today? It would be helpful if they arranged to return later with a team of specialists for a full inspection. Quite a lot later, if possible."

"I'll give him a long list of experts I think he needs. It'll take a week for him to get them together."

"Excellent. Thank you."

"That works for both of us."

"I suspect there's no real conflict here."

"I hope not. Okay, Sol, which way now?"

"Left."

Solomon trailed her from camera to camera, directing her through the corridors of the residential building. Chris had set up camp in one of the apartments that had been empty for years rather than one of the more comfortable recently-vacated ones, almost as if he didn't want to venture into someone else's territory. He was taking a shower. Solomon's rule never to enter private areas still stood. He waited for Kim to ring the buzzer and for Chris to eventually open the door in a blue Ainatio-issue bathrobe.

"Sorry," Kim said. "We've caught you at a bad time."

"We?"

"Sol and me."

"No problem." Chris ushered her in. "I'd be standing there all day. It's a novelty to have a shower with that much pressure."

"I think I've got you a twelve-week reprieve."

"That's great." He nodded a few times, looking a little awkward. "Thank you."

"Actually, I've come to ask you for a favour. In case we get overtaken by events and I forget to ask."

"Oh yeah. You said earlier. Well, if it's humanly possible, I'll do it."

She handed Chris the urn she'd carried carefully from the infirmary. "Will you make sure these get to Opis?"

Chris handled the urn with reverent care. He seemed taken aback. "This can't be your great-grandmother's ashes. You didn't have this when I found you."

"No, they're Mr Levine's. Would you scatter them for me when you land? He deserves to get to Opis after what he went through all those years. I don't know, maybe some on the planet, some into space... whatever seems right to you. Don't laugh at me, but I want him to reach Pascoe's Star."

Chris looked at the urn for a long time, jaw muscles working silently. It was one of the few times Solomon had seen his emotions anywhere near the surface.

"You have my word," Chris said. "That's an honourable thing to do, Dr Kim."

"I appreciate it. Thank you."

"Alex says you did right by us."

"I keep my word. I might need you to save my arse again one day."

Chris smiled. He wasn't quite the unredeemed, pitiless enforcer that he seemed to believe he was. "Any time."

Kim left, but Solomon finally broke his cardinal rule and hung around for a few moments. Chris sat down on the sofa and put the urn on the coffee table, then sat staring at it for a while as if he was working something out.

"So you won't be alone after all, Jamie," he said to himself. "You'll have company as soon as we get to Opis. That's better."

Solomon was both glad and ashamed that he'd heard it, and he would never intrude again. He withdrew instantly to wander around the site to think over the nature of grieving, and to watch humans doing what these humans did very well: organising themselves and making sure everyone was cared for.

He watched Annis Kim negotiating a passage to Fiji for Tev, courtesy of APS, to see the family he'd been separated from for so long. He watched Doug Brandt and the farmers working out what they could do for Marty Laurenson now that his sheep were gone. He watched Marc Gallagher cheering up little Jack Howard — Howie — with a story about his exploits with Tev in Washington, which was both thrilling and completely true. And he watched Zakko Chetcuti organising an APS medevac flight to Sydney for Dr Mendoza's patients, five elderly, terminally ill scientists, the people the doctor had refused to abandon.

"If they don't want to go to Sydney and they'd rather risk a space flight instead, I'll sign off on that and prep them for it," Mendoza was saying. "Their time matters a lot more than mine right now."

Solomon was intensely proud of them all, and didn't doubt his decisions for one moment. Trinder, Chris, and Marc had already formed a natural alliance built on the values Solomon found so appealing. These were the right kind of people. He'd had moments of doubt about his preference for the military because he'd read and been told so often that governance by it was dangerous and undesirable, but these men seemed not to want that kind of power. And that was exactly what qualified them for it. They were the heirs to *Cabot*.

Now it was down to Solomon to ensure that everyone reached Opis. He had twelve weeks to get this new community embarked in *Shackleton* and on its way to a new life.

After all the turmoil, death, and violence of the last few years, he wondered if the biggest risk was that the humans in his care might find Opis rather too tranquil by comparison.

* * *

MESS HALL, NOMAD BASE, OPIS:
THREE DAYS AFTER FINAL CONTACT WITH EARTH

"I think I miss Solomon more than Earth, you know," Haine said, stirring his coffee. "Very helpful with the morning crossword."

The view from the printed plastic cube now claimed as the mess hall reinforced the illusion of Opis as an Earth decked out with a few more exotic plants. Ingram had seen more alien landscapes in the Middle East. And that was the problem: illusion. She was still trying to reset to the expectations she'd had when she left Earth. The loss of FTL didn't matter a damn. What had they actually lost, other than Solomon? Nothing, just the fantasy that Earth was next door, which was dangerously seductive. They really were better off without it. Ingram had powdered scrambled eggs and drinkable coffee, and in a few months, when the agricultural projects ramped up, she'd have *real* eggs. When they took the hen embryos out of cryo, she was going to earmark one for herself and call it Mildred.

"You know what gets me?" she said. "The lies. They don't even have to be really big ones. The small ones pile up. It's a cumulative thing."

Any one of the deceits and secrets would have created bad blood in a working relationship, but this was a whole collectors' edition — telling everyone the crew was dead, turning foreign governments into potential enemies by stealing their technology, and then dangling the luxury of instant communications in front of an isolated crew before snatching it away. It wasn't Erskine's fault that the world had gone to rats in *Cabot*'s absence, but Ingram still felt that her crew had been abandoned. Being suddenly cut off without any explanation pissed her off. If Erskine had been that short of time, she could have sent a data burst instead of blathering on with stock excuses.

Based on Ainatio's previous form, Erskine was lying about something. It could have been anything from someone spilling coffee in the power supply to full-tar Armageddon. Not knowing which just left mistrust to ferment.

"Look at it this way." Haine seemed happier here already. He'd started sketching, and he hummed to himself a lot. "We can't reach Ainatio, but that means Ainatio can't reach us. We can live like pirate kings. Build our own empire. Have a bloody good laugh."

"Put it in the suggestion box and I'll take a look at it."

"You know something else? I just realised my ex must have been paid death-in-service insurance money, and possibly even my pension, but now she's ninety. Or dead. So there's that."

He laughed. Ingram, like everyone else, had put her financial affairs in order before she left, but after the welter of bad news from Earth, she hadn't given any thought to being declared legally dead. Just finalising everything before the launch had seemed like organising her own funeral. Now she was doubly dead.

"Hang on, are Ainatio still paying us?" she asked, going along with the idea. "Because they'd need to have us declared dead to keep the cover story going, but we're still working for them, so how did they hide the salaries? Or did they just stop paying us?"

"If we're dead, it should be tax-free. Ah, if only we could ask Erskine."

"See? What did I say? Everything they touch is a lie."

Haine started laughing. "Maybe that's why they cut the FTL link. For tax purposes."

"Hah."

"Piracy. It's all we have left. Mark my words. Buckle up your swash and prepare to board, me hearties."

Ingram cleared up her plates. "I think I'm going to take a rover out for a spin. See what's happening around our lovely new country estate."

"Look out for frisky wildlife."

"I haven't seen anything bigger than those rat-sized things," Ingram said. "Apart from the crows. I wonder if we've landed on the galactic equivalent of New Zealand."

"Well, there's a whole planet out there. It might not be all wall-to-wall paradise."

Ingram passed the bot hangar on the way to pick up a vehicle, but couldn't stop herself doing a quick detour. She walked along the bays of assorted bots, from shoebox-sized things right up to big excavators, and stopped in front of the four near-identical industrial quadrubots in their charging docks. They must have been part of the original cargo launched more than a century ago. The one that Solomon preferred was distinguishable only by the red logo on one flank, now partially chipped off by constant use. Ingram squatted in front of it, almost expecting to hear Sol's voice, but it was on standby like the others.

"I hope you're coming back, Sol." She wondered whether he ever amused himself by passing himself off as a regular bot to surprise the unwary. "And when you do, I want to hear everything that's happened."

The weather records that Solomon had provided showed rough weather in the cooler months of the year, but for the time being, Ingram could enjoy something that felt like a warm spring. The air was the freshest she'd ever smelled. She drove north towards the mountain range that hung tantalisingly in the distance like a permanent layer of purple cloud, flat-topped and constantly changing with the light.

The astrobiologists hadn't seen her sneak a high-powered rifle into the vehicle, so they weren't going to give her a hard time again about leaving the local wildlife alone. Ecological diversity was lovely, but she didn't plan on ending her days in the slavering jaws of some fascinating new species that she wasn't expecting to run into. If anything started on her, she'd shoot it and have it stuffed for display in the mess. There was probably a bot that could do that for her.

Half an hour out, she stopped the rover and got out to check whether the FTL signal had been restored. There was no reason to expect that it had, because Erskine had made the cut-off sound very final, but it didn't hurt to keep trying. She held the receiver up in the air, hoping for a comms miracle, but she was out of luck again. She even clambered onto the rover's flatbed to see if that helped. But nothing had changed. The display showed a flat line where the FTL signal had once been.

Standing on the rover's flatbed, she could now see down a gentle slope into the shallow valley shown on her chart. On the south side, there were signs of mining, where bots had excavated raw materials to build and manufacture for their human masters. Track marks had formed faint dirt roads leading back towards Nomad. Mankind had already left its mark on this world before the first human even set foot on it.

If Ingram ignored the tracks, the rest of the scene was postcard-perfect. A river snaked through the valley and disappeared into a forest the colour of red cabbage. The ground around her was covered with short, moss-like turf in a tasteful shade of sage green, dotted with delicate cream flowers. It was such a pretty landscape, so tidy and orderly, that it looked cultivated. She mistrusted it completely. It was the sea on a calm day, something to be enjoyed carefully before it turned on her and started rolling the ship, smashing fifteen-meter waves onto the bows.

She was wondering where all the inevitably poisonous, annoying, and aggressive insects were when she caught a flash of blue-black iridescence in the corner of her eye. She could guess who was keeping her company today. She turned slowly, hoping that the creature wasn't going to dive-bomb her again, and saw the big black bird, the one she thought of as the parent. She'd seen it a few times now and had spoken to it like a sparrow in the park back home begging for crumbs. Sometimes, when those piercing yellow, round-pupilled eyes met hers, she felt it actually understood every word. For all she knew, it was still sizing her up for lunch. But it did seem endlessly curious, and it always watched anyone it found walking around.

"Where are your babies, then, Mr Crow?" she asked. Maybe it was Mrs Crow. She had no way of knowing. "Have you grounded them?"

She hadn't seen the two smaller versions of the creature since the day the big one had strafed her, so it had either eaten them or it really was a parent that had warned its roaming offspring that humans were off limits. The bird settled on the ground about five metres from her, wings folded, bolt upright.

Ingram was tempted to get a little closer, but it was bloody big. She decided to give it a wide berth, ready to shoot if it went for her. She had the flare pistol, too, so she'd try to humour the astrobiologists and just scare the shit out of it if it looked like it was getting ready to attack. That big, black, toucan beak wasn't to be trifled with.

Don't stare at it. That provokes a lot of animals. They might not be any different here.

It just stood there, watching, making no attempt to move, the height of an adult human. Now that Ingram wasn't ducking to avoid it, she had a better chance to look at the detail, particularly the wings. That joint on the front edge reminded her of a bat's. What was that part in a bat, then, the wrist or the knuckles? She remembered the anatomical diagrams from biology class. The wings were modified hands with webbing between elongated fingers, so the knuckle that the bird appeared to be putting its weight on was the equivalent of the base of her thumb.

Ouch.

She wondered how it would react if she tried to record it. Slowly, she took her screen out and framed up. It was a real shame that she couldn't transmit any of this back to Ainatio.

The bird obliged and stood still while she filmed it. When she put the screen away, it seemed to relax, and draped its wings as if it knew its photo shoot was over and it could now bask in the warm sun. The biologists would have told her she was anthropomorphising, but this creature seemed as intelligent as any bird back home. For all she knew it was thinking the same about her.

"Damn smart plumage, Crow," she said. "Classy."

She was about to start backing away when she heard the rush of wings and caught a flash of shadow. She ducked just in time. It was one of the smaller birds. The big one made a long rattling sound rising to a crescendo and swiped at the small one, missing it by a good distance. Ingram couldn't see that as anything but a parent scolding a kid who was messing around, threatening a good spanking for misbehaviour. Mr Crow suddenly brought its wings together with a loud snap, like a Mandarin emperor cracking a fan open.

"Bloody hell," Ingram said. "You scared the life out of me."

"*Bloodyhellbloodyhellbloodyhellbloodyhell!*" It came out in a rush, in a voice so like to her own that she was rooted to the spot. "*Bloodyhellbloodyhell!*"

"Oh, you're a *parrot*. You're a mimic." She really wished there was someone else around to witness this. She hadn't even recorded it. Were the biologists going to believe her? "This is going to be fun. No learning swear words, okay? If some sailor tells you *sod off* is a traditional Earth greeting, ignore them."

"*Bloodyhellignoresodoff.*"

"That's right." Good grief, they learned fast. Or maybe it had heard the crew more often than Ingram had realised. "You're very clever."

"*Bloody hell bot.*" The bird's speech slowed down to a normal human rate. "*Bloody hell bot.*"

Bot. Had she heard right? There was something else going on beyond simple mimicry. If it knew the word, it might have heard it while hanging around the camp, and there were certainly plenty of bots at the site. Ingram tried hard not to imagine meaning that wasn't there, but it seemed to understand that *bloody hell* was her reaction to being startled. Maybe it was telling her that the camp's bots disturbed it or frightened its offspring. They'd been rolling around the area for years.

Damn, was it making a formal complaint?

"Bot," she said. She made a walking motion with her fingers, then decided to show the bird an image. She had no idea what its visual spectrum was like, but if it could see in this light, it could probably see at least as well as she could.

She took out her screen, found an image of a quadrubot, and turned it around so that the bird could see it.

"*Solomon Solomon Sol Sol Sol,*" said the bird, in Solomon's voice. It rustled and flapped its wings. "*Sol-o-mon.*"

"You're right. That's Solomon." The accuracy of the different voices was starting to disturb her. And how had the bird heard the name? Again, she'd had no idea that any conversations outside had been overheard, but she'd never looked up to check if there was anything sitting on the roof. "Sol's gone away now."

"*Ma'am,*" the bird said, in a voice she didn't recognise. "*Ma'am ma'am ma'am ma'am.*"

"Yes... that's what they call me." She tapped her chest. "My name's Bridget Ingram."

"*Briddd-jit.*"

"Bridget. Ingram."

"*Bridget Ingram Bridget Ingram ma'am ma'am ma'am. Yes.*"

This was getting bloody scary. She was obviously dealing with something a lot more intelligent than anyone had imagined, and that raised serious questions about colonising the planet. She had no choice, though. This was the real world, and she didn't have the option of apologising for turning up uninvited and offering to move elsewhere. Humans and crows would have to learn to get on and give each other some space. But one thing was certain: nobody was going to be shooting or eating these birds.

Ingram could have stayed there all day trying to have a conversation with the creature, but she'd reached the stage where she needed to talk to the biologists.

"You're fascinating," she told the bird. "I wish I knew more about you. I bet we'll get to know each other well, though. I've got to go now, but I'll see you later."

She felt so discourteous leaving it in mid-conversation that she gave it a little wave as she turned away. She could've sworn that it bobbed its head politely at her.

Now don't get stupid about this. Lots of animals do that bobbing motion. You don't know the first damn thing about avian biology, least of all here. Stop it.

She drove off, half-expecting Mr Crow to come flapping after her, but it stayed put and she finally lost sight of it in the rear-view as she drove over the crest of the hill. She rushed back to the mess, bursting to tell anyone who'd listen, but it was empty and this couldn't wait until lunch. She hunted for an audience. She found Bissey, Haine, and Jeff Aiken with one of the agri planners, Andy Braithwaite, in the dry lab. They were all leaning over a chart on the table.

"You're back early, ma'am," Bissey said.

"You're not going to believe this, but I've had a conversation with one of the locals."

"Of course you have, ma'am."

"The big black bird."

"Take more water with it next time, Bridgers," Haine said. He rarely called her that these days. "It worked for me."

"Come on, chaps, this is exciting science. The bird showed up and I started talking to it. And it mimicked me. Like a parrot. Only it didn't stop there."

They all straightened up and forgot the crop map for a while.

"Did you record it?" Haine asked.

"I was too gobsmacked, to be honest."

"What happened, then?"

"It reproduced my voice, and Solomon's, and it used his name. I didn't have to prompt it. I showed it a picture of a quadrubot and it said 'Sol.' It even called me ma'am."

There was a moment of silence. Then they all burst out laughing.

"It's encouraging that the local wildlife respects rank," Bissey said. "But I hope you're winding us up. Because that's too weird."

"You buggers don't believe me, do you? It even says *bloody hell*. I don't think it's just repeating what I say. It seems to understand context."

That just started them laughing uncontrollably again.

"All right," she said. "You try it. It's bound to come back and hang around, because it's curious, so if you don't believe me, go and speak to it and tell me what happens." Ingram turned to Jeff Aiken. "Chief, you were officially the most cynical man in the Royal Navy. What would convince you?"

"I'll engage it in a debate on Kierkegaard, ma'am. That's my litmus test."

She had to join in the laughter now or lose her dignity. She knew what she'd heard, but like all apparently impossible things, it made her doubt herself. The debate continued on and off for the rest of the day, and carried on in the mess in the evening. This time the astrobiologists joined in. They were buzzing with excitement, which made Ingram feel less like she'd imagined more comprehension on the bird's part than was actually happening. Nina Curtis kept going back to the image of the quadrubot.

"That's the significant thing," she said. "You didn't mention Solomon's name before you showed it the picture?"

"No, I just took out my screen. It definitely reacted to the image. It kept repeating *Solomon* and *Sol*, and it mimicked his voice."

"If it can understand that pixels on a flat piece of plastic are a representation of a totally different three-dimensional object, then there's some conceptual thinking going on. Dogs and parrots can do that. Many species can. It's still unusually intelligent, though. I'll reserve judgment until we see it, but I'm excited."

"I think you just had first contact, Captain," Haine said.

"No. I think Solomon did."

Now Ingram was worried that the bird wouldn't return and she'd have no way of proving its unsettling command of language. She looked out for it the next day, and even drove out to the site where she'd found it before, but there was no trace. The rest of the week turned into a vigil for her, waiting for it to show up and prove to her that she wasn't losing her marbles.

Maybe it only wants to know what's happened to Sol. We might not be as interesting as something that doesn't smell alive but acts like it is. Who knows? But isn't it amazing that it cares?

On Friday morning, though, Mr. Crow returned. Ingram was alerted to its arrival by Jeff rapping on the admin office door.

"There's a vulture here to see you, ma'am," he said.

"At last." She jumped up and grabbed her jacket. Now she'd either look like a fool or she could show off her wonderful discovery. "Have you tried speaking to it?"

"It asked for you personally."

"Hah."

"No, it really did. Commander Devlin was out front and it sort of ignored her, looked around, and then went back to her and said *Ma'am Ingram Bridget* a few times."

"Good grief."

"There's quite a crowd down there now."

"Don't scare it off, for goodness' sake."

Ingram walked out through the front doors with Jeff behind her. The bird was sitting in front of the flagpoles — or standing, it was hard to define — and gazing up at the flags. Nina and her team were standing back a few yards, videoing it and having intense whispered discussions. Ingram went up to the bird, still wary of the big beak and those strong wings.

"Hello," she said.

"*Ma'am hello. Hello hello.*" That elicited a collective gasp from the biologists. It cocked its head to look at Jeff. "*Chief. Chief.*"

Jeff, a man who would barely raise an eyebrow at an inbound missile on the radar, looked surprised. "Chief Petty Officer Jeff Aiken," he said.

"*Jeff Chief. Hello.*"

"Blimey." Jeff actually smiled. He looked at Ingram. "It's a shame Sol isn't around to see this. He never mentioned that these things talked. I assume he never knew."

"You make him sound dead, Chief," Ingram said.

The bird suddenly jerked its head up. "*Sol dead no no no.*"

Ingram realised she wasn't surprised at all by where this was going, but when she glanced up to make sure the biologists were getting all this, they looked as if they'd stopped breathing. Stunned didn't begin to describe it.

Jeff stood in front of the bird as if he was talking to a kid. "No, Sol's not dead. Sol's okay. But we can't talk to him. Radio. Broken." Jeff indicated the receiver in his uniform shirt pocket, held it to his ear, and shook his head. "No signal. No. Can't hear him."

The bird just looked at Jeff as if he was an idiot. "*Hear again,*" it said. "*Sol hear.*"

"I haven't got a clue what it means," Jeff said, "but I don't need a PhD in big words to realise that thing knows what it's saying. It's trying to communicate with us."

He detached his radio from the lanyard and held it out very gingerly. The bird rocked slightly like a man sitting back on his heels and lifted its wings. Now Ingram could see what that joint on the forward edge really was, and it wasn't like a bat's wing at all. What she'd thought was a claw, the equivalent of a thumbnail in a human, unfolded from the feathers, and it was something entirely unexpected.

This bird had fingers. It had *hands*.

"Oh my," Ingram said.

There must have been thirty people out there now watching the spectacle, but there wasn't a sound, not a breath, not a creak of boots, not a rustle of fabric. The world had stopped.

The bird took the radio very carefully, examined it, and somehow opened the plastic case to peer inside. It stared at the innards for a long time, then poked a thin, clawed forefinger into it, prodded it with the tip of its beak, and put it back together again.

"*Broken no*," it said to Jeff, holding the radio out to him. "*Broken no*." Then it jerked its head back and looked up into the sky. "*Up broken*."

Every bit of colour had drained from Jeff's face. He turned to Ingram.

"Ma'am, I think our friend here is confirming there's nothing wrong with the radio, but it might be a problem with the signal."

That was the only way Ingram could interpret it, too. She couldn't even look at the biologists. For all she knew, they could have fainted by now. And she had no idea where this left Nomad or anyone's view of humanity's place in the universe.

"*Friend*," the bird said, giving its wings a shake. "*Help friend — friend help*."

It was very early days, but that sounded a lot like a plea for co-operation. Ingram wondered what help an intelligent avian might need.

EPILOGUE

They're odd things, humans. It's their bones. The way that their skin stretches over their skeleton makes them look like something's trapped inside and struggling to get out. But I mustn't stare. We share this world now. We both have reasons for coming to this place.

But they do look so much like fledglings. It's that unfeathered skin.

Jeff is a human I like to speak with, but much that he says makes little sense. He's squatting on the hillside at the moment in the long garnet grass, glancing up and down between the sky and the device he's holding, searching for something. His arm moves slowly. I think he's looking for his link with home. But he puts the device inside his garment, gets to his feet, and stares into the clouds with one hand clutching the strap that holds his weapon on his shoulder.

Without taking his eyes off whatever it is he can see, he raises his other hand with the palm towards him. Then he extends his middle finger. He's so still for a moment that I wonder if this is some ritual I should copy to show respect. It takes some practice to mirror the way he isolates a single digit like that, but I manage. He doesn't look at me.

"You've got yours coming, arseholes." He's talking to the air. Perhaps I've misunderstood how their communications work. Can another human hear him? I thought their relay was dead. "Karma's a bitch."

Jeff has done this twice today. I understand how upset the humans must be to know that they can't talk to their comrades. I settle next to Jeff and try to coax out an explanation. Their language is linear and can be learned, but their thoughts... they're layered and tangled.

"Sad?" I ask.

"Annoyed. Angry."

"With?"

"Earth."

"Whole world?"

Jeff does a twitch of his shoulders. I've seen the other humans do it. He's still staring into the impossible distance between the hillside and his home world, which he can't possibly see from here.

"Feels like it."

He's talking to himself now, as humans seem to. He knows I can't work out what that might mean, at least not yet, so he's saying it to hear the words himself. I must study this habit. They'll be our neighbours for some time.

But it would be very good if they stayed. They're soldiers. Soldiers are good to have around when you have barbarians for neighbours. And they seem very like us in certain ways that matter. They watch out for one another.

"I don't think they're going to get here," Jeff says.

"How you know?" My English is much better now. "They say?"

"No, Fred, they *don't* say. That's the problem. Something bad happened, they wouldn't tell us what it was, and then they cut our comms link."

My name isn't Fred, but it's what he calls me. He can't pronounce our initial *hreh*, so that's as close as he can get. Humans are very poor at sounds.

"They have attack?"

Jeff looks at me and wrinkles the skin between his eyes, his sign that he doesn't understand. Then it vanishes. "We don't know. They just cut the link. So we still can't talk to them. And Solomon can't reach us."

I don't understand all the words, but I think he means that his people have abandoned him. Whatever the detail, he's angry and upset. Your kin should never leave you to your fate. This is wrong. I share his outrage.

"You ask others come?"

Jeff moves his head quickly from side to side. "We can't send a signal, but even if we could, it would take them forty-five years to get here."

"But talking link got here fast."

"Ah, but it's very small." He makes that smallness gesture, digits forming a circle, almost touching. "Our FTL's limited. No big ships." Then he holds his hand as if there's an imaginary sphere clutched in it. Humans are quite good at making signs. "Only small objects. And messages."

Have I understood him correctly? "But you here. How?"

"We set off a long time ago. Many years. Cryo? You understand cryo?" He puts his hands together and rests them against his cheek, head tilted. "Sleep? Suspended animation? Stasis?"

"Sleep through long go?"

"Yes. That's it."

"We help."

"Thanks." I know when he makes sounds to be friendly but doesn't mean them. I can see the muscles tense under that fledgling skin on his face. "We appreciate it."

Ah, he doesn't understand. I spread my wings and hold them level. Humans use that gesture to mean flying. "We know how make ships very fast."

"You've got ships, have you?" He wrinkles his skin again and looks me over as if I'm hiding something. "Do you build ships? Do you travel around the system?"

"Had ships. Many, many worlds." It's a lot to explain. I don't have the words for it. And perhaps I shouldn't tell him yet about the wars, the barbarians, and the hateful ones we won't work for. Would it do any harm to bring more of his friends here? We're clever, but weak and few. Humans, though — they're clever, they seem to be many, and they know how to wage war. I've seen their reverence for it. "We still know how move. We send numbers. And we get talk in the now for you to home again."

That sparks a light in Jeff's eyes. He looks right at me. He's suddenly very still.

"Do you mean drives? You know how to build FTL drives?"

Jeff makes another gesture, holding his arms out in front and skidding one hand across the other as if it's taking flight. Humans make much more sense with their hands and faces than they do with their words. Yes, we know what we both mean, more or less.

"Drives, gates, paths," I say. Does he understand what I mean by that? That we can show them how to travel timelessly, to move around and communicate as easily as we once did? "We know where. Ways from there to where to where, quick, safe."

"And you're willing to share this?"

I understand *share*. I've watched them eat. "Yes. Needs for friends."

"What can we give you in return?" He points from himself to me. "What we give? What you want? What you need?"

Ah, we're really making progress. "Be friends."

Jeff blinks and shows his teeth. This is a smile. It's the first thing I learned about humans. They smile when they mean well or when they like something. It goes all the way up to their eyes. Sometimes being able to see the beast trapped inside that featherless skin is very useful. I think we both mean the same thing by friendship.

"Okay." He folds his arms and nods. "Friends."

"Friends. We help."

Friends are important in this part of the galaxy. Sometimes the strife of the barbarians nearly catches up with us, and we need as many friends as we can find. Friends don't let you down. Friends stand by your side and defend the citadel, as we would defend theirs.

We will help the humans, and they will help us, and we'll both survive what's to come. We have an understanding.

The Nomad story continues in
MOTHER DEATH
Read an excerpt on page 573

ABOUT THE AUTHOR

Karen Traviss is the author of a dozen *New York Times* bestsellers, and her critically acclaimed Wess'har books have been finalists five times for the Campbell and Philip K. Dick awards. She also writes comics and games with military and political themes. A former defence correspondent, newspaper reporter, and TV journalist, she lives in Wiltshire, England.

WANT TO READ MORE?

For more information, visit karentraviss.com, where you can sign up for news and exclusive previews of forthcoming books, or contact Karen by e-mail. You can also follow her on Twitter via @karentraviss

ALSO BY KAREN TRAVISS

NOMAD
- Mother Death
- Here We Stand

RINGER
- Going Grey
- Black Run

(CONTINUED ON NEXT PAGE)

WESS'HAR
- City of Pearl
- Crossing the Line
- The World Before
- Matriarch
- Ally
- Judge

COLLECTED SHORT STORIES
- View Of A Remote Country

HALO
- Glasslands
- The Thursday War
- Mortal Dictata

GEARS OF WAR
- Aspho Fields
- Jacinto's Remnant
- Anvil Gate
- Coalition's End
- The Slab

STAR WARS
- Republic Commando: Hard Contact
- Republic Commando: Triple Zero
- Republic Commando: True Colors
- Republic Commando: Order 66
- Imperial Commando: 501st
- Bloodlines
- Sacrifice
- Revelation
- The Clone Wars
- No Prisoners

NEXT UP:
MOTHER DEATH
NOMAD BOOK 2

The remaining settlers now have a brief window to launch *Shackleton* and head for Opis. It's not going to be easy. They have guilty secrets to keep from APS, and some have to break painful ties to Earth. But that's nothing compared to what they don't yet know about the new planet, the struggle they'll face to reach it, and the hard choices they'll have to make when they get there.

* * *

"Look, you wanted the FTL. I got you the FTL. We don't have the working comms version, but we know more or less how Ainatio built it, and we can develop that into drives."

Tim looked right through her. "I think it's rash for anyone else to head for Opis until we've got more answers on this Nomad project. They're all going to die."

"Shit, Tim, we all will."

"But they needn't die that soon."

Tim didn't do concern for others. He just assumed everyone else was as devious as he was, which was probably sensible, but Annis had had enough. She wanted out of this game. She'd outlived her usefulness to him, so anything short of being shot or locked up was a bonus. If she lost her uni job and had to clean toilets, that sounded like a fair exchange to get out of full-time professional back-stabbing and never knowing what was true and honest and *real* any more. She was a physicist. Reality was her religion. Why had she let this job go on so long? Because she was good at it. Because Grandma Park had been wronged. And because having a clear-cut enemy to punish and defeat was comforting when you felt everything you cared about was under threat.

She also knew that quitting didn't mean she'd be free to leave.

"Everyone's going to die if they stay here," she said. "They'll starve when the food reserves run out. It wouldn't kill us to resettle all of them. You could keep an eye on them then."

Tim wrinkled his nose. "If the very worst happened, and they weren't able to launch *Shackleton*, of course we'd give them refuge."

"If you meant that, you'd have done it already."

"A lot of them *want* to leave Earth, Annis. They think this world's finished. They may well be right."

* * *

Printed in Great Britain
by Amazon